STORMLORD'S EXILE

STORMLORD BOOK 3

GLENDA LARKE

orbit

www.orbitbooks.net

Copyright © 2011 by Glenda Larke
Excerpt from *The Sworn* copyright © 2011 by Gail Z. Martin
All rights reserved. Except as permitted under the U.S. Copyright Act of 1976, no part of this publication may be reproduced, distributed, or transmitted in any form or by any means, or stored in a database or retrieval system, without the prior written permission of the publisher.

Orbit
Hachette Book Group
237 Park Avenue
New York, NY 10017
Visit our website at www.orbitbooks.net

Orbit is an imprint of Hachette Book Group. The Orbit name and logo are trademarks of Little, Brown Book Group Limited.

Printed in the United States of America

First North American Orbit edition: August 2011

10 9 8 7 6 5 4 3 2 1

**Two simultaneous strokes with his arms,
one on the right to sweep the oil lamp
at Elmar, the other on the left to
knock the zigger cage flying.**

Jasper hadn't anticipated it. Elmar had. He lunged in attack at the same moment as the lamp sailed towards him. Flames flared up in his face and burning fuel splashed onto his clothing. Mica dived at Jasper to escape being skewered, knocking him flat as he crashed into his knees. Jasper glimpsed Elmar's sword blade missing his brother's neck by the breadth of a finger. Out of the corner of his vision he saw the lamp roll on into the next bedroom, dribbling burning oil as it went. He and Mica rolled away from each other. Elmar was on fire, beating at his burning clothing, his sword dropped and forgotten in his fear. The ziggers screamed.

Jasper dumped the slab of water on them all without a second thought.

Elmar sagged against the tent wall, gasping, his hair and skin singed, his clothing charred. His armsman's instincts reasserted themselves. He crouched, his gaze sweeping the bedroom, his hand groping to pick up his sword. In this room the fire was out, but flames flickered in the room behind him.

That was all Jasper noticed before his brother punched him brutally hard in the stomach. He doubled over, appalling pain spasming through his gut and expelling the air from his lungs. Helpless, he lay on the floor, watching, yet unable to move. The smell of burned hair and ziggers was strong in his nostrils. He saw Mica whirling around, looking for a weapon. And he still heard ziggers.

Praise for *The Last Stormlord*

"What a tale...This is a GREAT book."
——*Aurealis* magazine

By Glenda Larke

ISLES OF GLORY
The Aware
Gilfeather
The Tainted

THE MIRAGE MAKERS
Heart of the Mirage
The Shadow of Tyr
Song of the Shiver Barrens

STORMLORD
The Last Stormlord
Stormlord Rising
Stormlord's Exile

WRITING AS GLENDA NORAMLY
Havenstar

for
Dylan Stukenberg
with love

May you always know the refuge of a good book.

The Quartern

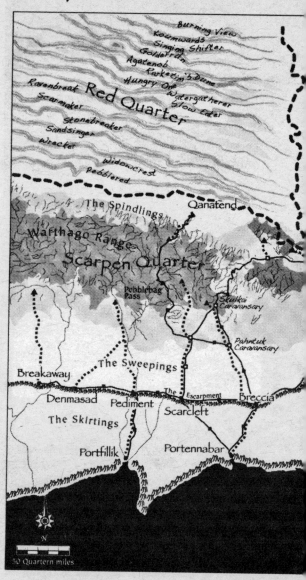

© P Phillips

Khromatis
Variega Mountains

White
Quarter
(Alabaster)

Borderlands

The Whiteout

*Rinra
Plurida*
Sylvine

*Fucoid
Mine*
*Uast
Mine*
*Lang
Beit*
*Sryput
Wells*
Samphire
*Mine
Emery*
*Mine
Silverwall*
*Chumut
Wells*

ycross
Border
Humps

*Drywater
Settle*
*Dopstik
Settle*
Edeopal

Shorl

*Quartzgran
Settle*
*Washm
Dribarra*

*Wash
Kering
Settle*
Gibber Plains
*Wash
Prase*
*Dollypot
Settle*

*Wash
Dryhone
Settle*
Gibber Quarter

The Edge

The Giving Sea

● town	■ caravansary	⋯ water tunnel
● settlement	⚒ salt mine	▲ mother cistern
— main caravan routes		▫ other cistern
		■ well

CHAPTER ONE

Scarpen Quarter
Qanatend City
Qanatend Hall, Level Two

Lord Jasper Bloodstone stood at the window of Qanatend's stormquest room. His eyes were closed, his mind focused, his body tense. He ignored the feel of small amounts of water on the steep slopes of the devastated city below, and scattered across the plains beyond the walls, and concentrated instead on the larger mass he had created.

When he opened his eyes, it was to gaze through the open shutters towards the peaks of the Warthago Range. A distant billow of dark cloud was a blotch on the blue, like the smudge of a god's thumb.

The strain eased out of his shoulders and his hands uncurled. Silly to tense up like that, but this cloud had been brought a long way from the sea. His toughest storm-shift ever. He glanced back at the waterpainting on the table behind him, then again at the scene outside; they were identical. "We did it," he said. Already someone in the streets below had spotted the cloud. He heard them calling out, drawing attention to it, followed by joyful laughter.

"More you than me." Terelle came up behind him to massage his shoulders, easing away the knots, the tenderness in her touch a balm to his worries. "Without you, my waterpainting would go horribly wrong, and you know it."

She sounded tired, and he was reminded how much shuffling up exhausted her. How long would they be able to continue to bring water to the whole Quartern? Two people, supplying everyone? It was impossible! "Why don't you rest for a bit," he suggested, indicating the sofa in front of the fireplace at the other end of the room, "while I get this rain where I want it?"

"Mm. I think I will," she said. She removed the painting from the paint tray, crumpling it in her hands. "Who's getting the water?"

"Golderrun. It's one of the far northern dunes."

He watched as she walked to the other end of the long room to throw the ruin of the painting into the empty fireplace. Using the contents of the tinderbox on the mantelpiece, she set fire to it. The paint curled, then crackled and sputtered, burning with rainbow colours as the resin within caught fire. He wondered if it assaulted her artistic soul to destroy her own creation, even though they'd agreed it was necessary.

"I wish I could just acknowl—" he began.

She silenced him with a gesture. "We've said it all before."

"*You* have, anyway."

"I'm a terrible scold."

People must have confidence in their stormlord, she'd

said. *Better they don't know about me, not yet.* All true, but to take sole credit for something they did together just felt...rotten.

"Wake me when you've finished," she said, and sank down out of sight on the sofa. She was asleep almost immediately.

Turning to his task of moving the rain-laden cloud, he concentrated on keeping it together on its passage over the dunes. Pebblered first, then Widowcrest, Wrecker, Sandsinger...He worked on, but was interrupted long before the storm reached Golderrun.

Someone knocked at the door with the imperious rapping of a person who did not intend to be denied entry. Jerked away from his focus, he almost lost his hold on the water vapour. Cursing under his breath, he halted the movement of the cloud.

He didn't need to open the door to know who was on the other side, or to know they were all people of power: Iani Potch, now Highlord of Scarcleft, Ouina, who was Highlord of Breakaway, and two other rainlords, both priests from other Scarpen cities. Finally, worst of all, Basalt. He called himself Lord Gold now, even though the Council of Waterpriests had not yet confirmed him as the Quartern Sunpriest.

Pedeshit, how he *loathed* that sanctimonious hypocrite. *You sun-fried idiot, Jasper. You forgot to bar the door.*

Terelle popped up to peer over the back of the sofa. She blinked sleepily at him, eyebrows raised in query. He shook his head at her and indicated she should stay out of sight. Eyes widening, she ducked down.

He steeled himself for what was to come. In theory, as

a stormlord and their only potential Cloudmaster, he out-ranked them all. In practice, they were all wealthy Scarpen nobility who were twice his age—while a few short years ago he'd been Shale Flint, Gibber grubber and waterless settle brat. Their respect for him was patchy.

Lord Gold didn't wait for him to answer the door but marched in, his priests and the two highlords trailing behind.

"You wanted to see me?" he asked, barely polite. "I'm stormshifting at the moment. Can't it wait?"

Basalt flushed purple. "No, it cannot!" he roared. "Do you think we can't sense what you're doing?"

"You're all rainlords, so I'm sure you can. But why should my stormshifting bother you?"

"You're sending water into the Red Quarter."

Jasper's mouth went dry. So *that* was it. "Yes. That's my duty, as Cloudmaster."

"You aren't the Cloudmaster yet, you sandworm!"

"There aren't exactly any other contenders for the position."

"And I doubt your piety, even though you call yourself Bloodstone and wear the Martyr's Stone as if you have a right to it!"

Jasper's fingers went to the greenstone pendant around his neck. Flecked with red, such stones were said by the pious to be stained with Ash Gridelin's blood. This one he'd found himself.

His baby sister, Citrine, had clutched it as she died...

"My lords, please," one of the waterpriests said, his tone placating. "That's not the issue here."

Basalt turned his cold stare on the man, who faltered. Iani stepped between the priests to speak, his palsied hand trembling like a sand dancer in a mirage, his lip weeping dribble.

Oh, sandhells, Jasper thought, steeling himself to meet the misery in the man's eyes.

"Jasper, look around you at what was done to this city," Iani said, pulling him to the window. "Where are the people? Where are the children? Where's my Moiqa?" The last question he answered himself, chin quivering. "They nailed her to the gate while she was alive. Did you know that? Her blood is still there, staining the wood. You can see it. Kaneth carried her remains up to the House of the Dead..." His voice trailed away. The tremor in his hand began to shake his body.

He swallowed the bile that rose in his gorge. "Iani, I am truly sorry, but—"

"How can you send those murdering red bastards water? How *can* you!"

His anguish made Jasper wince.

Lord Ouina took up the argument where Iani left off, her anger roiling behind the glint of her eyes and the contempt of her tone. "They'll think us weak, you sand-wit. They'll send their armsmen after us all over again. Their sunblighted army wrecked our tunnels and maintenance shafts, so why not make them thirst? Have you baked your brains too long in the sun? Do you *want* them to come back again and take whatever we have left? The next time it could be *my* city that suffers."

"Not all Reduners are coloured with the same dust," he protested. "They didn't all support Sandmaster Davim in the past and they don't all support Sandmaster Ravard now. Would you have them all thirst, even their children, because some among them are murderers?"

"Yes!" Iani's dribble spattered them both as he shook an agitated finger. "If they'd been kept busy hunting water before, they would never have had time to attack us. Qanatend would not have fallen, nor Breccia either. Moiqa would still be alive, and Highlord Nealrith and Cloudmaster Granthon." He dabbed at the spittle running from his permanently sagging lip.

"If I cut their water, they'll steal more from our cisterns," Jasper replied. "Then they'll come and batter at our gates."

"No they won't," Basalt said, "because now *we* are the victors. We should assert our strength and beat them into the ground, the godless heathens that they are."

"I thought the problem you had with them was that they had too *many* gods," Jasper said mildly and then berated himself. Being facetious might be satisfying, but it was only going to make Basalt hate him all the more. He hurried on. "If I cut their water, it'll be those who support us who suffer first and most. My lords, please, you're wasting your time. The moment we think it's all right for Reduner children to die by our actions because they are Reduner, we lose our own humanity. I won't do it."

"Children grow up," Ouina said. "Reduner children become the Davims and Ravards of this world."

"It's because of Ravard, isn't it?" Basalt glared at Jasper, his anger barely under control. "That's why you continue to water the dunes. Because he's your brother. Have your family ties warped your judgement?"

Jasper's eyebrows shot up, his astonishment genuine. "You're accusing me of being a traitor?" The surprise was followed by a stab of fear. Basalt was a powerful man, soon perhaps to be even more so. He needed to be careful, yet resolute. *Sunblast it, that's not easy.* Basalt was now in full spate like a rush down a drywash. *Damn whoever told him Ravard was my brother.* He had no idea who it could have been; a number of armsmen could have heard the tail end of his conversation with Mica during the battle for the mother cistern.

"My waterpriests saw you talking to Ravard during the battle," Basalt said. "Talking! When you should have been *killing* him. Maybe Lord Kaneth is hand in hand with you on this too—didn't he let the defeated Reduners ride by the walls of this very city without molesting them? And we know why, don't we? Lord Ryka persuaded him. Because she was sharing Ravard's bed!"

His reasoning was so outrageous, Jasper laughed.

"That's *enough*!" It was Iani who intervened. "Are you shrivelled, Basalt? If it hadn't been for Lord Jasper, there wouldn't have *been* a victory. If it hadn't been for Lord Kaneth, Qanatend would still be in Dune Watergatherer's clutches. Anyway, it was Vara Redmane who forbade the attack on the defeated dunesmen, not Kaneth."

"What makes you say that? You weren't even there." No hint of conciliation tinged Basalt's tone. "Now turn that storm around, Jasper, and put the rain in the Qanatend catchment area."

In answer, Jasper started the cloud moving again— towards the north. Basalt and Ouina immediately glanced to the window, outrage on their faces.

"You—you—Gibber upstart! How dare you defy a Sunpriest of the one true faith?" Basalt asked.

Jasper hoped the look he gave the Sunpriest was calm and steady, because it certainly wasn't how he felt. He wanted to slam his fist into the bastard's stomach. He wanted to tear off the man's priestly robes and tell him he wasn't fit to wear them. And most of all, he wanted to ram the lies about Mica and Ryka down his throat until he choked on them.

I will never back down on this. Never. And I'll see you in a waterless hell first.

"The storm goes north," he said. "Now, if you don't mind..." He gestured towards the door.

Iani took the hint and ushered the waterpriests out. Basalt and Ouina both stood their ground. Iani hesitated, then shrugged, saying as he left, "I hope we don't all live to regret your decision, Jasper, the way we lived to regret Cloudmaster Granthon's." The words were not so much accusatory as genuinely sorrowful.

Which hurts worse than anything Basalt could say. Jasper held the door open and looked pointedly at Basalt and Ouina. "I think we've said everything there is to be said, my lords."

"Well, *I* haven't," Ouina said. "You're witless, Jasper. You'd do well to look hard at your friends. Kaneth and Ryka have thrown their lot in with the Reduners. She always was a lover of all that was red, and sleeping in Ravard's tent has tipped her over the edge. Worse, Kaneth has a head injury and thinks he's some sort of mythical Reduner hero and your friendship with a snuggery girl of dubious origins is not helping you see things from a proper perspective." With that, she stalked from the room, her back rigid with indignation.

Jasper gaped after her. *Ryka and Mica?* Where did they get that idea? And Kaneth, crazy? He wasn't crazy; far from it. They'd spoken at length, several times, since his own Scarpen forces had descended from the Qanatend

But Terelle would never say anything unless it was true...

"Shale, she was a slave. Kaneth was too hurt to help her. She stayed for him, and the only way a slave gets to stay alive is to do what they're told."

Appalled, the pain more than he could bear, he jumped to his feet and strode to the window, to lean on the sill and drag in the air as if his lungs were starving. *This can't be right. If it is, I don't want to know it. I don't want to think of Ryka and—Oh, weeping shit, how could he?*

Deep, calming breaths.

"Don't forget the cloud," she said.

Terelle, ever prosaic and practical. He'd forgotten it. Cursing under his breath, he located it again and had to work to pull the teased edges inwards. She watched him, troubled.

He wanted to say loving things, but—convinced they would sound silly on his tongue—didn't give voice to them. All he managed was a softly spoken, "I don't know what I will do without you."

She gave a little nod, as if to tell him she understood, but she looked ill. "It won't be forever," she said. "I— excuse me." She walked to the door, smiling over her shoulder, but her posture was unnaturally stiff. "Be back in a moment."

He swore again when she was gone, at himself this time. His careless words had made her think about staying with him instead of going back to her great-grandfather. That was all it took to make her sick, all it took to make usset's waterpainted magic assert its domination over r. That horrible old man had painted her in Khromatis d the painting was pulling her there before she was er than his depiction of her.

mother cistern and found Kaneth and Vara a
possession of the city.

Basalt stared at him through narrowed eyes. H
clutched at the heavy gold sunburst hanging arou
neck, symbol of the Quartern Sunpriest. He held it
from him as if it was emanating rays of holiness fro
metallic heart towards Jasper. "A warning, Bloodsto
believe you've been influenced by evil ideas from the e
and I will battle to wrest you away from wrongdoi
Your duty is to men and women of the one true faith.
Those words said, he kissed the sunburst and marched
from the room, his embroidered robes sweeping the flagstones behind him.

Jasper closed the door with a sigh. "You can sit up
now," he said.

"Am / the evil influence from the east?" Terelle asked.
She looked shaken.

"Probably. Don't take any notice of him."

"He scares me."

He flung himself down on the sofa beside her. "H
can't hurt us. He can just make things withering irksom
But if that's all, why does he worry the innards ou
me? I don't understand where this silly idea about
Ryka and Ravard comes from, though."

She didn't reply.

"It's so ridiculous."

"Shale," she said, and then stopped.

He turned his head to look at her, rejecti
silence said. "No. I don't believe it."

"Kaneth's men, the ones who were slaves—
It can't be true. Ryka's a good ten years old
he's a rainlord. Anyway, he wouldn't do th

He dropped his head into his hands. When she'd gone, who would help him to stormshift? They—and the whole of the Quartern—were in such a mess, and no matter which way he looked, he couldn't see a way out.

The moment Terelle stepped outside the room and shut the door, she leaned against the wall with her eyes closed. Pain griped her stomach. She wrapped her arms around her waist and slid down the wall until she was sitting on her heels.

Think about going to Khromatis.,. Think about going to Russet. You'll feel better then. You'll meet him in Samphire as you promised...

"Terelle?"

She opened her eyes to see Feroze Khorash, the Alabaster saltmaster, looking down at her, his pale eyes concerned. "Are ye all right? Ye're as pale as my pede."

She shook her head.

"Russet's magic making ye ill again?"

She nodded. "I was on my way to the privy."

He reached down and helped her to her feet. "There's one just along here, if I remember rightly." Leaning on him and still clutching her stomach, she made it just in time.

After throwing up, she rejoined Feroze in the passage. He handed her a kerchief and his water skin. "What happened to make ye sick?" he asked.

"I just—just wanted to stay with Jasper so badly. It overwhelmed the feeling I have to get to Khromatis."

"A war inside ye, eh? Nasty. Terelle, our Alabaster forces will be leaving for Samphire soon. Ye could come with us."

"No, I can't. I have to complete enough waterpaintings to last Jasper while I'm gone and I must see the inside of the Breccian stormquest room to do them."

"Ah. So how long before we see ye in Samphire?"

"A third of a cycle perhaps? No more than half a year, for sure. When I left Russet, he said we had a year to get me to the place where he painted me." She handed back his kerchief and water skin. "Thank you. I'm better now."

"Jasper doesn't know ye get so sick still, does he?"

She shook her head, more vigorously this time. "And he mustn't. You mustn't tell him, Feroze, please. He has so many problems already. He already worries quite enough about me."

"Ye must learn not to be yearning too much for what ye cannot yet have."

They exchanged rueful smiles.

She watched him walk away, a kind man who held an innate sorrow within. As far as she knew, he had no family, no lover. His life appeared to be governed by his reverence for his God and his loyalty to his land and the Bastion. There must have been much more to him, but she'd never found it. As he vanished around the corner of the passage, she wondered, not for the first time, where she'd seen that same shrewd, amused look in another set of pale eyes rimmed with white lashes. Whose?

She couldn't remember.

An armsman brought Jasper a note from Terelle a little later, to say that she was helping out down in the kitchens and wouldn't be back. Without thinking—because thinking would have paralysed him into inaction—he asked the armsman to find Lord Ryka and ask if she had a moment to spare.

When she arrived a little later, his heart dropped queasily. Both of them had come. Ryka and Kaneth. He unbarred the door, bracing himself for an embarrassing, distressing conversation.

What am I to say? Sunblast you, Mica! You have made things so withering hideous for everyone. When he thought of his brother forcing a woman like Ryka into bed, he wanted to be sick.

He waved the two rainlords over towards the chairs at the table but didn't sit himself. "I got your message this morning about you both wanting to return to the Red Quarter," he said to Kaneth, postponing the need to bring Mica into the conversation. "The Scarpen needs all the rainlords it can get. Especially Breccia. With Davim dead, his forces defeated and in retreat, why go back to the dunes?"

Ryka sat, but Kaneth leaned against the heavy wooden lectern where the map of the northern dunes was unrolled. He was wearing a sword, and had a dagger thrust into his belt as well. With his scarred head and puckered face, plus his look of tautly curbed tension, he looked every inch a veteran bladesman before a battle. "If you think Ravard considers himself defeated, you're badly mistaken. Ryka knows what he intends."

"He'll fight to the bitter end," she agreed, looking down at her hands. "And he still has the men to do it. You defeated an army, true, but not all Davim's drovers were involved. Some of his marauding groups were over in Alabaster and another larger force was in the northern dunes looking for the rebels. They'll still be itching to prove themselves. The Reduners may coddle their bruises for a while, but the war's not over."

"Vara wants to return home, obviously," Kaneth added. "She wouldn't let me attack Ravard's defeated men because she hopes in time they'll desert to join her. She needs more men, and I have some—ex-slaves with revenge in mind. Better still, I can recruit more. Men of the dunes, Reduners willing to listen to me because they believe I'm Uthardim reincarnated."

"But you aren't. And encouraging them to think you are is dishonest."

"I've never encouraged that. In fact I deny it, and have done so ever since I regained my senses." He gave a lop-sided smile accompanied by a careless shrug. "But if they continue to believe it despite my denial, I will use that belief to help them. I've never been known for the niceties of my moral philosophy, Jasper."

Oh, waterless damnation. I've lost them both . . .

"Are you sure you aren't returning just to exact revenge on Ravard?" he asked. The words almost choked him.

Kaneth exchanged a glance with Ryka. "That's not my specific aim," he said after a long pause, "although I wouldn't mourn him if it happened, and you shouldn't either. Mica Flint is dead, and what you have in his place—Sandmaster Ravard—is someone else again."

Jasper felt ill. "You'll goad him into a personal fight, if nothing else."

"If I can. The Red Quarter needs a new sandmaster, a dunemaster if you like, to lead all the tribes on all the dunes; someone who regards the Scarpen and its storm-lord as an ally, not an enemy. Someone who won't raid the Alabasters or the Gibber and who doesn't hanker after the Time of Random Rain. In other words, someone who is *not* Sandmaster Ravard. I intend to be that person until such time as a suitable Reduner emerges." He paused, and tilted his head at Jasper in query. "I can't imagine that you'd object to any of this."

Jasper's stomach churned. Everything Kaneth said was true and logical. Mica had to be stopped. Somehow. He switched his attention to Ryka, but was unable, in his embarrassment, to maintain eye contact. "You're a scholar. You don't belong on the dunes, surely." *And Watergiver knows, I need your guidance, Lord Ryka.*

"Kaneth, Khedrim and I are a family, and I'll not have us parted again." Her reply was firm, allowing no hope she would ever change. "We'd like to have your blessing, and your aid, too, once you're back in Breccia. More pedes would be useful, for example. I've made a list."

A list.

He wanted to laugh, more in derision than amusement. *Waterless skies, now I know why Taquar thought I couldn't rule and stormshift too. How can I make decisions about what to do, organise a war, rebuild Breccia, arrange for Qanatend to be evacuated, all at the same time? And now Kaneth wants above all else to kill my brother—and I need to help him do it?* There were too many problems, and whatever he did, he was supporting his brother's defeat and death. Mica, always scared pissless, who'd nonetheless done his best to help him when Pa had turned on him with irrational savagery. He resisted an impulse to sink into the nearest chair and bury his head in his hands in maudlin self-pity.

Instead, he squared his shoulders and took a deep breath. "Leave me your list when you go," he said. "I'll see what can be done. But remember, I also have Breccia to consider. What's left of it. Oh, and Kaneth, why don't you take Davim's pede? It was one of those we captured. Burnish—magnificent animal. Can't hurt you on the dunes to be seen riding Davim's mount."

"Thank you," Kaneth said, obviously pleased. "If it's any help, we don't need storms sent to our rebel camp. The water in God's Pellets is permanent. Take some out, it refills."

"But I sense no touch of water out there, none!"

"It's encircled by stone hills and the water is actually inside a cave. I guess all that blocks your senses."

"Ah. Let's hope that keeps you safe from Ravard's water sensitives too, then. When do you want to leave?"

"Tomorrow morning. One other thing: Elmar Waggoner, my Breccian armsman. I'm leaving him with you."

"You are?" Jasper was startled. In the past, when it came to action, the two men had always been inseparable.

"Elmar is not that fond of the dunes. He's a good man in a fix, though, and a fine fighter."

"I remember. My gain, then." He hesitated, then added, "Bear this in mind: Mica was a victim."

"Perhaps. But he abrogated all rights to be treated as such the moment he threw in his lot with a man like Davim."

"What choice did he have? Kaneth, he was fourteen, maybe fifteen years old! He'd have been killed if he'd stood up to the sandmaster."

"And we'd have been a lot better off if he'd had the guts to do just that. Don't ask me to pity him, Jasper. Not after what he did to me and mine."

He turned on his heel and strode out of the room. Jasper suspected it was either that or throw a punch at his stormlord. With a grimace of annoyance, he turned to Ryka, but she forestalled anything he might have said.

"Jasper, the choices Mica made back then don't count any more. He—Ravard—has choices *now*, choices which could change his direction. Those are the ones that count, and the ones he will be judged on."

"The ones he'll die by?"

"If he makes the wrong choices, yes. Do you doubt it? Haven't you seen the look in Kaneth's eyes?"

"Did—did he treat you so very badly? He was once a gentle person. It was the war—" He almost took a step backwards when he saw the look she gave him. Spitting sparks, Terelle would have said. *You witless waste of water; where's your sense?* It was the kind of remark Shale might have made, but he wasn't Shale any more and he should have known better. He *did* know better.

But oh, it was Mica…

Ryka took a deep breath before she answered. "Did he physically mistreat me? No. In his strange way, he was at times even kind. But he took away both my liberty and my freedom of choice. He used my child to chain me for his personal use. Yes, while he was still a lad he was kidnapped and raped and whipped, forced to slit the throat of his best friend in order to save his own life."

·He stared at her, appalled. "Best friend?"

"Chert, I think he said it was."

Chert? Oh, weeping shit. Rishan the palmier's son from Wash Drybone. What the withering spit have you done, Mica? How could you?

Remorseless, she continued. "I know all that, so I can feel compassion. And because I do, Kaneth hates him all the more. I wish I did hate Ravard; it'd make things a lot easier for both of us. Don't mistake my compassion for lack of resolve, though. If Ravard continues down the

same path, I'll see him dead—by my own hand if
need be."

The look in her eyes was as hard as ironstone. Jasper
kept quiet.

"At this point in time, his fate is in his own hands. All
he needs to do is approach you with a plan for reconciliation, and his future—and ours—can be different. If he
doesn't, good men will continue to die until one of us
wipes him from the face of the dunes. Either way, Kaneth
is right. Mica Flint is dead."

She added, more kindly, "I'm sorry we have to part this
way, Jasper. What your brother did has made it impossible
for either of us to return to Breccia, to serve you as rainlords. Maybe... maybe, one day. But now things are too
raw."

He nodded dumbly, hearing what she did not say:
*Every time I look at you, I will see Ravard, and remember
what he did to me...*

Still she did not leave, and he waited, knowing she had
something else to say. Ryka always did.

"How long will you be able to keep up the storms?"

"I'm not sure."

"Terelle told me yesterday she has to leave for a time to
settle a family matter in Khromatis." She looked at him
quizzically. "Of all places."

He nodded, not making it easy for her.

"I'm beginning to think the most monumental mistake
we ever made was not taking you seriously when you
spoke of her talents."

"Yes," he agreed.

She came up to him, put her hands on his shoulders
and kissed him on both cheeks. "Look after her, Jasper.

I like her, and I don't think you should marry Senya Almandine."

He smiled slightly. "Neither do I. I'm sorry, Ryka. About everything."

"So am I." She grimaced, and was gone.

CHAPTER TWO

Scarpen Quarter
Qanatend City, Level One and Level Three

The windmill above their heads rattled and creaked in the wind, canvas and metal vanes spinning in the hot, dry breeze that swept down the northern slopes of the Warthago and across the Spindlings. Dust stung Terelle's face then was blown on, towards the Red Quarter. She covered her nose with her palmubra.

Of the six of them up there on the roof of Qanatend's waterhall, only Messenjer, the Alabaster mine manager, ignored the battering with unmoving stoicism. Jasper ducked his head as if he could escape the worst of it. Ouina, using words more appropriate to a pede driver than a highlord, swore as wind-blown hair whipped into her eyes. Iani was constantly brushing away the sand that stuck to his dribble-wet chin. Feroze had lifted an arm so that his loose white sleeve sheltered his face.

Squinting against the battering dust, Terelle looked up. She'd never seen a windmill until they'd arrived in Qanatend. In the other parts of the Scarpen and the Gibber, winds were unpredictable things, rare, hardly more than playful gusts soon gone, although sometimes they could be mischievous and destructive enough to be called spindevils.

"I don't understand how a wind can shift water," she remarked to Feroze. "I must ask someone to show me the workings."

"I wish we could use the wind in Samphire," he said.

"What *do* you use?" She hadn't thought to ask when she was in Samphire.

"You'll be finding out soon won't you?" Ouina asked. "I hear you are leaving for the White Quarter."

"Not yet."

"But the Alabasters leave tomorrow. You're going back to Breccia first?"

"Yes." *And I'll bet Lord Gold asked you to find that out.*

"The fewer people Breccia has to feed, the better."

"I suppose that means we won't be seeing you in Breccia for quite some time, then, Lord Ouina?" she asked sweetly. "That is thoughtful of you."

Behind Ouina's back, Feroze waggled a chiding finger, but his eyes twinkled. He waved his hand at the line of pedes now leaving the city to wend its way northwards. "There go Kaneth and Vara now."

They all lined up along the rooftop rampart to watch. In the late afternoon sun, the shadows of the caravanners were stretched thin, their skeletal shapes painting dark lines on the landscape. No one needed to ask why they'd chosen to leave in the evening; they all knew there was nowhere to hide out on the Spindlings in the daylight.

Those at the head of the column—Kaneth, Ryka and Vara Redmane—reached the top of the small ridge just to the north of the walls before the last of the followers were out of the northern gates. Ryka was sharing Kaneth's mount, her baby in her arms. Vara drove her own pack-pede. At the crest they all turned to raise their hands in farewell. Those under the windmill waved back, the pedes moved on, and Vara and the rainlords disappeared from sight.

"Kaneth and Ryka should never be going with that shrivelled old crone," Ouina muttered. "Let alone taking a baby who could be a rainlord, or even a stormlord. We have to build ourselves up into strength. How are we going to do that if rainlords like them spend their time in the Red Quarter?"

Jasper cleared his throat and said politely, "We still have rainlords."

"Breccia doesn't." Ouina made it sound like a personal triumph for her as the highlord of a city which did possess rainlords. "But never mind, I understand Lord Gold is offering you waterpriest rainlords."

Terelle resisted a desire to roll her eyes. *I don't like her. She has a mean heart.*

"I still think you ought to be leaving with us tomorrow," Iani said to Jasper. "It may not be safe here."

"I have fifty men with me and I'm not staying long. I have more stormbringing to do here before I go south," he added vaguely. Terelle, who tended to flush whenever she deviated from the truth, marvelled at the brazen way he could lie when he put his mind to it.

As they dispersed from the rooftop, Jasper detained Iani with a hand to his arm and she heard him say, "I'm sorry we have to abandon Moiqa's city. I know it seems like a betrayal of her, and all who died here."

"Yes," Iani agreed, his voice grim.

"One day we'll be back, I promise."

Iani gave a terse nod.

"On your way home to Scarcleft, look in on Taquar, will you?"

"I intend to."

"Be careful, Iani. Never underestimate him."

Iani gave a thin-lipped, twisted smile. It wasn't pleasant, and Terelle looked away with a shiver. Around them, the dust-laden air swirled; above, the windmill rattled.

Out on the Spindlings, the light began to fade.

Later that night, Jasper left Terelle sleeping and made his way out of Qanatend Hall onto Level Two. He stood for a moment in the middle of the paved street and roamed with his senses. There was no one to be seen, no one to be felt outside the buildings. After dark, Qanatend died. Few citizens remained to keep the streets alive. Even though he'd brought only the uninjured Scarpermen and Alabasters with him, most were still too exhausted to celebrate their victory over the Reduner forces. Of the usual haunts a bladesman might have sought at a time like this—a snuggery, a bar with good amber on tap, a bath house with hot water—none survived. Not any more. Not in Qanatend.

Descending to Level Three, he walked the main street seeking two men—his guardsman, Dibble Hornblend, and Elmar Waggoner, Kaneth's armsman—sensing the air for a hint of their water. His senses brought him ultimately to what had once been a luxurious villa and he peered at the gate, broken and hanging half off its hinges. A name had been carved into the bab wood. He ran his hand over it, reading it with his fingers: *Peridot*. A rain-lord family named, as many were, after a gemstone, all of them gone, slaughtered when the city fell. He touched the gouges in the wood where gems had been prised out. War didn't only devastate people, it destroyed all that was beautiful.

Inside what remained of the villa men slept and moaned in their sleep, their dreams scarred by war, their peace tempered by grief.

Elmar Waggoner... He suspected there was a story to be told about why Elmar and Kaneth had separated, but he wasn't about to puzzle over it. What was the saying? *Don't look for cracks in the jar when someone gifts you water*. He liked Elmar and trusted him; he'd seen him fight, too. That was all he needed to know.

He slipped through the broken gateway and started across the outer courtyard. The feel of water on the move alerted him; he looked that way and saw a shadow detaching itself from the darkness under the porch.

"Elmar," he said as he heard a sword scraping out of a scabbard. "No need for that, though I'm glad to see you're as alert as ever."

"*Shale?*" The name jerked out of the armsman in astonishment and for a moment Jasper was transported back to another city, to another fight, on the day they had met, before Shale Flint had become a stormlord who called himself Jasper Bloodstone.

"Oh—my apologies. Lord Jasper. Cloudmaster."

"Technically not Cloudmaster yet. Not until the Rain-lord Council decides I am. Come, can we go inside? It's withering cold out here."

"Oh. Of course." Elmar hurriedly went to open the

main door. The lock was broken and the hinges damaged; it scraped across the tiled floor. "But m'lord, you really oughtn't be wandering about like this without a guard, specially not at night."

"I *am* a stormlord. Outside of a battle, I have little need of guards." Not a boast, just fact.

Inside, Elmar led the way to the room he had appropriated, where he fumbled with his flint to light a tiny oil lamp on a table. "Is there something wrong then, m'lord? I mean, I could easily have come to see you."

"I'd rather no one knew what I was up to and I'd appreciate it if you told no one of this visit, except my driver, Dibble Hornblend. I need the two of you. You can tell him about it in the morning. Do you know him?"

"We've met." The wick caught and lamplight flickered. Jasper looked around, but its meagre glow showed only devastation. Broken furniture, cracked tiles, slashed carpets, wooden cupboards scarred with knife cuts, a pile of broken pottery shards swept into a corner. At some time past, flames had licked their way up a tapestry. The tattered, charred remains, hanging like an exhumed shroud, still smelled of smoke.

"Even their cat didn't survive," Elmar said, seeing him taking it all in. "Those withering dunesmen ate the wilted thing. I found its remains in the fireplace. A *cat*."

Jasper sat down at the table, careful not to disturb the pile of board-books propping up a chair with a missing leg. "I heard it was the same after the fall of Breccia. I suppose, to be fair to Reduners, cats aren't pets on the dunes. It breaks Terelle's heart. She rescued some kittens downlevel and brought them to the kitchen in Qanatend Hall." He smiled, recalling her attempts to carry six clawing bundles of fur wrapped in her cloak. "But now, to tell you what I want. I'm going to visit Dune Watergatherer, in secret, to talk to Sandmaster Ravard. I need a guide, an experienced armsman, who speaks their tongue better than I do, just in case it's needed. You, in fact. And I need Dibble to guard Terelle, who goes with us. And you may as well know this too: Ravard is my brother."

Speechless, Elmar sat down with a thump on the only other chair in the room.

Jasper explained. When he had finished, and as he had expected, the armsman dug out every reason he could think of to back up his assertion that going to Dune Watergatherer was an appallingly bad idea.

Jasper heard him out patiently. "Elmar," he said gently, "I am aware that the dune is in the heart of the Red Quarter and we have to cross a lot of other dunes to get there. I'm also aware that Reduners are dangerous, Ravard is an accomplished bladesman and a water sensitive, they guard their encampments, I've no right to risk Terelle's life and, um, what else did you mention? Oh, that my brother will turn down any offer of conciliation. You could be right about that too—but I have to try. Not only because he's my brother, but because a lot more people will die if we don't bring this foolish war to an end."

"Then maybe you'll think about the withering, sun-blighted *stupidity* of risking our only stormlord in something so weepingly sand-brained. If you'll forgive the plain speaking, m'lord."

"I'm not defenceless. Neither am I witless. And everything you've said, Terelle has also said to me, a lot less politely, too, if you can believe that. It was she who made me promise to ask you along, because you've been there.

Kaneth says you don't like the dunes and don't want to return. I'm hoping you can curb your dislike long enough to venture there again."

Elmar tensed at the mention of Kaneth's name, then shrugged. "Yes, of course. M'lord, we could all end up dead, easy as falling off a pede. We'll stand out on the dunes like shooting stars in the sky." He rubbed at his forearm, still stained red by the dust of the dunes. "None of you are red, for a start. None of us have braided hair. You don't speak their natter and my knowledge of it is not too good.

"And don't think you can dodge the tribesmen that easy either. These folk don't hang around in their encampments, you know. They're out there on the dunes: hunting, looking for plants and roots, herding their pedes from place to place, stuff like that. We could bump into a mob of chalamen, all armed to the teeth, long before we got near Watergatherer."

"I can understand quite a bit of Reduner. Mica and I used to earn tokens serving the dunes caravanners when they came to our settle when we were lads. But most of all you should have faith in my water abilities, Elmar. You do your part, and I'll get you there alive and undetected."

"There are bleeding few places to hide out there. And taking a woman along? Terelle's not like Ryka, a rainlord who knows how to handle a sword."

"Believe me, I don't bring her lightly. Unfortunately, she is necessary and I can't tell you why." *I wish I could, though.* However, hearing the malice in Lord Gold's voice had convinced him that he and Terelle had made the right decision. To Lord Gold and people like Highlord Ouina, magic that wasn't bestowed by the Sunlord faith was a canker on the face of the earth. To tell them that their stormlord was aided by Watergiver magic from Khromatis would be like asking them to trust a spindevil. The fewer people who knew, the better.

"What about settling for a more experienced armsman, rather than Dibble? He's a bumbler—trips over his knees, he does."

Jasper smiled, remembering the battle at the Qanatend mother cistern, when Dibble had saved his life several times. "Not when it counts," he said. "And he's my choice."

Elmar subsided into silence, considering. When he spoke again, he was resigned. "When do you want to leave?"

"Tomorrow night. Tell me, how long will it take to get there?"

"Depends on who we bump into on the way." He pondered the question further. "And how many times we bump into them. Ten days if we're lucky and have good mounts. More likely double."

"I leave the preparations in your hands. We take two pedes and we'll leave after dark, without anyone knowing which way we're going."

Even by the light of the guttering lamp, he caught the appalled look on Elmar's face.

"No one?" he asked. "You're not telling *anyone* where we are going?"

"No. Almost everyone leaves tomorrow anyway. The fifty or so men remaining will be under instructions to await my return, that's all."

Now Elmar looked horrified as the full import dawned on him: he and Dibble were to be completely responsible for the safety of the Quartern's only Cloudmaster on a trip across a hostile quarter to visit a man who wanted him dead. Jasper nodded sympathetically.

"Well, I'll be pissing waterless," the armsman said.

Only if I die, Jasper thought.

CHAPTER THREE

Scarpen to Red Quarter
Qanatend to Dune Watergatherer

Terelle had never been in the Red Quarter before. They travelled by night and slept by day, always tucked away in a dune vale as far distant as they could be from any encampment. On their first day on the dunes, Elmar was as tense and watchful as a pebblemouse away from its burrow until Jasper, exasperated by the armsman's extravagant precautions, told him to trust the extent of his stormlord powers.

They were sharing their morning meal and he handed a piece of damper to Dibble as he spoke. "I'm not Kaneth or Ryka," he said. "I can tell if someone's coming our way much further off than they can. If I know the person, I can even identify them at a distance."

He smiled at Terelle then, his look as sensual as a touch. She knew he was thinking of her, of the way he could sense her from the other side of the Quartern. The wonder of that skimmed shivers down her spine; he sensed only her so far away, no one else.

"Don't worry," he said, waving a piece of damper at

Elmar before popping it into his mouth, "I'll get you all to Dune Watergatherer in one piece. Where I'm going to need you most is in the sandmaster's tent."

Sneaking into Ravard's tent in the middle of an encampment? The thought of it scared her into a state of panic. "Why are we doing this?" she'd asked when he had first told her of his intention. "I don't understand. You told me you already spoke to Ravard—Mica—about this when you were at the mother cistern. You begged him then to reconsider—"

"Things are different now," he'd replied stubbornly.

"How?"

"Davim's dead. Watergatherer was defeated. Mica is Sandmaster of the whole dune. He will be more inclined to listen to reason."

She was not so sure, and from the look on Elmar's face, and the way he and Dibble exchanged a glance, she didn't think they were either. Finishing her damper, she said, "I'm going to do my waterpainting."

"*Waterpainting?*" Elmar asked. "You're going to be bleeding *painting* out here? Do we need our pretty portraits painted? M'lord, just what the pickled pede are you two dryheads up to?"

Dibble, still unused to Elmar's lack of deference to his superiors, winced and put a hand to his eyes.

Jasper just looked amused. "Elmar, are you going to grizzle all the way to Dune Watergatherer and back?" he asked.

"Probably," Elmar said, scowling. "You're both sand-crazy. You need me to bring some sanity to the party." There was a brief silence. Then he added, politely, "My lord."

Terelle hid a laugh.

"You'd better get used to it," Jasper said, his tone mild. "Terelle paints wherever we go. Why is none of your business."

Elmar snorted. "Of course not, m'lord."

"Don't you go all peevish on me, either. I think I'd prefer your swearing."

"Ah. Yes. So would I, m'lord."

Gradually, as the days passed, they became a team. Jasper trained with Elmar and Dibble every evening around sunset, before they moved off. During the day, they all shared the camp chores and the sentry duty. On the third day a meddle of pedes, under the care of several boys, approached the camp while grazing. Elmar suspected they were attracted by the presence of strange pedes, and told Jasper they would not change direction of their own accord. "M'lord, you'll have to work out some way of spooking them," he said.

"If I scare them, what's to say they won't run this way and flatten our camp?"

"They'll head for home if they can't see an attack from a particular direction."

"I hope you're sure of that." He homed in on the largest beast with his water-senses, and started to pull the water from the animal's gut through its cloaca. The pede panicked as its digestive tract spasmed, then thundered away, followed by the rest of the meddle.

"So?" Elmar asked. They couldn't see the pedes from where they were, but they could hear the shouts of the young meddle herders.

"You were right."

Elmar grinned at him.

It wasn't the only near-disaster they had. Several times at night they had to ride out of their way to avoid drovers and hunters or grazing tribal pede meddles. Several times they hunkered down and waited until people had passed. Elmar had been so sure something would go wrong that Terelle thought he must be in a pleasant haze of surprise when they arrived on Dune Watergatherer without ever having been seen by a Reduner.

They reached the dune at dawn and hid in a shadowed sand vale about five miles to the east of a large encampment, which Jasper said was Ravard's. They were still too far away for him to be aware of his brother's water, but he knew exactly how many waterholes the dune had, and his maps told him which one belonged to Ravard's camp, so he had no doubt he had brought them to the right place.

That was the easy part, she thought. And the easy part was over.

At sunset that day, Elmar walked to the top of the dune overlooking their makeshift camp. Jasper could tell him any number of times that there was no one else around, but every evening he checked for himself.

Reckon I got too used to Kaneth's unreliable water-powers all those years, he thought. *There's no changing that now.*

The fiery ball of the sun slid along the horizon as if it was reluctant to take the final plunge over the edge. The shadows along the lip of the dune had the rich colour of freshly spilled blood. On the plains between the Watergatherer and the Sloweater, the blaze of the last sunshine alternated with dark streaks of shadow from bushes and the occasional scrubby trees.

"I never guessed the Red Quarter would be so beautiful."

He started, but it was only Terelle, arriving to stand beside him. He thought of the day he'd first met her and Jasper, in Scarcleft. She had been, what, eighteen? Not beautiful, but serene. Calm. And then the day had exploded into bloody violence. Elmar had not seen her again until she arrived in Qanatend. She still possessed that cool exterior, but now he knew it concealed a sharp mind and an even sharper eye.

She said, "I thought it would be ugly, but it's not. In fact, I think it's the loveliest of all the quarters. The Scarpen is too rough. The Gibber is too flat. Alabaster is too . . . white. But this—" She gestured. "The way the sand folds and pleats and ripples. All those glorious flowers that bloom in a day and are gone by night. The creepers that hug the ground like snakes. The wind patterns in the sand, the play of light and dark. Look, see the crest of the dune there? It's so sharp, you would swear it'd been cut with a sword."

He looked where she was pointing, surprised. He saw nothing beautiful in any of it. It was Reduner territory, a harsh, garish place with no softness, just like the men who inhabited it. "It's time I was waking Lord Jasper," he said.

"Give him a moment longer. He needs his sleep. Especially tonight."

"Why did you come? He's worrying himself sick about you, not knowing if you'll be safer with him, or better off with Dibble. If you weren't here, he could concentrate on what he wants to do."

Her clear gaze did not waver. "Neither of us had any choice. Just trust me when I say it was unavoidable. And you shouldn't make him feel worse about it than he already does."

"You aren't afraid, are you?" He stared at her in surprise, suddenly knowing it to be true.

"Not for myself. My future is not one that includes dying yet a while." She glanced away from him towards the camp, and the look on her face told him more about her feelings for Jasper than words could have done. "But let me give you this before it gets too dark to see it." She held out her hand and he saw that she was holding one of her rolled-up paintings. "A gift."

He took it from her, astonished. After unrolling it, he held it up so the sun's dying rays illuminated the paint. His heart gripped, quickening his breathing.

She was silent, waiting for him to speak.

It was a long time before he could get the words out. *"How did you know?"*

"I'm a snuggery girl," she said. "Trained to see how people feel about one another."

He touched the face she had painted. "It's so real," he whispered. "So very real." Then he let it roll up again and his voice hardened. "Does it amuse you to see a tough-skinned bladesman love where he shouldn't? Do you giggle about it with your friends?" He shoved the painting back at her, pushing it against her chest. When she didn't take it, her passive resistance fuelled his anger further and he let the portrait fall to the sand.

She looked hurt. "I find nothing stupidly amusing in loving someone. I thought you might wish to have his likeness, that's all. It was—it was the only way I knew to say thank you for being here. For being prepared to look after Jasper tonight even though I know you think what he's doing is crazy. You're risking your life for him."

He shouted at her then, knowing all the while that it

was the wrong thing to do. Knowing he was wrong. "You sun-fried female! I *have* to keep him alive. We *all* have to keep the stormlord alive. Without him, we die!"

Upset, she whirled away and ran down the dune towards the camp. He stood there, watching. When she disappeared under the shade of the canvas, his shoulders slumped. He stooped to pick up the portrait. Unrolled it again. And there was Kaneth, so alive and real, not the way he was now, damaged and scarred, but the way he had been: handsome, younger, carefree, on the day Terelle had first met them both.

And he wondered why the waterless hells he loved a man who could never love him back.

She felt such a fool.

Stupid, sand-brained sand-tick of a woman! You should have known not to poke your nose into other people's business. Now you've just made him angry when he needs to be calm and focused.

She wanted to kick herself. Instead she went to wake Shale. Jasper. Remembering to appear cheerful, as if this might not be the last day of his life.

Elmar is right; what you are about to do is stupid and irresponsible. You're the stormlord. You shouldn't have a private life that means more to you than your safety—because the whole Quartern depends on you being alive.

It wasn't fair. It never would be fair. But he was slowly accepting that—and so must she. If the rest of her life meant painting him stormbringing every day, then that was what she would have to do.

Pain cramped her gut, doubling her over. Wilted damn, she had to be more careful with her thoughts.

Think of Samphire and Russet instead.

Slowly, the pain passed and she straightened.

Jasper smiled at her when he woke, and touched her arm in passing when he rose. A small gesture, but she read the love there. Was it too late to persuade him to turn back? She opened her mouth to speak, but he shook his head at her.

"Not now," he said.

"You're irreplaceable."

"Everyone is irreplaceable."

"But only you are essential to us all."

"Mica won't hurt me. Not when we are face to face, in his tent. He's my *brother*. We loved one another. In the heat of battle, everything was different. All I need to do is meet him not as an enemy bladesman, but as the only family he has remaining."

He sounded so convinced, so adamant, she knew she had no chance of shaking his belief. But she went cold all over nonetheless. *He is wrong. I know it. He is so wrong.* Not wanting him to see her fear, she stood with her back to him while he readied himself. No, not fear—her terror. *It means too much to him.* Memory of an older brother who had once loved him, memory of a time when the only person who stood between him and a miserable, unloved wretchedness was Mica Flint.

Ryka and Kaneth are right. Mica is dead. Abuse killed him and left a different man in his place. Her own certainty soaked through her, as potent as the fear it engendered; a certainty reinforced by a talk she'd had with Ryka before she'd left. *Ryka slept with him, night after night. She knows him in a way Jasper never can, and she didn't think he'd ever give up his plans for the Red Quarter.* She turned around.

"Don't go," she said. "Don't go." She was shaking with her knowledge of impending disaster. *Listen to me, please.*

But he was already striding out from under the canvas shelter, unaware of her increased agitation. "I'll be fine," he said over his shoulder.

He accepted a plate of food from Dibble and made a joke about the armsman's cooking. Elmar was stowing his bedroll. They all wore Reduner clothes salvaged from the ruins of Qanatend, but Elmar was the only one of them who really looked the part. His red stain was natural, the result of his time as a slave on the dunes; Terelle had made a stain from her paints for everyone else and it tended to streak.

"Are you clear on what to do?" Jasper asked Dibble.

"Ride like hell for Dune Scarmaker with Lady Terelle. It'll take us about three days. Wait at the waterhole there for you and Elmar. We'll know the place because you'll plant a cloud over the top of it on the third day. There'll be no one there because it's been deserted ever since Davim killed the men of the tribe." Vara Redmane's tribe.

Sure that Russet's waterpaintings of her future meant nothing too terrible was going to happen to her until she'd reached Khromatis, Terelle wasn't nervous, but poor Dibble was already worrying himself sick about her safety. She was tempted to paint the three of them safe, greeting another dawn, but waterpainting was double-bladed magic; it could cut the wrong way. *Remember the earthquake that killed the innocent . . .*

Quickly she turned away to pack her things. When she was ready, Jasper took her aside to speak to her. "If there's no cloud and no sky message, then you'll know something has gone wrong and it'll be up to you to find your own way back."

She stared at him, unsettled and miserable. "Shale—will you do something for me while you're talking to Mica?"

"What?" he asked, his tone neutral.

"Remember that he was young and confused and vulnerable when he was taken. Who knows how Davim played on that? Talking to Ravard may not be enough to bring the old Mica back. Can you remember that—for me? I want you alive tomorrow. You have to live, and not just for me."

She tried not to hear the misery in his reply. "I know. In a set of scales, Mica's life and mine are not equal. That's not fair to him, but it's true and I will remember it, I promise. You're right: no matter what, I have to leave his camp alive and free. You have my promise I won't make any assumptions. And I know for sure that Elmar won't either."

He walked with her to Dibble's pede, where he squeezed her hand, brushed her forehead with his lips, whispered words of love in her ear, and helped her up. He said to the armsman, "I am relying on you to take care of her."

She mounted, cursing her purloined pantaloons. They were several sizes too large.

Jasper drew rein in a dip between two folds of the dune. Mounted behind him, Elmar leaned forward to hear his whisper. "We're about a mile out from the encampment. There's a sentry directly in front of us, about half a mile away, but he is walking to the right. I think this is a good place to leave the pede. I don't want the camp animals to smell it and get restless."

Elmar slid down and started to hobble the antennae. "Shall we leave it loaded?"

"Definitely. I suspect we'll be leaving in a hurry. We'll leave our cloaks, too."

"Can you sense your brother?"

"Not yet."

Elmar swapped his scimitar for his sword, slipped a dagger into his cloth belt, secreted a smaller blade in his tunic pocket and took up his pede prod. One end of it was iron-tipped and sharp; the other end was weighted. Jasper lit a lantern and then closed the shutters. Designed to filter in enough air to keep the wick alight yet block the light, it was standard city guard issue. It meant they could walk in the dark, but if they needed light in a hurry they could get it by flipping the shutters open.

Elmar stared at him, squinting to see better in the star-light. "You aren't wearing your sword," he said.

"No."

"My lord—"

"I can't go to talk peace with my brother while openly wearing a blade. I do have a dagger hidden but I have a far more effective weapon. There is always water at hand." He turned and started to walk up the side of the dune that skirted the dip.

"From now on, over the top of each crest, we'll crawl, not walk," Elmar warned. "Against the slope no one will see us, but against the skyline, we block the stars. Enough to alert a good guard."

"Right. And Elmar, I don't want a trail of bodies. We sneak in and out, unseen."

"You going to talk to Ravard *unseen* as well, m'lord?"

Jasper gritted his teeth. When Elmar larded his conversation with "m'lord," it meant he was about to raise objections. Usually a lot of them. "Mica and I will either come to some sort of agreement, in which case we walk out of there openly, or we'll leave him tied up. Or take him with us and dump him away from the camp so he has to walk back before he can rouse an alarm."

"That easy, you reckon, m'lord?"

"I have my methods. And my weapon to achieve it."

Elmar nodded dubiously. "I heard the tales, back in Qanatend. They say you did a bleeding good job with water during the battle. But forgive me for a bit of blunt speaking, Lord Jasper, if I say you'd be better off leaving his corpse behind. That might be a more certain route to peace, if you get my meaning."

"I can't kill my brother."

"No, but I can. Do it happily, in fact. I owe the blighted bastard that much."

Jasper went cold. Had he made yet another mistake? "Armsman, you are in the employ of Breccia and your stormlord. Last I heard, that meant unquestioning obedience and loyalty. You will not kill the sandmaster without explicit instructions from me."

"Begging your pardon, m'lord, but given the choice between him running you through with a sword and him with my dagger in his guts, I reckon I'll choose the latter. No bleeding question. And I won't ask you first."

"I suppose that's fair enough. But I don't want you killing him out of revenge."

Elmar gave an exaggerated sigh. "Can't see why not. Frankly, you don't know the salted bastard. Not like me and Kaneth and Lord Ryka."

"You have your orders."

"Yes, m'lord."

"You understand them?"

"Yes, m'lord. He's safe enough unless he threatens you."

"Right. Now let's get going." Jasper rubbed his arms to warm himself up as they climbed the slope. He felt tight with anger all over. Trouble was, he was no longer sure who had angered him so: Elmar, Mica—or himself.

When they topped the rise, Elmar added, "This does look familiar. But then, the sandblasted dunes all look alike in the dark. In the sunlight too, if it comes to that. Shall we find a tent and knock on the door?" His teeth gleamed in the starlight.

"Sarcastic bastard, aren't you?" Jasper paused, tasting the air with his water-sense. "He's here. I have a hint of his water."

"That's simple then, isn't it? All we have to do is get through the guards without them being aware of it, hope there's no one getting up to water the plants or sneak into his girlfriend's bedroom, then tip-toe up to Ravard's tent and get inside without waking him. Then, of course, we wake him up."

"Is his tent likely to be guarded?"

"They never did that before. Now, who knows? Maybe things have changed now they realise slaves can be a danger. But then, Ravard never did like slaves. The slaves in his camp were Davim's, not his."

"Really? I didn't know that." The thought was comforting. "What about Ryka?"

"Except for Lord Ryka."

Sandblast you, Elmar. He tried not to think about that, and looked up at the stars instead to judge the time. "How long after sundown do they usually turn in?"

"When the fires die down. Maybe a run or two of a sandglass. They'll mostly be asleep by now, I reckon."

They moved on, without talking. Dodging the guards was easy enough when he could feel their water; it just took patience. About half the run of a sandglass later they were lying just under the lip of a sand hill, peering over the top to look down on the encampment. The sweet herbal smell of burning pede dung lingered on in the air, but the communal campfire had been dampened down. A shape nearby indicated someone had fallen asleep, well wrapped. When Jasper reached out with his senses, he discerned an entwined couple.

When some moving water attracted his attention, he shifted his awareness in that direction. Two men, walking together. He located them, but it was impossible in the dark to see who they were or what they were doing. His water-senses did better: men, not women. And their walking was no idle stroll. They were purposeful. Guards, then?

For a long time, he didn't move. One part of his mind continued to track the two men, but he shifted focus again, this time to the tents, studying each until he knew how many people they contained; who was restless, who was not; where the water jars were, and which jars were most accessible. A scorpion crawled within inches of his hand; he sensed that too, but paid no attention. Elmar grunted and flicked it away.

He widened the circle of his senses again, touching the pedes hitched on five separate tether lines scattered around the encampment.

Another widening out and he was back at the outer sentry posts. The guards were good, alternating their pacing with quiet listening and watching, not following the same routes or any regular path or direction. Unpredictable, and giving every appearance of being alert. If it hadn't been for his water-senses, there would have been little chance of penetrating their lines without them knowing. And those two men inside the camp? More sentries, he was sure of it now. They were making a circuit, looking at every .tent, checking the perimeter and the shadowed areas.

He switched his attention once more, this time seeking out the waterhole down on the plains. Sentries around there too. Gently, he pulled a skein of clean water out of the pool at the bottom of the rocky gully. He teased it to the lip of the gully, skimming it up the rock walls as it came. Pausing it there, he waited to see if the guards reacted. All was quiet.

Not water sensitives, then. He was in luck. He eased the skein a hand span or so above the ground, well away from the guards, towards the encampment. Beside him, oblivious to what he was doing, Elmar studied the layout of the tents.

Jasper whispered, "Mica is in the largest. He's alone."

Elmar nodded. He was impatient, but he was also an experienced armsman, used to long runs of the sandglass spent waiting, and his silent, mild fidgeting probably would not have been noticeable to the water-blind.

Refusing to be hurried, Jasper separated the water into two portions. Most he shaped into a thin sheet which he thrust high into the sky. Someone might see and be mystified by the distortion of the stars if they looked up, but he doubted anyone would guess the cause. The rest, about the size of a sleeping pallet, he secreted behind the largest tent. The two guards had just checked the area and moved on.

He whispered, "Let's go. And remember—we are not here to kill anyone."

"Right. We're just here for a friendly chat, like."

Jasper forbore to reply.

CHAPTER FOUR

Red Quarter
Dune Watergatherer

They reached the back of Ravard's tent without being seen, or sensed. Jasper paused to take several deep calming breaths. Behind the tent was an outhouse, then the valley slope with his water hovering nearby, but mostly his senses were overwhelmed with the feel of Mica's water. Worse, his longing for contact was a physical ache in his chest. What he wouldn't give to touch his brother again, in friendship. To hug him. Sunblast, it was hard to believe in the validity of Terelle's warning when he remembered a Mica who had been neither brave nor callous...

Beside him Elmar was taut and watchful, his dagger already drawn. He gave a nod, and Elmar inserted the point of his blade into the tent wall and began a vertical cut. The jute canvas was thick and tough; the noise was deafening. Wincing, Jasper gripped Elmar's arm to stop him.

Elmar stepped back and Jasper applied a small ball of water to the cut and then forced it, drop by drop, into the weave, gradually extending the dampness into a line until it reached the point where the wall disappeared into the windblown sand at his feet. When he'd finished, he stepped back and gestured to Elmar to continue. This time, the cut was completed in silence.

Nothing else had changed. His water-senses told him his brother was prone and unmoving, probably asleep, somewhere towards the front. Silence all around, not a sound to indicate anyone had seen or heard their foray into the encampment.

Gently, he pulled the slit canvas apart and slipped inside. Elmar followed, sword in one hand, dagger in the other, the wrist loop of his pede prod stuck through his belt so that the prod swung at his side, easily accessible. Jasper held the cut open a little longer to bring inside all the water hovering near the outhouse. Elmar grinned at him.

Salted damn, he loves this, Jasper thought. *The fear, the anticipation, the fight—he feeds on it.* And then, wryly, *I wish I could.*

The room they entered was small. The carpeting was firm under their weight. Jute, he guessed. Scarpen goat-wool rugs were softer. Carefully he unshuttered one side of the lantern to allow a sliver of light to escape, and followed its beam with his gaze. A bedroom with bedroll, quilts, an empty dayjar, a washstand and a wooden chest; nothing remarkable, nothing to fear—yet sweat rolled down the sides of his face, to peter away into the dryness of the air.

Silently he pushed through the door flap on his right, and found himself in the main hall of the tent, where visitors were received. The tent flap to the outside was laced shut. Woven wall hangings and carpets brightened the interior with vibrant colour and intricate pattern. More wooden chests, the kind the Scarpen imported across the Giving Sea from the Other Side, too many of them for the size of the room, and so very . . . Breccian.

His heart skipped a beat. *Stolen,* he thought. *Oh, sand-hells, Mica. Why?*

A large water jar squatted in one corner, tall enough for the lid to be level with his waist and too fat for a man's arms to encircle. Three-quarters full. Good, a weapon for him, if he needed it. He crossed the room and eased the lid back to expose the water, just in case.

He glanced at the other door in the room, closed by a canvas rolled down from the top. Behind that, his brother slept. Hesitating for no good reason, he stood irresolute and heard Terelle's warning in his head once more. He put the lantern down on a chest and wiped clammy hands down his trouser legs. Then he gave a nod, picked up the lantern and, with exaggerated care, Elmar moved to lift the canvas door for him to enter the bedroom beyond.

As he stepped in, more sweat beaded on his face and trickled down. Irritated, he tried to vaporise it, but it was too salty and in the end he had to wipe it away so it didn't sting his eyes. His old failing hadn't left him—he could only move clean water.

He let the narrow beam of lantern light traverse the room, to fall on the sleeping form. His brother, naked, lay on his side half-covered by a quilt, his breathing deep and even. *Mica.* In spite of the beaded hair spilling over the cushions, Jasper couldn't think of this man as Ravard. His water was Mica's, still tinged with the lad he had been when the two of them had run through the bab groves together.

The bed was some kind of stuffed quilt-like pallet, laid directly on the carpeting. He forced himself to look away, to scan the room for weapons. There they were, lying on top of a large knee-high wooden chest next to the bed: a scimitar, a sword, a dagger—and a cage of ziggers.

Mica and *ziggers*. His stomach heaved.

On the other side of the room another similar oblong wooden chest, a washstand with basin and ewer and towel, and some clothes and sandals carelessly discarded on the floor at its foot.

Behind him Elmar—looking meaningfully at the zigger cage—was still holding the door flap open for him to drag in the hovering block of water. Carefully he did so, placing it just under the roof of the tent, a slab hanging right over the sleeping man and his weapons.

Elmar sidled across the room to push aside yet another closed door. He looked through, then signalled that the two rooms beyond were empty. Jasper, who already knew that, reached across his sleeping brother to pick up the blades one by one. He gave them to Elmar, who disposed of them by stealthily shoving them into the connecting room and pushing them out of sight.

Elmar returned to stand by Mica's head, the point of his drawn sword almost touching the sleeping man. Jasper put the lantern down on the box, careful to ensure the light did not shine on Mica's face.

Elmar pointed to the ziggers. They were stirring in the cage, waking up in the light, then buzzing, excited. Their wing cases clicked and vibrated.

Loathsome things, Jasper thought, quelling a shudder. *We are prey to them.* Neither he nor Elmar was wearing the perfume that told the beetles otherwise. Mica would be, but even someone slathered in the right aroma was not mad enough to release them in a closed-in area where they could easily become confused and attack the wrong person. Still, he portioned off part of the water, preparing to drown the little bastards. Then he hesitated. They were no danger in their cage, and killing Mica's ziggers might not be the best way to start an amicable conversation.

Elmar glared at him. In that split second when his concentration slipped, the Reduner warrior in Mica—doubtless directed by his water-sense—plunged into action. In one violent movement, he twisted and yanked Elmar by the ankles with both hands. Elmar crashed backwards. Mica let go and rolled out from under the quilt to grab for his weapons. His hand groped along the top of the chest in vain.

Jasper grabbed the lantern away from his reach and unshuttered all four sides. Light filled the room. The ziggers beat against the cage bars in a frenzy. A sickly smell filled the tent as they signalled their agitation. Jasper hated them so much he nearly gagged on the smell, but resisted his urge to kill them.

"Mica," he said, his voice harsh with a welter of emotion, "we're not here to hurt you. Otherwise you'd be dead by now. It's me, Shale."

"What the—I'll be pissing waterless! *Shale*," Mica said, but his gaze was locked not on Jasper but on Elmar, who scrambled to his feet, wincing, his sword firmly in hand. "How the pickled pede did y'get in here?"

Groping for something coherent to say, his mind curiously blank, it took Jasper a moment to reply. "We need to talk."

The room was suddenly still, all three of them poised and watchful. Then Mica sat up slowly and moved to lean back against the wooden chest, knees drawn up, untroubled by his nakedness. The move was arrogant in its assurance, the smile he gave unperturbed.

Elmar jammed Mica's knees down with his foot and kicked his ankles apart. "Don't you move again."

Mica gave a crooked smile at Jasper. "I think he's looking for an excuse t'kill me. He didn't come out of our last fight too well, if I remember correct."

"Neither did you, you stinking—"

"He has his orders," Jasper interrupted. Mica tensed in a way that awakened old memories for him. *He used to do that when Pa scared us.*

"So what do y'want, little brother?"

And effortlessly, without planning it, Jasper slipped back into the Gibber accent of his childhood. "I want an end t'this war. I want the Quartern t'be at peace agin. I can supply you with water. In time, reckon I can give you all y'want—more than the dunes had under Cloudmaster Granthon."

"And in return?"

"In return, you continue t'sell us pedes, normal trade resumes, and you stop your incursions into the White and Gibber Quarters."

Mica snorted. *"Resumes? Incursions?* Fancy words from a Gibber grubber once no more important than a sandtick on a pede's arse. D'y'reckon you can upend a sandglass and everything'll go back the way it was? Y'know what we Reduners and Gibber washfolk learned under Cloudmaster Granthon, Shale? We learned if water is short, drovers and Gibber grubbers get the worst of it. And when we trade with th'Basters, we get the worst of that, too. Ask your fancy salted friends."

"The Red and Gibber Quarters didn't get the worst of it. *Everyone's* water was cut. Everyone suffered. Mica, Davim has snuffed it. You don't have t'follow his sand-brained dreams no more."

"Nightmares, more like," Elmar interrupted. His sword point was never far from Mica's neck.

Jasper shot a warning look his way, but said in agreement, "Nightmares. If you return to a Time of Random Rain, settlefolk and drovers'll be the ones snuffing it. Littl'uns. Your way of life would have t'change. You'd have t'wander the dunes. And you'll have t'fight us agin, if you continue t'raid other quarters. If you force your plans on other dunes, then you'll have t'fight Vara Redmane and...Uthardim. Why would you ever *want* t'do that?"

"Davim died for that dream, and it's worth fighting for. Our independence. Our true culture. Free of the likes of that lying Scarperman pretending t'be a Reduner hero from our past. Or his whoring rainlord bitch."

The sneering hatred in his tone was disconcerting, but the insult to Ryka, after what Ravard himself had done to her, was as painful as a physical blow. Jasper swallowed his fierce resentment. His hands were shaking, so he placed the lamp back down on the top of the chest, hoping Mica wouldn't notice his angry trembling. "*Your* culture?" he asked.

"Yes, *mine*! On the dunes we take in anyone prepared t'kneel to the sandmaster's law. *My* law, now. Everyone equal, sharing what we got. We don't care about the colour a man was born with, nor what natter he spoke when he was a lad. We're all red here. We speak the language of the dunes. And we'll fight t'get the freedom t'go where we please, when we please—the way drovers once did. The way we should've done in the Gibber, 'stead of being gormless dryheads, taking handouts from the bleeding palmier. When he felt like giving us something."

Jasper tried to keep his face impassive, but his heart was furious in its beating. *How can Mica sound like this? Mica, so bitter and hateful. Wilted damn, he has a sword at his throat and he's not even sweating. Yet he never had the courage to stand up to Pa. Mica was always scared witless! Where did my brother go?*

And then, a harsh acknowledgement of the truth: he'd heard the real voice of the new Mica back at the battle for the Qanatend mother cistern.

Withering spit. I was sand-witted to come here. Elmar and I could die because of it . . . His insides churned sickly.

"Look at the way we grew up, Shale. The Scarpen kept us thirsty, always in bondage t'them and their weeping law. Born waterless, 'cause Pa was landless and always slurped. Whose law was that? The Scarpen's! No way out for us if we'd stayed in the Gibber. We had t'steal t'stay alive. Remember that? The withering rainlords keeping us poor and thirsty, while they sat in their pretty buildings and forgot what it is t'feel the earth underfoot. Water-wasters and street grubbers all, never knowing the land."

Suddenly his tone perceptibly softened. "What did they know about feeling the way the wind clicks your beads as you ride the dunes? Did they ever scent the wildflowers in bloom? Or take pleasure in the hunt, in pitting wits against the cunning of the animal?"

Jasper started to reply, but Mica cut him short. "And you went and licked their arses for the water you drink. Where was your pride? Now you're a water-waster with the best of them."

"You think the stormlords had it easy t'bring water to the whole Quartern?" Jasper asked, livid. "A handful of men and women? Then only one—poor sick Granthon? And now, just me?"

"Listen t'yourself, Shale! You're telling me we're doomed if we rely on a stormlord. You die tomorrow, *no one gets watered.* You get sick, or fall off your pede, we all die. You reckon we ought t'risk that? Better we roam the dunes following random rain, like we used to, back when we ruled. Better we get used t'that way of life, never depending on no Cloudmaster, who'll put other people 'fore us. Here, everyone has rights to water. We don't have waterless babes on the dunes."

"No? That's exactly what you'll get if you continue Davim's mad scheme t'return to a Time of Random Rain! You baked your brains in the sun so long you can't see that?"

"We'll drink or thirst together. But I reckon we got a better chance looking after ourselves."

Jasper heard what he didn't say and shuddered inwardly. *He can't afford to let me live. While I steal the clouds forming along the coast, there'll never be enough random rain to support the tribes. He has to kill me and any other stormlord that comes along . . .*

And he knows it.

"Why don't we talk about this—"

"Get out of here, Shale. Leave us be. We'll take our chances. The only way we got anything t'talk about is if you promise t'let the Red Quarter go our own way. Out from under your bleeding stormlord magic. Free t'do what we want."

"I'd do that, if every dune agreed and if you stayed

within your borders, except for your trade caravans. What in all the Sweepings happened to you that you could think it right to attack a city? To kill and rape and maim and steal? To take *slaves*?" His gaze locked onto his brother's, begging him to say what he wanted to hear.

Instead, Mica smiled. "There speaks the stormlord again, eh? Didn't take you long." As he spoke he rested both elbows on the top of the box behind him, naked and unconcerned, head tilted and flung back, still a picture of arrogant relaxation. "You know the only way you'll get to live, lil' brother? If you stop stealing the natural clouds along the coast, and we start to get natural rain."

Grief-laden, Jasper swallowed back bile. "You can't win, Mica. You really can't."

"Shale, you remember how we went bathing in the pools after that huge rush came down the wash? D'you r'member how good it was?" And even before he finished speaking, he moved. Two simultaneous strokes with his arms, one on the right to sweep the oil lamp at Elmar, the other on the left to knock the zigger cage flying.

Jasper hadn't anticipated it. Elmar had. He lunged in attack at the same moment as the lamp sailed towards him. Flames flared up in his face and burning fuel splashed onto his clothing. Mica dived at Jasper to escape being skewered, knocking him flat as he crashed into his knees. Jasper glimpsed Elmar's sword blade missing his brother's neck by the breadth of a finger. Out of the corner of his vision he saw the lamp roll on into the next bedroom, dribbling burning oil as it went. He and Mica rolled away from each other. Elmar was on fire, beating at his burning clothing, his sword dropped and forgotten in his fear. The ziggers screamed.

Jasper dumped the slab of water on them all without a second thought.

Elmar sagged against the tent wall, gasping, his hair and skin singed, his clothing charred. His armsman's instincts reasserted themselves. He crouched, his gaze sweeping the bedroom, his hand groping to pick up his sword. In this room the fire was out, but flames flickered in the room behind him.

That was all Jasper noticed before his brother punched him brutally hard in the stomach. He doubled over, appalling pain spasming through his gut and expelling the air from his lungs. Helpless, he lay on the floor, watching, yet unable to move. The smell of burned hair and ziggers was strong in his nostrils. He saw Mica whirling around, looking for a weapon. And he still heard ziggers.

Disoriented, he sensed water falling above him and panicked because he didn't understand. A confused moment later he realised it was not inside the tent. He had lost his hold on the block of water far above in the sky and it was plummeting down, spilling as it came. Halting it by sheer force of will, he was left weakened and his pain increased. Gasping, helpless, he rocked to and fro, clutching his stomach.

Concentrate, dammit. Override the pain. He tried to pull water from the family jar in the next room, but his power was childlike, faint and wobbly. The water slopped and streamed away. He rested, took deep breaths.

Where had the zigger cage gone? Was it broken? He tried to see, but couldn't move more than his head. *Concentrate. Get air into your lungs. Get that water here.* He groaned as cramp radiated down his legs. Sunblast, how could one blow do so much damage?

He saw Elmar move towards Mica. A swordsman's stance. *Good, maybe he wasn't badly burned.* The tent walls were moving. No, not the walls. The light on them. Dancing? Flames in the next room. Pedeshit, the carpet on fire. Smouldering smell of burning fibres. And still the sound of enraged ziggers shrieking their savage fury. He managed to edge himself up on one elbow as Mica and Elmar circled each other. An unequal fight. Elmar had the blade; Mica had nothing. Elmar lunged, Mica ducked and dodged away, as graceful as a dancer.

Jasper tried to speak. Then he saw the zigger cage. It had bounced off the wooden chest on the far side of the room and was now stuck upside-down between the top of the chest and the tent pole that stabilised the centre of the canvas wall. It wasn't broken. Relief washed over him. How long had it been since Mica first made his move? It felt like an age, but he suspected hardly any time at all had passed. The pain was beginning to fade. He dragged more water up out of the water jar in the reception room and brought it as far as the door, but had trouble applying enough force to push the hanging canvas out of the way to bring it inside. Blighted eyes, why was he so wilted weak?

And all the while he watched, captive audience to a deadly fight.

Mica scooped up a wet cushion from the bed and hurled it at Elmar, then followed it with another and another. Elmar ducked and wove, but the fourth one caught him a glancing blow on the cheek, the impact splattering water into his eyes. He jerked his head as if it also pained his burned skin.

Taking advantage of Elmar's distraction, Mica flung open the lid of the second chest. Something cracked, but he didn't notice. In one fluid move he'd plucked up a pede prod from inside and turned. He spun the prod in his hand and let go. The weighted knob cracked Elmar on the temple and he dropped without a murmur. Mica dived back into the chest and drew out a sword.

Jasper dragged himself to his feet, still unable to stand straight. Taking a deep breath, he started coughing. *Smoke. Smoke in the air.* He groped for his knife with one hand and waved his other at the zigger cage, trying to draw Mica's attention. The cage had been squeezed between the chest lid and the tent pole, splintering several of the bars when the chest had been opened. "'Ware," he gasped.

With one last effort he pulled the water through the door and across the room, dumping it all on the cage where the ziggers were already crawling free.

Please let the shrivelled little bastards drown . . .

But one flew up before the water hit, slicing the air with its shrill keening. The tent was smoky and Jasper couldn't see where it went.

Mica smiled. The tip of his sword danced in the air. "That's all yours, brother. Can you kill it before it strikes you?"

"I can't pull water out of them," he said, panting as if he'd been running. "Not my skill." A desperate ploy for compassion, for aid, for some indication of a brother's concern. He didn't rely on it; he groped with his senses to gather fallen water into a ball before it soaked into the carpet. And caught sight of the adjoining room where the flames now licked the canvas ceiling. More smoke choked the air, acrid with the carpet dyes. It caught in his throat.

He began to move slowly towards Elmar. Very slowly.

He knew sudden movement would make him a target for the zigger. He hovered the water ball, unsure whether it was destined for the zigger or his brother. "I'm going to take Elmar and leave," he said quietly. "I suggest you pay attention to your tent. Once it really catches fire, you'll have no time to get out of here. The ceiling in there is beginning to char."

He searched for the zigger, but it had fallen silent, and in the flickering light and the drifting smoke it could have been anywhere.

Mica swung his sword to follow him as he moved. "I can't let you do that," he said. "If he's not dead already I'll make sure he is. He owes me a dent t'my pride, and tonight he settles it. And as for you—I'll give you a chance, Shale. If you can make it out that door without a zigger in your ear, you can go. Outside you'll just have t'hope you can escape my men. I doubt you'll get far. But you leave this fellow behind."

In that moment Jasper truly saw Ravard. Not Mica, but a ruthless Reduner sandmaster standing proud and unbending—and he thought in despair he could look forever and never find Mica in there again. He brought down the ball of water and fitted it across the man's nose and mouth, welding it to him with his power and his sense of water. He didn't even have to look to keep the ball in place.

Mica—no, Ravard—pushed at it, but his fingers moved through it without budging it in the least. His puzzled expression quickly turned to anxiety and then desperation. He opened his mouth and the water moved in. He choked, dropped his sword and tried in vain to splash the water away.

Pushing past him, Jasper bent over Elmar, panic giving way to relief: the armsman was still breathing. He grabbed him under the arms and began to drag him on his back towards the door, horribly aware the fire in the next room could explode into a conflagration at any time.

At the doorway, he hesitated. *Kill my brother, or not?* It was so easy to murder a man, and so difficult to decide to do it.

The naked Reduner dropped to his knees, eyes bulging as he began to die.

And that was when the zigger dived, screaming, straight for a horrified eye.

CHAPTER FIVE

Red Quarter
Dune Watergatherer
Dune Scarmaker

A tiny sliver of time, the length of the zigger's dive, the duration of its shrieking attack. That was all it took for Jasper to realise perfume meant nothing when it had been washed away.

He didn't think. Pulling the water away from Ravard's nose and mouth, he moulded it to shoot at the zigger, but he was too slow, too late.

Ravard, kneeling on the carpet, clutched at his eye, screaming, the kind of screams you heard on a battlefield. Jasper dropped Elmar and leaped to his brother's side, his hand reaching for his dagger. He knew if he hesitated he would never do it, so he grabbed Ravard's covering hand away and poked the tip of the blade into the damaged eye. It sliced through the zigger into the iris. In one sure cut, he killed the zigger before it could plunge deeper into the tissues. Ravard's remaining eye blazed into his own, his front teeth bit deep through his lower lip, his fingernails dug into Jasper's forearms leaving bloody marks. He no longer made a sound, as if he had gone beyond horror and agony into shock.

With one deft twist of the blade, Jasper dug out the beetle. His brother whimpered then, an animal-like sound that seared his soul. Sobbing, Jasper dropped the dagger, still with the zigger skewered on its point. Then he reached into Ravard's eye with his forefinger and thumb and ripped the eyeball out of its socket. Still attached, it hung on Ravard's cheek, raw and blood-covered, dripping zigger acid. Grasping it, Jasper slashed it free with the knife. He opened his hand and it fell onto the floor, a bloodied mess. His stomach heaved. Wiping his palm down his trousers to rid himself of the feel, he used the ball of water to rinse any remaining acid out of the eye socket and from Ravard's cheek. Then he pulled himself free and washed his own hand.

And Ravard knelt there, rocking to and fro and keening, his single good eye staring at him, relentless in its hate. Blood poured down his face.

Outside, someone was shouting to wake the camp, doubtless in answer to Ravard's previous screams. And at that moment, the tent roof in the next room burst into gouts of flame, sucking air from the bedroom. Jasper hauled Elmar into a sitting position and crouched so he could drape his unconscious body across his shoulders. He staggered upright and headed for the reception room. The shouts outside grew louder and more urgent. He dragged more water from the family jar and flung it behind and ahead of him, wetting the tent walls and roof in an attempt to slow the progress of the flames.

Just before he stepped into the room at the rear, he looked back. Ravard was on his feet in the reception room, blood still streaming down his face, coughing in the smoke, stumbling blindly towards the front door. Golden snakes of fire slithered up the tent walls. Someone was slashing the ties on the door flap from the outside.

Jasper ran, choking, leaving his brother behind. Gasping for air, staggering under his burden, he squeezed through the slit in the back wall. As he stepped outside into the cool of the night air, the whole tent exploded as a whoosh of flame burst through the roof.

He drew in a shuddering breath of clean air and stumbled away into the dark. Elmar was still unconscious. Above, the water from the waterhole hovered. He left it there. Behind him, the tent was aflame. He headed for the nearest pede line, not trying to hide. Men and women were running in all directions, yelling for water or grabbing up blankets to smother any cinders as a night wind gusted sparks in unpredictable eddies. Others were striking their tents to diminish the chances of them catching fire. No one took any notice of Jasper. In the confusion, he was just another Reduner, helping an injured tribesman.

There was no one at the pede lines. He bypassed the first two tethered animals to reach Mica's mount, the beast the two of them had saved from the rush in the drywash so long ago, the same one that had in turn saved his life when Mica first tried to kill him during the battle. He had no trouble remembering its water. The beast clicked a greeting, and ran its antennae along his body in delighted recognition. He hauled on its tether to bring it down into a crouch. Half dragging, half pushing, he manoeuvred Elmar up onto its back, draping him stomach-down across one of the segments. The wounded man muttered and groaned. Fortunately, the sound was lost in the pandemonium around them. The whole camp was awake now. Jasper wondered if Ravard was coherent enough to have told his men a stormlord was in the camp. He thought it probable; what he didn't know was what orders he would give.

> *Ravard, not Mica. Remember it.*
> *Oh, spitless hells. His eyeball on the floor.*
> *Don't think about it, you sandworm.*

Normally a driver would have untied the tether from the mouth ring; Jasper unhitched it from the picket line. There was no saddle and, worse, no reins. But he had a prod! He'd almost forgotten; Elmar had taken one as a weapon. It would be inadequate to guide the animal, but it was better than nothing. He unhooked it from Elmar's belt. At the head of the pede, he yanked on the mouth ring to persuade it back onto its feet, then urged it forward. When the beast was moving, he grabbed a mounting handle and pulled himself up onto the first segment.

"Elmar, can you hear me? Wake up! You've got to hold on."

Elmar swore richly, but his words were slurred.

"Hold on." He took Elmar's hand and placed it on one of the side mounting handles. "Grip that. We're heading out of here."

"What the...bleeding *shit*...happened? My head feels...hit by a hammer."

"Close enough."

"Withering mallet...banging my skull. And that bastard...set fire to me!"

"Quieten down, will you? I need to get us out of here

before someone thinks to release every damn zigger they've got."

"Told you...this was a bad idea...you withering louse of an upleveller." As this was punctuated by a series of groans, Jasper didn't take Elmar's lack of respect to heart. He urged the pede up the slope of the valley that sheltered the encampment. Once they reached the crest, he began to move the water in the sky after them. If the Reduners did want to risk their ziggers, well, he'd drown the whole lot of the flying horrors.

"We're being followed."

Elmar, battling his pain and aching head, did not reply.

Jasper had never felt so besieged. Just moments after leaving the camp and already people were on their tail. Problems, danger, distress, guilt, responsibility—he wanted to sink under it all. Just disappear. Pretend it had never happened. Send himself back to yesterday and start all over again.

But he couldn't. Elmar depended on him. Terelle would be waiting for him on Dune Scarmaker. He was the Cloudmaster and the whole Quartern looked to him for life-giving water. He wanted to scream: *I never asked for this!* Instead, he was left with a playful pede under him and a mob of infuriated tribesmen rampaging in pursuit, armed to the teeth and bent on revenge for the affront to their pride and the injury to their sandmaster.

Sunblast the pede. It was so happy to see him, it kept stroking him with its feelers. All he wanted was for the blighted animal to run fast in the right direction, but without a pair of reins, how was he going to achieve that? All his stupid fault too, just because he wanted to make a point to his older brother. Wanted to say: *I am the one that rescued this pede from the rush down Drybone Wash. It should have been mine from the beginning.* Stupid, stupid grubber that he was. He ought to have chosen an elderly staid hack that would have got them back to their own pede with a minimum of fuss.

"Elmar, don't pass out on me again. You have to hang on." He'd heard somewhere that you shouldn't let someone with a head injury and unfocused vision go to sleep, because he might never wake up. In Elmar's case, he'd be bound to fall off the pede.

He jabbed the pede again, and finally it rose into fast mode and raced across the dunes, its mouthparts angled into a prow at the front to push the low bushes aside, its feelers tucked along its sides to lessen the wind resistance. Jasper breathed a sigh of relief and began to calm.

More in control now, he used his senses to note that the chaotic confusion behind them was being straightened out. It had become an organised search on pedeback. He felt the mounted men heading out in all directions, most of them to the south—but not all. Five pedes were heading east lengthways along the dune, towards him.

He had to head back to where he'd left their own pede and all their gear. They couldn't leave those things behind; already Elmar was shaking with cold, a reaction to his injuries. Guiding the pede with his makeshift rein was difficult; he was constantly having to correct its path. Their pursuers were gaining.

Blighted eyes, we're in trouble. How the withering spit do I guide the beast with one flimsy line attached to a single mouth ring?

The answer was, he couldn't. There had to be another

way. There had to be, because otherwise they were going to be caught.

Think. A scattering of useless ideas flittered through his head. Use fear to keep the beast from straying? What would it be scared of? *A spindevil wind. Fire. Pain. Noise.* Nothing useful suggested itself. He lacked the ability to conjure up a spindevil and he could hardly start a fire on the back of a pede. He could shape water, though. Something the animal wouldn't understand and would therefore fear. *A ghost pede ...*

He pulled the water in the sky closer to make it more easily manageable. Splitting it in two, he moulded the halves into two huge pedes made of water and placed one on either side of his mount, each matching their speed a few paces away. Feet he didn't bother with, but he did fashion two feelers, solid-looking things that whipped this way and that. In the dark, the water-pedes partially obscured the scenery beyond and the ground under them. Their sides rippled in the wind of their movement so that they took on eerie life. Interested, the stolen pede swung its head one way and then the other to take a look. To Jasper's dismay, it wasn't perturbed, but reached out with a feeler in curiosity and stroked one of the ghost beasts.

Damn, Jasper thought. A pede depended more on smell and feel than on its poor eyesight, and all this one sensed was harmless water.

"What the spitless damn...are you doing?" Elmar asked. His voice was thin and weak, but at least he was coherent. And, by the sound of it, battling the pain of his burns and what must have been a colossal headache. "Did you really want to make withering playmates for the blighted animal?"

Playmate. Of course. Jasper increased the speed of the two ghosts so they started to draw ahead. The real pede gave an excited clatter of its mouthparts and doubled its pace to catch up. Elmar groaned as the speed doubled the roughness of their ride.

Jasper breathed again and thought of Mica. One-eyed Mica.

When he'd plucked out his eye, his brother had not made a sound. That was all Ravard.

His brother was really and truly dead.

They rode at a breakneck speed into the hollow where they had left their pede. Jasper hauled on his single rein, yanking the beast's head around so that it was forced to a halt. He jumped to the ground while they were still moving and roused their own sleepy animal.

At Jasper's direction, Elmar dismounted and climbed unsteadily onto the rear saddle of their own pede. "I'm going to drive you," Jasper told him. "I'm relying on you to hold on." He attached the lead from Ravard's pede to the rear saddle handle of their own, then handed Elmar his cloak. "Try to keep warm. If you fall off it's going to cost us time we don't have, so it's important you tell me if you're having trouble staying upright. That's an order, El. You understand?"

"Understood."

He mounted and turned to hand Elmar his water skin. "I'm sorry about this."

"I was right... wasn't I?"

"You were."

"Spitless sand-tick."

"Indeed." *And that's the unhappy truth. Well, I've*

learned my lesson, and you're paying for it. He gripped Elmar briefly by the shoulder, then settled into the driver's saddle and picked up the reins. They had a long way to go before they could feel anywhere near safe. But first he had one more thing to do.

He took the water he had used for the ghost pedes, merged the two, then pushed it through the air, faster and faster, just at the height of a man mounted on a pede. It was the work of moments to clear the saddles of the unsuspecting riders looking for them and to spook the five mounts into a panicked scattering.

That would slow them down.

Unfortunately there was a whole tribe out there, scouring the desert to the south, and he was far too tired to carry another drop of water with him unless it was stoppered tight inside a drink skin.

For Terelle and Dibble, travelling at night by starlight was not hard, even without a water sensitive with them. They had two occupied dunes to cross, Slow Eater and Ravenbreak, so they travelled only at night, hunkering down in dune valleys during the daylight hours. They arrived on the Scarmaker at dawn on the third night and rested until the sun was up and they could see Jasper's cloud. By midmorning they had found the waterhole. The water, the colour of emeralds, was easily accessible, and fruiting bab palms provided shade and fresh food.

No one was there. Terelle knew the story: Sandmaster Davim had slaughtered the men of the tribe who lived nearby and enslaved the women. The only one who had escaped that fate had been Vara Redmane.

The place was fine; it was the waiting that was tough,

the waiting and wondering if Jasper and Elmar were dead or injured or taken prisoner. Then, just two sandruns after they'd arrived, they saw dust out on the plains to the north, but even half the run of a sandglass later all they could discern were two myriapedes in the lead, while a mile or two behind, five or six pedes followed at speed.

"Something's gone wrong," Terelle said. "That can't be them in front. They don't have *two* pedes."

Dibble didn't waste time speculating. At the first sign of the dust, he'd started saddling their mount, and he had it all packed and ready to leave long before they could recognise the drivers. "I think we'd better go, Terelle," he told her.

She stared at him, heart fluttering in panic. "What if it is them?"

"What if it's not? There's nowhere to hide around the waterhole. What if it *is* them and those others are Water-gatherer warriors bent on killing them—and us?"

She nodded in reluctant agreement and mounted behind him. He turned the pede towards the foot of the steep north face of Dune Scarmaker, which began about half a mile away. It rose in a precipitous slope without vegetation or tracks, a red wave rearing above the plain like a drywash bore wave about to thunder down on them. From that angle it looked an impossible ride. She feared they'd have to dismount and walk.

Dibble looked back at the waterhole and his eyes widened. She turned and saw water being sucked up, spinning out of the waterhole into a twisting pillar.

"Shale," she said.

"Lord Jasper," Dibble said at the same moment.

"I don't think we should wait anyway," she said, suddenly even more anxious. "They *are* in a tremendous hurry."

He prodded the pede hard in answer, and it moved off at a smooth run. "We'll wait at the top. His instructions were for me to look after you and that's just what I'm going to do. Don't worry," he added with irritating cheerfulness. "There's a heap of water there in the waterhole still, and what a stormlord can do with water is withering marvellous."

He tried to guide the pede straight up the dune. The animal balked and for a moment they battled, driver and mount. When they slid backwards as much as they advanced, Dibble gave up and let the pede decide how to tackle the slope. It began to zigzag at an angle.

Terelle took little notice. Her heart was pounding in fear, not for herself, but for Jasper. She kept staring back at the scene as it unfolded below. The racing pedes looked as small as millipedes; the dust was a mere scuff on the landscape. They were too far away to make out who it was in the lead. To her dismay, she could now see that the first group of pursuing Reduners were not the only ones; further back was an even larger number, a mixed group of myriapedes and packpedes with multiple riders.

Oh, Shale, she thought in dismay. *How your brother must hate you.*

The waterhole ahead had blazed in Jasper's senses all the way from Dune Ravenbreak, like the distant flaming of a caravansary beacon. He knew its shape, its depth, its amount even before he reached ahead and hauled out what he needed. No subtlety, he just yanked. And it came.

He turned in the saddle to look at Elmar, still seated

immediately behind him. Elmar's face was ashen; even in this dry heat, his skin glistened with sweat. "I'm fine," he said.

A lie, my friend.

Such rotten luck. They had evaded their pursuers soon after leaving Ravard's encampment. They'd hidden out on Dune Sloweater during the day, and then crossed undetected to the other side of Ravenbreak in one intense overnight ride. Unfortunately, with the dawn, things had gone wrong. They'd been spotted by a local hunting tribal party, who—noting they were unbeaded—had proved unfriendly. Not wanting to lead the Reduners to Terelle, they'd taken a circuitous route south and finally shaken them off. They'd then risked riding across the plains to Scarmaker during the day, only to be spied by Ravard's men while they were out in the open, just a sandrun short of the waterhole.

Grimly, Jasper rolled the water he'd collected into a long cylinder, hollow in the centre, about as wide in diameter as a pede was high, and long enough to block those following him if he placed it across their path. After pulling it into place behind him, he hovered it ten or twenty paces across his trail, above the ground.

He gave a quick glance to the dune, still half a mile away. He could see a pede nearing the crest and felt Terelle's water there.

"Ziggers!" Elmar warned.

Jasper heard them too. A flock of them, by the intensity of their screaming, still distant and already audible. Fear ran shivers of cold sweat down his spine.

A man's eye on a knife blade. An eye socket ripped and bleeding. And for what?

Vile, horrible things.

They reached the edge of the waterhole at full speed. Elmar loosed the second pede to take care of itself and Jasper brought the mount they were riding at the time— the one he had stolen from Ravard—to a clattering halt. He leapt down, guided it into a circle and yelled, "Get down and into the centre!" He linked the reins from the mouth rings to the rear mounting handle, pulling them tight so that the pede's head rested against its rear in its normal sleeping position, with himself and Elmar inside the circle of its body. The beast shuttered its eyes, and hunkered down on its softer belly, adopting the posture that was its defence against ziggers.

"Blighted eyes," Elmar muttered, "I really wish you could kill the rainlord way." He flung his cloak over himself and huddled low, face buried in his lap, hand over his ears.

"So do I." Jasper knelt, but remained uncovered; his senses were with the water he had dragged from the hole, with the riders, with the ziggers, those speeding horrors, now well ahead of those who had released them. He dropped the roll of water until it almost touched the earth, then trundled it forward towards riders and ziggers, faster and faster, a giant spool rolling across the plains.

A few of the ziggers flew into it, and drowned as their wings were ripped away. Most simply flew higher over the top. He felt them coming. How many? Forty? Fifty? Hurriedly, he pulled more water out of the waterhole and formed it into a round slab big enough to place across the curled body of the pede, like a lid for a pot.

The next few moments were a chaotic hell within his head. The sense of water on the move bombarded him from all directions. The roll of water. Men on pedes. Some close, some still so distant. Fifty tiny bodies flying this way and that, visible in the air above them although distorted through the water, disappointed to find the soft, tasty human prey out of reach. Some crept into the crevices between the pede segments and pierced the thick skin with their pointed mouthparts to drink the blood. The pede clattered its segments in mild irritation. Other ziggers, frustrated by skin that was too thick for them to eat their way through, continued to seek a passage to their preferred human victims. Keeping track of them all, just in case, was like trying to keep an eye on individual ants after kicking over their nest. At least none headed up the dune towards Terelle and Dibble.

The roll of water was racing now, almost out of his control. Every now and then it skipped along the earth, collecting dust and grit, but it had its own momentum. All he had to do was keep it together.

Some of the Reduners faltered, slowing their mounts. One of their number yelled something, but he was too far away for Jasper to hear the actual words. He hoped it was encouragement. He hoped they'd think there was no reason they couldn't take a deep breath and splash their way through it on their pedes. After all, it was only water… People often underestimated the power of water, especially if they weren't Gibber grubbers who'd watched the rampage of a rush down a drywash.

In his head he pictured what he could feel unfolding. Reduner pedes churning full speed at the water. Then, at the last possible moment, every pede balking. They screeched their fear; he could hear them as they plunged and reared, careening sideways into one another as the water smashed into their faces, travelling fast. The force made it hard for the riders to stay in the saddle. Men fell and were trampled. Panicked animals scattered.

Further away, though, more were coming. He could feel them. *Damn you, Ravard. Why couldn't you just let it be?*

Oh, Mica. Mica.

He turned his attention to the ziggers, detaching pieces from the water over their heads to hurl at them. He chased them with water, damaged their wings, drowned them. Until every one was dead. He let the water fall, soaking himself and Elmar, unable in his exhaustion to return it to the waterhole.

Slowly he got to his feet, his sudden frailty sending him to the panniers for something to eat. "The ziggers are all dead," he told Elmar. "And we've got to get going before the next wave of men hits us."

Elmar stood unsteadily, then dragged himself back onto the pede, his soggy cloak around his shoulders. "I wish I could be of more help," he said. "It's this damned dizziness. The headaches I can put up with." He held up his cloak, heavy with water. "Why the bleeding hells did you drop the water on top of us?"

Jasper went to untie the reins. "I doubt you'll be much good until you can rest instead of riding long hours in the sun. You've managed well, Elmar. And no, I'm not drying your cloak for you." He glanced around for the second pede, only to find it already plodding its way up the dune after its stablemate. He patted Ravard's pede. "This fellow did well, too. Does it have a name, do you know?"

"Ravard called it Chert."

Chert. Blighted eyes.

To remember his friend? Or to show the world he didn't care?

He had no idea. He did not know this man, this Ravard. But then he wasn't sure he knew himself any longer, either. He'd taken the pede on the cusp of his anger as a petty revenge, a boy's silliness when he thought about it, yet he couldn't regret it. It was so withering satisfying to own that pede, to have shown Ravard he was not to be underestimated.

"Chert it is," he said.

He turned the beast towards the slope of the dune, eating as they went so he'd have enough strength to deal with what was to come.

When they were halfway up the wall of sand, he stopped a moment to look back. None of the first group of pursuers was following. They didn't have much choice; most of their pedes were scattered and riderless, heading north in their panic. The second group had arrived on the patch of wet land. Some were helping the injured; others were taking extra men on their pedes—and were turning towards the dune. Jasper sighed. They were going to follow. As he prodded his pede upwards once more, he wearily pulled more water out of the waterhole. The twist of it trailed them up the slope, droplets dripping on the sand to betray his fatigue.

Terelle and Dibble were waiting for them on the crest, their mount grazing in the dip behind them, joined now by its stablemate. Terelle's gaze sought Jasper's, her eyes anxious, as if she could sense the depth of his anguish.

"What happened to you?" Dibble asked Elmar, horrified when he saw the state the armsman was in. "What happened to your eyebrows? The front of your hair's all frizzled!"

"Charred by a flame. It'll grow back."

"You were *burned*?"

"Just...singed. It's sore, but no more than that. I also got clobbered on the head."

"He's been groggy and ill ever since," Jasper added as he slid off the pede. "You drive this animal, Dibble, so you can look after him. Terelle, you go with them. I'll catch up with you shortly. I have to deal with this other lot behind us." He smiled at her as he handed the reins to Dibble.

"Are you all right?" she asked.

"Tired, that's all."

"Is Mica among them?"

He shook his head. "No. And you were right, Terelle. He's not Mica, not any more."

"I'll take Elmar," she said. "Dibble will stay with you."

Without a word, Dibble gave her the reins.

"Don't either of you listen to a word I say?" Jasper asked him, exasperated. "I *am* supposed to be your Cloudmaster."

"Then act like it," Terelle snapped. "You're more important than any single person in the Quartern. Dibble will stay in case you need help."

"I am quite capable of—"

"Perhaps. And perhaps you'll need help," she added, mounting in front of Elmar. The look she gave him was calm and steady—and utterly determined. "I'll ride on slowly."

He watched her go, wondering if the way he felt about her was as obvious as he thought it must be. "Remind me never to argue with her once she's made up her mind," he said to Dibble when they were out of earshot.

"What are you going to do?"

"I am going to kill men," he said.

Them or us. He needed to sleep; the pedes needed time to eat and rest—and they still had a long way to go. The thought made him sick, but it didn't alter his intention by as much as one drop of water.

Lying flat on the sand, he peeped over the edge of the slope. The first pedes were already zigzagging their way upwards, sand sliding under their feet.

He waited patiently until they were three-quarters of the way up. Then he made another tube of water and rolled it downwards. They saw it coming, hauled their mounts to a standstill and tried to hold them steady and calm. Each driver instructed his pede to mantle its eyes, and obediently, they did.

More prepared this time, they might have succeeded in halting the panic if the only weapon coming their way was water, but it wasn't. As the roll descended, Jasper—in his fatigue—allowed it to roll over the sand. It collected more and more grains on the outside. He began to find it difficult to hold together, and water leaked from it in streams. The flow destabilised the slope, which started to slip.

For a moment Jasper watched. The sand-slide started as a small patch eating back into the slope. It widened, grains tumbling into the slide until a thundering wave of sand followed the water. The dune screamed. Water, then sand, hit the men and pedes. Jasper was no longer watching. He was running to join Dibble, vaulting onto his pede and shouting for them to go.

But he couldn't run from what he felt inside his head.

The water that was men and animals jumbled together, bodies contorted, breaking, somersaulting, plunging, suffocating—and dying. The water alive one moment and struggling to go on living...and then life winking out, leaving only something that was still water, but insensate.

One by one they died, and Jasper lived every death.

CHAPTER SIX

Red Quarter
Northern dunes, God's Pellets

Dune Koumwards was twice the height of most dunes. It was on the last stages of its journey towards the Burning Sand-Sea to the north, and it clung to its position within sight of God's Pellets with a tenacity few dunes had ever mastered. Twice its more southerly travelling companions had piled into it, raising its height and increasing its bulk. Each time, it had grown another crusting of plant life for stability.

Its future was far from sure. Perhaps, one day, a gale too strong to resist would come to breach that floral coat. The sand would shuck its skin and ease its way onwards. For now, though, Koumwards brooded over the north, wrinkled with ridges and rucks, frowning with creases and dips, a giant barrier containing a thousand hiding places for an army—but no water. Each plant on Koumwards eked out its existence on the moisture of dew and the skeletons of its predecessors. The dune had no waterhole, and a rain-lord had to dig deep with his power to gain even a hint of the dampness at its heart.

"We're too far north for stormlords," Kaneth said. "It never rains up on Koumwards or the Pellets, which is why Ravard has given only a cursory search for us here."

"And yet Vara found the place." Ryka was struggling up the steep slope of the dune's northernmost ridge on foot, her sandals entangling in the creepers, the thorny seed cases clutching at her pantaloons and digging into her calves. She cursed under her breath.

Far below her, Vara and their warriors were preparing the camp for the night and lighting fires to cook the evening meal. There were more of them than there'd been when they'd left Qanatend. They had not ridden straight for God's Pellets, but had visited numerous tribes on many of the dunes, recruiting more armsmen, with some success.

Nothing like a victory to persuade folk to join your side, the cynic in Ryka thought.

"She is wise, that old woman," Kaneth said, still speaking of Vara. "She remembered all the old legends of the Pellets and the Source she'd been told by her grandmother, and she set off to find it based on the descriptions in the stories. The marvel is that she found a band of young warriors to follow her on her quest. Of course, wind-whispers travel fast on the dunes. She is known as the woman who outwitted Davim and his warriors after they threw her husband's head at her feet. She has a reputation."

"I'm not surprised." *He is fond of her, even though they argue like horned cats in heat.*

He reached the crest and held out a hand to haul her the last pace or two. "That's it," he said with an expansive sweep of his free arm. "God's Pellets."

She gasped. But she was looking directly down, not at

the horizon. The flat plain was staggeringly far below, and it was the first time she had seen a dune with its front slope covered in vegetation.

He grinned at her. "Hey, you're supposed to be looking over there." He jabbed a finger towards the north where a distant grouping of rounded uneven knolls rose from the flatness of the land between Koumwards and the next dune, Burning View.

She squinted at the towering red rock humps that caught the light of the setting sun. "Well, you know I can't see very well. But they do look *huge*."

"Wait until you look up at them from below. Or until you climb to the top of one of those knobs."

"Climb them?" she asked, wondering if it was even possible. *The north is a place built on a grand scale. We are as negligible out here as sand-fleas on a pede, not even worthy of scratching.*

"It takes our sentries about half a sandrun. We have a lookout camp on eight of them. It would be hard for Ravard to creep up on us, even if he thought to look."

"What are your plans for the immediate future?" she asked, a wave of guilt taking her by surprise. Caught up in caring for a baby a mere quarter-cycle old, and sleeping whenever she could, she realised she had not lately played much of a role in Kaneth's life or in forming his vision of the future. "I'm sorry," she said. "I should have asked that question before this."

He placed a finger on her lips. "Don't ever apologise for taking care of our son. Not ever." He enfolded her in his embrace while he pondered her question, a faraway look in his eyes. "The answer? Patrol the dunes to contain Ravard's marauders, recruit as many new warriors as we can, catch and train more wild pedes for our recruits. Those are the short-term goals. Vara refuses to allow an all-out war, and possibly she is right. What's the use of a victory, if it leaves behind a world where there is nothing to salvage?" He paused again, then added, "Long term— once we have a new leader for the dunes and Ravard is dead and his warriors scattered—it will be time to go home, to be a father and a husband, to drink too much amber and grow fat and wise in my old age."

She laughed.

They stood hand in hand and watched the sun set and the shadows lengthen. A wind sprang up, twisting its way along the crest, rippling the leaves around their feet but failing to stir the few patches of exposed sand.

He said, "I'm sorry to bring you back to the dunes after what you went through, but I can't see any way we can stabilise the Red Quarter without this Uthardim fellow playing his part. We both know he's about as substantial as sand twirling in a spindevil, but men have been flocking to join us because of it. I never wanted this, but if I can assemble a real army, large enough to show Ravard he hasn't a chance, and if Jasper brings water to the dunes to show his good faith, well, we might have peace enough for the Reduners to find themselves a worthy sandmaster to rule all the dunes."

"A dunemaster."

"Yes."

"What's your greatest danger?" she asked, thinking of Khedrim's safety.

Again he waved a hand at God's Pellets. "It's a fortress, but fortresses can also be prisons. We bring in new warriors all the time. They are not allowed to go home again until they have proven themselves, and Vara or I grow to trust them, but even so our greatest danger is a traitor within." He paused to consider his own words. "Perhaps traitor is a harsh word to use. Spy, maybe. A hero for the wrong side."

She thought of another question she'd never asked. "Do you think your rainlord abilities will ever return?"

"No."

"Do you miss them?"

"All the time. We'd be a lot safer here if we had a few rainlords."

"Your, er, other ability?"

"It's unreliable. And weird." He ran a hand over the scar on his head. "That wallop on the skull just accentuated the oddness of what was there anyway. You remember how good I was at finding small amounts of hidden water when we were students?"

She nodded.

"I think that ability has edged out all the others. I can sense a tiny film of water, but not a dayjar. Sometimes it tells me about how a person feels. I can sense a frown, or tension in their muscles, or a heart beating faster than normal. I am assuming what I sense is a change in the water within. It is random and not dependable. It's how I found Vara Redmane—I somehow became attuned to the wrinkles in her skin. That's all I felt, but I knew there had to be an old woman up here somewhere."

"And the moving of sand?"

He tensed, and she knew he was remembering what his manipulation of the dune had done to her. She laid her hand on his arm in reassurance.

"When I didn't know who I was, I wasn't even sure I

was the one who was doing it. It was just—instinctive. Reaction rather than premeditated action. Now I've had time to think about it? Deep in the dunes the sand is damp. Perhaps that's the—the presence I feel and which I can move."

Sorcery, magic, or the Sunlord's blessing? Unnatural and blasphemous, or supernatural and blessed? Ryka was shrivelled if she could see the difference between water-sense and whatever it was that Kaneth had.

I'm scared of it, though, she thought. *It almost killed me and I don't believe he has the slightest idea of what he can unleash.*

But who knew? Maybe it would save them all in the end. Still, she shivered. She was a scholar, and scholars liked to understand things. She said, "If any other Reduners can feel the dunes the way you can, no wonder they speak of dune gods. This might be what shamans feel. After all, they are water sensitives. Maybe their ritual to find a new shaman is not so silly."

"How do they do it?"

"The men of the dune run down one of the steep slopes. If the dune sings under the feet of one of them, he's the new shaman. Maybe he actually starts the singing by touching the dampness within the dune."

He winced. "I'd rather be just an ordinary rainlord. Ry, I don't *want* to be Uthardim. I want this all to be over, so that we can be at peace again. I have you and Kedri. The idea that I might die in some pointless battle—" He gave a half-laugh. "Once it was adventure, and dying didn't seem to matter much. Now even the thought of it hurts because I have so much to live for."

"All the more reason why I don't want you to go after

Ravard just because you want revenge for what he did to me. It no longer matters, not to either of us."

He didn't speak, but drew her back into his arms and buried his face in her hair. "Don't ask me to forgive someone for hurting you, someone who tried to usurp my place as a father to Kedri. That's too much to expect."

And perhaps it was.

She changed the subject. "Do you mind that I named him after a Reduner boy?"

"Khedrim? That helpful youngster from Ravard's camp? Likeable, obliging lad, but a shade simple. I did wonder what made you choose the name."

"He's dead. I accidentally killed him when I escaped."

"Ah."

She waited for him to say something else.

"Ry, do you need the reminder of something so—so obviously tragic?"

"It's the least I can do for him. Khedrim the Reduner was a *nice* child. Bland words, but true. He would have made a fine, if simple man. He never will, because his path crossed mine."

"Ah. All right then. I call him Kedri anyway." The look in his eyes softened. "He looks like a Kedri."

She laughed again. He always could make her laugh.

They watched until the light dimmed, then walked back to the camp. She shivered in the evening chill and he draped an arm around her shoulders. "Cold?"

She shook her head. "Just thinking. Something made me remember Taquar. He's still alive, you know. Iani has him hidden."

"And you think that's a mistake?"

"Well, I understand why Jasper wanted it that way—in

case he needs Taquar to help him make storms again. But
for all that, I think it's a mistake. You don't put a man like
Taquar in a prison and expect him to stay there."

He didn't answer. It was a sobering thought.

The following morning they rode on to God's Pellets and
arrived just after midday.

From the outside, each entrance to the valley appeared
only as an indent among tens of such indents and creases
that led nowhere. Eight of these indents opened up to narrow canyons that led into the interior, four to the north,
one to the east and three to the south.

"How did you ever find your way in?" Ryka asked Vara
in the language of the dunes as she studied the approach
and failed to identify the entrance they were heading
towards. But then, with her poor eyesight, she didn't really
expect to.

"Saw wild pedes swallowed up by the rock, I did. Followed them. They were coming inside for the water and
the grazing. Still do occasionally, but they use one of the
northern entrances now, as far as they can get from our
camp. Got some of the lads taming the herd so we can
cull them every so often for mounts."

They rode into one of the indents, which opened out
into a narrow, winding crevasse. Ryka craned her neck at
the ribbon of sky above. The rock walls, fissured and
cracked, towered straight up. A prison, Kaneth had said,
but a trap was the term that occurred to her.

Her heart faltered. *Oh, sun-blighted damn*, she thought.
*Having a baby makes you a terrible coward. You worry
yourself sick about things that haven't even happened yet
and likely never will.* She looked down at Kedri's downy

head, peeping out of the sling she wore to hold him resting on her chest. He made her feel as soft as bab mush and about as vulnerable. Just looking at him could curl her lips into a smile.

The slim passage divided twice and finally opened out into the central valley. Her eyes widened in astonishment. She had never imagined anything like this. The valley floor was flat and green, the edges bobbled with clumps of trees. Ten miles or more in length, two miles wide, and as far as she could make out, the opposite side was just as steep and rocky as the one they had come through. These weren't hills so much as stone walls pockmarked with cave openings and decorated all the way to the rounded knobs on top with strange shadowed holes, like the artwork of a giant sculptor.

Mostly, though, she was overwhelmed with the feel of water all around her. The sensation was so new the hairs stood up on her arms.

"Wither me wilted," she murmured to Kaneth. "Everything is wet! And yet I didn't sense any of that from outside. There's water in the soil, did you know that? And in those grasses, too."

"The pedes love it. Although the wild ones never stay more than a day or two."

She looked around in awe. "I've never seen so much green. And look at the size of those trees!"

He nodded.

"I've read about places like this," she said. "But they were always on the Other Side, not in the Quartern. And Jasper told me Russet the waterpainter says there are green places in Khromatis, too. Which is the cave with the water?"

"The Source? There." He pointed to a large opening several miles away to the left, one of the few places where trees did not border the rock. When she frowned, trying to see it properly, he said, "I'll take you there." He urged their pede in that direction. The other riders all headed to the right, where a substantial encampment had been built in amongst the trees bordering the southern side of the valley. It seemed an odd place for a camp until she remembered Reduners allowed neither camps nor pedes anywhere near a water supply for fear of contaminating it.

"One day we should build a city here," Kaneth said. "When we have peace and all the uncertainty is over."

She stared at the back of his head, dumbfounded.

"Us? But you are a Scarperman," she said. *And I'm a Scarpen rainlord.* "And this is the Red Quarter."

"Yes, and I'm mist-gathering, I suppose. I would never spoil this place, the valley. This is somehow sacred. I don't know to whom or what, and I don't care, but I do know there are some places that shouldn't be changed, and this is one of them."

"So where would you put a city? Koumwards will eventually come and cover all this up."

"Not the valley. Look at it. It's never been filled with sand. If Koumwards does move, I think it'll flow around it, like the waters of a rush down a drywash parted by a rock. If a city was built on the northern side, it would be protected, too. And I don't mean a Scarpen city, either. It has to be Reduner." He added in a murmur more to himself than her, "There must be a way of piping the water from the Source without damaging the valley."

Drawing rein in front of the cave, he helped her down and they walked hand in hand up a slope of smooth stone into the mouth of the cavern. The opening was a vast maw, as tall as two pedes end to end, the roof behind it high and cavernous, the depth to the back perhaps as much as two hundred paces. The lake, the Source—according to the folk tales, the Over-god's gift to the dunes—lay as still as the rock itself. It covered the back half of the cave.

Letting go of Kaneth's hand, she walked deeper inside to see better. When she looked up, she could see glow-worms in the dark recesses of the roof, steely glints of light like a thousand distant stars. When she looked down at the water, each glimmer was caught in perfect reflection.

She knelt beside the water and cupped some in her hand to drink. The ripples raced across the surface like living things, splintering the reflections into dancing light and dark. Sipping from her hand, she drank. Cold and pure, some of the water splashed onto Khedrim's head and he startled, jerking his arms and legs in reflex. His eyes sprang open and he wriggled, twisting in her arms, squawking like an unfledged bird responding to its parent's return to the nest. She smiled and murmured words of comfort to him, but he turned and struggled still more. If he had been a little older, she would have sworn he was trying to wriggle out of her arms into the water.

"Look, Kaneth," she said, "I think he wants to dive into the lake!"

She glanced to where he was standing, further back near the entrance, a blurred silhouette against the brightness of the outside light. He didn't reply and his stillness seemed unnatural to her. Panicking, she hurriedly stood and strode to his side.

"What is it?" she asked. "What's wrong?"

"Memories," he said, his voice husky. "It was here that Vara brought back my memories of you. It was here she—she *altered* me. Changed me from Uthardim back to Kaneth." He reached out to grasp her hand, to draw her close and bury his face in her hair. "She saved me, Ryka."

"The god can cure you," she said from where she stood, next to that cold, still lake of water in the cavern. "Come, bend over the brazier. Inhale the smoke."

Old, wrinkled, nearly toothless, her red skin creped like the ridged crust of a salt pan, her dark bab-kernel eyes boring into him…Was she wise or misguided? He couldn't tell. Elmar was glaring at him, signalling him not to trust a Reduner. The herbs burning in the flames smelled pungent, heady. The dagger she wore was kept wickedly sharp and in constant use, whether trimming the point of her pede's feet or skinning an animal for the pot. Every night by the light of the campfire, there she was, playing with that blighted blade of hers. The warriors she led were polite and wary when they spoke to her. They knew she could be a dangerous woman, for all that she was as old and wrinkled as a dried bab fruit.

But his head ached so, and the fringe of memories tormented him, never coming into focus. Ravard's woman, Garnet—what had she meant to him? Was the child she carried really his? He sought the knowledge, but it slipped by, just out of reach. Somewhere inside, he knew he wanted to thrust Uthardim away, together with his strange abilities; he wanted Kaneth the rainlord back.

So when Vara had beckoned to him, he'd gone. And now, in further obedience, he knelt by the brazier and bent to inhale. The smoke swirled, entered his head and he was swept away in a hazy, potent mist.

Later—how much later?—he felt himself walking. Tentative steps, feeling his way. He was in a thick fog, strong with herb smells, too dense to see anything. He walked on, groping blindly mile upon mile through that eerie, drifting obscurity, only gaining surety when it finally thinned. Voices from the past called out to him. Long-forgotten family members, childhood friends, girls he had bedded, men he had fought, teachers he had learned from. Events jostled to be remembered; fun begged to be recalled. He ignored them all as he strove to find the present.

His tottering steps became the confident strides of a warrior. Freeing himself of the last curling wisps entangling his legs, he emerged into a sunlit world. In the distance, Vara's camp bustled in morning sunshine. But it had been evening when he had bent over the brazier...

He glanced back over his shoulder, expecting to see mist; instead he was gazing into the depths of the Overgod's cave through its huge maw. When he turned to face forward, it was to see Elmar hurrying towards him, anxiety written in every crease of his frown.

And in his head, he was Kaneth Carnelian. Where the hell was he? What was going on? His last truly clear memory was fighting a Reduner in the Breccian waterhall.

The Red Quarter, that was it. He was Uthardim. No he wasn't. He was a slave. No he wasn't—he'd escaped.

He battled to remember his time as Uthardim. Garnet was just a name. He struggled with that. But there was something he had to remember about her... something...

And then the horror hit him. Ryka. Blighted eyes help

*him, had she died there in the Breccia waterhall? He
reached out to find her water, to touch her presence—but
there was nothing. Just her absence. No, worse: no water
anywhere. No feel of it in people or pedes or anything. He
was as water-blind as a lowlevel street sweeper.*

*He grabbed at Elmar, desperate for answers. "Ryka?
Where is she? What happened to her? Do you know?"*

*But even as he asked the question, Garnet's face and
Ryka's melded into one. He struggled to comprehend.*

*Elmar opened his mouth to say something, but Kaneth
cut him short. "You lied," he said. "She would never
have stayed on the Watergatherer to have our child. Not
Ryka. Not with that man. Why did you lie?"*

*And that was when Elmar told him she had died. That
Ravard had murdered her.*

He looked over her shoulder to the lake. "This is where I
was reborn. Here is where I remembered you and lost you
in the very next moment, believing you were dead, and
Kedri with you." He wanted to say more, but couldn't.
Words and emotion seemed inextricably mired in his
throat, choking him. She looked away, as if she could not
cope with his pain.

Head averted, she said softly, "It's over now. We are
together and safe."

"Yes," he said.

But deep inside, he wondered.

Ravard was still alive.

CHAPTER SEVEN

Scarpen Quarter
Breccia City
Breccia Hall, Level Two
Sun Temple, Level Three

"Where the salted wells is my green silk?" Fuming, Lord Laisa Drayman, widow of the last Highlord Nealrith of Breccia and wife of Taquar Sardonyx, rifled through clothing, most of which was heaped on the floor of her wardrobes. "And my fox fur cloak? Did the servants steal the clothes I left behind? Even some of my underthings have vanished."

The middle-aged woman standing behind her didn't flinch. "I heard the hall servants got themselves killed or taken as slaves, m'lord. I doubt they had much of a chance to pinch stuff." She shrugged. "The Reduners, now..."

Laisa frowned, eyeing her with more attention. "Watch your tongue."

"You asked me something, so I answered. That's not being cheeky, I promise you. I need this job."

Laisa dropped the dress she'd been holding. "You

weren't a servant here before, surely. I don't remember you."

"No, m'lord. My name's Ara. I was the wife of a gold-smith down on Level Five. When the Reduners came, he died, as did my sons. The gold was stolen, the shop wrecked. Heard there was work to be had here in exchange for food and water, so I came. Can't say as the food is plentiful, though."

"We're all hungry," Laisa snapped. The whole city, once the richest in the Quartern, was now reliant on what help the other Scarpen cities would send, and it was infuriating.

The door to the adjoining room opened just then, and Senya Almandine stepped in, her brows drawn together in a glower. "Mama, no one has cleaned my room," she said in a tone of hurt perplexity. "There's blood on the floor and the bedding isn't clean and there's no fuel in the water room and someone peed in my—"

"All right, all right," her mother interrupted, flinging up her hands in exasperation. "No more." She nodded at Ara. "See to it that my daughter's room is cleaned first, then mine, and that we are both supplied with water and clean linen."

"Clean linen?" The woman snorted at the idea, but she bobbed her head in terse acknowledgement and left, shutting the door behind her. Laisa sighed. "I am afraid it will be quite a while before things are back to normal, Senya. We have to make the best of it. Come, let's see if we can find a meal somewhere."

Senya made no move to leave the room. She settled her-self on her mother's bed, her expression sour. "Why did we come here? Why didn't we go to Scarcleft instead? It's much nicer there. They haven't had a war, and Seneschal Harkel will see that we're properly cared for even though Jasper and Iani have Highlord Taquar imprisoned somewhere."

Laisa suppressed an unmaternal desire to shake some sense into her daughter, and regarded her with concern instead. *She lacks guile...but she is far from innocent. That's a dangerous mix. Sunlord love me, what did I give birth to?*

As if she'd noticed her mother's flash of annoyance, Senya added in concern, "There's not even a proper physician here to look after your arm."

"My arm is fine. It's healing nicely. But I do wish you would spend a little more time thinking things through. I imagine Seneschal Harkel is dead, my dear."

Senya's eyes widened. "He is? He was fine when we left Scarcleft, wasn't he?"

"He was a prisoner, and Lord Iani was in charge. Do you really think Iani the Sandcrazy would have allowed Harkel to live? Besides, you need to be here in Breccia because this is where Jasper will be. You two must marry very soon indeed."

"How can we, when that outlander snuggery girl hangs around him? He loves her, not me! She's the one who went to Qanatend with him."

"I'm afraid he does, but that has *nothing* to do with marriage. Do you think I loved your father? Of course not. One marries for position or wealth or security, not love."

Senya appeared unsurprised. Instead she remarked, "I did hear she was leaving."

"Who? Terelle?" Laisa looked at her with interest. "Who told you? And to go where?"

"Back to her grandfather." She pursed her lips in thought. "Or was it great-grandfather? Or great-great-grandfather?"

"Where did you hear this?"

"I hung around the back of Jasper's tent one night before the battle—she sleeps with him, did you know that? I told Lord Gold she was a whore. He promised he would see to it that she was sent back where she came from. But when he spoke to Jasper about it, Jasper was furious. He wanted Lord Gold to return with us to Breccia. Gold refused, of course, but he was in such a foul mood all the time." Her face lit up. "He hates Terelle."

"You spoke to Basalt? There are times when you truly surprise me. But you have to learn...*subtlety*. It wouldn't do to be caught eavesdropping."

Senya smiled, a dazzling smile of pride. "No one caught me!"

Forgetting her intention to seek out food in the kitchens, Laisa sat beside Senya on the bed. "Perhaps you should tell me all you overheard."

"Well, a lot of it didn't make sense. Stuff about those waterpaintings she does all the time. Terelle was trying to make them sound important so Jasper would think more of her. But she did say something about having to go to Samphire soon—that's in Alabaster, isn't it?—because her great-whatever-grandfather was there. It sounded as if he was ill. And then they talked about her going to Crow-wherever-it-is."

"Khromatis?"

"Khromatis. Is that the land on the other side of the White Quarter? I think I remember the name from history lessons. Lord Gold says they're all blasphemers there.

Anyway, I didn't understand what they were talking about. None of it made sense. Oh, Jasper was worried about whether he could keep shifting clouds."

"That's not good news," Laisa said in dismay. "I did wonder how he's managed as well as he has. Senya, there is something odd about that girl and her waterpainting."

"It's just stupid stuff. She's got sand for brains."

"I'm not so sure." She stood and began to pace. "I suspect this grandfather of hers is the outlander who did the waterpaintings for us in Breccia."

"The ones we had in the entrance hall?"

"Yes. Do you remember the last waterpainting we had? Of the woman riding a black pede across a white land? The woman it portrayed was Terelle, I'm sure. I finally made the connection."

"Really? How odd! But what does it matter?"

"Odd things have a way of being important." Laisa stopped her pacing and turned to face her daughter. "She took her painting things that day Jasper and Taquar had their fight in Scarcleft Hall. You were there, not me. Tell me, what did she paint?"

"It was so silly. She started painting before they even began fighting. She did a picture of the courtyard."

"That's all? No people?"

"Not that I saw. It was just the empty courtyard where they were going to fight."

"What was she doing while they were fighting?"

"Still painting, I think. But I didn't really look. I was watching the fight."

"What happened to the painting afterwards?"

Senya frowned, trying to remember. "I never did see it."

"Think, Senya. It was in a tray and the tray was full of water. What did she do with that?"

"Oh, I remember! She poured the water onto a potted tree near the gate. She carried the empty tray away. There was no painting in it."

"Was she carrying a rolled-up painting?"

"No. Just her painting things in that string bag of hers. If she had the painting with her, it must have been all scrunched up in the bag." She paused, then added, "That *is* odd, come to think of it, because she told Taquar she was going to do the painting as a record of the fight. Like it was important history, or something."

Laisa murmured, more to herself than to Senya, "Even more interesting is why she did all those weird paintings of dead ziggers *before* we enticed the little stinkers to the lanterns."

"You mean, like she was painting something that hadn't happened yet?"

Laisa stared thoughtfully at her daughter, her lips parted in wonderment. She said slowly, "That is an interesting way of looking at it. Jasper's explanation was that Terelle is superstitious and believes she can kill ziggers by painting them dead." She fiddled with the beads at her neck, her mind in ferment. *No one can paint the future, surely?* Whispers of sorcery always abounded among lowlevellers and the ignorant, but that was just superstition...wasn't it? "You know, I think I need to speak to Lord Gold as soon as he gets back from Qanatend. And I think perhaps you need to go and visit your cousins in Breakaway until Terelle disappears out of Jasper's life."

Senya brightened. "Oh, good! They give lots of parties,

and the market there is full of things from across the Giving Sea."

Laisa stared at her, wondering why her daughter was giving no thought to another reason she needed to disappear from Breccia for a while: her pregnancy would soon be obvious.

The Sun Temple, like most of the uplevel buildings in Breccia, was scarred with the marks of fierce fighting. The waterpriests had sold themselves dearly during the battle for Breccia. Except for Basalt, of course. He'd somehow managed to escape the city before it had fallen. Laisa felt her lip curling with disgust when she thought about it, but it was a pointless emotion. Like it or not, Basalt was an ally, and she would be foolish to antagonise him.

The day after he returned to Breccia from Qanatend, she made her way to the Temple. In the aftermath of the battle, anything valuable, especially if it had been trimmed with gold or gemstones, had vanished—yet when she was ushered into the Sunpriest's battered office, Basalt was clad in the full vestments of a Lord Gold and wearing a sunpriest's gold insignia. After greeting her, he spoke to her at boring length about his experiences in Qanatend, and it was some time before she was able to question him about Terelle's waterpainting of Jasper's fight with Highlord Taquar.

He replied readily. "Yes, I remember. Or rather, I remember her doing it. I didn't actually see the result."

The look Basalt gave her was avid with his love of intrigue and gossip. *Watergiver above, I do so loathe the man. He's genuinely nasty. And that makes him a fool. Nastiness is* such *a waste of time and talent unless it has a purpose.* If there was no point in antagonising someone, it was so much wiser to be pleasant to them. Still, she wasn't going to be so misguided as to underestimate the Sunpriest.

Elbows on the Sunpriest's desk, Basalt regarded her over his steepled fingers. "Why do you ask?"

"I understand Terelle has to leave to visit her ailing grandfather in the White Quarter. Lord Jasper hankers after the girl, although I find it difficult to see why. She may have had a snuggery background, but she hardly seems beguiling." The remark was honest rather than spiteful; but then, she wasn't a man. "However, that's beside the point. I just want to make sure that she does not feel free to return to the Scarpen once she's left. It's in my interest for my daughter to become the wife of the Cloud-master, and it may also be in your interest, too. That is unlikely to occur if he's constantly enticed to the bed of another."

"That's certainly true. But, forgive me, Lord Laisa, I fail to see the connection to her waterpainting."

"Senya tells me Terelle told you she was painting the fight to preserve the scene for posterity. Yet she destroyed the artwork."

He looked at her blankly. "Yes, that's right."

She kept silent.

"Ah, I see your point. If it was to record a historic moment, why did she not keep it safe?"

"Exactly."

"Maybe it was just poorly executed and she decided to throw it away."

"On the other hand, if it was some form of sorcerous magic, designed to influence the fight—"

Basalt froze. When he spoke again, his words and the anticipatory gleam of his gaze were at variance. "It would explain why a man of Taquar's skill and experience was defeated and sorely injured by an untried coward of a youth. Despicable!"

"Utterly."

Another pause from him, then he said, "The lords of Khromatis call themselves Watergivers, or so I have heard. A presumptuous, blasphemous race."

"They are indeed."

He fiddled with the quill on his desk, then began to trim the point with his dagger. "I have heard rumours that they are much feared for their power: that they hold sway over the commoners through forbidden arts."

"Is waterpainting one of those arts?"

He pursed his lips to blow the quill clippings away. "I don't know. I know no details of their sorcery. They hide what they are."

"Which itself is suspicious, surely."

"I've heard talk of Guardians who exist to keep Khromatians safe behind their borders. I've even heard that the salt-dancers of the Whiteout are the Guardians, taunting travellers until they lose their way on the salt and die."

Laisa assumed an expression of worried concern. "I have an uncomfortable feeling about Terelle Grey's waterpainting. There is—I hesitate to say it, for it seems ridiculous—some slight evidence to suggest that what she paints becomes the future."

Basalt's eyes widened. "Sunlord save us!" For a moment he was speechless, then added, "Surely that can't be right. Think of the *power* she would have." His horror was unfeigned.

"Exactly. And the stormlord is in love with her."

"If she's dabbling in such wickedness, she must be stopped. But how can we find out if it's true? She's hardly likely to tell us. I did hear she was returning to Breccia with the stormlord." He drummed his fingers on his desk while he thought over the problem. "Trouble is, the rules of our one true faith demand clear-cut proof when it comes to accusations of this nature. We'd have to be careful before giving utterance to any allegation. It would be a terrible shame to accuse anyone unjustly."

"Especially because soon there will be a meeting of the Council of Waterpriests to endorse your position as Lord Gold," Laisa said, careful not to allow any touch of her cynicism to tinge her tone.

"Indeed. I must find proof. Or at the very least wait until after the council meets before launching an official investigation."

"My understanding is that she won't be staying here too long. She has to leave for Alabaster and possibly even Khromatis. I'm not sure there would be time to find any proof before she goes, especially when it is a hard thing to prove anyway." She placed an elbow on his desk, balanced her chin in her cupped palm, and mused, "If a few wind-whispers were to be heard when she and Lord Jasper return to Breccia, it would be a shame, but I suspect it will happen."

"It could," he agreed.

"Of course, once she's gone to the White Quarter, it would be hard for her to refute anything of a more specific nature. She could be accused of blackening Taquar's name with her dark arts. Gossip is a powerful tool and it could cast doubts about my husband's guilt and his unjust and arbitrary imprisonment. If people fear her and her waterpainting, how will she ever be able to return to the Scarpen, let alone marry the stormlord? I imagine that priests might rail against waterpainting from the temple balconies on Sun Days, if the Sunpriest—after research into the phenomenon—uncovered the sorcerous nature of the art."

There was a lengthy silence. Then Basalt—Lord Gold and Sunpriest presumptive of the Quartern—gave a slow smile. "You could be right, Lord Laisa. Indeed, you could."

CHAPTER EIGHT

Red Quarter
Dune Watergatherer

The man praying at the shrine was the Watergatherer Sandmaster, master of every tribe on the dune. Praying to the dune god was expected of him. Everyone knew that if the god was respected, then the dune dwellers prospered.

And so he prayed. Sometimes he thought he even heard the god stir and murmur something, but whether it was a promise of victory or a prophecy of disaster and defeat, he had no idea. Most of all he wanted an answer, any answer, and it disturbed him that he never heard one, not really. Underneath the veneer of the warrior sandmaster, beneath the leader who strove to become the sandmaster of *all* the dunes, there was one part of him that was hardly more than a youth. One part of him that was a Gibber grubber who had become a tribemaster called Ravard.

Now Ravard One Eye. He touched the red eye patch he wore, and rose to his feet, dusting the sand from his knees.

He looked up at the finger of stone pointing upwards to the sky. It should have fallen in the landslip, but it had stayed where it was, rooted deep in the dune as the sands had slipped away from it. The visible part of the stone was now much longer than it had been, and the base wider. The dunesmen regarded that as a miracle, a sign that in spite of everything his tribe was still favoured by the dune god, and he was still the god's favoured son. The disaster of defeat in battle had been Davim's fault, not his, they said. That belief had become part of his legend, adhered to even by the men of Davim's tribe. Emerging from his tent alive after battling a stormlord was enough to further that legend; to have plucked out his own eye to save his life from a rogue zigger had made him an admired hero.

That was not the truth, of course; Ravard knew full well that Shale had been the one to remove the zigger and his eyeball. Just the sort of daft thing the Gibber grubber would indulge in—trying to help him, as if it was possible to go back to the past, to when they'd been brothers supporting one another. Those times had been nothing glorious anyway, certainly not anything worth remembering.

He hadn't told anyone he'd wrested Lord Jasper's dagger from his hand and used it to spear his own eyeball; they'd made that assumption when they'd found him clutching the bloodied knife and staggering towards the door of the tent. God save him, he remembered the horror of it yet, the appalling agony and matching despair that had gripped him so tightly he had not been able to move or cry out. Ironically, it had been that action of Shale's that made Ravard's continued position as sandmaster of Watergatherer so remarkably easy. He would have liked to tell his brother that to mock him for the stupidity of his compassion.

And yet...

And yet. His little brother, Shale.

No, he mustn't think about what might have been. The only way was the one that lay ahead. He was going after Uthardim and Garnet. Kaneth and Ryka, rainlords. His men would support him in that; less risky than challenging a stormlord. Time enough to think about the Scarpen when he controlled all the dunes . . .

He turned away from the shrine to see Kher Medrim plodding his way up towards him—Davim's uncle, still the Warrior Son just as he had been for Davim, although the man complained he was too old now.

He strode down the path to meet him. "Kher Medrim, welcome. I've been expecting you. Any success with the task I gave you?" He clapped the elderly man on the shoulder, genuinely glad to see him.

"The lad is yours." Medrim clasped his arm, smiling. "A clever plan to seek him out and offer something he couldn't resist."

He grinned. "Ah, just a matter of blood running true. How could a son of Davim's be anything but ambitious and brave and a leader? Come, have a drink with me and tell me all about it." He led the way to the bench and chairs in the covered area next to his new tent. It was cooler there as the breeze skittered down the slope of the vale and funnelled between the tents. His latest bed mate, without being asked, brought them both a steaming mug of herbal mix and fresh-grilled yam crisps, then left them to talk.

"A better cook than your Breccian slave," Medrim remarked, tasting a crisp. "What was her name? Garnet?"

"That wouldn't be difficult," he said dryly. "Come, tell me about this eldest son of Davim's from Dune Hungry One."

"Promising lad. Eighteen, nineteen. That randy bastard of a nephew of mine sired him when he was no more than fourteen!" He chuckled, showing teeth yellowed and cracked with age.

"A warrior?"

"Indeed. Skilled. Arrogant as a half-grown horned cat, and as dangerous. Ambitious as ever Davim was. Resentful, just as you thought he'd be. In that particular tribe, his father is despised as the man who refused to marry one of the tribe's daughters even though he got her breeding. The lad's mother, a bitch called Robena, keeps her humiliation alive, fool that she is. He's more than ready for a woman in his bed, and blood on his blade. Instead she keeps him at her side. The other youths tease him, the girls laugh. Yet he's all Davim's son. Strong, tough, unsentimental, a fighter who'll leave bodies in his wake like a pede trampling a pebblemouse den."

"You offered him the post of my Warrior Son if he proves his worth in Uthardim's betrayal?"

"Yes. I gave him a year. He has to give us the location of their camp and all their weaknesses in less than a star cycle. He jumped at the chance. Brilliant strategy, Kher. Damned if I can figure how you knew it would work." He raised his mug to his sandmaster. "How's the eye?"

"The socket doesn't trouble me. Being without an eye does, though. It hampers my ability to fight. I'm learning to compensate by using my water-senses. I took your advice and have been training a battle partner to cover my left-hand side. But tell me more about this get of Davim's. His name? And what are his beads?"

"Clevedim. Calls himself Cleve." He chuckled again. "Because it makes people think of cleaving, I suppose.

And his beads are devil's dice. Young men—they're all the same. Scrambling after names and symbols that make them seem bigger men than they are. Devil's dice are just lemonite. Like Jasper Bloodstone." He snorted. "Why Bloodstone? It's just another name for green jasper with red spots, but it makes him sound bloodthirsty. Misnamed, if ever there was a misnaming. The fellow won't even stop our water because he can't bear the thought of children thirsting. He forgets children grow up into warriors or become the mothers of warriors."

Citrine, Ravard reflected. And then wondered why he had suddenly remembered his little sister. Not giving himself time to pursue the thought, he asked, "How does this Cleve think he's going to get into Uthardim's camp? We've had no success with anyone we've tried to plant among them."

"He reckons all he has to do is wait for Uthardim's men to come to him. He's not going to hide his parentage. Apparently, the rainlord Kher has recruiters visiting all the camps that aren't wholehearted in their support of us. He's taking their strongest and best, and Clevedim is certainly that. They haven't been to his tribe yet—it's one of the most remote." He drained his mug, took another piece of yam and added, "Now I must be on my way back to my own camp if I am to arrive by nightfall."

"I'll come with you," Ravard said, standing up at the same time as the older man did. "I want to see Islar."

"But if we have Cleve, we won't need Islar."

"If one sand-tick hidden on a man's arse can draw blood where it hurts, what do you think two could do?"

Medrim chuckled. "Give him more to itch?"

*   *   *

Islar, the older of Davim's two legitimate sons, had newly
been accorded warrior status. At fourteen cycles in age,
he wasn't old enough to challenge a tribemaster, let alone
to think he could be sandmaster. Yet Ravard had the
uncomfortable feeling that such a challenge would occur
one day. People expected it and many of them would urge
Islar to try when the time came.

To stave off any jealousy in the lad, he'd promised Islar
the position of tribemaster of Davim's tribe as soon as he
was eighteen, but already he'd seen the first signs that
Islar was becoming a focal point for the disaffected of the
dune, which was annoying. He *liked* Islar. He was enthu-
siastic, a hard worker, a talented fighter. Quiet, serious
and tough, too.

As he sat with what had been Davim's family—his two
sons, his wife and his brother—eating a meal and speaking of general tribal matters, Ravard thought of what Kher
Medrim had said about the choice of beads. Islar, he was
amused to note, had threaded his hair with ice quartz.
The crystals, clear and cold, were supposed to be a focus
for visionary wisdom. They were generally not favoured
by warriors though, not when they so easily caught the
sunlight and could send a flash across miles of dune. Not
something you wanted to be wearing if there was tribal
rivalry or dune wars.

As the afternoon cooled, he indicated to the lad that he
wanted a private conversation and suggested they take a
walk. Islar agreed with alacrity, obviously proud to think
the new sandmaster wanted to consult him.

Ravard curbed his amusement, wondering just when
he himself had suddenly become old enough to notice
such things and find them entertaining. As they followed

the path the women took to collect water, he remarked, "So now you're a true warrior of the tribe. And I hear good things from your uncle about your progress on the training grounds. He says you're becoming renowned for your extraordinary courage."

"You honour me, Kher." The boy's admiring glance went to Ravard's eye patch.

"There are other tasks that need courage, ones even harder to perform. It's one of those I want to ask your advice about."

"I—well, of course. Anything."

"Here's the problem. Your uncle Kher Medrim and I have a plan to bring down the rebel Reduners, but to make it work we need someone who doesn't look like a threat to them. A woman, perhaps. Or a girl. Or at least, someone obviously not an experienced, battle-scarred warrior. Someone who understands the Quartern tongue as well as ours. And the person must be unknown to any of the warriors who are with this fake Uthardim and Vara Redmane."

He paused to let Islar think, then added, "This person would be going into the enemy camp to serve the enemy in whatever way they to use him or her. Cleaning the out-houses, maybe. Think about that. They'd be friendless and alone, cut off from all family and help and comfort. And once they learned information of use to us, they'd have to find a way to escape. They could die in the attempt. In fact, they could die in the attempt to *enter* the rebel forces. We do have a plan for getting in, but it'll involve an injury."

"Isn't it, er, dishonourable to spy?"

"It's dishonourable for a man to pretend to be a

reincarnated Reduner hero and to divide the dunes against one another! It's dishonourable to take water handouts from Scarpen street grubbers who sleep between walls and use water to keep themselves rich and powerful."

They had reached the camp's waterhole, and he guided Islar to the rocky edge. At one end, bab palms thrived in patches of soil. Along the rocky sides, jute plants grew in every pocket of soil they could find. A creeper of desert runner cascaded in a shower of red blossom from the rim downwards, falling free until it touched the surface of the water.

Ravard continued, "All that water, every drop of it, was sent to us by men who gifted it with generous smiles and sweet words, even as they stabbed us in the back. We can't ride our land any longer, free to come and go where we want. They wall us in with rules and taxes and laws and their water gifts. We grew soft and forgot how to find our own water, forgot how to roam as the dune drovers we are: nomads, free and untrammelled. To cast off those shackles was your father's dream. Now it's mine. But the rainlords and the stormlord combine to prevent it ever happening. How can we find random rain if all random clouds are seized and used before they ever come our way? They're the dishonourable ones, and if we must use a spy to purge ourselves of their dishonour, then we will."

Islar glanced at him, and his voice held a tinge of awe. "You can feel that way, even though you weren't born on the dunes?"

"It's the dune gods who make Reduners, not where we were born. That's the true glory of the dunes. Remember, the gods guided the original Uthardim here from the white-skinned south." He smiled. "In the end we all share a red skin and red hair, a red land, black pedes and the language of the dunes. That is what makes you and me drovers.

"And now we seek a new hero. Or heroine. Islar, we don't even know where these men hide. They must use rain-lord sorcery to conceal their camp and supply themselves with water, otherwise we'd have found them before now. Your father hunted for Vara's camp, and now we're trying. We've decided the best way is to plant a spy. I have men who'd be delighted to try—but every one of them would run the risk of being recognised as a Dune Watergatherer armsman. The rebels would never trust a recruit from our dune."

"They don't know *me*," Islar said quietly.

Ravard allowed the silence that followed to extend until Islar began to fidget. Then he gripped the lad's shoulder. "Well, I must admit your name did come up when Medrim and I were discussing this. But we decided that it was too dangerous to risk a son of Davim's." He touched his eye patch in wordless illustration. "You will one day be my Master Son. These are dangerous times and I need an heir who's near grown. Besides, over the years, people have seen the sons of Davim. You could be recognised."

"Look at me, Kher. And remember Islar as you knew him when you lived in my father's encampment. I was not in the battles for the Scarpen because I was too young. I'm only recently braided, fully armed and mounted. A cycle back, I was a child. Since then, I've grown a hand span taller, broadened at the shoulder and built muscle. A cycle ago I looked like a boy. Now I am a youth—not old enough to be feared by a man, true, yet changed enough to be unrecognisable by those who once saw a child playing around a camp. And unlike my little brother, I don't resemble my father."

"That's true. Your voice is breaking, too." He paused again, as if to consider.

"Really, if I was to join the rebels, no one'd know me. And Father insisted I learn the Quartern tongue from our caravanners."

For a moment Ravard was washed by an irrational wave of jealousy; he wanted to be like Islar, young and free and brave and in search of adventure...Instead, he was weighed down by decisions and troubles, water shortages and the desertions of dune warriors, the divisions between the tribes and their differing visions for the future. He released his grip on Islar's shoulder and infused his tone with doubt. "I suppose it could be possible, if we thought of a good story."

Islar leaned forward and said passionately, "I want those people *dead*. That man who pretends to be Uthardim the hero. The whore with him, who revealed herself as a rainlord. And Vara, that withered old woman, pretending to be a dune warrior! She mocks us. If I cannot escape and get information back to you, then at least I can kill them, or even just one of them. Without their leaders, they'll be no more than a meddle of traitors running in circles. Sandmaster, I ask your permission to do this."

"Talk it over with your uncle, then we'll discuss it some more. We mustn't make hasty decisions. The planning has to be thorough. Besides, there's no hurry. Our men are still recovering from injuries, and we need to obtain more pedes and weapons and ziggers to replace those we lost. It'll be more than half a cycle, perhaps a full cycle, before we meet Uthardim head on."

As they walked back to the encampment, he was careful to treat Islar as a fellow warrior, telling him all he knew about the rebels and Uthardim, and a few sketchy ideas that he and Medrim had discussed about how to introduce a spy into the rebel camp. They parted then, Islar to attend to his evening tasks at the pede meddle while Ravard sought Medrim.

He found the older man seated under the veranda of his tent, surrounded by blades, various grades of whetstones, a pile of tartsip creeper leaves for cleaning, a small jar of bab oil and a polishing cloth.

"Here," Medrim said by way of welcome, "you can oil the blades I've already sharpened. What did the lad say?"

Ravard sat, took up a wad of leaves and began to work on the scimitar Medrim indicated. "He jumped at the chance."

"Knew he would. Are you going to tell him his half-brother will be doing the same thing?"

"No. If the two of them don't know about each other, one cannot unintentionally betray the other."

"And I have your promise?"

"About Islar? Yes. If he comes back safely, no matter the outcome, he'll be my Master Son. And when I become sandmaster of all dunes, Islar will be the sandmaster of Watergatherer."

"I think we should think of a new title for you, when that happens. Dunemaster. Ruler of every dune."

Ravard smiled. It had a good sound to it.

Yet, as he bent to clean the blades, and the long shadows of evening cooled the canvas, he felt only sadness. For a moment he couldn't have said why. Then he knew.

Ryka, oh Ryka. Why couldn't you have stayed? You'd

have made a fine wife for a dunemaster. We could've
started such *a line of Reduner warriors...*

And then hate overwhelmed his desire. The bitch had
made a fool of him, and she would pay. Oh, she'd *pay*.
He'd take her son, and make him his own, he swore it.
And he'd laugh when she begged for his mercy.

CHAPTER NINE

Scarpen Quarter
Breccia City
Level Thirty-four
Breccia Hall, Level Two

Dibble sat quietly in a corner of the Keg & Cask, a Breccian pothouse on Level Thirty-four. He was off duty but suspected if he drank any more he would have a headache in the morning severe enough to interfere with his ability to perform any duty at all, so he sat nursing his mug of amber and pondering just what Elmar Waggoner was up to.

He watched as Elmar, on his way back from the pisshouse, wended his way through the crowded room. The careful way the armsman walked, the slight stagger which he corrected with a hand on an arm or the back of a chair, told him Elmar was drunk again. It seemed so out of character for someone so canny to be drunk so often. Every night lately, lurching from pothouse to pothouse, dragging Dibble along in his wake…

Not that he minded spending time with Elmar. He'd admired him from the moment they had met in Qanatend;

the man was a legend, after all. Since then, the hero worship from afar had changed to something more informed and more personal. In fact, he'd become weeping fond of Elmar. Probably not a good thing. Some said the armsman was a man betrayed. Lord Kaneth Carnelian had thrown him out of his bed to take a wife and that was why he was plunging into the seedy side of the city, drinking and visiting the male snuggeries.

Dibble didn't know if he believed it. All he'd ever heard about Lord Kaneth indicated that he'd always been a nipple-chaser, not one for men at all. True, Elmar did go quiet whenever Lord Kaneth's name was mentioned. And he'd once caught Elmar looking at a portrait of the rainlord that Terelle had painted, but somehow it was hard to imagine a man as tough as Elmar ever succumbing to a broken heart.

He sighed. Sometimes he felt as if he was drowning in quicksand, not knowing how to keep his nose up. He and Elmar weren't sharing a pallet, not yet anyway, so just why in all the Sweepings was an experienced armsman like Elmar dragging a fellow like Dibble Hornblend around every pothouse and male snuggery and bath house from Level Ten downwards?

Dibble knew he was still as green as a bab-palm sucker, naïve as a cleanskin pede, plunging into trouble with embarrassing regularity because he tended to believe everything he was told. Maybe that was it. Maybe Lord Jasper wanted his personal bodyguard to be sharper. More perceptive. So he'd asked Elmar to give him an education?

It seemed unlikely.

Still, the post of bodyguard *had* grown into something

of huge importance. Sometimes Dibble would wake in the middle of the night, sit bolt upright and think, *I am responsible for the safety of the Cloudmaster. What if someone is attacking him right now?*

Although Lord Jasper had not repeated anything as silly as his sand-brained ride to talk to the sandmaster of Dune Watergatherer, Dibble worried that he would, and the thought made him ill. He still wondered exactly what had happened that night. Jasper could have told them, but hadn't. Elmar Waggoner had been unconscious for the last part of the fight and even his memory of what had happened immediately before his injury was patchy. The armsman was only now, almost half a cycle later, finally free of his headaches and dizzy spells, but Dibble wondered if the enforced rest was doing him any good.

Face it, he thought. *As far as understanding what's going on around you, you're as good as buried in sand up to your sunblasted eyebrows.*

A burst of laughter on the other side of the room made him idly seek the cause. Nothing much; just two men at a table sharing a joke. Or so he thought until one of them looked up. He was missing half his nose, as if it had been cleanly sliced away by a sword cut and then healed leaving his nasal passage exposed.

The hairs on the back of Dibble's neck stood up. Sunlord be frizzled—he knew that man. One of Seneschal Harkel Tallyman's enforcers from Scarcleft. The guards had called him Snotnose. He switched his attention to the second man, fear still pricking at him. Yes, him too, another enforcer.

Shocked, he darted glances their way every now and then, trying to seem uninterested. Laughter over, the two men bent their heads together as if they did not mean to be overheard. One of them dipped a finger into his amber and wrote something on the tabletop with a wet fingertip. The other nodded and wiped it out. They were both armed and neatly dressed. There was nothing about them to suggest poverty or troubled circumstances. Worried, Dibble wondered how they had escaped punishment in Scarcleft. Highlord Iani would never have let enforcers loose, surely? He tried to attract Elmar's attention, but the armsman had his arms around the shoulders of two people at the bar, a man and a woman, and wasn't looking his way.

Another man joined the two enforcers, someone Dibble didn't know. It had the look of a planned meeting, a discussion, not an idle drinking session.

This is not good. Enforcers are Lord Taquar Sardonyx's men... Their prosperity had been linked to the Highlord of Scarcleft.

He was about to leave the table to tell Elmar when he saw the armsman was on his way back, carrying the man and woman along with him by the force of his personality and, perhaps, by the promise of a free drink. Nothing new in that; Dibble was used to the way Elmar flashed his tokens around and then sat back with a fatuous smile on his face and listened to the drunken conversation that ensued.

"These are my new friends," Elmar said tipsily as he pushed the newcomers onto the bench at their table. "Cuprite and Trundle. *Reeve* Cuprite," he added, pointing to the man, who couldn't have been more than thirty-five but had an elderly man's paunch and sagging jowls. By contrast, the woman was tall and slim.

"So I'm buying him a drink," Elmar continued. "Got to

support our new reeves, right? And this here is Maddy Trundle, who reckons she knows the reason Breccia's in such a mess. Maddy used to be a dyemaker."

"A mess? The city's in better shape than it was," Dibble replied, indignant. "Elmar, tell them!" But Elmar had wandered off in the direction of the keg to buy some more amber. Dibble didn't know where to begin. Jasper had achieved so much since he had returned from Qanatend, and he'd worked day and night to achieve it. "There's water in the cisterns, and the groves are being watered. The trees are being replanted—"

"We're all wilting beggared!" Maddy cried. She had the deep voice of a man. He blinked. Salted damn, but she was pretty. She continued, "How long do we withering have to wait for them trees to fruit? Takes five cycles, that's what. What we going to do in the meantime?"

"The stormlord is doing his best—" he began, and then corrected himself. "I mean the Cloudmaster." The Council of Rainlords had confirmed the title, but he forgot to use it sometimes.

"Sunblighted upleveller, what does he know about hungry littl'uns?" Maddy cried. "And no work to be had for the likes of me. Who wants anything dyed these days? No one! They're all too busy trying to find food to put in their stomachs. And in the meantime the streets run wild with armed thieves attacking us honest folk in our homes, taking what little we got. And what's the Cloudmaster doing while we suffer? Bet he don't go hungry."

If he did, you wouldn't get any water, he thought angrily, but before he could express the thought, Cuprite weighed in with his own complaints.

"The Cloudmaster's only answer is to get us deep in

debt to the other cities, buying food," Cuprite said sourly. "Even if we get out of this mess we're in, our young'uns'll be paying back the debt till they drop dead of old age. He ought to up the price of their water, but he won't." He leaned forward and waggled his forefinger at Dibble. "The fall of Breccia was the fault of you Breccians. Over in Breakaway, where I'm from, there weren't no Reduners, and you know why? 'Cause we're a pious folk. We sacrifice to the Sunlord, never stinting. Our highlord most of all. Never misses a Sun Day service, or a holy day thirst, she doesn't. And the Sunlord protected us. You was warned. It's all in the holy book. Wish I was back there, but the Sunpriest said he needed help here, so here I am. Doesn't mean I like the place."

Trundle nodded sagely as Elmar came back with the amber. "'Strue," she agreed. "Remember them uplevellers before Breccia fell? Sodden water-soft lot, decked out in silks they bought from outlander traders 'stead of honest workers like me, the men spending their time in snuggeries and such, while we down here on the lower levels worked our hands to the bone for them. And now we got a cloudmaster what won't set foot in the Sun Temple."

"He's too busy calling up storms so you'll have your water to drink, that's why!"

The reeve took a swig of his amber and addressed Elmar, who was edging his backside on to the bench as much as Cuprite's ample backside would allow. "Yon lad's a hatchling, as innocent as sunshine." He switched his attention back to Dibble, saying, "Look, you salt-head, the Cloudmaster might be bringing us water, but he's not bringing us good times like we had before. The Sunlord's not pleased. His rays burn, where they used to give life.

We shrivel under the heat of his disgust. And you know why?"

"I can't imagine," Dibble said, trying to rein in his rage. Several people had grouped around the table to listen, and there was a murmur of agreement.

"Cuprite has the right of it," said an elderly man, his face flushed red with drink. "We've run foul of the Sunlord, for sure. So who's to blame for that?"

Reeve Cuprite warmed to his subject. "It's all the fault of that outlander who lives up in the hall with the Gibber grubber. The waterpriests say she's a blasphemer from the land of the profane across our borders. Polluters all—look what they did to the 'Basters! Perverted them until they deny the Sunlord, though the Lord shines bright in all his glory for all to see. She should be sent back where she came from, the lying, snuggery harlot."

"Ought to be thrown out into the Sweepings," someone said. There was a murmur of agreement.

Dibble went cold. "She's Gibber born," he protested. "She's not like that at all. And how can you be so insulting to Gibber folk? I fought alongside Gibbermen who came to defend the Scarpen and you dare—" He gasped as Elmar drove the heel of his sandal into his instep, hard.

"Friends, I think we must be going," Elmar said. "This lad has had far too much to drink, methinks. He'll be imagining he knows the Cloudmaster next."

Elmar hauled him off the bench and pulled him towards the door, saying, "You really ought to learn to keep your mouth shut, you sand-brain." He suddenly did not sound at all drunk as they stepped out into the night air.

"But people talk such a load of pedeshit. Shouldn't I tell them they're wrong?"

"And end up getting yourself scragged and dumped in the garbage? You have to learn to be more clever, m'lad! This is the thirty-fourth we're on. Come on, let's go back to the barracks."

"Why are we doing this, Elmar? Listening to all these low-lifes every night..."

"You're getting a bit big for your sandals, aren't you? Didn't you tell me you're a Scarcleft lowleveller and your pa was a shoveller in the smelters?"

"Yes. Nothing wrong with that, and I'm not ashamed of it. But I've learned to think better since then, about the world. And about people. And thinking about stuff is better than throwing mud at folk 'cause someone says you ought."

"Pity someone didn't knock some sense into your skull along the way," Elmar said cheerfully.

"Terelle's in trouble, isn't she?"

"Possibly. No, probably. Lord Gold has his claws out. He wants a cloudmaster under his thumb; instead he has one who doesn't even go to temple if he can help it. He can't be too critical of Lord Jasper, so he looks for someone to blame. What we don't know is how dangerous he is."

"What if he had Taquar's enforcers to call upon?"

Elmar snorted. "And where would he get them from?"

"I saw two of them back in there. Fellow with half a nose, together with a mate. What in all spitless hells would they be doing in Breccia? I'd have thought Lord Iani would have slaughtered the whole bunch. Or at least imprisoned them."

Elmar stopped and turned to look at him. "Someone else told me the other day that he thought he'd seen a man who'd been an enforcer. He wasn't certain, so I didn't take much notice. Pedeshit. We could do without scum like them in the city at a time like this."

"Yes. Did this other fellow mention a man with half a nose?"

"No."

"Maybe there's more than these two, then?"

"I'll see what I can find out. I wouldn't have thought Lord Gold would stoop that low, though."

"Who else?"

"Maybe no one. Maybe they just escaped." He started up the street again. "Come on, now. I want to get a good night's shut-eye. Tomorrow, we're having a chat to the Cloudmaster." As he marched on up Main Way to the next level, his gait was as steady as a sober waterpriest on a Sun Day.

They reached the fourteenth before comprehension dawned on Dibble. "Oh! I get it now. You mean we've been doing all this to collect information for Lord Jasper? Why didn't you tell me?"

"That's right, my boy, all those morning headaches were in the interest of Scarpen security. You can blame Lord Jasper, not me, all right?"

Dibble briefly closed his eyes. Sometimes he was so weeping sand-witted.

Terelle sat at the end of the shaded curved front row of the balcony overlooking the Sun Temple courtyard. If she looked to her left, she knew she'd see Jasper sitting next to Laisa in the middle of the row, but she carefully avoided doing so. After the news Elmar and Dibble had brought, Jasper didn't deem it wise for them to demonstrate their friendship too publicly, especially while they were meant to be demonstrating their piety. Well, pretended piety. Jasper didn't believe in the one true faith, and never had; she at least had once been sincere. It had been a long time since she'd sacrificed water to the Sunlord, though, and she was none too sure what she believed any more.

Below, in the full sun, stood some of the pious citizens of Breccia, those who could not afford to pay for seats. Even as she watched, priests passed water jars around and the congregation poured water into them from their drink skins.

The wealthier patrons and the higher members of the priesthood sat where she did, on the shaded balcony, and were expected to give tokens, not water. The priests said it was for the poor, but she was no longer naïve enough to be sure that was the case. She squirmed uncomfortably in spite of the padded chair and the woven palm shading. Ceremonies were always held at midday, to give appropriate honour to the Sunlord, but it wasn't the heat that made her uneasy; she just felt out of place among priests and reeves and overmen and the wealthier uplevellers.

A little later she discovered the worst disadvantage of being in the front row of the balcony: once Lord Gold mounted halfway up the tower to the open stage from where he gave the Sun Day sermon, he was precisely level with them. If she looked straight ahead, she was the target of his disapproving stare. She dropped her gaze and resolutely stared at her knees as he began to speak.

The first part of the sermon was dull, full of homilies about the worth of sacrifice and the essence of charity. Her mind began to wander, returning to some of the things Elmar and Dibble had said to her and Jasper. "Stinking rumours being spread about like manure in a bab nursery," was the way Elmar had described it. What he'd said next was more disturbing. "Basalt is dangerous because he has the backing of the whole Scarpen priesthood. He had to get new priests to replace the ones who died here in Breccia. Trouble is, he's handpicked his own mates: narrow-minded bigots, every last spitless one of them. And these are the men people listen to nowadays. Worse, they are the only rainlords we have here in Breccia, besides Lord Laisa and her daughter. Instead of leaders like Lord Merqual Feldspar and Lord Kaneth and the old Lord Gold, we have this lot. Water-wasters, every bleeding one of them! And they're not just dealing with religious matters. Because there aren't enough reeves and ordinary rainlords, they are also taking the water of the dead and giving rulings on all matters concerning water, from bath houses to buying extra water allowances."

Terelle had added the obvious. "People don't know you, Jasper. They don't know what you do. They only see the waterpriest rainlords." And so Jasper had decided to make more public appearances, including Sun Day religious services.

About halfway through the service, she knew it had been a mistake.

After a lengthy discourse about the ethical obligation to set a good example, followed by a long digression on the slipping moral standards of Breccian society during which he recounted a list of particularly nasty crimes committed in the past ten days, Basalt launched into his attack.

"Our leaders have to set an example for all. Only then will the Sunlord truly smile on us! Only if our rulers spend time in public prayer setting an example others can follow will we have a city of wealth and prosperity."

He was staring straight at Jasper while he said this, so there could be no mistaking his target.

"We should of course be generous with our understanding. Not everyone has the advantage of a truly moral upbringing by Sunlord-fearing families. But we who have possess a moral duty to teach those less fortunate. We have a moral duty to point out to the transgressors their transgressions. We have a duty to identify those among us who would lead us astray."

With those words he shifted his gaze to her, the movement of his head so abrupt and the gesture of his hand so precise it was clear he was identifying the source of his ire. Heads craned to look. People twisted in their seats. Those below tilted their heads to seek out his target. Appalled, Terelle reddened and ducked her head.

"We have among us those who would corrupt our leaders with their foreign godless heresies!" He dropped his voice to a softer tone, "Brethren, I would beseech you, seek out the sedition and cease its influence. Be watchful—"

There was a murmur in the crowd, a fluttering rustle of movement.

"—of all outlanders preaching religious sedition—"

She looked up to see that Jasper had stood.

"—whether it be behind closed doors or not—"

With a glare at Basalt, he strode towards her, forcing everyone else in the front row to hastily pull their feet out of his way. He gestured for her to precede him and she didn't argue.

"—and be ready to tear the heart of blasphemy out of our city—"

She stood and dashed for the stairs, Jasper following close behind.

"—no matter how high they stand—"

Dibble, who had been lounging there with three of his fellow guards, sprang to attention before falling in, two behind and two in front. As they left the temple, Jasper's face was darker than one of his own rainclouds.

Behind them, Basalt's voice still sounded. She caught the words, "Alabaster heresy... Ash Gridelin... vile lies from a godless, bloodless people... punishment..."

It was only when they reached the peace of the Cloud-master's sitting room that either of them spoke. Jasper closed the door and took her in his arms. A scurry of half-grown cats came to greet them, but she barely noticed. In horror, she realised she didn't feel safe, even there. *He cannot protect me*. The thought, thorn-sharp, scored her peace of mind.

"I'm sorry," Jasper said.

"What will you do?"

"I'm not sure. But I want that man out of Breccia."

"The city has always been the seat of the Sunpriest," she pointed out.

"Time that changed."

She took a deep breath and gave voice to what she knew needed to be said. "We've completed enough paintings. And I always had to be in Khromatis where Russet painted me within a year. This time we've had together in Breccia, it's been precious, but we both knew it'd have to end. I'm ready to go." She had accumulated everything she needed, from clothes to paint-powders. She had even been revising all that Russet had taught her of the Khromatian language.

She half-expected Jasper to say no, he couldn't part with her yet, but he was silent, thinking. When he broke the silence, it was to say, "I made up my mind some time ago to send someone to assassinate Russet."

"*What?*"

"I didn't do it in the end. But he did tell you that if he died, the magic in his painting would die too. So I thought you wouldn't feel compelled to leave if..." He shrugged in an embarrassed fashion.

"Well, yes, he did say that. But he might've lied."

"There was no reason to. In fact, it encouraged you to kill him."

"He knew I wouldn't," Terelle said. "Don't do it, Shale."

"I wouldn't do it without telling you, but Terelle—I'd murder him, if you agreed. Myself, personally, if that's what it took."

"No." She shook her head vehemently. "We don't do that sort of thing. It makes us as bad as he is. Anyway, I've another reason to go. To bring back Khromatian storm-lords, if I can."

"Yes. But I want you to know you have a choice."

"Committing murder is not a choice."

"No. But being forced to leave because of his magic is no choice at all."

"I don't want to talk about it."

He sighed heavily. "I suppose you're right. And the sooner you go, the sooner you'll be back." He turned from her and struck his palm against the wall of the room in a sudden expression of rage. "Now I have another man I'd happily slaughter. How dare he stand there, with his sanctimonious ranting—"

"What about these enforcers that Dibble mentioned?

Do you think I—I'm in danger here? Do you think Basalt would actually send someone to harm me?"

"Well, seeing as you hardly leave the hall, no, not really. And we don't know that those men Dibble saw had anything at all to do with the Sunpriest. Or anyone else here, for that matter. But I don't like the thought of them turning up in the city nonetheless. My men are out looking for them. I've already sent a note to Iani to ask if he knows anything. I thought the enforcers were all arrested when Taquar was defeated."

"They were bullies. Ruffians with bad reputations."

"I know. But quite apart from them, I don't want you to be subjected to this kind of vile innuendo. We'll let the whole thing die down, as it will. When they see that you aren't here, they can't blame you for whatever goes wrong." Exasperated, he added, "It's all so stupid."

"Part of the problem is you're trying to be cloudmaster and highlord, and it's just too much."

"Do you think I don't know that? But there's nothing I can do about it. There's not a single rainlord suitable for the post of highlord who wants to come here. And I can hardly blame them. We are short of labour, physicians, food, pedes, reeves, rainlords, guards—you name it, we don't have enough. What rainlord with half a brain wants to take on all that? Oh, there are some, I suppose, but they are hardly suitable." He made a sound halfway between laugh and snort. "Laisa, for example."

"Laisa wants to be highlord? After she betrayed you to Taquar? I trust you aren't thinking of allowing that!"

"Hardly. I couldn't trust her even as far as I can spit a bab seed. She's been nagging me about it, though. I'm just grateful Senya hated it here so much that she agitated to go to her Breakaway relatives before we came back. I'm hoping she *never* comes back. But those two are the least of my worries. Of course I wish I had the time to walk the streets, to talk to people, to let them see me and my concern for them. But I have neither the time nor the strength."

"And no one knows that you have to do double the normal stormshifting." Together they had been trying to fill every cistern in the Scarpen and White Quarter to the brim before she left. Once she was gone, Jasper would have to work from the limited number of paintings she could leave behind, using most of them to form clouds for the Red and Gibber Quarters, which didn't have as much storage. "But what could Lord Gold's motive be for attacking us like that? He can hardly want to replace you!"

"It's not me he's after. It's you. Ironic, isn't it? You were the one who always sacrificed to the Sunlord, and prayed at the temple. I was the sceptic who questioned everything."

"What are you going to do?"

"After today's little episode, I refuse to play the hypocrite again. It was hard enough before, pretending piety when the Alabasters say they have proof that our Watergiver was no more than an ordinary man who seduced every halfway passable female he could persuade into his bed. Sunlord above—his blood even flows in my veins, it seems!" He gave a lopsided grin. "I'm glad I have an excuse not to step into a temple and pretend to believe he's our link to the Sunlord."

"Maybe the Alabasters' proofs are forgeries."

"Do *you* think so?"

"Their beliefs are sincerely held, if that means anything. But then, it was all a long time ago."

"At least the Alabasters wrote things down at the time.

Here, according to what Ryka once told me, most of our people back in Ash Gridelin's day were illiterate. Society had broken down. They were wanderers—hunters and gatherers and herders following the random rains. It was at least a thousand cycles ago, probably more. Nothing about the Watergiver was written until years after he died, when the tunnels were already built and folk were more settled. Who knows if they remembered correctly when the time came to transcribe oral teachings?"

She slumped down into her chair. One of the cats clambered up to sit on her lap and she petted it absent-mindedly. "I wanted so much to believe it was true, that there was a greater being who cared. That all I had to do was pray and help would come."

"Just because they were wrong doesn't mean everyone was. Maybe the Alabasters have it right. To me, it does sound like a much more rational and tolerant faith."

She brightened a little. "You're right; it is. But you aren't going to believe in it, though, are you?"

"I don't think I am a very believing sort of person. I just wish people could believe what they want and tolerate what other people believe. Oh, blighted eyes, I'm going to miss you."

"What if I can't get back in time? What if you run out of waterpaintings while I'm gone? What if no Watergivers will come back with me?"

"Hush." He came over to her and pulled her to her feet. The cat clung on till the last minute, then jumped to the floor. He put his fingers flat to her lips. "We'll have done our best. You won't be gone forever anyway. And I'm going to send both Dibble and Elmar with you." He put his arms around her, as if he could keep her safe.

Her eyes widened. "Oh, no, you can't! The two people you trust the most? Send a few guards with me as far as Samphire by all means, but not your best men. Feroze said he'd make sure I had Alabasters to take Russet and me the rest of the way."

"Yes, I know. But he also mentioned that no Alabaster is allowed deep into the heart of Khromatis. You'll still be on your own there. We know the odds are you'll arrive safely because Russet's painting says so. What we don't know is whether you'll get *back* safely. It's of the utmost importance you do, not just for me, not just for yourself, but for the Quartern. I must know that two people I trust implicitly will be there, looking after your safety. In fact, I'm going to tell them exactly why you're so important."

"But what about *your* safety?"

"Terelle, for all their complaints about me, believe me, no one is going to so much as cut a hair of my head. First, most people are scared silly of rainlords, let alone a stormlord. Second, they all need water and no one is going to hurt the person who keeps them alive. But I tell you what, if it makes you any happier—I'll keep unused the last of the stormshifting paintings that you complete before you leave. It will be your guarantee that I'll be here, waiting for you, when you come home." He smiled at her. "I'll even promise to look after your cats."

He reached up and took off the bloodstone pendant he wore around his neck, and hung it around hers. "Wear this, to remember me by. To know that I'm waiting, and that I care. I'm—I'm not much good at saying the right things, so I want you to wear it, and when you touch it, I want you to hear the sweet things that I ought to say, but which get stuck somewhere before I can get them out."

She wanted to protest, to say that the pendant might be stolen on the journey, that it was too valuable, but he stopped her words with what he said next. "When you return," he said, "the first thing we'll do is marry. And I don't care what anyone else says."

His hand slipped from her neck to her lips, tracing the curve of her smile, and then trailed down to the fullness of her breast, the touch light and exquisitely tantalising. Without shifting his gaze from her face, he flipped the bar on the door with his free hand. Then he lowered his head to kiss her, and she had no opportunity to say another word.

Not once in the next sandrun did she give a thought to Lord Gold or leaving Breccia or anything other than how much she loved Jasper Bloodstone.

"The insolent mongrel!"

Lord Basalt was pacing his office in the Sun Temple, apparently unable, in his rage, to sit.

Laisa, listening, knew better than to interrupt.

"How dare he walk out on my sermon." He marched across the large room, turned on his heel at the window, and strode back the way he'd come. "Humiliating me before the faithful. An insult to the Sunlord! And this man dares to wear a martyr's stone around his neck, flaunting its holiness, when he himself is without faith!"

Laisa, whose immediate thought was that Basalt had been abominably rude to Jasper first, still said nothing.

"How can I chastise him in the manner he deserves for his lack of respect to the one true faith and its Sunpriest?"

As this appeared to be a genuine question, she ventured a reply. "I think you already did. The remainder of your sermon was very much to the point, even if he wasn't there to hear it. I'm sure someone will relate the salient points to him. However, you're right if you're thinking it difficult to, er, *chastise* the Cloudmaster. You can't do much to the only stormlord we have. I suggest you turn your attention to the only woman he apparently cares for. If today is not enough to send her on her way—and I suspect it will be—then I think you ought to consider something more persuasive."

"I've been working on gathering evidence of the sorcery component of waterpainting in general."

"I assume it's against the dictates of the one true faith, but is it against Scarpen *law* to use sorcery?"

"Black magic is illegal. It's the same thing," he added dismissively.

From what little she'd heard about black magic, Laisa thought it little more than a desperate attempt by superstitious people to influence events, with about as much success as could be achieved by crossing one's fingers for luck.

"It is one of the few crimes which can be tried by the Council of Waterpriests. The guilty party can be tried in absentia and the penalty is death," he continued. "There hasn't been a case for over a hundred cycles, so the law has been highly successful in stopping it."

She blinked at his remarkable logic, but didn't comment. Instead, she said, "In that case, I think you have the perfect method of chastising the Cloudmaster, don't you? He would be most upset if his lover was…threatened with such a substantial penalty. It would, I think, make him amenable to being more than reasonable."

"It's not so easy. Convincing evidence must be presented and the verdict must be agreed upon by three-quarters of the council."

She waved her hand in airy dismissal of his objections. "Threats, my lord. *Threats.* You don't have to actually proceed. I have every confidence in your ability to persuade."

CHAPTER TEN

Scarpen Quarter
Breccia City
Breccia Hall, Level Two

It was so lonely without her. So solitary.

By all that's holy, why is it when I like and trust some-one, we're always parted? In his family there'd been Citrine and Mica. Among the rainlords, Nealrith, Kaneth and Ryka. Within his staff, Dibble and Elmar. All of them had gone, one way or another. And now, Terelle. Terelle, who was part of the person he was. Jasper calculated, not for the first time, how long she'd be away and had to admit that it could be as long as a full cycle. A year without her, and only fifteen days of it had gone by.

He sat at his desk and contemplated the letter Iani had sent him. When he reached the part about the enforcers, it wasn't reassuring. *Harkel Tallyman,* he read, frowning over Iani's shaky writing, *and his enforcer officers were all found guilty of crimes against the people of Scarcleft and sentenced to life imprisonment in the punishment quarries. I checked and they are all still there. I wonder if it is some of their underlings who have turned up in Breccia.*

To save on flax paper, Iani had written the continuation crossways over the previous lines. Jasper turned the sheet sideways and puzzled over it some time before he worked out what the highlord was saying. When he did, it unnerved him. *After Taquar's defeat, these men were locked in several rooms within Scarcleft Hall as a temporary measure. Sometime during the next few days, the men in one room vanished, some twenty or so of them. By the time their escape was noticed, there was no sign of them. They must have left the city. Maybe the men seen in Breccia were some of these. My belief is that someone let them out.*

He sighed.

Sandblast you Iani; you could have told me this earlier. He'd already ordered his guard to arrest anyone suspected of having once been an enforcer, but the days had gone by and no one was found, not even the man with the missing nose.

Jasper turned his attention to other troubles.

Stormshifting was not on his agenda that day. He had enough paintings for just over a full cycle if he delivered one storm every three days, and this was a day he had allotted to spend on the administration of the city. He began to deal with a heap of petitions, few of which he was able to do anything about. There weren't nearly enough staff to help him. The unpalatable truth was that Highlord Nealrith's seneschal, his scribe, his actuary, his registrar and other key functionaries of Breccia, had been killed, along with all the rainlords and most of the reeves. The educated uplevellers who would once have stepped forward to fill such posts were mostly dead as well, or had gone to live elsewhere.

Immersed in problems, he almost didn't notice the knock at the door. "Come in," he said, his mind still on the document he was perusing, an appeal from a metal merchant complaining about the state of the caravan routes to the White Quarter.

Laisa entered, smiling at him in a way that instantly aroused his suspicions. She was dressed in dusty riding clothes and carried a palmubra. "Just thought I'd drop by and tell you we caught that band of water thieves who were raiding the tunnel to the north."

"Excellent news. They weren't Reduners, were they?"

"No. Breccia folk. Six men and three packpedes they had rented from Portennabar. The guards are questioning them now."

"Thanks for your help." Weird, that. He'd found himself turning more and more to Laisa for help. Her advice was often sound, and she used her considerable rainlord skills to prevent theft, track leaks and to do many of the mundane tasks once done by city reeves. Jasper still didn't trust her, but he didn't know what he would have done without her, either.

She perched on the edge of his desk. "Finances bothering you again?" she asked, waving a hand at his accounts.

He nodded.

"You're too generous with the tax tokens you collect, especially when there's hardly anything coming in from the Red Quarter now. People don't value what they get for free. They waste it, for a start."

"Don't be silly. Nobody is wasting anything."

"I don't understand why you're still rationing at below a dayjar per person per day when our cisterns are full."

"Because it will be a long time before they are full again,

and so I have told all the Scarpen cities. My next storms go to the Gibber and then the White and Red Quarters."

"Your choice, I suppose." She shrugged. "Another piece of news. Senya should be here tomorrow."

He winced. "Don't expect me to be overjoyed."

"Nothing's changed, Jasper. You still have to have stormlord children. And you have a better chance of doing that if you marry a rainlord."

"She's a lousy rainlord and I told her before she left that I have no intention of marrying her."

"Well, we'll see." She slipped off the table. "I am going to have a bath."

"Don't waste water."

"I never do." She grinned at him, and left.

Irritated, he turned his attention to how to pay the workers for the replanting of the bab groves. A cat rubbed against his shins. He lifted it onto his lap and patted it, but his thoughts were elsewhere.

Late the following morning, after a celebration at the smelters to mark their first firing since the sacking of the city, Jasper was met by Breccia Hall's seneschal as he entered the main doors. He'd had to upgrade Cottle Chandler from junior steward, and the man had about as much idea of how to run a building the size of the hall as Jasper did, but he did his best.

"Lord Senya has arrived back," Chandler said. He blushed furiously as he spoke, mystifying Jasper. "Lord Laisa asks that you meet with them both in her quarters. Oh, and Lord Gold is there too, m'lord." His expression conveyed warning, but that was not much help when he uttered no words of caution.

Jasper's stomach churned nonetheless. *Sunblast them.* When Basalt and Laisa got together, the outcome was never good. Smoothly, without the slightest sign of consternation, or so he hoped, he said, "Present my compliments and say that I'm dusty and I'll join them once I have cleaned up."

"Lord Laisa did seem to think it was urgent."

Quickly he sent his water-sense ranging over the city. As far as he could tell, everything was as it should be, so he said, "I'm sure it cannot be so urgent that I have to drop everything immediately. I wish to wash and I'll be there when I have."

Chandler looked as if he wanted to say something further, but then thought better of it.

"Is there something the matter, seneschal?"

The man cleared his throat, embarrassed. "Nothing urgent, m'lord. I think you had better see for yourself."

Jasper felt as if doom was sitting on his shoulder. He cleaned up and changed and was about to leave his apartments when his glance alighted on his sword hanging in its scabbard by the outer door. Normally he would not have worn it inside the hall, but Chandler's edginess made him uneasy. He strapped it on with no anticipation of using it, but rather with the idea that it made him appear more authoritative, and walked the short distance to Laisa's apartments.

Ara, Laisa's dour maid, opened the door, ushered him into the reception room and quickly disappeared to leave the four of them alone. Lord Gold was standing by the window, wearing the overly ornate robes of his office, his face etched with an expression of distaste. Nothing new there. Laisa was as serene and as beautiful as ever, fault-

lessly dressed, also as usual. Senya, however, glowered at
him in murderous rage from where she was seated in an
armchair.

She was fat. Her face was plump, her arms more
rounded than he remembered. Her waist—she didn't even
have a waist. And then—oh, Sunlord save him. A moment
of incomprehension dissolved into shock as he finally
grasped the cause of the changes. She was *pregnant.*
Worse, she looked as if she was due to give birth any
minute.

For a moment he couldn't think. Couldn't *breathe.*

And then thoughts tumbled through his mind without
order or coherence. It wasn't his. This was a trap. He'd
have to marry her. No, he couldn't. He *wouldn't.* It was
Taquar's. No, Taquar couldn't have children. Maybe that
was a lie. It could be someone else's. Anyone's. But the
timing would be about right…No, he wouldn't marry her.
Ever. She'd planned this. *Oh, weeping shit, Taquar planned
this.* But *why*? What possible benefit could that bleeding
bastard of a rainlord have thought to derive from Senya
having a baby? *His* baby? It didn't make *sense.*

The three accusing faces stared at him, then Laisa
said coolly, "I think, Lord Gold, that his shock is a mark
of his guilt, don't you?"

Jasper took a few more steps into the room. "Shock is
just that, no more, no less." He fixed his gaze on Laisa.
"Why have you kept this a secret all this time?"

"I wanted your little snuggery whore gone first. So
that you can devote all your attention to the problem at
hand."

"Problem?"

"Yes. An innocent, unmarried girl is pregnant. And

you have no choice about the solution, as we all know you're the father. You have to marry her. As you can see, it's not only a matter of necessity, it's also a matter of some urgency."

He turned his stare, as cold as he knew how to make it, to the Sunpriest. "Lord Gold is not involved in this and I don't know why he's here. In fact, I suggest he leave."

Basalt did not move. "I'm guardian of the morals of this city and I will see that right is done."

"I asked for him to be present," Laisa said. "Marriage is a matter for the one true faith."

He hesitated, wondering whether to make an issue of the Sunpriest's departure. Loathing the man as much as he did, he found it anathema to think Lord Gold was about to be privy to this humiliating situation. But was it worth it? He resisted a desire to stuff water down all their throats and spoke to Senya instead. "What do *you* want, Senya?"

"To be the Cloudmaster's wife," she said, without hesitation. "This baby is your daughter."

The word "daughter" hit him like a plunge into cold water. It gave life and reality and substance to someone whose existence he had not yet fully registered, let alone acknowledged. A *daughter*. A rainlord would know the gender of her own child. He could probably confirm it himself, if he wanted. Suddenly it was not just a concept, but a flesh and blood child to be considered. Very possibly his child. Probably his child. Abruptly, the idea that someone else might raise any offspring of his came to appall him. The thought was more than he could bear.

"You despise me. Why would you want to marry me?"

She shrugged. "For the position, why else?"

"To cover your shame, child!" Basalt snapped. "To pay the price of your sin. That's why you must marry without delay. And as for you, Lord Jasper, I am utterly *shocked* by your reaction. Have you no shame, either?"

"Not much," he admitted with honesty. "It was Senya who crawled into my bed without an invitation, after all, and at the time I did intend to marry her. I've only her word that I'm the father—I certainly was not the first to bed her."

Basalt's repugnance for him increased, visible in his eyes, in the outraged way he drew back as if he was in danger of contamination.

Well, good. I have managed to surprise him, Jasper thought with satisfaction.

"That's enough," Laisa snapped. "I will not have my daughter's moral character denigrated by—"

"Oh, Laisa, don't give me a load of pebbles and sand and expect me to swallow it! Try to tell me *you* have some sense of honour and I'll throw it back in your face."

Basalt, who had been spluttering in his attempt to express his disgust, found his voice again. He pointed a finger at Jasper as he spoke, his spittle flying. "You *dare* to malign this delicate young woman with your filth? How dare you insinuate that Lord Sen—?"

"Lord Gold!" Jasper bellowed.

They were silent, but he knew it wouldn't last. He lowered his voice, making no attempt to curb the fury in his tone. "I do not know why you are here. This is a private matter. Since when have waterpriests concerned themselves with the morals of the bedroom?"

"You should be apologising to Lord Senya—"

"Why? She wanted this. She planned for it."

"You—you are despicable!"

"No, I'm honest." He marched to the door and threw it open. "Leave."

"Jasper," Laisa said, her calm apparently still unruffled, "I regret the need to say this, but I think you must hear what Lord Gold has to say before you do anything precipitate." She crossed the room to shut the door. "Sorry, but you really must listen. Firstly, your marriage to Senya is not the only thing we want."

He stood there, looking at her, his heart racing in growing horror. *She knows she's won*, he thought. *But what makes her think I will cave in so easily? What are they up to? Sweet water, save me...* A nauseous certainty that there was going to be no way out shredded the last of his hope.

"What do you expect to get out of this?" he asked at last.

"I want to be Highlord of Breccia."

"Very well, tell me just how you intend to force me into a marriage I do not want and how you're going to impel me to give this city into the hands of a woman with as few scruples as you, Laisa."

She turned to Basalt. "Perhaps you'd like to start by explaining what you've found out about waterpainters, my lord. And do try to be civil. There's no need for this to become a brawling match to see who can shout the loudest."

Jasper, restraining a desire to wring her neck, gave Basalt a terse nod. "I'm listening." *They had to bring Terelle into this, didn't they? The bastards.*

"My concern is ever with the spiritual well-being of

the Quartern. As Lord Gold that's my duty. It should also be yours." He glared at Jasper. "One of the prerogatives I have as head of the Council of Waterpriests is to ensure that all forms of unholy magic are dealt with promptly and the perpetrators severely punished. These things do not come from the Sunlord, but from the evil existing in the world. They can be used to coerce decent citizens, and worse. All such forms of unnatural practices must be rooted out and banished, the very knowledge of them wiped from the minds of men."

Jasper glanced over to Senya. She was sitting calmly, watching him, her head to one side and a small smile on her lips.

She smells victory too, he thought, and felt again that groan welling up inside. He made balls of his fists, digging his nails deep into his palm. "Please get to the point, Basalt. I know of no magic."

"Waterpainting is such a magic."

"Placing paint-powder on the surface of water is evil? Don't be daft."

Basalt bristled and Laisa glared at Jasper.

"For the past half-cycle, I've put my priests to work researching all that is known of waterpainting," Basalt continued. "Firstly, it's an art that's not known in the Quartern. It comes from the land of blasphemers to the east."

"Have you been there, Basalt? Have you ever heard a person of Khromatis utter blasphemies? Where is your proof of that assertion?"

"They call themselves Watergivers, do you deny that? The 'Basters themselves admit that they have their faith from Khromatis, and they've stated openly in the past—although they're more circumspect now—that they believe Sunlord worship to be a fallacy. They've said clearly that our Watergiver, Ash Gridelin, is not a holy figure who sits at the right hand of the Sunlord, but rather one of *them*. The Khromatian heretics. An ordinary person! Do you deny that?"

"I know little of their beliefs and care even less."

His mouth dry, Jasper walked to the dayjar in the corner and pushed back the cover to take some water. He made every movement with studied casualness, but sunblast it, his fingers were trembling with anger as he lifted the ladle to drink. He was furious, but he was also cautious. Basalt had the power of every waterpriest in the Scarpen behind him, and he controlled every rainlord Breccia had—even, it seemed, Laisa.

He added, "I still don't know what your point is."

"My waterpriests have been researching the archives in our libraries. They have found assertions that waterpainting can be used to fix the future. We're of the opinion that Terelle Grey used the medium to kill ziggers during the battle for the Qanatend cistern. Worse, we have evidence that you used this painting sorcery—and the sorceress—to defeat Highlord Taquar during your fight with him at Scarcleft Hall. I myself saw her painting the scene; so did Lord Senya. Anyone present that day will tell you that they were astonished you won against such an accomplished and experienced bladesman as Lord Taquar Sardonyx. Now I believe we know *how* you won. You used iniquitous, immoral methods."

"I see. So we all have to be kind and considerate to our enemies, do we? Why, then, is it all right to take a man's water, to kill in the rainlord manner?"

"That power is Sunlord-bestowed. And the Sunlord does not give such power to just anybody."

"Oh? And yet the two most powerful of such lucky lords I can think of are myself and Taquar. Taquar was instrumental in wiping out a Gibber village, including killing my baby sister and other members of my family—all to gain himself power over a stormlord. But that's fine because he didn't use sorcery? And now you accuse me—who, also according to you, must have been chosen by the Sunlord as a recipient of his blessings—you accuse me of immorality and iniquity because you think I *did* use sorcery? And what are these supposed crimes of mine and Terelle's? Let me think…" He started counting them off on his fingers. "Killing ziggers sent against an army of which you were a part, m'lord. We were preventing the second invasion of the Scarpen, I believe. And, oh yes, deposing a rainlord who betrayed our people to our enemies. Your logic seems a little askew, Lord Gold."

The Sunpriest's face mottled with purple blotches. "You're clever at playing with words, but it doesn't alter the fact that I have sufficient evidence to charge Terelle Grey with the use of sorcerous magic. Her favourite painting appears to be of you—we believe that you're the innocent party here. You don't understand what she has done to you. She has been changing your future to suit herself. Forcing you to do things without you being aware of it. To turn from Lord Senya to her, for a start—"

"Well, I can tell you *for a start* that Laisa doesn't believe a word of that nonsense."

"The penalty for guilt is death."

"What?"

It was Laisa who answered. "The penalty for using

sorcery, such as waterpainting, is death. Jasper, the Council of Waterpriests has already met and passed judgement on Terelle Grey. She's been found guilty and the punishment is for her to be taken to the House of the Dead, to have her water publicly extracted. The rainlord death."

CHAPTER ELEVEN

Scarpen Quarter
Breccia City
Breccia Hall, Level Two

"What? Are you both sun-shrivelled?" Jasper took two strides to where Lord Gold stood. He grabbed the Sunpriest by the neck of his robe and jerked him forward until they were almost nose to nose. Through gritted teeth, he said, "You'll be weeping lucky if I don't strike you dead right here and now. I don't need the ability take your water. I can use this sword of mine. Or I can stuff you head first into that family jar in the corner. And right now I can't see one reason why I shouldn't."

"I can give you several, Jasper," Laisa said, still apparently unruffled. "Have you *no* idea of the power of waterpriests in the Scarpen? People see them as their conduit to the Watergiver or the Sunlord. Kill the Sunpriest and you'll find yourself having to watershift from a prison like the one you put Taquar in."

He answered her without shifting his gaze from Basalt, still wriggling ineffectively in his grasp. "You're sun-fried. Waterpriests may have power, but without me *you're all dead.* I never wanted this, but the truth is I am the only stormlord you have. How can you threaten me or the woman I love and expect to achieve anything beyond my rage? I will not marry that woman"—he still kept a hold on Basalt's collar as he pointed at Senya with his free hand—"and I will not give this city to a ruthless, conniving bitch!"

He flung Basalt from him. The Sunpriest tripped and fell backwards onto the floor. Gasping, he struggled to prop himself up on one elbow but made no attempt to rise to his feet. Even half-prone, he continued to berate Jasper. "We can't do without you, no, but we can do without your snuggery harlot! She has been condemned by the Council of Waterpriests. If she sets foot back in the Scarpen, the sentence will be carried out by the first waterpriest who sees her."

"Jasper, Jasper," Laisa said, placatingly, "we don't really want Terelle or you dead. Her sentence has been suspended, pending a decision as to whether she is to be granted a stay of execution in the interest of mercy. And that, Jasper, depends on Basalt. He—we—are willing to forget all about Terelle as long as you marry Senya, as long as Terelle stops her waterpainting, and as long as I have Breccia."

He was seized by an intense desire to laugh uncontrollably. He tried to subdue it, but a loud guffaw burst out of him anyway. "You sand-brains! You don't get it even now, do you? Without Terelle and her waterpainting *there is no cloudshifting.*"

They stared at him, Senya still in her chair, wide-eyed and puzzled, Laisa frowning as the truth began to dawn on her, Basalt in shocked disbelief.

"That's right," he said, with a harsh laugh. "Your *sorcerer* has been using her talent to bring you the water you drink, and I hope you choke on it. The truth is, I cannot raise water vapour from the ocean without her. With her, I can just manage to water the whole Quartern, more than I could ever manage with Taquar's help. It leaves us both exhausted, but we can do it. So tell me, you petty little man, is this so-called sorcery evil, or is it a blessed Sunlord-given talent to save us—to save you—from thirsting to death?"

"You—you're lying!" the Sunpriest said.

"No. There's not a drop of rain will fall unless she helps me. You want proof? Senya, go into the Stormquest room. Here's the key." He took off the leather thong around his neck and gave it to her. "There are shelves on the left-hand wall as you go in. Bring me one of the paintings you see rolled up there. Any one, and be careful with it."

Sulkily, Senya unfolded herself from the chair. She was ungainly with her advanced pregnancy, and once again he was hit with the reality of a child. Their child. He was soon to be a father. *Oh, waterful mercy. Why her?* The answer came all too readily: because he had been a witless, sand-brained fool.

She left the room. Basalt climbed to his feet and moved to sit in the chair she had vacated. Jasper was glad to see he was shaken. *Blighted eyes, I still want to kill the bastard.*

Laisa shook her head, bemused. "That explains *such* a lot. Why didn't I see it?" She looked over at Basalt. "He's telling the truth. Are you sure you've got the religious aspect correct, Lord Gold? Perhaps waterpainting is not such a bad thing after all?" When he didn't answer, and in fact looked as if he was about to have a seizure, she reproached Jasper. "You should have told me."

"Would it have made a difference to anything?"

"Who knows? I don't think it makes a difference now, unless I am very much mistaken."

He regarded her, hoping they could read nothing on his face. She was talking about Basalt of course, telling him that the man was not about to change his mind. Something shattered inside him. This was a nightmare beyond imagining. All his fault. Because he'd bedded Senya in a moment of weakness. And now Terelle had to pay for it.

As if she knew what he was thinking, Laisa came close enough to lay her hand on his arm again and dropped her voice so only he could hear, "Lord Gold would have gone after Terelle no matter what, you know. He hates all 'Basters with a passion, let alone someone from another land."

"She was born in the Gibber," he snapped, addressing Basalt rather than Laisa. "She's sacrificed precious water to the Sunlord all her life."

Basalt was scowling as Senya reentered the room. Jasper took the key first, hanging it around his neck again, then the painting. Unrolling it and holding it up in front of his chest, he showed them. "Me, stormshifting," he said. "In the stormquest room. You can see clouds out of the window, storm clouds that will bring water. Using the power that is in this painting, I am able to draw water vapour from the ocean and make the clouds you see here." He wasn't about to explain to them the secrets of water-painting and how it fixed a single point in future time, or how he could ensure the arrival of that time by putting the same objects in the right places on the table, the way Terelle had painted them. "Of course not all waterpaintings are imbued with power. The ones that used to adorn the houses of the rich were no more than paintings on water."

Basalt was ashen-faced, and Jasper knew he had convinced the man of the truth of his explanation.

"I want this verdict of guilt against Terelle withdrawn," Jasper said. "Immediately."

"Never," the man replied, standing. "All unnatural power not stemming from the Sunlord must be forbidden sorcery. So say the holy writings bestowed through the medium of the Watergiver that we may know the path of righteousness. They are never wrong. Besides, we prayed to the Sunlord to give us guidance to make the right judgement. The verdict still stands."

Laisa, in alarm, intervened. "My lord, it seems that if Terelle does not return to Breccia we're all going to die."

"You must have more faith, Lord Laisa. The Sunlord will provide the means to help his chosen. Have no fear." He gave Jasper a hard stare. "You have strayed from the true path. You were chosen by the Sunlord as a recipient of his power, but you have been found wanting. This is why your power is inadequate. With prayer and sacrifice and atonement, I see no reason why the Sunlord's face of light will not bring a full stormlord's strength to you. If you are not worthy, well, the Sunlord has already shown us an alternative path. If Lord Taquar is released, and water is bestowed only on the faithful of the Scarpen instead of the heathens elsewhere, then the Holy One's will shall be done."

Jasper blinked, flabbergasted. "Do I hear you rightly?

My method of bringing water to the whole Quartern with
Terelle is sinful, whereas if I supply only half the water
required, but do it with the aid of a multiple murderer like
Taquar, it's somehow *holy*?"

When the Sunpriest did not answer, he added, "You are
sick, Basalt. Now, revoke this sentence of death on Terelle
or you'll not leave this room alive."

"Come now, Jasper, let's be sensible. Together Basalt
and I can prevent you from harming him. And I hardly
think you want to be accused of murder anyway."

When he opened his mouth to tell Laisa what he
thought of Terelle being murdered, she intervened hastily.
"Look, I'm sure we can come to some sort of agreement."

"I want to be the Cloudmaster's wife," Senya said.

Laisa nodded. "And I want to be the highlord. Lord
Gold wants an end to sorcery. And you want to save
Terelle. It should be within our abilities for us all to
work out an agreement where we all get what we want."
Jasper started to speak, but she forestalled him again.
"You marry Senya immediately. You declare me highlord
immediately. Lord Gold announces to the Council of
Rainlords that the verdict against Terelle has been nulli-
fied in exchange for her agreement—which we will assume
you can persuade her to follow if she ever returns—to use
her waterpower only to do pictures like this one, in the
service of the Quartern and its Cloudmaster." She indicated the painting he was still holding. "She will undertake never to do any other waterpainting that involves
sorcerous magic."

She looked at Basalt. "Is that agreeable?"

He didn't answer the question, but, sounding petulant,
said to Jasper, "I don't see that such an agreement is neces-

sary. I'm confident that the Sunlord will find a way for us to receive enough water for our faithful. I'll send out my men with ziggers to find and kill the sorcerer woman, even if they have to go all the way to Samphire. She may have been Gibber born, but her blood is tainted by her ancestry. Lord Senya says she is the granddaughter of that old water-painter, Russet. I *warned* the previous Lord Gold about him; Lord Nealrith, too. Neither of them would listen."

How could he protect Terelle? She was already ten days into her journey, close to Samphire. Even if the Sun-priest's agents missed her while she was still in the Quartern, they could easily find her on her way back to the Scarpen. He could send her a cloud message, warning her—but she had no rainlords with her. No one who could stop an assassin with a zigger. His desire to strangle Basalt was so strong he had to put his hands behind his back.

"If you kill Terelle, you'll die the moment I hear of it," he told Basalt.

The Sunpriest shrugged. "Then it will be the Sunlord's wish." His tone told Jasper the threat meant nothing. He believed his deity would protect him.

For a moment everyone in the room remained poised, tense, silent. Senya chewed on her lip, unusually subdued. Laisa, more alarmed than confident now, was staring at him. Basalt was openly seething.

Jasper knew his future was in ruins. He had to salvage what he could; he had to decide what was most important. And what he could jettison. Words streamed through his head: *I have to keep Terelle safe...I have to be able to water the Quartern...I have to prevent any return of Taquar to a position of power.*

He made his decision—*he* would determine the outcome, not Basalt or Laisa. And he would pay the price. He dropped the painting.

In one fluid move, he wrenched water out of the family jar and as soon as Laisa, Basalt and Senya swung their heads to look towards it, he had his sword out of his scabbard. Even as Laisa began to utter a warning a cube of water was encasing Basalt's head. The Sunlord immediately used his rainlord power to push it away—but just as quickly, Jasper circled it around to cover his face again. Basalt repulsed it all, only to find streams of water coming at him from behind and above and below. His ability to react succumbed to his panic. He began to choke and splutter.

Senya screamed. Laisa lent her power to help Basalt, shoving water away from his nose and mouth. He began to run for the door, his wet clothes flapping, his hands flailing ineffectually at the water that followed him until—coughing and sputtering, desperate for breath—he fell to the floor gasping.

Laisa rushed at Jasper to slap him with an open hand; she never reached him. He swung his sword up and she only just stopped before impaling herself. Senya's hysterical screaming was loud enough to bring people to the door. A guard threw it open, his sword already drawn. Several others crowded into the opening behind him. They took in the scene, gaping in varying degrees of horror.

Probably related to the extent of their piety, Jasper thought, surprised at his own calm. "Guards," he said with the same restraint, "please escort Lord Senya to her room and ask her maid to attend to her. And shut the door when you go, would you?"

For a moment the guard in the lead stared, nonplussed. Jasper could almost see him considering whether it was better to obey the bringer of his water or help the man who was the spiritual leader of his faith. It didn't take him long to decide. He snapped his mouth shut and signalled the guards behind him to assist Senya from the room. As there was no way she was in any state to be cooperative, they complied by bodily lifting her by the arms and carrying her out. The first guard followed them and closed the door behind him. Senya's screams continued outside, growing fainter as she was borne away.

"Laisa, would you mind sitting down and staying there for a moment, while I attend to Lord Gold?" Jasper asked.

She was gaping at him, for once at a loss for words, but when he didn't lower his sword, she shrugged and did as he asked.

He stood over Basalt, who was still on the floor trying to regain his breath. The water hovered in the air not far from his cheek. Exhausted, Basalt was no longer trying to push it away.

"Lord Gold," Jasper asked, trying to sound as pleasant as possible under the circumstances, "do you doubt that I can kill you?"

The man, chastened at last, shook his head.

"Good. Then remember that, because if you threaten the woman I love again, you will die and I will work to demolish every trace that the Council of Waterpriests ever existed. Understand?"

Basalt gave the minimum movement he could to indicate a nod.

"Excellent. Now perhaps we can come to an agreement. I'll grant you most of what you want; you'll grant me much of what I demand. On the rest, we compromise. If you break this agreement, I'll carry out my threat to you and your Council. If I break my side of the agreement, then I understand you'll go ahead and attempt to kill Terelle Grey. And I suspect this would be followed by some considerable unpleasantness on both sides, which any rational man would want to avoid."

Basalt nodded again.

And I trust you about as far as I can throw you, Jasper thought.

"Laisa," he continued, "tomorrow I will appoint you Highlord of Breccia, as long as you endeavour to make sure Lord Gold doesn't harm Terelle. And I think I should also warn you I'll not countenance any attempt by you to control the water matters of this city. They are my affair."

Cautiously, she murmured her assent and added, "What about Senya? This *is* your baby."

"I will talk to Senya about the conditions of this proposed marriage. It will have to be in name only, but I don't believe she'll regard that as onerous. If she's still agreeable after our discussion, I'll marry her the day after she has given birth to a healthy child—assuming that there's nothing about the baby or the date of its birth to indicate it's not mine. I'll then acknowledge it as mine. If I remember correctly, that will legitimise the child under Scarpen law."

She considered that briefly, then nodded. "Agreed. And I assure you that, to best of my knowledge, the child *is* yours."

Throughout this conversation, Basalt had been struggling up into a sitting position. Jasper now stepped back to give him room. "And as for you, my lord, you'll extend your mercy to Terelle Grey, acknowledging to your council that she was working in the service of the Quartern and its Cloudmaster, not indulging in evil sorcery. In return, when she comes back to Breccia, I'll undertake to see that she uses the magic power of her waterpainting only in the service of the Quartern. I'll make sure she doesn't diminish religious faith in the Scarpen or threaten anyone's belief in the Sunlord."

For the third time Basalt nodded.

Jasper continued. "There is one other suggestion I'd like to make. Given our antipathy, perhaps you would consider removing the seat of your Council of Watergivers, and indeed the seat of the Sunpriest, to another city of your choice. Considering the poverty of Breccia at the moment, this might well benefit you anyway. At the beginning of every cycle, as long as you keep your side of the bargain, I'll make a substantial donation to the Sun Temple of whichever city you choose, as long as it is not this one, to last throughout your lifetime.

"Now, will those terms be agreeable to you?"

He reached out and helped the Sunpriest to his feet. Once up, Basalt shook him off. "The conditions are acceptable," he said with little semblance of civility. "Rest assured that I'll be delighted to establish the main Sun Temple elsewhere. I wouldn't want to stay in the same city as a ruler of your moral depravity!"

"Then we're in accord," Jasper said. "I don't particularly want a man of your ridiculous unbending moral rectitude in my city. Laisa, would you be so kind as to dry Lord Gold's clothes?"

While she obliged by extracting the water and returning it to the family jar, he returned his sword to its scabbard and gave orders to the single guard still outside the door, telling him to see Lord Gold out and to offer him a chair back to the temple. "There was a minor accident with the family jar and he is a little shaken," he finished.

The guard's lips did not twitch even the slightest. "Yes, my lord."

As the Sunpriest brushed by them both on his way out, Jasper added, "By the way, armsman, I would hate to hear that an insignificant incident like this has become the subject of gossip."

"Yes, my lord."

Jasper closed the door, took a deep breath and turned to Laisa.

CHAPTER TWELVE

Scarpen Quarter
Breccia City
Breccia Hall, Level Two

Jasper was shaky, as if his knees had turned to water. He sat down in a straight-backed chair opposite Laisa.

She said, "That was very smart of you—offering him compensation to move. Sometimes you surprise me, Jasper."

"Bribery works wonders with criminals," he snapped. "Now, two things for you, Laisa. First, a warning. I expect your rule of this city to be in its best interest. I'll not take kindly to any attempt by you to grow rich at the expense of the city's poor. If I'm unhappy, I guarantee you won't like the way I remedy the situation."

She didn't react, so he moved on. "My second point is more a question. Do you know why Taquar was so set on Senya seducing me? Did he intend me to father her child, and if so, what was his motive?"

"I'm sorry, Jasper, I don't know. I'm as intrigued as you are, and as mystified. If he ever told Senya the truth, she didn't confide in me. From something she said once, I think he just spun her a tale about how he wanted more stormlords born as soon as possible, and she was fool enough to believe it." She shrugged, hands held palm up. "But we both know that's unlikely to be the real reason."

He suspected she was telling the truth, and that unsettled him. Taquar had been up to something. It would pay him to find out what, before it was sprung on him as an obnoxious surprise. Picking up the waterpainting he had dropped, he left her for the stormquest room without saying anything more. Once there, he leaned back against the door and took a deep breath. Nothing would ever be more painful than seeing Citrine killed, but betraying the woman he loved came close.

Terelle. You don't deserve this. He closed his eyes, picturing her face, remembering the feel of her water against his, the sound of her voice, the touch of her hand. And that bastard had *threatened* her. No, worse, he had persuaded the Council of Waterpriests to condemn her to death. And because he'd made it a religious matter, the Council had the legal power to do it, leaving Jasper with no real choice.

Marriage to Senya. He could hardly think of it without feeling sick. How would it make Terelle feel? To save her life, he was going to betray her! Utterly and damnably. How was it possible to love her so much, and yet do something that would make her so wretched?

Damn you, Jasper Bloodstone. Damn you, damn you, damn you.

He didn't know if she'd ever forgive him, but he did know he would never forgive himself.

That evening, Jasper sent a message to Senya saying he would like to dine with her alone. She duly arrived in his private dining room, unsmiling and wary.

"I have asked the servants to leave the serving dishes on the table so that we have some privacy." He pulled out a chair for her, and she seated herself without greeting him. She looked tired and ungainly, and not particularly triumphant at her victory. He wondered if she was regretting her decision to seduce him now that she was dealing with the reality of a pregnancy. That she had intended to fall pregnant he had no doubt.

She waited for him to serve her, but he didn't oblige. He put food onto his own plate and poured himself some water, wishing it was wine. "When is the baby due?" he asked.

"As if you don't know," she sneered.

He didn't. For a start, he was a little vague about the exact length of a pregnancy. More to the point, he was vague about the actual date of the seduction; so much had happened since then. A war. So many deaths. Finding Mica and losing him all over again. Finding Ryka and Kaneth—and losing them all over again too. Finding Terelle. Being made Cloudmaster. Learning how to stormshift with Terelle. *Losing Terelle, all over again.* He felt like getting up and walking away, not stopping until he was back in the Gibber...

Instead, he said evenly, "No, I don't know."

"Any time now."

"I would apologise, if I didn't know that you and Taquar planned this together, and that he showed you how best to make it hard for me to say no at a time when I was vulnerable and friendless."

She pouted. A year earlier it might have appeared attractive; now it just appeared childishly silly. "You did say you would marry me."

"Yes, I did. I apologise for changing my mind. Frankly, though, I don't understand why you *want* to marry me. After all that has happened to Breccia, no one cares about propriety any more. And you are the last cloudmaster's granddaughter, young, attractive, a rainlord. There must be many young men in other cities who would love to marry you. If you don't want to be bothered with this child, I'll see to it that she is properly cared for."

She spooned food onto her plate while he was speaking, as if she was not paying attention. He blinked at the amount she took.

He pushed on as she started to eat. "I guess what I'm trying to say is, why in all the Sweepings do you want to marry a man who doesn't love you and doesn't want you?"

"You wanted me once," she said with a sly smile and licked some gravy off her lower lip.

"Believe me, that's never going to happen again. If you want to be bedded, you'll have to go elsewhere and I won't acknowledge any more children you may have. They certainly won't be mine."

"In the Gibber and on the lower levels here, maybe it doesn't matter if unmarried women have children, but if you think it makes no difference to uplevellers, you have sand for brains. If you don't marry me, I'll never be accepted back into Breccian society."

"There isn't much left of Breccian society," he pointed out.

"There will be once Mama is in control. And I'll see to it that there is, too. But I must be married to the father of this brat, and you know it. Oh, people will forgive us— you and me—because of the war and everything, as long as in the end you do the right thing. But if you don't, your daughter will be a bastard, and respectable families will cut her dead in the streets if she as much as smiles in their direction."

His heart missed a beat as he thought of his unborn daughter. *Sunblast it, the little bitch is probably right. I might be able to do it to Senya, but I can't do it to a child. Any child.*

She chatted on, sampling the dishes as she talked, oblivious to his sudden disinterest in his food. "I don't want to bed you, so that part doesn't matter. And I'm never going to have another child." She shuddered. "To puke up my breakfast and to look like a pregnant goat all over again? Never!" She waved a fork at him. "I want to be the stormlord's wife, just like you promised back when we were in Scarcleft. Only now it's not just the storm-lord's wife, it's the Cloudmaster's wife. That makes me the most important woman in the Quartern."

He frowned and pushed his plate away. Did she really think being someone's wife made her more important than, say, Lord Ouina ruling a whole city, or the woman physician he'd recently met down on Level Twenty-nine, treating the ills of the sick and injured without asking for any payment?

"I suppose it could be an important job, if you wanted to make it so," he said with as much neutrality as he could muster. "What were you intending to do? Perhaps you could establish more schools for lowleveller girls. That would be more than just a worthy cause. Or—"

She flicked away any idea he might have had with a wave of her hand. "The Cloudmaster's wife doesn't work. Her job is to . . ."—she hunted for the right word—"set the tone for upleveller society."

"Tone?"

"Yes. Fashion and society. People need someone to look up to. To emulate. It's what makes society work properly. There has to be a—a—hierarchy. A ranking. Proper standards."

He stared, wondering if she was mocking him, but all he could see in her eyes was guileless anticipation. "Who told you that?"

"Lor—Lord Taquar," she replied, faltering a little under his stare.

"Senya, does it ever occur to you that you were manipulated by Taquar into doing what he wanted rather than what was in your own best interest?"

"He loves me. And do you think I'm so stupid that I don't know what is good for me?"

He almost said he was certain of it, then thought better of it. There was nothing behind that gaze of hers except self-interest. Once, he'd thought it was just her immaturity that made her that way. Now he wasn't so sure.

She smiled across the table at him. "I don't think we need do this sort of thing very often, do we? Because I find you as boring as the booming of a night-parrot. Oh, and one other thing—I don't ever want to see Terelle Grey anywhere near Breccia Hall again. If ever she comes back to Breccia. And if you break your promises, I'll make sure Lord Gold takes it out on her."

"And I will make sure you regret it." He stood up, driving his dagger into the wood of the polished table top in front of her. She leaped up with a squeal, her eyes round with shock. "But you're right. This is a pointless activity. I suggest you leave."

She threw down her napkin and ran from the room. He

sat down again, head in his hands, hoping she had not seen the panic he was sure had flashed across his face when he thought of Terelle never returning, or if she did, of being subjected to Senya's malice and Basalt's twisted idea of justice. He schooled his expression into a mask of placid calm, then climbed to his feet and went to look for Laisa.

She was in her apartments. Once her maid, Ara, had left them alone, he said, "I've just come from my attempt to have dinner with Senya," then stopped, not knowing quite how to continue.

Laisa had been sewing, but she now laid her work aside. Not embroidery, he noted with a modicum of surprise, but mending a tear in a dress. Laisa was nothing if not practical. A cargo of new fabrics had recently arrived to replace all the sheets and chair covers and similar furnishings ruined or stolen during the occupation of the city, so he guessed the seamstresses were overworked attending to that.

And you are thinking of everything except what you should be talking about.

"And . . . ?" she asked, waving him into the chair opposite.

When he still didn't say anything, she sighed. "It's taken you a long while to wake up."

"I haven't seen her for months," he said sourly. "Before, I thought—I thought she was just immature. But it's not just that, is it?"

She shook her head but said nothing.

Damn your eyes, Laisa. "Why did you insist on my marriage to her as part of your bargain?"

"Because if I didn't, I'd have had to bear the brunt of

her revenge. Her water-powers are fortunately small because she has steadfastly refused to work at them—for which I'm now suitably grateful—but make no mistake about it, Jasper, she is a rainlord, and she could be dangerous. I would not leave your Terelle alone in the same room as her, if I was you."

"What's wrong with her?" he asked bluntly.

She sighed. "I have no idea. I used to think it was because Nealrith spoiled her rotten. Now I know it's more than that. Is it possible for someone to be born without a conscience? Without the slightest interest in anyone else's well-being?" She shrugged. "If so, then Senya is that person." She stabbed at the fire with the poker. "I may be a bitch, but I'm a rational, thinking bitch. At times, I even have a conscience. She doesn't."

"And this is the woman you'd have me marry?"

"You're the only person who has the power to dominate her. And you're the only person who can give her what she needs to be happy—and when Senya is happy, she doesn't cause trouble. Give her money for luxuries, position to lord it over others, all with no responsibilities, and she won't bother you."

"Apart from the fact that there are precious few necessities around, let alone luxuries—" he began.

She cut in. "Jasper, if you don't want your daughter to be treated like a snuggery whore behind your back and ridiculed as the Cloudmaster's by-blow, you *will* marry Senya. What's the problem anyway? Terelle is a snuggery lass. She won't put any store by a marriage ceremony. But take my advice, if she returns, keep her privately, well away from your wife."

Scrambling to his feet to stare down on her, he wanted

to let loose his rage, yet knew there was enough truth in her words for him to be wary of the penalty for not heeding them. That, he decided, was the trouble with Laisa. She was often wise, she often gave astute advice, and it lulled you into believing she was on your side. He didn't know who was worse: Senya with no conscience at all and no understanding of her lack, or Laisa who knew exactly what was morally right, but was quite prepared to ignore it any time it interfered with her plans.

He left the room, aware he was missing something. There was a lurking danger he hadn't identified, and those two women lay at its heart like scorpions hiding in his clothing.

The trouble was he had no idea when they would sting, or why.

Ten days later, Jasper's daughter was born.

Outside the birthing room, he took her in his arms for the first time. He folded the swaddling cloth away from her face and arms, marvelling at her tiny perfection. She mewled, clasping and unclasping her minute fists as if she wanted to grasp the world. The stir of love he felt was immediate and as potent as amber on an empty stomach. He had no trouble believing she was his daughter. Her skin was more golden than his natural brown, but her hair was black, her eyes dark. She was perfect and vulnerable and his heart was irretrievably hers.

When the midwife took the baby back, he felt her absence as a loss. He attuned himself to her water so he could track her presence and watched as she was borne away.

"Satisfied?" Laisa asked.

He nodded, not caring that he had no real way of knowing she was his. "Tell Senya to send for me as soon as she's ready for the wedding ceremony."

"Aren't you going in to see her? It *is* customary for the father to acknowledge the woman's role in all this."

"I have nothing to say to Senya, and I'm quite sure she'd be happier not seeing me. And please, Laisa—don't ask Lord Gold to return to wed us." The Sunpriest had already left to set up the main Sun Temple in Pediment.

The midwife returned from Senya's bedroom just then, still bearing the baby. "She won't put the babe to the breast," she said with a puzzled air. "She said to give her to you, m'lord."

Startled, Jasper took the bundle he was being handed and the woman bustled back into the bedroom. "She won't—? Laisa? What am I supposed to do?"

"Don't look so horrified. She told me long ago she wouldn't feed the child. I arranged for a wet nurse, and another woman to help out as well, and I sent for them both this morning. They should be here any moment. Senya also said they—the nurses and the child—were to be quartered with you."

His eyes widened. "With *me*? In my apartments?"

"I have an idea she is getting her revenge for those tedious months of pregnancy. She wants you to be the one woken by a crying baby in the middle of the night. What are you going to name her?"

"*Name* her? I have no idea." He paused to look down at the tiny face now surrounded by the goat-hair blanket. "She's so golden…" He considered that and thought of Citrine, named for the yellow quartz around Wash Drybone. But no, there would only ever be one Citrine for him. "I'll call her Amberlyn." It was the name the Gibber folk gave to citrines that were more orange than lemon-coloured.

Laisa snorted derisively. "She's probably got jaundice."

Amberlyn didn't have jaundice, and soon proved herself to be a normal, noisy baby. In the meantime Senya decided to postpone the marriage until she could have a wedding dress made. Paradoxically, her stalling irritated Jasper; he wanted the ceremony over and done with.

She ignored her daughter. Laisa didn't seem particularly interested either, and neither of them ventured into Jasper's apartments to see Amberlyn. He liked it that way. Now that Laisa had taken over the running of the city, he had more time on his hands, and he often spent it rocking his daughter to sleep in his arms, stroking her face with his finger, in a state of total wonder.

"All fathers think their daughters are perfect," the nurse, Zirca Throbbin, told him, amused by his infatuation.

Her daughter, Crystal, was the wet nurse. To his initial horror when he met the girl, he realised she wasn't much more than a child herself. "People survive however they can," Zirca told him when he questioned her privately. "Crystal was raped by the Reduners. Baby stillborn, Sunlord be blessed. Don't you be worried, m'lord, I'm here to keep an eye on her and your daughter."

Waterful mercy, he thought, *have we come to that? Where children end up being wet nurses to survive the bad times?* Still, he was glad Laisa had found the pair. They were cheerful and loving and they doted on Amberlyn.

Sometimes he would stand out on the balcony holding his daughter, shading her from the harshness of the sun, while he sensed for Terelle. She was still in Samphire and had been for some days. He contemplated sending her a cloud message, telling her of what he had done—but how could he put news like that up in the sky for all to read? He had already written her a letter. No excuses, just the bald facts of why he would soon be a married man, with his most heartfelt apology to the woman he loved. And with it, a warning to beware, just in case Lord Gold did not keep his side of the bargain. He'd written another letter, to Elmar Waggoner this time, telling him of the Sunpriest's threats.

He sent them both with armed couriers to Alabaster.

Twenty days later he and Senya were married in the courtyard of the Sun Temple. The latter part of the ceremony seemed endless. They stood in the full sun holding hands across the shallow pool while they waited for the Sunlord to give his blessing by evaporating the sacrificed water. Her hand was small and soft in his. She bestowed delighted smiles on him, for the benefit of the audience, he assumed. Under the covering of the yellow cloth the priest had wrapped around their hands, she was digging her nails into his palm until they cut the skin and drew blood.

He felt besmirched.

It should have been you, Terelle.

And then, another painful thought, *Oh, Amberlyn, I could never wish you away, not now. But I do wish you were Terelle's daughter.*

Several days after the wedding, Laisa went to see Senya. She found her lying on a divan on the balcony with her hair, just tinted with rubyleaf paste, spread out in the sun to dry while she was in the shade. Laisa took the parasol from the servant girl and waved her away.

Senya pouted. "What's wrong now?" she asked. "And don't let the sunlight on my face. I don't want freckles and you know I hate brown skin."

"I want to talk to you about freeing Lord Taquar."

"Well, it's about time. I thought you'd forgotten all about him."

"I couldn't see much reason to risk my neck trying to free him before this. Now we have a motive. A very good one."

Senya blinked doubtfully, trying to follow her reasoning. "I give up. Why now and not earlier?"

"Why do we have to put up with Jasper being the sandgrouse cock in the roost, my dear?"

"Because he's the only one who can bring us water."

"Right. Either with Taquar, or with Terelle. We know stormshifting doesn't work too well with Taquar, so when it was working without him, it seemed best to just accept the situation, at least for the time being. But now..." She smiled. "There's another player." *And I think I have finally realised what Taquar was up to...*

Senya still looked confused.

"Oh, never mind, Senya. Let's just get Taquar back, shall we?"

"How? We don't know where he is."

"I've been trying to find out."

"In the Scarcleft mother cistern where Jasper was? After all, that's Lord Iani's city now and he's Taquar's gaoler."

Laisa coughed to hide her irritation at her daughter's

unintentional obtuseness. "Senya, use your brains. You can't keep a rainlord somewhere like that. Especially not one with Taquar's skill. He'd mess up the water supply of the whole city and probably drown Iani while he was at it. Besides, when we were leaving Scarcleft to fight Davim, we saw Taquar—obviously drugged—being loaded onto a pede, remember? And then Iani and Jasper and Terelle all vanished. When they caught up with us, days later, we were near Pebblebag Pass. And Taquar wasn't with them. They have him imprisoned somewhere north of the Escarpment. But where?"

"Oh. So now what?"

"Not much point in trying to follow Iani when he takes Taquar supplies. Iani's a rainlord and he'd know if he was followed. I have spies in Scarcleft, men who tell me what they can—but none of them have seen anything that might lead us to Taquar. Iani has been too clever."

Senya held up a tress of hair to admire the highlights gleaming in the sun. "But you have another plan."

"A chance, yes. I think Terelle's paintings are worth investigating. We know she helps him make it rain. We know how hard it must be to imprison a rainlord, especially one as good as Taquar. What if she used the power she has and painted him imprisoned? I want you to help me look for a painting of Taquar. You're Jasper's wife; guards aren't going to question you if you enter his apartments. Especially not if Amberlyn is there. You have to start taking an interest in your daughter."

Senya pulled a face. "I don't care if I never see her again."

"Then pretend! You're very good at pretending. Think, Senya. If you're wandering around with a baby in your arms, who's going to question you? Just choose times when Jasper is not in Breccia Hall."

"Her paintings are kept in the stormquest room. I can't get in there; he wears the key around his neck. How can we get it without him noticing?"

"Well, you could—"

"No, I could not! There is no way I'm climbing back into his bed. I hate him."

"I don't suppose he'd have you anyway. I'll think about it. In the meantime, just get the guards accustomed to you coming and going in and around his apartment, all right?"

"All right. For Taquar." Senya smiled, dipping her head and looking up through her lashes.

Trying to let me know she could take Taquar away from me as easy as sipping water. Withering lot she knows. I never owned Taquar in the first place, and never have. No one has, least of all Senya Almandine . . .

Then why the hell do I want him back?

Laisa answered that question to her own satisfaction as she left the room a few moments later. *Because Taquar Sardonyx needs me. Because . . . my feeling for him is the nearest I'll ever get to knowing what it is to love someone. Stupid, sand-brained choice, but the heart doesn't follow the head. Unfortunately.*

CHAPTER THIRTEEN

White Quarter
Samphire

"Another day or two of rest won't hurt him," Physician Errica said as she and Terelle walked away from the Physician's Hall, trailed at a discreet distance by Elmar and Dibble. "An untreated scorpion bite is no little thing for such an old man. He was doing well until just before you returned, when he had a bout of congestion of the lungs."

They had just spent an irritating run of a sandglass with Russet. He should have been glad to see her; instead he'd scolded her for the length of time she'd been gone, and then railed at Errica because she'd told him he couldn't leave for Khromatis until he was stronger.

Terelle glanced at the Alabaster physician, trying to look blandly neutral, and refrained from commenting.

She suspected she hadn't succeed when Errica pulled a face at her and said sourly, "Ye're lucky he's still alive, but he'll never admit it."

Terelle wasn't surprised the physician was more than a little tired of Russet's constant grizzling. "Lucky? If he'd died, I'd be free."

"That's not a very charitable statement."

"Why should I be charitable when he imprisoned me with his magic just so he can take me to his land against my will? And does he have an altruistic reason to do that? No! He thinks it'll bring him back into the inner circle of power in Khromatis. I'm withered if I know *why* he thinks that'll work. I don't belong there. I don't know anything about the place or the people, and I care even less."

"Kermes," the physician said. "That's why. The name. It is a famous one. People will respond to it."

"My name is Grey."

"Not unless you can prove your mother wed your father. Take my advice and call yourself Terelle Kermes while ye're in Khromatis."

Inwardly sighing, she acknowledged the advice was probably good, but she resented the further rejection of her father, a man she would never know because Russet had killed him. "Why won't any of you tell me about Khromatis? Why are you all so secretive?"

"It's forbidden."

"You mean you know what it's like there, but aren't allowed to tell?"

Errica nodded, but said nothing. She was guiding Terelle up a narrow staircase shaded by the tall salt-brick walls of houses, to show her the view at the highest point in the city.

"Who forbids you to talk?" Terelle was all out of patience and it was difficult not to let her irritation spill over into her tone. "You trade with them, don't you?"

Errica was silent. She was puffing slightly as she toiled up the steps; she was a large woman and did not move with the ease of the young or slim.

Terelle persisted. "Do you speak their language? Can you teach me a little in the time we have before I go?"

"We all learn the language of Khromatis. Our written language is theirs," Errica admitted. "But there are better teachers than me. I will arrange someone."

"For Elmar and Dibble as well, please." She glanced behind to where the two guards followed. They were the only members of their party remaining; the rest had already returned to the Scarpen.

At the top of the steps, they emerged into the full sun on the flat roof. Blinking in the brightness, Terelle was astonished by the size of the area. On the far side, two white myriapedes plodded stoically around in a circle under shade awnings. They were harnessed to a beam of wood, far too solid and straight to have ever been part of any Quartern tree. Their constant pacing had worn a groove in the rock-hard salt blocks of the rooftop. Several Alabasters tended to two more beasts chewing on cut samphire while resting in the shade.

"It's the way we draw water up to the top levels of the city," Errica explained. "Pede power."

"You bring the animals up the *steps*?" she asked, incredulous.

"When they are still second-moult youngsters, yes. After that, they stay here the rest of their lives."

"Oh." *Those poor things, spending their lives walking in circles . . .*

Behind her she heard Dibble exclaim as he and Elmar arrived at the top of the steps, "I'll be spitless! It's bigger than the roof of Breccia Hall back home."

Much bigger, she thought. She walked to the closest edge and looked over the parapet.

Samphire was a white city with glittering walls, a sparkle of towers and domes stepping elegantly down the slopes of a conical hill. The city buildings, built of blocks of hewn rock salt and baked in the dry heat of an unforgiving sun, blinded with their whiteness. The outer walls, built of salt blocks larger than she was tall, melded with the stone of its foundations in seamless unity, then towered up high and steep. The city as a whole emerged, pristine as frost, from the sea of green and purple samphire surrounding it. The single gate was made of huge logs of wood.

The view extended in all directions. To the north, the expanse of sparkling salt that was the Whiteout; to the south, the plains pockmarked with clumps of scrawny bushes, stretching towards the Border Humps. No wonder Reduner marauders preferred to attack mines and caravans.

The wall won't help them if the Reduners attack their water supply, she thought morosely. Always, always, water was at the heart of everything, and Samphire's water was tunnelled in from the Border Humps. She could see the towers of the inspection shafts striding away in a straight line towards Senruk Wells, which they had passed on their way in from Breccia.

Unlike Scarpen cities, no smelters or firing kilns belched outside the walls. Instead, fields of samphire came right up to the foot of the ramparts. She could see workers bending and straightening, harvesting the succulent stems and loading the pede panniers. At this distance, the pedes were so small they appeared hardly larger than desert millipedes. The city itself was built with pede transport in mind: streets wide enough for laden packpedes to pass, squares large enough for the animals to turn around. Street lads armed with brooms and scoops waited on almost every corner to collect pede droppings for fuel.

And as for their people, where were all the poor? Or, for that matter, the rich? Everyone dressed more or less the same. Plain white robes for indoor use and for manual workers; mirrored robes at other times. The mirrors flashed irritatingly when they caught the sun, but Errica had given her one such robe to wear, so she did. She didn't like the weight of it tugging at her neck and it didn't make her blend in any better. The brown of her skin would always make her conspicuous among pale-skinned Alabasters, like a dark sand-flea on a white cat.

People in the street stopped to stare when she passed. There was a clannishness about them that excluded the outlander, even when they were welcoming.

Their sameness—it has a price. The different don't fit in. I wouldn't like to live here.

As she wondered just how to extract more information from Errica so she could arm herself for her trip to Khromatis, she absent-mindedly fingered the wall next to her. It was smooth and dry, yet it glistened in the light as if wet.

"This is the one place in all the Quartern where we don't want it to be raining." The voice that spoke at her shoulder was not the one she had expected; when she turned it was to find Errica had disappeared. Instead, she was being addressed by an elderly Alabaster man leaning on a walking stick. He was vaguely familiar, but for a moment she couldn't place him. *Must be someone I met last time I was here.*

"Salt dissolves in water. Samphire City would melt if it rained," he explained. "Eventually."

"Oh! Yes, I suppose so." She looked at the wall uneasily. "I find it hard to think of salt as building blocks."

"The original city was built of stone. It's still there, under our feet. What's left of it is now our cellars and cisterns. Nobody used salt blocks back in the days when it rained, any more than they lived in the mines, either. The rain turned the Whiteout into a lake back in those days."

"So I've heard." Then she remembered who he was and flushed hotly. "You're the Bastion. Forgive me—"

"Nothing to forgive. I asked to see ye informally, like this. Errica and Feroze have both told me that ye've been asking many astute questions—which they aren't able to be answering. The law forbids it."

Flustered and at a loss, Terelle wondered in a panic if she'd broken the law by asking.

He saw her confusion and smiled. "Come. There are stairs over there leading down to my offices. Dismiss your guards. I'll see that ye are returned safely to the Emery Townhouse."

She did as he asked and followed him down the steps that led inside the building, assailed by loneliness and a wild moment of unreality: she, a snuggery girl, about to chat to the ruler of one of the quarters?

"I am . . . not above the law," he was saying as he limped downwards, "but I am in a position to be bending it a little. And I happen to be thinking ye deserve that much."

The room they entered at the bottom of the steps was small and cramped and contained no luxuries except board-books and scrolls. Of those, there were plenty, filling the shelves carved into the thick walls. The Bastion waved her into one of the half dozen chairs—the usual heavy armchairs carved of rock salt. At least these had cushions. She sat, feeling herself dwarfed by its size, and he sat opposite, sitting back with a sigh of relief. The smile he then bestowed on her was benign, but his milky bluish eyes, small in their age-shrunken sockets, shone with a sharp intelligence.

"I trust your journey here was more pleasant this time," he said.

"Much, thank you. Jasper—the Cloudmaster—was worried about Reduners, but we saw none. We did see signs that they've been raiding caravansaries, though. Mostly to take water, I suppose."

"But ye found enough to water yourselves?"

"The Cloudmaster supplies the caravansaries," she said vaguely.

"A talented young man."

"A solitary one, unfortunately. He cannot manage to water the whole of the Quartern alone forever."

He stopped moving, stilled so suddenly and unnaturally that she was shocked, wondering what she'd said. When he spoke again, and it seemed a long time afterwards, his words were oddly flat, yet she felt an undercurrent of anger. "Does he think to be stopping our rain?"

"No. But there is a limit to what one man can do."

"Ah." There was another silence, then he said, "I've never been to the true heart of Khromatis, up in the mountains. None of us have. Alabasters are forbidden past the Borderlands and the administrative ward called the Southern Marches, as are all foreigners."

She blinked, struggling to cope with the sudden change of subject. "Why? What do they have to hide?"

"Nothing that I know of. But the early history between Khromatis and the Quartern was fraught. Wars, invasions from this side—I speak of the days before we Alabasters lived here, ye understand—terrible, terrible times when ferocious tribes pillaged the land. In the end the Khromatians decided this land was the dwelling place of evil and their engineers flooded the Borderlands to be making the crossing difficult. They diverted a river, I believe. The marshes ye'll cross were originally man-made. This happened around the same time we Alabasters were exiled here. About two thousand years ago."

"You were exiled from Khromatis? Why?" she asked.

"To become the guardians of their borders. To be making sure that people don't enter Khromatis from the Quartern. We take that task seriously. Ye and Russet are Watergivers, so of course that does not apply to ye, although Russet may have broken some Khromatian rules by coming here in the first place. However, that's not our business."

"Why do *you* have to protect *their* borders? It's not your land any more!"

He looked down at his hands. He had long thin fingers, and his skin was paper thin, his blue veins knotted and uneven under the fine mesh of wrinkles. "It is our burden. Our duty. Our atonement for a great sin committed long ago. When our penance is done, we will go home."

She stared at him in bewilderment. "Home? To *Khromatis*?"

"Yes. One day we will be forgiven and be permitted to return."

"You were exiled—and you remain in exile—for something that happened so long ago? Why, that must have been before the Time of Random Rain."

"It was. In an age of regular rain, when the Giving Sea

didn't exist and there were no Scarpermen, or Gibber folk, just the ancestors of the Reduners."

"That's incredibly silly," she said, so taken aback that words slipped out before she'd thought about what she was saying. "How can you—and your people alive here and now—be guilty of something that happened so long ago? And why should it still be your home after all those years? Why, I don't feel the least bit like a person from Khromatis even though my parents grew up there."

He looked pained. "For us, it is just so."

She almost laughed, then realised her mockery was rude. "I'm sorry. That was ill-mannered of me." Her mind was racing. Why had he told her what he had? She now knew more about Khromatis and the Alabasters than anyone she'd ever heard of! *They keep a secret for two thousand years and then blurt it out to me? Because I'm supposedly from Khromatis and should know it anyway? No . . . there's more to it than that.*

Diplomatically, she asked a more neutral question. "Will I be able to take my two Scarpen guards to Khromatis? I don't want to travel with Russet without protection. I don't trust him. And from what you've just said, his people aren't all that hospitable."

"We'll not stop your guards, but what happens on the other side of the Borderlands we've no control over. We'll deliver ye all to the Khromatian authority in Marchford. That's one of the three border towns. Many Alabasters work there and in the surrounding fields and farms. If the Khromatians refuse to be allowing your two guards any further, there's nothing we can do."

He stood up. His movements were slow and deliberate, his balance unsure. He took up his stick again and headed towards the door on the other side of the room. "Come with me a moment. I want to be showing ye something." He turned to leave without waiting to see if she followed.

Wincing every step of the way, he led her down several flights of stairs until they emerged in a narrow room with curving walls, lined with recessed shelves full of scrolls and books from ceiling to floor. She looked around in awe. It was so dim and cool, she wondered if they were partially underground. The numerous light wells at the top of the outer walls were angled upwards through the salt.

"The library is circular," he said. "It goes all the way around the hill. In the centre is our main water cistern. That's the pumping mechanism ye can hear."

"I didn't know there could be so many books in the world," she said. "No one could possibly read all these, surely?"

He laughed. "Probably not in several lifetimes. These are our history. The oldest of these documents, a copy of the Rules of Faith, dates back several thousand cycles to our exile. The originals are even older and still to be found in Khromatis. They are the actual words of God, recorded on clay tablets by the scribes who heard Him speak from the waters of the Source."

Terelle gave him a blank look.

"The Source is the spring feeding all the rivers of Khromatis. The Quartern priests tell ye the source of all life is the sun, but we know the sun is our enemy and it would shrivel us if the earth had no life-giving water. God lives within every drop of water on this world—including the water within our bodies. We are mostly water; did ye know that? And of all people, those of Khromatis are the closest to the Source—the true heart and purity of God."

"The Reduners use the same word about a natural water supply in the dunes," she said.

"Perhaps they are wiser than the Scarpen folk."

"So you believe the Sunlord is something evil?"

He shrugged, indifferent. "Perhaps. But our writings do not say that. They do not mention him."

"Why are you telling me this?"

"Because I want ye to believe your waterpainting power comes not from the Sunlord, but from God, the real living God, part of whom flows in your veins, in the water of your blood. We want ye to know ye are a Khromatian, a Watergiver lord, born of our faith, and God has His purpose for ye."

Her head was reeling. "Which is?"

He laughed. "I am not God! How can I say what His purpose is? He will let ye know, all in good time." He waved a hand at the shelving. "I could prove much of what I say, if ye could only read our script. At the end of each star cycle, a history of that cycle has to be written by the Bastion's historian and kept here. I could show you the very one describing the coming of Ash Gridelin and how he passed on water skills and sensitivity during the Time of Random Rain. It was quite deliberate, ye know. He promised his lovers they would have special children who would save the world, and they did."

She frowned. "You recorded things from *before* the Time of Random Rain?"

"Indeed. From back when only us and the original plains dwellers lived here. The Scarpen and Gibber folk came later and built their mines and their towns and traded the minerals back to their home cities. Still later the sea rose up and cut them off from their origins. By then, the original people had already retreated to the dunes. The seasonal abundant rains ceased and the Time of Random Rain began. The only way to live was to follow the rains. Most people died and they were still diminishing in number when Ash Gridelin happened by."

"How did the Alabasters survive before he came?"

"We raised white pedes and farmed samphire. In the Time of Random Rain, we dug for underground water near the Border Humps and built the first water tunnels. Later, even that water began vanishing, but by that time Gridelin had come and the first of the Quartern stormlords had been born. Unfortunately for us here in Alabaster, his behaviour was considered so outrageous he was forced to be leaving before he fathered even a handful of children. That's why our water sensitives are rare. We haven't had a rainlord or a stormlord born in several hundred cycles." He waved a hand vaguely around the walls of books and scrolls. "The story is all in there."

"*Alabasters* built the tunnels?"

"We built those in the White Quarter, certainly. Later we taught Scarpen folk how to be building their own." He paused to ease himself into a chair. "When the water vanished and they were cut off from the outside world, Scarpen folk thought they were being punished for their sins. They tried to placate a ferocious sun with their water sacrifices. When Gridelin turned up, they were sure the Sunlord had sent him."

"And he didn't tell them otherwise?" she asked in distaste.

"Who knows? It was a long time ago, and although we have good records from Alabaster, our forebears knew little of what went on in the other Quarters. Our God is gentle and giving, and perhaps he instigated Gridelin's restless need to be exploring, which resulted in his succour of the Quartern. They were different times. Pointless to be judging them by our standards." He smiled at her. "If ye like, we will teach ye more of our faith. Ye will find it a kind one."

She shook her head with sudden violence. "How do I know it's not all spindevil dust in the wind? Tales to pacify children? I sacrificed water all my life to the Sunlord and now you and Feroze have convinced me there is no Sunlord, and never was. But you can't make me believe *another* lie." No sooner were the words out of her mouth than she reddened at her own rudeness and rushed from the room, running up the stairs. At the top she came face to face with Feroze.

Her anger drained away as if it had never been. "I think I've just been unforgivably rude to the Bastion," she told him miserably.

"Ah."

"I ran out on him. He's down in the library."

He smiled at her. "Wait here, Terelle. Maybe I can sort it out, and then I'll walk ye back to the townhouse. All right?"

She pulled an unhappy face and nodded. He disappeared down the steps and she leaned against the coolness of the salt wall with her eyes closed.

Why does it feel as if someone wrenched the heart out of you? You loathe the Quartern Sunpriest, and you've known for ages about who Ash Gridelin really was...

The answer, when it came, surprised her. B*ecause you need to believe in something. You're not like Shale. You need to know that you aren't alone, that there is a purpose to this life that is bigger than you are.*

The smile Feroze gave her when he returned was wry. "Don't worry," he said, "he understands."

He led her out into the streets again by another route and as they began the descent, he said, "The Bastion told me he never did say what he really wanted to tell ye. He has asked me to be saying it instead."

"So he had his reasons for telling me things that no one else in the Quartern knows?"

"Yes, I'm afraid so. Terelle, if there is limited water to be had, then we are the ones who'll suffer most. If Lord Jasper has to be making choices, then he will choose to be watering the Scarpen first. And ye are leaving. We worry that ye'll not return."

It was her turn to be silent, to wonder what he had not said. After a moment she sighed. "You know, don't you?"

"That the only way Lord Jasper could have been bringing water to us all is with the help of waterpainting? *Your* waterpainting? Yes. We understand the limitations of a stormlord better than most, and we understand the abilities of a waterpainter. He could not have overcome his problems with cloudmaking so quickly. We put two and two together."

She stopped in the shade of a wall to look at him. "And what is it you want from me?"

"Poor Terelle. There is always something, isn't there? Last time it was to use your powers to be fighting the Reduners. Now it's stormshifting."

"I have every intention of returning."

"I know. We want more. We want ye to be bringing another Watergiver back with you. In fact several, if possible."

She was silent.

"Ah," he said. "That wasn't a surprise to ye, was it?"

"Jasper has already asked me. But nonetheless I *am* surprised to hear it from Alabasters. Why in the sweet waters do you think Watergivers would listen to *me* rather than you? You know them, mix with them in the Borderlands, work for them, trade with them, worship the same god, know how to speak their tongue. Why haven't *you* asked them?"

This time the silence was so long she was sure he wasn't going to reply, but she held his gaze. The flow of pedestrians in the street passed to either side, making an island of them. She was unsettled and angry, hating her ignorance. Feroze may have seemed his usual calm self, but the artist in her saw the tautness of his shoulders and neck, the tense clenching of his jaw, the trouble that clouded the sparkle in his eyes.

"They despise us, Terelle," he said at last. "We are the abomination cast out by their ancestors, never to be heeded again. Our crime was beyond forgiveness. Were we to be asking a boon, they would refuse it without thought. Why do ye think they've never sent us water? So many of them are waterlords! Stormlords. They could send us rain on a regular basis."

"What did you do?" she whispered.

He shook his head and turned away. "It matters not," he said as they continued on their way. "What matters is your ability to persuade them to come. Three or four of them—best not waterpainters, perhaps. Ye're right; that's a dangerous art, better left alone. No, we need more of those ye would call stormlords. Khromatians call such folk waterlords. Waterlords and waterpainters together are the Watergivers. Of course, most people are neither, being water-blind just like most Quartern folk."

"Do you think they'll listen to *me*?" she asked again. "Leave their homes and their land because the Quartern asks?"

"I don't know. But every land has its adventurers, the people who want to be exploring, seeing new places, trying new things. There'll be such among the waterlords. I'm not expecting a man with Gridelin's answer to the problem, mind you. No, just people who could help us all over a rough spot for a short time until more stormlords are born."

She was silenced, feeling unbalanced. *As if I was sucked up into a spindevil,* she thought. *As if my feet can't reach the ground. I am too* ordinary *for all this.*

"Would ye like me to be coming with ye as far as the Borderlands?" he asked. "The Bastion suggested I do so."

"I—yes. Yes, I would." It was the truth; of all the Alabasters she had met, it was Feroze she trusted most.

"Then, with the Bastion's permission, I'll do so."

When they reached the townhouse and Feroze turned to leave her, she laid a hand on his arm to delay him. "There is one thing I'd like to understand. What was the sin that your ancestors committed? What could be so terrible that you're all still ashamed of it two thousand years later?"

He took a deep breath, as if he needed to steady himself. "I suppose ye'll find out soon enough. They silenced God," he whispered. "They silenced the voice of God."

He turned and walked away, but not before she had seen the tears in his eyes.

CHAPTER FOURTEEN

The White Quarter
Samphire and the Whiteout
Borderlands
Khromatis, Southern Marches

"I don't like this city," Dibble said quietly from where he sat on his bunk in the dormitory of the townhouse. There was no reason for him to speak quietly; there was no one else there, but the two of them were perpetually cautious. "I don't like it at all. And I don't trust these people."

Elmar, lying down on his bunk next to Dibble, turned his head to look at the young guard. *He's just a lad,* he thought, even though he knew that patently wasn't true. Dibble was as old as Jasper Bloodstone and, by all reports, had distinguished himself as an armsman of calibre in battle. Dibble Hornblend deserved to be called a man, but he was twenty years younger than Elmar, and that was enough to have him seem ridiculously youthful for the responsibility of this expedition. "They are just...different," he said. "A dour folk."

"Yes, that's it. They don't laugh much, do they? They

don't drink much, either. And I haven't seen a single snuggery anywhere."

"That shouldn't worry you. You got me," Elmar said.

Dibble flashed a grin, but then grumbled, "Right—but no weeping privacy. I don't want to go to a snuggery; it just seems weird that there are none."

Elmar snorted. "You may not see them, but they'll exist, I'll bet."

"El, seriously, is she safe among these people? And the old fellow is the Bastion? He doesn't look like a ruler!"

"These aren't safe times."

"This whole trip scares me waterless," Dibble said, starting to clean his fingernails with the tip of his dagger.

"It should. I reckon we've as much chance of getting Terelle home safely as a sand-flea has of lasting a day on my arse."

"But we have to."

"'Sright. We do."

"I heard that."

Elmar sat bolt upright and bumped his head on the bunk above. The figure—a silhouette against the light—was unrecognizable, but the voice was indubitably Terelle's.

"Can you try being a little more cheery about my chances?" she asked. "You know, like telling me that this is going to be as easy as adding salt to a cooking pot out on the Whiteout."

Elmar swung his feet to the floor, rubbing his head. "Wish I believed that, but it's not weeping likely. If Russet could paint your future, then what can all these other Watergiver folk do to you—to us—if they put their minds to it? And we not only have to get you home safe, but bring some of them back, too."

"Not good odds, huh?"

"No. But maybe we can do a bit to make them better."

She crossed over to sit on the end of his bunk. "Like what?"

"Been thinking about it. A lot. Maybe it might be a good idea for you to divide your paints, in fact all your painting stuff, into three equal lots. Then we each carry one."

She frowned. "Why?"

"Terelle, the paints are your power, and they can be taken from you. You need a back-up. We'll carry it. Them. Two back-ups."

"Ah. Yes. What else?"

"I want to teach you and Dibble the sort of thing that Lord Kaneth and I used out on patrol. How to leave messages for one another in case we are separated, how to leave a trail and how to follow a trail without alerting others. How to use hand signals without speaking."

"That's also a good idea," she agreed. "And we all need to learn as much as we can of the Khromatian tongue. I've arranged lessons while we're still in Samphire. And then the guards who ride with us to the border will teach us more."

Dibble groaned. "Lessons. I've never been much of a one for lessons."

"These ones might save your life. Or mine," she told him with a severity Elmar knew was only half a joke. "And now I am—without the slightest compunction— going to tell you all the secrets I've learned. Just remember they are secrets."

Elmar hid a grin. *I do so like a practical woman,* he thought.

*   *   *

The first part of the journey north-east was easy enough; stones across the salt marked the trails. They picked up water two days out at Fucoid Mine and then several days later at Mine Sylvine. Besides Feroze, there were ten young armed Alabaster warriors with them. Russet, in a shaded basket chair made for the elderly, rode on the baggage pede.

Oddly enough it was Dibble who did best with learning the language of Khromatis. Sitting around the campfire of a night, with the flames spitting like water on a griddle because of the salt mixed in with the pede droppings, the Alabasters vied with one another to give the most memorable lessons. The pedemen had decided that teaching Dibble and Elmar was an amusing way to pass the time. Dibble played the role of a sand-witted armsman, diverting them with his outrageous mistakes and never taking it amiss when they made fun of him.

"It's actually easy," he confided to Terelle and Elmar. "There's a music to it. All you have to do is remember the words, like memorising a song..."

Elmar did try, but was forced to admit he had no ear for a tune and kept forgetting the words. Terelle had her waterpainter's memory. When she wrote words down, together with their meaning, she remembered them forever. Feroze was her teacher, and he appeared to enjoy the lessons, so her progress was rapid, although he did complain her accent was woeful.

A day out of Sylvine, they hit the first of the salt marshes that began the Borderlands. They camped there at the edge of the marsh, near a band of samphire about fifty paces wide, after which the land gradually became grey and soggy, indented with shallow puddles covered in greenish slime. Half a mile in, there was no more samphire, just a salt and mud bog.

"Don't walk into it," Feroze warned Terelle as she stood in the samphire looking across to where they would be travelling. "Under the scum it becomes clingy wet glue. Step in it, and ye'll sink to your knees and, believe me, it's no joke trying to pull a person out again."

"So much water in there," she said, incredulous. "Just lying around?"

"Yes, but it's as salty as can be, and quite useless."

"It smells awful."

"That's the scum. Horrible stuff."

"Wet ground," she said, marvelling. "It seems..." she hunted for a word to describe the profundity of her shock, "sacrilegious."

She glanced around the camp, at the fire sparking and spitting in blues and greens, at the guards cutting fresh samphire for dinner, at the pedes grazing hungrily among the plants. The scene was safe, reassuring, even familiar. And that safety, that familiarity, would soon be behind her, inaccessible. She was going to a place where water lay about on the ground, and flowed past as rivers.

"How do we cross the Borderlands if it's all so gluey?" she asked.

"Oh, the pedes have no problem. Their weight—and ours—is spread over all those legs, and onto their bellies too, when the going gets very soft. As long as we stay on their backs, we'll be fine. The problem is always to find dry land to make camp in the midst of the muck."

"When I was talking to you back in Samphire, you told me the Alabasters were exiled for silencing God. What did you mean?"

He looked stricken. "It is difficult for me to speak of such iniquity. Ask Russet." With that, he strode away to where the pedes were munching the samphire, and a moment later she saw him grooming one of the animals.

She sought Russet, who was huddled by the fire on his colourful woven mat, and sat down beside him, directly on the salt.

"The Alabaster won't be telling ye what ye want to be knowing," he said with a touch of his malicious glee. "Upset him, did ye?"

"Feroze suggested I ask you to explain about the Alabasters silencing God."

He gave a high-pitch chuckle. "Such silliness. Superstition! Old myths the Khromatians would be forgetting long ago, except—" He dropped his voice and beckoned her closer. "—'cept it suits Khromatis for Alabasters to believe it." He poked her in the ribs with a sharp finger. "Ye not be worrying over such. Worry about the Verdigris, if ye must."

"Verdigris?" It was the bright green colour in one of her paint pots. She wondered if his mind was wandering.

He poked her again, grinning. "Your worst enemy, girl. Verdigris family. Ye'll see. Get hold of ye, and they'll throw ye off the walls of the Peak."

She knew he was waiting for her to ask what the Peak was, but she would not give him the satisfaction. Revolted, hating him, she stared silently back into his small green eyes.

"Just as well I be painting ye, no? Ye be safe. For a while."

And for the rest of the evening, he refused to say another word.

*   *   *

Terelle was awoken in the middle of the night by the touch of gritty fingers on her face. She shrieked and sat upright, her heart hammering wildly.

No one was touching her. Elmar lay on one side of her, snoring gently, wrapped tight in his cloak and blanket; Russet lay on the other, but not asleep. From the glint of starlight in his eyes, she knew he was looking at her.

She touched her cheek. Under her fingertips she felt the roughness of salt grains. Calming her beating heart, she looked around. Two rows of sleeping people lay stretched out on the salt, none of them more than a few paces from her, with Dibble on one end. Further away, Feroze stood next to another guard, holding a lit candle lantern high. They were both staring away into the darkness behind her head, bodies rigid with tension. She looked over her shoulder to see what made them stare so fixedly—and froze in terror.

Towering over her, only a few paces away, was a salt-dancer. She'd seen such dancers before, swirls of salt caught in a spindevil, but not one like this. It was three times as high as a pede was tall, its body wavering, arms shivering and undulating. Further away, several others cavorted across the plains, the salt of their ghostly bodies sparkling in the starlight. These were not the usual amorphous shapes, nor mirages either, but fearsome human-like monsters with holes for eyes in elongated faces. The hair stood up on the back of Terelle's neck and her heart pounded even harder. She wanted to reach out and shake Elmar awake, but she was too scared to move.

The nearest dancer bent and reached out a hand to touch her. Panting in horror as fingers dragged across her cheek, she gasped and slapped the ghostly fingers away with both her hands. Her blow scattered the salt, leaving the arm truncated at the wrist.

She scrambled up as Feroze approached and Elmar woke. "Don't worry," Feroze murmured as Elmar tumbled out of his blankets, already grasping his sword. "They can't hurt ye. They're just salt."

"No. S-salt-dancers are just salt flurries, sh-shapeless wisps scurrying this way and that. These are *people*! Huge people. But…" They were made of salt. Anxiety made her voice quaver. Next to her, Elmar gaped at the salt-dancer, then poked it tentatively with his blade. Nothing changed.

"No. Not people. Water sensitives mixed that foul water of the Borderlands with salt, so that the salt flurries can be manipulated."

She shivered. "That's impossible! No water sensitive can do that."

"These are waterlords especially trained to sense those who don't have the peculiarities of Alabaster blood. They've grouped together to be menacing ye—the four of ye. They've jumped to the conclusion ye and Russet are Quartern folk too. They want to be scaring ye away from the border. Don't worry, they can't hurt ye."

"You won't get into trouble with them, will you?"

He shrugged. "They need us, as much as we need them. They need all the other minerals we mine here in the Whiteout and the Border Humps. They need what we import from the Gibber. They need our labour for their manufactories and their fields. Go to sleep, Terelle. Salt-dancers have no power except to scare." He smiled and walked away, the light from his lantern swinging the shadows as he left.

She snuggled back down into her bedding, wrapping herself against the cold. "Did you see that?" she asked Russet. "Your people welcoming us. What makes you think they'll greet us with affection when we cross the Borderlands?"

"We are Kermes. Your grandmother married a Verdigris," he said. "Rulers, all. Watergivers. Waterlords. Deserving of respect."

But she didn't believe it, not the part about respect. Elmar snorted, indicating he didn't think much of the reasoning, either. She'd already known that her grandmother, Russet's daughter Magenta, had married the ruler of Khromatis, the man they called the Pinnacle, but now he had given her another piece of the puzzle. The Pinnacle's family name was Verdigris, and Russet thought they were his enemies and therefore hers too. *Sunblast you, Russet. Why can't you just say things outright?* She wondered if perhaps he was growing senile; he seemed worse now than he had been before. Being bitten by the scorpion and then almost dying of thirst had aged his mind as much as his body.

She dropped back into an uneasy doze, her last thoughts of Khromatian Watergivers who hated strangers so much they used their energies to scare them away. The nearest of them must still be over a hundred miles away, and yet they'd not only manipulated water with finesse, they'd used it to manipulate damp salt.

The power they must have . . .

The pedes didn't seem to mind the salty stagnant water or the greyish mud that sucked at their pointed feet and oozed up between their segment plates, but Terelle hated it. The stench of wet rot, the grey drabness of the mire, the horrible viscosity of it, the weird salt mists that blanketed them for long periods while the pedes picked their way across the marsh: she loathed it all. The smell not only permeated the air, it seeped into the fabric of their clothing and clung to their bedding; it contaminated their drinking water with its stench and made their food taste mouldy even when it wasn't.

No permanent paths crossed the Borderlands. As fast as a track was made, it was swallowed up by the shifting pools and mud ponds and sluggish trickles of water welling up from underground. Apart from birds, the only living creatures were grey mudworms, some of them as long as an arm, basking in the pools as they digested the soil and exuded long lines of waste behind them. Herons and stilts feasted and screeched with annoyance if the caravan came too close. Nights were cold and damp, full of sucking and slithering sounds as worms pushed their way through the muck. Feroze used his water-senses to find patches of dryer soil where they could light a fire or sleep, but the mud and stagnant water were never more than a few paces away.

"Give me a battle any day," Elmar said at breakfast after their first night in the marsh. "This place belongs in a nightmare."

"The worst is the water," Dibble grumbled. "It's supposed to be precious, not *rotten*."

Terelle glanced at the horizon. It was jagged with far-off mountains. Another strangeness, that white capping of—what was it Russet had called it?

"Snow," he said when she asked again later that morning. Their pedes were ambling along side by side, their

feet making odd plopping noises as they lifted, followed
by a squelch as they sank back down. Elmar was driving
her, with Dibble behind, and Feroze was driving Russet.
"To be getting to the Peak, ye'll cross those mountains."

"Why would I want to go there? Is that where you
painted me?"

He shook his head. When she said nothing, he added,
"The Peak be the main city of Khromatis. Seat of the Pinnacle."

Fear dried her mouth and lips. She'd thought initially
that if she was to bring waterlords to the Quartern, she'd
have to visit those close to the Pinnacle. Now it was
sounding more and more like a bad idea. She'd be damned
if she'd go to the Peak or to the Pinnacle just because Russet wanted her to, for some selfish reason of his own.

"There's no point to secrets anymore," she said. "I'll
see for myself soon. I need to know as much as you
can tell me. What will we find on the other side of the
Borderlands?"

"Nothing ye've ever seen before," he said. "A place
where soil burns in fireplaces, where Alabasters be
labouring like animals for us, where water is for wasting,
where land be growing green."

"Oh, for once in your life, can't you say something that
will be of *use*?" she cried. "Your secrecy might cripple
me. If you want my cooperation, you have to tell me what
I'm supposedly heir to. You have to tell me all you know.
Where is the place you painted me? What can you tell me
about our family?"

"Your tongue be too sharp, girl!"

"And yours too twisted. Russet, I am out of patience.
Tell me what I need to know."

"Ye be too like your mother. Magenta be always rude, like this. She be not disciplining ye, as the Pinnacle be wanting."

"I'm not Sienna. Magenta was my grandmother, not my mother. And I never knew her."

He looked shocked, then said, snappishly, "Of course I be knowing who ye are." Then he mumbled something she couldn't catch.

Oh, weeping hells, what will I do if his mind goes?

She said, more politely, "The Pinnacle was your son-in-law when you left Khromatis. But do you know if he's still alive? Maybe someone else is the Pinnacle now."

His face paled and he swayed. If it hadn't been for his chair, he would have fallen.

Feroze glanced behind to make sure he was all right and answered her question. "The Pinnacle is never called by name, any more than we call the Bastion by name. I believe, though, that there was a change of ruler about ten years ago and the present Pinnacle is the brother of the last."

Russet brightened. "Ochre be dead then? Good!" He directed another of his gleeful smiles at Terelle. "Then Pinnacle now be usurper. Ye be Pinnacle!"

She snorted. "That's daft." *You were just told your son-in-law is dead and you're happy about it?* Thinking about it made her go cold all over. Did he have a heart in that scrawny body of his?

Mother, I never knew you, but I understand why you ran away.

"Feroze," she asked, "is the Pinnacle ever a woman?"

He shrugged. "I don't know. Terelle, ye have to be understanding that Khromatians *never* discuss such matters with us. They don't think it…" He searched for the right word. "Seemly. To them we've no right to be treated as equals or informed about anything."

"That's disgusting. You Alabasters work for them and they don't want to talk to you?"

"That's right. Unless it's to give orders, of course."

Russet laughed.

Terelle was so furious with him she didn't look his way. "Do any of them speak your tongue?"

"Oh, everyone does in the Southern Marches. That's the area where Alabasters work," Feroze said. "Even though we speak their language, and it's not necessary for them to learn ours, they do. Every household has an Alabaster tutor to teach the children."

"We be not trusting ye," Russet said, still grinning. "Want to know what ye be saying."

"Your problem with the language will be once you leave the Southern Marches," Feroze added. "Khromatians from the north don't bother to learn."

"Like me," Russet said. "Be not knowing till learning in the Quartern. Sienna, ye do what I tell ye, there be no problem."

"Who's he talking about?" Elmar asked, puzzled, when the other pede drew ahead and Russet was out of earshot.

"My mother. He's getting us muddled. It's not the first time, either."

Elmar turned to look her full in the face. "That's *not* good."

"No."

"I'd rather take you home. Terelle, are you *sure* you can't withstand his painting?"

"I'm sure."

"Best then you concentrate on getting him to tell you exactly where this place is, the one where he painted you. We go there, then leave for home."

She smiled at him. "And try to pick up some stray waterlords looking for adventure along the way?" It wasn't much of a joke, but it was the best she could do. Inside, her apprehension swelled, threatening to consume her.

Even though she knew the power of the painting would see to it that she ended up in the right place whether she liked it or not, she took Elmar's advice and continued to question Russet about the location. Finally, in their last camp inside the Borderland marshes, he told her the place was close to Kermes Manor, the house owned by his family.

"Born there, me," he said. "Magenta born there too, but she was a beauty." He looked her up and down in scorn. "Not plain, like ye. So I be taking her to the Peak, to meet the Pinnacle. He liked beauties, that man."

"Ochre Verdigris?"

Out of the corner of her eye, she saw Feroze's head swing up in shock to stare at them.

Russet nodded. "She married him. But only one child living. Sienna Verdigris, the silly frip." He shook his finger at her in sudden anger. "Ye—ye—"

"I am *not* Sienna," she said and quickly changed the subject. "Where is Kermes Manor?"

"The Slew."

"And that is . . . ?"

"The ward above Southern Marches."

"Will Kermes Manor still be in your family? Who will live there now?"

"What? What? Why asking, eh? Ye live in the Peak soon! Ye the Pinnacle. Rule the land. I teach ye." He grasped her arm, the grip of his bony fingers painfully tight.

Feroze stepped in and led him away to sit down by the fire, telling him it was time to have something to eat.

Elmar exchanged a look with Dibble, then shook his head at Terelle. "I don't like this at all. I think we're going to be up to our ears in politics when we get to Khromatis. And politics anywhere is a midden of garbage. Tread in the wrong spot and you fall straight into a waterless hell."

"I want to know why Feroze startled like a pebblemouse when I mentioned the name Verdigris," she said.

She bided her time and grabbed him later that night to ask.

For once he was forthcoming. "I didn't know the Pinnacle's family name was Verdigris," he said.

"What does it mean to you?"

"The military governor of the Southern Marches—that's the man who both commands the armed men and administers the ward—is a Verdigris. He's been there in the south for the past eight years. I suppose the Alabasters who work across the Borderlands might know if he is related to the Pinnacle, but I don't. They hate him."

"Why?"

"I've heard he's a cruel man."

She shivered.

They emerged from the marsh at the base of a small rise. Without stopping, they rode on. Another quarter-run of a sandglass brought them to the top of the rise to overlook a small valley. Perhaps two miles away below was Marchford, buildings jostling on either side of a ribbon of water. Chimneys smoked and belched from a jumble of outlying smelters and ovens, furnaces and manufactories. Terelle wrinkled her nose. An acrid smell hung on the air, tainting the valley and subduing the lingering stink of marshland rot. The river below the town ran brown and oily, soiling the banks.

"We have company," Feroze murmured and held up his hand to halt the caravan.

She hardly heard. She was still overwhelmed by all she could see: clouds, grass, trees, slopes rising to a background of impossibly high mountains—and water. Water running over the land, through the town and out the other side, just sliding away, untrammelled, uncaught, made dirty as if it didn't matter. Wasted. The sight was so shocking, she could hardly catch her breath. The two sides of the town were linked across the wash by a stone road. A bridge, Feroze called it.

"Is that like a drywash when the rush comes down?" Dibble asked, wide-eyed in shock.

"No," she replied, her tone as unforgiving as granite. There was no comparison and there never could be. "No, *nothing* like."

"That's a river," Feroze said.

"That's Khromatis," Russet said with smug satisfaction. "Civilised life again." He shot a glance to where she sat on her pede. "Your home."

She snorted. This was even more alien to her than the Whiteout. Leafy bushes. Trees, so tall. Grass. All *green*. And dirtied water running to waste. She shivered. The wind, blowing from the direction of the mountains, was cold and she wasn't used to it being cold during the day while it was still sunny. At the Bastion's request, Alabasters in Samphire had given them warmer clothes and strange shoes that covered their feet to the ankle. Now she understood why.

"All that green, it looks *sick*." Dibble was grinning, so she guessed it was an attempt to joke.

"Snap out of it, you two," Elmar said. "Feroze is right—those people down there are on their way to intercept us." He used his pede prod to point at a group of men riding up the valley slope towards them. They were still some distance away, riding in orderly formation. The spears they carried, held upright, bristled above their heads.

"Border patrol," Feroze said. "Water sensitives among them."

"Withering winds," Elmar muttered as they approached, "as formidable an array of sharp points as the thorny lizards of the Gibber."

"Forty men," Dibble said. "Riding…animals. What *are* those things?"

"They look a bit like the donkeys I've seen in Portennabar," Elmar said. "Hoofed. These are larger, though. And…different."

"The tails are different. These are all hair. And they are bred to be ridden," Feroze said, "not to be pack animals. They are Alpiners. I'm told there's something similar found across the Giving Sea, but they are different colours, from what I've heard." He gave a grunt of disparagement. "Alpiners would be useless in the Quartern. Always wanting to drink."

Large men sitting on small mounts—they looked ludicrous. Nervous, Terelle wanted to giggle, but curbed the desire. The animals were covered in reddish-brown hair, but had tails and neck hair that were long and white. Muscular beasts, sinewy things to look at, yet they hinted at hidden strengths and speed.

Her heart thumped as the men rode closer. There was no mistaking their intention to intercept the caravan. There was no mistaking their occupation, either: these were professional armsmen. Their metal helmets had plates curving across the cheek and extensions to protect the nose. Their leather breastplates were metal-studded; their biceps and forearms were armoured with metalled links. They wore swords, not scimitars.

"Men dressed to fight," Elmar muttered. "I am liking this less and less."

"They don't need to use swords to defeat us. They have stormlords a lot more powerful than Jasper." *They can make salt dance a hundred miles away . . .*

"They won't all be stormlords," Elmar said, probably to make her feel happier.

"In fact, very few of them," one of the Alabasters said in agreement. "Wouldn't be more than twenty waterlord armsmen among those patrolling the whole border, from north to south."

The riders weren't sitting on their saddles; they rode astride them, which didn't look comfortable. They wore tunics over trousers that fitted into solid leather footwear of a kind Terelle had never seen before. And over their left shoulders, slanting across their chests and pinned under a belt at the waist on the right, they all wore a kind of woven and knotted scarf of a vividly patterned weave that reminded her of Russet's clothing. The draped ends that hung loose at a man's right hip anchored the scabbard for his sword.

That's just Russet's wrap, but worn differently.

Feroze, at the head of their caravan, twisted in the saddle to signal for Dibble, who was driving Russet, and Elmar, driving Terelle, to bring their pedes forward to flank him on either side. The others arrayed themselves behind while they waited.

The armsman in the lead was taller than any man Terelle had ever seen. His helmet made it hard to see his features, but there was one thing certain: he was not smiling. He shouted a command and the troop reined in. Terelle looked from one impassive face to the next but it was hard to distinguish much under those helmets. When her glance fell to the backs of their hands she could see a few were tattooed with patterns, just like Russet's.

No, not quite. The patterning is different.

The leader snapped out something to Feroze that Terelle did not understand.

Calmly, Feroze introduced himself as Saltmaster Feroze Khorash of Samphire, advisor to the Bastion, then introduced Russet by his full name and status, Lord Russet Kermes, waterpainter of Khromatis. He waved to indicate Terelle and was about to name her, but was stopped by the astonished murmur that ran through the group of riders. The leader stiffened in the saddle, the harsh lines of his face deepening into a frown. A moment later he reached up and removed his helmet. His brown hair was long and curly; unrestrained, it fell to his shoulders. His brown skin and green eyes were a match to Terelle's; for the first time in her life she gazed on the face of someone alike enough to have been her brother or cousin, albeit tattooed. She guessed him to be in his early forties.

And she didn't like him. It was not the harsh lines of

his face that made her mistrust him, but the gesture of removing his helmet. It was done as a mark not of trust, but of arrogance, as if he wanted to say: *Remember this face? You should know me and bow. And you should know that I do not fear you, or your puny armsmen.*

Behind him, three of the men exchanged glances, then as one, they also removed their helmets. At first Terelle could see no significance in this. Then she realised: each one of the four was tattooed across the cheeks, and the pattern on each—a swirl of blue curlicues—was identical. She suspected the four of them were proclaiming their common lineage. She guessed the leader was the father, and the three others were his sons, the oldest perhaps in his early twenties, the youngest seventeen or eighteen.

Terelle looked over at Russet. He was sitting as motionless as a chameleon, eyes hooded, hands gripping the chair arms tightly. *He knows what those tattoos mean,* she thought.

The leader stared at Russet, his eyes as hard as emeralds. When he spoke, Terelle struggled to understand, but managed to catch the gist of his words. "I thought you were dead, long since," he said. "And what of my cousin, Sienna?"

Russet glared at him in silence. Terelle wasn't sure if he was angry at the question or confused by it. She asked, using her own tongue, "Your cousin? Are we related then? I am Sienna's daughter. She died many years ago."

The man swung to face her, his eyebrows snapping together in a glower. She had the feeling he'd understood her. "My name is Terelle," she said, avoiding the tangled issue of her family name. "What's yours?"

CHAPTER FIFTEEN

Khromatis
The Southern Marches
Marchford

Terelle didn't like the Khromatian leader.

She didn't like the way he sat motionless and stared at her. There was no warmth in his eyes, no welcome in the harsh lines of his face. Only when Elmar and Dibble both started to fidget did the fellow answer the request for his name, and this time he used the language of the Quartern. "Lord Bice Verdigris. Commander of the Southern Marches."

Oh, hells.

He followed that statement up with an order. Four of his men rode forward, two to where Dibble sat, two towards Elmar, their belligerence expressed in lowered spears aimed at the two armsmen.

Feroze spoke again, in Quartern, still calm. "These two Scarpen men are the personal bodyguards of Lord Terelle. And Lord Terelle is the betrothed of the Cloudmaster of the Quartern. She is his envoy and he has asked that her attendants be granted a special dispensation to enter this land, in the interest of friendship between neighbours."

She gripped the saddle handle as her blood ran cold. For a moment she couldn't identify what disturbed her so. Feroze was putting words into Jasper's mouth, but it wasn't the words that panicked her, it was the way he said them. The way he lowered his eyes and folded his hands in his lap. The unspoken deference and submission in the way he held himself. That wasn't the Feroze she knew.

Russet spoiled the effect of the words anyway, by glaring at Terelle and then spitting out words as if they were poisonous, "Betrothed? *Betrothed?* What? Who said? Ye belong here!"

Elmar winced and swore under his breath.

Terelle, trying to match Feroze's calm, said merely, "I will marry whom I please, when I please." She turned her attention to Lord Bice. "Greetings, cousin. I would like to keep my two guards. The Cloudmaster might take it amiss if they were to be sent back without me." She was trying to sound both imperious and unruffled, but had no idea if she'd succeeded.

Lord Bice met her gaze, but there was no softening there. "Very well. They can come with ye for the time being while ye are under my *kharits*, my...my care. But if ye and Lord Russet want to be riding further into Khromatis, ye'll have to be doing so without them, or any Alabaster. For now, we will escort ye to my quarters beyond the town." His heavy accent told her he had not learned the Quartern tongue as a child.

While he was speaking, the Khromatian armsmen, in answer to some unseen signal, lined themselves up on either side of the travellers. It should have felt like an

escort to honour them, but it didn't, not to her. It felt like
an armed guard for prisoners.

Elmar made a small gesture of warning to Dibble that
meant, *Be alert!*

No one talked much as they descended into the town.
They were travelling too fast for normal conversation
anyway. Assaulted by new impressions, assailed on all
sides by new sights and smells and sounds, Terelle felt a
heightened tension.

Wild trees grew on the hill slope, not the widely scattered, scraggly, twisted things of the Quartern, hardly
taller than a pede; no, these were neatly grouped together,
tall, leafy and plentiful. Even the town was odd to her
eyes. The buildings were made of stone, not mud brick or
salt, and were roofed with some sort of pale grey material.
The streets were paved with stone, which the pedes hated.
They clicked their mouthparts in irritation and would
have swung their feelers about in outrage if their drivers
had not hobbled them to the side mounting handles.
Smells were strange, an irritant in her nostrils. Acridity in
the smoky air, the unfamiliar odour of alpiner droppings,
the all-permeating sweetness of water that was strange
only in its abundance, the tickling perfume of flowers and
grasses wafting from the hillsides and gardens—it all
made her want to sneeze.

The place was grimy from all the smoke, yet ablaze with
colour—flowers, clothing, ornate decorations on the
wealthier houses in the form of carved and painted patterns
under the eaves. And wood: there was wood everywhere.
Carts, barrels, doors and window frames, seats, bridge railings. Chopped wood neatly stacked in house yards, which
puzzled her, until she realised it was for burning.

Sweet waters, they *burned* wood.

Abundant wood, abundant water. By all that's sunholy, do these people know *how lucky they are?*

They did not stop on that side of the river, but rode straight through the town to the bridge. As they crossed, Terelle stared through the railings and, disoriented and dizzied by the sight of sliding water, clutched the saddle handle tight. On the other side, they entered a busy street market and were surrounded by a bustling, hustling jostle of people. Colourful stalls blocked half the roadway, and people thronged what was left. The way they gazed at Lord Bice and his men was neither cheerful nor admiring. Bice, she decided, was not popular. Alabasters used pedes to come and go across the Borderlands, so Khromatians were accustomed to seeing them, but they stared hard at her and Russet, and registered shock when they spotted Elmar and Dibble, too dark to be Alabasters, yet too fair to be Khromatians. Many wore colourful wraps similar to Russet's; others, mostly workmen and tradesmen, wore plain trousers and tunics.

In the market the crowd slowed the column to a crawl. Several itinerant vendors made the most of the moment and started to pester the Alabaster guards to buy their goods. One seller approached Elmar and Terelle in an attempt to sell a large cloth pouch full of the tiny mirrors that the Alabasters sewed to their clothes. She was about to dismiss the vendor with a shake of her head, when Elmar asked how much they were. After bargaining that didn't seem much different from similar haggling back in a Scarpen city, he negotiated the purchase.

"What do you want these for? They're as heavy as a stone mortar," she asked as he handed them to her to put in a saddle bag.

"They're for you," he said quietly. "Just in case. Tiny, yet easily seen."

"Ah." She knew what he was suggesting: it was likely they'd be separated and mirrors could mark her trail. Now that she'd met the first of her relatives, the thought was disturbing. To be alone with Russet in this land? She shrivelled inside.

As they continued on in single file through the streets, Elmar said to her over his shoulder, "If they do separate us, Dibble and I won't give up, I promise you. No matter what happens, remember that and take heart."

She leaned forward so she could speak into his ear. "Be careful, Elmar. This Bice scares me. I'd never forgive myself if something happened to either of you."

"Maybe we're both trembling at nothing more dangerous than salt-dancers."

But she didn't think so. She'd seen the flash in Lord Bice's eyes when he realised who she was: shock had been closely followed by rage. Worse, it wasn't the momentary rage of a hot-tempered man, soon over. No, his was a cold fury that would stay beneath the surface while he made his plans.

She knew his kind.

The residence of the Commander of the Southern Marches was beyond the town on the eastern bank of the river, a mile upstream. It was as large as Breccia Hall, but surrounded by gardens. Terelle had never seen a building as beautiful, or as extravagant. Elegant pillars, archways and polished stone walls were punctuated by doors and windows trimmed with polished wood; straight pieces of wood, too, not gnarled and twisted like Scarpen wild wood, or soft and patterned like bab palm. Windows were not just shuttered openings, but were glassed. She couldn't think why anyone would want to do that. And then there was the garden. Trees that appeared to serve no purpose beyond their looks. Open ponds, exposed to the greed of the sun.

Sunblast it, she thought, disgruntled. *I will never see a Scarpen city the same way again.*

The Alabaster guards, together with Dibble and Elmar and all the pedes and the luggage, were whisked away to the barracks at the back of the house. Lord Bice handed Feroze, Russet and Terelle over to servants as soon as the rest of them arrived at the main door, then disappeared himself together with the young men she'd thought might be his sons. He had not introduced them.

Anxious, but trying not to show it, she followed a dour young man wearing a uniform similar to the Khromatian armsmen, although without the armour or the impressive footwear.

Feroze spoke to him in Khromatian and then dropped back to whisper to her as they trailed the man upstairs, "He's an army orderly. This is not Bice's personal manor house, although he and his sons treat it as such. It belongs to the army, and is the residence given to the commander."

Behind them, Russet struggled to keep up. Terelle hesitated, about to offer to take his arm, but he glared at her, apparently affronted that she thought he needed aid. She shrugged and hurried after Feroze. At the top of the stairs, they were met by more orderlies in uniform, who fussed around them, showing them to their separate rooms, providing each of them with a change of clothes, readying baths and serving food on trays. Everything was overly comfortable, more opulent than needed, more confusingly complex than necessary. For her, the worst was tramping across wooden floors. In the Scarpen, even small items such as bab-wood chests were not all that plentiful. Imported wood for building was formidably expensive. To wear it out by *walking* on it felt like blasphemy.

A Khromatian woman came to help her dress; she wanted to laugh and send her away. When she held up what she was given to wear, she was glad she hadn't because she couldn't decide how to put it on. "What happened to our bags?" she asked in halting Khromatian.

"The orderlies will bring them up later, I suppose," the woman said, and added scornfully, "They are military men, you know. Won't do anything unless they get a direct order. Here, let me help you." She took the clothing and began to wrap the fabric around Terelle, pleating and tucking the ends in. Terelle had seen women in the town wearing wraps, and had thought them pretty, but when she took a step, she half expected the whole thing to fall off. As she made her way to Russet's room next door a little while later, the feel of the skirt flapping around her ankles was irritating.

Feroze was there before her. Russet was sound asleep, snoring noisily. They stood by his bed, looking down on him, but he didn't stir.

"I think we had better leave him be," Feroze said. "He's worn out."

"What does this Lord Bice intend to do with us?" she asked as they moved away from Russet's bed. "He's hardly said a word, and yet he's apparently my cousin. That's hardly making me feel welcome."

"I dragged some information out of the orderly who

was attending to me." To Terelle's ears, Feroze sounded
unsettled and worried. "Hard work, but here's what I
found out. The Pinnacle—the one who was Russet's son-
in-law and your grandfather—he was the older brother of
Lord Bice's father. Because your grandparents had no
children other than your mother, and she disappeared, the
position passed to Lord Bice's father after your grandparents died. He's the present Pinnacle. Those armsmen with
the tattoos are Bice's three sons, by the way. Hue the
eldest, Jet the middle one and Rubric, the good-looking
young one."

"Is Lord Bice next in line?"

"Yes." His agreement sounded dubious, his tone wary.
"He was an only child."

"Until suddenly I pop up, in theory a pretender to the
position. Which I don't want." She sighed. "I have to talk
to Bice. To explain things."

"I agree, ye need to be emphasising that ye're here at
the request of the Cloudmaster, in order to invite waterlords to the Quartern. Perhaps that will get his attention,
more than anything else." He shot a glance at Russet and
lowered his voice still further. "Play down Russet's part."

She nodded.

"Would ye like me to be talking to Lord Bice first? I
could look for him, ask him to see ye. I suppose ye could
mention the waterpainting that has dragged ye here. It
would tell him ye didn't have a choice."

She matched his whisper. "I'd like to. Then maybe
he'd take me to where it was painted, so I could turn
around and go home again." She walked over to the window and looked out, thinking. Evening was approaching,
speeded on its way by a cloud-covered sky. The glass

squares distorted the landscape, blurring outlines and smudging colours. Someone crossing the grass appeared as a moving smear of hues across a static background. *Why do they bother with glass when it is so hard to see through?* "But it could be a lot more complicated than that. If I tell Bice about being coerced by Russet's painting, he'll guess Russet has plans for me, and for himself."

"Which might put ye both in jeopardy."

They looked at each other, their indecision shared. "Do you think I should go with you to see Bice now?" she asked.

"Not yet. I don't want his contempt for Alabasters to be influencing his attitude to ye."

"Surely you exaggerate."

"Terelle, look around at this room. Yours I imagine is similar."

She glanced around: two beds, a large fireplace, a woodpile beside it to burn—*wood!*—elaborate moulding around the top of the walls, waterpaintings long since parted from their trays now hanging in frames on the panelling. A ewer and wash basin on a stand. The glassed windows. "It's luxurious. And so is mine. So?"

"A lovely room, fit for a lord. I told Lord Bice I was the advisor to the Bastion, and he put me in the windowless box room across the passage, with nothing more than a trundle bed and a single blanket. I suppose I'm lucky he didn't put me down in the barracks with Elmar and Dibble."

That shocked her more than anything else he'd said. "I don't understand. That is—is—is discourteous, to say the least."

"Deliberately so. They feel it is deserved."

"No," she said in revulsion. "What happened long ago should no longer have consequences. Worst of all is that you all acquiesce in your own punishment!"

He gave a faint smile, and something told her that he was not mocking her. Her words troubled him, she guessed because in his heart he agreed with her.

"We may never achieve a fair world, but it doesn't mean that we shouldn't strive for it," she said. "Are there any Alabaster servants in this house?"

"No. This is the heart of their rule in the Southern Marches. They don't want Alabasters privy to their secrets."

Someone knocked at the door, and as Russet didn't stir, Feroze went to answer it. Dibble and Elmar were both there, the strain on their faces easing when they saw Terelle and Feroze. The servant who'd brought them to the door left, and Feroze waved the two men inside.

"We brought up the rest of your baggage," Elmar said, dumping his load on the floor. He and Dibble exchanged unhappy looks, then Elmar continued, "Lady Terelle, I apologise for not—not succeeding in my duty."

"Pardon? In what way?"

"The guards insisted on searching all our bags, including yours and Russet's. They removed all the paint-powders. When I protested, they said it was Lord Bice's orders."

"They threatened us," Dibble added sourly. "Said if we made a fuss they would bundle us up like roped baggage on our own animals and send us back to Alabaster."

"*All* of the paints?" she asked, dismayed.

"They were thorough," Elmar replied. "I'm sorry."

"Not your fault." She sat down on the second bed and

tried not to feel sick with apprehension. "I hid some powders in the personal things I have with me. It's enough for one painting. For emergencies." When she saw Feroze's face she felt even worse. He was looking at her in horror.

"We never thought—" he began, then stopped. "Neither the Bastion nor I dreamed they would treat ye and Russet with anything less than respect. Ye are Khromatians. And lords."

"Bice is a lord," Elmar said. "Does that make him a stormlord or a waterpainter?"

"Either," Feroze replied. "There's no way of knowing. Either way he could be dangerous, even though those possessing any water talents are bound by strict rules here. Watergiver family names are usually colours, and their personal name is always a colour, bestowed when they manifest their water skills, so you can tell them from ordinary folk."

"Bice is a colour?" Dibble asked, surprised.

"There's a bice green and a bice blue," Terelle said. "Rubric is red ochre, jet is black. Hue seems to cover everything. What about their tattoos?"

He shook his head. "What you would call an upleveller thing. They indicate which of the fifteen aristocratic families a man is from. Meaningless, really. As for being a waterlord or a painter: from my meagre knowledge of Khromatis, I think waterpainting is a rare talent."

"That's handy to know," she said.

"It's the kind of thing that Russet should have told ye, the old spindevil of a man."

She shot a look at her great-grandfather, asleep with his mouth half open. "He's always kept secrets, right from the beginning."

"Gave him a sense of power over you," Elmar said, his contempt for Russet obvious. He looked around for somewhere to sit, but there weren't any chairs. Dibble was standing at the window, trying to see out, but it was dark and only his own face looked back at him. Elmar settled himself on the edge of the second bed. "You could have told us more, too," he said to Feroze. "I'm fed up with secrets."

"We know less than ye may think," Feroze replied. "Some Alabasters live here in the Borderlands, certainly, but they are kept separate. Khromatians don't mix with them, or talk to them, other than what's needed for their work."

No one said anything. *Alabasters could still have told us more,* she thought, *if they could free themselves of their stupid ties to their past.*

To break the embarrassing silence that followed, Feroze said, "I think ye two armsmen ought to be staying here the night. One on duty in the passage outside and the other asleep here with Lord Russet. Right now, I want to be locating and talking to Lord Bice."

"You aren't taking your sword?" Elmar asked as Feroze headed for the door.

"The orderly took it away from me, on Bice's instructions. Alabasters are not permitted to go armed. But I do have my dagger."

"Be careful," Terelle said. Silly words, she knew. Careful of what? Careful how? He gave her a sad smile as if he was not looking forward to the conversation and left the room.

"Have you eaten?" she asked the two men as she closed the door behind him.

"Yes, if you can call their food fit to eat," Dibble grumbled. He'd gone to the fireplace to light the lamp on the mantelshelf. The room was growing dark as the dusk closed in. He fiddled with his flint and steel, saying, "No bab anywhere."

"The meal wasn't that bad. Better than samphire, samphire and more samphire," Elmar said.

"Blast, I think my tinder is damp. Now that's one thing that doesn't happen much back in the Quartern. Tell the truth, I don't mind staying up here all night if they'll let us. You'd have thought we were covered in sand lice with a bad case of desert peel, the way they treated us down there in the barracks. Not friendly, that's for sure. One of the men said they'd be escorting us to the border tomorrow."

"He did?" Elmar asked. " 'Us'?"

"Well, I think that's what the fellow said. Don't know if he meant just us two, or us two and the other Alabaster guards, or the whole lot of us, but he sounded like it was definite."

Elmar swore. "Blighted eyes. That's not good news."

"Better than hearing they were going to gut us both while we're asleep," Dibble pointed out.

Terelle went to help him with the lamp. "Well, we'll see what Feroze can do."

"If they send us back to the border, we'll pretend to go back—and follow you instead." Dibble had the tinder alight at last, and Terelle held a taper to the flame. He sounded utterly confident and she envied him the certainty. She felt mean as she reminded him that water sensitives would notice their return.

"We'll dodge them," he said cheerfully. "After all, no water sensitive can possibly keep track of all the water they feel, can they? I mean, Lord Jasper told me he blocks it most of the time back in the Quartern, otherwise he'd go mad."

That was true; he'd said much the same thing to her often enough. And in a place that had so much water like Khromatis, it must be even worse. And more difficult to track the water of individuals.

As he lifted the lamp glass for her to put the taper to the wick, she told them what Feroze had said about her relationship to Bice and the Pinnacle. Elmar's expression became more and more grim.

"If your cousin is unscrupulous, he could well be planning your death right now. It'd certainly be in his interest." He made an expression of disgust at the snoring Russet. "That old man's a sun-fried fool."

"At least I'm probably safe until the painting he did becomes real. Trouble is, until then, I'm not free to go where I want. It tugs at me all the time."

"Can we have a look at it?" Elmar asked.

"If it's still in the baggage." She rummaged through the bags, found and then unrolled it so that they could look. She knew every nuance of it—the running water of the river, the way the grass appeared to be wind-ruffled, the clothes she was wearing, Russet's clothes and his pair of sandals lying on the grass.

Dibble brought the lamp over to take a better look. "This is not going to give him much protection," he said, studying it. "Those *are* his sandals, though. I saw them when the Khromatians were rifling through his things."

"I did wonder why he bothered to bring such old, battered things with him," Elmar said and gave Russet another look, but the man was still snoring, his mouth open, his face slack. "Besides, everything here is too damp and soggy for sandals."

"And cold. How long ago did he do this?" Dibble asked Terelle.

"I was not much more than fourteen at the time."

"So he was just guessing what you would look like, years in advance. Bit risky, wasn't it?" Elmar asked.

"You know, I'm not sure anyone really knows all the risks. Perhaps his doing the painting determined what I would look like now. On the other hand, if you paint the impossible, it won't come true. I guess that's why he has my hair blowing across my face and my head ducked down so it's shadowed a bit. He wouldn't want to get my looks too wrong."

Outside a wind had picked up and the casement rattled. The reflections of the lamp flame in each small pane cavorted in unison. Terelle remembered the salty fingers trailing across her face and shivered.

Dibble went back to the window and touched a pane with a finger. "It's freezing out there and the sun has not long gone down." He put his nose to the glass and peered through, then gave a grunt of surprise.

"What is it?" she asked.

"Water falling. Just like before the battle for the mother cistern when Jasper made it rain."

Elmar was off the bed in a flash, striding to the window to peer out. "I'll be pissing waterless," he whispered. He hadn't been at the battle.

She came to look as he opened the casement. A blast of cold air and water gusted in, whipping her hair back from her face. She touched the dampness on her cheeks. "Random rain," she whispered.

"Not random, you silly frip!" Russet said suddenly from his bed. He sat up to stare at them all. "Regular rain. Be happening all the time. And have some sense, eh? Be cold and wet out there. Shut the window!"

At least now I know why they put glass in them, she thought.

The idea of not wanting water to enter was so alien to her she wanted to laugh, in hysteria rather than amusement.

It was Dibble, edgy and restless, who sobered her. "How long will we give Feroze to come back before we start getting jittery?" he asked.

They exchanged glances, but there was no way any of them knew the answer.

CHAPTER SIXTEEN

Khromatis
The Southern Marches
Marchford, Commander Bice's manor

Feroze headed for the main stairs, driven partly by guilt.

They're right. We ought to have told them more. He might not have known all Terelle needed to know, but Alabasters living and working in Khromatis could surely have supplied additional information.

As he walked down the long passage, his booted footfall echoing in the empty hall, he saw the Bastion in his mind's eye. Old, fragile with age, making mistakes as his mind lost its acuteness. He loved that man, but knew he could have handled this better.

We have lived too long attached to our past, a past that should mean nothing any more. Alabasters are good people. We may not have been so once, but now we seem to be better people than these Khromatians. And yet we have convinced ourselves otherwise. Even our faith is gentler, kinder than theirs...

It was twenty years since he'd last crossed the Borderlands. Now that he was experiencing Khromatian arrogance and prejudices at first hand once again, he was remembering his distaste for the place. Worse, as he walked this passage, he felt far too close to death. His rational voice said, *Surely not. Bice is still governed by the law, and laws are strict here.* His gut told him something else, and he didn't like the words it used. Bice was an angry man. A man who'd thought for years that his future claim on the Pinnacle's seat was secure. An angry man could be dangerous in his rage.

I have to convince him Terelle is not interested in staying in this land, let alone ruling it.

An orderly, replacing a burned-out candle in a holder along the passage, informed him that at this hour of the evening, Lord Bice and his sons would be dining in the room directly to the right at the bottom of the main staircase. As Feroze descended, the wood creaking under his boots, three men started on their way up. Young men all, finely dressed, laughing and jostling one another. Without their helmets and armour, with their shoulder-length hair loose about their shoulders, they bore little resemblance to the armsmen of Bice's troop, but there was no mistaking their face tattoos. These were Bice's three sons.

How they love colour, Feroze thought. *They're like noisy parrots swooping and quarrelling around a waterhole. So different from us.* Colourful knee breeches tucked into long white stockings, gold-buckled shoes, shirts tied at the neck in elaborate bows—and for warmth, a vibrant, rough-spun Khromatian plaid thrown about their shoulders.

The oldest of them was the first up the stairs, and he stopped when he saw Feroze, deliberately blocking his passage. "What are you doing down here?" he asked, speaking his own tongue. His aggressive tone grated. "Weren't you told to stay in your room?"

He had been, but he wasn't going to admit that. Instead, he said smoothly in the same language, "I wish to see Lord Bice."

"Well, maybe my father doesn't want to see you."

"Oh, stuff it, Hue," the youngest of the three said, the lilt of his voice more that of a boy than a man. "Leave him be."

Without waiting for Hue's reaction, Feroze stepped around him. He half expected a hand to fall on his shoulder to wrench him back, but Lord Bice was now standing at the foot of the stairs anyway, dressed in a similar fashion to the others. Feroze stopped one step higher, so their faces were level.

Bice ignored him to say to his sons, "You have your orders. Get ready now." The three turned without a word and continued up the stairs. When they were out of earshot, Bice turned his cold-eyed gaze to Feroze. "How dare you interrupt my evening with my family! Is it not enough that I am forced to offer hospitality to you as one of my great-uncle's party, without having you presume on the relationship?"

"I see little of your hospitality," he said, fighting the instinct that told him to lower his gaze in the submission due from a morally inferior race. "Confiscating material that belongs to the guests is not good manners to me."

Bice drew himself up as if he wished to appear both larger and still more menacing. A servant, bustling out of the room behind with a tray of rattling dishes piled high, ruined the moment as she bobbed and passed noisily by. Even this appeared to further infuriate Bice. "Come with me," he said as he strode to a nearby door, wrenched it open and gestured Feroze to enter.

When he stepped inside, the odour of burning wood assaulted his nostrils, coming from logs in a fireplace lit to warm the room. He'd forgotten how much that smell was part of Khromatian everyday life. He glanced around. Light from the flames was augmented by a lamp burning on a table, a carafe and glasses next to it. Taking in the soft-stuffed chairs grouped in front of the fire, he guessed that although the room was empty, it might be where the men of the household congregated before or after dinner. Shelving along the walls was stuffed with board-books, tied shut with ribbon to keep the pages safe between the decorative ends.

He should have been safe, protected by the Kermes name, even by his association with the Bastion. In another place, in such a pleasant room filled with books, he might have felt at home. Instead, his skin crawled with dread.

Exuding aggravation, Bice marched to the table and poured himself a drink. He did not offer anything to Feroze, nor did he indicate they should sit. "Did you think I'd tolerate renegade waterpainters under my roof, possessing the power to command my future? If so, you're a lack-wit! Russet Kermes was daft before he left Khromatis twenty or so years ago; Sienna Verdigris was wild and uncontrollable without a shred of gentility. We thought she and Russet were both dead! You Alabasters told us they'd disappeared without a trace in your barren lands. And now he reappears with this girl. A mongrel of God knows what ancestry, brought up among the barbarian heretics of the Quartern! I wouldn't trust her with a dagger, let alone the power of waterpainting. I have no intention of falling under the evil magic of a half-breed recreant. Of course I made damned sure she wouldn't be able to use her powers in this house."

"She is your cousin, not some wild animal. She is also a deeply moral woman, here at the behest of the Cloud-master, to ask aid of the Pinnacle and his waterlords. Treat her with the respect she deserves."

"She deserves nothing!" He spat out the words, his hatred as deep as it was irrational.

Feroze refused to show the despair that was seeping into him with every word the man uttered. He said quietly, "If you are concerned that she's here to seek her position in Khromatian hierarchy, let me assure you that she has no interest in any such thing. She wishes to return to the Quartern to be married as soon as she can. She does not feel herself to be Khromatian."

"And what of her brats?"

Feroze was mystified. "Pardon?"

"Her children, you dimwit!"

"I'm sorry, I don't—"

"Are you such a total fool? Don't you know the laws of inheritance?"

"How can I? You keep these things a secret. I didn't even know who the present Pinnacle was until I set foot in this house."

Bice listened, his face changing from anger to disbelief to amusement. "That addlepated old fool, Russet keeps Khromatian secrets yet, does he? He may not have known his son-in-law was dead, but he certainly knew who was in the line of succession."

"The rules of succession can be changed, surely."

"You blaspheme! The Pinnacle is such by divine right.

Only God can change the succession—by choosing who is to die, and when. The line of the Pinnacle passes from eldest child to eldest child, as long as they are Watergivers. The only way it can be broken is by death."

Bice was making an effort to control his temper, but the look in his eyes was deadly.

Feroze stood motionless, taking care to show nothing on his face, but his mind was racing. He knew now that he—no, all of them—had miscalculated the extent of their danger. *That's what happens when you make assumptions about people you've never met.* He began to assess the room from a new point of view—that of an Alabaster warrior.

"That grubby bogworm of a woman upstairs *is* the Pinnacle," Bice continued bitterly, "whether she knows it or not. *Every single man who was with me the day we met knows it.* And so, of course, does my dear great-uncle Russet. Even if she says she doesn't want it, her children would have the option, then her grandchildren, and their children—as long as they have water-power. And of course they would. The Verdigris and the Kermes lines usually breed true. And you tell me she's marrying the Cloudmaster? Of course her children will be water talented." He paused to drink and to take a deep breath, as if he wanted to control his anger.

Why is he telling me this? Because Russet knows it anyway? Or—

His heart skipped a beat, then speeded up. *Oh, God, because he's already decided to kill us? What was it he'd said to his sons? "You have your orders."*

What orders?

Keep calm. You have to get out of here. You have to warn the others.

"Then I suppose there is nothing more to talk about. I will take Lord Terelle back to the Quartern in the morning. What you do with Lord Russet is up to you." Even as he spoke, his gazed roved around the room and his fear built. The casement windows were closed. So was the door. The wood in the fireplace was well alight, the sap occasionally exploding in showers of sparks that died on the stone floor. He edged closer to the grate, his back to the flames, and almost knocked over the brass poker set. The sofa, facing him, was now between the two of them. Bice, he noted, was not wearing a sword.

Bice dropped his voice until it was almost a whisper. "The only thing that could have saved her is if she had no water-powers. That is why I had the baggage searched. And there they were—waterpaints. In her baggage, and in her guards' bags. So I can't just throw her back over the border as I'd like to do with the whole damned lot of you."

Feroze stared at the man, his heart plummeting still further with sickening suddenness. He'd just heard his death sentence, and he knew it. Worse, he had just heard Terelle's. No, everyone's. Everyone who had crossed the border was doomed by this man's ambition, and Lord Bice had even given himself a religious justification: if God wanted Terelle's line to sit on the Pinnacle's seat, then God would not allow her death.

"You can't kill Lord Terelle," he said, proud to hear that his voice was steady. "She is protected by waterpainting magic. Possibly Lord Russet is too."

"And you?" Bice asked softly. "What about you, Feroze Khorash, advisor to the Bastion? Did they paint you and your men, to save you? Or did they not care about the life of a sickly-white salt-man?"

Feroze didn't answer. He felt the tug of Bice's power against his skin and willed his water to stay with him. Was Bice just testing his abilities or wanting to kill him? He had no way of knowing, but his fear increased tenfold. *God, I have always followed Your way; care for me now, hold me in Your palm or lead me to the waters of the afterlife…*

And then the door opened and Bice's three sons came in. The room shrank and left Feroze claustrophobic. Gone were the soft evening clothes. They wore utilitarian brown garb, their identical plaids now draped over the shoulder tucked neatly under the belt to leave their swords easily accessible. Their expressions were sober and only the youngest glanced his way; the other two ignored him. All three were on the far side of the sofa, with their father.

"Rubric," Bice said, addressing the youngest, "go tell Greven the time is now and to go ahead. And lend him what help you can."

The young man looked baffled by the message, but nodded and departed.

"Hue, you and Jet take this 'Baster out and dispose of him. Strip the body and dump it in the river. Then come back and we will deal with the others upstairs."

Before Bice had completed his orders, Feroze was already moving. His fear melted away into fury and desperation. In one fluid move he had his dagger out of concealment and he'd grabbed the poker in his other hand. He took one step forward as the two remaining sons drew their swords and separated to approach him from either side of the sofa. Feroze placed a foot in the centre of the front of the seat and pushed as hard as he could. The sofa slid, then toppled, catching Hue as it fell, but missing the middle brother, Jet.

Hue tumbled sideways, the sofa on top of him.

Jet took no notice. He lunged forward, eyes gleaming with anticipation. Feroze guessed he expected a parry with the poker in return. A poker against a sword? Fool-hardy. He ignored the lunge and leaped onto the toppled sofa. From that vantage point, he jumped straight onto Hue who was wriggling out from under it. Boot heels driving in, he had the satisfaction of feeling ribs cave. Just to make sure the man would be out of the fight, he trod on the middle of his face and broke his nose.

And turned his attention to Jet and Bice.

Jet, momentarily stymied by an opponent who had jumped out of his way and then ignored him, was now approaching more cautiously, his sword weaving. And Bice, unarmed, was groping under the sofa for Hue's sword. Feroze thought furiously, weighing his chances, blessing the fact the heavy wooden door was closed. There was unlikely to be interference from the servants. But Bice would be a hard man to defeat.

Alternating knife and poker, he lashed out at Jet in a furious flurry of feints, slashes and jabs, to drive him back, confused, against the bookshelves built along the wall next to the fireplace.

I'll bet all you've ever done with a sword has been in a practice yard, he thought.

Bice shoved the sofa out of the way, grabbed up Hue's sword and came at him, but Jet was closer. Feroze hurled the poker at him. Without waiting to see what happened, he ducked to grab the shovel from the poker set and thrust it deep into the burning embers. As he straightened up, he hurled the heap of red-hot coals in a sweeping arc of cinders and flame.

Jet flinched and his sword point went wide. Both he and Bice were showered with hot ash and coals. Jet jerked backwards, brushing at his smouldering clothes, and jostled his father who was still thrusting forward. For a precious moment they tangled.

Feroze leaped for the nearest window, knife still unused in his hand. A brief moment of triumph, of knowing he had succeeded. He'd bought the few moments he needed to reach the window. He undid the latch, threw open the casement, leaped onto the sill—

And a thrust of pain speared him from spine to chest. He tottered, wondering why he was unable to move, and fell back into the room.

Landed on his back. Pain dragging through his innards. Jagged pain so intense it stopped his breath. So severe he couldn't scream. *God, the pain. God the pain God the pain God, God, God. Take it away. Just take it away.*

Something snapped. The pain disappeared. Vanished. Took everything with it. Lying there. No feeling. Nothing.

Gasping, he dragged air into his lungs.

He moved his head. Watched as Bice and Jet exchanged victory smiles. He tried to lift his hand. Nothing moved. He couldn't feel anything. *He couldn't move.* He tried to speak, but all his effort was going into taking a breath. Then another. And another.

Leisurely, Bice walked across the room to his side and snorted as he looked down on him. "Alabasters! They don't even have a real man's red blood." He bent over to pick something up. "Blast, he landed on my dagger and snapped the blade off in his back." He held up the handle.

And Feroze Khorash knew he was dead. As hard as he tried, no breath would come.

CHAPTER SEVENTEEN

Khromatis
The Borderlands
Marchford, Verdigris Manor

"I'm going to take a look around." Elmar stood up. "They wouldn't let us in with our swords, but I still have my dagger."

"They disarmed me," Terelle said mournfully, thinking of her paints. "Or very nearly. Somehow I think that emergency I mentioned might be closer than we imagined. You be careful, Elmar. You don't want to create a problem where we have none, by creeping around someone else's house."

"I'll tell them I can't find the privy." He grinned at her.

The worse their situation, the more Elmar seemed to find to joke about. She didn't smile back. "If they separate us," she said, "don't worry. The magic will get me where I have to go. Follow me if you can, but if you can't, go back to Samphire."

Elmar snorted. "We're here to protect you. I don't fancy telling the Cloudmaster that we just didn't feel like it."

"El, you may not have a choice."

"We'll see, won't we?"

Once he'd gone, she stood by Russet's bed. He was still awake. She said, "You made a big mistake. Bice Verdigris is not going to help us get to where we've got to go. Quite the opposite. I suspect he's going to force us back over the Borderlands. Is it possible for us to go on, by ourselves, on the pedes?"

"Pedes be sick in the cold up in the mountains. Even here, they soon die if not kept inside."

"So we need these—what were they called? Alpiners? Where do we get them?"

"Can be buying. Have gold." He patted his money pouch, which he had worn to bed.

"And who's going to be selling them to us?"

"Have faith in my waterpainting! It be getting us there. Not worry, silly frip of a girl. Now go. Leave me in peace."

She sighed with deliberate exaggeration and turned to Dibble. "Let's get my baggage to my room."

"Your things and Russet's are all mixed up with ours," he said. "That's why we brought our things up as well. After they searched everything, they just piled it all back in any old how."

"Then we'll take it all to my room and sort it out."

Outside in the passage, all was quiet. "I don't think anyone else has rooms along here," she remarked as they carried the baggage from Russet's room. Once in her room they barred the door and began to sort out all their belongings.

"Where did you hide the paints you kept?" he asked when they had everything in its correct pile.

"I have two water skins. I hid the paint-powder in one

of them. Anyone picking it up casually would think it has water in it."

Dibble gave her a baffled look. "You mixed all the colours together?"

"No, of course not. They're in waxed cloth sachets, in case our baggage got wet. Russet suggested that, actually, back in Samphire. They were each small enough to fit down the spout of the water skin. Look." She showed him the skin and shook the sachets out onto her bed. She looked around. "I wonder if—"

Before she could finish the thought, Dibble hushed her with a finger to his lips and a tight grip to her arm. She listened. Somewhere distant, someone was screaming.

No, not one person. Several people.

Dibble went to unbar the door and eased it open. The cries were still faint.

"Try the window," she said.

He nodded, closed and barred the door, then crossed to open the casement. Screams, shouts, running footsteps, the clash of metal on metal, all much louder now. There was nothing to be seen, but somewhere people were fighting.

"Sunlord save us," Dibble muttered. "What the withering spit is going on? Elmar and Feroze..."

Waterless hells. "Could it be the Alabaster guards in trouble?" She hesitated. "I think we have to go and find out."

"Elmar would feed my liver to a horned cat if I left you unguarded."

"You don't have to. I'll come with you."

"Then it'd be my heart he'd feed to the cat!" In his agitation, he strode to the open window to look out and then to the door to listen.

"If the rooms across the passage are empty, maybe we can see from there what's happening at the back of the house."

She threw one of Russet's plaids over her paints and they returned to the passage, leaving the lamp behind. The door of the room opposite opened easily onto another bedroom. It showed no signs of occupancy, present or past. Once Dibble opened the window, the sounds from outside trebled in volume: shouts and banging and screaming.

"I'll be shrivelled," she whispered. The screaming was horrible, the appalling agony of someone who no longer had existence beyond their pain.

They were looking down on a cobbled yard separating the house from a line of one-storey buildings. Torches placed at intervals in wall brackets lit the scene with flickering light and tainted the air with the acrid smell of burning pitch. Armsmen—Bice's men—were milling around the end of the building opposite, trying to batter down the huge doors. They weren't having much success.

"That's the stables," Dibble said.

Terelle searched for the source of the screaming, and located a man lying on the cobbles. A woman was kneeling beside him, wringing her hands. He'd been speared, and the spear was still in him.

"Not an Alabaster or Elmar," Dibble said. "The barracks where the Alabasters ought to be are at the other end. The doors these fellows are battering at lead into the last of the stalls where we left the pede tack. What the frizzled hell is going on?"

"There are other bodies on the ground," Terelle said, almost choking on her fear. She was looking directly underneath their window. Two, three—no, five bodies lay on the paving. Two were wearing Alabaster white, their blood staining the cloth, pooling along the joins between the cobbles. No one was taking any notice of them. Further away, another wounded man, a Khromatian, was seated with his back to the stable, clutching his leg.

"That's Evert," she said, looking at one of the Alabaster dead. "I'd know his head of hair anywhere. He was talking to me about his children only this morning..." She swallowed, afraid she was going to be sick.

"I think the remaining Alabasters must have barricaded themselves inside that stall. Terelle, we're in trouble."

She forced her gaze away from the dead, still trying to take everything in, to make sense of the disaster unfolding. A woman, not part of the purposeful activity around the stable door, stood further to the left, closer to the house wall. No, not a woman, a man. He was motionless, so still that he blended into the background, and she had to blink to make sure he was there at all. She was too far away to have any idea who he was. *Sunlord help us, that's probably one of the Verdigris family.* Watching, waiting for the moment he could use his power to empty the Alabasters of their water.

"Where are the pedes?" She was whispering, although there was no need.

"Behind the stables. We rigged up a tether line. They're too big to fit into these alpiner stalls. We were told a few days in the open wouldn't hurt them." His voice shook with rage as he added, "I have to get down there."

"Wait—look, there's someone flitting through the shadow. To our right. Trying to get to the back of the stables."

He stared for a moment, then said with certainty, "Elmar. Terelle, go back to the room and bar yourself in."

As he turned to go, his sword already drawn, she called after him, "Dibble, think. Odds are they want us all dead. Bice and his sons are either waterpainters or stormlords, probably the latter. They can kill the rainlord way." She nodded to the window. "They might have already sensed Elmar's water, even know who he is."

He paused in the doorway to look back at her. "I know." His voice was rough with fear.

"What can you do? There's too many of them!"

"What can I do if I stay?" he asked. "Terelle, they're our guards and they're being killed."

She glimpsed the misery in his eyes as he turned away. Hurriedly she said, "I'll paint you out of there. Just stay alive long enough." She swallowed her terror. "Please." *It's worth the risk. It is. This time, it truly is. Otherwise they'll die.*

"Thank you. Don't open the door except to one of us, for any reason at all."

"I won't. I promise." And her promise was heartfelt. She was scared witless. "Dibble, wait. You need to take some things with you."

"But I'll be back—"

She grabbed him by the arm, and pulled him to her room. "You know the rule: never go anywhere without a water skin." Hurriedly, she ransacked Elmar's pack, then her own, and stuffed some items out of each into Dibble's. "There, take this. And remember, I am protected. They can't kill me. Hold onto that knowledge."

He pulled a face, grabbed the bag and hurried to the door. "May the Sunlord's light shine on you," he said over his shoulder and was gone.

He's so young, she thought, worrying, then remembered he was several cycles older than she was. *How do men manage to be so withering brave?*

She wanted to warn Russet, but every moment was precious and she pushed him out of her mind and not only barred the door, but moved the bed so it was wedged up against it. Turning the lamp up as far as it would go, she glanced around the room. Her paint tray—she had brought only one—was still in her baggage, but she didn't have enough paint-powder to paint a picture that large. She cast about for something else to use.

The water ewer on the wash stand sat on a matching round dish with a raised edge. She couldn't have asked for anything better. She moved the ewer aside and filled the dish with water. Her fingers fumbled with the ties of the paint sachets in her hurry. If she was slow—or inaccurate—she might be too late. No amount of waterpainting could bring back the dead. Even as she opened up the motley base, she was sifting through all the possibilities for her painting.

Feroze, Dibble and Elmar. But what about the others? What would give them all the best chance of living? With a sinking heart she knew she'd have to abandon the Alabasters who had barricaded themselves in the stable. Painting three figures in such a small bowl would take all her skill and she had no idea which Alabasters were still alive anyway. She couldn't do everyone. *Sweet water save us, sometimes there are only bad choices.*

With a sob, she began to paint, afraid her desperation would wreck the only chance she had.

When Elmar left Russet's room, he headed towards the back staircase, the way he and Dibble had been brought up to the second floor. Through his friendship with Kaneth, he knew enough about how the wealthy lived to be aware there would be another set of stairs for the more privileged of the occupants, but right then the servants' stairs seemed a better option. The last person he wanted to meet was someone with stormlord or rainlord powers.

There was no one about. He heard nothing until he reached the ground floor, where noise issued from the kitchen: dishes being stacked, running water, chatter. He dodged that area and continued on his way, growing increasingly unhappy as he realised he had no clear idea of where to start looking for Feroze. He emerged at the back of the main entrance hall. At the far end were the huge front doors, and the bottom of the main stairs. Along the sides were doors leading to various rooms, all of them closed. Somewhere there was a murmur of conversation. His hand fell to the hilt of his sword. Which way to turn?

One of the doors opened on the right, not far from the front door. The conversation went from muffled to audible speech. Elmar dived under the sweeping curve of the staircase.

He recognised Lord Bice's voice. He was speaking Khromatian, and Elmar wasn't sure he understood correctly. He thought he heard, "Yes, he's dead. Luckily. Take my arm, Hue. I'll help you to the stairs."

The next part he couldn't understand, but he heard Feroze's name and something about a knife. Hue replied, and although Elmar understood only every second or third word, it was clear he was swearing. And in pain. His voice sounded odd, as if he had a stuffed-up nose.

"Take his other arm, Jet," Lord Bice said.

Two of his sons, Elmar thought. He'd found out their names by listening to the talk in the barracks earlier. *The handsome one is missing. Rubric. Sunlord save us. Who's dead? They wouldn't kill Feroze, surely!*

He heard the approach of footsteps and hunkered down under the lowest steps, frozen, willing himself not to make the slightest sound. Sweat broke out along his brow. *They'll sense me. Sunblast.*

Bice spoke again, closer now. "Take your brother up. I'm going out to…" The rest of the sentence was once more unintelligible to him.

"What about the body?" Jet asked.

Those words hit Elmar so hard he didn't even hear the answer, let alone comprehend it. *Body? Whose body? Watergiver have mercy, please don't let it be Feroze.*

The two brothers continued on up the stairs, Hue complaining with every step, in too much pain to sense anything, Jet too focused on his brother to notice Elmar's water. Or so he hoped.

Bice is another matter, Elmar thought and almost groaned as the man came closer. He was going to pass by the staircase and walk to the back of the hall. He'd be so close Elmar would be able to reach out and touch him; there was no way he would not notice a man crouched under the stair well, especially when his water was no longer masked by that of Jet and Hue.

Just then someone hammered at the front door. Bice cursed, and his footsteps turned and moved away in that direction. Elmar heard the door open, and the sound of voices. From the tone of the speaker, he guessed it was a guard making some sort of report. Hue and Jet stopped on the stair to listen. Bice said something, they continued on their way, the front door closed and there was silence in the hall. Bice had gone out.

Hue's progress up the stairs was painfully slow. At last their footsteps faded away and Elmar was alone in the entrance hall. He let out the breath he had been holding and ran softly across to the room the men had vacated. The door opened silently when he raised the latch. He slipped into the dimness within and closed the door behind him.

For a moment he stood, stilled by terror. He didn't know why. There was nothing moving. No soft sounds of breath or the tiny creaks caused by someone shifting their weight. The room was empty. Coals glowed in the grate, giving some light. More filtered in through the window glass from torches burning outside, enough to see the dark shapes of table and sofa, chairs, shelves. A casement window was open, which was odd because it was cold and wet outside.

The smell. The smell was all wrong. A battlefield smell. Intense, disgusting. Human waste and fresh blood—that horrible stink of violent death he knew too well from the skirmishes and battles of his lifetime. But more than that too, for there was also the stench of burned cloth and paper.

Cautiously he walked further into the room, his eyes adjusting to the dim light. Grit crunched under his feet as he went. As he rounded the sofa, moving towards the window to look outside, he stumbled over something on the floor. He saved himself by grabbing an armrest but still half fell, one knee dropping down into a pool of something wet. Shocked, he grappled with the horror of what he saw. A white-haired, white-skinned, white-clad

Alabaster; even in the dim light, he could tell that much. And he was kneeling in the man's spilled and congealing blood.

He swore, every foul word he could bring to mind, then his initial shock melted into a more considered wariness. And a ferocious anger, a coiled-up desire to smash someone. He pushed the sofa over to block the door. Next, using the fire tongs, he took a coal and lit the lamp on the table. He returned to the body with the light.

Feroze.

You murdering bastard, Bice. In your own home. The man wasn't even wearing a sword.

He knelt again, to examine the body. A dagger blade had broken off in his back. A Khromatian knife. He'd been killed from behind.

Those bleeding bastards, he thought. *Those wilted, shrivelled-souled bastards. I hope they rot in a waterless hell.*

He went cold at the implications. Bice and his sons had murdered a guest in their own house, which boded ill for the rest of their "guests." Once thing was certain: Feroze had not started this fight. He was not a warrior at heart, preferring consensus and reconciliation to violence. *A gentle, kindly, generous man…* This was pure murder, nasty and sudden.

Ever practical, he patted Feroze down, found his purse in the pocket of the robe and dropped it into his own money pouch. There was nothing else. When he rose to his feet, his only certainty was that he had to get out of there—fast.

As he stepped away from the body, more grit crunched underfoot. He bent to pick a little up in his fingers: a piece of charcoal. A glance around the room told him there was spent charcoal everywhere. It hadn't done much damage to the stone floor, but books had been charred and a hole burned in the sofa.

I'll be sunblighted, he thought, then muttered affectionately, "You almost did for the whole blasted house. I'll miss your salted carcass, Feroze. I hope you found the God you were looking for somewhere."

He gave a grim smile and returned to the fire. Using the shovel from the poker set, he tossed live coals onto the sofa and in amongst the books on the shelves. When he was sure he had the beginnings of what would be a future conflagration, he turned to go.

And that was when the screaming started. He jerked his head up to listen. A door slammed above somewhere, there were questioning voices, yelled orders, feet running on the stairs and across the hall. He ran for the open window and climbed out. From there he raced for the barracks, knowing then that he was already too late.

The Alabaster guards had been betrayed. The screams were those of a man dying in agony.

The manor house was large, and even though he raced around it, the worst was already over by the time he arrived. Flattening himself in the shadow of the house wall where two corners met, he watched and assembled an idea of the situation. The Alabasters had probably been surprised in the barracks, but those who still survived were now barricaded in part of the stables, where Bice's men were attempting to batter down the door. Fortunately the planks were thick and stout. He guessed the Alabasters were prepared to sell themselves dearly, hoping, perhaps, that their sacrifice would enable the rest of the party to escape.

He'd come to know them on the journey: good men, every one of them, but men who took orders. It had been Feroze who led them, Feroze's example they followed. *Which means it's up to me to rescue them—or abandon them, and get Terelle to safety. No, wait. Terelle's the only one who's safe for the time being. Maybe Dibble can get her down to the pede while I try to extract the Alabasters from this mess. At least they'll have a better chance then.*

He sneaked back into the deserted barracks. Four men lay dead in there, three of them Alabasters. Weeping shit, with the bodies he'd seen outside, that meant there were only five still alive, and odds were some of those were wounded. He snatched up all the spears and cloaks and water skins he could find, plus two swords abandoned on the floor, then topped up the pile with a few blankets and shoved them out of the back window of the barracks, letting them fall to the ground. He climbed out after them and looked around.

No one was looking his way. The only people visible were two men with their backs to him. They were watching the rear of the stables, at a guess in case the Alabasters broke out through the roof, there being neither door nor window at the back.

He picked up the bundle of clothes and weapons and headed away from the buildings, half expecting one of the men to yell at him, asking what the salted hells he was doing. To his relief, he reached the pede lines about fifty paces from the stables without being questioned. Several sets of the panniers were still there, upended on the ground, and he blessed the carelessness of the men who had not put them under cover. He loaded up his pede, then extracted four of the spears and stuck three of them in the soft ground. He hefted the fourth in his hand, sighted along the shaft at one of the men, and prepared to launch the weapon. The Khromatian guards still had their backs to him.

"Need some help?" a soft voice asked from the other side of the pede.

Elmar almost impaled himself under the chin.

"Only me," Dibble said in a cheerful undertone. He came forward to pick up one of the spears. Weighing it in his hand, he asked. "Where's Feroze?"

"Murdered."

"Watergiver be damned! Are you *sure*?"

"Yes. Where's Terelle?"

Dibble swallowed.

Elmar gave him a moment to gather his wits.

"Locked in her room doing a painting of us getting out of here alive," Dibble said at last. "I don't know about Russet. You want these fellows dead?"

"For a start. You take the one on the left."

Together they hoisted their spears.

The two Khromatians died together, side by side. If they called out in their death throes, the sound was lost in the yelling and battering of the stable door on the other side of the building.

Elmar plucked the two unused spears out of the ground and gave them to Dibble. "Keep these handy. Select a pede to ride. Fashion the tether as a temporary rein and we'll each put a pede on a leading rein as well. We're going to ride those bastards down, halt for a moment in front of the stable to get the others out of there—there'll

be five of them, I hope—and then ride for our lives."
He handed over the extra sword he'd taken from the
barracks.

Dibble followed his lead and began untying his mount,
feeling his way in the dark to loosen the tether knot.
"Terelle?"

"We're leaving her behind, at least for now. And that
bastard Russet."

"You can't be serious! She's the reason we're here."
Dibble gaped at him in disbelieving shock.

"Dibble, she wouldn't come with us anyway. We can't
take her to where she needs to go. Russet has to do that.
And we can't go with them, because these armsmen will
kill us. We'll follow her later, I promise. Now fix that
leading rein and let's be gone from this stink heap."

Unhappily, Dibble did as he was told. "Bice is out
there. He just arrived as I snuck by. Talking to one of his
sons. The youngest, I think. Rubric, is it? If they're rainlords, they can take our water. I gave 'em a real wide
berth, but they may have sensed me."

"Ah. Guess we'll have to hope Terelle gets that painting done. I don't suppose you know exactly what she was
portraying? It wouldn't have been a fire, would it?"

"She hadn't even started when I left."

"Hmm. All right. You pull up immediately in front of
the stable door. Poke your beast and get him thoroughly
riled so he's flinging his feelers around. I'll go after Bice
if he's still there. Forget about what I'm doing; just concentrate on getting the Alabasters out of that blighted stable and onto the pedes. Then head for the river, not the
bridge. I figure our pedes will cross water better than
them silly alpiner things."

"These animals have never seen water like that," Dibble protested, bridling the myriapede he was to lead as best he could, then tying the other end of the rope to one of the saddle handles of his own mount. "They might panic."

"But they won't drown. Jasper once told me he saw one swimming in a rush down a drywash. Hey, don't make that knot too difficult to undo," Elmar warned as he mounted. "One of the Alabasters might prefer to ride it than to sit behind you. Ready?"

Dibble climbed up onto his pede. "Yes."

Elmar looked across at him. "Good luck, Dibs."

Dibble nodded. "You too, El." His voice was husky.

"Oh, and one other thing: the house is on fire. Don't let that bother you. Terelle won't get burned, but it might keep the Khromatians occupied for a bit once they realise." No sooner had he said the words than there was panicked yelling in the distance. "Reckon someone just realised. Let's go. Good luck, m'lad."

"Same to you, old man," Dibble said cheekily, and the two of them prodded their mounts into action.

CHAPTER EIGHTEEN

Khromatis
Marchford
Manor house of the Commander of the Southern
Marches

When Terelle started on the painting, her concentration was total. She had to do this right. If she'd had more time she might have thought of something better—but every moment she spent thinking was another step closer to death for Feroze, Dibble and Elmar. Always, always she was hemmed in by the limitations of waterpainting: you couldn't paint yourself and you couldn't paint the impossible. And worse than the limitations was the viper under the rock: the unexpected result that the artist hadn't anticipated.

And so she painted the most harmless thing she could think of: the three men standing together in front of the huge gates of Samphire.

She'd almost finished when there was a knock at the door. For a while she ignored the sound, and painted on. The knocking grew louder.

Feigning befuddlement, as if she'd just woken, she asked sleepily, "Whatissit?"

The reply came in the Quartern tongue. "Cousin, it's Jet Verdigris." *The middle son.* "Can I talk to you?"

"Yes, of course. Just a moment." She worked on, frantic.

He was silent for a while, then knocked again. "Hey, it's cold out here."

"Just a moment. I'm not dressed. I'd gone to bed."

Apparently taking her at her word, he was silent. She finished some of the finer details with the tiniest spills and manipulation of powder.

"Come on, cousin, this is ridiculous! You don't need to dress up." He started banging on the door, hard.

"All right, all right, I'm coming." Her heart thumped. He no longer sounded friendly. "What's all that noise outside?" she asked. "What's happening?"

"That's what I want to talk to you about."

She examined the painting and could find nothing else that needed doing. Shutting out the pounding at the door and stilling the hammering of her heart with willpower, she reached down into the depths of herself, touched the essence of the painting and shuffled up the motley.

Immediately, she knew there was something wrong. Something botched, as Shale would have said. Terror prickled, shivered through her body, paralysed her. She forced the shuffling upwards, manipulating the paint to work its magic.

It ripped. Tore widthwise as well as deep into its heart. Tore part of her soul. The battering, the angry sounds outside, all faded into the background, almost unheard. The painting in its bowl rippled, created a wave. She felt as if the world had tilted, then rearranged itself, but the new configuration was wrong. Botched.

Oh, Shale.

Confused, she thought she smelled smoke, then saw wisps creeping into the room through the cracks in the wooden floor. Fire? Had *she* done that?

She looked back at the painting. Feroze, in the centre—or rather the paint that had formed him—had sunk to the bottom of the bowl. For a moment she stared in horrified shock, then a wave of nausea curdled her insides as she realised the meaning. *Oh, Feroze, not you. Not the kindest man of all. Seeking, ever seeking to know God.* Even as she watched, the bowl cracked and the water ran away. It sizzled on the floorboards, as if they were hot. It couldn't be her fault, surely. Her mind refused to work.

The thumping at the door was deafening. The room shuddered under the blow. The door burst into shards of wood. *A rain of splinters,* she thought. *How funny.* The bed rocked and scraped across the floor. Men pushed their way in: Jet, his dark eyes savage with the triumph of the hunt, then three other men, armsmen, their swords drawn.

Maybe Elmar and Dibble are safe. They didn't sink. Maybe for them, the painting worked. Maybe.

"Kill her," said Jet, in his own tongue.

Harkel Tallyman had said that too. Last time she'd run, and escaped. This time there was nowhere to go. And the room was stifling. As if it would burst into flames any moment. The air could have been a blast from a furnace.

"My lord, are you sure?" one of the men asked. He swallowed uneasily and glanced at the armsman next to him. "She's all yours," he muttered.

She looked—almost dreamily—across to her pack. Thank goodness she had stuffed the waterpainting, the one Russet had done to control her future, into the bag Dibble had taken.

None of the Verdigris family must see that, she thought, but was no longer sure why. She began to cough. *Why is it so hot? They wanted to kill her, just like Harkel. Simply because she lived. They didn't need any other reason.*

The men in front were looking at one another in dismay. Jet snatched up the painting she had just done, stared at it and then thrust it into his pocket. "Get on with it!" he growled at one of the others. "Let's finish this so we can get to the old man."

She understood the words but couldn't move. Where to go anyway? Under the bed, like a frightened mouse? Try to open the window before they stopped her—and then what? Dive to the ground from the second floor? Hardly. Fight? She had no weapons, nothing but the hope that Russet's past waterpainting power might protect her. Perhaps.

The second armsman came towards her, his sword raised. She didn't move, so he put the point to her throat.

"Do it," Jet said coldly.

Terelle stared at the owner of the sword, meeting his gaze with her own. "Can you?" she asked, her voice thready with terror.

The point of the sword wobbled. The man started sweating. His breathing speeded up, yet he still didn't drive home the point.

"Oh, for crying out loud," Jet said. "Let me do it." He drew a dagger from his belt.

Relieved, the man with the sword dropped the point away from her throat and stepped back, seized by a bout of coughing.

She started to laugh. "That's right. Kill me. If you

can." She wasn't sure if it was bravado or hysteria. "By the way," she said, hoisting her pack onto her back, "I think the house is on fire, don't you?"

Elmar and Dibble and the four pedes swept around the corner of the stables. There was no sign of any of the Verdigris family. The smell of smoke was everywhere.

Good, Dibble thought. Being waterlords, they would be busy with the fire. *Terelle, thank you. Your magic is keeping us safe so far.*

The Khromatians battering at the stable door whirled to face them in shock. The pedes plunged into their midst, knocking men aside, trampling them. In the mêlée, Elmar wielded his sword, slashing at anybody in range. Pede feelers whipped the air to rip anything they hit with their serrated edges. One moment a Khromatian was hurling a spear, the next the skin opened up on his face like fruit peel and the spear was knocked off course by the flailing feeler.

Dibble drew rein in front of the stable so abruptly the pede segments compacted with an audible clatter. He snatched at the saddle handle to prevent himself from being flung to the ground. The stable door, made of thick boards, was partially staved in and the gap was defended by the spears of the Alabasters inside. Dibble found himself looking in on the men he had come to rescue, his heart racing.

"Briass," he yelled, naming the first man he identified, "quick! Grab a couple of bridles and get out here, up on the pedes."

They didn't wait for a second invitation. Briass unblocked what was left of the door and four men emerged, one of them wounded.

"No one else?" Dibble asked, his heart sinking to see so few. Briass, Dondon, Carventer and the lad everyone called Saltlip because he had a downy white moustache.

"Dead," Briass said. He always had been laconic.

"So is Feroze."

Briass swore but didn't waste time. With Dondon's help, he hoisted Carventer, who had a wounded leg, onto the spare pede, then casually speared a Khromatian who came barrelling towards them with a roar of anger. Saltlip scrambled up behind Dibble; Dondon and Briass bracketed Carventer. Dibble undid the leading rein and tossed it to Briass. Fixing the bridles they'd grabbed would have to wait.

"Lord Terelle?" Briass asked.

"Explain later!" Dibble was already prodding at his pede with the butt-end of a spear. Dondon kicked out at another Khromatian, who had recovered from his surprise enough to climb the mounting handles of the pede, and his boot heel snapped a couple of teeth. Saltlip launched a spear that pierced a man through the thigh. Dibble grinned. They were giving these spitless bastards a beating. The joy of battle was on him. He was invincible. He looked around for someone else to hit.

Instead, he spotted Elmar on the other side of the yard, pulling his pede around in a tight circle. The pede, goaded by pokes of the prod, beat the air with its feelers, mowing down any man who hadn't thrown himself flat to the cobbles. Several spears were launched at him from further away, but they all bounced harmlessly off the pede carapace. With an odd breathless regret, Dibble was reminded they had to get out of there. When Elmar's pede flowed past him, heading for the river, he prodded his mount after it. They headed straight for the meanders marked by a band of trees growing thickly along the banks.

"Will we be followed?" Saltlip asked Dibble.

"Don't know. Not yet, I think. The waterlords will be busy with the—"

Even as he spoke, something swooshed over their heads and they were sprayed with droplets of moisture. By the time they looked up, there was nothing to be seen. "Busy with the fire," Dibble finished. "Reckon they're taking water out of the river."

They looked back at the house. The fire at the front had been doused but flames burst through the roof towards the back, and a gyre of sparks spiralled into the sky.

"Serves you right, Bice," Elmar said grimly. "And Feroze, we'll remember you. You didn't deserve to die in such a godless place."

Oh salted wells, Dibble thought, thinking of the fire. *Terelle's at the back of the house.*

Some time later they pulled up among the trees. Elmar peered down at the river sliding slickly through the gloom in near silence. *Sunlord be withered. Why couldn't the Khromatians give some of this water to the Quartern, blast them?*

He pointed further to the north. "Look, up there it widens out. Shouldn't be so deep."

"What are we waiting for, then?" Dondon asked. "I want to be going home!" Briass nodded and urged their mount upstream along the bank.

"I'll be pissing wilted," Saltlip muttered, echoing Dibble's thought. "All that water going to waste. Just... flowing away. And the pedes are going to get *wet*?"

Elmar, who had seen the rush down a drywash often

enough, was not so impressed. "If that's what it takes. But I don't want them to spook." He paused, then asked, "Dibs, are you feeling anything . . . odd, at the moment?"

"You mean, like . . ." His voice trailed away as he tried to find the words. "Strange."

"Yes."

"All I can think about at the moment is getting back to Samphire."

Elmar heaved a disgusted sigh. "So it's not just me. I was right—That sun-shrivelled *idiot* of a woman."

Dibble's eyes widened. "You mean . . . ? Waterful mercy. Terelle painted us *there*?"

"I'm afraid so."

"But—but how can we follow her, if . . . ?"

He left the words unspoken, but Elmar heard them anyway: *if we feel like this?* If we have this ache in the gut, this pressure on the heart, this overwhelming desire to be somewhere else? No, not a desire. A *drive*. Like a desperate thirst. He could no more have resisted it than he could have stopped breathing. Whether he liked it or not, they were heading towards Samphire, and they were going to do it as quickly as they possibly could.

"We'll come back, I swear it," he said to Dibble.

"But she . . ." Dibble looked back at the house, now just a distant glow on a knoll. "Watergiver help us, that's why she made me bring the pack. She knew."

Elmar nodded. "She *made* it that way."

Saltlip, following the conversation without really understanding, asked, "Ye're talking about Lord Terelle? She's not alone. Lord Russet is with her."

Elmar grunted. "Might as well sprinkle salt in the sea for all the use he'll be. She's on her own, and there is nothing any of us can do about it, because you Alabasters can't stay either. You stand out amongst these brown-skins like a white pede in a Reduner meddle. There is no way you could follow her." He prodded the pede to set it in motion after the others. "We have to head to the White Quarter fast, but first we have to take on board as much water as we can. And fix on the bridles."

Where the river widened, it was only knee-deep for most of the way across, with one deep channel that wasn't wide enough to worry a pede. They paused in the shallow part to encourage the animals to drink as much as they could hold. When Dibble opened up his pack, he found three water skins—Terelle had packed not only his, but Elmar's and her own. Saltlip had his because he always wore it. The others had left theirs in the barracks, but Elmar had picked up three of them.

"We are going to need more water," Dondon said morosely.

"We have one set of panniers," Elmar said.

"Take out the blankets and cloaks. The blankets we can sit on. The cloaks we can wear."

While the men filled the panniers, Dibble examined the contents of his pack. "Two palmubras, squashed. Skin paste to prevent sunburn on the salt. One bag of dried bab fruit. One knife. And a painting. Two tinderboxes with flints. Three candles. One bowl. Some leather strips to mend broken tackle or sandals or whatever. Some twine. That's it."

"What's the painting?" Elmar asked.

"Can't see in this light."

"She's given us the one Russet did," Elmar said, with certainty. "So the Verdigris don't take a better look at it."

"You reckon she knows we'll come back?"

Elmar gave a harsh laugh. "She knows. Tell me, do you want to go back to Lord Jasper without her and tell him what happened?"

"Not weeping likely!"

"Exactly. She knows. Tell you one thing, unless we can spear some birds on the way back, we're going to be very hungry by the time we get to Mine Sylvine. That bab fruit goes to the pedes. Now fill those water skins and drink as much of this river as you can get down your gullet without throwing it back up again, because water is going to be in short supply too."

With that dour remark, Elmar picked up the bowl and went to top up the panniers now that the men had replaced them on one of the pedes. Every drop was going to count.

Terelle, he thought, *when I see you again, I'm going to wring your neck. Couldn't you have thought of a better way of saving our worthless hides?*

If she survived this, Terelle knew she would look back on it and wonder if she'd been more than a little mad. Out of the tangle of emotions and regrets and fears, a thought emerged that was as coherent as it was pointless: *the imminent prospect of death fries your brain. You can't cope with the idea that in a heartbeat you'll be dead, so you waste precious time thinking things that don't matter . . .*

"I really do think the house is on fire," she said as Jet grabbed her. "See the smoke? It's seeping up through the floor. Which is rather hot. Don't you think we ought to leave here and go downstairs?"

Jet pressed the point of his weapon into her throat, but his fingers trembled and he didn't seem able to force it home. The tip barely broke her skin.

"Honestly, I don't think you can kill me," she said, her confidence growing. For the first time, she was grateful for Russet's painting of her. "Do you?"

He tried then. The effort to ram the point into her jugular shook his body, but nothing happened.

"My lord!" one of the men cried. "She's right. The floor is burning!"

The men backed out of the room, coughing, jostling their way through the door. Jet looked around, confused. The dagger point dropped away from her throat, so she grabbed up Russet's plaid from the bed and held it over her mouth and nose as she headed for the door and the smoke thickened. Jet started coughing then as well, and grabbed her arm, digging his fingers in. She tried to pull herself free, but he was far too strong. He pushed her from the room, shoving her and roughly scraping her arm on the door frame. She yelped, furious. He took no notice. In the passage much of the smoke was coming from the direction of the main staircase, so he turned the opposite way. His men had already gone.

"Russet," she said urgently, her eyes streaming. "In the next room!"

"Who cares? I was supposed to kill him too." He dragged her in his wake, her arm gripped tight.

As they passed Russet's door she lowered the plaid to scream with all the volume she could muster. "Russet! Fire, fire! Get out of there!" In the distance she could hear similar cries. *What's the matter with him? How can he sleep through all this?*

Jet tugged at her and she struggled against him. When he pulled her onwards, she bit his hand, ripping into his flesh savagely until she tasted the tang of blood. He slapped her face, hard, the blow making her ears ring. She pounded his nose, then pulled his hair. His eyes teared.

He hauled her up until her face was level with his. "I may not be able to kill you, but I still have my dagger, and I'll cut your tits off if you try any more of that. Understand me?"

Wracked with coughing, she couldn't struggle any more, or reply. She covered her nose with the plaid, then once again she was running after him, hauled along in his grip. When they reached the head of the narrow back stairs, they were slowed by a rush of six or seven servants and orderlies coming from the opposite direction to use the staircase. For a moment the smoke thinned out and she looked back the way they had come.

Russet had stepped out of his room. He stood there looking at her. In the dark, he was only recognisable by his silhouette, backlit by a candle burning in a wall holder. She called out to him, and he raised a frail, shaking hand in reply. He took a step towards her, a black shape stooped with age. Smoke swirled. He tried to bat it away, coughing. Then, without warning, the background to his silhouette became a brilliant wall of yellow flame, erupting through the floor somewhere behind him in a whoosh. Gone in a flash, it was replaced by showers of sparks, cascading, twinkling, dying in a crash of broken timber. Another roar of flames. Slowly, oh so slowly, he turned to look.

She screamed his name. And he vanished. Disappeared inside flames whipping up to the ceiling from the level below. There was no floor, no silhouette, no Russet. He had been obliterated, the hideous roar of flames and the shattering of the floor wiping him out as if she had dreamed her vision of him.

Where he'd been, the air burned.

Jet's grasp on her wrist was the powerful hold of a warrior. He plunged down the stairs, jerking her off her feet so that she almost fell. A blast of flame and smoke burst along the upper passage. The roar of it followed them down the steps as if attached to their heels. She flung the plaid over her head. The ends smouldered.

Everyone was coughing, screaming, shouting, pushing. She tried to wrench herself free, but Jet's hold never weakened, never wavered. As they passed the kitchens he dragged water from there and threw it up and over the stairs, drenching them and those behind them. And then they were outside, in the cobbled courtyard between the stables and the kitchens.

After the heat of the house, the cold of the night was biting; after the noise of the fire and the sounds of a house dying, the shouts and sounds of men seemed puny. She drew breath, sucking in clean air.

Russet is dead.

I can be killed.

CHAPTER NINETEEN

Khromatis
Marchford
Manor house of the Commander of the Southern
Marches

Jet flung her into the arms of someone wearing a Khromatian uniform. "You," he ordered, "keep her close. Your life if she gets away from you. Understand?"

The man nodded, quickly pushing her to arm's length in embarrassment, although he kept a grip on her upper arm. He looked at Terelle blankly as Jet hurried away. "Who are you?" he asked in Khromatian. He was not a young man and she did not recall seeing him among the men who had ridden with Bice.

"Lord Terelle. What's going on here?" she asked in the same language.

Her accent gave her away as much as the name. "Oh," he said, and started speaking Quartern. "The house is on fire."

"I know that," she said, curbing her irritation as he guided her further from the house. "What happened?"

"How should I know?" He stared at her, still at a loss,

still holding her arm as if he thought she'd run off if he let go, and yet there was fear in his eyes. "Ye're the woman who says she's the daughter of the Pinnacle's heir, the heir who was lost?"

"Well, Sienna Verdigris was my mother," she agreed cautiously.

He snorted as if he didn't quite believe any of it, but she could still see the caution in his eyes and there was a tinge of embarrassment in his voice as he added, "Reckon I got to be tying ye up."

She touched the bloodstone pendant hidden under her neckline, seeking reassurance that it was still there. Her connection to Shale. "I don't want to run away." *Or did she? Russet was dead...*

"Well, can't say I'm going to be believing that, lass." He pulled her into the last stall of the stables through the broken doors. There was a corpse on the floor, which he ignored.

When he released her arm, she knelt and touched the dead man's face. Tromward, an Alabaster guard from Samphire. *He loved to sing as he rode...*

The Khromatian fumbled around in the dimness until he'd unhooked a bridle from the wall. "Step outside," he said. "I can't see what I'm doing in here."

Outside again, the area was brightly lit by flames. Tiles on the roof had caught fire, which seemed odd to her. Whatever were they made of? *Wood?*

"Put your hands behind ye," he ordered. "Sorry about this, but duty is duty."

"That's uncomfortable. Tie them in front." She slid her pack to the ground, blessing her foresight in picking it up before leaving her room, and wrapped Russet's plaid around her shoulders against the cold of the night air.

He assessed her quietly, then shrugged and did as she asked. "Now we'll go and sit on the edge of the water trough over there in the yard and wait for the waterlords to be putting out the fire. Shouldn't take long."

The stone trough was empty; they must have already removed the water to use. Sunblast, she could have used a drink, a wash. Her throat felt raw. Her skin was dusky with soot, her clothing stank of smoke. From where she sat, she could see water sailing through the air from the direction of the river.

The image that kept returning to her, though, was her last view of Russet. Befuddled, old, not quite understanding, and then he had...vanished. *The floor,* she thought. *The floor disappeared under his feet.* A truss had burned through somewhere, and so part of the passage had collapsed into the fire. *He's dead. Just like that. All his greed-driven dreams gone in a moment. In the end he'd returned home to die, chasing what he could not have.*

She felt no regret, no love, no satisfaction. He'd caused her so much grief, and it was far from ended. Perhaps the only emotion his death engendered was relief. And a worry. He'd told her the death of a waterpainter meant the death of his magic. If he'd told the truth, then she was free. She could go back to the Quartern without becoming ill. She'd no longer have to fight the desire to press on who knew where. But that would also mean she had no protection. His death placed her in jeopardy. If Jet wanted to murder her now, he could.

She thought of returning to Breccia and felt nothing. Perhaps the compulsion had already faded. *How ironical is that,* she thought. *I wanted to be free, and now that I am, I'm in the worst danger I've been for years.*

Pushing all thought of Russet away, she turned her attention to her immediate predicament. *I can't waste a moment. I have to find out as much as I can about this place. About these people. That's what's important now.*

"What's your name?" she asked. "You speak very good Quartern, by the way."

The fire was dying, but pitch torches in holders still burned on the outer wall of the stable. By their light, he looked at her with a puzzled expression. She was the granddaughter of a Pinnacle, but he'd been told to treat her as a prisoner. For all he knew, she was a waterlord with the power to take his water, so he was cautious. After a moment's reflection, he shrugged. "Eden Croft," he said. "M'family's always had Alabasters working for them. My da's a farmer."

"But you joined the armsmen? You don't wear a sword."

"I'm an army groomsman."

"Tell me about my cousins. Jet, for example. Is he married?"

He stirred uneasily. "None of my business," he said at last.

"Where do the Verdigris family live when they aren't here?"

He waved a hand vaguely in the direction of the mountains. "Long ways off."

"In the Southern Marches?"

"Further. Another Pale."

Well, that didn't get her very far.

"Do you know where the Kermes' Manor is?"

Silence.

Salted wells, this is like trying to squeeze water from a stone. "Is there some objection to me knowing all this? What's the big secret?"

"We don't gossip with Quartern folk." He softened the words with his apologetic tone, still obviously confused about how to treat her.

"I'm not Quartern folk. My mother was Lord Bice's cousin. And my father was an eel-catcher from around here somewhere. His name was Erith Grey."

The man gaped. "Ye're one of the *Greys*?" he asked.

"So Lord Russet told me. That's the old man—my great-grandfather." She looked at the burning house and rubbed at an eye. Obligingly, it started to water, more because of the soot on her finger than any grief. "He—he died a few minutes ago, in the fire. I'm—I'm all by myself now."

He looked horrified. "I'm sorry. I didn't know anyone had died." When she silently brushed away a tear, he added, "The Greys are famous round these parts. My sister married into the family."

"Really? Can you tell me anything about my father? I know nothing! I'd love to meet his family."

He eyed her cautiously. "I didn't know Erith. My sister might have done, but—well, her husband isn't a waterlord or anything like that. He doesn't see much of that side of his family."

She stared at him. "Waterlords?" she asked, incredulous. "Erith was a *waterlord*?"

"I didn't say that. He can't have been, not with a name like Erith. But he was from that branch of the family. Ye'd have to ask m'wife." He shrugged. "What do I know of lords? I'm a simple man who tends the alpiners. Listen, lady, I reckon ye're in a heap of trouble here, specially if Lord Russet truly is dead. If ye have a chance, go back across the border."

And I think I would if I could—but I've sent away the people who would have gladly helped me. At the very time it might just have been possible to leave. Sunblast it, the timing is ridiculous! Russet had thwarted her even by the hour of his dying. She closed her eyes briefly and felt herself sway as loneliness and fear engulfed her.

No. She mustn't give way. She opened her eyes. "I came here to beg help on behalf of the Cloudmaster of the Quartern. We need waterlords to come to us, to bring water from the sea to our mother wells. Do you think any waterlords would want to aid us that way?"

"We Khromatians don't mix with others," he replied after pondering the question. "It's a contamination."

"You employ Alabasters."

Uneasily, he nodded. "I was even raised by an Alabaster nurse. That's how most of us learned to be speaking your tongue. But Alabasters are servants. We call them the Forbidden People. They are not even supposed to profane our language by using it, although they do. And none of our people are supposed to be crossing the Borderlands."

"And yet one of your—*our* people went there once and taught the water sensitives of the Quartern how to storm-shift."

"Ah, ye mean Ash Gridelin. He's much looked down upon here for deserting his people and his land. We don't do such things. No, m'lord, ye'll not find waterlords here who'll go to your land." He paused, then added with a shrug, "But then, who am I to be speaking for lords? They're as far above me as the stars are above the mountains."

After that he became taciturn again, although he did promise to ask his sister to find out what she could about Erith Grey. "But I'm not like to be seeing ye again, m'lord, to tell ye what she might find out."

About the run of a sandglass later, when the fire was completely out, Bice came around the corner into the yard, his face grim and besmirched with ash and soot. Jet and Rubric were with him. Bice dismissed Eden Croft with a brusque wave of his hand and the man scurried away, his speed indicating that he knew better than to be in the commander's vicinity when he was in a mood like this.

"I want to talk to ye," Bice said to Terelle. "Now." He spoke to her in Quartern, for which she was grateful, even though his accent was thick and hard to understand.

"Good," she said, "I always wanted to talk to you. You're the one who preferred to murder us rather than hear what we had to say. And don't try to tell me differently. Jet made his intentions quite clear when he came to kill me."

"Your damned Alabaster set fire to my house!"

"Feroze? What were you trying to do to him at the time? You can't tell me he would do anything like that deliberately unless it was to save his own life, and ours."

He smiled, a grim smile that bordered on a sneer.

Her heart turned over in dread. "He's—oh, hells. He really is dead, isn't he? He is—was—a gentle man, and his death is on your conscience. What is the *matter* with you? We came in peace, to ask your help."

"Ye came to be usurping my father's place."

"Twaddle! I've never had any intention of staying here. I wanted to see the Pinnacle and bring the request from the Cloudmaster. Our land is in trouble. Once before one of your people saved us. We were hoping that some of your waterlords could find the compassion to do the same again."

Even as she spoke, she was trying not to blush, remembering just how Ash Gridelin had set about giving help.

"That's a likely story," he said, his tone thick with contempt and disbelief. She knew he wasn't speaking of Ash Gridelin. "Anyway, we don't give a spit for your problems. Ye're no concern of ours." He drew his sword and placed the point at the base of her throat.

Terror burgeoned inside, overwhelming thought. *I've no protection . . .*

"Do we have to go through this ridiculous charade all over again?" she asked, surprised to hear how steady her voice was. "I have had my future painted. Are you prepared to have the magic twist back to hit you because you try to kill me? Ask Jet what happened. He tried to murder me and the house caught fire."

"You can't kill her, Pa," Jet said in his own tongue. "I tried. So did my overman. It was impossible. She's telling the truth—someone must have painted her future. And mother has said often enough that waterpainting magic has a way of biting you in the nose if ye try to circumvent it."

She was about to nod, and changed her mind. *Moving your head up and down isn't a good idea when you have a sword poking you in the throat, you daft woman.* Then she realised what he'd said. For some reason it wasn't obvious to Jet that it must have been Russet who painted her. Why not? *They think that the Quartern has water-painters?*

"Yes," she said. Her mind raced, then everything slotted into place, explaining so much, even Russet's arrogance. They were so self-contained that outsiders were irrelevant to them. The Alabasters they tolerated because they needed them and Alabasters had once been Khromatians. Beyond the White Quarter, they had no interest in anything. They knew the Quartern had stormlords, but they'd never bothered to find out enough to discover that waterpainting was unknown there. Doubtless they thought Ash Gridelin had passed on both talents to his descendants.

"Yes, someone did paint my future," she said, taking care with her choice of words. "To make sure I would return safe to the Quartern."

"Where did he paint ye? What were ye doing? Where's the painting?"

"Don't be ridiculous. Where do you think it is? I left it with the Cloudmaster."

The point of his sword dropped away from her throat. Bice turned to Jet, reverting to his own language again. "You said she did a waterpainting?"

He pulled the painting she'd done of Feroze, Dibble and Elmar out of his pocket and smoothed it out.

Bice glared at her and tapped the painting. "Where is this place?"

"Those are the gates to Samphire."

Jet snorted. "She's been clever in her choice of scene. She made it so there's no point in going after them, Pa. With the magic on their side, chances are we couldn't catch them, not when they've already had a good start, and we certainly couldn't kill them." He turned to Rubric. "And you're off the hook, brother. Not your fault you made such a mess of killing those Alabasters. The magic wasn't on your side."

She was struggling to follow the conversation and couldn't interpret the odd look on Rubric's face, nor the quick perplexed glance he shot at his brother.

"Have you removed her paint-powders?" Bice asked him.

"If she or Russet had any more in their rooms, they burned up. We did take a lot out of their luggage earlier. I'll give them to Mother; she'll appreciate having them."

"Yes, yes. Good idea." Bice slid his sword back into its scabbard. He looked at Terelle thoughtfully and switched languages. "So we can't kill ye. But we can imprison ye until ye die." He smiled. "A disagreeable death, I believe—the magic kills ye in the end, because ye cannot obey it. Ye end up being torn in two, so to speak." The pleasure in his smile splintered what was left of her composure. "That will teach ye to be threatening me."

"I wasn't threatening you," she protested. "I don't care a grain of sand for being the Pinnacle. I am about to marry the Cloudmaster of the Quartern. All we ever wanted was the help of a few of your waterlords. Which is in your interest, if you think about it."

He snorted and was about to cut her off, so she rushed to say all she needed. "You trade with us. You buy our salt and minerals. You use the labour of the Alabasters who are part of our land. Somehow, I think you'd find it hard if we didn't exist. And that's a very real possibility. We've only one stormlord at the moment. What happens when he dies? Even now he cannot bring enough water to the Quartern on his own."

"Your waterpainters can bring you rain."

Sunblast. It's so hard to keep track of lies . . . "You must know that using waterpainting is not so simple! The consequences can be disastrous. The truth is the Quartern is dying of thirst and the Stormlord'll cut water to the Alabasters first. What then for you? One day you'll be the Pinnacle. How will you manage here in the Southern Marches without Alabaster labour? Without our minerals and salts and metals?"

There was a moment's silence when she'd finished, so she knew she'd said something to give them pause. In the end, though, Bice just shrugged and turned to his sons, speaking in his own tongue. "Have some waterlords go after the Scarpermen as far as the Borderlands to be making sure they don't double back. Then you, Jet, and Rubric depart tomorrow for Verdigris Manor. It's time you both saw your mother anyway. Take this woman . . ." He paused, then asked in Quartern, "What's your name again?"

"Terelle."

"An outlandish, meaningless name. Take her with ye. I want her imprisoned in the manor, far away from the Borderlands, where we can keep an eye on her. She can't possibly make her way home from there." He was speaking to his sons, but he was looking at her. He enjoyed her knowing his plans. He liked seeing the fear in her eyes.

"We get to go home?" Rubric was grinning. Jet looked pleased.

"Tell everyone ye are taking her to see the Pinnacle. I'll send a message to him later. Doubt he'll actually want to be meeting her, but it be his decision. No paint-powders, so she's harmless—but keep a close watch anyway."

"She may be harmless, but waterpainting isn't," Rubric warned, switching his speech back into Khromatian. "Mother won't like it."

Bice replied in the same tongue. "Your mother is always fussing about something. Once ye reach the manor, put Terelle in the tower. She's not to meet anyone but us. Choose guards who don't speak the Quartern tongue. We don't want too many people to know about her."

Jet looked doubtful. "A lot of the men already know who she is."

"I know. Best we spread it around that the fire was started by these foreigners, that Russet was killed and Terelle injured. We want a way of explaining her death later."

Rubric frowned. "We *are* going to kill her?"

"No, of course not," his father said impatiently. "We don't have to do anything. She'll die because she was painted. Torn in two by her inability to do what the power of the painting wants her to do."

"It won't kill her on the way home, will it?" Jet asked.

"Hardly. She might even last a year or two past the time portrayed in the painting."

Terelle clenched her jaw tight, wishing she hadn't understood this last exchange. *You utter bastards. You're enjoying this, aren't you? I now absolutely understand why my mother left this place.*

She raised her chin and glared at Bice. "You're making a big mistake. Do you think the Cloudmaster will take my disappearance lying down after the others reach home?"

"And do ye think that will worry us? Your Cloudmaster has less power than a salt-dancer if he can't bring water to all the Quartern." He added a sentence or two in Khromatian, something about clearing out all the water that had been dumped on the house, then turned on his heel and left.

Jet and Rubric exchanged glances. Jet grinned. "Good to be going home, eh?" he said in Quartern. "Been a whole season since I saw Azure. Hue will be in a spitting rage—he gets to be staying here mending a few broken ribs. Let's get this waterpainter tucked away out of sight, shall we? We can put her in the salt store for the time being. No windows, good stout door."

He said that bit about going home deliberately, Terelle thought. *Well, they're not going to cow me. I've been imprisoned before and I escaped then. I can do it again.*

She started plotting. It was better than thinking about the bleakness of being alone. About Feroze.

At least I have some of my things in my pack. I wonder if I can steal back my paints? They will be somewhere in the baggage. And I have to contact the Alabasters somehow. They're the only people who can get me back across the Borderlands.

When the two young lords led Terelle away, Eden Croft stepped out from inside the stable where he had been hiding. *I must be crazy,* he thought. *Why did I do that? I should have walked off, not stayed to listen. None of my business what men of the upper pales do. And no dustblower lass from across the bog is any concern of mine.*

And yet...his wife would say differently. Had a tongue on her, his wife, and she didn't mind using it. She was keen on family, and damn proud that her husband was a Grey. Of course, there'd been one devil of a hullabaloo about one of them running off with the heir to the Pinnacle. Eden had been ten or so, and he remembered it clearly. Erith Grey's immediate family had not come out of it at all well. The father had been brutally beaten by members of the Verdigris clan and was never the same man after that. Erith's brother had been forcibly conscripted to serve along the northern borders and he'd never come home.

It hadn't paid to rub the Verdigris family up the wrong way back then. Still didn't.

Sheer curiosity and a spur of the moment decision had prompted him to step into the stable through the broken door and listen. It had been a daft thing to do.

No, he didn't think he was going to mention it to the wife.

He left, heading out to check on the alpiners he and the other groomsmen had released from the stables into the home paddock when the house caught fire. He had some explaining to do about why he hadn't been there, helping to calm the animals spooked by the flames.

CHAPTER TWENTY

Scarpen Quarter
Breccia City, Breccia Hall
Warthago Range, Begg's Caravansary

"I've looked everywhere in his apartment for an extra key or a stray painting," Senya said. "It's easy enough to look. He pretends to be glad I'm taking an interest in the brat, but if I come, he leaves. The nurses don't take any notice of me when I'm not with Amberlyn, so I go through all his things. Do you know he doesn't have much? Anyone would think he was still a Gibber grubber! His clothes are practically rags and he doesn't even own so much as a ring. I'm fed up with looking. The paintings must all be in the stormquest room, and we both know where he keeps the key to that. There were piles and piles of paintings on the shelves there."

Laisa, reclining on the divan in her apartment, nodded. "Yes, dear. I'm sure you've tried hard. I think I might have the solution to getting the key. The seneschal's office is supposed to have duplicates."

"Oh, so we can just ask Chandler for the key then?"

"No! We don't want Jasper to know we were in there.

I've told Seneschal Chandler I'm going to check that every door in the hall has a key, and that he has a spare, and that they both work. I told him I'd do it myself because we didn't want just anyone to have access to all the rooms. He thought it a good idea."

Senya laughed. "You're the highlord! He couldn't say no, even if he wanted to."

"Exactly. Today, I spent a very boring day looking at the linen cupboards, the pantries and the cellars. Unfortunately, Chandler thinks it his duty to accompany me. He regards the security of the hall as his special domain, with the keys as the symbol of his office." She rolled her eyes. "Tomorrow, Jasper leaves early for a Rainlord Council meeting in Scarcleft and won't be back for a few days. Chandler and I will start upstairs and come to the stormquest room in due course. The next room we come to will be yours. I'll have the bunch of keys, including the one to the stormquest room. I'll slip it off the ring and pass it to you when the seneschal is distracted. Hide it. When we move on to the next room around the corner in the passage, you run out, unlock the stormquest room, and then run after us, waving the key and saying we dropped it.

"In the evening, we'll both retire early, dismiss our maids—and take a look at what's inside that room."

"But how will we lock the door again?"

"We'll take care to leave everything the way we found it and hope Jasper will think he failed to lock it properly."

Senya clapped her hands, smiling happily.

Laisa, regarding her, experienced a moment of profound misgiving.

*   *   *

The first part of their plan was executed smoothly. Senya obtained the key without Seneschal Chandler having any idea it was gone. Laisa continued to accompany him, checking other doors, chatting about minor problems pertaining to Breccia Hall as they proceeded. After a while, however, she began to be uneasy about how long Senya was taking to bring the key back. By the time they'd checked all the bedrooms on that storey, there was still no sign of her.

"I think we've finished here," the seneschal said. "Shall we go up to the next storey?"

"Yes, but tomorrow, I think, if—"

Just then Senya appeared, the key dangling from her hand. "You should be more careful!" she said, glaring at Chandler. "I found this one on the floor! And I had to come all this way, running after you."

The seneschal looked astonished. "I didn't drop a key!" he protested and held out his hand to take it. "Which room is it for?"

Laisa stepped forward hastily and took it from her instead. She looked at the label. "Senya's," she lied and slipped it onto the ring. "My fault. I must have been careless. Here," she said, giving it to the seneschal, making sure the position of the errant key was lost to his gaze as the keys bunched up. "We've done enough today. I am sure we both have other things to do."

As the seneschal started down the stairs, she ushered Senya away in the opposite direction. "What *took* you so long?"

"When I went back to the passage, the maid was washing the flagstones in front of the stormquest door! I couldn't unlock it in front of her, so I had to wait." She shrugged sulkily. "I don't see why we can't just be open about it anyway. What's the point of being the highlord, or the Cloudmaster's wife, if we can't do whatever we like?"

Laisa didn't even try to answer.

After dinner, when all the servants were either busy or having their own suppers, the two of them slipped into the room and barred the door. They'd brought a lamp and Laisa quickly stuffed the draught snake along the bottom of the door so none of the light would show in the passage. The shutters were already closed tight.

"I'll light the candles," Senya said, heading towards the candelabrum on the table.

"No!" Laisa said. "Nothing must change in here, not even the height of burned tapers. We'll have to make do with the lamplight. Perhaps it'd be better if you sat down at the table and watched. Maybe you can come up with some good suggestions?"

"There must be at least a hundred paintings on the shelves," Senya pointed out as she sat. "Maybe he just hid it in full sight, mixed in with the others."

"Possible. Although I suspect they may have hidden the one we want very carefully." She looked around. No cupboards, no chests, no carpets. Much of the furniture and ornamentation had been destroyed during the Reduner occupation. Fortunately the invaders had never found the original stormshifting maps; Jasper had carried those away to safety.

The floor was laid with flagstones and there was nothing to suggest any of them had been lifted in the past couple of hundred cycles. She bent to look at the underside of the table, the map lectern, the sofa and the chairs. Nothing. Methodically she began to check each shelf, even

looking inside every board-book and studying every map
and painting.

Two runs of a sandglass later, she'd been through every
one of Terelle's paintings and replaced them exactly as
she'd found them. Senya was snappishly bored. "I'm
freezing in here. Why don't you look on top of the shelving?" she asked. "Some of them don't go all the way to
the ceiling."

Laisa, who had already glanced up there and noted
there appeared to be nothing on top, nodded. Anything to
placate Senya. "Good idea," she said and dragged a chair
across so she could take a better look.

The surface was still too high for her to see anything,
so she began to run her hand along it. She was about to
complain of the dust, when her fingers encountered a
raised surface. "There's something here," she said softly.
She stepped down from the chair and began to pile books
up on the seat, taking care to remember which shelf they
came from and in what order.

Senya smiled. "Told you so."

Laisa climbed up on top of the books and looked. "It's
a flat piece of slate, I think." Inserting a fingernail under
one corner, she levered it up. "And something underneath
it." Carefully she laid the slate to one side. "A painting,
right-side down." She wiped the dust from her hands onto
her dress, lifted the painting with exaggerated care and
brought it to the map table.

Senya examined it, her interest avid. "Is that a mother
cistern?" she asked.

They were looking at a painting of a cave. The entrance
was protected by an iron grille, and the door in the grille
was standing open. Taquar was there, face shadowed by a

palmubra, dressed in a garish red outfit, but still vaguely recognisable. Five other men were portrayed only from the back, one wearing the yellow robes of the Sunpriest's office, and four dressed in the uniform of Scarcleft guards. To the left of the cave a word was painted on the rocks in large white letters: *Shale*.

"If it is, I've never seen it before." Thoughtfully, Laisa placed a finger on the mountains in the distance. "This scenery means it has got to be up in the Warthago somewhere. But it can't be a city's cistern because Taquar would mess with the water."

"What about a caravansary cistern?"

"Risky. Who knows who might happen along and let him out?"

Senya looked up with a puzzled frown. "What does the painting mean, anyway?"

"As far as we know, a waterpainting can be either be an ordinary painting or a magical one. We don't know how Terelle makes it magical, but if she does, what is portrayed becomes reality sometime in the future."

"So this is a painting she did of Taquar to make sure he was imprisoned in this particular cistern?"

Laisa frowned in thought. "No, it can't be, surely. Lord Gold was with us when they took him off to imprison him, remember? And she's painted Taquar outside the grille, free. I wonder why? I would have thought—no, of course, that's it. This has yet to come true. It's her way of keeping him imprisoned, because no one could free him unless they reproduce this scene, and that would never happen exactly this way unless it was reproduced by someone who had seen the painting. Only she and Jasper know, so they are the only ones who can do it."

Senya looked confused. "But what's to stop someone finding him by accident and breaking open the grille without bothering with all this silly stuff?"

"If they were able to do that, then this scene would never happen. So the magic won't allow his release any way except this one." She tapped the painting. "Clever."

"But *we* know now," Senya said, smiling as she began to understand.

"There are maps here, and cisterns are always marked. Let's see if we can find this particular one." Trying not to change the position of anything, Laisa hunted through the maps for the ones she wanted, then spread them out on the table side by side. "Look for one that's neither on a caravansary route, nor supplying a city."

It was Senya who found it. Her finger jabbed at a triangle deep in the Warthago. "Here. It's a caravansary, but there's no trail to it. Look."

Laisa peered at the tiny writing next to the triangle. *Landslip, Cycle 1-958,* she read. Further below, there was a tiny symbol of a hut, used to denote caravansaries. Beside it were the words *Begg's C.* "I remember my father speaking of this," she said softly. "Begg's Caravansary. It was on the route between Pebblebag Pass and Breccia. There was a massive landslide and a whole caravan was lost, back before I was born. The slip was so bad they had to change the route, so the caravansary was no longer used either. Senya, I think you've found the place."

"And we have the painting of how to get him out of there."

"Yes. Or rather, a painting to make sure he doesn't get out of there until all these conditions are met. If we want him to be free, we have to replicate this picture. Someone

wearing Sunpriest's garb, four men wearing Scarcleft
guard uniforms, the word Shale written on that rock
there—and Taquar wearing red." She laughed. "That's a
lovely touch. Terelle's, I bet. She knows he'd not be seen
dead in a ghastly suit of bright red like that if he could
help it. The little jade. I almost like her at times."

Senya glared. "She's horrible."

"Actually she's made it nicely easy for us. None of
these people have their faces painted; they could be anyone. We can use those enforcers of mine, the ones I rescued from Iani. Easy enough to find someone to sew new
Scarcleft guard uniforms for them. We don't even need
Lord Gold. We can borrow one of his robes. We'll have to
plan it very carefully so that neither Iani nor Jasper hear
a wind-whisper about it."

She studied the details of the painting, memorising it
all. When she glanced up again at Senya, she was smiling.

"But then what?" Senya asked. "I mean, when we have
Taquar free again—what happens? Iani rules in Scarcleft—so who will support Taquar's return? He doesn't
have an army or a city or anything. I don't suppose he
even has his money any more. Iani stole everything. How
will he take care of us?" She pouted. "I'm the Cloudmaster's wife here. I have money and power and now people
are beginning to be nice to me. And you're the one married to Taquar, not me."

"My dear, I don't suggest that you involve yourself
with Taquar again. You're right: here you have everything
you'll ever need. I, on the other hand..." She pondered
her predicament. To be the wife of the highlord in prosperous Scarcleft, or to be the highlord of a ruined city
with destroyed groves like Breccia? It would take ten

cycles before Breccia would be back to what it had been, with a great deal of hard work in between. Worse, Jasper supervised every move she made to be sure she was fair. *Fair!* She snorted.

"I want to swap this tedium for what I had with Taquar. A rich life, living in Scarcleft." But even as she said the words she felt her own doubt. In Breccia she had power and the potential for even more...

"Yes, but how can you do that? Iani rules there and Jasper will never allow it."

"If Taquar gets out, Iani will die. Taquar will see to that. And we have the means to persuade Jasper to support Taquar's rule in Scarcleft, I promise you. But not yet. This must be timed exactly right. We must strike the moment we hear that Terelle is on her way back."

"But why? That will be ages yet. Maybe a whole cycle!"

"Because after we act, Jasper needs to be kept busy stormshifting. The main reason, though, is that I want to give him time to be utterly wrapped up in his daughter first. That is the key to our success. And babies get cuter the older they are. I think the best plan is for you to drop all interest in Amberlyn. Stop visiting her. Ignore her. That'll make him feel sorry for her."

Senya shrugged. "Good. I hate babies. They smell horrid and spit up all the time. But I don't understand why you want Jasper to become besotted with her."

"Senya, when you want someone to do something that they will hate doing, you must give them a reason. A very good reason. Amberlyn will be that reason." She looked back at the waterpainting. "I think I had better do a drawing of this, so I don't forget the details..."

Taquar Sardonyx was sure he was slowly going mad. At first he'd thought it would be easy enough to escape. Now he knew he'd been too complacent. His jailers had anticipated every possible weakness of his cage and taken steps to strengthen them.

After his first optimistic days he'd swiftly descended into the grimmest black of despair, until he'd even lost track of how long he'd been imprisoned. Half a cycle, perhaps? Although it seemed much longer. At first he'd marked off the days. Then he'd had days when he'd forgotten if he'd done it or not. After a while, he decided it didn't make any difference whether he knew how long he'd been there or whether he didn't. What did it matter?

Days passed when he didn't care about anything much. He stopped taking pains with his appearance, stopped washing his clothes, stopped cleaning his teeth. Then one day he'd thought of Jasper, spending four years in a place not much different. *You are not weaker than Shale Flint,* he thought. *You are twice the man he is.*

Enraged by his own weakness, he began to climb out of the abyss. He developed a strict regime of exercise and cleanliness, of reading and writing to stimulate his mind. He climbed the grille every day, using only his arms to carry his weight. He sacrificed a plank from the wooden table in order to carve a wooden sword with the small table dagger he'd been allowed to keep. Using the pede kibble left behind by the men who'd rebuilt the grille, some sacking and the cord that had tied the supplies together, he constructed a quintain, which he strung from a projection on the roof of the cave. He practised swordplay with it every day.

His frustration and fury did not diminish, but he was pleased with his new leanness and toughness. His muscles were as hard and strong as they had been when he was eighteen. He examined every inch of the cave looking for a way out, and every time Iani came, he waited for him to make a mistake. But Iani was too canny. He would not deliver the food and other items to the front of the grille until Taquar had retreated to the back. He listened to Taquar's requests, and usually brought what he asked for on the next trip—but he never answered a question, nor did he engage in any conversation. After dumping the supplies, he'd leave in as short a time as possible.

Whenever Taquar felt him coming, he hid the quintain and the wooden sword, but Iani must have noticed how fit his prisoner was becoming. He never remarked on it, and his indifference was an insult. Of all the people who had been involved in his incarceration, Iani was the only one Taquar actively wanted dead. He wasn't even sure why; it was just something in the way Iani looked at him, a visceral emotion so appalling that Taquar knew he would take pleasure in seeing it die along with the man.

As for the others who had put him in this cage—Terelle and Jasper, even Ouina—those people he could in some perverse way admire for the way they had turned the situation to their favour. But not Iani.

And then there were Laisa and Senya. Senya he dismissed as of no import. She was immature and ridiculous, easily manipulated. Her mother was another matter. He smiled when he thought of her, remembering the angry passion of her sex, the way she could both love and hate him in the one moment. Laisa was not easy to categorise, and he wasn't sure he liked that. He preferred to be able to predict people and felt safest around those he could manipulate. Laisa was many things, but he was never quite sure of what she would do next—and he was relying on her. Unwise? Probably. But what choice did he have?

In the end, she did not fail him. She came alone, riding a myriapede, unruffled and competent and calm. At the time, he was stripped to the waist, glistening with sweat from a vigorous bout with the now-hidden quintain.

"Hello, Taquar," she drawled by way of greeting, her gaze roving over his body in open admiration. "Who would have thought a hermit's retreat could be so beneficial and . . . invigorating?"

"Shut up and get me out of here."

"Now that's no way to greet your rescuer." She slipped down from her mount. "Pump some water through to the trough for the pede, will you?"

He did as she asked, and he knew she was assessing his awkward gait as he limped his way to the back of cave.

As she opened the trough spigot outside the cave, she said, "Don't get your hopes up. I am not here to rescue you—yet. It is going to take a while to organise."

"What the withering blazes do you mean? Just get a prybar and a mallet and from the outside you can bust these locks wide open—"

She didn't reply. Instead, while the pede drank, she began to take things out of the pannier. "Does Iani ever search your, er, quarters?"

"No, he doesn't dare enter. He knows I'd kill him in an instant."

"Good. Then here's some wine I managed to find. It's withering scarce these days. So be suitably grateful." She passed two bottles through the grille. "And a sword. Some silk sheets." When he regarded the latter with blank astonishment, she said, "A little luxury never goes amiss."

"You're weeping sandcrazy."

"Don't be rude to your saviour."

"Silk *sheets*? Laisa, I just want to be *out* of here!"

"And you will be. Eventually," she said calmly. "Here, take this." She handed something else through the bars.

"What is it?"

"A suit of clothes."

"*Red*? You're sun-fried!" He was more angry than puzzled now and had to force down an impulse to grab her through the bars and wring her neck.

"Calm down," she said. "They have to be red for a reason. I have a lot to tell you. You'd better draw up your chair and listen, very, very carefully. This is going to take a long time. How much do you know about what has happened since you left Scarcleft?"

Through gritted teeth, he said, "Nothing. Absolutely nothing."

"Then make yourself comfortable."

He took a deep breath and fetched the chair. She took the saddle from the pede to sit on and settled herself before she began. Then she told him how Davim had been defeated, and what Terelle was, and how Amberlyn had been born. And then, right at the end, she told him he might have as long as another half-cycle before she thought it would be safe for him to venture out.

No matter what happened, no matter what she did for him, he knew he would *never* forgive her for the delay.

Right then, he hated not just Iani but the whole world. Iani would be the first to die, but he suddenly had enough savagery to wreak vengeance on them all. Especially on Terelle and Jasper. Oh, yes, especially those two.

CHAPTER TWENTY-ONE

Red Quarter
God's Pellets

The table under the canvas shade was spread with a map, weighted down at the corners with small stones. Ryka had her index finger resting on the red line of a dune sketched across the sheet of paper, and blessed the fact that she had no problem seeing things under her nose. "This is Dune Agatenob, pedemaster. This tent symbol here marks the position of your tribe's encampment."

The man she was addressing, a Reduner pedemaster called Gilmar who had just ridden in to bring them news from his dune, nodded sagely, although she doubted he had much understanding of maps.

She was proud of her mapmaking; she'd spent hours talking to those who knew the dunes, asking them about the distances between camps and dunes and waterholes, about where the sun rose and set as seen from their encampments at different times of the year, about the valleys and slopes of the sands. In addition she had organised some of the women to make paper from the jute plants growing in the valley. Reduners usually cultivated the plants to make canvas and cloth and rope, but she needed paper if she was to devise better maps than the atrocious things the Scarpen had relied on for the Red Quarter.

Gilmar was not the only person looking at the map. Also grouped around the table were Kaneth, Vara Redmane, Davim's illegitimate son Cleve and, hovering in the background, Cleve's mother, Robena, joggling a restless Kedri up and down on her shoulder.

"And you say that Ravard has emptied your waterhole, pedemaster?" Kaneth asked Gilmar.

"Almost, yes. Seemed like every bleeding pede on Dune Watergatherer descended on us one night, with every pannier they own, with every warrior—and all their allies likewise." He shook his head at the memory. "Too many of them. No point in resisting. By the way, did you know that Ravard has lost an eye? He wears an eye patch now."

"We did hear that, yes. Rumour has it the Cloudmaster was responsible." He faked disinterest. Ryka was not fooled; Kaneth was pleased to have Ravard's loss of an eye confirmed. He asked, "How much water does your tribe have left?"

"Barely enough to last another five days, Kher."

Vara stared at the listeners, unblinking, like a lizard awaiting prey. "Reduners do not steal water. Ever. If Ravard's done this thing, then he's gone to a place where no true warrior of the dunes would tread."

"Seems he's taken half the Reduners of the Quarter with him," Kaneth said dryly. "Draining a waterhole was not something he did alone."

Vara's scowl was ferocious. "He leads the tribes astray, into outlander crimes. He must be stopped. Soon! Before he diverts all drovers into twisted ways." She switched her gaze to Gilmar. "We'll send you water. Better still, bring all your tribe here until the Cloudmaster sends more rain."

"Will that be necessary?" Ryka asked. "Jasper will surely have sensed a huge movement of water like this theft. He'll replace it as soon as he can."

"I don't think so," Kaneth said, "because he won't know it was *stolen*."

"We have to stop Ravard," Vara growled, "or he'll do this again."

"We need more rainlords," Ryka said. She gave Kaneth a meaningful look. "If we had more, we could intercept Ravard every time he and his warriors leave Dune Watergatherer."

He ignored the look and said in reply, "Unfortunately, no rainlords seem to want to join us, or so Jasper said in his last communication. Anyway, I agree with Vara on this. Bring your whole tribe here, Gilmar."

"That's a decision for my tribemaster and our sandmaster," he replied, but he smiled his thanks. "I'll return to my dune to tell them of your generous offer, Kher."

"No, some of us will go," Kaneth said. "And we'll take water, too, so they have enough for another few days while they consider the suggestion. The rules here are that newcomers such as yourself are not permitted contact with dunesmen from outside until we're sure of your loyalty. If you leave God's Pellets, it'll only be with our trusted men."

"Ah. And how can I become one of your trusted warriors?"

"Kill some of Ravard's men in one of our skirmishes," Clevedim said with the easy pride of a man who had done just that. "Simple enough."

Gilmar glared at him. "You're Davim's get, aren't you? From Dune Hungry One? With your parentage, you have a lot of killing to do before you prove your loyalty to me."

"He had more than one parent!" Robena snapped, eyes flashing dangerously. "And I'm the one who raised him, you sandworm."

"That's enough," Kaneth said. "We have enough enemies outside the valley without making more within." He fixed Gilmar with a piercing gaze. "Is that understood?"

Gilmar looked down, contrite. "My men and I came to fight for Uthardim. We're willing to fight alongside anyone who fights for you, Kher. My apologies."

Robena opened her mouth to say something more and Ryka hastily stood on her foot.

"We'll be warriors together," Clevedim said calmly.

"Good. And Gilmar, you don't fight for me," Kaneth said. "You fight for the dunes. For Reduners everywhere. For yourselves. Cleve, can you see that Gilmar and his men are settled, and that they're fitted into the roster of duties?"

Cleve nodded and led the pedemaster away, apparently without rancour, while Vara and Kaneth discussed the logistics of transporting water to Agatenob. Ryka held out her arms to take Kedri from Robena, and the older woman relinquished him reluctantly. "Any time you want me to look after him," she murmured, "you have only to say. And any advice you need on raising a son, I can help there too." Her gaze followed Cleve, as if to say, *Look at what a fine job I did with my own.*

"I know. You've been so helpful," Ryka replied, feeling guilty that she didn't like the woman more than she did.

"You'll learn," Robena told her. "I'm sure you'll do a

good job in the end. It might help if you were more focused." She glanced at the map on the table, her meaning clear. "One of the other women was telling me you were intending to start teaching the boys to read and write. That's Scarpen thinking. On the dunes, it's not proper. Scribing is for the learned shamans who've been blessed by a dune god."

"Actually I wasn't thinking of teaching boys," she answered sweetly. "I thought maybe the girls would be more interested." That wasn't quite true—she had wanted to teach any child who professed an interest—but her wicked streak couldn't resist the temptation to shock Robena. When she was rewarded by an appalled look, she sighed at her own lack of restraint. The woman was so pretentious, and so easily shockable.

Kaneth grinned at her as Robena and Vara left together some time later. "Not the easiest of women, is she?"

"I swear, if she wasn't so utterly devoted to Kedri, and so good with him, I'd pull her nose. How is it that someone so helpful can also be so blasted irritating? She's like a stone in your sandal when your hands are full. It's not that she *tries* to be obnoxious, it's just that, well, she *is* obnoxious."

"I feel sorry for Cleve. Poor fellow, when we dropped by his tribe he jumped at the chance to join us, but then she was equally adamant he wasn't going without her. He would have liked nothing better than to leave her behind. What do you think of him, Ryka?"

"I haven't made up my mind yet," she admitted. "I've noticed you're trying to include him as an observer to your decision making, but I'm not sure he's the potential leader for the dunes you've been hunting for."

"He's young yet."

"True. Nineteen?"

"About that, yes. The young men from his tribe admire him, look up to him. You'd think that because he's Davim's son they'd resent him, but it doesn't work that way. Reduners respect lineage. They like it when a position passes from father to son."

"I do know that," she said wryly.

"Sorry. Of course you do. He's a fine fighter. One of the best. Marvellous rider, too."

"Hmm."

"Are you dubious because he reminds you of his father?"

"No. He's not Davim. Davim was cruel by nature. Cleve is not."

"Come on, Ryka, what's your problem with him?" He followed as she turned to enter their tent strung between the trees behind them, a spacious pavilion of several rooms.

Inside, she removed Kedri's dirty clothing while he gurgled at her happily. "Well, for a start, he doesn't respect Vara," she said at last. Handing a naked Kedri to his father, she went over to open the family jar, scooped out a basin of water and dropped Kedri's clothing into it.

"That's it?"

"That's it. So far." She rinsed the clothing, then extracted the pure water and returned it to the jar.

He grinned at her. "Maybe that's his mother's fault."

She smiled back at him as she shook out the dry clothes. "Possibly. But he'd better learn to be adaptable—that's the mark of a good leader. Here, let me have the lad back so I can dress him again."

He handed Kedri over and took the basin out onto the veranda, where he threw the dust it contained into the wind. When he returned, she said, "Kaneth, it's time I was riding out with you."

"No."

"You're in danger when you don't have a rainlord with you. I'm a rainlord. So—"

"No."

"Sooner or later there'll be ziggers out there. The main reason tribes in the past didn't make full use of ziggers is that they knew other tribes would turn around and do the same thing back to them. *But we haven't got ziggers and we don't use them.* The only reason Dune Watergatherer and their allied dunes are not using them against us now is that they don't have enough of them to risk, because we destroyed so many during the battle. But they will have been breeding them up again. When they have sufficient they will turn them on us. When you meet an armed force out there, they won't attack; they'll open cages instead."

The look he gave her was stricken. "Ryka, love, your poor eyesight makes you especially vulnerable to zigger attack."

Her tone gentled. "Kaneth, I love our son and I want him to grow up with a living father as well as a mother. And the best way to make that happen is for me to ride with you. I make use of my water-powers, not my eyesight, to sense ziggers."

His gaze dropped away from her to look at Kedri. The boy was sitting on the carpet, unaided, looking up at his father in an interested way and drooling over his clean clothing. Ryka was certain he was getting his first tooth.

"Kedri needs you still. At home. With him every day.

Ride out with me and you'll be gone for twenty days at a time! And you know your water-senses aren't that brilliant."

"You'd never be ambushed if I was with you," she persisted. "I may be a lousy rainlord, but I can still give warning of people sneaking up on you. And I can suck the water out of ziggers. That's all the edge you need."

"Ry, to have both Kedri's parents riding out would mean he could end up an orphan. Besides, you're still breastfeeding."

"I can wean him. And I'm not going to be sidetracked. Kaneth, think about what you've been achieving here, and what you've *not* achieved. Your forays have kept Ravard so busy he has fewer men to spare to raid the White and Gibber Quarters and he's not getting supplies in the form of stolen weapons and other useful stuff. That's a big plus. But you're not causing him real harm, either. And now he's just pulled off a huge raid, designed as much to insult you as anything else."

She hated herself for the look that flitted across his features just then. She'd heard wind-whispers about how Dune Watergatherer warriors laughed and boasted that their sandmaster had fucked the wife of the rainlord. There were even whispers that Kedri was his son, not Kaneth's, and that was why he had a Reduner name. She didn't know if it was Ravard who'd promoted those rumours, or whether they'd just taken on a life of their own. It didn't matter. What mattered was how each whisper, each mocking word of ridicule, sliced into Kaneth's heart, leaving a trace of pain behind, visible to her in his eyes, etched into the lines of his face.

He never blamed her, not by his words or his actions.

When he smiled at her, his abiding love was there for all
to see. When he touched her, she felt his yearning, his
desire, his admiration. But she knew his hatred for Ravard grew. She knew a sliver of jealousy had splintered
somewhere deep inside him. He wanted her to hate Ravard with an all encompassing fury and didn't understand
how she could feel sorry for this Reduner sandmaster—
because he had once been a settle lad called Mica Flint.

She said gently, "I can give you the edge."

"In time, I promise."

His tone told her she wasn't going to win this argument. Not yet. Nonetheless, she gave him a look intended
to tell him the final decision was only deferred, not
decided.

Please don't let it be too late.

Kaneth left the next morning with a band of twenty
men and fifteen water-laden pedes. At least he took Cleve
with him, which pleased her. The young man was a water
sensitive, which gave them some protection against
ambush.

Fifteen days later he was back with the whole of Gilmar's
tribe, and the following few days were hectic as men,
women and children had to be settled in. Ryka was so
busy that it was two days before she heard about a young
lad called Guyden.

It was Robena who told her.

"Poor boy," she said, "the only one of his tribe left
alive, and now the injury he got while escaping is infected.
They say you're skilled with such things. Could you come
and take a look?"

She was no healer, but she'd always had an interest in

medicinal possets and poultices, and she'd gained a reputation around the valley for her minor successes with cuts and wounds. "Who is he?" she asked as Robena showed her which tent the lad was in.

"You know what happened to Dune Scarmaker, years back?" Robena asked.

"Vara's dune? Yes, of course. Davim made an example of it. He killed the sandmaster, then wiped out most of the dune's warriors. The women and children were given the choice of death or submitting to his authority. Vara Redmane escaped, but most changed their allegiance."

And Ravard, a youth trying to prove himself, must have taken part in the massacre.

"Well, this lad, name of Guyden, was one of Bejamin's tribe."

She thought back. Tribemaster Bejamin had been Vara's brother-in-law. His tribe had chosen to die and to kill their children with them, down to their smallest babies. The deaths had been unfortunate for Davim, because when the news leaked out, many young men of other tribes had been enraged and ridden off to join Vara.

"How did Guyden escape the suicide?" she asked.

"He hid in the dunes," Robena said. "Came back to find them all dead. Kher Davim made him a slave and by all reports used him badly, even though he was still a child." She clucked, shaking her head at the idea. "As usual, when he was old enough, Davim gave him the opportunity to be a warrior, or to remain a slave. And he chose to be a slave."

"Brave lad. So how come he's here with Gilmar's tribe?"

"The Watergatherer drovers often carry their slaves with them on raids, to groom the pedes, do the cooking, fetch and carry. This time he escaped. They speared him in the leg as he ran, but he managed to hide in the dark and made his way to Gilmar's tribe."

She was taken inside to one of the inner rooms and Robena introduced them. His look of quick interest told Ryka he had heard of her. He was still a youth but already had the look of a warrior, even though his hair was unbraided. He was nearly as tall as she was, broad across the shoulder and muscular, doubtless from his slave labour. "I'm told you were speared. May I see the wound?"

He was bare-chested, and when he rolled over onto his stomach to show her the injury to his calf, she saw his back was a mass of bruises, the mark of a beating.

Oh Sunlord, she thought in disgust. *Have you come to this, Ravard?*

The leg wound itself looked nasty, but not yet dangerous.

"You are Lord Ryka who was the slave Garnet?" he asked. His tone was neutral.

"Yes," she said. "I don't remember ever seeing you in Ravard's camp."

"No. I never went there," he said. "Can you do something for the wound?"

"Yes. It's not too bad. I shall have to clean out the foulness first though, which will hurt."

He shrugged. "I've been through worse."

I'll bet, she thought.

She tried to chat with him while she worked. He seemed indifferent to the pain, but his replies, although polite, were monosyllabic. His main aim, as far as she could tell, was to be braided as a warrior and start fighting for Uthardim. When she asked him why he wanted to be a warrior, he replied without hesitation, "Revenge. Why else? My father would expect it, were he alive." The rage in him was hot and passionate, yet also very much under control.

"Kher Vara will see to it that you are braided," she said. "Tell her what your bead preference is, and if they are obtainable, she will supply them."

"Ice crystals," he said, without hesitation.

She thought it an odd choice. The white polished sides of such crystals caught the sunlight; it wasn't the selection of someone who wanted to be inconspicuous.

Leaving the tent some time later, she was unsettled. *War,* she thought. *It does things that never go away while memory lasts. We will pay for Davim's ambition for a generation or more.* It wasn't the way things should be, but it would be so. People found it hard to let go of the past when it seared their remembrance.

Shrivelled hells, Kaneth, I hope you can let loose the spindevils in your head before Kedri grows up. I want peace for him, not this.

Outside she bumped into Vara. The old woman was chewing a wad of keproot, the same stuff people smoked in Scarpen snuggeries. It stained her remaining teeth brown. "So," she said, "you've met Guyden."

"Yes. You remember him?"

"The child? Yes. I knew his parents well enough. But he's no child now. This one's a man, bitter. Even looks different. He's a warrior, just like his father, Dorwith." She sighed. "We're all that's left of our dune, Ryka. Him and

me and people like us. An old woman who chews keproot
to forget, and a lad already older than his years, possessing a heart brimming with hate. That's Dune Scarmaker.
Our legacy." She plodded away, in Ryka's eyes suddenly
no longer a battler but a tragic figure.

CHAPTER TWENTY-TWO

White Quarter
Samphire

"This is it."

Elmar craned his neck to look up at the top of the gate to Samphire and said the words with flat certainty.

Dibble nodded in agreement. "You're right. I feel... lighter."

Glancing at Dibble, Elmar raised an eyebrow. "Ah. I suppose it's true we've been a mite hungry lately."

When they were crossing the Borderlands back into Alabaster, they'd had no food at all. Across the Whiteout, they'd had only what they could find in the abandoned mine towns: mostly dried samphire and strips of pede meat jerky.

Dibble snorted and regarded the huge gates. "Y'know what I mean. Lighter in... spirit. This must be where she painted us, standing in front of the gates to Samphire. Now we're free to go back." He shook his head sadly. "I've hated feeling I had to go somewhere when I really didn't want to."

"Like being rent in two," Elmar said with a nod. "And

that's the way Terelle has been torn for years. What Russet did to her was horrible. I had no idea." He looked at the space between them, a gap large enough for another man, and gestured with his hand. "She painted *him* here, too. Feroze. I can almost feel him. Almost." An oddness, as if the magic was trying to make something true, but couldn't and never would be able to do so. Terelle had done the painting to save them all, not knowing that Feroze was already dead. He'd probably been dead even before Elmar had left her. He glanced to where their four Alabaster companions were still seated on their pedes, regarding them with varying degrees of impatience. "I think we'd better go."

Saltlip, wearing a long face, asked, "Have ye two finished with your sightseeing then? Can we now proceed into the city, perhaps?"

"Sorry. Just something we had to do." He and Dibble scrambled onto their pede.

"I'll drop ye off at the same townhouse as ye were in last time," Briass said. "Then I'll talk to my overman 'bout ye meeting the Bastion. He'll fix it for ye. The Bastion—he'll take the deaths hard, I'm thinking. Feroze especially."

Briass was as good as his word. That evening Elmar and Dibble were escorted up to the first level, then passed to a servant who took them to see the Bastion.

Terelle had once mentioned that Alabasters were not bothered by protocol, but the lack of security and the absence of formality surprised Elmar nonetheless. The room he and Dibble were ushered into was small and stark, with few decorations. The only other person there was Messenjer, once the manager of Mine Emery and now apparently the Bastion's aide, who greeted Dibble as if he was a friend and nodded to Elmar whom he had met briefly in Qanatend.

No guards anywhere. Sun-fried 'Basters, he thought, *don't they give their ruler any protection?* The Bastion indicated they should be seated, but they were both uneasy about sitting in the presence of a ruler and exchanged an embarrassed glance.

"Or stand if ye prefer," added the Bastion with a sad smile. "So, I've been informed by Briass that Feroze Khorash didn't return with ye, and neither did several of the guards. That they're dead. I want your account of what happened."

"Feroze and the others were *murdered,* my lord." *Waterless hells, is that how I should address him? I forgot to ask!* "Cold-bloodedly murdered. Feroze and six guards, taken by surprise. The only reason Dibble and I got to escape was because Terelle Grey painted us out of there. On the way we rescued those Alabasters still alive. I feel sure she painted Feroze as well, but she was too late. He was dead when I found him."

He was angry just thinking about it and was about to give voice to his opinion of Khromatians in general and the Verdigris family in particular, when he realised the Bastion was weeping. Appalled, he watched as a trickle ran down the man's wrinkled cheek. He looked away, moved. He'd heard about people who could cry tears of grief, but he'd never seen it before.

"I've known Feroze since the day he was born," the Bastion said softly. "Ye saw his body? There can be no doubt?"

All Elmar's belligerence leaked away. "None," he said. "I'm sorry. I think he was murdered by Lord Bice Verdigris and his three sons. Bice is the Commander of the Southern Marches. I gather that he both rules the ward and commands the guards there."

"I've heard of the man. The Alabasters working in the Marches bring back news from time to time."

Elmar thought peevishly that they could have done with that information before they'd entered Khromatis. *What fools these folk can be. They put more store by the restrictions of the past than the safety of their people. It's ridiculous!*

"Start at the beginning," the Bastion said. "And tell me everything ye remember."

With the occasional contribution from Dibble, Elmar related the events from the moment they'd set foot on the other side of the Borderlands. When he tried to skimp on the details, the Bastion demanded a more precise account. As he described his discovery of Feroze's body, the Bastion listened with his head bowed, his hands gripping tight to the arms of his chair.

It was two runs of a sandglass before the tale was finished, and Elmar was wishing he had taken up the offer to sit.

"So then ye rode back. No problems with the rest of the journey?" It was Messenjer who asked.

"No. As far as we could tell, we weren't followed. We were short of supplies until we reached Mine Sylvine. We raided the stores there."

The Bastion stirred, as if his back was hurting him. "And what do ye want to do now?"

"Go back and get Terelle," he said promptly.

"Ye'll have our aid."

Messenjer looked shocked. "My lord! Who are we to interfere in the affairs of the Khromatians? We've no rights in their land. Our involvement in this affair to date must have been deeply offensive to them."

Elmar flushed in anger. "I hope you're not saying that the murder was justified because someone was *offended* by Feroze's presence?" He held himself rigid. It was either that or bury a fist in the man's self-righteous expression.

The Bastion made a calming gesture with his hand. When he spoke his voice was firm but conciliatory, and it was to Messenjer that he addressed his remarks. "It's not us who've behaved badly. This Lord Bice Verdigris has committed a crime of the most despicable nature. He's killed one of our own, the most honest of men, as well as some of our guards, and he's done it to be maintaining his position as heir, even when he was assured no one had designs on his claim. He'd have killed Terelle, too, if he'd had the means to be doing it. Messenjer, can ye doubt that Feroze Khorash would *never* initiate a fight against his host, in his host's home? *Feroze?* If ever there was a man who put conciliation before violence, it was Feroze."

Messenjer stirred uncomfortably, abashed. "Yes, that's true. But we don't know for sure what happened. Neither of these men actually saw how Feroze died."

"No, we didn't," Elmar agreed, his voice harsh with fury. "But I heard Bice say it was lucky he was dead. I saw them—Bice and his two eldest sons—leave the room where I found Feroze with a Khromatian dagger in his back. He'd barely stopped bleeding! And I know what your own men, our Alabaster guards, told me about how they were attacked without provocation in the barracks.

Some of them died before they could even rise from their beds."

This time Messenjer could not meet his gaze.

Dibble shot a look at Elmar and then addressed the Bastion. "My lord, at least we know what *not* to do now. And we have an idea of where Terelle will be taken. We won't take Alabasters with us this time. We want to blend in."

"Ye don't speak the language," Messenjer said.

"We've been working at it," Elmar told him. "Hard. The guards have been helpful. On the way back they wouldn't speak to us in the Quartern tongue. Dibble's better than me; he *sounds* right. I may say the right words, but it sounds horribly wrong. Maybe—maybe I could pose as someone with a speech impediment."

The Bastion nodded. "I'll send a teacher to work with ye both for as long as ye're here. In the meantime, what would ye need? We'll do everything in our power to help. Messenjer?"

Messenjer cleared his throat and said unhappily, "We can supply guards and guides and pedes to the other side of the Borderlands bog. Whatever supplies ye want."

"Their money tokens are different from ours," the Bastion added. "We have a lot in the treasury. Ye can take as much as ye need."

Messenjer's still didn't look happy, but said nothing.

"We need paints," Dibble said. "For Terelle. They confiscated hers."

Messenjer looked even more displeased, and this time he spoke up. "Now that is difficult. We don't have water-painters here. The paint-powders they use are special. Perhaps ye can buy them already made in Khromatis, if ye know what to ask for."

"Sounds risky," the Bastion said. "I'll give it some thought. When do ye want to be leaving?"

"As soon as we can," Elmar said. "But we also want to be as prepared as we can. Do you have maps of Khromatis?"

Once again it was Messenjer who answered. "Not that I know of. None of our people ever leave the Southern Marches, ye know."

"I'll have the library searched," the Bastion said. "And I tell ye what else we can do, Mez. Call all the Alabasters who have worked in Khromatis lately for a meeting." He turned to Elmar and Dibble. "I'll tell them they must answer whatever questions ye ask."

Messenjer's appalled expression was a statement by itself.

The Bastion continued to address Elmar, but his next words were probably more for Messenjer's benefit. "We've spent generations working for the Southern Marches, making their goods there, mining their needs here in the White Quarter. We've guarded their borders. We've kept their secrets because they asked it of us. We've exiled ourselves because they demanded it of us. We've held ourselves in readiness to be returning because they said one day it'd be possible. But now the covenant between us is deeply and irrevocably shaken." He turned his faded pale blue eyes on Messenjer. "I want to be calling a council meeting. There are decisions to be made and they cannot be mine alone."

"Which council?" Messenjer asked.

"Both. Combined." He added for Elmar and Dibble's benefit, "We have a Traders' Council and a Miners' Council."

"I'll see to it," Messenjer said. He looked shaken.

The Bastion tried to smile, but the curl of his lips was

more sad than joyous. "When she was here, Terelle spoke thoughtless words in haste, but they were words said from the heart, and they've eaten into my certainty ever since. She asked me why Khromatis should still be called our home after so long. It was ridiculous, she said. In her words: 'I don't feel the least bit like a person from Khromatis even though my parents grew up there.'"

Messenjer paled. "My lord!"

"Yes, Mez, I hear ye. But Feroze is dead. He's dead because we trusted people who despise us. And I think it's time we change. Time we challenge what they've done to us."

Messenjer was outraged. "It's God's will! And we shouldn't speak of such things in front of outsiders."

"God's will? I wonder. However, ye're right about one thing; this doesn't concern outsiders. Elmar, Dibble, the city is yours."

Elmar bowed his head. The interview was over.

After the two Scarpen armsmen had left, the Bastion interviewed Briass and the other three Alabasters, one by one. As he had expected, they confirmed Elmar's story. When the last of them had left, he sat slumped in thought. Then he looked up at Messenjer. "Ask the scribe to be attending me, please. I want to be telling the Cloudmaster about this."

When the mine manager gave him a look indicating the depth of his continued unease, the Bastion shook his head at him. "People who don't change stagnate, Mez. It's time we looked to the Quartern."

"Ye haven't asked the advice of the councils yet!"

"Do I need their permission to be writing to a fellow

ruler about the fate of his prospective bride? How'd ye feel if I knew Errica was in danger but didn't tell ye? Lord Jasper has a right to be knowing."

"Then it's up to Elmar or Dibble to be telling him."

"They're not men who think in terms of letters. They serve their stormlord in the way they best know: action. The letter is my task. When ye've brought me the pen and ink, go make your preparations to call the councils."

Messenjer left without another word. The Bastion sank back against the cushions, remembering the past: that other world when he had been young and in love, and his wife had held in her arms the only child they were ever to have.

She'd looked up at him tenderly, not knowing that one day he would walk away from her and his son, to serve a larger master. "Can we name him after my grandfather?" she'd asked. "He was a wonderful man, and I miss him and his wisdom."

And so they had. They'd called their son Feroze, after her grandfather. It was a bonus that it fitted so well with his own family name, Khorash.

CHAPTER TWENTY-THREE

Khromatis
Marchford to Verdigris Manor

Terelle was utterly miserable.

She would *never* get used to riding an alpiner. After pedes, they seemed such *inadequate* animals. So ridiculous, only a single person being able to comfortably ride at a time. And all the food they ate, just to carry one person with a minimum of baggage. Besides, riding one made her so *sore*. Her mount was on a leading rein, so she didn't have to do much, but she wasn't used to riding with her legs spread out on either side of a beast. She was jolted and bumped and bounced until she wanted to scream. Each time she dismounted—awkwardly because there were no mounting handles—her buttocks and thighs felt as if they were on fire. And this was only the first day of her journey. Waterless skies, how would she survive?

And that was another thing, the skies *weren't* waterless. They dripped water like a cracked pot, for long periods at a time. *Rain*. It was one thing to know it existed, quite another to experience it—dripping down her back and off her nose. Running down inside her boots. Soaking everything. Water falling from the sky and running away into the soil, nobody caring enough to catch it in containers, everyone cursing it...Didn't they know how lucky they were?

Fortunately, before they'd left Marchford, Rubric had seen Terelle's cloak and decided it was totally inadequate for the journey. He'd replaced it with something called a mantle, made of wool that was matted and slightly oily. The water tended to run off it and at night its warmth was welcome.

It was a kind gesture from Rubric. This youngest cousin of hers was a puzzle. He spoke rarely, even to his brother. If she'd had to describe him, she would have called him watchful. His eyes were never still, his head was often cocked as if listening to distant conversations, his whole posture was vigilant and guarded. He was also beautiful in a way neither of his brothers were. More elegant in action, his toned muscles sleeker, his features more refined, his lips fuller, his tattoos more intricately done as though he'd cared for the artistry. He turned the heads of women without even trying to catch their attention. It was the combination of hard male strength and refinement that was so attractive, she decided. That and the streak of compassion she hoped she'd detected.

That's a dangerous thought, you stupid female. He is probably the one who slid his blade into Feroze when the poor man wasn't expecting it...

"I thought your waterlords stopped it from raining," she grumbled to him.

"Only if the rain is unseasonal or excessive," he replied. "If it didn't rain often, how could the plants grow? Besides, it's tiring to move rain just because we don't want to get wet."

She had no answer to that.

Ten people made up their party. Besides Jet and Rubric, there was a groom to care for their mounts—not Eden Croft, unfortunately—five armed guards, none of whom spoke the Quartern tongue, and a woman called Mauve who did. Terelle wondered why Mauve was there, until the first time they dismounted to rest the animals and relieve themselves. When she made her way into the bushes for some privacy, Mauve followed her.

"You could at least look the other way," she said to the woman sourly.

Mauve shrugged. "All right, but I'm a waterlord, so don't think ye can move an inch without me knowing it."

The words dismayed her. How was she ever going to search the baggage for her waterpaints if she was watched every moment of the day? Sunblast it, escape was impossible. Rubric and Jet were Watergivers of some kind, probably at least as powerful as Jasper. They could all track her water. They could ride alpiners; she couldn't. She had to ride with them, learn all she could and watch for opportunities, especially for any way to recover her paints. A waterpainter with paints and prepared to take the risks that went with shuffling up had myriad ways to outwit a stormlord.

As she walked back to the alpiners, Mauve trailing her like a trained pede, she reflected that things could have been worse. No one had made another attempt to kill her. She was sure it would not have been difficult now. The constant need to travel towards the place where Russet had painted her was gone; he'd told her the truth when he said that if he died, she'd be free. The feeling was extraordinary. Only once the compulsion had been stripped away did she realise how much it had dragged her down over the years. It had lurked there, just under her skin, a constant irritant she could never banish.

And now? The Khromatians' mistaken belief that she was invulnerable to sudden death was the only thing keeping her alive. The irony of that forced a wry smile from her.

When she and Mauve rejoined the others, Rubric gave her a sharp look. "What's so funny?" he asked.

"I haven't had someone watch me pee since I was two years old," she said. "What a humiliating task you have given Mauve, watching me in my most intimate moments. Have you all no shame?"

He reddened as she'd hoped he would. What she didn't expect was the twitch of a smile at the corner of his lips, as if he appreciated her attempt to embarrass him. "Ye have a way with words," he said.

Jet was less appreciative. He glared at her. "Be respectful to your betters," he said.

She glanced around. "My betters? I see none."

As if he sensed that bandying words with her would be undignified, he stalked away to attend to his mount.

"A way with words indeed," Rubric said softly. "I can see this is going to be an interesting ride."

It had stopped raining, so she took off her mantle to shake it, only to find the water flying away from it in a shower of droplets. She blinked in surprise and looked at Rubric. His lips twitched as he dried the rest of her clothes.

She blushed at the casual intimacy of it and looked away.

Just before they mounted to ride on, she walked over to

the track, bent down under the pretext of adjusting her boot and placed a tiny piece of mirror in the dirt at the side, just as she had done all along the way, especially whenever the road divided. The bundle of mirror pieces had been one of the things she had placed in her pack before leaving her room.

When she looked back as they moved off, she could see the mirror piece twinkling in the meagre sunlight. However, it would probably be twenty days or more before Elmar and Dibble even made it back to Marchford, if they ever did, or could. If they had even reached Samphire safely in the first place.

If. If. If.

For the next three days, they rode fast on the flat roads of the lower river valley, bypassing the towns and staying in wayside inns. Mauve not only shared her room, but slept in the same bed as well, to make sure she didn't try to sneak away during the night. Whenever Terelle tried to find out more about her, or have any kind of conversation that was not necessary, Mauve refused to answer. In the end she gave up and ignored the older woman, looking through or past her as if she had no physical presence at all. A petty revenge, but at least she felt she'd won a small battle.

I'll show them, she thought. *They can't cow me, and they can't control me even though I am a prisoner.* And just to confuse Mauve she spent the fourth day grinning in apparent delight every time she saw her watching.

After the third day, the terrain changed. Towns dwindled to villages, the inns were further and further apart. They slowed as the road grew steeper. Still following a river, the track began to climb past farms of steep fields where farmers tended orchards and goats and similar animals she had never seen before, covered in wool rather than hair. Later, the farms alternated with forests of trees. Not that she'd had any idea what a meadow or a forest was until she'd seen one. She hadn't even seen trees that tall before, let alone so numerous and varied. All that green. Dibble was right; the scenery was bilious.

They started to sleep in what the Khromatians called bivacs. Apparently anyone could use them, although they were built by the military for armsmen on the march or officials on the Pinnacle's business. Basic structures constructed beside the track, they were little more than walls and a roof to keep off the rain. Most of them did have a privy at the back, although she sometimes decided she'd rather not use it.

They bought fresh food from the farms they passed, simple fare that she ate heartily. Under Rubric's tutelage she was even beginning to understand how to ride the alpiner without bouncing like a bag of bab fruit on the back of a handcart. At times like that she thought him genuinely kind. But trust him? No, that would have been a step too far.

On the morning of the day after their first bivac, she was overwhelmed with the oddest feeling that she was returning to a place she'd seen. The flow of the river, the way the grass rippled in the wind, mountains in the distance...then she realised. This was where Russet had painted her. They didn't stop. As they rode past, she thought she felt the last traces of the magic of his painting as tiny flickers of unease, so light they slipped away into nothingness.

Further down the road they passed a manor house on a hill overlooking a bend in the river. The alpiners were walking at the time and she glanced at the building in mild interest. It was by no means the only manor they had seen, and she would have dismissed it from her mind if Rubric had not ridden up beside her and said, using Khromatian as he usually did, "That's the Kermes family house."

She didn't reply, but studied it with more interest. *Elegant,* she thought. *So different from Scarpen houses always joined to the next.* And then, *My grandmother was born here. Grew up here. I suppose my mother came here too, sometimes. I wish I'd known her. I wish I'd known them both.*

Rubric said, "I wasn't born when Russet and Sienna Kermes vanished. But I do know it was a great scandal in their family, and ours too. A dark secret everyone tried to hide. Then you came to tear it all open, and now it seems my grandfather shouldn't be the Pinnacle, but you should." He chuckled as if that amused him. "And you don't even speak the tongue of the land properly! Did you really expect to be made welcome?"

"I didn't even know I was in the line of succession. Who lives there now?"

"Oh, another branch of the family. You didn't *know*?"

"No. Russet never told me."

"You must be missing him."

She almost laughed. Instead she shook her head. "I didn't like him. Why should I miss him?"

He blinked in surprise, as if that had not occurred to him.

"I seem to be extraordinarily unlucky in my relatives.

Do you like yours?" she asked, shooting a look at Jet. Although he was not in earshot, she wondered if Rubric would reply.

He didn't. Instead, that same play of secretive amusement twitched his lips. More, she thought, for himself than for her.

Then, suddenly serious, he slipped easily into the Alabaster dialect of the Quartern tongue to say, "I'm sorry ye're in this predicament. I'd go to the Quartern with ye, if it was allowed. But it isn't, not for anyone. Ye were mad to be coming here, and that old man should have known that. Must have known that. Ye were wise not to like him."

She gaped at him in amazement. "Did you have a hand in killing Feroze?" She had no idea why she blurted out the question just then. It had popped into her head, unasked and unconsidered; it suddenly seemed important that she know.

"No," he said. Just that: no explanation, no excuses. Then he allowed his mount to drop back behind her again.

Sunblast it, Elmar, you had better come after me with some paints, because I'm wilted if I know how to get out of this mess without them.

They climbed on and up. It rained more, and grew colder, day by day. The trees were shorter, more stunted, more like the trees she knew from home. She learned to appreciate the muscular strength of the alpiners as they plodded upwards without complaint, fuelling themselves with grass or small plants every time they stopped. Each day they ate a handful of some special kibble the Khromatians gave them.

They'd left the Southern Marches and crossed the next

ward called the Slew, to enter a ward called the Wilder
Pale. Here the bivacs became more elaborate, with cover
for the animals, and feed left for them in bins. The single
room for travellers contained a fireplace and blankets.
Although they lacked caretakers, all seemed in good order.
Several times they passed through small villages scraping
a living from woodcutting and hunting, and when they
bypassed the manor house of the Commander of the
Wilder Pale, guards rode out to collect a toll for use of the
track, only to exempt them when they found the party was
led by the Pinnacle's grandsons.

After that, the valley they were in narrowed, the river
grew more tumultuous, the forest more eerie. Short,
twisted trees had trunks thick with moss and branches
draped with lichens called old man's beard.

The mountains frightened Terelle. These were nothing
like the Warthago; they were so high they scratched at the
sky with snow-topped edges, so stark their ridges were
blades to cut the clouds. They glistened with wet black
rock, their sheer walls wept water. They shut out the sun
and funnelled the wind into freezing gales. Barren of people,
they were wild with game, furry things she'd never seen
before. Voles, the Khromatians said. Marmots, hares. The
guards hunted and cooked them, stews of meat and roots
that were thick and rich and tangy.

One night it snowed. When they stepped outside in the
morning the world was white, sounds curiously muted.
She was dumbfounded. Nothing Russet had told her—
and not even the glimpses of white on the peaks—had
prepared her for the wonder and beauty and sheer impos-
sibility of fresh-fallen snow. It melted quickly when the
sun shone, taking with it much of her confidence. How

could someone like Elmar cope with a world so different, so strange? She was expecting too much. She began to hope the two Scarpen guards wouldn't try to follow her; this place would confound them even if they never met an enemy. Still, she stuck pieces of mirror into the bark of wayside trees, and worried she would run out of them.

Ten days after they'd left Marchford, they entered the gap between two peaks leading into the valley of the Low Plateau Pale.

At the top of the pass they halted and Terelle walked to the northern edge. It was a fine, clear day, and below she could see the flat floor of the valley spread out like a map. Tiny villages, threaded through with roads and stone walls, were so far away and small they could have been painted on a flat canvas.

"We stop in a bivac here tonight. We'll be home by nightfall tomorrow," Rubric said, coming to stand beside her.

"Where do you live?" she asked.

He pointed with his riding crop. "See that bunch of buildings to the left of the road? The ones with the orange roofs? That's Verdigris Manor. You will die there one day."

She rolled her eyes. He was like that, kind and helpful and pleasant, and then he'd throw her an upsetting statement or an unexpected remark. "So nice to be reminded," she said. "You have a charm that's all your own."

"We own all the land you can see between the river and the mountain wall. We raise alpiners. See the herd?" She squinted against the slant of late evening light, to see moving dots in a walled meadow. "My mother manages the stud when we're gone," he added.

"I thought she was a waterpainter."

"Yes. A healer."

She frowned, wondering if she'd misunderstood the word.

"Don't you do that in the Quartern?" he asked. "Use waterpainting to heal illnesses, at least those sicknesses that respond to it?"

She was confused. "No," she said. "Would your mother teach me?"

"Are you daft? No one would allow you near a grain of paint-powder. Mind you, you could ask her. She is like me," he added obscurely. "Not a Verdigris."

"I don't understand," she said.

"Jet, Hue, Father, my grandfather—they are Verdigris to the bone. My mother is a Lustre. Jade Lustre, before she married. My name may be Verdigris, but I take after the Lustre side. They're granite to our glass."

Granite is hard, glass transparent and clear... Glass breaks so easily...

What is he trying to tell me?

He asked, "If you don't heal illnesses, what do you do with your waterpainting in the Quartern?"

"Stormshift," she said. "What else when water is scarce?"

"Ah. Here we stormshift, too. We move the storms away when they bring too much rain or wind or snow."

She shook her head, indicating her wonder at the idea. "Are you a waterpainter too?"

"No. I am an ordinary waterlord. I'm not sure what you'd call it."

"Stormlord, I suppose. We have stormlords and rain-lords, and then reeves. Reeves are the folk with lesser abilities. Why not go to the Quartern?" she asked. "See for yourself. There, you would not be just the youngest son. You'd be rich, if that's what you want. Powerful, if power is what you seek. Revered, if you want respect." She took a guess at his dreams. "There you could be a Lustre, not a Verdigris."

He turned abruptly away from her and went to join his brother. Sighing, she wondered if she'd made a mistake. He might not have murdered Feroze, but he was one of the men who had killed the Alabasters at the barracks... She pushed the thought away and continued to stand at the edge of the pass, studying the valley, imprinting the detail forever on her waterpainter's memory. Her purpose was important; if she was to escape from the edifice she could see below, she needed to know every inch of the building, its surroundings, and the way out of the valley.

If only I could get hold of my own paints...

She thought she'd identified the saddlebag they were in, but the knowledge had not been much help. Jet carried it on his mount and slept with his head on it at night. Although the guards were friendlier than they had been at first, their vigilance had not decreased to the point of allowing her anywhere near Jet's belongings.

When the light was gone, she returned to the bivac in the pass. It was bitterly cold and her breath clouded on the air.

"I know what ye were doing," Rubric said in her ear when she came close to the fire to warm up. This time he chose to speak Quartern, perhaps because he didn't want the guards to understand.

"Looking at the scenery?" she suggested.

"No, remembering. So ye can escape. And if ye're not,

ye should be. I wonder how long we have before the painting that was to be taking ye home will pull ye apart
instead."

"Perhaps it'll just pull your house down around your
ears to set me free."

He stared at her.

"Don't tell me you haven't thought of that."

He still didn't speak.

"You haven't, have you? Are you all so…ignorant?"

"We know waterpainting can have unexpected results,
but ye exaggerate."

"I was imprisoned once before. In Scarcleft, to be exact,
by the highlord, the city's ruler. So someone painted a
picture of me free. The magic worked. I wasn't pulled in
two; it pulled down the house instead—a very large house,
like your manor houses. In fact more than one house was
damaged. With an earthquake. People died."

He looked shocked.

She was merciless. "You have no idea who painted the
picture of my return to the Quartern, so you have no idea
how powerful they are. But I think it would be wise not
to imprison me, or try to kill me."

And I wish that was true…

"I think ye're bluffing," he said.

"Do you? We'll find out, won't we?" She smiled, trying to rattle him.

Jet glared at them from across the room, as he always
did when anyone spoke to her more than was necessary.

Rubric laughed and walked away. She wasn't sure
whether he was laughing at her or just annoying his
brother. She'd decided there was little affection between
the two, and a great deal of something else less pleasant.

Rivalry? Hatred? Bitterness? Jealousy? No, something different. Something she couldn't put her finger on. Jet appeared contemptuous of his younger sibling, poking fun because he wasn't as tall or broad-shouldered as the rest of the family. She'd noticed that the guards, perhaps following his lead, sometimes sniggered about Rubric behind his back.

Nice family, these Verdigris. On a par with the Kermes. She decided she now loathed the expression Quartern people used about inherited traits: *Hide your blood and it still speaks.* Pellets and nonsense—she might share Verdigris blood, but she was withering sure she shared nothing else.

Later that evening, after walking outside to visit the privy, Mauve trailing a discreet distance behind her, Terelle overheard the two brothers talking. They were standing deep in the shadows a little way from the bivac. She caught only snatches of the wind-borne conversation.

"I hope...in order to learn more," Jet said, "so that we can control her better."

Rubric gave a low, mocking laugh. His reply was slightly more audible. "Of course! What else? She's a sand grubber. You can't think I...surely? Or do you... interested...because she's a woman who doesn't yet know what I am, perhaps?"

She had no idea what he meant.

Jet urged his mount to a gallop as soon as they hit the flat road on the valley bottom, and most of the guards followed, whooping and shouting. Mauve had already left them at a crossroads to head home herself. Rubric and two of the older guards continued at a more sedate pace. He

made no move to speed up; in fact he dropped back to ride
at a walk beside Terelle.

"They haven't seen their families in a while," he
explained. "Jet is passionate about his wife, Azure. Funny
that. He usually gets his thrills from hurting others; around
her he's a spring lamb."

"Lamb?" Her Khromatian had improved enormously,
but that was a word she didn't know.

"Baby sheep."

She snorted. "I find that hard to believe."

"So, tonight you begin your imprisonment."

"I have been imprisoned before. I'll survive."

"You think you'll escape, don't you? You puzzle me,
Terelle. Why are you so calm about this? You know my
father and brothers want you dead, and I'm quite sure my
grandfather will concur, when he hears. What chance
have you got?"

"If it worries you, then help me escape. Come with me.
Imagine the adventure, Rubric!"

"No one has painted *me* into safety," he said.

She stared at him. "They'd kill you for helping me?"

"For attempting to leave Khromatis. Possibly. No one
ever leaves, so I don't really know. Your mother was the
last to go." His voice was thick with bitterness. "If I was to
leave, it might be the last straw for my father."

"What did you do that he could hate you so much?"

"Not be the person he wanted." He shrugged, as if it
meant nothing.

Then I will paint you there, she thought with her own
layer of bitterness. *As soon as I have my colours again,
I'll paint you all there. You Verdigris killed Feroze and all
those young men, strangers who never hurt you. They*

never hurt any of you. You would have killed me, if you could. Sandblast you all—you will serve us in the Quartern.

But even as she thought the words, she wondered if she could do it. She had suffered so much herself from the compulsion of waterpainting. *You are weak,* she thought. But deep inside, she was not ashamed of that. Besides, of what use would an unwilling stormlord be?

Then, as she thought it through, it occurred to her how much danger she could be in—for the rest of her life. People in Khromatis knew what she looked like now. If one of them was a waterpainter, they could paint her dead. As far as she knew she had not yet met one, but she soon would: *Bice's wife, Jade Lustre Verdigris.*

She went cold all over. How could she escape if all this woman had to do was waterpaint her back in captivity? Come to think of it, why didn't Bice just ask his wife to picture him as the Pinnacle to ensure his succession? No, wait, that could mean his father's sudden death.

"Why so thoughtful?" Rubric asked.

"How many waterpainters does Khromatis have? And how many other kinds of waterlords?"

"Waterlords, I've no idea. Never thought about it. Waterlord families tend to intermarry in order to keep the power within those families."

"It's the same in the Quartern."

"Water sensitives never seem to have very large families. Is it the same in the Quartern?"

"Yes. I've wondered why not."

"Not sure. It just doesn't happen. Perhaps that's just as well; God's way of not spreading the power outside the main families. It would be too difficult to control. Too easy to kill others. Or to force them to do things. Water-painters are the most dangerous of all, of course, because not only is it possible to kill someone anonymously and destroy the proof you did so, but it is so easy for there to be backlash from a painting."

"Like an earthquake. And people dying. Yes, I know."

He ignored her sarcasm. "There are only five families that reliably produce waterpainters—the Kermes and the Lustres are two of them. I doubt that there are more than fifteen waterpainters alive at the moment." He looked across at her. "Quite enough to keep Khromatis safe if anyone was to attack us, if that's why you're asking. Did your Cloudmaster send you to spy?"

She snorted her scorn at that idea.

Just then they turned off the road to ride through a gateway. A gravelled track, raked smooth, led onwards through trees. Surreptitiously, she dropped her last mirror pieces.

"We've just entered our property," Rubric said. "Welcome to Verdigris Manor."

"You want me to say thank you?"

She glanced at him and caught the sardonic curve of his lips. "We have a great many rules for waterpainters, of course. I suppose it's similar in the Quartern."

"What are yours?" she asked.

"Well, all waterpainters have to be..." He paused. "I suppose you would say 'registered.' Registered with a central guild, after testing shows they possess certain artistic talents. That's a start. If anyone isn't registered, it is against the law to teach them to shuffle up. If a guild member was rash enough to do that, they would have their hands cut off. I don't think I've ever heard of it happening though."

"We don't have enough waterpainters in the Quartern to have a guild," Terelle said blandly. "Go on."

"Then you have to pass a test after training. And the test includes knowing all the rules about usage. You are not permitted to kill or maim or coerce by means of waterpainting. Anyone pictured in your painting must give their consent, or you must obtain the guild's permission, or their parents' consent in the case of children. Things like that."

"And no one breaks the law?"

"Now? Not often. History, alas, is rife with waterpainting wars and usurpers and political murders."

"We don't have fifteen waterpainters," she said. "Imprison me, and thousands of people will die in the Quartern because I'm not there to bring the water. And you could find a very powerful stormlord on your doorstep in a terrible rage. You might point that out to your grandfather if you get the chance. The present Cloudmaster is one of the most powerful we've ever had." *Apart from the slight problem he has with salty water.* "But he doesn't particularly want to spend all his days stormshifting. And what if he should die? We have a lot of rainlords as well, of course. They're usually trained in warfare, among other things." She tried to make it sound vaguely like a threat, while still accounting for the need the Quartern had for Khromatian waterlords, but had an idea she was digging herself a hole with the contradictions.

She ploughed on, "Because you have so many rules, you've forgotten just how dangerous waterpainting is."

"We have the rules *because* we know how dangerous it is."

"Rubric, I'm not panicked about being imprisoned. I'll

get home one way or another, and anyone who tries to stop me might end up dead."

He appeared to be pondering this while they rode on, but she couldn't tell what he was thinking. She couldn't help remembering what he'd said to Jet. *She doesn't know what I am.*

They scared her, those words.

When they emerged from the woods, it was to see fields cleanly sundered from the trees by a stream and, beyond that, the manor house, a stone building surrounded by lavish gardens.

I'll never get used to this, she thought. *The extravagance of growth, the abundance. They really have no idea of what we face in the Quartern. No wonder they don't care.*

"Rubric, what can I do to change what your family is doing to me?"

She expected him to laugh at the naïvety of the question, but instead he paused, then said, "I don't know. It's pointless to ask to see the Pinnacle. You've met my father and brothers. They're made in the same mould as my grandfather. None of them will ever trust your motives, and my grandfather will never let you see his face for fear of what you might do. Because you could paint him dead, at some future time."

"I don't want him dead! Why the withering spit would I want him dead? I don't give a salted damn about being the Pinnacle. And I don't have any paints anyway, and I'm weeping sure your mother won't lend me any."

"Terelle, by your own admission, someone painted you apparently safe back in the Scarpen. Sooner or later, the magic is going to start working to get you there. You're going to be very sick. My father doesn't doubt you'll die. True, you've made me wonder just who will emerge victorious. Us, with our imprisonment of you, or the magic to get you home. If we win, you sicken and die. If the painter back in the Quartern was very powerful, then you'll escape."

"And how does that make you feel?"

"I think my father is a fool. He'd have done better to trust you. Instead he has threatened his home and his family. He is small-minded enough to pour scorn on the skills of the Quartern. He thinks you're all as weak as crickets in winter."

Instinct prompted her to silence.

Another long pause. Then, "I didn't kill any of those Alabasters. I was supposed to take their water. But I couldn't. I couldn't use my power. I stood there and felt waves and waves of sickness hit me until I thought I was drowning. I didn't know what was wrong with me. Now I do—it was the strength of the power in your painting. Those Alabaster guards were necessary to get the two Scarpermen safe back to Alabaster, so their lives were spared. I *know* how powerful you are."

There was something wrong with that assessment, she knew, but right then she didn't want to think about it. She said, "I'd talk to your father again, if I were you. I don't want anyone to die this time, just to free me." She swallowed. "Sometimes I wake in the middle of the night, after a dream. It's always the same dream, only it wasn't a dream the first time. It was real. A child, dead in his mother's arms because part of a falling house crushed him."

"Talk to my mother," he said, troubled. Then added, "She doesn't speak your tongue, but your Khromatian is really good now. Your waterpainter's memory, I suppose." He gave her one of his horrid mocking grins as he urged his mount ahead at a trot, pulling hers behind. The conversation was at an end.

CHAPTER TWENTY-FOUR

Khromatis
Low Plateau Pale
Verdigris Manor

When Terelle entered the manor with Rubric, Jet was standing talking to a middle-aged woman in the large main entrance hall. A small boy clung to his boots and an older girl had a grip on his plaid scarf, while another woman had hooked her arm through his.

"My mother," Rubric murmured in Terelle's ear, "and that's Jet's wife, Azure, and their two children."

Pleasant domesticity was not what she had come to expect of Jet. When she felt her lip begin to curl in cynicism, she hastily turned her attention to Lord Jade. Tall, dark-skinned and beautiful, she resembled Rubric the most of all her sons. Rubric went straight to her and kissed her hand and then her cheek. Her smile was pure pleasure as she murmured a greeting Terelle didn't catch. Then she turned to Terelle and the smile dropped away.

As Jet said nothing, Rubric introduced his mother and sister-in-law.

"Jet tells me you are Sienna Verdigris' daughter, and a

waterpainter," Jade said, her tone flat. "I'd have bid you welcome, had not Jet told me we're to imprison you here. I dislike the idea of Verdigris Manor becoming a jail to one of our own family, even if your party did attack my husband, even if you came to assert your right to be Pinnacle."

Hunting for the right words to say, Terelle ended up merely blurting out, "That is a terrible lie."

Lord Jade raised an eyebrow. "You are very bold." Her tone was coldly furious. She lifted her hand to show a letter she held. "I have my husband's account, right here."

"He's a murderer and a liar," she answered, equally cold. She was so furious she couldn't think, and her Khromatian deserted her. Turning to Rubric, she spoke in her own tongue. "Are you going to lie too? Are you going to say that poor Feroze attacked first? That those Alabasters killed by your men—"

"Say no more," he said, cutting her off. "No more, Terelle." He looked at his mother then and said, in Khromatian, "My mother knows the truth."

She thought he meant his mother would believe her husband, but Lord Jade went deathly pale at his words.

Something in Terelle snapped. All the anger and grief she'd shut within her since Feroze's death erupted from that dark place, overwhelming her. Somehow she dredged up the Khromatian words to say, "I don't want to be a Verdigris. I'm Terelle *Grey*. I don't want to be the Pinnacle. Why would I? This is not my land. And the Verdigris family are murderers. My Alabaster friend Feroze went to your husband to ask him to come and talk to me. And Bice *killed* him."

"Threw a dagger into his back when he was fleeing,

that right, Jet?" Rubric said, accompanying the statement with one of his mocking smiles.

Lord Jade looked from Terelle to her sons, horrified. Jet grew even angrier. His wife—who had not said a word—took one look at his face, released her hold on his arm and quickly drew the children from the room.

Snarling at his brother and speaking in Quartern, Jet said, "Shut your bleeding mouth, ye fool!"

Terelle shifted her gaze to Lord Jade and waved a hand at the brothers. "The Verdigris men murdered Feroze and six guards. Jet came to kill me. Tried and failed. I am safely waterpainted."

As she struggled to find more words, Jet launched himself across the room and smashed a fist into her nose. It happened so fast, she was only beginning to react when his fist connected. She heard her nose break, the crunch of it grating inside her ears. Pain exploded across her face, and an instant later agony radiated outwards into every part of her skull.

She was lying on the floor, blood everywhere, with no memory of falling. Choking and trying to breathe, she strove to conquer the engulfing pain. Jet stood over her, his sword in his hand. His face was contorted with murderous rage. Her first coherent thought—as she swallowed her blood and started dragging in air through her mouth—was that he would be successful this time.

Then Lord Jade's voice, filled with outrage. "Put your sword away, Jet!" The ringing in Terelle's head wouldn't let her understand the rest of what the woman said, but it was clear she was berating her middle son in no uncertain language. She had not raised her voice, yet her words seemed to fill every corner of the hall.

Rubric bent over her and helped her to sit up. "Are ye all right?" he asked. For once, he sounded genuinely concerned.

"Hardly," she said, spitting out blood. "De bastard broke dy dose." Speaking hurt so much that tears ran down her face.

"Ye're braver than me," Rubric said cheerfully, "poking Jet like that until he reacted. He's not known for the sweetness of his temper. We tend not to be provoking him."

"Oh, frizzle you," she said, nauseous and dizzy. She clutched at him to pull herself to her feet. Moaning, she wiped away the tears with the back of her hand, to see that Jet had vanished. Lord Jade pushed a kerchief into her hand and she used it to stem the bleeding. Touching her nose started the tears flowing again. *Blighted eyes, but that is weeping painful.* She couldn't even think straight.

"So, Mother," Rubric asked, "where do we imprison this vicious enemy of ours, my cousin Terelle? I believe Jet was suggesting the ice house."

Terelle glared, but doubted he noticed her expression behind the now-bloodied kerchief. *Withering shit, this is agony!*

"Certainly not," Lord Jade said. "Take her up to the tower room. I will bring my paints."

Rubric seized her by the elbow. "Let's go," he said. "It's a long climb."

"Goin' t'be sig," she said.

"Sig?" he asked, puzzled.

She took a deep breath and enunciated carefully. "Sick."

"Do ye think you could wait till we reach the garderobe?" he asked in Quartern, but the last word he used was a Khromatian one she didn't recognise. She nodded anyway.

Disoriented, she leaned on his arm, too ill even to notice the way they took. Something told her she should be paying attention, but her head was spinning too much to obey her instinct. She was vaguely aware they crossed a number of rooms before they arrived at the foot of stone steps spiralling upwards. Every step sent pain stinging into her cheekbones. The steps were too narrow for two people, and only his solicitous hand on her back as he walked close behind her enabled her to continue upward.

At last they stepped onto a landing at the top. In front of them was a thick wooden door with a bar on the outside.

"This is it," Rubric said. "Your home for the remainder of your life. Used to be the lookout post for our sentries in days gone by. When we had enemies." He unbarred the door and made an extravagant bow to usher her in.

"One od dese days summun is goin' t'wring your deck, Rubric," she told him.

"Not sure what ye just said," he responded, still infuriatingly cheery, "which I suspect is probably just as well." He took a look around. "Ah, I'd better send up a few comforts I suppose. Like linen and firewood and a lamp. No glass in these windows unfortunately, but the shutters close tight. Only thing is it's rather dark with them shut. Ye won't go jumping out, will ye? I mean, ye wouldn't want to oblige my father by committing suicide, would ye? There's the garderobe over there in the alcove behind the curtain. When she looked blank, he said, "Ye know, outhouse. Or whatever ye barbarians call it.

At least he wasn't using Khromatian. She didn't think her brain could cope with their language right then. Abruptly, she sat down in the room's only chair.

"Do ye still want to be sick?"

She shook her head, which was a mistake.

He turned as a servant girl stepped through the door carrying a bundle of bedding. "Ah," he said. "Mother is one step ahead of me, as usual." He looked Terelle up and down in assessment. "Can ye survive a moment longer while Vittia here makes up the bed with mother's best lavender-scented linen? Ye do look awful!"

Tentatively, she removed the cloth she had been holding to her nose to see if it was still bleeding. It was.

Vittia busied herself with the bed, every now and then shooting interested glances at her, and looking away immediately if she caught Terelle's eye.

"Ye were terribly muckle-headed to bait Jet like that, ye know," Rubric said. Arms folded, he was leaning against the fireplace. He sounded irritatingly smug. She closed her eyes, not caring. When she opened them again, it was to find a succession of servants parading in and out of the room, bringing oddments Lord Jade evidently thought she needed. Besides the bed and chair, the room already had a floor rug and a small table. To this was now added a wash stand with ewer and bowl and towel, a bar of soap, a jug of drinking water and a mug, a lamp, all Terelle's baggage, wood for the fireplace and a tinderbox with its own flint and steel.

When the servants stopped coming and Vittia left as well, Rubric helped her over to the bed and she lay down. A moment later, Lord Jade entered, carrying a paint tray and other painting paraphernalia, which she placed on the table. She filled the tray from the ewer and began to sprinkle the water with the motley.

Terelle's mouth went dry with fear. *She could kill me so easily... I said dreadful things about her sons and her husband.* They were true, but that wouldn't make them any less hurtful.

"Don't look so nervous," Rubric said. "I imagine Mother is just going to mend that nose of yours."

What if something went wrong? "We doan use wadderpaiding to heal," she said. "How duz id work?"

He relayed the question to his mother, but left Terelle to understand her reply. "You can't make the impossible possible," Jade said. "The bone in your nose, if it is broken, will mend in its own good time. But using waterpainting magic, I can immediately set the bones in their right place, reduce the swelling and stop the bleeding. I do it by painting your nose looking normal. Vittia is bringing up a herbal drink to ease the pain. Ah, here she is now."

The servant came in and gave the mug to Terelle. Rubric raised her up enough for her to drink. "All of it," he said. "Remember the adage—if it tastes like poison, it's a medicine. If it tastes like honey, it's poison."

I do want to wring his neck, she thought, deep in her misery. *He's a snide, sarcastic little pest.*

She drank the medicine, trying not to pull a face at the awful taste, because that hurt, and trying not to wince at every swallow because that hurt too. When she lay back on the pillow, she watched as Jade painted with quick sure placements of colour, then concentrated to shuffle up. From where she was lying, Terelle couldn't see the artwork. Through the haze of her discomfort and nausea, she wondered if she ought to be scared silly. This woman could do whatever she wanted, and who would report her if it was against the law?

As if Lord Jade understood what she was thinking, she caught and held Terelle's gaze. "Do not fear me. Healers swear not to kill or harm. First, I want you to look at yourself. At your face."

She held out a looking glass, the surface so beautifully wrought that when Terelle gazed on her own image there was no distortion other than the damage Jet had inflicted.

"Weebing shid," she said. "I am such a mezz!" Her nose was swollen, misshapen, red and crooked. Her top lip was split, which she hadn't even realised. She handed the mirror back, not wanting to see.

"I have to wash off the blood," Rubric said. "It's going to hurt, but I'll try to do it gently."

While he was dabbing at her nose and she was wincing, Lord Jade reached up and took an intricately woven gold and silver chain from around her neck. She dangled it on her fingers, showing it to Terelle. "This is my holdfast. The magic won't work until I place it where it is in the painting." She laid the pendant on the pillow next to Terelle's head, once Rubric had finished cleaning her skin. "Understand?"

She'd never heard the word "holdfast," but she'd used similar items to create a unique situation. "Yes."

"I'm afraid it will hurt. You must not touch your face. You must try not to move." She aligned the holdfast perfectly, so that it matched her picture.

Terelle tensed. It didn't help. Her nose felt as if someone had pushed a hot poker up a nostril. Her cheekbones screamed their agony. Beneath her skin, bone took on a life of its own and moved like worms writhing. She wanted to scream, to snatch at her face.

Jade placed a hand over hers. "A little longer." Her voice, her beautiful voice, was sad, yet firm. "Keep still."

She struggled against her desire to scream. And then Rubric was on the other side of her, calming her with gentle words so different from his usual snide cynicism. She felt his hand on hers, comforting yet steely, stopping her from raising her fingers to her face. Her eyes watered, and she looked at him through the blur of tears, his features softened by the mistiness of her vision. He was beautiful, and she felt an urge to paint him one day.

Then all stilled. Her skin stopped crawling. Slowly, oh, so slowly, the pain began to diminish. She could suddenly breathe through her nose, and the drip of blood rolling down the back of her throat stopped. She closed her eyes and relaxed for the first time since she had entered the manor.

"It looks good," Rubric said. He sounded pleased. "You were never exactly pretty, but at least you don't look like a goat's arse any more."

"Rubric!" his mother said, shocked.

"Sorry, Mother."

To Terelle's surprise, he did sound contrite. She opened her eyes, to find Lord Jade handing her the painting, freed from the tray. It showed only her face, and a little of the pillow, with the chain resting next to her head. Lord Jade had portrayed her much as she would normally look, although with a healing cut on her lip, and with her skin discoloured over a slightly swollen nose.

"To lessen the risk of anything going wrong, I made the area of the painting no bigger than is needed." When Terelle looked blank, she added, "I only portray your face and the pendant. Nothing else."

Rubric explained more fully. "If she was to include more stuff—the bed, your body—then there would be more opportunity for something to go wrong with the magic. Healers paint only the area to be healed, detailed enough to identify the person. Plus the healer's personal holdfast, which fixes the moment the painting becomes the truth."

"Now look at yourself," Lord Jade said and gave her the mirror.

Wonder consumed her. Her nose was almost the right size. The skin was discoloured as if bruised, but her nose was as straight as it had ever been. The cut on her lip was still there, although it seemed to have closed up. She was the woman in the painting.

"Thank you!" Her delight and wonderment momentarily overwhelmed her commonsense and she asked, "Could you teach me to be a healer?"

A shadow passed across Lord Jade's face as Rubric translated. She replaced the pendant around her neck, picked up her painting things and left without a word.

"I've upset her," she said to Rubric, her enthusiasm draining away. "Didn't mean to."

He was scornful and this time he did not deign to use her tongue. "Terelle, since you arrived, you have told her things she didn't want to hear about her husband and sons. On top of that, she's had to imprison you, knowing that you are either going to die horribly or—according to your version anyway—cause the fall of her family. She's a healer, sworn to help the ailing; yet her husband has asked her to play a part in a murder. And she just watched her son hit a woman and come close to following that up by plunging his sword into her. How did you think she was going to feel about all this?"

And in all that, you didn't tell me what in particular I said to upset her. He was hiding something. "I didn't *insult* your father or your brothers. I told the truth. And surely she knows it. She can't have been married to a man—for what, thirty years?—and not know the sort of person he is. And I think that Jet at least proved what sort of monster *he* is."

He looked at her with a half-smile. "And what about me? Am I one of your murderers too?"

She knew what he was now. It came to her in one revelation, the explanation for the things that had puzzled her about him, what he'd referred to when he'd been talking to Jet. It was if a mist was wisped away and she could see him clearly for the first time.

I do know what you are, Rubric. Or at least, what you were.

Jade had once hankered for a child who would become another waterpainter in the family, but Rubric's desire was to be as his brothers, an armsman. That was why Jade had been upset: Terelle was an outsider gifted with something Jade had desired—in vain—for one of her own children. But Terelle's understanding encompassed more than that. So obvious. How had she not seen? She, snuggery handmaiden and waterpainter, should have realised; Rubric's past had left its history. So much about him suddenly began to make sense. And Jet had mocked him, asking if he was interested in her because she was the only woman around who didn't know his past.

Rubric Verdigris had once worn another body.

But now is not the time to mention it.

She chose her words carefully. "Marchford. I watched from upstairs. You were outside the stables while your men tried to batter down the door. You say you tried to kill the Alabasters and couldn't because my magic wouldn't let you. But, Rubric, I hadn't done my painting then. It wasn't the magic that stopped you."

He paled, then colour rushed back into his face.

"It's nothing to be ashamed of."

"Ah," he said. "I guess you've just answered a question I had about myself."

For a moment she thought that was all she was going to get in answer, but then he continued, his words tentative, stumbling, apparently irrelevant.

"When I was young I watched my brothers learn their sword play. I longed to join them. Mother wanted—she wanted me to be her assistant, even when it became obvious I was not a waterpainter. But me—I wanted to be my brothers. I argued with my parents for years. In the end, my mother—she, er, helped me and I joined my father's guards. I am quick and skilled, a clever swordsman rather than a powerful one, but mostly we are a peaceful land, with not much call for an armsman's skills. The occasional rape or murder or theft to investigate, the occasional hunt for a criminal. And then came the first time I was asked to kill my fellow men."

His gaze held hers, and she heard resignation in his voice, as if he had lost the idea of hope. "There, that night, in the barracks and the stable as you saw—that was the first time, and it was in an unjust cause."

He peeled himself away from the wall. "But armsmen aren't supposed to question causes. They are supposed to obey orders. So I tried to use my powers to kill men who didn't deserve to die, and I couldn't. I just couldn't. At the time I did think it was my failing. Later it was easier to think it was your painting making a different future for those Alabasters. That it was their luck they were needed to get your two Scarpen guards back to Samphire. Now you tell me that wasn't so." He paused, looked away, embarrassed, and then back again. "Make no mistake Terelle, I'm no innocent standing here. My water skills made it easy for others to do the killing." He gave his irritatingly sardonic smile, but this time the sadness in it made her heart turn over. "I did find out one thing that night: maybe I'm in the wrong trade."

With that parting shot, he let himself out and closed the door. She heard the bar across the door fall into place. In her head she heard what he hadn't said: he'd thought he'd wanted to be an armsman, when what he really wanted was to be his brothers.

Rubric Verdigris had been born a woman and had grown up to know himself to be a man.

She sighed. Life was so stupid sometimes, and so unjust.

She considered getting up to explore her room, but the moment she lifted her head from the pillow she felt so bad and the pain was so severe, changed her mind. Not long afterwards, the soporific properties of the posset took effect and she slept.

CHAPTER TWENTY-FIVE

Scarpen Quarter
Breccia
Level Two, Breccia Hall

Sunlight streamed into the stormquest room. Amberlyn
was in her cradle, enjoying the feel of the sun on her bare
legs, while her father just enjoyed watching her. He could
tick off the precious moments of wonder: the first time
she stopped crying the instant he picked her up, the first
time she turned her head to look at him when she heard
his voice, the first time she smiled at him and captured his
heart all over again, the first time she made a wild clutch
at his face and bopped him on the chin. Every moment
was magical.

Selfishly glad that Senya never came near her now, or
even cared enough to ask anyone about her progress, he
sometimes thought of Amberlyn not as Senya's child at
all, but as Terelle's. And then he would be awash with
horrible wrenching guilt, made all the worse because he
couldn't explain to her in person. Whenever he thought of
her receiving and reading his letter, he would break out in
a cold sweat. He had a distaste for making excuses and

suspected his account just made him appear pathetically guilty.

And then news came from Samphire. The bearer was Sardi, the younger son of Messenjer, and he brought a letter from the Bastion. Jasper greeted the man, took the letter and sent him down to the kitchens to get some food. He sat down on a chair next to Amberlyn's cradle and broke the seal.

Two sheets of linen paper unfolded on his lap, written in spidery black script horizontally, then crossways over the top to save on paper, all in the shaky lettering of an old man with arthritic hands. With wrenching disappointment, he realised there was nothing from Terelle.

He read the sheets through, scanning quickly, then went back and read each line with care, absorbing every nuance, every hint, every scrap of information he could extract. The news was no better the second time around. Feroze had been murdered. Terelle and Russet had been seized. Killed? No one knew for certain. The Bastion was working to send Elmar and Dibble back to rescue her, better prepared this time.

The words danced and blurred. In his frustration, he wanted to pound his fists against the desk, or fling water from one end of the city to the other. Most of all he wanted to grab his palmubra and his water skin and ride for Khromatis.

He forced himself to calm. To consider the other thing in the letter that leaped from the page at him. The Alabasters had changed their policy. They had made the decision to withdraw all their workers from Khromatis and to refuse trade with their neighbour, until such time as an apology had been received in Samphire, Terelle had been returned, and the families of the Alabasters who had died were compensated. If these terms were not met, then all ties with Khromatis would be permanently severed.

Frowning, he pondered what impact such a policy would have, but had no answers because he had little idea just how much trade or contact the Alabasters had with their neighbours.

Sandblast you for being so secretive, he thought. *We could pay heavily for your mistakes.*

No, more than that. Terelle had already paid dearly. He closed his eyes in despair. Trembling, he laid the letter down and sank his head into his hands.

She's all right, you have to believe that. They can't kill her because of the painting.

But what if that future had already been fulfilled?

Oh, my blighted eyes, why did I ever let her go?

But then, he'd had no choice, and neither had she.

Amberlyn gave a little cry, wanting his attention. He picked her up and laid her against his shoulder, rubbing her back and smelling the baby scent of her hair against his cheek. She pulled at his ear.

I must go after her. What can Elmar and Dibble do? They're not rainlords. They're not even reeves. How will they ever even find her? But I can. If I get close enough, I can.

He'd lost track of her when she'd begun to cross the Borderlands; the distance had become too great.

But if he left the Quartern, who would bring water? Terelle's paintings showed him stormshifting in the storm-quest room; he couldn't use them elsewhere. Then again, if Terelle died, how would he bring water in the future?

Taquar.

Oh, shrivelled hells, not with Taquar.

Terelle. Terelle, you must return. You must.

Perhaps he should leave it up to Elmar and the Alabasters.

His thoughts spun out of control, battering him with contradictions and grief and alternatives, none of them good.

If I go, what of Amberlyn? Oh, sweet waters, is there anyone I can entrust her to? He'd be damned if he'd leave her to Laisa and Senya.

Iani, of course. He'd send her to Scarcleft with the two nurses.

He took a deep breath. There was no point in flailing around like a child with too many choices. He was the Cloudmaster. A land depended on him for wise decisions. He walked to the door, still holding his daughter, and spoke to the guards outside. "Call the nurse to come and take Amberlyn, please. And ask the man who brought this letter from Alabaster to come and see me when he has eaten."

Zirca appeared within moments and he handed Amberlyn over to be taken back to the nursery in his apartment. By the time Sardi arrived, Jasper was seated behind the map table and had composed himself. He hoped he looked more like a cloudmaster. "Sit down Sardi. I have a few questions."

"Yes, m'lord."

"Do you know if a courier caravan reached Samphire after Terelle? I sent letters to the Bastion and to Terelle and Elmar Waggoner, her guard. I was hoping they would arrive before she left."

"There hasn't been a caravan in from the Scarpen in the past quarter-cycle."

His heart sank. "You're sure?"

"M'lord, if a caravan arrived, the whole of Samphire would know. But…" He stirred uneasily. "We did see a dead pede between Skulkai and Fourcross Tell. A recent kill. Had mouth rings, so it was a domesticated beast. It'd been carved up for meat."

"No signs of men? Tents? Other pedes?"

"No, m'lord. But Reduner marauders usually take everything, including men, if they attack a caravan. We didn't see any graves."

"Are you still suffering Reduner raids into Alabaster?"

"No. In fact, the Bastion was talking of allowing the mining settlements to be reopening. We assume Lord Kaneth has the Reduners contained."

"Not entirely, perhaps." He thought of the courier and his guards, and felt ill. Dead? Slaves? He'd probably never know. "Sardi, how much is this new Alabaster policy—not trading with Khromatis, and not supplying labour—going to affect Khromatis?"

"A great deal, m'lord. At least, that's what people say in Samphire. Most of Khromatian mills are in the south, and almost all the workers are poorly paid Alabasters. If they employed Khromatians, everything'd cost more. And where would they get their salt and potash and soda? Of course, it'll be a while before shortages are felt. And we haven't acted on this yet; the Bastion is still awaiting an answer to his ultimatum. It could take a while, if Lord Bice sends to the Peak for advice."

"Do people feel the Khromatians will eventually give the Bastion what he wants?"

There was a short uncomfortable silence before Sardi said, "Most do. A few, like my father, think the Khromatians will attack us."

"Go to *war*?"

"Yes, m'lord. The Bastion doesn't think that'll happen, because of the difficulty of crossing the Borderlands and the Whiteout. They don't have pedes. There's no way they could use alpiners, though maybe they could seize some trade pedes already in the Southern Marches if they're quick to be realising the Alabasters were leaving, once the exodus starts."

I'll be spitless. Another weeping war. "So you don't think the Khromatians would win?"

"M'lord, if they were to send continuous storms they could melt Samphire to the ground. They don't need to be crossing the Whiteout."

"Do they *know* Samphire is made of salt?"

He shrugged. "If the Southern Marches are typical— well, they're ruled by an armsman, commanding mounted fighting men. They've got waterlords trained in warfare. And they've got waterpainters, though not in the army. Everyone there fears waterpainters most of all. Not sure why. I've never heard of them being anything except healers, but there are tales about using them in battle. They've never been invaded, y'know. Another point is all our spear shafts come from Khromatis and all our iron is worked in the Southern Marches, because we don't have fuel for furnaces and such. We'd soon be in trouble. But then, so would they, without our labour and skills."

"Is the Bastion willing to go to war over this matter?"

Sardi looked down at his feet and fidgeted. The silence was in danger of becoming uncomfortable when he spoke again. "My father thinks the Bastion believes war is unlikely because Khromatis has a lot to lose, but that he's willing to be risking it. Feroze was the Bastion's son, ye see. One of the family he was forced to be abandoning in order to become the Bastion."

When Jasper gaped, Sardi explained. "We believe a ruler shouldn't have divided loyalties. A Bastion has to be relinquishing all ties to his family, to his home, to his wealth, even to his name. The present Bastion left his wife and young son, but Feroze sought him out when he was an adult. Some now say it's the Bastion's love for Feroze driving him to this confrontation with Khromatis."

"Do you think that's true?"

"I don't know. What the Bastion says speaks to many, particularly young folk. Some of us are sick of believing Khromatis has the right to be despising us, to be using our labour and be paying us so little, to be buying our goods for a pittance while we're the ones risking our lives in the mines and making the goods they want. We tend their flax fields, stoke their furnaces, dig their drains, protect their borders, keep their secrets. They tell us that's our penance and our only way to heaven and God. Well, there are many who now say: enough."

Jasper thought in wonder that he'd learned more about Alabasters in a half-run of a sandglass than he had in the previous twenty cycles. *I cannot let there be another war within the Quartern. I cannot. There has to be a better way.* "Sardi," he said, "I am going to Khromatis. In fact, I intend to be in Samphire before you are. I'll leave the day after tomorrow, and I'll take a shortcut across the Border Humps."

"There's a problem with water that way—"

"Not for a stormlord."

As Sardi made his way out of the door a little later, Laisa arrived in front of it. Without waiting for an invitation, she entered saying, "I heard there was a letter for you from Samphire."

"That's right. And you decided you have a right to know what's in it?"

"Oh, don't be such a sand-tick, Jasper. I'm a highlord and responsible for this city. Is there anything I should know about?" She sat on the edge of the table and neatly crossed her legs.

She loves doing that, he thought. *Because men always focus on the view it gives them...And to think there was a time when she could stir my desires.* Right then, his adolescent days seemed a long way in the past. He said, "The Bastion is preparing for a confrontation with Khromatis."

"That shouldn't be any concern of ours, should it?"

"The White Quarter is usually considered to be part of the Quartern and therefore part of the Cloudmaster's responsibility."

"I suppose," she said indifferently, "as far as water matters are concerned. And trade. But for protection against outsiders?"

He raised an eyebrow. "Didn't you notice that we had help from the White Quarter when *we* needed it?"

"All right, all right, I see your point. But what's all this about? The Alabasters are hardly known for their aggression."

"Whatever the reasons, we can't risk a Khromatian invasion of the Quartern."

Sliding down from the table, she sat in the chair opposite him. "I don't understand why you're so concerned.

Just because Terelle's in Samphire? Surely not. She could leave. She could even come back here, as long as you keep her well away from Senya."

"Nonetheless I'm going to Samphire."

"What? *Why?*"

"They need a stormlord."

"What is it you're not telling me?" Her foot tapped irritatingly against the chair leg.

"Oh, waterless skies, Laisa, will you stop trying to see mysteries where there are none? Now if you don't mind, I've a lot to prepare, so could you go and attend to your highlord affairs and leave me to mine?"

She stopped then, but not because of anything he'd said. Her lips parted in an "oh!" of surprise. "I've been so stupid, haven't I?"

"I wouldn't know. But you are certainly annoyi—"

"You asked Terelle to see if the Khromatians would help us by sending us some stormlords. She and her grandfather. They're in Khromatis, not Samphire! That's it, isn't it?"

"Stop jumping to conclusions." The words sounded normal enough, but he couldn't stop the flush rising in his cheeks. And she saw, of course.

For a moment she was speechless, then said, "You're mad. Given what our one true faith thinks of the religion of the 'Basters, you suggested that we import some of their sorcerers to manage our storms? And you sent the one person who was invaluable to your cloudshifting and has been helping to keep our cisterns full? Jasper, did you take leave of your senses?"

There didn't seem much point to any further denials; she would never believe them. He said, "They took her prisoner and killed some of the Alabasters with her. Including Feroze Khorash. Terelle is in danger, and the Bastion is risking a war on her behalf."

"She's in Khromatis? And you intend to go after her? What about your stormshifting?"

He heard real horror in her tone and winced. "Thanks to the rationing, we're not short of water yet. In fact, I'm going to spend the rest of the time before I leave stocking Scarpen and Alabaster mother wells, and watering as many of the Gibber washes as I can. But please send a message to all the cities not to assume that my filling their cisterns now means they can abandon rationing. Supplies will be short over the next cycle."

"Sunlord damn you, Jasper—"

"I trust it has not escaped your notice that I have been managing without Terelle."

"Yes, I've noticed. And I have also noticed the number of your storms has been reduced since she went. Jasper, you can't risk yourself for her. You can't. You're all we've got!" Her voice shook with fury.

"I have to bring her back. Without stormlords or Terelle, or someone like her, we go thirsty."

"Jasper—no. Without *you*, we all die. You *cannot risk yourself.* That's not just foolhardy, it's beyond stupid. Criminal!" She stared at him, white-faced.

"If she doesn't come back, then we die."

"No, we don't. As long as we have you and Taquar, we're safe."

"Safe? Relying on that man? He brought us to our knees! Look at this city."

"*He* didn't do that."

"No?" He took a deep, calming breath. "I'm going to

Samphire the day after tomorrow. I'll send Amberlyn to
Iani with Zirca and Crystal. Fortunately they're devoted
to her, so there should be no problems. I doubt that Senya
will object. And may I suggest that you send no messages
telling Lord Gold about my intention to bring Khromatians here? It's never going to happen, so there's no point
in arousing his religious ire."

"I agree, it doesn't seem wise." She shook her head in
disbelief. "One thing about you, Jasper—you have enough
gall to match Lord Gold any day."

*That's not quite a commitment to keep it quiet is it,
Laisa? You're the snake under the rock. Harmless until
you bare your fangs . . . Just what are you up to now?*

She continued, "Is there nothing I can say to deter you
from this course? Go talk to the Bastion, by all means.
From what I hear the roads are safe enough now. But don't
cross the Borderlands. You may never come back. Send
some rainlords instead."

"They would be helpless against the waterlords of
Khromatis. And obvious too; our rainlords are all fair-
skinned people, which Khromatians are not. They look
more like me. Now please leave. I have some more stormshifting to do."

She gave him a look full of doubt and irritation, and
left the room.

Briefly, he closed his eyes, as if shutting out the visual
world would also shut out his problems. *At least,* he
thought, *I can tell Terelle in person about Senya and
Amberlyn.*

Oh, Terelle.

Missing her was an ache that wouldn't go away.

*   *   *

Laisa went straight to visit Senya and found her entertaining some of her friends from the city. *Lording it over them,* Laisa thought, and sent them packing with a sweet smile and an implacable look in her eye.

"Senya," she said once they were alone, "we have a problem."

"Can't I even have my friends visit without you—"

"Listen. I have to get Taquar out of that cave in a hurry, much earlier than I thought."

"Why? What's happened?"

"Jasper has decided to go to Khromatis."

"Why? Don't tell me his snuggery slut went there!"

Laisa decided it might be more diplomatic not to mention the danger Terelle was in. "To try to bring back some stormlords to help him shift storms. Trouble is, he'll be putting himself in danger and we have to stop him. So I want Taquar out of his prison, living in Scarcleft again. Thank goodness I have all the uniforms and things I need ready. Even Lord Gold obliged with a full outfit for us to use." He'd wanted something in return of course: a promise that his allowance would be continued and he'd be permitted to return to Breccia if Jasper was ousted from the city. Laisa had shrugged and acquiesced.

Senya frowned, trying to take all this in. "And then what? I don't understand."

"I can't stop Jasper leaving Breccia. But I can make him come back in a hurry, before he leaves Samphire for Khromatis."

"How?"

"By sending him a message telling him Taquar is free and has killed Iani. The timing is crucial, and I am not sure if we can get it all done in time..."

"Is that enough to bring Jasper back?"

"I certainly hope so. We have the right bait."

Senya pouted. "You keep saying that, but I have no idea what you mean."

"Amberlyn, my dear, Amberlyn. If Taquar has Jasper's beloved daughter, we can get him to do whatever we want. For the rest of his life. And Jasper, very kindly, is sending her to Scarcleft."

"Oh! But what would Taquar do with a baby?"

"Nothing, as long as Jasper behaves himself. With Amberlyn in his hands, Taquar will get to stay in Scarcleft, with all his privileges returned to him. He might even be able to wrangle his way back to being the Cloudmaster. So, my dear, I hate to upset your pleasant life here, but as soon as Jasper leaves for Samphire I think you must make a visit to Scarcleft. When you get there, you tell Lord Iani in a panic that your sandcrazy mother found out where Taquar is hidden and has gone to release her beloved husband. That will send Iani racing up to the Warthago to stop me."

"And then?"

"We'll leave that up to Taquar."

"Won't Jasper just attack Taquar like he did before?"

"Think, Senya. All Taquar has to do is threaten to cut off Amberlyn's nose or something, and Jasper will do as he is told. In the end, Jasper will live in Scarcleft, doing the stormshifting we need—which won't include the other quarters—while Taquar manipulates him through Amberlyn."

"And you?"

Laisa paused. "I'm not sure," she said slowly. "I'm rather coming to like being a highlord. Perhaps I'll stay here and rule the city, especially if I don't have Jasper looking over my shoulder all the time. I am not sure that Taquar is worth giving up a whole city..." She shrugged, wondering at herself. She was not usually so indecisive about what she wanted. "We'll see."

"And me?"

"You can decide when the time comes. Scarcleft or Breccia."

And I wonder how long it will take you to realise Taquar manipulated you into having a baby by Jasper, just so he had a hold on the stormlord. My poor dear daughter. You haven't a moral thought in your head, and yet it never occurs to you that there are others just as amoral.

CHAPTER TWENTY-SIX

Khromatis
Anderfoot and Variega Mountains

Elmar had trouble sleeping. He and Dibble were lying on the ground in a copse of trees just over the Khromatian border, wrapped tight against the cold, huddled together. Around him the noises of the night—things snuffling through the fallen leaves, clicking in the trees, hooting in the sky—were as unfamiliar as the far-off murmur of flowing water. Still worse was the damp. Neither of them were used to that. But it was not the sounds, or the damp or the chill of the air that kept him awake. It was the task they had ahead of them.

He may have thought of Terelle as a friend, but he could never forget that she was also Lord Terelle, one of the most important people in the Quartern. She had to be brought back so they had a chance. Just thinking of the responsibility made him tense up.

At least, this time around, the Alabasters had helped as much as they could with information, clothing, money, food and advice, but now the two of them were on their own.

I could do with Kaneth at my side. Withering hells, I miss him.

Dibble grunted in his sleep and flung an arm across him. The armsman was a fine man to have around, but he was so…so damnably young. He still jiggled around like an ant caught in a sandpit when he was excited or tense; he still talked too much and asked too many questions. Although maybe that was not such a bad thing. Not shy about asking what things meant, or trying out what he'd learned, Dibble had turned his verbosity into an asset when it came to learning Khromatian. He could even crack a joke in the language when needed. Elmar knew he was going to be grateful for that skill, but oh—it would have been good to just follow along after Kaneth, instead of being looked up to by Dibble, as if he had the slightest idea of what he was doing.

I want to have a quiet life for a change. He pondered that, then muttered, "Waterless damn," he muttered. "I must be growing old to think like that."

They had arrived in Khromatis without being detected, thanks to the Bastion's ingenious idea of filling the whole of the Borderlands up with people riding pedes in every direction. Two thousand men and every mount in Alabaster had criss-crossed the bog, aiming to confuse the Khromatian water sensitives while Elmar and Dibble headed for the other side. They'd hoped the border patrols would be spread thin, and that was exactly what they found. The Alabaster water sensitive with them had dropped them off in Khromatis far from the nearest sentries.

Sandblast, why can't I sleep?

He tried to concentrate on the star river winding its way across the sky, just visible through the leaves, but his mind wandered. Were they going to get away with this? They both had the right clothes, had dyed their hair black and stained their skin brown. Fortunately their blue eyes were not so very different to the Khromatian green.

And if they found Kermes Manor but Terelle wasn't there? What then? What if she hadn't left a trail? He had no idea. No plans. Just a wild notion that they would find her somehow and launch a rescue, then escape, probably with every withering Khromatian Watergiver at their heels.

Simple, right? Something he and Kaneth would have done for fun in their younger days...But no, not even half-asleep could he convince himself of the truth of that. He'd never done anything as sun-fried stupid as this, never embarked on anything that had so little chance of success. Especially not when the price of failure was unthinkable.

Fear skimmed through his thoughts at regular intervals like birds crossing a waterhole to drink. At each touch, he pushed it away, but it always returned.

And Dibble, the dryhead louse, looked up to him as a warrior hero.

Little did he know.

The next morning, having washed and eaten, they walked into the nearby town of Anderfoot, in search of an inn called Bogger's Tavern. According to the Alabasters who'd helped them with information back in Samphire, the owner was a Khromatian dealer who could find anything, no questions asked, if the price was right.

Elmar trailed behind Dibble, carrying the bigger pack, his clothing awry, his mouth hanging open. If anyone appeared to be taking too much interest in them, he tripped over his staff or dropped his pack, grinning inanely or grunting as he gathered things together again. It wasn't long before Dibble was wearing an expression of long-suffering that was only partly play-acting.

"Don't overdo it," he growled when Elmar flapped his arms like a demented sandgrouse in order to scare a cat sunning itself on a doorstep. He had to ask for directions five times before they finally found a poky little pothouse squeezed between a cooper and an apothecary. Neither of them could read the sign creaking monotonously over the door.

"Bet they sell plenty of headache remedies," Elmar muttered. Besides the noise of the squeaky sign, the cooper in his yard was pounding a hoop onto a barrel with a mallet, while inside the pothouse several drunken patrons were arguing. Or maybe singing. It was hard to tell.

"Makes you feel at home, eh?" Dibble asked, his grin broad.

He'd have clipped Dibs over the ear, except it would have been out of character.

They entered and looked around. The drunken singers staggered past them on their way out. The place smelled of vomit, brewed alcohol and cat piss. A pot-bellied man sweeping the floor of the otherwise empty room looked up. "Wanting something?" he asked. Then he spotted Elmar, who let his mouth sag open and his tongue loll out. "The idiot with you?"

"M'brother. This Bogger's Tavern?" Dibble mumbled.

"That it is." The man left the broom propped against the wall, wiped dirty hands on an equally dirty apron and walked behind the bar counter. His stare swept over them, shrewd and assessing, from head to boots and back again.

Elmar lounged against the wall near the door, all

senses alert. He dribbled on his tunic, wiped his chin with the back of his hand and then settled for picking his nose. His instincts were already screaming at him not to trust the man and his staff was close at hand.

"Want to talk to Master Basker," Dibble said.

"That's me."

"Got a package waiting for us," Dibble mumbled, hoping to cover any oddity of his accent. "Paid for in advance." He placed a silver coin on the counter top as he had been instructed to do. If the town's Alabasters had done their part, he was about to be given the paint-powders Terelle needed. He added the exact words he had been told to say. "A little extra for your trouble."

"And the contents?"

"Paint-powder."

The man picked up the coin. "Right. And I was told to ask your name."

"Denker."

"That's the one." He hefted a bundle from somewhere down at his feet. "Crushed sea urchins, cadmium, cinnabar, ochre, umber, sienna, chalk, indigo—someone has a well-lined money pouch. This stuff cost as much as a pair of boots made of seahorse leather!"

Dibble shrugged. "I'm just the delivery boy." He picked up the bundle, nodded in a friendly fashion and pushed Elmar out of the door in front of him. Once outside, Elmar opened the packet and quickly thumbed through the contents.

"Not everything's there," Elmar said.

"Huh?"

"That stuff about the money pouch and expensive boots? That was a hint. He wants more money. Go back inside, but don't say a word. I'll stay here. You put another silver coin on the counter and wait. He'll say something about how he has another buyer for what he didn't put in the parcel, or some other excuse. Just stare at him and wait. Look as if you aren't going to budge."

"How the withering winds do you know all that?"

"Dibs, he may be a Khromatian, but I've met his double back in the Scarpen twenty times over. He knows there's something that doesn't smell right about this deal and he intends to make some money. If you're too long, I'll come in and strong-arm him. Otherwise, when you come out of the door afterwards, run and join me. I'll be behind the cooper's gate."

As soon as Dibble disappeared inside, Elmar scampered clumsily to the left, past some amused women walking by with their market baskets full of greens. Outside the cooper's he waited for a moment until no one appeared to be looking, then stepped behind the gate to the yard, which opened outwards, so that he was hidden in the triangle between gate and plank fence. It wasn't much of a hiding place, but it had the advantage of not being visible from the tavern door or the cooper's yard.

Dibble emerged a while later and jogged to the left. When he drew level, Elmar pulled him behind the gate.

"You were right," Dibble acknowledged, holding up three small packets. "What now?"

"Check what's in them and wait. Unless I'm much mistaken, someone's going to take a look out of the tavern door in a moment, to see which way we went." He peered though the hinge crack. "Spot on!" he whispered. "Basker himself with a boy he wants to send after us."

"Why would he do that?"

Basker walked into the middle of the street, looking first one way, then the other. Finally he shrugged and said something to the boy and they both disappeared back inside.

"Good. He was probably thinking he'd alert the local guard, but now he doesn't know which way we went, it's hardly worth the trouble. I hope. Is everything there?"

"As far as I can tell." Dibble stuffed the packets into his pack.

"Then let's get out of here as fast as we can." He pointed up the street towards the mountains. "That way," he said as he shouldered the bundle. Now that they had a weapon for Terelle, all they had to do was find her. "We have to reach the road heading north-east. Once we're on it, keep an eye out for those mirror pieces."

A sandglass run later, they were walking briskly away from the town on the main road. They were already north of Marchford, and if Terelle was on the way to Kermes' Manor, this was the route she would have taken. The Alabasters, who had been exchanging information to and fro across the border, said two of Bice's sons had been seen heading north after the fire, but no one knew if she was one of the party.

Elmar felt sick, thinking about all the possibilities. *We know so damned little about where to look. We're probably many days behind.* And there was still no glint of a mirror to be seen.

All they had to go on was the knowledge that Russet's magic would work to bring her to where he'd done the painting, near his family home of Kermes Manor. *Thank the Sunlord I overheard* that *conversation.*

Shortly before midday, they caught up with a farmer on

his dray going the same way. Having sold his farm produce at the market, he was on his way home and offered them a ride for a couple of coppers. Dibble was scornful; they could walk faster than the alpiner was pulling the dray, but Elmar frowned at him and indicated they should take it.

Underway once more, with them sitting on the empty sacks, he said quietly, "We've a long way to go and a pack gets heavy. We'll take rides whenever we're offered them. Ask this fellow how far to the Kermes Manor."

"Kermes?" came the answer when Dibble asked. "The Watergiver family? They don't live in the Southern Marches. Don't you know that, lad?"

"Never had nothing to do with lords," Dibble muttered.

"Ah. Suppose not. We're the tiddlers, scraping for a living, we are. Soft-handed fellows don't have aught to do with the likes of us. They live up the heights."

Sounds like a Scarpen city, Elmar thought, and wondered just how high "the heights" were.

Shortly afterwards, the farmer dropped them at a divide in the road, and it was there that Elmar spotted the first of Terelle's mirror pieces, catching the sun where it lay. He pounced on it, grinning, as the cart disappeared down the branch track.

"How can we be sure the mirror was one of hers?" Dibble asked.

"We can't. But only Alabasters use these bevelled pieces and they're unlikely to be dropping them along a road."

"There are some Alabasters working in the fields," Dibble said, pointing to where white-skinned men were harvesting the crops growing on either side of the road. "Are those plants flax?"

"I don't know. But by all that's holy, don't go asking any Khromatian that. It would be a dead giveaway that we don't belong here."

"No one we've seen so far seems suspicious of us. Except the tavern keeper. The town was full of folk, but no one gave us a second glance."

"They've never seen folk from the Quartern who aren't Alabasters. I reckon it just never occurred to them that's what we are."

He was glad to see the panic at the back of Dibble's eyes ease a little. *Not that we'll be very happy in a while,* he thought, glancing up at the sky. *When clouds get that dark, it rains.*

It was weird having to consider the weather. Back home it was either hot or cold, depending on whether it was day or night. Here, there were so many variations. Dry, wet, cold, windy, hot, warm, cool, damp, and blithering freezing enough for him to worry his balls would drop off.

He sighed. He so much wanted to go home.

Elmar glanced over at Dibble. He was wet. They both were, but Dibble's body shivered with cold. Every so often he hunched over to sneeze and wiped his nose on his sleeve. At least their hair dye and skin stain seemed water-fast.

Four bleeding days of rain, on and off. Water running away into the soil as if it was useless stuff. And no one on the road to give them a lift either. Strange how odd the rain made him feel, as if he was complicit in the wicked waste of water. Pity it also made them so thoroughly miserable.

"I don't think we should sleep out in the fields tonight," he muttered. "We'll pay for a room in a roadside inn if we find one."

Dibble blinked in surprise. "That'll take a lot of coin."

"Thanks to the Bastion, we have a lot. If we get sick because we're wet and cold, we won't be of any use to Terelle. Later on there'll be those bivacs things the Alabasters told us about, but here near towns there's only inns, so we'll get a room, pay for a fire and eat some meat hotpot. Do you remember all that the Alabasters told us about what to ask for and how much you should pay?"

Dibble nodded. "I also remember they told us it'd be more normal for travellers like us to rent floor space in front of the taproom fireplace after the drinkers go home."

"Yes, I remember. But tonight we're going to spoil ourselves."

Some time later, with full stomachs, a warm fire and beds that did not appear to have any bugs, Elmar was rewarded by the sight of a relaxed and cheerful Dibble. His own spirits lifted in turn. *Blighted eyes,* he thought, *once I left it up to Kaneth to make all these sort of decisions. Maybe I've finally grown up myself.*

He grinned at Dibble. "Let's turn in," he said, and blew out the candle.

CHAPTER TWENTY-SEVEN

Scarpen Quarter
Begg's Caravansary
Warthago Mountains

Taquar, bare-chested, was exercising when he felt the water that told him he was about to have visitors. He was startled. Usually it was just one man—Iani—and one myriapede. This time it felt like a small army.

He washed and dressed, then sat down to wait. As the party on its way up the ravine grew closer, he counted two packpedes, two myriapedes and over twenty people. He was no stormlord, so their identities remained a mystery until they were in sight.

Laisa. He hadn't expected her so soon, not from what she'd said previously. *I'll be wilted—where did she get all those men from?*

It wasn't until they were closer still that he recognised some of them: they were his own water enforcers from Scarcleft. Or had been, until Iani had taken over.

When they halted in front of the cave, Laisa came forward while the most senior among the enforcers, a nasty piece of work who went by the nickname of Savage, organised the men into unpacking the panniers.

"You're a welcome sight," Taquar said, inclining his head to Laisa with a smile as charming as he knew how to make it. "Where the withering hells did you get this crowd of reprobates from? Don't tell me you managed to free Harkel, too!"

She smiled back. "No, sorry. Although I did hear recently that he was still alive. Apparently Iani thought dying was too easy a punishment. Harkel and the rest of your enforcers are working in the quarries just to the west of Scarcleft. When you're home again, you can release them. As for this lot? Jasper and Iani were stupid enough to allow me to sleep in Scarcleft Hall before we rode out to fight Davim. I made the most of my time. In the confusion, I helped myself to your stash of jewels and tokens, let these miscreants out, paid them off and told them there would be more if they wanted to contact me later. When I turned up in Breccia, most of them did. They have proved themselves invaluable."

For a moment Taquar was torn between cursing her and laughing at her audacity. She had turned his misfortune into her profit and that was hard to forgive, even though he would have done exactly the same thing had their positions been reversed.

"So what's the situation?" he asked. "What changed to bring you here earlier than anticipated?"

"Let's get you out first. We have to reproduce Terelle's waterpainting exactly, which means you must wear the red clothes, and one of these men must wear Lord Gold's vestments, and we have to paint the name 'Shale' on the rocks over there."

"What's the matter with bringing a sledgehammer and knocking the lock to pieces?"

"I have no idea, but I suspect something would go wrong. Because we'd be working against the magic, instead of with it."

He snorted with disbelief.

She said softly, "You haven't seen what I've seen. Terelle Grey and her waterpaintings have done things that I would not have thought possible. Tell me, when you imprisoned Terelle in Scarcleft did you give her back her paints just before the earthquake?"

He stared at her. "You can't be saying..." He went cold, remembering the painting she had done of him dead.

"I think we are very lucky that she's such a moral person. She painted something intended to free her from Scarcleft Hall and it brought down walls. That made her a great deal more cautious, which is just as well for us. I suspect if I'd come up here with a sledgehammer and tried to get you out by breaking the lock, something would have happened to stop us."

"How are you intending to open the grille if not by breaking it open?"

"With a picklock, of course. One of this disreputable band is an expert, apparently. Now go and put on those dreadful red clothes."

He obliged, noting with enjoyment that she watched him as he changed. "And once I'm out of here?" he asked.

"We set an ambush for Iani. If Senya has done as I asked, he's on his way here to check on you. When he's dead, you head back to Scarcleft. Amberlyn will already be there, thanks to Jasper."

"Amberlyn? Sunblast it, Laisa, tell me what the salted hells all this is about."

By the time he was fully dressed, she'd updated him with a broad summary of events.

He came back to face her through the grille, not sure that he liked this overly confident Laisa. She'd become too independent for his taste, too forceful. He said, "One can't ambush a rainlord."

"Iani'll be alone because he dare not bring anyone else here. I have people ready to move up behind him. He won't be able to turn back, and if he comes here, we'll be waiting for him. Not so much an ambush as a trap."

Struggling with his illogical fury, he said, "May I remind you he's a rainlord and not all that easy to kill?" He was amazed at the intensity of his desire to strangle her for no reason other than her efficiency.

You've been too impotent for too long, he told himself.

"It's only Iani," she replied. "Don't tell me *you* fear that silly old crippled man, because I won't believe it."

"Fear him? Hardly." Savagery surged somewhere within his chest, needing gratification. "But he can turn on those following him and dry them to dust and bone."

"There are two water sensitives among them; he can't take *their* water."

"And what if he doesn't come at all? He may not believe Senya."

"Possible. In which case we'll have to go to him. It would be more complicated, doubtless, but we can find a way to kill him. We have to infiltrate his city with the enforcers and then seize the key places anyway. Once we have Amberlyn, any resistance will collapse."

"We can't let Jasper go to Khromatis."

"No. I've already sent a letter to him, to tell him you are free, Iani is dead and you have Amberlyn." She smiled at him. "A little premature, but he's not to know that. I've sent the letter to Samphire with a couple of trusted cara-vanners. It should arrive immediately after he does."

"You can't be sure he'll get it before he leaves for Khromatis."

"No."

"That's a weakness of your plot."

"Perhaps, but my men are fast."

"Will he believe what you say? That's the second weakness."

"Oh, I wrote the letter in such a way that he will have no doubt I am familiar with this place. That's all I need to convince him that he's in enough trouble to come back immediately."

She grinned at him. "Stay here while I get everyone arranged the way the painting was done."

It was galling to know she had planned everything with-out consulting him, especially when, if he was honest, her plan was a good one. He needed to get back to Scarcleft. Iani needed to die. They all needed Jasper back, and the only way to be certain of that was to threaten his daughter. The man was sandcrazy; how could he ever think that it was wise behaviour for the Quartern's only stormlord to risk himself in a hostile land they knew nothing about?

As he waited, Taquar pondered his future. With Amberlyn in his care, he could force Jasper to water only the cities of the Scarpen that he authorised, which meant that he wouldn't be tired all the time because of the cloud-making. Yes, this could work—as long as Jasper returned.

*   *   *

As she painted Shale's name, Laisa was intrigued to find she didn't have to think about the right way to do it. It was as if something was guiding her hand. Similarly, when she went to give instructions to the men about where to stand, she found it unnecessary. They were already in position, without any guidance at all. If she'd needed confirmation of the power of waterpainting magic, she certainly had it now.

When the painted word was ready she nodded to the picklock to open the door in the grille and a short while later Taquar stepped out of the cave, a free man.

"Is there anything you want to take with you?" she asked.

"Not a thing," he said. He didn't look at her, didn't smile, didn't thank her.

She was assailed with that all too familiar feeling: Taquar was not a forgiving man and she was sandcrazy to want to have anything to do with him.

He walked over to where the men were waiting, down at the ruins in front of the cave. One of them gave him a broad grin. "Good to see you again, m'lord. Reckon we need you back in Scarcleft so as we lot can go home."

Uneasily, she stared after him. And made up her mind: she was never going back to Scarcleft to stand at his side again.

They waited out the rest of the day in the ruins below the cistern. There was no sign of Iani. Taquar paced to and fro and practised his swordplay with his enforcers. Laisa watched, aware that his impatience was barely under control, troubled to see how much his damaged knee slowed him down and limited his flexibility.

That night he led her into the ruins, stripped her naked and took her there, on the ground, his passion brutal and uncaring. She matched his desire the first time, even gloried in his need, but by dawn, she was bruised, aching and sore. He left her where she was without a word and went to wash at the trough. There was a finality to what had occurred, and she knew it. She picked herself up, dressed and leaned against the wall, eyes closed, thinking of all the things in her life that might have been, had she made different choices.

Mid-afternoon, while she was watching Taquar where he sat drawing patterns on the earth with a stick, his head swung up to look down the track. "It's time," he said. "We have company coming. Get those saddles on."

The men scurried to obey without even looking her way. *And I'm the one who's been paying them this past year,* she thought. *What a fool you are, Laisa Drayman.*

She attuned her senses down the track but still could not feel the approach of water. "How many?" she asked Taquar.

"Only one pede. Too far away to say how many people."

He mounted the driver's saddle of her pede without asking, then, to further wound her feelings, did not wait for her to mount but rode away. By the time she and the rest of the men were ready, he was already out of sight around the first bend.

Fuming, she scrabbled up on to one of the other pedes. "Catch up," she shouted in the driver's ear.

Taquar looked back just the once. The grille to the cistern cave stood open. *I am free.* Waterless soul, he would never let anyone confine him again, in any way. *You will pay for this, Jasper. You will pay for the rest of your life. And no matter what you do, you will never see your daughter again, unless it suits my purpose.*

He read the road ahead as if it was a picture unfolding before his gaze. One man alone on a pede, riding at a steady pace, oblivious to Taquar's approach. Iani, he assumed.

Vengeance, at last.

Iani, finally aware that someone was riding towards him. Iani, deciding to halt. Iani dithering while he wondered what he ought to do. Iani, turning back—perhaps because he sensed there was not one pede descending the trail, but many. And stopping again, because he felt riders following him from below.

Taquar rounded the bend and saw the rainlord halted in the track ahead of him. A killing rage surged in his blood and he rejoiced. This was what it was like to be alive, to be Taquar Sardonyx, highlord, rainlord—and free. Laughing, he drew the sword he had borrowed from one of the men—*his* men—and urged the pede into fast mode. His flaming passion to kill this man ripped through him, every nuance of it a pleasure. He saw the look of shock on Iani's face and revelled in it.

And then his headlong attack came to an abrupt end, as if he'd ridden into a stone wall. The pede dropped in full gallop, crashing to the ground with a suddenness that sent him flying over its head. He had a horrified glimpse of the earth coming up to meet him before he slammed into the ground. At the last minute he managed to twist his body slightly to take the brunt of his fall on his shoulder. He tucked his head in and rolled, breath driven from him, sword lost, in panicked acknowledgement that he had miscalculated. Iani had taken the water from his pede. The man might be crippled with a weak hand and leg, but he was both rainlord and warrior.

Taquar scrambled to his feet, gasping but alert. A spear came hurtling at him. He ducked and the spearhead seared his neck in passing, furrowing a shallow cut. Smiling, he pulled the water from all the legs on the far side of Iani's pede. *Two can play at this game, you spitless bastard.*

The animal toppled before Iani could throw another spear, and he tumbled with it. Taquar found and scooped up his sword, then leaped onto the carapace of the help-less pede. He looked down on Iani where he lay with his crippled leg twisted at a weird angle, bone poking through the skin. With leisurely contempt, Taquar jumped down to the wounded man, barely aware of the pain of his own bruises.

"I think your life is over, you shrivelled shell of a human being. I am taking it all back—my life, my free-dom, my city."

Iani levered himself up into a sitting position. He gripped his leg above the break, as if that could stop the pain and raised his gaze to stare at Taquar. "Shrivel you! There are others who will bring you down, you wilted excuse for a man."

Casually, Taquar flicked the tip of his sword across Iani's cheek, opening up a cut. "We'll see about that. Per-sonally, I think I have all the water I need in my jar, while yours is stone dry. Shall I play with you for a while, do you think?" He trailed his sword point across Iani's cheek to the corner of his eye. "What do you think it would be like to be blind?"

"That's enough, Taquar."

Laisa, the words snapping out of her in the imperious tone he hated.

One part of him had been aware of her approach with the rest of the men and pedes, but he had dismissed them all as unimportant. He didn't look at her. "Or shall I ruin your good hand?" he asked Iani.

"End it!" Laisa again.

"You are going to kill me, so what does a hand matter?" Iani batted the sword away from his face as he spoke. "Or an eye? Or anything else? Come to think of it, I'm not so enamoured of life that anything matters much any more. Not even Scarcleft. Take it, if you like. Take it all. I know you won't be holding it long."

Taquar swung his sword, intending to remove Iani's nose, but the man flung himself flat on his back and the blade whistled harmlessly through the air. "I'm going to dismember you piece by piece," he began, but Laisa interrupted.

"Oh, spindevil take you, Taquar, what are you doing? Kill him and be done with it!"

"Laisa," Iani said from where he lay. "Might have known you'd be involved in this. You have a knack for choosing the losing side."

"He took everything away from me," Taquar told her. "And now I intend to make him pay."

"Withering spit," she responded, "what did you expect? You took his daughter from him."

"I'll do what I like," he said, and slashed Iani's other cheek. Iani gritted his teeth and jerked his head away.

Laisa raised her voice. "I'll not stand here and see you torture someone," she said.

"Try to stop me." He drove his sword through the centre of Iani's hand, pinning it to the ground.

Iani made no sound. Instead he turned his face to Laisa, still mounted on her pede. One side of his crooked mouth quirked up and he said, "You do it."

Not understanding, Taquar shot a glance at Laisa, but she didn't reply, and her gaze didn't shift from Iani. Taquar turned his attention back to the trapped rainlord— only to find him lying motionless, water pouring from his nose and mouth and ears, draining away into the dust.

For a moment he couldn't comprehend it. A rainlord could hold onto his water. Iani couldn't be murdered the rainlord way . . . And then he did understand. He turned on Laisa, but she met his fury with icy calm.

"He allowed me," she said calmly. "A brave man."

"You bitch!"

"There was a time when you would never have considered torture worthy of you, Taquar."

"There was a time when I hadn't been imprisoned in a cave," he snarled. He walked over to her mount, gesturing for the driver to descend so he could take the man's place and climbed up onto the saddle. "Bundle up Iani's body into a pannier," he said to the man and prodded the pede away, heading down the hill slope. "And as for you, Laisa, you do anything like that again, and you'll be the one tortured to an early death."

"You can hardly stop me seeing my own daughter and granddaughter!"

The armsman in charge at the gate of Scarcleft Hall shone his lantern down on their party, doubt etched into every line of his face. "'Scuse me, Lord Laisa, but Lord

Iani gave no orders 'bout you coming to the hall in his absence. I can fix rooms for your party at the inn on Level Five..."

"That's what the man at the city gates suggested," she said, "but I've a mind to see my daughter tonight."

"'Pologies, my lord. 'Spect Lord Iani tomorrow and reckon he'll see you then—"

Taquar, the hood of his cloak pulled up to shadow his face, turned away to murmur to Laisa. "Tell him yes, you'll go to the inn, but you expect his personal assistance to see to your comfort there."

Laisa made the request, her tone deliberately imperious. The armsman, a half-overman, agreed after some more initial hesitation, and a few moments later he was stepping outside the postern gate, accompanied by a lantern carrier. By then, Taquar had dismounted and was waiting for him. He took the man by the arm and at the same time pulled the hood down from his head so that both men could see who it was.

The lantern carrier gasped. The half-overman paled and stuttered, "L-l-lord Taquar!"

"I have something to show you," he said. Without waiting for a reply he indicated the place where one of Laisa's men had tipped the cloak-wrapped contents of a pannier onto the ground. "Unwrap it."

The half-overman obeyed and the lantern carrier shone the light onto the desiccated remains thus exposed. It was undoubtedly a man.

"That gold bracelet," the lantern carrier whispered, referring to the jewellery hanging on a chain around the neck of the corpse. "Lord Iani always wore that. And them's his clothes."

"It is Lord Iani," Taquar agreed. "Or it was. Now you have a choice. You can order your men to open the gate and resign yourself to having me back as your highlord, or you and your lantern bearer die right here and now. And I assure you, your deaths will be in vain because I *will* return to Scarcleft Hall. In fact, I will sleep in my own bedroom tonight. Your decision."

The half-overman and the lantern carrier exchanged shocked looks.

"He's right. Your choice will make no difference to the outcome," Laisa said. "You face two rainlords here. But we'd prefer to make this simple rather than messy. Better for everyone, don't you agree?"

The half-overman swallowed. A long silence ended only when he found his tongue once more. "Of course, my lords. If you'll wait just a moment, I'll have the gate opened." He looked up at the top of the wall where a guard was watching what was happening. "Armsman, open the gates for the highlord!" he called out.

"Wise decision. You'll find my men of great use to you in your future duties," Taquar said to the half-overman as they rode through the gate a moment later. "Please see to their comfort. And tell the seneschal and the overman I'd like to see them in my quarters immediately."

"Perhaps," Laisa added, "you'd see that Lord Iani's remains are handed over to the House of the Dead for burial rites, and arrange for someone to show me to my daughter."

"Of course, my lord."

The man looked sick, but he was as good as his word. Within a tenth of a sandrun, the pedes were led off to the stables, the enforcers were re-establishing themselves throughout Scarcleft Hall, Taquar was talking to a terrified seneschal and an overman already resigned to his own likely death, while Laisa was opening the door to Senya's rooms.

Senya looked up as she entered. "Oh good! You've come," she said. "Can we go back to Breccia now? I am *so* bored here."

It wasn't quite the welcome Laisa had hoped for, but she smiled and said, "I rather think we shall, very soon. I want to go home, too."

And she meant it.

The two men carrying Laisa's letter to Samphire only learned that Jasper had taken a shorter route after they arrived. He'd reached the city four days before them—and he had already left for Khromatis.

CHAPTER TWENTY-EIGHT

Khromatis
On the Variega Mountains
Southern Marches, Salted Pan Pothouse
and Grey Manor

"These make the Warthago look like something a pebblemouse constructed," Dibble said, gazing up in awe at the Variega Mountains ahead of them. "Look at the size of the things! And we're supposed to *cross* them?"

"Verdigris Manor is over there somewhere, beyond the pass," Elmar said. He was just as impressed as Dibble, but he wasn't about to let on.

They'd had two pieces of luck on their journey, both beyond price and both quite accidental. The first had been when they bypassed Kermes Manor without realising it. By the time they did find out, several villages further on, they had already seen a number of mirror pieces, enough to tell them that Terelle had also bypassed the manor. A little casual conversation between Dibble and a man building a stone fence alongside the road confirmed that a party of armsmen with two women had passed that way, and the two officers had borne Watergiver tattoos.

"I suppose that makes sense," Elmar said. "After all, Russet is her family, nothing to do with the Verdigris folk, except that his daughter married one. Those Verdigris lice are taking her either to their own property or to the Pinnacle. The problem is that somewhere back there she must have fulfilled the future of Russet's painting. She has no magical protection now."

"They'd not do that," Dibble said with certainty.

"Not do what?"

"Take her to the Pinnacle. Because if they did, and she ever got hold of waterpaints, she could paint him dead. Strikes me that it's a bleeding dangerous thing to do, to meet a waterpainter. They could kill you whenever they felt like it. Unlike us. An armsman has to be face to face with his enemy, risking his own life. A waterpainter can do it from the other side of the Quartern." He sighed. "El, they're taking her to their own place. And they don't ever intend to let her go."

He's probably right at that, Elmar thought.

"Do you think they dropped Russet off back there at his family home?" Dibble asked. "The fence-builder was sure there was no old man among them."

"I bleeding hope so. I don't want to meet that sun-blighted old niggard again."

"Me neither. I don't think I like these Khromatian waterlords very much."

Elmar looked across at him. "They aren't much good at showing a fellow a good time, are they?"

For a moment they stared at each other, deadly serious, and then simultaneously guffawed.

Three days after that conversation, they had their second piece of luck. They were trudging along in the interminable

rain, their boots clogged with mud, the bottom of their
trousers clinging wetly to their legs, the rain dribbling
down their cloaks in cold rivulets. After spotting what
appeared to be a shelter of some kind at the side of the
road ahead, they quickened their pace.

The shelter was occupied by a farmer and his son,
waiting out the worst of the rain before returning to the
fields. The farmer plied them with bread and cheese and
conversation while they waited for the shower to pass.
The rain stopped, and after they were on their way again,
Dibble could barely contain his excitement.

Elmar kept silent until the farmer was out of earshot.
"All right," he said, "what did he say? You mentioned
Terelle to him!"

"Yes. Seems one of their mounts dropped a shoe. I'll
be withering witless, though: did you notice the alpiners
wore *shoes*? I certainly didn't. But I'm sure that's what he
said."

"Go on, go on. I'm not interested in animal boots!"

"Well, apparently they had to stop to put the shoe or
sandal or whatever back on, otherwise the beast would
have started limping. So they came to the farmer's place
and he did it for them. I thought he said he nailed it on, but
that can't be right."

"It doesn't matter! What about Terelle and the Verdigris bastards? Was she with them?"

"He said there were two tattooed waterlords, two
women and a number of armsmen. He said one of the
lords told him he was Rubric Verdigris, and the other was
his brother. The farmer asked the women if they would
like a glass of milk and one of the women sounded real
funny when she replied. Lord Rubric called her Lord

Something, but it was a really odd name he couldn't remember. I asked if it was Terelle, but he still couldn't recall it."

"It would be her, all right. You asked how long ago this was, didn't you? What was the answer?"

"It was the same day as the goats at Hassle's farm got out and ate all the apples in his orchard," Dibble said dryly. "That's as close as he could say."

"Wonderful. And what about where they were going?"

"Ah, now there's the good news. The farmer asked Rubric where they were heading, and he said to Verdigris Manor. The fellow doesn't know much about where that is, but he said he's heard that if you get to the top of the pass, and look down the other side, you can see the roof."

The taproom of the Salted Pan in Marchford was full, as usual for that time of night. It was the only place in the town that sold amber, imported from the Gibber Quarter through Samphire, and it was the only place close to the foundries where the Alabasters could gather without being hassled or pointedly ignored. The inn was owned by a Watergiver, but the man behind the bar was an Alabaster, and so was every other person in the building, from the scullery skivvy to the chambermaid.

Until the door opened and the stranger stepped in.

Conversation died as if someone had closed a spigot on the spoken word. Heads swivelled. Movement ceased.

The man stood for a moment in the open doorway, then carefully pulled the door shut. He was not a large fellow, but his cold dark eyes and the authority in his stance made him a commanding presence. The pack on his back he allowed to slip to the floor, placing it against the wall, together with his staff. He shrugged off his cloak to hang it on one of the many hooks around the walls.

His gaze roved round the room, shifting from face to face, hesitating where anyone dared to hold his stare, only moving on when the person looked away. His eyes were brown, his skin too—a combination common in the Gibber Quarter, but rare in Khromatis. Still, Gibber grubbers were unheard of on this side of the Borderlands, so the fellow was doubtless Khromatian. Certainly, the cloak and garments he wore spoke of Khromatian weaving and the boots were the product of a Khromatian bootmaker. Worse, he wore a sword, and no one was permitted to do that unless he was a Watergiver or an armsman of the forces. Yet neither would ever deign to enter this taproom, surely. The Alabasters regarded him cautiously.

Once he had scanned the whole room to his satisfaction, the man spoke, and the language he used was their own.

"I'm looking for Marrake Khorash," he said.

Heads turned away from him then, and gazes sought and found a man seated at the bar. "I'm Marrake," said the target of their combined gaze. "Who wants me?"

The stranger threaded his way through the tables. "I have a letter for you." He dug into his belt bag to produce a small piece of parchment closed with a wax seal and handed it over.

Marrake took the letter, his astonishment clear. He fumbled for his knife, broke the seal and read the letter. Then he handed the sheet to the man behind the bar so he could read it as well, saying, "A room where we can be private, please, Breth." He slipped off the barstool to stand. He was short, barely taller than the stool itself.

Breth read the letter, nodded at the newcomer, and said, "That way." He indicated the stairs to the right of the bar. "The room at the top, to the left."

The stranger indicated that Marrake was to precede him and held out his hand to take back the letter as he passed the barman.

Only when the two of them had disappeared upstairs did anyone speak.

"*Who* was that?" someone asked.

The barman shook his head. "I've no idea. But the script was signed and sealed by the Bastion, saying that he expected everyone to be giving the lord who was bearer whatever he wanted any time he wanted it, in the name of God."

Upstairs Jasper turned to face Marrake. "I need help."

"I assumed that," the little man said wryly. He waved a hand at the letter Jasper held. "Ye know he's my cousin?"

"Yes, he told me."

"A bastion is supposed to be cutting himself off from his family."

"He's not that sort of man."

"No. Is this about Feroze's death?"

"Yes, in a way. I didn't know if you'd heard about that."

"Oh, bad news travels fast among the Alabasters here. Him being a relative of mine, I'd appreciate hearing the details, though, if ye know them. I take it ye are a Gibber-man, not a Watergiver."

"That's right."

"And a lord?"

"Of sorts."

Marrake climbed up onto the bed to listen, sitting with

his feet dangling because they were too short to touch the floor. His size made him seem childlike, but Jasper sensed that to underestimate this man would be a mistake. His eyes were shrewd, and there was something in his voice that told of an innate belief in his own value. Jasper related as much as he knew of how Feroze had died and the unknown fate of Terelle.

"And who are ye, that ye've the Bastion's ear and support?" Marrake asked. "And what, for the love of God, is your mission here? If ye're caught, the penalty is surely death."

"They'll not kill me so easily. My name is Shale Flint, and I'm a...a rainlord. I don't speak the language of Khromatis, and I need a guide and a mount to travel to the north, into the mountains. That's where they've taken Terelle. I intend to fetch her home. Ahead of me are another two Scarpermen with the same aim."

"You want a *Khromatian* guide?"

"The way I understand it, it's not possible for an Alabaster to go further north than the Southern Marches. So, yes, I do."

Marrake frowned in thought, swinging his legs. Once again Jasper was reminded of a child and had to thrust the thought away.

"My lord, the people of this land aren't brought up to treat outsiders with compassion or equality. Outsiders are inferior; it's as simple as that. To be finding someone who'll not betray ye will be difficult."

"There are always people who can be bought, surely?"

"Yes, and they're the same people who'll take your coin and then betray ye."

"Then I'll go alone. I'm not without a talent for mayhem, if need be."

"A man after my own white heart."

"But what about a mount? I need something to ride. I must catch up with the men ahead of me."

"And ye've never ridden an alpiner before?"

"No. I've never been to Khromatis before."

Marrake's smile spread into a gleeful grin. "That should be very funny indeed." Just when Jasper was wondering if he should revise his opinion of the man's maturity, the grin vanished and Marrake said with renewed seriousness, "That gives me an idea. My lord, tell me about this woman. Ye said Terelle Grey is a waterpainter because she has Watergiver blood?"

Jasper nodded.

"Grey is the name of a family from around here. They breed alpiners and manage eel-beds." When Jasper looked blank, he added, "They raise eels for food. Used to be quite prosperous, but not so much now. All because of a scandal a long time back, before I ever came to Khromatis. One of their young lads ran off with a woman from one of the waterlord families. Heir to the Pinnacle, she was."

"Sienna Kermes. No, Sienna Verdigris. Kermes was her grandfather."

"I don't remember her name, but the lad she ran off with was called Erith Grey. The joke around these parts was that she preferred 'perspiring in an eel-bed in the peat' to 'aspiring to be Pinnacle in the Peak.' Ye telling me it's their daughter ye're chasing?"

"That's right." Jasper still had no idea what an eel was, but he didn't bother to ask.

"No wonder the Verdigris family wants to kill her. She could claim the Pinnacle's seat."

"That would have no interest for her."

"No, but it might be of interest to the family Grey."

"In what way?"

"Lord Shale, the Greys were ostracised and much of their business ruined when they crossed swords with the Verdigris lot. I'm only an Alabaster, and no one tells us much, but it's common knowledge that the Grey family was darned upset when Lord Bice Verdigris was made Commander of the Southern Marches and he showed up here with his three sons and started lording it over folk. Never missed a chance to be humiliating any of the Greys, I can tell ye. Refused to be buying their alpiners for the Verdigris armsmen, stopped the barracks from buying their eels. The Verdigris family are not well liked around here in general, and they're hated by the Greys."

"So you're saying the Greys might be prepared to rescue one of their own?"

Marrake swung his legs up to sit cross-legged, then propped his chin up on a hand. "Exactly. And they have alpiners, too. Think, Lord Shale. If they can show everyone that the Verdigris family is after murdering the real ruler to the land, there'll be a far bigger scandal than Erith Grey's misdemeanour ever was. It'd be the end of Lord Bice here. Oh, yes, I think the Grey family might just be delighted to be meeting ye."

"Good. When can you take me to meet them?"

And I wonder what the waterless hells Terelle will think of this? In his gut he knew she wasn't going to be at all happy to be welcomed by her father's family because they thought she was going to be their saviour.

Oh, spitless damn. Why is nothing ever simple?

*   *   *

Terelle's uncle now ran the Grey farm.

For some reason, Jasper found it odd that Terelle should have close relatives, ones she knew nothing of and had never cared to find. She'd had only poor experiences with the single relative she'd known.

Her uncle, Gelder Grey, was a muscular farmer of sixty, heavily tattooed on the face and hands the way Russet had been. His sad eyes and weak, tremulous voice didn't match his bulk. His character was similarly conflicted, or so it appeared to Jasper. He loathed the Verdigris clan with a passion, yet cowered before their power. He delighted in the idea of having his brother's daughter in a position to topple the Pinnacle, yet was reluctant to help her.

He was welcoming to "Lord Shale," jumping to the conclusion that he was in a similar position to Terelle—a Khromatian who had, through no fault of his own, been born in the Quartern. His Quartern language was ungrammatical but understandable.

While they were talking, a large, broad-shouldered man of about thirty appeared, lightly tattooed on the face, whom Gelder introduced as his son Umber. "He cares for our alpiners. Umber, this fellow be looking for Erith's daughter. Wants to be taking her back. He's a waterlord. Marrake says the Bastion be vouching for him."

"I heard what happened at the Commander's manor in Marchford," Umber said, greeting Jasper with a friendly smile. "Did my father tell ye?"

"I was surprised he knew so much," Jasper said, sizing the son up as a bluff, amiable man in spite of his intimidating size. "He's just told me a groom there was married to one of your family and he actually spoke to Terelle." The rush of joy he'd felt at the news was still with him.

"Yes, Eden Croft. He was there. Saw what happened. His wife wheedled the story out of him and told him to be telling us. The Verdigris took your lass to their family manor. That's up on the Low Plateau Pale, on the other side of the pass."

"I hope she's still alive." He couldn't sense her and her absence was a constant ache to his soul. *It's because she's too far away. It must be. The mountains block her, and there's too much water.*

"Well, the old man certainly isn't. The Kermes fellow. He died in the fire. Eden Croft found out that much. They tried to be killing your Terelle, but couldn't because she'd been waterpainted. That true?"

"As far as I know, yes." But even as he said the words, he knew that had changed. Russet was dead. *Sunblast. That means she could be free of the magic—but vulnerable. Oh, sweet waters.* "Where is she now?"

"Jet and his younger brother Rubric left with her the next day, apparently heading for their home on the other side of the mountains."

"I need to rescue her, urgently. I need mounts and a guide and I need to leave as soon as possible and travel fast."

"He says he can pay," Marrake said from where he had perched himself on the back of a sofa. Jasper guessed that he liked to sit up high so he could look people in the eye.

Gelder leered at Jasper. "Want us in danger? Cost ye plenty!"

"I have coin. I also have a sapphire or two. Valuable, good-quality ones you can have instead of the coin."

"Let me look."

Jasper dug in his purse and produced two of the gems

he had there. The rest he had secreted in various seams of his clothing. "Near perfect," he said. "For these, I need four mounts, with tackle and feed, and a good guide who is familiar with the trail and knows where Verdigris Manor is. Someone who can speak my tongue. He would have to get me there and bring me and Terelle back again. I'll pay for any other food or accommodation along the way."

Gelder rolled the gems in his fingers and held them up to the light. "Good gems. But dangerous work. Armsmen know we be helping outsider, we in trouble." He turned to Umber. "We keep in the family, eh?"

To Jasper's surprise, Umber grinned. "Gladly."

Gelder looked across at Marrake. "And I don't want to be hearing any rumours, understand?" He added something in Khromatian that was probably a threat.

Marrake nodded and smiled, but no amusement reached his eyes. He slipped down from the sofa. "My job is done. I'll leave ye here," he said to Jasper. "Good luck. Ye'll need it." He clasped Jasper by the hand and while Gelder and Umber were conversing in their own tongue, he whispered, "Trust the son, not the father."

After Marrake had gone, Gelder took the sapphires and left Umber and Jasper together to plan their departure.

"Ye overpaid him, ye know," Umber said. "So come with me while I choose the best damn hacks we have in the stable to be making up for it."

Jasper smiled slightly as they left the house in the direction of the stables. "I hope you're telling the truth because I wouldn't know the difference. I've never ridden an alpiner before."

"Really? Well then, ye're going to be the sorriest young

man this side of the Variega Mountains by the time we reach the pass. Ye'll be sore enough to be killing your mount and walking."

"I'll survive."

"I'll get ye a steady beast with no tricks."

"Why did you just tell me your father is a cheat?"

"Perhaps because I loathe the bleeding rotten bastard. I stayed on the farm up till now because of my mother. If I'd left, he'd have beaten her to death one day, and I couldn't persuade her to be leaving. But she died earlier this year, and now I'm looking for a way to get out of here without losing everything that's owed me." He grinned at Jasper again, but the expression held more grimace than joy. "There's never been much love in his pile, I can tell ye. Why do ye think young Erith skedaddled? My grandfather was even worse than Gelder. People in these parts say Erith was the best of the bunch, but wild." He waved a hand at the building they were heading for. "Generally the Greys treat alpiners and eels better than themselves. We'll ride out of here without showing Gelder which hacks we take, I think. When do ye want to leave?"

"Now." Jasper pointed to the pack he had with him. "I have everything I need."

"I haven't even had my breakfast yet!" Umber protested, and then he threw back his head and laughed. "Lord Shale, I believe ye're a man after my own heart." Suddenly sober, he added, "Ye do know we could die? The Verdigris family are strong in magic. Ruthless, vicious bastards. The moment your girl doesn't have the protection of magic, she's dead. If we're caught, we're dead, too."

"Then why did you agree to guide me?"

"Because I want out of this place. Because the idea of a man so in love that he'll risk everything for his woman appeals to something in me. Maybe the same thing that had Erith die for Sienna. Because for once, I want to be doing something other than feeding eels and breeding alpiners." He shrugged. "I've always wanted an adventure, and now I've got it. I'm good with a sword, by the way. And I'm a waterlord, so I suppose we can give them a fight if it comes to a confrontation."

Jasper, who'd made no mention of Terelle being "his woman," blushed and hastily changed the subject. "You're a Watergiver?"

"Yes, didn't ye know? If a person's personal name is a colour of some sort, ye know they were granted that name as a youngster, when they were identified as a Watergiver."

"I know umber is a colour, but Bice?"

He laughed. "Yes. And Jet and Rubric and Hue." He glanced at Jasper as they walked up to the stable entrance. "We usually choose our own names. Umber is a clay pigment. Heat it up and it becomes more intense. That still describes me. Jet has a black heart, as his name implies. And Hue? Not one colour, but all. Delusions of grandeur even in his name. And ye, Shale? Rainlord, huh?"

Jasper nodded, but his heart sank. *Salted hells, what have I got myself into now?* He had to trust a Watergiver, and it felt like a rotten idea. "Stormlord, actually. One step up."

"We don't make that distinction. I guess I'll find out your skills as we go along. And ye don't speak our tongue?"

He shook his head.

"Never mind. I'll do the talking along the trail. Dressed

like that, ye can pass for one of us—just don't open your mouth."

As Umber turned to give orders to the stable hands about the alpiners, Jasper raised his gaze to the distant mountain peaks. Somewhere on the other side of them was Terelle. Soon he'd feel her presence again, like a tantalising whisper on the wind, a whisper that spoke to him of her water. He must, because if there was no touch of her, it might mean she was dead...

CHAPTER TWENTY-NINE

Khromatis
Low Plateau Pale, Verdigris Manor

Rubric always knocked and waited for Terelle to give him permission to enter. He came every day, usually staying the run of a sandglass. Vittia came at the same time to clean, to bring Terelle clean clothes and more water, but her tasks were quickly done. Sometimes Rubric also came when her lunch was delivered, choosing to sit and eat with her.

Terelle had to admit it was the highlight of her day; ironic when she considered how much he exasperated her, always irritating but rarely explaining anything. He was like an itch you couldn't scratch. She did bless his kindness, though, in bringing her board-books to read. Without those, she might have been bored out of her mind. They were written in Khromatian, but their alphabet was similar and deciphering it helped her to learn the language. Rubric continued with her spoken lessons, drilling her over and over until word patterns became automatic, until she was actually thinking in Khromatian, even dreaming in it. Occasionally they dropped back into the Quartern tongue, but it was no longer necessary.

At first, she concentrated on resting and healing; later she returned to her old dance routines to keep her muscles toned. And every day she begged to see Lord Jade again.

"She'll come one day," Rubric assured her every time she asked. Once he added, "When she comes to terms with seeing one of her sons hitting a woman in the face, with knowing her youngest and most beloved offspring has been a party to killing a number of innocent Alabasters, and with her husband having revealed himself to be the unscrupulous monster he is."

And still the days went by without her seeing the waterpainter again.

"What about the danger I represent by being here?" she asked. "How can she not worry over that? Rubric, I've no desire to hurt you, or her, or Azure and the children. Yet everyone here is in danger from me." It was a lie, but she put into her voice all the horror she remembered from the Scarcleft earthquake. "You have to let me go, or risk your house falling down around your ears in order to free me from this room. You *have* told your mother this?"

"Yes. She'd never heard of anyone causing an earthquake with paint before."

"Oh, stop being so flippant. Perhaps your waterpainters are more ethical and cautious about what they paint and how they paint it. The person who did the painting that caused the earthquake wasn't. And he's the same person who did the last painting of me."

"I'll pass that on to my mother."

"When are you returning to Marchford?"

"Soon. We've only lingered this long because Jet caught the grippe from the children and has been too sick and feverish to ride. Fevers can't be cured by waterpainting. He's getting better and we should be off in a day or two."

Her heart lurched sickeningly at her anticipated loneliness. "I'm not sure why, but I'll miss you," she said.

"Really? Come to think of it, I'll miss our conversations too."

"There is so much I still don't know."

"Like what?"

"Like why Khromatians hate Alabasters so much. Like why you are so secretive and protect your borders from intrusion so assiduously. So many questions."

"You never stop trying to learn things, do you? Always probing and digging and looking for rational answers. I bet you're more often disappointed than satisfied."

"Only when Rubric Verdigris won't tell me stuff I want to know."

He laughed. "Oh, all right. Here's a summary of our religious history to answer your first question. And bear in mind that this is boring stuff I had to listen to in school when I was more interested in beating the mockery out of other boys in the playground.

"Our faith started in the highest mountains, where all our rivers originate, among the Alabasters, did you know that?"

Terelle shook her head.

"They were the pious ones who taught us to stop worshipping devils and demons, and turn to the one true God, the Source of all water, the giver of life. Men made pilgrimages there to hear God speak in the Source, where it bubbled from the mountain as a small stream. All this is several thousand years ago, you understand."

She nodded.

"In those days, God really spoke to people. His voice issued forth through the water. Thousands of believers went on pilgrimages there and heard the voice of God. The Alabasters grew rich on the gold brought by the pilgrims. They built cities. They mined the mountains. They made things from the metals they found. They changed from simple mountain folk to greedy merchants. They tossed their rubbish and their poisons and their sewage into the rivers so that it spread throughout Khromatis, into every corner of the land. People died of poisoning and in plagues spread by the filth. The Alabasters said we brown folk didn't matter, only the white-skinned were pure.

"So God became angry. He told pilgrims he would not speak to them until the land he had granted them was pristine again. His voice vanished from the Source. In their anger at the Alabasters for what they had done, the lowlanders rose up against them. Wars were fought. The Alabasters lost because we had Watergivers and they didn't. Their cities were razed flat to the ground and their mines were closed. They were banished from the mountains they had defiled. Religious leaders say that when God speaks again, it'll mean the Alabasters are forgiven and can return. The stories say the Alabasters were remorseful and agreed to their own punishment and exile. They have lived in the hope of their return."

"Let me guess what happened next—the Khromatians suddenly found they missed all the metals and metalworkers. That was when they brought back the Alabasters to do the work in the Southern Marches. Right?"

"Something like that."

"I hate to tell you, but your manufactories are making a poisonous mess of the Southern Marches."

"Ah, but those lowlands weren't part of our original land at the time when God spoke to us, so our leaders—in their infinite wisdom—don't care about the pollution down there."

"Nice." She sat pondering the story in view of what she knew about the Alabasters.

"Nothing else to say?" he taunted. He sat on the window ledge, precariously balanced yet wholly at ease.

"A harsh sort of god," she said, "one who punishes generations that had nothing to do with the crime."

"People do that all the time. Punish you for things you've no control over. Like being born poor or...different." His sardonic bitterness was back.

"Do you believe the story you just told?"

He shook his head.

"What do you believe in, then?"

"I guess...in justice. That somewhere after this life there is justice. Compensation for suffering." He laughed. "How mad is that?"

She didn't think it was mad at all, but said nothing.

"Your second question—about why we protect our borders so...assiduously. That has a history, too. It comes from the time when the world changed. You had your Time of Random Rain. Over the Giving Sea, whole cities vanished under the oceans. To the east of us, people starved because they were sea fishermen and there were no fish to catch. Terrible things happened. The priests say we were protected from the worst of it by God because we'd exiled the Alabasters. I think it's more that we were sheltered by the mountains. Anyway, the only thing that threatened us was all the people trying to come into our land to save themselves from thirst and starvation—or drowning by the oceans. Watergivers and the army served to keep all comers out. A simple story."

"A cruel one."

"It is, isn't it? When starving people knock, you lock the door. We've been like that ever since."

She changed the subject. "You've never told me the real reason your mother was so upset when I asked if she'd teach me how to use painting to heal."

He altered his position to lean back against the window frame, one foot on the ledge and his hands clasped around his bent knee. He gazed out over the garden, but his eyes were devoid of any awareness of what was out there. Then he sighed and turned back to her. "She dreamed once of having a daughter, one who would be a waterpainter. Someone she could teach, not just to heal, but also to produce paintings of beauty and intensity. I failed her on both counts."

"Those are her works on the walls downstairs?" She had a vague recollection of seeing paintings in the entrance hall.

He nodded. "She is the greatest artist of our Pale. She is also our greatest healer."

"Oh? Then I'd have thought people would flock to your door. But I haven't noticed that you have many visitors." From her room, she had a near perfect view of who came and went.

"My father doesn't like it, but she did convert a room at the back of the house where she does her painting, overlooking the kitchen gardens. It's quiet and she can receive patients there without them coming through the main part of the house. Mostly they're just friends and neighbours."

She blinked, hiding the burst of joy inside her. *I know where to find paints.*

He didn't notice. "It's sad my father won't let her pursue her talents—to run a hospice, perhaps, or to exhibit her art in the Peak. He thinks it beneath the dignity of a Verdigris to be an artist, let alone heal any farmer or ditch digger who needs it."

"And she accepts the limitations he places on her?"

"What else can she do?"

She snorted. "I can think of plenty of things I'd rather do than stay married to Bice Verdigris."

"It really is none of your business."

"No, you're right. But don't expect an apology. She could teach *me*."

"Instead of me? You think you'd make up for a son who was so—so disappointing to her? Besides, what use would it be to you to know how to heal? You're going to die right here, in this house."

Terelle glared at him. "Well, I don't believe that, do I? I believe the magic of a waterpainting will get me out of here—possibly to the detriment of the Verdigris family."

He slipped down from the sill to lean against the wall, arms folded, feet crossed at the ankle, one of his favourite postures: the couldn't-care-less-pose.

She reverted to what they'd been talking about previously. "Your mother loves you deeply as you are. She changed your appearance, didn't she? To match what you know yourself to be. Is that not an act of great love?"

He paled and stood bolt upright. "I don't know what you mean."

"No? Doesn't your mother's waterpainting skill have something to do with the way you look now?"

His silence lasted so long she wondered if he was going to reply at all. Finally, he whispered, "How did you know?"

"I'm a painter. I see things most don't. And then, I was also brought up in a snuggery. One of the handmaidens there was more feminine than me. And yet her body wasn't female."

"Ironic, isn't it? At my birth, my mother thought she had what she wanted: a daughter. Trouble was, the girl grew up to be a boy in all ways—except the ways that count for men like my father. My mother? She loved me enough to waterpaint me the way I want to be, the way I felt myself to be, at least externally. Hundreds of paintings. Tiny little changes, year after year after year. Or sometimes not so much changes but keeping me the way I was." He ran a hand over the flatness of his chest. "And I worked hard to become the swordsman I wanted to be. The muscles are real."

"She did a wonderful job. You both did." She tilted her head appreciatively. It was a snuggery handmaiden look.

"Stop it!"

She flushed. "Sorry. I must admit I'm amazed your father ever allowed you to become an armsman."

"My mother said he had to, or she'd leave him and..." He paused. "Let's just say there are things he wouldn't want the world to know about his business dealings; things my mother knows."

"She must love you deeply. And yet you aren't happy."

"Why should I be happy? I'll never be completely the person I want to be." He shrugged. "I could live with that, be happy even, if everyone else could accept what I am. But the world doesn't work that way. My religion tells me I sin, although I'm blessed if I know how. My father loathes me. My brothers think I'm a joke. If I display compassion or mercy, they call me girlie. My fellow armsmen ridicule me to my face even though I can match them in half a dozen ways. No matter how good I am, it's never good enough. And have you any idea how many times I've had to ward off unwanted attention from other males who profess to be better men than me? The only way I've saved myself from rape is with my waterlord power. What I am grieves my mother. Should I be happy?"

"I'm sorry. I guess it's hard for me to imagine what your life's been like. Back where I come from, it wouldn't matter. Not even the waterpriests care about such things. Oh, there'll always be some who are contemptuous of snuggery men and women, but mostly who you are, and what you do with who you are, is no one's business but your own—unless you interfere with the worship of the Sunlord. Then it becomes the business of the waterpriests."

He was interested, she could tell. Intrigued. She said softly, "There's no need for you to put up with being ridiculed or despised. There are other places to live. Come with me back to the Quartern. You can marry and live an ordinary life."

He didn't quite believe her; his gaze was wary. "Well, maybe not ordinary if you are a stormlord," she amended. "That puts you at the top of the uplevellers. Richer, more revered. You can move clouds, right? And make clouds? Even from salty water?"

"I suppose so. Though here we don't usually need to do that. It is not considered proper for Watergivers to interfere with God's weather unless folk are in danger. You know, from flooding or avalanches or something."

"We are in danger of dying of thirst. And you'd be happier in the Scarpen Quarter, really."

He was silent.

"You could be totally yourself."

"Stop it! You people are—"

But he couldn't finish the sentence. She guessed the word he had been about to say was "barbarians," and that he had halted himself when he'd realised how ridiculous that would sound.

He threw himself out of the room, and she heard him clattering down the stairs. She raised an eyebrow and waited. A moment later he sheepishly reappeared.

"I thought it was too much to hope you'd forget," she said as he shut and barred the door.

Alone again, she crossed to one of the windows. She'd flung Russet's plaid over the windowsill, anchoring it inside by squashing the end between the bed head and the wall. The remainder flapped outside in the breeze. She placed it there every day, bringing it inside at dusk to put around her shoulders in the cool of the evening when she closed the shutters. So far, no one had commented, or thought to wonder why she did it. It was her hope that Elmar and Dibble would see it.

If they returned.

If they ever found her.

She wasn't relying on them, though. Every day she watched the world through the windows, studying the movement of people and farm animals until she thought she knew the routines. Part of every day she spent unravelling the wool of one of the thick knitted blankets on her bed, then plaiting it into strings and finally replaiting the strings into rope. She disguised the absence of part of the blanket by making her bed herself every morning.

The rope itself she hid under the bedclothes, blessing the fact that there was no way she could be surprised at the task of making it. Not only was the unbarring of the door noisy, but she usually heard the footsteps on the stairs.

Later that day, as she was about to finish her rope, she heard someone coming, a light step that was definitely not Rubric's. By the time Lord Jade entered, Terelle was sitting in her chair, reading.

Standing in the doorway, her expression haughty, Lord Jade looked formidable. "Leave him alone. You unsettle him."

"He's old enough to make his own decisions."

"He's not even twenty."

"He's hardly a child. He's a soldier for pity's sake! A man who's had to kill other men."

"He's not a—!" Lord Jade stopped, stricken.

"He *is* a man. Don't tell me you don't know that. Not after how you have helped him over the years."

"He'll be happier if you don't tease him with the absurd."

"Pardon?"

"The idea of going to your barbarian land? It's impossible."

Surprised he'd mentioned it to his mother, she said, "On the contrary. You're a mother trying to protect a child, but he's old enough to make up his own mind."

"And do you really think his father will allow that?"

"Why should Rubric listen to his father? Come to think of it, why should *you* listen? Do you love Bice? Is he good to you? Is he good *for* you? Time to take a stand, don't you think? Your children are grown, you have a way of earning your own living. You can even paint your way to freedom."

"How *dare* you make insinuations about my family! Who are you to talk to your elders like that?"

Terelle interrupted her with a burst of laughter. "Don't be ridiculous, Jade. Can you think of a single reason why I should respect anything at all about you? You keep me a prisoner here, shut in a single room, believing that I'll one day die, horribly. You haven't done anything at all to earn my respect. Or even my good manners. Yes, you healed me, but your son was responsible for the injury in the first place."

The woman stared at her in shock, then walked out of the room, barring the door behind her.

Well, Terelle thought, *I guess I just sabotaged any idea she might have had of teaching me about water-painting. Let's see if I have at least got her to* think *about things.*

That night Terelle didn't close her shutters. She sat at the window late, watching and waiting while the activity around the house and stable ceased, the gleam of lamplight dimmed and vanished, doors closed and bolts were shot.

She already knew that the house remained unguarded at night. The Verdigris family didn't fear attack and they didn't fear robbers, either. Wondering about that, she decided there really wouldn't be much point in robbing a waterpainter's house. The painter could always paint the stolen items back again and the thief would be obliged to bring them back.

When she guessed everyone was in bed asleep, she attached the rope to the bed frame and flung the rest out the window. The tower was too high for the rope to reach the ground, but all it had to do was get her as far as the roof of the storey below; after that she would find a way down. She had to. She swung herself up onto the window sill. In her money pouch she had her tinderbox and a candle. Over her shoulder was slung her water skin. The tray from under her water ewer was stuffed down the front of her tunic. Barefoot, she paused on the ledge, steeling herself for the worst part of her climb: scrambling over the edge.

Deep breaths, Terelle. You can do this.

One leg, then the other, feet scrabbling desperately to find a toehold roughness of the stone, hands grimly gripping the rope. Prayers, to a god she wasn't sure existed, that the rope was strong enough. Heart somewhere in her throat, beating like a Gibber war drum as she unhooked the fingers of one hand to move her grip down. She hung there until she could gather enough courage to move her other hand. Or a foot. One at a time.

Oh, wither it, I hate this.

Finally, her feet hit the roof below. Quickly she half slid, half scrabbled down the slope to the guttering. Bracing herself against the gutter itself, she looked over the edge. The ground was a long way down, and a glance was enough to tell her both the creepers along the wall were far too flimsy to take her weight.

She edged herself back, and half-crawled, half-scrambled towards the back of the house. Here, the first storey below extended further behind the house than the second storey she was on—and there was a ladder attached to the wall separating the two roofs. Once she was down on the lower roof, a look over the edge revealed a large water barrel on the ground below. A drainpipe ran down the corner of the house between the roof gutter and the barrel.

Taking a deep breath, she swung herself over the edge and shinned down the pipe, scraping her hands and knees on the way, to land on top of the barrel.

Down on the ground a moment later, she leaned against the wall, knees wobbly, waiting for her pounding heartbeat to subside. Once she was in command of herself again, she went off to explore, fear replaced with a thrill of excitement. After all the days of inertia and all the time she had spent helpless at the mercy of others, the feeling of taking charge of her own destiny was exhilarating.

She flitted from window to window, from door to door, looking for one that was not barred. When a small entry door at the back of the house yielded a little to her push, she risked a shove and the faulty latch pulled out of its slot. Again her heart thumped and goosebumps prickled. She paused to listen. All was silent. Inside, she found herself in a scullery that gave on to the deserted kitchen. She tiptoed through to nearby rooms, finding the cool-room, pantry and meat larder, stillroom and cellarage, before she found what she was looking for: the room where Jade received her patients.

She entered, closing the door behind her, lit the candles on the mantelpiece and looked around. A waterpainter's room. Everywhere she looked, there was the paraphernalia required for the art. Paint pots and labelled powder jars, trays and water, paint spoons and cleaning cloths, mortar and pestle, rolls of finished paintings. She wouldn't need the tray from under the ewer; she needn't have brought her own water.

Lighting some more candles, she set to work.

*   *   *

So engrossed was she in the joys of painting again, so focused on her one chance to free herself, that if there were any signs she was in trouble she never heard them. The first she knew was when the door burst open to slam against the wall.

She spun, a paint spoon sailing out of her hand to land on the polished wood floor leaving a splash of vermilion like a spray of blood.

Jet. Jade. Rubric. Standing there in the doorway, frozen in their consternation.

For a moment she didn't move, either. Fear glued her there, mouth open, paint pot in one hand, eyes staring, breath halted. And then she felt it, the horror reaching into her to seize her water, tendrils tugging deep inside. Someone was trying to kill her the rainlord way. She flung herself under the table, as if she could stop the process by putting the wood of the tabletop between her and Jet. It was him, of course. She sensed his rage in the clutching wrench of magic.

Rubric yelled at him. "Stop it, you numbskull! You want to kill us all?"

She resisted, but still felt the tugs of his killing power until Jade snapped with all a mother's exasperation for a wayward child, "Halt that this moment! You'll make things worse!"

Slowly, cautiously, Terelle crawled out on the far side of the table and stood up. *He can't kill you anyway, not now. Have faith in yourself. In the magic.* A few deep breaths quietened the thudding of her heart. *One of them must have awoken and sensed me down here.*

The three of them entered and spread out. Jade, untidily

dressed, was carrying a lighted candelabrum. Jet was barefoot and had not yet done up the ties on his shirt. He held his sword in one hand and his unbuckled scabbard in the other. The murderous expression on his face reflected hate back at Terelle. Rubric, also barefoot and carrying his sword, wore only a nightgown. He was white-faced with shock.

For a moment she was puzzled at the extremity of their fear. Then it struck her. They thought she might have murdered them with her magic. Rubric had been worried Jet's action would prompt her to shuffle up their death—if she hadn't already done so. In disgust she flung the paint pot she was clutching onto the table. "I'm not like you," she said. She waved a hand at the two trays on the table. "I don't wantonly kill people. Come have a look. And no, you can't undo it. I've already shuffled both pictures up."

They moved as one to the table edge. Jet was still holding his sword as if he was looking for an excuse to run her through. Jade brought the candelabrum up to the first of the two trays Terelle had completed.

They wouldn't know it, but both paintings showed the interior of the Breccian stormquest room. She had used the bloodstone pendant Jasper had given her as a holdfast in both. In the first painting, it lay on Jasper's map table next to the picture of another painting in a tray depicting Jasper controlling a storm—one she had not yet painted, and would not until she was safely back again. It was—or so she hoped—enough to make sure she would return to Breccia healthy enough to paint. She couldn't paint herself there, but she could paint her holdfast and her own artwork.

Jade frowned at it, not understanding, then moved the

candelabrum onto the next tray. She stared at it, her two sons by her side, taking it all in but without the knowledge she needed to comprehend what it meant. She raised her gaze to meet Terelle's across the table. "Where is this place?" Her voice quavered with dread.

"It's the Cloudmaster's stormquest room in Breccia. Breccia's the main city of the Scarpen Quarter."

With a crash, the candelabrum dropped out of Jade's nerveless fingers onto the table. Terelle jumped. The candles blew out, but she didn't need their extra light to see the woman's shock.

"What have you done?" Lord Jade whispered. "By all that's holy, *what have you done?*"

Jet stared at the second tray, which showed Jade and Rubric side by side inside the stormquest room of Breccia Hall. Then his head jerked up and he launched himself straight across the table at Terelle, sword raised.

"Die, bitch!" he yelled.

CHAPTER THIRTY

Khromatis
Low Plateau Pale, Verdigris Manor
Wilder Pale, on the road

Terelle stared across the width of the table between herself and Jet. It was too wide for him to reach her, so he leaped up onto the tabletop via a chair seat. Her first instinct was to stand still with her mouth wide open, but she conquered her paralysis and ducked to scramble back underneath. Jet could either come down and crawl after her or wait for her to come out. She hoped he was left looking foolish.

Head swivelling in panic, she watched for his descent from the table. *I could have just stood there and let him skewer me, I suppose. My painting would mean he'd fail*...She swallowed, knowing she lacked the courage. Just because he couldn't kill her didn't mean she couldn't be hurt.

Then Lord Jade spoke. In freezing tones she addressed her son. "Have you *quite* finished, Jet? Is it possible for you to have a calm conversation on a serious topic, or are we always to be exposed to your histrionics?"

Terelle didn't know the final word, but breathed a little easier anyway. There was no mistaking the tone.

His sword now sheathed, Jet jumped down and went to stand near the window. Indicating the trays, he said in a fury, "She painted both of you in her God-forsaken city on the other side of their land. You *know* what that means!"

Terelle clambered out on the side furthest from him. Jade ignored him and turned to her in anguish. "Why? What you've done is unethical and cruel. You would force us away from our homes and family?"

Calmer now, Terelle answered directly in Khromatian. "Why not? That's exactly what you Verdigris did to me."

Jet made a sound of disgust, but Jade exchanged a long, wordless look with Rubric. At last she turned back to Terelle and waved a hand at the paintings. "This place is in the heart of the Quartern?"

"Yes. And if I don't return home, people will thirst to death in time. They may anyway, if the Cloudmaster and I can't bring them enough water."

Rubric gave a sudden frown. "Wait a moment. Something's not making sense here. Why didn't I think of it before? If you're so necessary in the Quartern, why are you here? They could have sent anybody."

"I'm Khromatian. Lord Jasper was under the obviously mistaken impression that I might be welcomed by my family and you might listen to me. But you're right—he would not have sent me under normal circumstances. My great-grandfather Russet waterpainted me here in Khromatis, so I had to come whether I wanted to or not."

Rubric gaped. "Lord *Russet* painted you?"

"Then I can kill you," Jet said. He sneered at her from

the other side of the room. "We could have done that any time after Russet's death!"

"Not any more. Now I really do have a painting that ensures my return." She indicated the trays on the table.

"I don't think so," he said, suddenly gleeful. He pointed at the first of the trays. "Not if you mean that one. I know that jewel. You have it around your neck. I suppose it's your holdfast." He looked at his mother. "If I killed her now, then the effect of the magic of her paintings would lessen enough for you to avoid going to the Scarpen at all. Isn't that right?"

"Yes, but you can't kill her because the painting won't let you," Lord Jade replied impatiently. "Her future is to return to that place, because her holdfast is there."

"We can send it there with an Alabaster!" Jet said, his smile full of malice.

Terelle's mouth went dry. Oh, sweet water. "But not just anybody can do that waterpainting on the table portrayed in the picture," she pointed out. "There are no other waterpainters in the Quartern. None. I have to go home to do that painting."

Jet looked at his mother. "You could do it."

"Yes," she said, "I could. But I'd have to be in Breccia first."

"No, you wouldn't," he said, his grin triumphant. "You can do it here. And we can send it back along with the holdfast. The Alabaster we sent could replicate the scene. There's nothing in what she has painted to indicate the picture is still floating on water, is there?"

They all looked at the first of the two waterpaintings on the table. What he said was correct; it could have been a dry painting dumped in a tray. *And that's not the worst.*

Terelle thought. *I know what he's getting at: a way to kill me right now. Then the magic would die and Jade wouldn't even have to do the painting. The holdfast wouldn't have to be sent to Breccia.* Desperate, she shot a glance at Rubric.

His expression went from puzzlement to comprehension. "Mother, don't! If you decide that's what you will do, it frees Jet up to murder Terelle. And to do it *right now.* Don't you see? Your intention would provide the magic with another way for the picture and Terelle's holdfast pendant to get back to Breccia! If you agree to it, then Terelle would no longer be protected. Jet kills her, and it all becomes irrelevant anyway!"

Lord Jade stared at him. Terelle felt sick.

"Mother," Rubric said. He'd injected a wealth of meaning into the single word, but Terelle wasn't sure how to read it. "You can't have the intention to go at the same time as you have the intention to thwart your going."

Jade considered Terelle angrily, then fixed her gaze on Jet. "You are your father's son. Now get out of here."

"Pardon?"

"Do you know your mother so little?" She seemed to grow in stature, to become suddenly more imposing. Her voice was steely once more. "I'm a healer, sworn never to misuse the power of waterpainting. A healer, sworn never to kill or hurt or maim. *And you would have me murder.* Oh, it might be your hand on the hilt, but it'd be *my* decision that killed Terelle. You're due to leave for Marchford. Rouse your armsmen and leave as soon as you've eaten and packed. Tell your father what happened here and why. Tell him Rubric and I are leaving for the Quartern and that we'll take Terelle with us."

"But—"

"There are no 'buts,' Jet. Your behaviour has been reprehensible and your way of thinking disgusts me. Now go."

"I know what Father would want," he said, drawing his sword. "He'd tell me to kill this barbarian, and that's exactly what I'm going to do."

"Then you'll have to go through me," Rubric said. He raised his blade into a fighting stance.

Terelle frowned, concentrating hard to understand the conversation when the impassioned words were uttered so fast.

Jet's expression was one of amused contempt. He strode across the breadth of the room towards his brother, saying, "I've got better things to do with my time than fight my pathetic little sister. Get out of my way, little girl."

Rubric hurtled at him in a rage. Jade shrieked at him, without effect. At the last moment, Jet realised Rubric was in earnest and parried the stroke heading for his chest. Terelle spun on her heel, thinking to head for the door, but Jade was blocking her way. Terelle grabbed up the nearest chair instead, using the upholstered seat as armour for her chest. She pointed the chair legs at Jet.

Jet feinted and Rubric lunged, to be disarmed by a clever twist of Jet's blade which sent the sword spinning through the air to hit the far wall. "White-hot anger is never the way to win a fight," said Jet, mocking.

Turning his back on Rubric, he advanced on Terelle, only to find she was already running straight at him, still clutching the chair. Before he could decide how best to deal with chair legs, she was on him. The force of her attack bowled him over flat on his back. His sword jammed into the wood of the seat and, as she fell, her full weight crashed down on him with the chair between them. The blade bent, twisted, then snapped.

To complete Jet's humiliation, Rubric used his water-lord skills to dump the water from the paint trays and the ewer on his brother's face.

For a long moment no one moved.

Jet lay on his back with the chair on top of him, as if he couldn't believe what had just happened. Rubric looked shame-faced as he calmed down. Terelle stared at the water trickling across the floor. *I wonder if I will ever get used to folk being so careless about wasting it.*

"It's almost dawn," Lord Jade said to Jet, her tone still without compromise. "Collect your men and leave."

Drying himself with his water talent, Jet climbed to his feet, broken sword in his hand. For a moment Terelle wondered if he'd defy his mother, but in the end he headed for the door. As he passed his brother, he flung the broken sword at him and snarled, "Don't bother coming back. And I promise you, this half-breed cousin of ours will never cross the border to the Quartern alive. Father and I'll see to that."

Terelle picked up another chair defensively and positioned herself behind Lord Jade, but Jet let himself out without looking at her and slammed the door behind him.

Jade turned to face Terelle, who took a deep breath and replaced the chair at the table, right side up. "And so all along you lied about the possibility of wrecking the house?" the woman asked, her tone heavy with loathing. "And now you've wrecked my family instead."

"Your family was wrecked long ago," Terelle replied, more comfortable with speaking Khromatian now that the immediate danger had passed. "And you know it."

"You're rude and ill-mannered. As it appears we have to travel together, I'll endeavour to be civil, but don't ever expect me to forgive you. We'll leave tomorrow." She turned to Rubric. "You should know me better than to think your warning was necessary. And Jet was right about your temper. Learn control, or you'll be the next one breaking noses." She turned on her heel and left the room.

Terelle and Rubric eyed one another warily.

"Are you mad at me, too?" she asked.

He walked over to retrieve his sword. "I love my mother; never doubt it. And I'll defend her over you any day. But I hate my two brothers, despise my father and loathe my grandfather who runs this whole muck pot of a country." He snorted. "We Verdigris are the slag heap of a family on top of the midden. You know what? I'm *glad* to go. But it'll be a long time before I forgive you for involving my mother. Do you think my father will ever forgive her? It's not in him."

"It's not her fault she'll have to go to the Quartern."

"That won't count with the rotten bastard." He slid his sword back into his scabbard.

"I had to paint her. If I hadn't, she could have worked out a way to paint something to undo what I was doing or to prevent my escape, or something. I couldn't risk it. It's not as bad as it looks. She'll have to go to Breccia, but then she can return here, I promise. If that's what she wants."

He didn't comment. Instead he sighed and asked, "Tell me, how the blighted hells did you get out of the tower?"

"I made a rope and climbed down a ladder and a drain-pipe. How did you know I was down here?"

"Jet woke up and sensed you. He woke Azure, and

Azure woke Mother and she told me. A rope and a drain-pipe, eh?" He raised an eyebrow. "Now that's not bad—for a girl."

"Oh? I can't say I was overly impressed with your manly efforts as an armsman."

"I thought the water was a nice touch."

She stared at him and then started to laugh. "Rubric, in another time and another place and under other circumstances, I might have liked you."

"Likewise. Terelle, take my advice, go on up to the tower and barricade yourself inside until such time as you see Jet ride out, all right?"

She nodded soberly. "I think that might be a good idea. In fact, would you mind escorting me there?"

Elmar stared at the pass ahead of them, a hollowed-out scoop between two mountain peaks. Heaped on either side were piles of what he now knew was snow. Mist seeped through the gap like fingers blindly seeking to clutch passing travellers. It had snowed the night before, a first for him and Dibble, and when they'd woken up that morning and ventured out of the bivac, it had been into a soft white world. The starkness of the mountains and rocks was mellowed by their white blanketing and sounds were muted. Snow made the stunted trees more resplendent than grotesque.

"What did that last wagoner say about the next bivac?" he asked Dibble. "I imagine the wind sweeping through that pass would freeze our balls off overnight without one."

"Should be there any minute now. Has blankets, but firewood scarce." Dibble looked miserable.

Desert chill was bad enough, but this icy air was something else. It seeped into Elmar's cheeks and froze him from the inside out. It chapped his lips and numbed the tips of his ears and the end of his nose. Putting one foot in front of the other in the snow was exhausting. It was a long while since they'd been able to hitch a ride; wagons didn't travel in bad weather, unless they could afford their own waterlord to push the snow aside and dry out the road. He spared Dibble a glance, careful not to show sympathy. If there was one thing he knew, it was when to be a friend and when to be the overman in charge.

Dibble saw the look and pulled himself together. "We're losing the light," he said, his tone carefully neutral.

Elmar looked up at the sky. The peaks and the pass had all disappeared, cloaked by cloud. Lower down, mist wisped across the face of the rocks and the gnarled trunks of the trees. A capricious wind whooshed and gusted down the slopes, only to die and leave the air still, awaiting the next freezing blast.

"We won't be able to see the road soon," he predicted, his own disgust barely under control. *Give me the Quartern any day. Dry heat and no ridiculously lavish excess of water.* "Almost enough to make me want to worship the Sunlord. How are we off for food, Dibs?"

"You can choose between dinner tonight and breakfast tomorrow morning, but you won't get both. Elmar, what's the matter? You've been as scratchy as a pebblemouse in a sand patch ever since you woke up this morning. You should be feeling happy as a frog in a dayjar. We must be almost there."

He stifled a sigh. "I'm fine." He wasn't though; he was worried. Travelling was one thing; deciding how to rescue Terelle from a place he knew nothing about was another.

Trudging on, he childishly enjoyed stomping pristine snow into muddy slush, even as the road ahead disappeared into a white nothingness. Damp began to bead on his coat as the air around them blurred.

"Is that a building ahead?" Dibble asked.

But when Elmar looked, the mist swirled thicker and he couldn't see anything. He ducked his head and plodded on. In the end they missed the bivac altogether. It was set a few paces off the road to the right, half-buried under a thick layer of fresh snow, and they passed it in the mist. Luckily a gust of wind sweeping through the pass cleared away a patch just as Elmar looked back. He glimpsed the unmistakable shape of the chimney about two hundred paces behind. Stopping dead, he called to Dibble, now slightly ahead of him. "Hey!" he said.

"Did you hear that too?" Dibble asked. He was looking towards the pass. The road rose steeply just past the bivac, then dipped again, so they could see nothing of the track ahead even as the mist began to clear.

"No. What? I just wanted to say we passed the bivac." He pointed behind him. "It's back there."

"I thought I heard something ahead."

Elmar cocked his head to listen, but the mist dampened sound. When riders burst over the crest, they were already on top of them, taking him by surprise. He glimpsed alpiners, armsmen, spears, alpiner breath on the cold air; heard the snorting, the jingle of harness, the swearing of startled men. He flung himself to the side, but the lead mount shouldered him anyway, sending him staggering. Dibble leaped the other way and tumbled awkwardly.

Alpiners propped and reared and veered around them.

One of the riders failed to keep his seat and crashed to the ground.

"What the wilted hells do y'think you're doing, you water-wasting scum!" Dibble yelled in shock.

Elmar could have throttled him. He had used the language of the Quartern. Then he realised it was even worse than he'd thought. The man Dibble had singled out to swear at was Lord Jet Verdigris.

Thoughts poured through his head in a jumble. *Jet's a stormlord . . . he'll recognise us . . . I'm dead . . . we're both frizzling snuffed . . . and I don't have my blighted sword.* He already knew there was no escape route. To the left of the track, a steep slope tumbled down to the icy mountain torrent. To the right, behind the bivac, a rock cliff slick with ice and snow formed a barrier wall. It was fight—or nothing. He moved with lightning speed. He flung off his cloak and yanked his pack from his back to heave it at Jet.

Caught unawares and still trying to calm his spooked mount, perhaps not yet fully understanding who they had run down, Jet was hit in the face by the flying pack. He lurched half out of the saddle, and the alpiner reared to toss the waterlord the rest of the way to the ground. Before Elmar could get to him, another rider pushed his mount in front to protect his lord. Elmar, knowing what Jet could do with his power, ducked and rolled under the animal. A hoof caught him painfully in the shin, but he uncurled on the other side and cracked Jet on the skull with the heavy end of his staff.

He had no time to see how effective the blow was. The rider pulled his mount around to shoulder him away from the fallen lord. Elmar backed away, just avoiding the swish of a blade past his ear. A glance around told him the rest of the riders were gaining control of their mounts. Two who'd evidently ridden on in the initial rush were now stationary down the track, mist swirling around them. They had two pack alpiners and they blocked the escape route downhill. *That makes, um, ten of them altogether.*

Someone yelled, "It's those blasted barbarian salt-lovers!"

We're shrivelled.

He glimpsed Dibble standing on the other side of the track, his back to a wall of mist which covered the edge of the road and the steep fall into the ravine.

He fluttered a hand signal to Dibble and then eased his fingers into a good grip on his staff. On the other side of the mounted man, Jet was dragging himself to his knees. *Sunblast. We'll be so much carved-up meat by nightfall.*

Dibble didn't fail him. He brought his staff up under the alpiner closest to him, whacking the beast in the delicate underbelly and raking the end, hard, towards its rear. The poor animal screamed and bucked. Its rear hooves slammed into another mount. In a moment the riders were once again in chaos. One alpiner backed over the edge of the road and disappeared soundlessly with its rider into whatever lay below. Another man lay senseless on the track bleeding from the head, although whether Dibble or a hoof had been responsible, Elmar didn't know.

While the man shielding Jet with his mount was distracted by the commotion Dibble had achieved on the other side of the track, Elmar smacked his mount on the rump with the staff. The animal slewed sideways, eyes rolling. Using the end of the pole, he then jabbed Jet hard in the stomach. The Watergiver doubled up, enabling

Elmar to thwack him over the back of the head, hard.
This time he made no mistake. The man was out cold.
Three down. Two spears from different directions sailed
through the air. He ducked, just avoiding being impaled
by the first. The second ripped through the flesh of his
upper arm. He glimpsed Dibble being downed on the
other side of the road, but couldn't be sure if he was killed
or not.

Please don't let there be another waterlord in this lot.

It was hopeless, he knew that. On foot, armed only
with knives and staves, an injured arm... *Watergiver save
me.* A spear grazed his leg, leaving a furrow of blood. A
man dropped dead in front of him. A cloud of vapour
burst forth in the air around his body.

What the—? For a moment he didn't understand. Then
he realised. He'd seen rainlord kills often enough, but
never into cold air... A dead man's water. A blossoming
of vapour to signal death. *But who—?* He had no idea
who'd killed the fellow.

Three dead and Jet out of it. Ignoring the blood, not yet
feeling any pain, he swung his staff at an alpiner bearing
down on him, swinging the wood across the animal's
nose.

Sunblast it, I hate hurting animals...

The alpiner reared, and the rider leaned forward, still
in control, readying his scimitar for a slash. He never
completed the stroke. A block of snow struck him from
above like a boulder, knocking him to the ground. Elmar
finished him off with his staff. What the pickled pede was
going on? No time to work it out. *Four down. No, five.* He
wanted to check to make sure the waterlord was dead, but
Jet's men—those who were left—kept him away. There

seemed to be suspiciously few armsmen still mounted and fighting. Maybe Dibble had taken care of another one or two when he hadn't been watching. No, Dibble was only just scrambling to his feet.

The flow of blood from his arm made his staff slippery. And another armsman was trying to ride him down.

He turned and fled. Just as the alpiner drew level, Elmar used his staff to vault out of the way. Pain shot through him from his wound, making him grunt. Plunging feet first into another armsman running towards him was pure serendipity. He stomped on the man's head, breaking his nose and cheekbone. *Good one, El.* He turned to see what the mounted man was doing, just in time to see more snow, a lot more snow, fly through the air, hitting the man's alpiner this time. Alpiner and rider fell. The rider appeared unhurt, but the moment he stood he sagged like wet paper and crumpled, dead, at Elmar's feet.

Another explosion of warm water vapour into the cold air. Mounts were bolting in all directions and they all seemed to be riderless. The only men who were still mounted were the two down the track, and neither of them had moved. Dibble sat up, looking dazed. The two men on their feet were assailed on all sides by flying clumps of snow. They started running down the track, all thought of fighting apparently abandoned. The air was thick with chunks of white, but none of it hit Elmar, which seemed odd. Dibble, upright once more, someone's sword in hand, was gazing around, his mouth hanging open. Elmar dodged a riderless trotting alpiner, its head flung up in terror as it passed, and made his way to Dibble's side.

"You all right?" he asked, clamping his hand over his

own bleeding arm, trying to stop the flow. The leg could wait.

"I think so. Head aches like sunfire. Might have cracked a rib, and my left hand is going to swell up like a melon, but I'm still alive. Thought I wasn't going to be. What the sunblasted hells is going on? This snow stuff—is it normal for it to fly off cliff-sides and clobber people?"

Elmar laughed. "Somehow I don't think so. Snow's just water in another form. Reckon we have a rainlord around here somewheres, one who's on our side."

"Is Jet alive?"

"Unconscious at least. Maybe even dead. Won't be bothering us for a while."

"Did you see either of the other brothers?"

"No. No Terelle, either. Reckon we're safe for a bit, though we'd better work out what's going on. Work out why those two back down the track haven't done a scarper too." He stared in their direction, but the mist still swirled around them. "One of them the waterlord, you reckon?"

"Reckon so. Whoever they are, let's hope they haven't got us on their death list."

Using his dagger, Dibble hacked some fabric from the clothing of the dead man next to him. Elmar sat down and Dibble knelt beside him to bind his arm.

Elmar didn't take his eyes off the waiting riders. The light had faded fast but he could just make out the shapes of several bodies lying in the snow at their feet. The two running men, he assumed. He raised his gaze to stare at the riders as they urged their mounts forward. The mist blurred their outlines and curled around the feet of their alpiners in a way that could not have been natural.

"El," Dibble whispered. "I think we're the only ones

left alive." He gazed around, troubled. No one was stirring and the cries and grunts of the wounded were stilled. "And we didn't kill most of them."

"No."

They both climbed wearily to their feet. Elmar leaned heavily on his staff, with Dibble supporting him under one arm. He could not have battered away anything larger than a butterfly right then; it was all he could do to stand upright.

"Elmar," one of the two riders said, as the last of the mist drifted away, "it's all right. Sit down before you fall. We'll attend to any problems left here."

He gaped. And sat down so suddenly he nearly pulled Dibble off his feet.

I'm delirious, he thought. He blinked, but the man coming towards him was indubitably Lord Jasper Bloodstone. Who should have been back stormshifting in the Quartern. Finally he blurted, "Lord Jasper! What the weeping hells are you doing here?"

"Saving your disrespectful arse, I hope. Although by the way you're bleeding over everything, I'm not so sure."

"Lord *Jasper*?" the other man asked, turning to look at the Cloudmaster.

"Ah, well, yes, actually. I'll explain that later."

"Yes, I rather think you'd better!"

"Umber, there's one still alive over there..."

"Lord Jet," the other man replied, without even looking at the fallen waterlord as he dismounted. "I think he might still be breathing."

He's the watergiver, Elmar thought. *And one who knows Lord Jet, too.*

The man called Umber walked unerringly to where Jet

still lay. With an ease that spoke of a confident familiarity with his mount, Jasper dismounted. Elmar rested by the roadside, his head spinning, feeling sick.

"I've tied up the arm," Dibble said, "But it really needs stitching, I think. The leg's not so bad."

Umber looked up from where he was kneeling by Jet's prone body. "Fractured skull, I would think. He may make it."

Who the sandhells is he? Elmar grimaced. Pain was finally making itself felt, and he couldn't decide which injury hurt the most.

"No chance," Jasper said. He started to draw his sword.

"No need," Umber said. He sounded surprisingly cheerful. "Never did think he was much of a human being."

Then, as they all watched, Jet's body shrank. His bones danced and jerked as his flesh and sinew dried. His water melted the snow around him, until he was a twisted carcass, as dry as carrion scorched in the sun and draped with his clothing, in a patch of bare earth. The cloud of vapour that had been his life wisped away in the wind.

Dibble looked utterly shocked.

Umber grinned at him. "Easy when a waterlord is unconscious."

"I was told he tried to kill Terelle," Jasper said, unrepentant. Without sparing Jet a further glance, he cut away some cloth from the garb of one of the dead to bandage Elmar's leg.

Sunlord save us, Elmar thought. *Has the Cloudmaster found us another stormlord?*

"Umber and I will throw the bodies off the road into the ravine," Jasper continued. "Better do that first in case someone comes. Dibble, see what you can do about the alpiners. Perhaps we could keep two for you and Elmar, then unsaddle the rest and set them free to find their own way home?"

"Not if home is Verdigris Manor," Umber said. "We don't want any hint of this getting back there as a warning that we're on our way. I'll check their branding."

Half-unconscious with fatigue and pain and blood loss, wrapped against the cold in his own cloak as well as Jasper's, Elmar watched as the large man checked the alpiners he and Dibble managed to catch, decided they were all army mounts from the Southern Marches, and shooed all but two of them further down the track by lobbing snowballs at them.

He was no longer sure what was real.

CHAPTER THIRTY-ONE

Red Quarter
Dune Singing Shifter
God's Pellets

If only we had rainlords.

How many times had he wished that in the past half-cycle or so? Kaneth wasn't sure, but too many to count. His requests to the Cloudmaster had been in vain; Jasper had replied saying there simply weren't enough rainlords in the Quartern. Those they had didn't want to come to the Red Quarter. And Jasper wasn't going to force them.

I wish they knew what the Red Quarter is like, he thought. Hauntingly beautiful, a tough red land that spoke to anyone who loved to ride and hunt, a place for a man who didn't like hard streets beneath his feet and walls blocking the view, for a woman who liked the open skies, for people who liked the idea that children could never be born without the right to water. A world where the youngsters ran free as they grew.

He smiled, amused. It was also a place where a man like Kaneth Carnelian was prompted into the poetical.

Still, who would blame him if they could see things like this? His pede, Burnish, had topped the rise of a dune, and he was looking across the expanse of Dune Singing Shifter. Fire creepers covered the slope in front of him, their ruby blossoms spilling like gemstones down the incline. In between the creepers, the furry white flowers of the smoke-bush were ruffled by the breeze. He listened, expecting the gusts to bring the wispy sound of the dune wren's song from a perch at the top of a prickly bush.

But there was only silence.

His body tautened. His hand dropped to his scabbard and he loosened the tie at the top to make his scimitar easily accessible. Next to him, Cleve drew rein. Burnish greeted the newcomer pede with its feelers.

"You see something?" Cleve asked quietly.

"More what I don't hear. The birds are silent. Signal to expect an encounter."

Cleve raised his hand to make the signs, while Kaneth scanned the bushes ahead, peering into the folds and twists of the sand valleys. "Must be over the next rise," Cleve murmured. "I can't see anyone from here, but there are bodies of living water out there."

"How many?"

The man shrugged. He may have been a water sensitive, but Kaneth already had ample evidence that he wasn't a particularly good one, although his mother thought otherwise.

"Want me to take a look on foot?" Cleve asked.

He nodded. "Take two men with you. Leave your pedes at the base of the slope. And remember they may sense you." *And how I wish we had a rainlord!* He thought of Ryka, safe back in God's Pellets, and pushed the thought away. *Let's hope their sensitives, if they have them, are no better at the details than Cleve...*

Cleve signalled two of the warriors to leave their own pedes and mount up behind him. No one spoke; from now on they would use only signs. The three men rode into the valley, dismounted, hobbled the pede's antennae and began to climb the opposite slope.

He's good, Kaneth thought. *Just as good as Elmar, although he doesn't have the experience yet. So why don't I like him much?*

The answer came swiftly. *Because I don't trust him.*

And yet the man had never given him reason to wonder about his trustworthiness. He'd killed enough of Ravard's men to prove himself several times over. *I have to give him the benefit of the doubt.*

Gesturing for the rest of the troop to follow—thirty men, five myriapedes besides his own—Kaneth urged Burnish down into the dune vale. After hobbling the two packpedes and leaving them behind to graze, he deployed the troop in a line halfway up the slope to the next rise. He himself sat alone on his pede in the centre. He watched as Cleve, with his two men well spaced, approached the crest of the dune. Uneasiness lifted the hairs on the back of his neck. He hefted his spear. Behind him, his men did likewise.

Before Cleve was able to peer over the edge, the whole ridge vanished behind a wall of heaving pedes and armed men.

Weeping shit, Kaneth thought. *The bastards must have had a sensitive, too.* They'd been waiting just on the other side of the crest. He stood, foot wedged under the saddle handle for stability.

Wait for the moment. Time it right. Wait...Now!

He launched his chala spear at the driver of the pede bearing down on him. It ripped out the man's throat. Blood spurted, a shower of it. The pede, a young one, balked, then reared. It didn't like the smell. Two of its riders were unseated; all the spears thrown flew wild.

And then he was in the middle of a whirling mass of men and pedes and flashing scimitars. Thought didn't exist any more, only reaction. And determination that he wasn't going to die, not this time. Yet somewhere he must have been noticing the things that mattered: how many pedes they had, how many men—and who their leader was. Not Ravard. A bald man. Probably a fellow nicknamed Redpate then, a pedemaster from one of the nearby tribes of the dune. Their numbers were evenly matched with his God's Pellets troop, but the attackers had the advantage of the higher ground.

"*'Ware ziggers!*" someone yelled.

A high-pitched shriek in the air, rising still higher. No, not one, several shrieks. The heart-stopping, fear-inducing shrilling of ziggers on the move. *Shrivelled hells.* Were these tribesmen sand-witted? In close combat, a zigger was easily confused and didn't much care whose nose or eye it ripped open.

No time to worry about it.

If he died, he died.

A screaming red figure leaped from a pede onto Burnish, jabbing spear in hand. Kaneth flicked the reins and Burnish slewed. The warrior was jerked off balance. With his pede prod, Kaneth parried the clumsy thrust coming his way. He tucked the reins into his belt and drew his scimitar. With a savage swipe of the blade, he slashed at the man's wrist, almost severing his hand. In silent shock, the warrior toppled.

Unrestrained, Burnish bolted free of the melee. It took Kaneth a moment to retrieve the reins and haul the animal back into the fray. At least the manoeuvre gave him a clear view of the battle. It wasn't going well.

A zigger homed in on him. He whipped his palmubra from his head and slammed the beetle into the hard segments of his pede. He saw one of his warriors cut another zigger in two with his sword; not a bad stroke from the back of a pede in the middle of the battle. Bleeding miraculous, in fact. He couldn't hear any more of the little monsters.

His gaze sought and found Cleve. He was still on the ground, attacking the enemy tribesmen from below by hacking at their legs. Effective, especially when their pedes were fully loaded with riders and therefore sluggish. Dangerous, though. A pede used its mouthparts as weapons.

Yelling the man's name, he gained Cleve's attention and signalled him to kill Redpate's mount. Cleve hesitated. Annoyed, Kaneth tried to approach closer, but the pede was flanked by others and no one was slipping through. He yanked Burnish to a halt and, needing more mobility, leaped to the ground, scimitar in one hand, jabbing spear in the other. He dodged through the battle seeking Redpate's mount, then attacked it head on. It sought to run him down, so he ducked first under the flailing feelers, then dived to the ground, rolling onto his back with his jabbing spear held to deflect the snapping mouthparts. The pede couldn't stop in time and it flowed over him, instinctively drawing its low-slung body upwards by straightening and pulling its legs inwards.

The soft belly was an arm's length above his prone body as it passed. When the last segment brushed overhead, he jabbed his scimitar up and used the momentum of the beast to rip it open. The blade was wrenched out of his hand. Hot guts spilled, writhing like worms, rich-smelling, dragging through the bushes. The beast bellowed and reared, throwing itself sideways. Kaneth emerged from under the rear end, nicked by a sharp-pointed foot. He jumped to his feet and looked back.

The wounded pede thrashed. Its riders toppled. It flung its feelers around, slicing through the fallen. Redpate scrambled out of the way, his face white with shock. Kaneth felt a moment's pity as he spun his dagger into the man's neck and watched him topple. To make sure he was dead, Kaneth grabbed up a fallen scimitar and slit his throat. Glancing around, he saw Cleve dodging the whiplash of the antennae as he fought another of the unseated men. Before Kaneth could go to his aid, Cleve finished him off. Another armsman put the pede out of its misery.

"Dune god save you, Sandmaster," Cleve said, as they ran for Burnish. "You should've been squashed as flat as a sand-louse." It could have been a joke, but the deep anger in the man's voice told Kaneth otherwise. Another thing he needed to think about when he had time.

"Sound the retreat," he said as Cleve mounted behind him.

"Why? We got them beat!"

With an effort, he restrained himself and the sharp retort on the tip of his tongue died unspoken. "Do it." As he swung Burnish back towards the bottom of the gully, Cleve unslung the bullroarer from where it hung on the carapace. Kaneth slowed briefly to give another of his own unseated warriors a chance to climb up. The man grinned his thanks.

As they rode on, the bullroarer circled over his head with the rhythmic sound unique to the tribe of God's Pellets. His men pulled out of the fight, and the attackers let them go. The fatal wounding of the pede and the death of their leader had turned the outcome of the battle Kaneth's way, as he'd known it would. As far as he could see, the attackers had no extra mount to replace the one that had been lost, and Redpate's death had rocked them. He suspected they had been on a day's foray out from their encampment, perhaps just a hunting trip, when they had sensed the God's Pellets men.

Once Kaneth reached Cleve's pede, he halted to let him dismount and to wait for everyone to reassemble. "What happened to the rest of the ziggers?" he asked.

"It was an accidentally broken cage," one of the men replied. "I think most of them were squashed, lucky for us. One of their own men got one in the ear." He grinned and added, "Serves him right."

"Are we missing anyone?"

"Yes, Benwith," another said, naming one of the men Cleve had taken on foot to the ridge.

"You certain?" Kaneth asked.

"Unless you can live with a spearhead buried to the haft in your eye."

"Blast it. That was rough luck. He'd just got married too." *Pedeshit, I hate that.* He would never get used to it, never. "Any others?"

"Pol here has a broken arm," Cleve said. "And his brother was smashed in the mouth with a pede prod. Lost some teeth."

Before he could respond, a pale-faced Pol said, "The lad, Guyden. He fell off my mount right early and I lost sight of him."

"Anyone see what happened to him?" Kaneth asked.

"I can see those white beads of his," one of the men replied. "They've put him up on one of their pedes—look!"

Kaneth stared back at where Redpate's men were still milling around what had been a battlefield, collecting the wounded. One thing, with those damned white beads of his, Guyden was easy enough to spot. He sighed. "Right. Let's go get him. Pol, you and your brother wait here." Everyone knew his policy: it was paramount that prisoners be either rescued or killed. They couldn't afford to have someone tortured to reveal the secrets of God's Pellets.

"Crescent!" he shouted, indicating the configuration he wanted. "We'll try talking first." He took the centre and as they advanced upwards, the pedes on the two wings paced faster and further out until they cupped the attackers. Kaneth pulled off his tunic, wrapped it around his scimitar and held it high as a sign they were ready to parley.

The warriors mounted as they approached, neither showing aggression nor accepting the parley by similarly sheathing a scimitar.

Kaneth halted some distance away. He spoke into the silence. "I am Lord Kaneth Carnelian, otherwise known as Kher Uthardim." Glibly lying, he added, "I can take your water." While speaking, he glanced to where Guyden was mounted, apparently unharmed.

"Give us the lad and we'll let you return to your camp."

The men exchanged glances, hesitating, then one of the older warriors gave a nod, and gestured to Guyden. The lad dismounted and ran to climb up behind Cleve. Kaneth signalled his men to leave. He waited until they were clear, but still didn't move himself. He had no intention of turning his back on any of their attackers and he just had to hope that none of them called his bluff. There was no way he could take anyone's water, although he supposed he could move the sand under their feet—and probably bring the whole dune down on top of himself as well.

They took the hint and urged their mounts up the slope, bearing their dead with them. When only the slaughtered pede was left to mark the battlefield, Kaneth rode after his men. Sometimes, he reflected, it was handy to have your enemies scared of you.

.

The troop arrived back at God's Pellets just as the sun was setting the next day. Burnish was about to enter the canyon leading to the inner valley when Cleve dismounted, sent his pede onwards with his riders and approached Kaneth to ask if they could talk. Kaneth curbed his annoyance; he wanted to see Ryka and Kedri. He wanted a bath and a meal and time to be with his family. But the young warrior had been brooding ever since the fight on Dune Singing Shifter, and he knew he had to deal with it now, or face worse problems later.

"Of course," he said, then added with slight hope, "if you feel it can't wait."

Heedless of the irritation in Kaneth's voice, Cleve continued, "You know what will happen the moment we enter the camp. My mother will hover and Lord Ryka and your son will have all your attention. But I need to ask you to explain why you did what you did on Dune Singing Shifter."

"Very well." He gestured to the driver on the pede behind him to lead the way in, saying, "Tell the camp Cleve and I will be there shortly." He stayed where he was as the others filed past into the canyon. "I'm guessing you want to know why I asked you to kill the pede."

"More than that."

"Well, get it off your chest and we'll talk about it. We'll walk the canyon." He tied the reins to the saddle handle and slid down to the ground. He poked Burnish with his prod and it ambled happily after the others in its meddle, dreaming perhaps of green grass and rest and as much water as it could drink.

"Kher Uthardim," Cleve began as they walked into the entrance of the canyon, "it's no secret my mother dreams I'll be sandmaster one day. But I know—unlike my mother—that I've much to learn. I know I'm a fine warrior. But I also know there's much more to being a sandmaster than fighting. A sandmaster has to know how to keep the tribes together, how to lead men the way you do."

Cleve paused, perhaps hunting for the right words. Around them, the darkness deepened as all light was cut off by the steep walls of rock on either side. "I was brought up on the dunes. You weren't, so maybe you feel differently. We survive here because of the pedes. They make us what we are. We don't kill them. And here within God's Pellets, we don't have enough of them anyway. We must have more if we're to win this war. And yet you deliberately killed one, a fine beast that belonged to the pedemaster of those warriors. Then, once it was dead and you'd killed Redpate, you didn't take advantage of their confusion or their leaderless state. You withdrew! Even when you returned to pick up young Guyden, you could've brought them to their knees. You could've drowned them in sand. It could've been a great victory, instead of a small one. Benwith's death would have counted for something."

"Benwith's death did count for something. And perhaps that is the difference between you and me."

Cleve looked blank.

"For you, the worst things that happened were the death of a pede and the lack of a huge victory that would have sent a message to the tribes?"

"Yes."

"To me, the worst thing was Benwith's death. I liked the man. Young, had a bright future. When I asked you to take two men, you chose him because you had confidence in him. That man is no more."

Cleve glowered. "Of course it was a tragedy. I know that. I don't need telling, as if I'm a child."

"Then think about it. If we'd gone on fighting, more would have died. Our men, as well as theirs. Never underestimate the determination of armsmen who think they're trapped with no way out. Yes, we could've beaten them. Yes, we could've seized their pedes and if any men escaped, they'd have had to walk home. Once there, they'd have taught their children and their children's children to hate us. If you become sandmaster of all the dunes in the future, that would have been your legacy to resolve: resentful men bowing to your will only because they'd been humiliated in defeat. You'd be your father, all over again. Successful—and hated by half those he ruled. Is that good governance?"

Kaneth suspected Cleve was staring at him with a

complete lack of comprehension after that last sentence, but it was too dark to tell. He'd concocted a Reduner word for "governance" out of words meaning "clever" and "ruling," because as far as he knew the language did not have such a word of its own.

Sunlord damn it, Reduners all need schooling...He sighed inwardly. Ryka was always saying the same thing, and she did her best with the children, but they both knew there had to be peace first.

Picking his way over the stones littering the way, he said, "To me, people will always be more important than pedes. If the death of a pede turns a desperate fight into a victory, then it is justified. More of our men would have died or been badly injured if I hadn't slaughtered that animal and downed their leader. The men retreated, leaderless and in trouble. They were defeated. Because I was merciful, they'll be grateful, rather than bitter."

"They'll think you weak, and laugh."

Kaneth shrugged. "I don't agree. And you have to realise the middle of a battle is not the time to ask for explanations of an order given by the person in command. Do that again, and you'll be working as the camp cook's boy. Understand? I mean it. There won't be another chance."

"Yes, Kher. I—It won't happen again."

"It had better not. If there's anything else, get it out in the open now."

"Just that lad, Guyden—he's not working out."

"Isn't he? I was watching his training session the day before we left the valley. I thought he was doing well."

"Oh, he's a fine fighter, and he works hard. None of that is the problem. But out there on Dune Singing Shifter, he froze. Then apparently fell from his mount without any reason. The time before that, he didn't fight well, either. He's a coward at heart, I think. When it comes to the kill, he wavers."

"He's young yet. Put him on valley duties for another half-cycle. Perhaps what he needs is more maturity."

"Possibly."

His tone told Kaneth that he was dubious. *I'm going to have to deal with this,* he thought. *It goes deeper than just this incident.* "Cleve, I don't think we share the same vision for the dunes."

"You can't think I believe in Davim's dreams of random rain!" He looked shocked.

"That's not what I meant. I'm sure you must have given some thought to how we can move from what we are now, a small band of men and women with insufficient warriors and weapons and food, to being the main tribe of the dunes. With someone of our choice—let's call him dune-master—ruling all the dunes."

"Yes, of course."

"Then tell me, what would you do differently, if you ruled God's Pellets instead of Vara and me, and people looked to you for leadership?"

Cleve hesitated.

"It's not a trick question."

"Will you hold what I say against me?" Cleve asked, his tone heavy with caution.

Kaneth gave a low laugh. "I'm not a man who bears grudges. If I was, this fight would be personal and Ravard would already be dead in his own tent, with his throat slit. And I'd probably be dead too, but with a smile on my face."

"I think you're too soft," Cleve said at last. "We should

strike the tribes who support Ravard, one by one. Swift raids, plundering their stores, killing their sons, stealing their pedes. Quick retreats back to the safety of the Pellets. We hit them at their tents, at their waterholes, when they graze their meddles. They should fear us, more than they fear Ravard and Dune Watergatherer. Then they'll support us, not him." His voice warmed, animated. "Instead, what are we doing? We patrol the dunes to prevent Ravard's raids of the White and Gibber Quarters. We harry him before he comes near so he doesn't discover where we are. We attack only armed troops who are looking for us. And it gets us nowhere."

They were reaching the end of the canyon. Ahead of them, Kaneth could see the twilight sky. He said, "You're right about one thing. If we followed your way, the tribes would fear us. But that's not the way to strength."

Scorn seeped into Cleve's tone. "I don't think you're right. I think the only reason you don't lose the respect of others is because people think you're Uthardim returned. If it wasn't for that, you'd be derided as a coward."

He was amused. "Do you think I'm a coward?"

"No, of course not! No one who saw what you did today would think that. But most tribesmen out there don't see you as a fighter. They don't see you at all, because you leave their encampments alone even if they support Ravard. So they suspect you're cowardly, or at least weak. Why by all the withering winds don't you declare yourself Uthardim returned, reincarnation of our greatest hero? Warriors will flock to your banner."

"Because it would be dishonest. I am not that Uthardim. If people want to call me Uthardim, that's fine—but I won't pretend to be what I'm not."

Cleve shrugged. "What does it matter?".

They emerged from the end of the canyon. Their two pedes grazed nearby.

"It matters to me," Kaneth said. He whistled to Burnish. Reluctantly, the beast eased its way across the grass to his side. "Cleve, sooner or later you are going to have to commit to my policies—or repudiate them publicly. Make sure you choose the right path. Because if you don't, you die. Let's ride on. I'm hungry, if nothing else."

Robena met them at the first tent, demanding to know why her son was the last into camp on the very day she'd prepared his favourite dishes for dinner, insisting he'd better come and eat before it was spoiled.

Kaneth dismounted and handed over the reins to a pede boy who came running up. As he threaded his way through the tents, he was remembering that Cleve was Davim's son. He contemplated the idea that the man was the stone in his sandal: the enemy within who could leave you lame and dying.

CHAPTER THIRTY-TWO

Red Quarter
God's Pellets
Dune Watergatherer

"It was just a skirmish. I'm not hurt."

Kaneth was trying to sound nonchalant, but Ryka knew him too well. He had that haunted look in his eyes, blast him, the same one that appeared every time one of his men died. She glared at him from across the bedroom of the tent. "A skirmish? That's not what I heard. Warriors don't get killed in mere skirmishes."

"It was unfortunate. A tragedy. But it happens, Ry."

"It wouldn't happen half as much if you had a rainlord with you, and you know it. And what about the ziggers?"

"What about them? No one was killed."

He removed his scimitar and knife and began to undo the ties of his tunic. "How's Kedri?"

"He's completely weaned now." She smiled fondly at her son where he sat on the carpet doing his best to ruin the embroidery on a cushion. "He loves his mashed yams and—" She stopped. "You're getting that glazed look again."

"I love him dearly, but I don't believe I'll ever find the

contents of his stomach fascinating." Kaneth dropped his tunic on the bed and poured water into the washbowl. He bent to wash and, when he finished, she used her power to dry him, returning the pure water to the jar.

She said gently, "You'll have an edge when I ride with you." She stood close to him and ran fingers down his chest. He kissed her forehead and whispered his love for her. She was right, and he probably knew it too, in his rational mind. She just had to get him to admit it. "No more discussion. I'll be riding out with you from now on, and that's final."

"But—"

"Kedri is well on his way to being a cycle old—"

"Ryka, I can count. He's still, what, eighty days short of a year?"

"Pernickety detail! The women in camp fight over who's going to care for him. Robena is so besotted, I'm worried she'll obsess over him the way she does with Clevedim. He won't miss me. The time has come for me to make sure Kedri's father stays safe."

Kedri lost interest in the cushion and crawled rapidly over to his father's feet. Once there, he pulled himself up by gripping the leg of Kaneth's trousers. Then he raised his head to stare at his father, making a series of noises that Kaneth swore meant Papa, but Ryka maintained were probably, "Lift me up right now!"

Kaneth bent and picked him up, a besotted expression on his face.

Blighted eyes, she thought, *how I love them.*

"You win," he said. "But if you ever let anything happen to you, I'll kill you myself. Ryka—if I take you along, and there's fighting, you're to stay out of it as much as humanly possible. Will you promise that much? For his sake?" He tapped Kedri on the nose. The boy giggled and demanded more. "Besides, if we have a rainlord, we don't want her to die any time soon."

"I promise. I just want to be there so you can use my rainlord powers. That's all, I swear. No sword play. No risks. I want Kedri to have a mother."

"I'd never forgive myself if anything happened to you."

"Then I'll definitely endeavour to stay unscratched." She shooed him out into the main room of the tent where she'd laid food on the low table in the centre of the carpet, a compromise to Reduner-style eating. "My own cooking. See how domesticated I'm getting? It really is time I climbed onto a pede and rode out onto the dunes."

He lowered himself onto the cushions, dumped Kedri beside him and gave him a piece of crust from the freshly cooked damper to chew on. "You'll miss him."

"Like someone has torn the heart out of me. I know. But still: it is time. And now—tell me why Cleve just wanted to talk to you and why I detect a note of exasperation in your tone when you mention him?"

He helped himself to the food. "I find him hard-hearted and unsympathetic. He doesn't care about people. Men are just so many shells on the game board to be moved about, with him as the gamemaster. Women are just bed partners, no more. And you were right, he can barely contain his contempt for Vara—after all that remarkable old woman has done."

"Yet he seems to have the respect of the young men around him."

He answered her in between mouthfuls of his supper. "Oh, yes. Especially those from his tribe. He's brave and intelligent and he inspires those who follow him. But if they die, he cares not at all, except perhaps if their deaths upset his plans. Are you sure *you* cooked this damper? It's really good."

"It's that mother of his," she said, pulling a face at him. He was always teasing about her lack of culinary skills. "Robena has taught him that nothing else matters except victory against Dune Watergatherer and replacing Ravard as the sandmaster. Cleve has as much chance of being normal as a water drop has of lasting in the midday sun."

Kaneth laid his spoon down as Kedri, his face smeared with masticated damper, climbed into his lap and started bouncing up and down. Wiping the child's face clean with his kerchief, he said quietly, "I love this place. I love the dunes. I like the life—or I would if I wasn't having to fight to keep it all the time. It troubles me to think that if we succeed in ridding the dunes of marauders, we could be handing them over to someone like Cleve. Yet he has a strong following. And I worry sometimes if it's a fault that I still see things from a Scarpen point of view. I'm stained red and I've beaded my hair, but there's part of me that remains a Scarperman."

"Compassion is never a fault. Perhaps when Cleve's older, he'll mellow?"

They exchanged sceptical glances that didn't need any words. She poured him a mug of water as he settled Kedri down in his lap and started bouncing him up and down. Kedri chortled. "Cleve's already pressing me to be more aggressive. And in a way, he's right. So far no one has found us here, but sooner or later that'll change. Today, for example—that lad from Scarmaker was almost captured."

"Guyden?"

He nodded and took the mug of water from her. "Yes. We

rescued him, but he could have been tortured and forced to reveal where we're hiding, if we hadn't got him back."

"I don't think he'd tell. Too much pride, that one."

"Pride?"

"Yes. Odd lad. Intense. Watchful. Quiet. Doesn't seem to make, or even want to make, friends. Helpful around the camp. Hard working. Well liked by the adults, not so much by the lads."

Kaneth tried to drink his water, but Kedri was making grabs for the mug. In the end Kaneth placed it on the table out of his reach.

"Does anyone have a problem with Guyden?" she asked.

"Cleve thinks he's a coward. He froze during the fight today, then fell off and was briefly taken prisoner. Cleve doesn't forgive mistakes easily."

"No, he wouldn't." She snorted. "Being scared seems very sensible to me."

"A dunes warrior is expected to fight, not freeze."

"He can't be much more than fourteen. Give him a chance."

"I will, but not yet. I'll put him on valley roster for the rest of this star cycle. He can hone his fighting skills and make himself useful as a sentry on the knob tops. I've noticed that he's not in the least bit worried by heights. Scampers up to the lookouts faster than anyone else."

Kedri leaned forward to take another swipe at the mug, so Kaneth settled him further back from the table while he finished his meal. He was just cleaning his bowl with the last of the damper when excited voices outside indicated something had happened.

Ryka drew back the door and Vara came straight in

without waiting for an invitation. She wasted no time coming to the point. "Party of four coming in," she said. "Heading straight for us, as if they know where they're going. The sentries spotted them. Two white pedes. I sent some warriors out to meet them."

"*White* pedes?" Ryka looked back at Kaneth and raised an eyebrow. "Some *Alabasters* have come visiting?"

"I told Feroze how to get here. He said he'd pass on the information to the Bastion."

"Those high and mighty salt-diggers coming to visit Vara Redmane?" Vara grinned, displaying her woefully broken and yellowed teeth. She gave Ryka a nudge in the ribs that almost sent her flying and hobbled away.

"This can't be good news," Kaneth said. "No messenger comes this far to deliver happy tidings." He returned to the table to finish his water. The mug, still where he'd left it, was empty. He looked down at Kedri, who gave him a beatific smile. "You spilled my water, you rascal?" he asked with mock seriousness. Kedri gurgled happily. "You little water-waster!"

Ryka dug with her toes at a wet patch on the rug. "All the way over here, by the feel of it. Now that's really clever. He must have tossed the water and put the mug down afterwards. This boy is getting a great deal too clever for his britches." She picked him up and gave him a hug. "Shall we go and welcome the newcomers?"

As they left the tent, Kedri looked back at the mug. If it was possible for a baby not yet a year old to look smug, then Kedri Carnelian did just that.

Much later that night, after the encampment had bedded down for the night, Ryka lay sated and naked in Kaneth's arms. Kedri was sound asleep on his sleeping mat in the inner room, and all seemed right with the world. The Alabasters had brought an innocuous message, offering gifts of salt and thanking Vara and Kaneth and their men for bringing an end to the raids by Reduners into the White Quarter.

And yet Kaneth lay next to her as tense as a pebblemouse smelling a snake. His skin, sheened with sweat, glistened in the lamplight. He said quietly, "We'd better get dressed. We're going to have a visitor."

She didn't argue but rolled out of bed and reached for her clothes. "I can't feel anyone moving this way."

"He'll come."

"Neztor?" He was the leader of the Alabaster party, a middle-aged man who'd been a mine manager until ordered to abandon his mine because of Reduner raids.

Kaneth began to dress. "Yes. I suspect he has a personal message for me and wants to seek out a private word."

She hadn't left his side and she was sure no one had said anything to him that she hadn't heard, but she knew better than to dispute his assertion. He'd be right. He always was. Frustrated, she asked, "*How* do you know these things?"

He shrugged and gave her the same sort of unsatisfactory answer he always did. "He was as tense as a tent rope in a wind. It was the way his muscles reacted to different things said, and to different people. The tiny shifts in the way he sat, or the way his eyelids moved, the way his gut moved along."

She looked revolted. "Are you about to tell me you know what my gut does? Kaneth, that is horrid!"

He grinned. "No, because I don't want to know. I don't

pay attention, any more than you pay attention to every-one's water as they walk around the camp."

"But you know the miniscule rearrangement of Nez-tor's water."

"I don't think of it like that. I just feel he's tense, impa-tient, anxious. So I guess he wants to tell me something, but not in front of everyone else."

"I don't understand how you decide what those tiny adjustments mean."

"Neither do I," he said, "and I find the more I think about them, the less I know. And although I can tell some-one is tense, there is no way I can be certain why, so I can be quite wrong in my interpretations."

"He's on his way now."

"Told you."

She wanted to throw something at him; instead she hurriedly tied her hair back and finished doing up her breeches.

It was Neztor and he was alone.

The letters he brought—there were two—were sewn into the back of his vest, between double layers of leather. One was from the Bastion; the other was from Jasper.

"Do you know what's in these letters?" Kaneth asked as he took them.

"I'm afraid I do," he said. "Everyone in Samphire knows the gist of what's happened."

Kaneth shot a glance at Ryka, and she leaned over his shoulder to read them with him. When they'd finished Jasper's, she said, aghast, "So, in summary, Feroze has been murdered in Khromatis, Laisa is Highlord of Brec-cia, Jasper has married Senya, Terelle is missing in Khromatis, apparently kidnapped and in danger, and I was right: Jasper does need her waterpainting in order to make storms. Elmar and Dibble have gone after her but haven't much idea of where she might be. And that withering idiot Jasper then decided he would go after them."

She didn't mention the main reason for Jasper's letter: to ask Kaneth to look after the water supplies of the entire Red Quarter. She didn't even want to think about what would happen if Jasper and Terelle didn't return at all. The Source would be the only reliable water in the whole Quartern. At the moment, or so Jasper wrote, the Scarpen and the White Quarter had sufficient water for more than half a cycle with the rationing they had in place. He did not mention the plight of the Gibber. He didn't have to; they both knew that even at the best of times, the settles only stored enough for half a cycle. Ryka felt sick. The news was dire, and there was very little they could do.

Kaneth crumpled the letter in his hand, half in anger, half in grief. "Sunblast, Ry," he whispered, "I think this is the worst news I've had since I was told you'd died."

I'll be waterless, she thought. *Maybe Ravard will get what he and Davim wanted after all: a return to a Time of Random Rain.* She swallowed back her fear. "What does the Bastion's letter say?"

Kaneth scanned it quickly. "He's giving his assurance he'll help Jasper and Terelle as much as he can. Oh, Sunlord above! He's preparing for a possible war against the Khromatians. The Alabasters are contemplating a refusal to work there if Terelle and Jasper aren't returned safely and unless Khromatian Watergivers undertake to supply water to Alabaster."

He looked up from the sheet of paper. "Has everyone gone *mad*?"

Several men rode in from the north, sent by the Sandmaster of Dune Singing Shifter, to tell Kher Ravard they'd fought Lord Kaneth but failed to kill him. Worse, they had failed to retrieve the object of their ambush. They had been after either Islar or Clevedim to bring them home with all their knowledge of where Kaneth's camp was hidden, how many men and pedes he had, and how best to defeat him. A youth beaded with ice crystals, whom they'd assumed was Islar, had allowed himself to be captured, but in the end they'd had to give him up. If Clevedim had been with Uthardim, they didn't know it. They had no idea what he looked like.

Ravard swore. *Patience, patience,* he told himself. *You are young. You can wait.* Eventually one of them would find a way to escape. Or someone would find out where Vara, Kaneth and their men were hidden.

Where Garnet is.

What no one understood was where they were getting their water. Water sensitives had roamed the northern dunes for any whiff of static water and found nothing that did not belong to a long-established tribe. No hint of extra or unexpected water, either from people, or pedes, or a waterhole. True, Ravard's men didn't have rainlords skilful at sensing over long distances, but if there'd been anything out there he would have thought that a normal water sensitive would have found it.

Never mind, he told himself. *Islar is a brave and resourceful young man. Clevedim is ambitious. One of them will escape soon and tell us all we need to know.*

CHAPTER THIRTY-THREE

Khromatis
Wilder Pale
Low Plateau Pale

"Are you warm enough, Elmar?" Jasper asked him.

"Warmer than I've been in days. Better fed, too."

Jet and his armsmen had brought packs and supplies fresh from Verdigris Manor. They hadn't gone to waste. Elmar turned his head to look appreciatively at the crackling fire. With the damp weather and the snow, he and Dibble had always had problems lighting a fire in the bivac. With Umber's stormlord skills, that wasn't a problem. He could even dry out a fresh branch snapped from a living tree.

The advantages of being a waterlord, Elmar thought sleepily. He tried to sift through the stray facts drifting through his head. All the men Jet had brought with him were dead. Umber was Terelle's cousin. A stormlord. Jasper was here because the Bastion had written to him in Breccia. While the Cloudmaster was gadding about Khromatis, the Quartern was getting no water at all.

Above all, we have to get him and Terelle home safe.

"How are the wounds?" Umber asked, breaking into his train of thought.

"Throbbing a bit. But whatever you put on 'em last night worked wonders. Hardly felt a thing. Managed to sleep well. Thank you for stitching them up, by the way."

"Ye can use more of the liniment. Good stuff. Kills pain and aids healing. Great for sprains, too. No rider should be without it."

He absorbed that. "You mean it's for the *animals*?"

"Sure. Ye didn't think I carried all that medicine stuff for us, did ye? Liniment, needle and thread, it's all for them. Blithering beasts are always doing dumb things and cutting themselves..."

Dibble muffled a laugh. Elmar glared at him.

"Lord Umber and I will be off now," Jasper said. "If he's forgiven me for deceiving him about who I am."

Umber grinned amiably. "Never was one to care overmuch about titles."

"We should be back in three or four days, at the most, with Terelle. If we aren't, then you'd better turn around and go home because there won't be anything you can do."

"We should be going with you," Elmar protested. "Nothing must happen to you!"

"With your injuries, you'd be more of a hindrance than a help. Even Dibble is still groggy."

"Just remember," Umber added, "ye tell anyone who comes that ye're Lord Umber Grey's men, and ye're under my instructions to be waiting here for my return. Anybody gets nosey, tell him to be sticking his questions up his arse. All right? Oh, and I've disguised the alpiners we purloined and temporarily altered the brands with a bit of clever shaving. I hope it's enough that they won't be recognised."

"People can tell them apart from one another?" Elmar was astonished. The animals were all the same colour and shape and, until then, he'd thought of them as more like birds—virtually indistinguishable from each other once fully grown.

"Of course! But I've cut their manes and tails into a bit of a mess, stained some of their hair and shaved other bits. They don't look like neat military mounts any more. Make sure they are fed and watered. I've shown Dibble how much to be feeding them, and he knows to be warming the water slightly first." With those words he smiled and left the bivac. Dibble followed him out, limping slightly from his bruises, but Jasper lingered.

"Get a good rest, El," he said. "We need you fit for the return journey."

"I'm sorry to have let you down, m'lord."

"Let me down? Salted wells, have you *no* idea how much you achieved? You got back to Samphire and told the Bastion what happened in Marchford. Which is why I'm here. Your news turned *everything* around. The Alabasters went from being secretive lackeys for Khromatis to being our allies. Anyway, I reckon this was always a job for a stormlord, but we just didn't know it." He patted Elmar's shoulder. "Rest and heal, so you'll be able to go back with us."

He let himself out, and a while later Dibble returned. "They've gone," he said. "It's beginning to snow again."

"He's changed," Elmar murmured.

"The Cloudmaster?"

He nodded. "To think I wondered once if he was strong enough to rule the Quartern. He ordered Lord Jet's death like it was nothing. No second thoughts, no agonising over the rights or wrongs."

Dibble shrugged. "I suppose it's no different from running a sword through an enemy in a fight. You didn't see him at the battle for the Qanatend mother cistern."

"Yet Jet's death bothered you. I could see it on your face."

"It was just...the fight was over. We'd won. And then, well, throwing the bodies into the ravine. It was disrespectful. They were armsmen, like us, El. Just fellows trying to earn a living. Fighting them is one thing, not burying them with proper respect is another. You're right; he has changed."

"You want him back the way he was?"

Dibble sighed. "No, I reckon not. Times are bad. We need a strong man. Reckon I'd always follow him to a waterless hell and back, and it helps to know he has the kind of flint to get us home again too."

"The ground's frozen. Would have been withering tough to dig a grave anyway, if that makes you feel better."

" 'Specially when I'd have been the plodder digging the bleeding things, eh?"

They grinned at each other companionably.

Sunlord save me, if the whole ride is going to be like this, I'll end up sandcrazy by the end of it.

An armsman and a groom led the way; another armsman and another groom brought up the rear with the pack alpiners. Behind her, Rubric was silent, out of loyalty to his mother perhaps. Terelle shot a sidelong look at Lord Jade riding beside her. Her stony look of grim anger and determination appeared permanently fixed to her face. Since they had all left the waterpainting room two nights previously, Lord Jade had not spoken to her once, and Rubric had been reticent and distant.

Well, too bad, she thought. Bice had ordered her death and then imprisonment, Jet had tried to kill her and broken her nose, Jade had collaborated in her incarceration. Rubric would be better off without the rest of his poisonous relatives—so was there some reason she should feel guilty about coercing the two of them to Breccia?

Inwardly, she didn't feel good about it. What Russet had done to her was not reason enough to do it to someone else. Yet she had. And she'd have to live with it, because there was no way she could reliably undo the future except by helping them to reach it. Or by dying.

"Have you forgiven me yet for painting your mother in Breccia?" she asked when Jade swapped places with Rubric. "She's a waterpainter. I was afraid of what she might do if she didn't come with me when I escaped."

"She would never have hurt you. I thought you had a good grasp of what people are like under their skins."

"Usually I do. I was brought up in a snuggery. It was the world in miniature."

"You've mentioned that before. What *is* a snuggery?" Then, when she told him, he exclaimed, "Oh, you mean a bawdy house! Really?"

So she told him about her early life. From the way that Lord Jade turned her head slightly Terelle guessed she was trying to hear, so she continued the story past her childhood and pitched her voice to carry. She wanted both of them to know about life in the Scarpen. By the time they stopped for lunch at a shelter along the track, she had covered much of her history, including her part in the war against Davim.

It was a clear day, crisp and cold, but the view was spectacular. After she'd eaten, she approached Lord Jade, who stood at the edge of the road looking down on the valley of Low Plateau Pale.

"It's beautiful," Terelle said. "And you've so much more than we have. Rivers, water falling down from the top of mountains, lakes, ponds, rain, snow, so many different trees. Your waterlords use their power to *stop* it raining. Would it be too much to ask that some of you could find it in your hearts to help us? Send us unwanted water, perhaps?"

Jade's head whipped around. "Do you think I care?"

She didn't answer.

"You don't know what you've done to me," Jade said. "You've wrecked my life. Bice will blame me for this. When I return, he'll make my life hell. You've destroyed all I have; don't ask me to care about your land."

"And you want to stay with a man like that? For what? What does he have that makes it worthwhile?"

Jade turned and walked away.

Rubric watched her go, then marched up to take his mother's place. "Are you trying to upset her?"

"Not deliberately. Look down there, at your home, Rubric. You won't return, not even when you can. You'll like the freedom the Quartern gives you, I promise you. And so would she, if she could untangle herself from her position as Bice's wife. It doesn't sound much better than being a snuggery handmaiden, and believe me, that wasn't much of a life."

"You're *that* sure I'll like it?"

She nodded. "Although maybe not Breccia. It still suffers the effects of the siege and occupation."

"Well, we'll see, won't we?"

As they walked back to the alpiners, a rider came around a corner of the track further up the slope. Terelle felt a tightness in her chest, and thought of Jasper. A resemblance. Same build, same hair, same colouring. But Jasper would never have ridden an alpiner as if he belonged on it, would never have been here in Khromatis, would never have abandoned his duty to the Quartern. Wishful thinking, that was all. She was a dreamer...

Another rider followed, but all her attention was still on the first. He was so like Jasper. And then she was running, feet scudding, oblivious to the danger of falling on the loose stones, not caring, knowing only that it was he, and that he had come. That he had come for her.

He vaulted off his mount, ran towards her, grabbed her up in his arms and whirled her around, saying her name over and over and over as if he wanted to hear it forever.

A moment.

The run of a sandglass.

A sliver of time. How long? She could not have said. But when she emerged from the cocoon of safety where nothing mattered but that she was safe and loved within the circle of his arms, the others were there with the alpiners, regarding them both solemnly. He released her, reluctantly, to return their regard.

"Introduce me," he said.

She wasn't sure she could speak. She was too breathless, her thoughts too confused, her heart too overwhelmed. When she found the words, they didn't sound as if they were coming from her at all. She looked at Jade and Rubric. "This is Lord Jasper Bloodstone, Cloudmaster of the Quartern, and the man I'm going to marry."

She knew there was something terribly wrong when the blood drained from his face and he stood staring at her as if she had sentenced him to death.

The conversation flowed on around her, over her. Introductions: her newly found cousin giving her a hug, his exuberant welcome a distinct contrast to that of the Verdigris family; Jasper trying to be polite to Rubric and Jade when he clearly would have liked to wring their necks; Jade reciprocating his initial antipathy as they sized one another up like frilled lizards in a threat display; Rubric ambivalent, caught in the middle.

Jasper told them how he'd met Umber, how he knew what had happened to her and Feroze, how Elmar and Dibble were now in a bivac because Elmar had been injured in a rock fall. Terelle explained that Rubric and Jade were going to the Quartern because she'd painted them there. Jade asked Umber if he'd seen Jet and his company of armsmen, and he said yes, they'd passed one another without stopping.

And in all the explanations, nothing told her why Jasper had looked at her with such sorrow and dread. All she was sure of was that it was going to hurt her, hurt her terribly. She'd seen it in his eyes. He was never going to marry her.

Within the run of a sandglass they were on their way upwards again. Private conversation was impossible because they had to ride in single file. Once they reached the top of the pass, they were pelted by wind-blown snow, and by the time they reached the bivac they would have been wet and shivering if the two waterlords and Jasper had not done their best to divert the worst of the flurries and keep their clothing dry. The place was packed; not only were Elmar and Dibble there, but so were the drivers of a wagon bringing bolts of linen to the upper pales. Any chance of private conversation was stalled. Terelle acknowledged that the cowardly part of her was glad, because she could go on pretending that everything was going to be all right. She was safe; Jasper was there. And it seemed her cousin was a waterlord too, and no friend to the Verdigris family.

The weather for the next two days kept them confined to the bivac. By the third day, which dawned sunny and warmer, Dibble was wholly recovered and Elmar was well enough to travel. The linen wagon departed that morning after Rubric and Umber had used their power to clear the worst of the drifts all the way to the top of the pass. Immediately afterwards, Terelle and Umber, as the translators, found themselves in the middle of an argument between Lord Jade and Jasper. Jasper was quietly insisting that Jade send her servants back to Verdigris Manor, and that she surrender her paints to Terelle's care until they reached Breccia.

"I don't trust you," Jasper said. "It's as simple as that."

"Terelle took my choices away," Jade said. "What can I do to harm you?"

"I've no idea," he conceded, "but I don't know you well enough to trust you. And you're a waterpainter."

Jade turned to Rubric for support, but he advised her to do as Jasper asked. "We don't need the servants," he said. "And you weren't going to use your paints anyway." He turned to Jasper with a murderous look. "My mother is a healer. She doesn't go around hurting people."

"I'm glad to hear it, but I don't know you well enough to trust you, either."

In the end Jade capitulated, and it was a smaller party that headed off down the mountain towards the Southern Marches.

The next four days of the descent were wet and blustery and unpleasant riding. They were worried about Elmar whose leg had developed an infection. Lord Jade agreed to help him with her healing, and Terelle gave her the paints back so she could use them, then observed the process close-up. Afterwards, wordlessly, Jade surrendered the paints to her once more, anger raging in her gaze. With all that, plus the worry and more inclement weather and the lack of privacy in the bivac, the conversation Terelle both ached and dreaded to have was never initiated.

It wasn't until they were crossing the lower slopes of the Slew Pale towards the border of the Southern Marches that the weather changed. They had a sunny day riding under a blue sky, the air was warm, the alpiners had a spring in their step. After their midday rest, Jasper told the others to ride on, as he and Terelle would walk for a bit.

When they were alone, Jasper came and sat next to her on the rock she had chosen. She pulled off her cap and spread her hair over her shoulders, enjoying the feel of the sun.

Vivie would scold me and say I'll get freckles...

"I think Elmar is going to be all right," she said. "It's wonderful what waterpainting can do. But Lord Jade told me afterwards that she thought his injuries weren't caused by a rock fall. How did he really get hurt?"

"Jet and company. They literally bumped into one

another. And, of course, Jet recognised them. Umber and I—fortunately—rode up just as they were getting tucked into a fight."

She looked at him in horror. "What happened to Jet and the others?"

"They're all dead."

"*All* of them?" Even now some things still had the power to shock her. Men she had known and travelled with, gone.

"We threw all the bodies into the ravine. We couldn't leave anyone alive to say what had happened. They attacked Elmar and Dibble."

"Jet's dead?"

"Yes, I'm glad to say. That was personal. Do you remember the groom, Eden Croft? He told his wife what happened back in Marchford, she told the Greys and they told me."

"Sweet waters, how can you look his mother in the eye day after day without flinching?"

"Easily. Especially once you told me about your broken nose. His father didn't tell him to do that—he did it all by himself."

"Are—are you ever going to tell Jade or Rubric?"

"No, we've all decided never to mention it. Better that way, surely. We've been lucky they didn't spot the alpiners we loosed."

She was silent, absorbing it all. *You've changed, grown tougher. And I wish you'd tell me what you've done to me…*

"Don't ask me to feel sorry, Terelle. The Commander of the Southern Marches declared war on me when he murdered Feroze and the other Alabasters. You'd be dead too, if Russet hadn't painted you. It's my duty to get you safely back to the Quartern. It's my duty to get Rubric and Jade there too, now, in the hope that I can save our land, and I'll do whatever it takes."

"Do you think they'll help us?"

"I don't know about Lord Jade yet, nor Umber either, but Rubric will. You *do* know that he's a woman, don't you?"

She gave him a quick look. "Yes. Except he's not. I mean, he's not trying to deceive anyone. He's a man to himself, and therefore he's a man to me."

He shrugged. "That's fine with me. All I want is another stormlord."

"How did you know?"

"His water. It's, um, not shaped right inside." He sighed. "Sometimes I know things about people I'd rather not be aware of. I like him, you know, and I hope he'll stay in the Quartern." He paused. "And now there's something else I have to tell you. I don't know how to say it so that it won't hurt. There *is* no way."

"When I mentioned we were to marry, you looked as if I'd struck you. Have…have you committed yourself to marrying Senya?"

"I—" He choked and cleared his throat. "Worse."

Sunlord save us… Sorrow scored her heart, robbed her of breath. She couldn't speak. She pulled back a little, removed her hand from his.

"Terelle, I love you. I want to spend the rest of my life with you. I intend to do just that. I didn't bed Senya while you were gone, you must know that."

"You've married her already." A flat statement of fact. She didn't need his confirmation. Sunlord help her, it hurt. *"Why?"*

He had difficulty forming the words. His voice sounded thick. She ducked her head so she didn't have to look at him.

"When Senya came back to Breccia, she was expecting my child. After the baby was born, I married her. It's a girl, Amberlyn."

Each word hammered her thoughts. She swallowed. *I will not cry. I won't.*

He plunged on. "Senya's not interested in Amberlyn, so I've been caring for her. There was a time when I'd have done anything to undo what happened—but I can't say that any more. I love Amberlyn; she's my daughter and she always will be. But none of that is the real reason I married Senya."

"You mean—you mean there's more?" The words half strangled in her throat. *What could be worse?*

He nodded miserably. "Laisa talked to Lord Gold about you and your waterpainting. He decided you were a blasphemous heathen using sorcery." Briefly he sketched all that had happened before he'd left Breccia.

She stared at him in horror. "Are you telling me I can't even go back to the Scarpen? That I'll be *killed* if I do?"

"No, no. It is part of my bargain that charges against you are not pursued. Besides, I'm still the Cloudmaster and Lord Gold has gone to live elsewhere. When we go back, I want Terelle Grey, waterpainter, to have her rightful place in the Quartern, acclaimed for the part she's played and will play to bring us water. We could live in Scarcleft. I—I'd like to have Amberlyn with me, too. If ever I set eyes on any of them again—Laisa, Senya or Lord Gold—it'd be too soon. Terelle, please, please tell me that you can forgive me."

She stood up abruptly, tears wetting her eyelashes. "Of course. But, blighted eyes, this is all too much. Give me time, please. Let me think. No answers now. No discussion now. Just...oh, withering pebbles and sand, I can't *think*."

He rose to face her, and she was grateful he didn't touch her. "I never wanted to hurt you. Never."

"I know. I know. But maybe we were never supposed to be together. You're the Cloudmaster. An upleveller lord. Senya is—"

He snorted. "I'm a settle brat, with a drunk for a father and a whore for a mother. I'm just me, Shale Flint. Never lose sight of him, Terelle. Please. He's what I am under this shell."

"You're also the father of a child I didn't give birth to. I don't want to discuss this. Not yet. Let's catch up with the others." She walked away to where her mount grazed.

"I love you," he said to her retreating back.

"I know."

He came forward to hold her stirrup. She hauled herself up into the saddle and looked down on him. The tears on her lashes still hadn't fallen, and his face blurred. "And I love you, too. I didn't stop loving you when you bedded Senya, so it would be illogical to stop loving you because she had a child as a result. But right now, I just can't handle talking about this. I'm sorry."

She turned her alpiner and headed down the road after the others.

That was when the tears started to fall.

CHAPTER THIRTY-FOUR

Khromatis, en route to the Borderlands
White Quarter, Samphire

"What in God's name do you think you're doing?"

Terelle woke to the outraged words, uttered just outside the bivac by Lord Jade, of all people. For almost ten days—ever since they'd left Verdigris Manor—the woman had hardly spoken to anyone unless the words were essential. But now, at last, something had aroused her to passion. Terelle rolled off the grubby straw pallet and emerged into the dawn light, bleary-eyed.

Jade, hands on hips, was addressing Jasper, who could hardly string a sentence together in Khromatian. The others were attending to their normal morning chores. The smell of hot porridge drifted past from the roughly built rock fireplace.

Terelle smiled at Jasper and said, "She asked you what in God's name you were doing." She looked around and was unable to see that he'd been doing anything at all.

"Ah. I thought it might be something like that. Tell her I'm collecting some water to save the lives of thousands of people in Alabaster in the coming weeks." He waved a hand at the sky in explanation.

Above, bruised-purple clouds gathered, moving in from the direction of the mountains. Terelle relayed the message.

Jade glared at them both in rage. "He's stealing from us!"

Jasper's reply was mild. "I asked Dibble to chat to some of the farmers yesterday along the route. They all say it's been a very wet season this cycle, and they're worried about the pastures failing to bloom, the crops going mouldy and the sheep getting foot rot, whatever that is. They're all wishing the rain would stop and have sent a request for waterlord intervention. So I'm stopping it. I'm taking the clouds to Alabaster with us. I doubt that it'll make much difference to anyone in Khromatis in the long run."

Jade stalked off after Terelle had translated, her back stiff with outrage, muttering something about sacrilege. Rubric and Umber, back from washing at the stream, both studied the clouds and, Terelle guessed, the feel of the way the water was moving, because they gave each other an amused look, followed by Umber's, "Can I help?"

Jasper grinned. "Of course!"

Intrigued, Terelle regarded the men while they pulled water vapour across the sky, and played—on a sky-wide palette—with the clouds they made. *As ever, boys will be boys,* she thought, hiding a smile of delight, and wondered how many farmers would notice the astonishing number of vulgar-shaped clouds in the sky that day.

When they passed the border stone to the Southern Marches, still trailing the thunderclouds after them like a dark frown on the face of the sky, they also left the main road. Under Umber's guidance, they took to the back paths as far as possible from Marchford in order to avoid the remote chance that Hue and Bice might sense Jade nearby. The tracks were lonely and the farms they passed appeared oddly empty of farm labourers. Still more strange, no one was on the road. They passed no carts, no alpinermen, no trudging workers. Umber frowned as they rode, remarking that he'd never seen fields look so unattended.

"No Alabasters," Jasper observed. "Interesting."

Terelle gave him a quick look, but he didn't say anything more. That night they camped in a small wood next to a stream, but the next night, they decided to eat an evening meal and stay at a ramshackle wayside hostelry. The owner informed them in outraged tones that his two Alabaster servants had run away, but if they were prepared for the service to be slow, they were welcome.

As they were about as close to Marchford as they were going to get, it was no surprise to anyone when Lord Jade announced over dinner that she wanted to see her husband and sons.

"Jet will have already told him that you're on your way to the Quartern," Umber said calmly as they sat at a table eating a plain and tasteless supper, a meal which led them to believe the cook had been one of the runaways. Terelle sat close to Jasper and murmured a translation into his ear. When another platter of food was delivered to the table by their host, they all fell silent.

"If you go to see Lord Bice," Umber continued when the man had retreated to the kitchen, "he'll in all probability try to stop you from going to Breccia. Physically. I think you know how difficult that'd be for you. Possibly fatal. I wouldn't do it if I was you."

Rubric nodded in agreement with Umber. "He's right, Mother. Best we don't go there, really."

Abruptly, Lord Jade stood up. For a moment Terelle thought she was going to argue the point, but then all her courage seemed to leak away and her shoulders slumped. "I'm going to eat my meal in the room," she said. She took her plate of food and walked to the stairs.

"She's not going to run away to your father, is she?" Umber asked Rubric.

He shook his head. "No. In her heart, she knows better than anyone what would happen."

"Then why . . . ?" Terelle asked.

"She wants an excuse not to go to him, so she feels less guilty. She was raised to do her duty. Marrying and obeying my father are all part of that." He sighed. "That's Watergiver families for you! Why else did Russet make such a fuss about his granddaughter running away?"

Poor Mother. I wish I'd known you.

Later, as Jasper and Terelle made their way upstairs, he said quietly, "An unhappy waterpainter could do a lot of damage."

She nodded, miserable. "I know. I'm hoping she'll want to stay in the Quartern of her own free will. She may never forgive me, though, which is sad. She could teach me so much."

"Is it even *possible* she'll want to stay?"

They halted outside the cubbyhole she shared with Jade. "I grew up with many women who'd settled for second best because there was no alternative. They made the best of what life dealt them because they had no other way to live. No skills, no money, no benefactor. The cage was comfortable, usually—but it was still a cage. Lord Jade's no different, for all that her cage was luxurious. She still bruised herself against the bars, without even realising they were there. Once she sees them vanish, she'll be a lot happier, you'll see." *I hope*.

The next night they spent at Grey Manor as a guest of Umber's father. Gelder greeted them sourly, immediately berating Umber for lending Jasper his best alpiners and tackle. Umber grinned amiably and let it flow over him, although Terelle caught a glimpse of burning resentment in his gaze. She liked Umber and thought him slow to anger, but this wasn't the first time it had occurred to her that, once roused, his temper would be formidable.

Only when he had exhausted his ire on his son did Gelder turn to Lord Jade, Rubric and Terelle. "You're Sienna's daughter, I suppose," he said, looking Terelle up and down in scorn. "Caused a great deal of trouble to my family, your silly frip of a mother." He shifted his gaze to Lord Jade and Rubric. "And who, by God's lost voice, are you?"

"Lord Jade Verdigris," Jade snapped, "and this is my youngest son, Lord Rubric, as I am sure you can guess from his tattoos. My husband always did say the Greys were ill-mannered farmers, and I can see he spoke the truth."

Gelder looked torn. From the look on his face, he would have liked to toss Lord Jade out of the house, preferably into a midden heap, but common sense recommended being obsequious to the wife of the Commander of the Southern Marches. He opted for the latter. He gave orders for rooms to be prepared and a meal cooked, and then said, "I do humbly apologise if my hospitality is lacking. Half our household staff were Alabasters and they disappeared three nights ago. Along with most every other Alabaster in the land."

"What do you mean?" Jade asked, her gaze flying to his face in startled surprise. "Disappeared?"

"They just upped and left in the middle of the night. Most of them. And not just mine, either. Everyone's. Organised it was—there was an unusual number of pack-pedes in the Marches, because a huge delivery of iron ore and several other overdue shipments of various things came in at the same time. They unloaded, but when they went back they ferried Alabasters to the border. Ungrateful wretches. They've all gone home. Some say war's on its way."

"That explains the empty fields," Umber murmured while Terelle translated to Jasper. "Khromatis is in trouble." He gave Jasper a sharp look. "Sometime, ye'll have to tell me why ye aren't at all surprised."

Shortly after Jasper entered his bedroom that evening, Terelle knocked on his door. When he opened it, he stood in the doorway, not saying a word. His body ached, just to look at her. She was so beautiful, so composed. He stared, unable to give voice to his longing.

She said, "I'm sharing with Lord Jade. The atmosphere is as cold as that bivac up near the pass." Her head tilted in unspoken enquiry.

"Huh," he said, and tried to think of something intelligent to say.

"I thought I'd look for something a little warmer."

His lips twitched. "Did you now? Come in, come in—I'll, um, put another log on the fire, shall I?" he asked, shutting the door behind her.

She made an exasperated sound and went to pummel his chest with her fists, but he caught her up in his embrace instead. His hunger—hot, desperate, greedy—plunged him deep into a kiss, into wondrous joy at her instant response. They fell in a tumble on the floor in front of the fire, tearing at one another's clothes, consumed by need, by passion, by grief.

And afterwards, long afterwards, they talked, lovers' talk of a combined future, of dreams of a life together, of Amberlyn. Deep into the night they made love again, leisurely, with tenderness, and slept only when it was already close to dawn.

I'm going home.

Terelle had to subdue the urge to dance with happiness as they said goodbye to Gelder and Umber the next morning and set off for the Quartern. All six of them were riding, the white myriapede Jasper had brought with him to Khromatis. A full load.

"I had hoped Umber would be coming with us," Rubric said, as they turned out of the main gate onto the road towards the Borderlands. "He seemed so interested in the Quartern."

"I thought he would too," Jasper said. "I guess I wasn't as persuasive as I thought I was." One more stormlord in addition to Rubric would have made a difference.

"Wait a moment—isn't that him?" Rubric asked, indicating a man standing by the roadside ahead.

"How did he get out here so quickly?" Like Rubric,

Jasper had no trouble recognising Umber's water long before they were close enough to see his features. The Watergiver was seated on his alpiner, apparently waiting for them.

"He obviously knows a shortcut we don't. Must have cut through the farm and jumped a few fences, I guess."

When they stopped alongside him, Umber was grinning affably. "Thought I'd like to be seeing the world. Thought it might be better if I just left a note for my pa. Easier that way. Ye reckon that ugly beast of yours will take my weight once we reach the Borderlands?"

"I'll stuff you in a pannier," Jasper said, his spirits lifting. "After all, we don't have to take any water with us, do we? We already have our own supply." He pointed upwards where their stolen storm still loomed, gravid with rain. They had been taking it in turns to keep it together.

"I'm far too large to fit into a pannier." He surveyed them all with a critical eye and switched languages. "Jade, my dear, I am coming with you. I think you might be the smallest. *You* can take the pannier."

"You, Umber Grey, can walk as far as I am concerned! At least I've had it confirmed that you're an idiot. Volunteering to go to the Quartern? Are you out of your eel-catcher's simple mind?"

"You're *such* a high-nose, Jade Verdigris," he told her, still cheerful, and turned his mount to face in the same direction as the pede. "I'll ride my alpiner for the time being." He smiled at Terelle. "Cuz, I've not long found you—how could I let you ride out of my life so soon?"

Affection for him made her smile. "I'm glad you didn't."

"Well, what are we waiting for?" he asked Jasper, beaming at them all. "Let's get going!"

*   *   *

They waited in the woodland until the darkest part of the night and then headed for the Borderlands. They aimed to ford the river well away from Marchford, but it wasn't long before Umber, still on his alpiner so as not to burden the pede until necessary, rode closer saying, "Ye feel what I'm feeling?"

Jasper was terse in his reply. "Yes."

"What is it?" Terelle asked. She was sitting directly behind him, with Jade behind her, then Rubric, and Dibble as rear man. Elmar was driving.

"Mounted men," he replied. "About thirty of them. Moving fast this way. If they're after us, they must have a waterlord among them."

"Why would they be after us? We're *leaving,* after all."

"My eldest brother's there," Rubric said. "I can feel him."

"Jet has told Bice what happened at home," Jade said. "He's ordered a border watch for us."

Terelle translated and Jasper swore. Neither Bice nor his eldest son would have heard from Jet, of course, but if Hue was on duty looking for the water of runaway Alabasters attempting to cross, he would recognise his mother's. And his brother's. This was probably no more than bad luck. At a guess, border patrols would have been stepped up and waterlords assigned to all the night-time ones—even, it seemed, someone with a recently broken collar bone. "Elmar, move it. As fast as you can!"

They plunged down the grassed slope to the river in fast mode, blessing the ability of a pede to flow smoothly across the roughest of terrain.

Jade gripped Terelle's shoulder, crying out in alarm.

Rubric said, "It's all right, Mother. These aren't alpiners; they won't break a leg in the dark."

Without halting, the pede plunged into the river. Elmar hadn't even slowed the pede down, or attempted to see how deep the water was first. The animal accepted his guidance and headed for the other side, its feet scrabbling for purchase on the riverbed. Jasper nervously eyed the water sliding past in the darkness, but it never rose high enough to wet them. He looked back over his shoulder, looking for Umber. Some way behind them his alpiner was skidding down the bank and into the flow. It soon had to swim. Umber dismounted into the water and clung to the saddle as the animal valiantly battled the current. They ended up further downstream than the pede but made it safely up the opposite bank.

Elmar drew rein at the top to give the pede a chance to shake its head and rattle its segments to rid itself of water. Jasper called back to Rubric, "Are you with us on this one?"

"I won't help ye kill my brother," he retorted, "if that's what ye mean."

"No. I thought of using water to slow them down. That way we can avoid a fight and unnecessary deaths. Are there going to be any other waterlords besides your brother?"

"I doubt it."

"Clueless clods," Umber said as he trotted up, streaming water as he dried his clothes. "They don't know who they face here."

"Let's throw some river water at them," Jasper said.

"Fine with me!"

"Elmar, get us started for the border again. Not too fast this time."

With Rubric helping, Umber and Jasper lifted water from the river and heaved it at the men approaching on the other side. No sooner was the water in the air than it started shooting off in all directions. Hue had no intention of getting wet.

He's powerful, Jasper thought. *This is not going to work, and Rubric knows it. Which is why he was happy to oblige, of course.* He sighed inwardly. Hue might be a murdering bastard, but it was unfair to ask his brother to fight him, especially when his mother was there. Fortunately, because she didn't understand the language they were using, she had little idea of what was going on. And the good thing was that Hue would probably not want to throw water at her.

He leaned forward to speak into Elmar's ear. "Fast mode," he said, reaching for the raincloud up in the sky to make it rain.

He waited until the Khromatian armsmen were crossing the river before he dragged the rain he'd created down as fast as he could, building up a wind with the force of the drag. Rain and wind barrelled sideways at the men in the river. Hue must have felt it coming and he did his best, but he was no match for a many-pronged attack. Water assailed him from Rubric and Umber, and from Jasper's wind-driven sideways assault. Worst of all must have been the sudden rise of the river as the wind pushed against the current and water built up, swamping the alpiners. In his mind, Jasper felt the troop fall apart into a number of struggling individuals, all fighting to stay afloat. As he'd never met Hue, he had no idea which of them he was.

He heard Rubric cry out, anguished, "They're wearing armour!"

Another thing he hadn't known. And he didn't need to be told why it was important. He began to feel men dying. Drowning, dragged under by the weight of what they wore. Rubric was silent. A while later, two riderless alpiners galloped past, panicked and dripping. Behind him, Terelle leaned forward to whisper into his ear. "The armsmen were Rubric's comrades. They may have mocked him, but maybe he called some of them friend. And then there's his brother, of course."

He nodded, his victory subdued. The Khromatians wouldn't be following them, but perhaps the price had been high.

Elmar drove the pede on, and by the time they reached the beginnings of the marsh of the Borderlands there was no pursuit. He reined in, and Umber dismounted. Jasper climbed down as Umber began to unsaddle.

"Hue?" he asked in a whisper.

"One of the dead," Umber whispered back.

He was shocked. "Are you sure? A waterlord should be able to stop himself drowning!"

"An alpiner landed on him in the water. I think he must have been knocked unconscious."

"Rubric must know he's dead. He'd have felt it."

"Of course."

Jasper looked back at the pede. "Rubric? Here a moment?"

Rubric dismounted in silence and came to join them.

"I'm sorry. I didn't mean anyone to die," Jasper said, keeping his voice down so Jade did not hear.

By starlight, Rubric's face was stony. "Ye can't expect me to believe ye're sorry Hue died."

"No, I'm not. He was involved in Feroze's murder. But

I am sorry to give you and your mother more grief. Would you like me to tell her?"

"Don't ye dare. She must not know. Not—not now, not yet. When she returns to Khromatis it will be soon enough for her to know two of her sons are dead."

He reeled under the impact of the words. *Rubric knows about Jet?*

"I know my alpiners, Jasper. And Dibble and Elmar were riding two of the beasts that left with Jet's party. Ye killed all of them, didn't ye? It's unlikely Jet would ever have ridden past Elmar and Dibble. He'd have recognised their water."

Jasper had to swallow before he could reply. "They recognised Elmar and Dibble and attacked. Your mother...?"

"She hasn't thought it through and I'm not telling her."

Jasper bowed his head, oddly ashamed, yet knowing he would do the same again in the same circumstances. "I don't know what to say to you."

Rubric shrugged. "Say nothing. I didn't love my brothers. But for all that, they were my mother's sons, and I dread facing her grief."

"I promise I'll see you both returned to Khromatis with every assistance, if that's your wish once the painting is fulfilled."

Rubric turned away without another word and remounted, fumbling for the carved foot slots in the dark. His mother spoke to him and he replied, but Jasper had no idea what was said. His stomach churned. *Weeping hells, I hate war. I hate what it does to us all.* Even the victories could make bitter memories.

Umber retrieved his belongings and abandoned the

saddle, bridle and saddle bags. His placed his personal things into a pede's panniers. "Now, he said cheerfully, "Jade . . . ?"

She glared at him and shifted onto the same segment as her son. "Sit there, you horrible man," she said, indicating the place she had vacated.

"Elmar, you swap places with me," Jasper ordered. Right then he wanted to distance himself as far as he could from all three of the Khromatians. "I'm driving." When they were all settled, he said, "Everyone comfortable? Then let's go home!"

Crossing the Borderlands was never pleasant, but having a stormlord in charge of the mount made a difference. Sensing far ahead, Jasper could select the best route through the stagnant ponds and had no trouble finding dry land when they needed to rest. When Bice—they assumed it was Bice—tried to make it rain there to bog them down, Jasper and Umber stole his clouds, combined them with what they already had, and kept them intact and overhead to shade them from the ferocious heat of the sun.

Unfortunately, there was nothing any of them could do about the boggy stench of the miasma they inhaled with every breath, or the niggling hunger from their half-rations because they carried more oats and beans for the pede than food for themselves. In addition, Jasper, Umber and Rubric were constantly having to protect them all from a continual barrage of water attacks and attempts to disrupt their own theft of Khromatian clouds. No one complained, though, not even Jade, but the three water sensitives were exhausted by the time they finally emerged on the far side several days later.

It was dawn on the Whiteout, when the salt pan was at its most beautiful, but even so, it looked to be what it was: a barren and hostile land, where men did not belong.

"God be voiceless," Umber said, horror in his voice. "Alabaster's *live* here?"

"They do indeed. This is where you exiled them to," Jasper answered, deliberately grim.

Again, even Jade couldn't think of anything to say to that when Rubric translated for her.

When Umber spoke once more, he sounded subdued. "Father said some of the Watergivers were talking of invading to be bringing the Alabasters to their knees. To force their agreement to be returning." He winced as a spindevil sent a flurry of salt battering against his face. He gave a bark of humourless laughter. "They have no idea. No alpiner could survive out here. We could bring water, but…" He gazed around at the colourless landscape ahead of them. "What would they live on? Alabasters import grain from us. What, by all that's holy, will people *eat* if trade ceases?"

"Samphire and pede milk," Jasper said, his memory of the Alabaster diet all too fresh.

Umber didn't look happy.

"What do you want to do with the cloud now that we're here?" Rubric asked Jasper.

"Hold on to it for the time being. It's the only thing that's going to save us from being hot and burned over the next few days. Besides, I'd like the Alabasters to see with their own eyes what Khromatian Watergivers could do for this quarter if they put their minds to it." He smiled. "I think a regular water supply for the White Quarter will be a non-negotiable demand once they see what's possible."

Terelle translated for Jade, who turned away as if to avoid the words. Jasper watched and knew her preconceptions about Alabasters had been shaken. *Good,* he thought, but he couldn't rid himself of the guilt he felt. His rational mind told him two unpleasant brothers had died, and the world was a better place because they had gone—but he had to look Lord Jade in the eye every morning and pretend he didn't know he'd been instrumental in killing her sons.

The Bastion asked to see both Jasper and Terelle the moment they arrived in Samphire. They found him sitting in his cramped study, a shrunken old man dwarfed by the huge hewn-salt armchair. The steady sound of the capstan burred in the background as it moved the levers and shafts to draw water up to the cistern. Messenjer was standing behind the Bastion's chair, his long fingers fidgeting with the embroidery on his white robe. One look at the Bastion's face was enough to tell Jasper something was seriously wrong.

"I'm relieved to see your return, my lords," the Bastion said. "Remarkable. Remarkable, what ye've done. There has never been a Khromatian visitor here in my lifetime. Never. Watergivers at that. I hope to be meeting them later. And of course, we saw the clouds over the Humps. Thank you for your rain. I admit I doubted the wisdom of your journey until then."

Jasper inclined his head and wished the man would get to the point. Whatever was coming was going to be bad, but he wanted to know.

The Bastion picked a flat package up from the table beside his chair and handed it to Jasper. "Taquar Sardonyx has escaped and killed Highlord Iani."

In shock, Jasper took the letters. *Amberlyn.* "That's—that's not possible," he stuttered. *Escaped? Taquar couldn't escape, not without knowing how . . .*

Oh, withering hells. Amberlyn! Taquar *has her?* He felt ice through his veins as the horror of the thought spread. Terelle grasped his hand, held it tight.

Pale-faced, she whispered, "My painting *failed*?"

"It happened not long after your departure. Lord Laisa sent a letter which just missed ye. It's in this packet. Other people have written since, some to me, some to ye. The last is the one from Lord Kaneth Carnelian; it arrived only a few days ago."

He looked up at Messenjer. "Get someone to be showing them to their rooms, Mez. Lord Jasper will need time alone to read these."

Grim-faced, boiling to read whatever was in the letters he carried, yet dreading the moment, Jasper strode behind the silent Messenjer, Terelle equally silent at his side, holding his hand tight.

"I've asked the servants to prepare a bath, clean clothes and a meal," Messenjer said as he showed them their rooms, side by side. "If there is anything ye need, just ask."

Jasper nodded and entered his room, untying the cord around the packet to extract the separate letters inside, six of them. Terelle disappeared with Messenjer and Jasper hardly noticed. He sat on the bed, leafing through the sheets of paper. From Breccia there was a letter each from Laisa, Senya and Seneschal Chandler; from Scarcleft there was one from Taquar, and from the Red Quarter there was one each from Kaneth and Ryka. For a moment he dithered between them, his hands trembling, bile bitter in his gorge.

In the end, he opened Laisa's first.

Hurriedly, he skimmed her neat concise writing, skipping the inessential to hunt out the essence.

...Regrettably I decided that, owing to the uncertain nature of your powers and the disappearance of Terelle, the future of the Quartern would be better served if Taquar was free. If Terelle doesn't return, you can work with him to produce storms—serving only the Scarpen. That way, neither of you will be worked to exhaustion.

Terelle entered the room and closed the door. "Read it to me," she said.

"From Laisa. *And therefore I found the painting of Taquar's prison that Terelle left behind. Using that picture, I located the place and released him. You were both clever and yet careless, Jasper, and you underestimated me.*

"*Sadly, Iani was killed—*" Stricken, he raised his head to look at her. "Oh waterless hells. It's true!" The sheet of parchment shook in his hand. *Iani suffered so much in his life. How could they? And I wasn't there. I didn't hide the painting well enough. But we needed to keep it. And Terelle's never been sure what would happen if we destroyed a painting before it became real anyway...* "The withering bastards. The withering bastards. I'll kill them, I swear I will."

She came closer to sit beside him and laid her head on his shoulder. "I'm sorry. I'm so sorry. We—we'll decide what to do later, when we know everything. Go on."

"She's a sunblighted monster. Listen: *Your combined stormbringing with Taquar was never enough before, because you foolishly insisted on watering the other quarters. This time Taquar has the means to force you to do exactly what he says.*"

He halted, in his dread not wanting to read the next sentence. The words danced; the meaning made his breath catch. "*Senya gave Amberlyn into his care.*"

He stared, hearing the echo of his own voice before the crushing reality hit. *Ah, Watergiver save her.* Perhaps it wasn't true? But he knew it was, and it was Taquar's scheming mind behind it. Abrading pain followed on the heels of the realisation that had slammed so belatedly into his mind. Only now did past events make sense. Only now did he understand how foolish he'd been. Always thinking he had the upper hand, when it was Taquar who had laid the foundations of what would count in the end.

This was why Senya had come to his bed. *This* was why Amberlyn had been born. To make a slave of Jasper Bloodstone, who was really only Shale Flint, Gibber grubber. They had dangled his child in front of his eyes, encouraged him to love her, to feel responsible for her, to pity her because she had a mother who didn't care. Because there had once been Citrine, and a boy laden with guilt.

And they were right. He would do anything for Amberlyn. Anything.

I'll be pissing waterless . . . what can I do? His helplessness was agony.

Beside him, Terelle bit her lip and was silent. He read on. "*He will kill Amberlyn unless you do exactly what he wants. I know him, Jasper. Do not take this lightly. He burns with anger over his humiliation. He is back in Scarcleft now, running the city once more. He has gathered his old water enforcers around him again. Even Harkel Tallyman, whom Iani was silly enough to imprison rather than execute.*

"*He is content to stay there and do nothing if you and*

Terelle can keep Scarcleft supplied with plentiful water and free of taxes. He will not interfere with the running of the Quarter or with you. Amberlyn will be kept within the confines of the city, not accessible to either you or, he assures me, Senya. The same two nurses, Crystal and Zirca, are with her still. Where you live with Terelle, or what you do, he doesn't care, as long as Scarcleft has all the water it needs.

"If, on the other hand, Terelle does not return and you need him to help you stormshift, then you will have to live permanently with him within the confines of the city and accept his overlordship in all things. Amberlyn will be moved elsewhere, and should you approach to attempt a rescue, she will die.

"If neither of these alternatives is acceptable, he will kill Amberlyn and leave the Quartern to cross the Giving Sea. If you deceive him in any way, then her death will not only be inevitable, it will be prolonged. The choice is yours."

He fell silent. The rage in his heart would not let him speak.

Terelle wiped a tear away and asked quietly, "Where does Laisa stand in all this? She is his wife, after all."

He scanned the rest of the letter hurriedly, then Senya's. "Laisa wants to remain as highlord in Breccia." He swallowed, forcing himself to think rationally. "That's... interesting. She's abandoning her marriage with Taquar." He read some more and shook his head over Senya's childish demands. "Senya wants to stay there in Breccia, too, with the allowance and status of the Cloudmaster's wife. Neither of them care what I do, as long as their lives are comfortable and the city gets its water." Bitterness coursed through him. Amberlyn was daughter and grand-daughter to them, and they didn't care. He swallowed back the wave of hatred that threatened to drown him.

He forced himself to pick up Taquar's letter.

It was much shorter; just a paragraph. He read it to himself. *I am not a cruel man, as you have cause to know. I can, however, be cruel, if cruelty attains results. I do not care for children, least of all babies. Amberlyn will be safe in the hands of her nurses for as long as you do as I ask; every time you defy me, I will take it out on her. Do you think it ever worried me when Iani's six-year-old daughter begged to see her mother and father? Do you think it worried me that she cried herself to sleep night after night? Not only Amberlyn's safety is in your hands, but her happiness.*

Jasper felt all the blood drain from his face as he read. He couldn't speak. He handed the note to Terelle in silence.

She read it and then it slipped from her grip, floating lightly to the floor as if there was nothing whatever of import written on its surface.

"Oh, waterless soul," she whispered.

"He's telling the truth about himself."

They exchanged a look. He hoped she would contradict him, but she glanced away without speaking.

He capitulated to the inevitable. "Which means I have to give him what he wants. At least for now." *Shut away the love I feel for my child in my heart. I must will myself to do nothing, for fear that what I do will harm her. Sun-blighted sands, can there be anything worse?* He wanted to ride straight to Scarcleft. He wanted to blast the gates open, to pull Taquar to pieces with his bare hands . . .

And he mustn't.

His thoughts felt as if they were mired in mud, as if he was walking through the Borderlands bog and each new step was a dragging effort. He stared at Terelle but couldn't think.

Amberlyn.

Terelle didn't even know her. How could she possibly know what he felt?

But then she said, "We will win this one. We'll win because the idea that such a man would so manipulate a child—*any* child, least of all one of ours—is unthinkable."

Her gaze was clear-eyed and implacable. *Ours.* She'd said "ours." He heard her conviction. And his mind cleared. Ideas formed and jostled, were considered and accepted or rejected. He *would* get Amberlyn back. He would. But first he'd lull Taquar into thinking he'd won.

Still groping among the ideas, he said, "I'll send Lord Umber to Breccia with Lord Jade. I'll ask him to stay there for at least a cycle. I think he's strong enough to bring sufficient water for the Scarpen. If the Scarpen has what it needs, Laisa and Taquar and Lord Gold will keep off my back long enough for me to—to fix other things."

I'll send them both a cloud message tomorrow, he thought. *One to Laisa in Breccia and the other to Taquar in Scarcleft. And I don't care who reads them.*

He looked down at the other letters on the bed beside him. "Let's see what Ryka and Kaneth have to say."

They dined together that night: the Bastion, Messenjer and Errica, Terelle and Jasper, Umber, Jade and Rubric. Terelle had little to say and Jasper was preoccupied.

He didn't have any choice, she told herself. *He had to*

marry Senya. Accept it and don't think about it. Simple.
Only it wasn't simple. It was hard. It hurt even when she
understood the manipulation. She shoved the unpleasantness away and concentrated on translating for Jasper
because the dinner conversation soon lapsed into Khromatian, to accommodate Lord Jade. The waterpainter
was determined to extract as much information as she
could from the Bastion about his intentions towards her
land.

"Yes," he was saying, "it's true. Almost every Alabaster worker has returned safe to us. Some did choose to
stay in Khromatis. Nursemaids, perhaps, grown attached
to their charges. Others have just been there too long and
can no longer contemplate the hard life here. I do not
judge them."

"And now?" Jade persisted.

"Now the Khromatians will pay a price for rarely making friends with those who worked for them. And for murdering some who went there in good faith."

There was a telling silence. Lord Jade flushed but she
persevered. "You'll suffer more even than us—you rely
on us for trade goods."

"Yes, but you rely on us, too. We are prepared for suffering. I doubt you Khromatians are."

It was Jasper who broke the silence that followed. "Perhaps the Quartern can help Alabaster out. I have a dream
for the Gibber. I'd like to see it as prosperous as the other
quarters. But it will need help, especially with the things
Alabasters know how to do well: mining, working with
minerals to make things, building water tunnels. We'd be
willing to pay for it."

Terelle blinked, startled. *We?* What did he mean, we?

The Bastion gave him an interested look. "Sharing profits?"

"I'm sure we could work out something to our mutual benefit."

"Indeed. But first we must settle matters with the Khromatians. They have to send us water on a regular basis if they want our labour and our trade."

Jade said, "My husband's father will never accede to that. There will be war."

He shrugged. "Your alpiners cannot cross the Borderlands and the Whiteout. Besides, who will make your weapons, and shoe your mounts?"

"Do you think we cannot cross the bogs?" she asked, scornful. "We are Watergivers! We made the bogs; in a couple of days we can make dry paths for the alpiners to pass, surely. Our waterlords can kill with their powers. Who will you throw against them?"

"It won't come to that. Do you think your mounts will be in battle condition when they come to the gates of Samphire? After crossing the Whiteout? They won't eat the kind of samphire we have here; we know that already. It's too salty for them. Alabasters in Khromatis have checked for us."

She appeared worried, as if she had just understood that this was not a spontaneous decision, doomed to failure. "We can make it rain if we want water. We can shade the army."

The Bastion shrugged. "Then we'll scatter, leave you the salt and even the city. We know how to live here. What will you do, occupy Samphire? Then what? Do you really want this land? You have no skills to use it. We'll return here once the land has defeated you. Anyway, the Pinnacle and his advisors make the decisions, not such as Lord Bice Verdigris. Decisions will come from the Peak, not from the Southern Marches, and I doubt the Pinnacle will view things the same way as Lord Bice does."

Umber nodded. "Lord Jade," he said, "if the Pinnacle has a brain in his head, he'll be more interested in having willing workers return than in ensuring their hatred with a costly war."

The Bastion turned his attention to Jasper and reverted to the Quartern tongue. "Go. Return to the Scarpen. Solve your problems there, and don't worry about us. Thanks to ye, we have water to last for the remainder of this cycle. Thanks to Lord Kaneth, we're free from attack and we'll run our caravans once more. We'll fight our own battles, and we'll triumph, God willing. And yes, if the Gibber wants our skills and our workers, pay them well and they will come."

Terelle felt a lightening of her heart. *Changes indeed. This can only be for the better, surely.*

They left Samphire a day later.

CHAPTER THIRTY-FIVE

Red Quarter
God's Pellets
Dune Watergatherer

Vara Redmane was seated on the carpet in Kaneth and
Ryka's tent, minding Kedri. At almost a cycle old he could
not only stand now, but take a few wobbly steps as well.
After plopping down on his well-padded bottom, he
clambered laboriously back up, stubbornly refusing assistance. "Bleeding pede-headed ornery sandworm in
the making, you are!" she told him. "Going to be poking
your dad in the balls one day just for the fun of it, I can
see."

He looked up at her and smiled.

She snorted. The little bastard had charm aplenty.
"You can't fool me, you squirmy little sandworm."

"Play water," he said firmly.

"No one plays with water. What are you, a bleeding
fish?"

"Water!"

"You can have a drink."

She levered herself to her feet, sighing because her

joints pained her, and went to the family jar to bring back a mug of water. He accepted it gleefully.

A shadow fell across the light streaming in through the open flap; someone had walked into the shade of the veranda. She looked up to see Guyden, the Scarmaker youth who wore the white beads. She didn't like him, didn't like his self-contained arrogance or the way his gaze was always hooded by half-closed eyelids, as if he kept secrets within.

Smug, she thought. *Always so smug. What does he have to be smug about, ever?*

"I've been looking for you, Kher Vara," he said politely. Always polite; she had to give him that. "Riders approaching. Small group."

"Kaneth and Lord Ryka are due back today."

"The numbers don't match. Only two pedes, three people. And they're wearing white, not red."

White? Thank the dune god, not that shrivelled son of a sand-tick, Ravard. "What colour pedes?"

"Black. My guess is Scarpermen."

"Everyone alerted? Extra men up on top?" They had an established sequence of procedures for when strangers approached, and everyone knew what to do and where they were to be.

He nodded, but he was looking past her to where Kedri played. His eyes widened, then narrowed. "That's Lord Kaneth's son? I'll be spitless! He's grown since I saw him last."

Doesn't ever call the sandmaster Kher Uthardim, either. I really wonder about you, young Guyden. You're from my dune and I should feel close to you, but I trust you about as much as a fly trusts a spiny devil lizard.

"Babies have that habit. Like youths rubbing their sticks to see who's got the longest."

He shrugged and turned to go.

"You're one of Dorwith's sons, you said. I don't remember you."

"He had eight," he said dryly. "Hardly to be wondered at that you can't remember us all. I was the youngest."

"Eight, that's right. Humph. My dugs might be withered, but my mind's not. I remember there was one called Guyden, too. You don't have the look of that child. Scrawny bunch they were, Dorwith's litter."

"Boys grow. Like him." He nodded at Kedri. "I'm expected back at my post." He turned and walked away.

She looked back at Kedri. He waved the empty mug at her. Water dripped from his chin and his clothes were wet.

"Finished that, did you?" she asked.

"Play water!" he said. He grabbed at the air in front of him, then opened his hand to show her what he had caught. The centre of his palm was wet. He frowned. As she watched, a small pool of water reformed in his cupped hand—and his clothes were dry.

"I'll be pissing waterless," she said, and her jaw dropped.

They stared at one another, the old woman speechless, the boy happily impressed with his own cleverness.

Finally Vara found her tongue again. "No, no play water. I'm going to take you to Merish next door. I have to see who these people are heading our way." She shook her head mournfully just thinking about it. Strangers had a habit of bringing more bleeding trouble. "And some time soon, I think I need to talk to your ma about you."

*   *   *

That evening, the encampment inside God's Pellets cele-brated the arrival of the Cloudmaster and his party, as well as the return of their own Kher Uthardim and Lord Ryka, arriving a couple of sandruns after the Cloud-master. They'd been out with a band of warriors deliver-ing a caravan of water to Dune Agatenob. As usual there'd been a skirmish with some of Ravard's men along the way, and initially the tales around the campfire were about that.

Now, though, the fire had died down and people had dispersed to their tents. Ryka sat with Kedri on her lap under their canvas veranda in the cool, leaning back on the cushions heaped on the carpet, listening to the three men sitting there: Kaneth, Rubric the Khromatian and Jasper. The desert night was domed by a starry splendour, the air scented with the perfume of flowers mingled with the lingering smell of roasted goat and the herbal sweet-ness of burning pede droppings. An oil lamp hanging from the tent rope gave a dim glow to the area.

Replete, with the tang of quandongs soaked in pip-berry juice on her tongue, Ryka was drowsily content. Her son had survived his first long separation from her with a minimum of fuss, yet had been suitably glad to see her return. Against all odds, Jasper and his driver Dibble Hornblend had returned safely from Khromatis, and with him there was this other young stormlord, brightly inter-ested in everything around him. A smart young man, she guessed; he had that sardonic gleam in his eye that usu-ally warned of someone not easily fooled by pretensions.

Everything felt peaceful and right—if only she could block her ears and not hear what was being said. Lord Rubric didn't contribute much, but Jasper and Kaneth had plenty to say, much of it not good: Taquar living in

Scarcleft threatening Jasper's daughter; Ravard, as usual, building up his armsmen and his ziggers while stealing water from his enemies; the White Quarter seeking to obtain future water from Khromatis at the risk of war. Still, the knowledge that another two stormlords and another waterpainter were now in the land eased her worries about the future.

Jasper had given them a full explanation of how waterpainting worked, and Ryka was quick to see the implications. "So that means you both have to be back in Breccia soon?" she asked Jasper. "Otherwise you'll start being sick, like Terelle was, because you both have unfulfilled paintings of you in the Breccian stormquest room."

Jasper nodded. "There's some leeway for us. Perhaps even as long as a year, especially as we have every intention of going there. We both feel fine at the moment."

"And Terelle is protected until such time she does the painting of you stormshifting, the one that she pictured in a tray, inside the waterpainting she did in Khromatis."

Jasper nodded.

"I'm not so sure," she said slowly. "A waterpainting within a waterpainting. What if that constitutes some kind of paradox? Or the larger painting cancels out the power of the second within it, or the other way around? I don't like it, Jasper. I don't think Terelle should rely on it making her safe."

Jasper and Rubric exchanged worried glances. "We have no reason to think it won't work."

"You've no reason to think it does, either, unless someone else has tried it before."

"Rubric?" Jasper asked.

"I've no idea."

"And," Ryka continued, "I don't much like the idea that Terelle could be at the mercy of Laisa and Senya. If Laisa gets her claws into Terelle, she has a hold over you."

"I'd rather trust a scorpion in my bed than Lord Laisa somewhere in the same city as me," he said, "but do I think she would hurt Terelle? No. She knows what Terelle and I can do together to bring rain, and she is far too much a rainlord to want to jeopardise that. A drought would hurt her personally, and Laisa likes her comforts. The main reason she released Taquar was to force me to work with him to bring water. Thanks to Rubric and Umber, that's not necessary. Secondly, in Amberlyn, she and Taquar already have the perfect way to control me." He paused, then added, "I sent two sky messages; one to Laisa, the other to Taquar. They were simply worded: *If Amberlyn dies, so do you.*"

He frowned unhappily. "Senya is another matter. She— she is not rational. However, Umber knows all about that and he will keep an eye on Terelle. He's delighted to find he has a relative he actually *likes*. And you know, Ry, Terelle is very capable of looking after herself."

"That's true," Rubric said. "As we in the Verdigris family found to our cost." His smile gleamed at her out of the darkness.

"Why didn't you bring her here?" Ryka asked.

"Do you think it's safer here?" he asked.

She didn't reply.

He added quietly, "I needed someone there to help Jade and Umber, and I didn't want to bring her into the midst of a war in the Red Quarter."

War? Is that what he and Kaneth are calling it now? She hugged Kedri tighter. "So what are you going to do about the three of them—Laisa, Senya and Taquar?" The teacher in her was intrigued: this thoughtful, mature man was the same lad who had once wrestled with his feelings of incompetence? And here she was, not offering advice now, but asking what he was going to do.

"For the time being? Nothing. My personal priority is to keep Amberlyn safe. And, ironically, probably the best way for me to do that is to do nothing."

It almost killed you to say that. Watergiver damn, but it's hard to believe rational arguments when your heart is involved. I know what you're suffering, Jasper...

"She has the same nurses she's had since the day she was born, so she's likely to be content. I don't expect her to be ill-used by Taquar for no reason; that's not his way. His cruelties always have a purpose." In the dim light she could see no change in his expression, but the tone of his voice was as cold and unforgiving as a stone bitten between one's teeth.

"I once promised Nealrith that I would look after Senya," he said a moment later. "But I don't think that's possible. Or even something I want to do. So I'll leave her to Lord Laisa's care." He gave a grim smile. "A just punishment for Laisa, perhaps. Terelle will show Umber where all the maps and coordinates are for the Scarpen stormbringing. Cottle Chandler, the seneschal, has my instructions to offer them every aid. Laisa might be highlord, but I've sent personal orders to my guard there to refer all orders to Chandler." He paused, his face clouding. "As long as Taquar gets his water without having to work for it or pay for it, he will be content—for a while. And so my priority as Cloudmaster has to be elsewhere, not with Amberlyn."

"Here." That was Kaneth, injecting the word into the conversation as fact. "Your priorities are here. You have to deal with the dunes first."

Jasper nodded. "You're walking a fine line between disaster and maintaining what you have. Ravard will find you here eventually. It's inevitable."

"Of course." Kaneth shrugged. "I'm surprised we've gone undetected this long. We're building up our forces hoping to match his, but it's too slow. Sandmasters and tribemasters fear Ravard too much to support us openly. So Ravard commands many more men than we do," Kaneth continued. "And we've had to devote a lot of our energies to bringing water to the northern dunes."

"At least you won't have to do that any more now that Rubric and I are here," Jasper said. "Two stormlords, one rainlord"—he nodded at Ryka—"and you, a man with the ability to move the sand beneath their feet. I think we can tip the odds in our favour."

Kaneth grinned at him. "Now that's what I've been waiting to hear." He clapped Rubric on the back. "Welcome to the dunes, my lord. We need you."

Ah, Ravard, why wouldn't you listen to me? Ryka thought. *They plan your death, and it could so easily have been otherwise.*

"Someone's coming at a run," Jasper said, even as Kaneth was saying, "Something's wrong." They both scrambled to their feet, looking in the same direction.

Ryka strove to feel what they did, but as usual she was the last to sense anything. A moment after she became aware of a running man, Cleve jogged up out of the darkness. "Could be a problem," he told them, panting. "It's Guyden. Rode out at dusk."

Jasper looked at Kaneth in question.

"A youngster from Scarmaker," Kaneth said. "We restrict coming and going to prevent betrayal. What happened, Cleve? In the Quartern tongue, please."

The man looked embarrassed. "Everyone's attention was on your visit. The guard on duty at the canyon entrance said Guyden gave a plausible reason: he had to make sure you'd left no tracks on your way in. Thing is, he never came back. They didn't realise he had no right to leave until their stint of duty was over. I'm sorry, my lord."

"Doesn't sound good," Jasper murmured.

"How long ago was this?" Kaneth asked Cleve.

"Four runs."

"Any point in following him?" Jasper asked.

"Could you sense him?" Kaneth asked him.

"I can't pinpoint someone who's had a start of four sandglass runs! An armed troop, maybe, but not a single man on a single pede."

"Then no, there's not much point. One person taking care not to leave tracks?" Kaneth shook his head. "I'll send a small fast band including a water sensitive after him, but I suspect they won't catch up. He's well on his way to Dune Watergatherer, I'll bet."

"Not just a runaway?" Jasper asked. "You think he's a spy?"

"Of course he is! Probably my father's son," Cleve said, and his voice was riven through with bitterness. "My half-brother. Islar. Why didn't I see it? Right age, and Vara didn't think he looked like the lad he said he was. Ravard sent him! That treacherous water-waster—"

They all stared at him in shock.

Finally it was Jasper who spoke. "It seems we both

have interesting brothers, then, Cleve. A mistake to underestimate either of them." He must have been delivered a heavy blow with the news, but his tone never wavered. "We'd better assume Ravard will soon know where to find us, how to get in here, and every detail of your camp, strengths and weaknesses."

Kaneth turned back to Cleve. "Double the guards from now on. Send out two pedes and ten men, a water sensitive among them. If they haven't found Guyden by the time they cross the Hungry One, they're to return. I'll be along in a moment to discuss plans. Rubric, go with Cleve. You may as well learn as much about God's Pellets as you can."

The two men left, Cleve already launching into a description of the camp's defences while Rubric listened.

Kaneth turned to Jasper. "Seems your arrival was opportune."

"Seems our arrival prompted this Guyden to action!"

"Possibly. I liked the lad." Being Kaneth, he shrugged and moved on. "Anyway, I'm glad you're back, Jasper. Glad enough not to slaughter you for risking your life in the first place, crossing the border like that. Tomorrow I'll need to alert our dune allies. Can you write some cloud messages for us?"

"Certainly. Just remember that they can be seen by everyone, not just those you want to tell. I'll need any maps you have."

"I'll get them. And another lamp." He disappeared inside the tent.

Jasper looked at Kedri on Ryka's lap. "He's grown so much. I've been thinking of him as a baby, and here he is walking."

Kedri promptly scrambled off her lap and crawled to Jasper's feet. He hauled himself into a standing position. "Up!" he said imperiously. "Want up!"

Jasper grinned and lifted him into his arms. "Leadership qualities, definitely."

"A despot in the making, you mean."

"Far too much charm for that."

"A charming despot. The worst kind. He's a stormlord, you know."

He thought she wasn't serious. "How can you possibly tell that at this age?"

"He moves water. For a long time I couldn't be sure, but I am now, and Vara agrees with me. We have to watch him like an eagle to make sure he doesn't play with it."

Jasper looked at her in shock, then smiled delightedly. "Is that normal for a stormlord? To develop skills so young?"

"No. He's just a precocious brat."

"I think that's the best news I've had in half a cycle." He swung Kedri up over his head and the boy chuckled. "You are our future, my lad. A cloudmaster in the making."

"More, more!" crowed Kedri, but then caught sight of Kaneth inside the tent. "Down! Want Dada. Dada play!"

As he toddled off, Jasper turned back to Ryka. They stared at one another in silence for a long while before he spoke again. "Tell me I did the right thing, coming here first." His voice was ragged with grief, with remembered horror.

"You did the right thing." She whispered, as if to say the words too loudly would be to make them untrue.

"Then why does it feel so bad? Sandhells, Ry, I love

them both so much I'd die for them without a second thought. I swore I'd take care of them. And all I've done is send Terelle into danger and allow Amberlyn to remain in the hands of my greatest enemy. I want to tear Taquar in two with my bare hands. I want to trample him into the ground. I want to hold my daughter, I want to see her smile once more. And what do I do instead? Come here to fight my brother who was once my only friend and protector. It all feels so blighted *wrong*."

"Mica had a number of chances to change direction. This is his choice."

"Is—is he a bad man, Ry?"

She looked down so she didn't have to see the pain in his eyes. "No. But bad things were done to him. Some people come out on the other side of horror better men; others don't. Mica coped by becoming a man called Ravard. Mica's never coming back, Jasper. I'm sorry. I didn't hate him, you know, even when I hated what he did to me. I'm sorry for him even now. He saved my life several times, at cost to himself. He was prepared to raise my son as his own. But he was warped by his past. He just…" She hunted for the right word. "He just couldn't see the world as other people do."

"Now people will die so needlessly because of his choices, and I don't know how to stop it."

"You can't."

She looked at him then, and wanted to weep.

The next morning, Jasper asked Ryka to take him and Rubric to the top of the highest of God's Pellets. He needed to develop a feel for their surroundings, and to climb the steep-sided, rounded hump offering the best view to the south was one way to do that. Some of the twenty-two hills surrounding the valley were connected to others; some were separated by narrow canyons. Eight of these canyons led into the central valley, many others were dead ends, twisting and turning until they gradually became narrower and narrower and finally petered out.

The highest knob was the favoured lookout; from the top it was possible to see both Dune Koumwards to the south and Dune Burning View to the north. It was a long, hot climb via ladders and roped steps, and the final stage was inside a natural pipe hollowed out by ancient forces.

"I have an idea that climbing down again is going to be even harder than coming up," Rubric remarked as they emerged into the sunlight close to the two sentries on duty.

Jasper unrolled the map he had stuffed into his small pack and anchored it with some pebbles. When the sentries came in to look, he scolded them and sent them back to their watch. They couldn't afford to be lax, not now. "So, Ry, where are we?"

She tapped the map. "Here. We're looking out towards Dune Koumwards, which has no tribes of its own. It's an exceptionally tall dune, otherwise you might be able to see the peaks of Singing Shifter on the other side." She added, for Rubric's benefit, "Ravard's dune, Watergatherer, is the seventh one to the south. If none of our men can overtake Guyden, it'll take him several days to get there, and presumably a few more for any attacking force to prepare. So we have some time to perfect our defences. Our men are blocking up most of these entrance canyons at the moment."

"How?" Rubric asked.

"Stones, traps, drop nets, stakes, deadfalls. We have sentries on top of every high knob, and water sensitives on pedeback patrolling all the way around. Unfortunately Guyden had plenty of time to explore and find out which canyons are dead ends and which ones go all the way through to the valley."

"Even if we had enough food, we don't want to hunker down here," Jasper said. "We need to defeat Ravard, not be cowed by him." He was aware of Ryka's sympathetic glance and ignored it. He found it easier to say Ravard, rather than Mica. He could pretend that way, pretend that the sandmaster was not the brother he'd once loved. "We will ride out after him."

"Fight somewhere on the dunes? Wouldn't we lose the advantage?"

We? Sweet waters, he's almost one of us already.

It was Ryka who answered. "Up to a point, yes. We have assets in two stormlords, a rainlord and Kaneth. And all they have is water sensitives. But we have only four thousand armsmen here. Out on the dunes I have no idea how many we can count on. They make promises, but who knows? Dune Watergatherer has about eight thousand fully trained, disciplined battle-experienced warriors on their own dune and could probably muster or coerce several thousands more, all experienced, from other dunes. And I'm not counting the camp followers— the lads or old men who look after the pedes, the slaves and so on."

"Ah. The odds suddenly don't look so good." Rubric was pensive. "So why not wait and ask for help from the other quarters as ye did before?"

"We tried," Ryka said, her expression wry, "immediately

after the battle at the Qanatend mother cistern. They turned us down. To most Scarpen folk, Reduners are the enemy. *All* of them."

"Those who came to help us from the Gibber suffered terribly," Jasper added. "They died, they were injured, they lost their pedes. I'd never ask them to come again. Never. We sent them home with all we could afford to give them, but the Scarpen folk were not as generous as I hoped." He waved a hand at the plains and Dune Koumwards. "We'll fight out there on the dunes somewhere. Two armies, Ravard's and ours. And we'll win because to lose will mean that this war will have to be fought over and over again, with the Reduners wanting random rain and trying to kill every water sensitive and rainlord and stormlord we have. I want peace on the dunes. A lasting peace."

"And how will ye bring that out of war?" Rubric asked. He sounded more puzzled than critical.

Jasper's heart thumped unpleasantly fast. *I don't know. Damn you, Rubric, you have a talent for asking the wrong questions.* "I have no idea. Right now I have to write some sky messages to all the dunes asking the men of other dunes for their help. It's a beginning."

"Islar's back."

At last! Ravard, seated at the communal table between the tents, looked up from his breakfast at the warrior who had brought the message. "Bring him here," he said, careful to sound unhurried and calm. When Islar came, he eyed the water on the table before he even appeared to notice his sandmaster. Wordlessly, Ravard handed him the water skin. "Drink," he said. "And eat. Then tell me all you know. You're a welcome sight."

Once Islar began his story, Ravard marvelled. God's Pellets was a hollow circle of hills and not solid as they had all supposed? The rock itself blocked their water-sensing powers? And there was water there. Endless water! Truly a dune god's miracle.

The worst news was the arrival of Shale. Jasper. He hadn't expected that. The last he'd heard, his brother had been in Breccia playing at being the saviour of the land. Why the waterless hells did he have to interfere in Reduner affairs? If only he'd decided to stay in the Scarpen, their paths need never have crossed again.

Having to contend with a stormlord was going to be tough. At least the rebels had only two rainlords: Ryka—and Uthardim, with his additional strange talent for moving sand. When Islar mentioned there was one other dark-skinned stranger in the party, he decided it was doubtless just another Gibber grubber, probably a friend of Shale's.

Over the course of the day, Kher Medrim, in his capacity as Warrior Son, set in motion plans to call up dune warriors, while he himself teased still more information out of Islar. How many warriors did Kaneth have? What weaponry did they possess? How many pedes? How could they enter God's Pellets? Would it be better to trap them inside or entice them out?

He already knew sky messages had been sent. Those that had been read didn't make sense. It didn't take him long to realise Kaneth had already communicated some kind of code to those dunes he knew would support him. With the arrival of the Cloudmaster, he had an easy way of sending a coded message. At a guess, he was calling for an assembly of their forces somewhere or another.

That evening, he told Islar and Medrim that he was declaring Islar his Master Son, as he had promised.

Islar, his dark eyes gazing at the sandmaster with a steady arrogance, said, "It's my due."

"Careful," Ravard said, glowering at him, "or you'll be thinking your prick is too big to fit in your trousers."

"I suffered the mockery of men inferior to me. I played a coward, swallowed the insults, hid my intelligence. In battle I risked my life to avoid killing those allied to us; I risked my life to escape, not once but twice. And I have done it all alone. I've *earned* the right to lead men."

"Maybe. This coming battle will prove your mettle, or otherwise. Now I want you to tell me about the rainlord. Ryka Feldspar."

"The woman who made a fool of you? I've met her. She's taken to riding out with the false Uthardim. I'm not sure he has rainlord powers. I've watched him carefully. Some of the men almost *worship* him, like he was some sort of god. Not because he moves water, though. Some of them reckon he reads their minds. Black magic stuff. Gives me the shiver-shudders, he does."

"He was a Breccian rainlord. Of course he has water powers! And the child?"

"Kedri?"

"Khedrim."

"I don't know much about babies. He's walking and talking now." He stirred uneasily as if something bothered him.

"What is it?" Ravard asked.

"When do rainlords first show if they have water sensitivity?"

"Maybe younger than us. Reckon Shale knew when he was ten or so, but he didn't let on, not even to me. Why?"

"It's that baby, Kedri. I saw him once, playing on the floor with a cup of water. Maybe I was wrong and the water just splashed, but I thought he pulled it out. Got it all over his face. If he can do that so young, I reckon he might be another stormlord in the making."

The hurt of longing welled up in Ravard. *He was supposed to be mine. He* will *be mine!* "Could be," he said with a calm he didn't feel. "One more thing—did you come across your half-brother?"

"Clevedim? That traitorous son of a whore? Yes, he's there. Always at Kaneth's elbow, spindevil take him!"

"He's on our side."

Islar's eyes widened. "That's not possible. Dune god be my witness, I saw him kill our warriors in battle! After every trip he boasted about how many men he'd brought down."

"It was our plan to get him into a position of trust."

Islar blanched. He shot a look at his uncle.

Medrim shrugged.

"You think being a sandmaster means easy decisions, Islar?" Ravard asked. "Sometimes we sacrifice warriors, fine, brave men. In our hearts we honour them. At the prayer stones we ask the dune god to guard our bravest in their final rest. But none of that makes decisions any easier. Clevedim is one of ours. In the final battle, he will be the man who turns the wind of victory in our direction."

Islar sat motionless as the colour slowly returned to his face.

Ravard waved a hand to dismiss the subject. "Forget him for the time being. Right now, we have plans to make.

You and I are going to penetrate God's Pellets. Do you think it's possible? Without the guards being aware? Bearing in mind that, since your disappearance, they will have guessed that their hiding place has been revealed?"

Islar smiled, and the gleam in his eyes was triumphant. "Of course!"

CHAPTER THIRTY-SIX

Scarpen Quarter
On the Skulkai Caravansary route
Breccia City

When Jasper, Rubric and Dibble headed into the Red Quarter shortly after leaving Fourcross Tell, the rest of their party, driven by Elmar on his own black myriapede picked up in Samphire, stayed on the caravan route that wended its way south to the Skulkai Caravansary and thence to Breccia.

On that ride from Samphire, Terelle had grown fond of Umber. Ever since they'd left Khromatis, he had done his best to tell the family stories about her father and his parents, about the life they'd led in their more prosperous days in the Southern Marches. Jade, on the other hand, was cool and aloof, although never impolite.

I don't suppose I can blame her, Terelle thought as they began their descent from the high trail of the Warthago. *I didn't like being coerced, either.* She was seated behind the waterpainter, and Jade's back was spear-haft straight, as if she refused to relax for a moment.

They topped a rise to a point on the trail with a view

clear south through the range to the Skulkai. Umber exclaimed, "Dear sweet God, look at those ridges! Like bear claws scratching at the sky. They have a godly magnificence, don't you think, Lord Jade?"

"A barbarian god," Jade said in answer. "Savage mountains suitable for a land that worships the sun."

"Not everyone does," he rejoined. "Terelle here follows our faith now, don't you, cousin?"

"You do?" Jade asked in surprise as she clutched at the saddle handle. She always rode the pede with an air of unease. She turned to look at Terelle, as if she half expected her to have visibly changed.

Terelle shrugged. "The Alabasters proved to me that the Sunlord is just a figment of men's imaginations. Physician Errica taught me something of the form of your worship." She could have added that she needed desperately to believe in something. She needed it to give her courage and hope, and most of all, meaning—but that need was private, so she fell silent.

It wasn't much of a conversation, but it must have had an impact on Jade because that night, as they sat around a small campfire and two horned cats caterwauled in a gully nearby, the woman thawed enough to ask her about the way in which she had been using waterpainting to stormbring. "You must be very careful," she said when Terelle described her methods. "You never know what the magic will decide—and the larger the painting, the more that can go wrong. That's why we have such strict rules in Khromatis, and the penalties are dire. There's no mercy when someone abuses waterpainting, even if they didn't intend to harm anyone."

Umber smiled benevolently on them both while they

chatted, as if the thaw was his doing, and he could well have been right. He'd tried hard to be pleasant to Jade, and to make her journey as comfortable as possible. When Terelle turned in for the night, she grinned at him, and he winked back.

The next day, Jade asked to learn the language of the Quartern.

Four days later, Elmar was reining in the pede at the top of the Escarpment to show Jade and Umber their first view of Breccia. At least the rooftops were green with plants, and a little of the skirting of the bab grove was visible at the foot of the slope, but still Lord Jade asked in a shocked voice, "This is the main city of the Quartern? Surely not!"

"You can't see most of it," Terelle said.

"I can see the land around it. There are no farms. What do you live on? Not even a sheep could find enough to eat here."

Elmar said defensively, "We don't have sheep. There are goats; they eat the bab fruit mostly. The groves are at the bottom of the scarp."

"This is not a land where it ever rains without the intervention of a stormlord," Terelle reminded her. She waved a hand at a straggly thorn tree growing alongside the track. "Out here, if a plant can't survive on dew, it dies."

Lord Jade shook her head in bemusement. "I had no idea," she whispered.

At least she sees the problem now, Terelle thought.

"There's a cloud there," Elmar said and pointed ahead with his pede prod. "Lord Rubric and Lord Jasper must be stormshifting."

Terelle squinted against the light. "It's a message cloud."

"A message cloud? What's that?"

Terelle explained and the two Khromatians glanced at one another, eyebrows raised. "You mean you write letters to one another in the sky?" Jade asked.

"You mean you don't?"

Umber laughed. "One up for the barbarians, eh, Lord Jade?"

Terelle relented. "They aren't exactly long communications. That would be far too difficult. And only Jasper has enough talent to do it."

"What does this one say?" Jade asked.

"'Highlord, treat the visitors at your city gate with honour, or learn the meaning of regret.' He has signed it." She'd felt bereft and afraid, and now she had proof she was never forgotten, or unprotected. He had been following her with his senses. He knew exactly where she was.

Thank you, Shale.

"I'll scratch her eyes out if she comes in here."

"No, I'm afraid you won't." Laisa smiled at her daughter benignly to cover her exasperation, then opened the letter from Jasper that the steward had just brought her. Terelle and her mysterious companions had been conducted to the guest apartments and Laisa had no intention of meeting them until she knew a little more about what was going on. She laid aside the letter opener and began to read.

Her mother's attention to the letter did not stop Senya from voicing her opinion. "I don't understand how she can have the *gall* to come back. She wasn't *supposed* to, not here. Can't we ask the waterpriests to charge her with sorcery? That's what Lord Gold wanted."

"Senya, please. Let me read this and then we'll decide. You saw the sky message today. That was a very public threat, and I tend to take such things seriously. You should never forget caution when you are dealing with a stormlord."

Senya sulked while she waited. Laisa took no notice. When she'd read the letter through, she flicked it with a fingernail and said, "It seems one of the people with Terelle is also a stormlord. They're from Khromatis."

"Blasphemers! Lord Gold will be *furious*. You must write and tell him. They'll be arrested and executed." She beamed at her mother. "How exciting."

"They've come here to stormshift while Jasper is busy with the battle in the Red Quarter." She looked across at her daughter. "So if we want water in our cisterns, we have to keep quiet about who they are and be polite to all of them, including Terelle. Understand?"

Appalled, Senya said, "Polite to that Gibber-grubbing snuggery slut? Never!"

Laisa sighed. "Yes, I suppose that's too much to ask. Better you don't meet her. I'll keep her out of your way and get her out of Breccia Hall as soon as possible." She regarded her daughter carefully. "If you are bored, my dear, may I suggest you take a trip to the coast or visit Amberlyn in Scarcleft?"

Senya looked at her, astonished. "Why would I want to do that?"

"She is your daughter."

"She's Jasper's daughter, not mine. If you're so worried about her, you go see her."

"What do you *want*, Senya?"

For a moment she looked stricken. "I want everything to be back the way it was. When we were rich and comfortable and people were always courting me and saying nice things. When Daddy was alive. Jasper *murdered* him; it's all his fault. And that snuggery whore of his."

Sunlord help me, I don't know what to do with this daughter of mine. Aloud she said merely, "I wish we could bring that life back too. For now, however, the only way we'll get anywhere near that time again is to have reliable water. Which means treating our guests with courtesy as Jasper asks and not telling the waterpriests who they are. Understand?"

"That Gibber grubber sleeps in my husband's bed, and we have to be nice to her?"

Laisa was taken aback by the venom in Senya's tone, but said calmly, "You are still the Cloudmaster's wife. You have the status. You have power here; she has none. We can both afford to be gracious."

Senya regarded her with eyes narrowed, then stood and left the room.

No, she didn't just leave. She flounced. This time Laisa didn't stifle the sigh. She walked out onto the balcony in an attempt to dismiss her daughter from her mind. She leaned against the railing to look out over the city. *Her* city; who would ever have thought that would happen?

Ah, Senya, I wish I could put things back the way they were, too. I'd even like to be married to Nealrith all over again. How strange is that? What a fool she'd been to hanker after Taquar. Her desire for him had brought her to the edge of ruin. Worse, his ambition had brought this disaster on them, and Sunlord only knew where they'd end up now.

Sometime later she became aware she was not alone. She whirled to see Terelle just inside the sitting room doorway, hand on the doorknob, regarding her with a neutral expression. Evidently Senya had not shut the door properly on her way out.

"I sent a message to suggest we meet over dinner," Laisa said.

"I know. The steward told me. But I thought it better we talk first. I don't want any trouble, not with you or Senya or with the temple priests."

"As long as you stick to the bargain Jasper made on your behalf—that you don't use waterpainting except to bring water—I suspect the waterpriests won't be moved to do much. Your guests are another matter. The priests in Breccia are all Lord Gold's men. Eventually they'll find out who your companions are, and they'll tell the Sunpriest everything. None of them will like the idea of Khromatians becoming a power in the land. Which they will be if they're our stormbringers." She shrugged. "You and Jasper have knocked the top off a wasps' nest."

"The Sunpriest would rather be without water?"

"Who ever said that Lord Gold was a rational man?"

They stared at each other, sharing a silent moment of agreement. "I owe Jasper an apology," Laisa said, breaking the silence. "Had I known your journey to Khromatis would yield a stormlord, I wouldn't have released Taquar."

"You've had a change of heart?" Terelle looked disbelieving.

Laisa didn't answer the question, saying instead, "I

think it best you have as little as possible to do with Senya."

"I agree. I have to show Lord Umber how Jasper goes about stormshifting, and where the maps and such are, which means using the stormquest room. Several days work, I imagine. I have Jasper's key. And then I will take Elmar Waggoner and find some lodgings downlevel. Lord Umber Grey and Lord Jade Lustre will be safer if they stay here. Jasper wanted me to warn you that if you fail to protect them, he will see you suffer for it."

"So he said in his letter. He was quite clear on the matter, never fear. How long do you intend to be in Breccia?"

"Until Jasper comes back."

"But in his letter he said he wasn't intending to live here again! That he would settle in the Gibber with you and concentrate on bringing them their water."

"First, he has to complete the series of waterpaintings I did of him here in the stormquest room. I'm not sure how many are left."

"Ah. I'm glad he saw the sense of leaving Taquar alone. Or was that your doing? I don't suppose you have any interest in looking after Senya's child, after all."

"No, perhaps not, but I can't say I like the idea of any child being a piece in a horror of Taquar's making."

She's fearless, I'll give her that.

"Will Taquar hurt the girl?"

Terelle sounded indifferent, but Laisa wondered if she was. Maybe she just wanted information to pass on to Jasper. "Taquar never does anything without a reason, and that includes murder and cruelty. The nurses look after the baby and he doesn't concern himself. Of course, that may change if either of you gives him reason."

"I'm surprised you elected to stay here. He *is* your husband."

Laisa smiled faintly, but didn't reply.

Terelle nodded pleasantly and left the room as quietly as she'd entered.

Elmar was waiting for her outside Laisa's door. Terelle smiled at him as they walked away from the highlord's quarters. "Did you hear all that?"

"I did. You be careful around that bitch."

"Don't worry about her. We've work to do. Jasper's orders."

He brightened. "Good. I'm bored to tears. I want to spit when I think of Dibble getting to fight Reduners while all I have to do is bleeding fend off Senya Almandine."

"We have to start telling the people of Breccia we have two new stormlords bringing us water. We won't mention that one of them is actually in the Red Quarter, just hint that he's in another city. We're going to praise Lord Umber Grey to the skies. We're going to visit every snuggery and taproom and gambling den and market from here to Level Forty-two, dropping hints about how wonderful these two men are, and how water talented and how they're going to save us from this wretched water rationing.

"The one thing we aren't going to do—yet—is tell anyone that the new stormlords come from Khromatis. Oh, but first we're going to get Umber and Lord Jade the most Scarpen-looking clothing we can find. I've already told Lord Jade to keep her mouth shut in public and not to speak to the servants, but I want you to work with Umber to get him to stop using 'ye' and not sound so withering *un-Gibberly* when he speaks."

Elmar grinned. "You want me to turn him into a Gibber-settle grubber?"

"Exactly. And Elmar, don't underestimate Lord Senya. She's a rainlord, and rainlords can suck the water out of you. Never forget that."

"Lord Jasper did say she never got that far in her studies."

"We can hope not, but don't rely on it, all right? That woman is missing something, and what is missing makes her dangerous."

"Missing something?"

Terelle considered her memories of Senya. "Logic. She's illogical and can't therefore be relied upon to do what we expect. That's dangerous."

They looked at each other soberly.

Then she laughed. "Never mind, Elmar. As we spread the word about the new stormlords, you'll enjoy the carousing and all the rest, won't you?"

"So that's what a bab grove looks like." Umber stood in the shade of the southern wall of the city and surveyed the rows of trees trimming the city with green.

Terelle, remembering how it had once been, was less impressed. "The Reduners destroyed such a lot."

"I'll admit I expected the groves to be greener," Jade said. "I didn't realise what a struggle life here is."

She sounded saddened, and Terelle felt a twinge of hope. Jade had also accepted Rubric's decision to accompany Jasper, which meant that she had to wait for him to return before they could duplicate the waterpainting that would free her to go home. Which was another good sign.

"Let's go and have a drink," she suggested. "Lord Jade has not tried bab amber yet."

They walked upwards, through the almost deserted lower levels, into the more prosperous parts of the city, now tattier than they had once been. She smiled grimly; one good thing about the city was that there was plenty of work for those who wanted it. They entered a tavern on Level Fourteen, and found a vacant table. Umber and Jade sat while she and Elmar elbowed their way to the bar. Elmar leaned on the counter and lowered his voice. "See the brown man over there?" he asked the barman.

The man nodded without interest as he busied himself filling flagons. "Gibber grubber, is he? Don't see many of them these days. What's with them bleeding funny tattoos on his face?"

Elmar leaned in close and dropped his voice to a conspiratorial whisper. "Eh! Watch your language, my man! That's the new stormlord, bringing you every drop of water you'll be getting through your spigots. Living up there in the hall he is, bringing clouds for the whole Scarpen. Name's Lord Umber Grey. Came here to save our hides. Nice fellow, too, would you believe? Not the ordinary upleveller with his wilted nose held so high he'd trip over his own knees. But then, Gibber folk are mostly humble, to my mind."

The man looked back at Umber with renewed interest. "Gibber, is he? Looks like one, 'cept for those tattoos. But I heard tell the priests are worrying about stormlords coming in from the heathen land on the other side of the 'Baster place. Blasphemers there, they say. In the temple on Sun Day the priest reckoned we ought to nail them all to the gate if they come here preaching their heresies."

"Don't know anything about that," Elmar said cheerfully. "Haven't heard any preaching out of this fellow. Looks like a Gibber grubber and speaks good Quartern, just like you and me, too." *Well, he does when he remembers...* "All I know is there's been rain over the Warthago every bleeding day he's been here. So I reckon I don't care where he's from, so long as he wants to help. Do them priests think we ought to kill folk decent enough to come to aid us? Blighted eyes, are they sun-fried?"

As Elmar counted out the tokens, the innkeep put the filled mugs on the counter. "Reckon you've got the right of it, armsman. Anyone who brings us water ought to be respected, right enough. Gibber is he? The Cloudmaster's Gibber too, after all. That's good enough for me."

Elmar handed two of the mugs to Terelle with a wink. She grinned as they walked back to Umber and Jade. "You're getting good at this, El."

"Secret is to tell the truth and imply the lies. Sounds as if the waterpriests might have figured out where Umber's from, though. Pity."

Over the next run of a sandglass, they watched while the barkeep passed on the gossip to everyone who entered. Appreciative looks were sent in Umber's direction, but no one approached the table.

Elmar bent to murmur in Terelle's ear, "I think we've won this one, at least. Lord Gold is going to find it hard to get approval in this city for a pissing stupid idea like bad-mouthing stormlords."

"I hope so," she said.

*   *   *

It was already dusk when they stepped outside.

A large crowd of boisterous men had just entered the outer courtyard, and they had to step aside to allow them to pass into the inn. As she stood there, Terelle swayed, suddenly dizzy. She put her hand out to steady herself against the wall, but misjudged the distance and almost fell. Her vision blurred. Pain stabbed her skull. Disoriented, she tried to cry out, but made no sound. Something pulled at her. Pulled at her skin, at her body. Her heart started to pound against her ribs. She panted, startled by the need to do so. Clutching at Elmar's arm, she tried to tell him something was wrong, but her mouth had dried out and her tongue was sticking to her palate. Sweat ran down her forehead into her eyes, gummed her hair to the sides of her face, dripped off the end of her nose.

Elmar looked down, then his eyes widened in shock. "What's wrong?"

She increased her grip on his arm, but her muscles cramped and she couldn't speak. Nor could she let go. Jade and Umber loomed up at the edge of her vision. Terrified, she wanted to scream.

Vision.

Something was wrong with the way she was seeing. Her eyes felt wrong. Dry. She started blinking, rapidly. Her arms and legs were tingling. She staggered against Elmar.

Jade clutched at her wrist to keep her upright, but her grasp was slick and her hand slipped. "She's sweating," Jade said. The concern in her voice was alarming. "It's pouring off her."

What's wrong with me? She wanted to ask the question aloud, but the words wouldn't come.

Then Umber answered anyway. "Dear God, someone's taking her water!" Then he was gone, beyond her vision.

Oh, she thought, with a remote calm that astonished the panicked part of her mind. *I'm dying. I bet it's Senya. The little bitch.*

CHAPTER THIRTY-SEVEN

Scarpen Quarter
Breccia, Level Fourteen
Breccia Hall, Level Two

"Drink this." Jade forced the mouth of her water skin between Terelle's lips. "Small sips. One after the other. Don't stop. Whatever you do, don't stop." Her consternation, badly concealed, terrified Terelle.

She was cold. And the woman was covering her with wet cloths. *Blighted damn, that is withering icy! Can't she see I'm shivering?*

Sip, more sips, pushed against her lips.

Mustn't stop. Hold on to my water. Hold on to it. I can do it. I did it when Jet tried to kill me. Waterlords can hold on to their own water. Stormlords can. I can. If I try.

Sip. Some more.

Jade cradled her tight, murmuring in her ear. "Hold on, Terelle. Just a little longer. Hold on to your water. You can do it. You have to because I won't do that painting. I won't, I swear. You have to. You have to live to do it."

Her brain wouldn't work. *What painting? There was something she should understand...*

She swallowed more water. Hold on to her water, that was it. Don't let it go. Fight it. Fight whoever was doing this to her.

Then, suddenly, it was all over. That horrible, deadly pull was gone. Vanished, as if it had never been.

She took a shuddering breath and gulped more water, long draughts until she had finished all Jade had. "I'll be all right now," she whispered as Elmar pressed his water skin into her hand. "I think." Trying to sit up, she was surprised to find how weak she felt. And was surprised again when she realised her head was resting in Jade's lap. "They stopped. And I'm alive."

"I've heard that taking a waterpainter's water is tough. I guess you just proved it to be true," Jade said, speaking in her own tongue, but keeping her voice low.

"She just fainted," Elmar said, shielding her from sight with his body as he answered a question from some of the inn's patrons. "Nothing to worry about." He waited until they'd gone before he turned back to Terelle. "Keep drinking."

"I am." She looked at Jade. "I don't think it was me that stopped it. It was you—by deciding you wouldn't do that second painting." She took Jade's hand and squeezed it. "Thank you."

Before Jade could reply, Umber reappeared. "I think ye, um, you'd all better come and look," he said in a low voice. "This is not good."

Elmar helped her up and they all crossed the courtyard to the side of the building. Empty barrels and casks were stacked there in a narrow laneway, hidden from view. Tucked away out of sight behind one of the stacks was the body of a man.

"Dead?" Jade whispered.

Umber nodded. "Stabbed him. Quickest way to stop him. I was scared she'd die if I wasted time arguing about it." He shrugged. "I'm no military man, but I don't make mistakes when I slaughter an animal."

"I'll keep watch to make sure no one comes this way," Jade said and went to stand at the corner of the building.

"He was a rainlord waterpriest," Elmar said quietly. "They're the only men who wear that kind of robe." He knelt by the body and went through the man's belt pouch and clothing. "Nothing much. A handful of coins. A water skin. A kerchief. And this." He extracted a small piece of folded parchment from the pouch, sniffed at it, read the words it contained, made a face and handed it to Terelle.

She raised it to her nose and said, "Senya."

"Not Laisa?" Elmar asked.

"No. That's Senya's perfume. Nothing to say Laisa didn't use Senya's scented note paper, though, I suppose." She unfolded it, held it up so it caught the last of twilight and read the contents aloud. Her own name was written in large, childish letters, followed by the address of the rooming house where she and Elmar were lodged. "Definitely not Laisa's handwriting. I don't know Senya's." *I don't need to. Laisa didn't know about this. Not her style. But it is Senya's.* She shivered, reaction setting in. She'd almost died. Senya had given her address to a priest and told him to murder her at the first opportunity he had. *And he'd obeyed.* Which meant that Lord Gold had sanctioned it.

"Now what?" Elmar asked. "Not good if it gets known that a Khromatian killed a waterpriest. Not weeping good at all. In fact, we'd all be salted."

"Then no one must know," she said.

Elmar tapped a barrel on the lid. "They're empty," he remarked. "Good. Probably waiting collection to be taken back to the amber brewery."

"Nice and large," Umber added.

The three of them exchanged looks.

"I'll strip the body of everything so he can't be identified," Elmar said. "We'll bring his clothing back to our lodging and burn it in the fireplace tonight."

Umber said, "I'll take his water and then we'll stuff what's left of him in the barrel. I doubt the men who'll come to pick it up will notice the extra weight."

"And once it's one of hundreds at the brewery, they won't even know where it came from," Elmar said. He began stripping the corpse.

"Thank you, cousin," Terelle said. "I owe you my life too, it seems."

"Terelle, that alone makes my whole trip here worthwhile."

For a moment it felt as if they were the only two people in the world. In their silence, within their gaze, a connection was made and approved; her heart lightened and her tension eased.

"It's good to have family again," she said. "Especially since I like you *much* better than my great-grandfather."

His smile broadened into a grin. "Me too." And he turned to attend to the corpse. She watched and thought of Jet Verdigris. *Another man who just disappeared. Yet I know what happened to him. I'm standing next to his mother, who doesn't know—and I can never tell her, not about Jet or Hue. Why does necessity sometimes make such liars of us all? I never want to hurt anyone, but I do.*

And then she remembered that both Jet and this nameless priest had tried to kill her, while Hue had participated in Feroze's murder, and she was glad they were dead.

When finally the dried-out skin and bone of the priest was stuffed into one of the barrels and his water was stored in their respective drink containers, Umber raised his water flask towards the barrel in macabre homage. "May God forgive us all," he said cheerfully, then winked at Terelle—and drank.

Two sandruns later, Umber was surveying the new set of rooms Elmar had rented for Terelle. "I suppose it'll do," he said to Elmar, but he hated the idea that he couldn't keep an eye on Terelle. "Ye pull your truckle bed across her door so anyone entering her room will have to go through ye first."

Elmar rolled his eyes. "M'lord, are you teaching an old spear how to fly true?"

"I'll see ye demoted to camp-pot scrubber if anything happens to my cousin."

"Oh, for goodness sake," Terelle said. "I'm sure my main problem will be lack of sleep because Elmar snores. Jade, take Umber away. I have enough problems with Elmar clucking over me without him as well!"

Still, she gave him a hug before he left for Breccia Hall. He didn't like living under Laisa's roof, but there was nothing much he could do about it. He needed the facilities of the stormquest rooms.

Damn it, when water-power is so valuable, Umber thought, *you have to lie down with whoever has it, be they pious or pernicious. It's ridiculous that Senya can't be brought to book for her crime.*

He looked across at Jade as they entered the hall. "Do you think we could tackle Laisa?" he asked. "I'm feeling in a fighting mood."

"Gladly," she said. "Although I suspect this will be another time when I'll regret my lack of proficiency in the language."

They found Laisa in her sitting room, and Umber wasted no time getting to the point. "Someone tried to murder Terelle this evening."

Laisa paled. There was no doubting her shock. "You don't think—" she began, then had to clear her throat and start all over again. "If that's so, it was nothing to do with me."

"The murderer was found to have this note on him." Umber gave her the folded parchment. "The address is the place where Terelle was staying."

She opened it up and read it. When she raised her head again, she was even paler. For a moment he thought she might faint, and Jade came across the room to hold her by the arm and lower her into the nearest chair.

Umber looked at her with more interest than pity. "I assume the handwriting is Senya's."

If Laisa had any thought of denying the idea, it didn't last long. She nodded.

"The murderer was wearing priestly garb. Which leads us to believe this may have been part of a larger conspiracy."

"I'll talk to her."

"*Talk,* Lord Laisa? Where I come from attempted murder is dealt with by more than conversation."

"I am the highlord here. This is my concern."

Her voice was calm, her tone even, but she'd clutched at the chair arms until her knuckles were white.

He said, "May I remind ye that the protection of Terelle Grey is also your concern? Ye were given a direct order by your Cloudmaster. The watering of your land depends on Terelle and Jasper and myself and Jade's son. Ye'd do well to be remembering that. And at the moment, none of us are happy with you. Ye'd also do well to be thinking very carefully about your next move. Do ye think ye'd get support even from your own guards if the water were to stop flowing through your pipes?"

"Jasper always puts the welfare of the people of the land first."

He leaned towards her, thrusting his face unpleasantly into hers, forcing her to press back against the chair. "Maybe. But I'm *not* Jasper. And right now ye—*you* are this far away from death." He held his thumb and fore-finger the width of a pea apart, right under her nose.

"You're a guest in this land, this city and this building! How *dare* you speak to me like that. And Senya is Jasper's wife."

"Ah. So she is." He straightened but didn't move away from her. "All right then. Show me that she has no contact with the priesthood nor anyone else until such time as Jasper arrives in Breccia once more, and Jade and I *may* allow her to continue breathing. Perhaps ye'd also be kind enough to send a message to this Sunpriest fellow, suggesting he tread carefully, because if he doesn't, ye'll get no water. Jasper may have scruples. I don't. And at the moment, it's me that's bringing the storms. Oh, and just to make sure ye understand the whole situation: ye do know about the power of waterpainting, don't ye? Er, you?" *Damn it, I think I'll give up with this ye or you stuff.*

"A waterpainter can make the future?"

"Think about what that means, if ye will. Terelle can paint Senya dead in her bed. Or you. Or both of you. And ye wouldn't wake up tomorrow morning. I wouldn't annoy Lord Jade, if I was you. Because she can do exactly the same thing. And she is *seriously* annoyed at the moment."

Laisa ran her tongue over her lips. She glanced at Jade and then rose to her feet. "What happened to the priest who—?"

He smiled as unpleasantly as he knew how. "What do ye—you—think?"

She hesitated momentarily and then left the room without a backward glance.

"I think you just ran the highlord out of her own sitting room," Jade remarked, amused. "You must tell me what you said to her."

"I was very polite," he protested, "and reasonable. Though I can never remember to speak like a Scarperman."

She snorted. "You may have the smile of a frog in a water jar, my friend, and jokes to match, but you have the teeth of a river gharial. And I think you just bared them." She took him by the arm. "Come, let's leave this room so you can tell me all about it."

Livid, Laisa bundled the maid out of Senya's apartment into the passageway and stormed inside. She slammed and barred the door and stood, hands on hips, glaring at her daughter.

"Were you out of your tiny mind?" she raged. "Trying to kill Terelle when the very water you drink in the future may depend on her? When Jasper made it quite clear we'd suffer if she was not welcomed?"

Senya looked up from the table where she was toying

with her jewellery. "Oh! You mean Lord Scriven didn't kill her? The stupid man!"

Laisa felt her rage swell inside her. She'd hoped there would be an explanation; instead here was confirmation of her worst fears. "No, he didn't, Sunlord be thanked. How did you get him to do it in the first place?" Nausea warred with her despair as her fury built.

"I sent one of my guards to Portennabar to tell Lord Gold about Terelle and the other two blasphemers. He ordered Lord Scriven to speak to me. So when Scriven came, I told him Lord Gold wanted the blasphemers dead, and the way to do it was to have them blamed for Terelle's death."

"And he *believed* you?"

"Why not? I am the Cloudmaster's wife! I have the ear of Lord Gold. And Lord Gold told him to speak to me. So I gave him the order to kill her."

"Lord Gold didn't order Scriven to kill her?"

"No, of course not. He wants her to stand trial for blasphemy or sorcery or something. But I was afraid Jasper would rescue her if that happened. My way was better. But now you're telling me Scriven mucked it up, confound him."

Laisa swallowed back her anger and sank into a chair opposite her daughter. "Senya, what you did was not—not *wise*. It will have repercussions you won't like."

"Only because it wasn't successful. That fool of a priest. Anyway, it doesn't matter. I have another plan. Look!"

She opened up one of the jewellery boxes in front of her and took out a small onyx perfume vial. Holding it up to show her mother, she asked, "You know what this is?"

"Perfume?"

Laisa took it from her. She was about to open it when Senya said, "Poison! It's triple-concentrated keproot. Put a drop of the unconcentrated liquid in a censer and burn it, everyone in the room feels relaxed and happy. Put five drops of this concentrated stuff into someone's drink, they won't taste it, but they'll stop breathing within a quarter-run of a sandglass."

"That—that sounds dangerous."

She shrugged. "It is."

"And *Scriven* gave this to you?"

She nodded happily. "Apparently hunters use it in animal baits." She picked up a necklace. "Have you seen this one? I found it in the Level Four market. I think it used to belong to that stuck-up Sattie Marker. Do you remember her? She died in the siege. I always liked it." She smiled. "And now it's mine."

"That's—that's nice. Senya, I think you had better go and stay with Taquar for a while. Until this whole affair blows over."

"No."

"Senya—"

"No. Taquar was so nasty to me last time we met. He said he wouldn't bed me if I was the last woman alive in the Scarpen." She pouted. "I won't go. Jasper's not going to do anything to me."

"Lord Umber is not quite so forbearing, and Terelle is his cousin."

"Who's going to listen to him?"

"He's a *stormlord,* you fool!" Her anger threatened to overwhelm her calm.

"He can't do anything to me. I'm the Cloudmaster's wife. Besides, Lord Gold will protect me. This is all his fault."

Laisa was speechless. Despair was a tight knot in her chest alongside the fury, and nothing she could say, at least nothing that Senya could understand, would make it go away. She could see all that she had rebuilt on the ruins of her world crumbling.

"We'll talk again in the morning," she said and rose to leave. On the way out she took the key to the outer door of the apartment and turned it on the outside. The maid was hovering. "Senya has gone to bed," she said. "You may retire yourself."

The maid happily disappeared towards the servant quarters; Laisa, swallowing back her nausea, headed towards the seneschal's rooms. She had orders for him, and they were all about limiting Senya's freedom. Opening up her clenched hand, she looked at what she held: the onyx vial. She desperately wanted to throw it away, but knew she wouldn't. Just in case.

She continued on her way. Somewhere in the back of her mind, she heard Nealrith weeping.

CHAPTER THIRTY-EIGHT

Red Quarter
God's Pellets

"No. No, no, no." Vara, hands on hips, her mouth pulled into a mulish line, glared at Jasper and Rubric and Ryka.

Kaneth and Cleve, on the other side of the stone camp table, exchanged glances. Shading them all, a thick red canvas in two spaced layers kept off the worst of the midday heat, but it was still stifling.

That's one not-so-good thing about this valley, Ryka thought, her mind wandering because she didn't want to absorb the import of Vara's words. *No breezes, the way there are out on the dunes.*

"Never," Vara said, just to make sure they all understood.

Ryka subdued a desire to throw something at the old woman. Ten days since Guyden had ridden out, and only now Vara was being difficult. Preparations were complete for their army to march. Forces from friendly southern dunes were gathering to the south of Dune Watergatherer, awaiting Jasper's cloud messages to advance on Ravard's forces from that direction. Allied armsmen from more northerly tribes had been riding in, arriving at God's Pellets in small groups for days, until the arrival of the Watergatherer army on Dune Koumwards had finally cut off the stragglers.

Some were well armed, well mounted and well stocked, others woefully ill-prepared. There had been headache after headache of logistics. She'd hardly seen Kedri, as she wrestled instead with pieces of parchment covered with figures and names and amounts—supplies, men, armour, weapons, pedes, food, water panniers. She'd struggled to have it all at her fingertips so that armsmen were fed and clothed and armed appropriately, pedes were fed, groomed and accoutred. And now it seemed their assumption that they could use water from the Source as a weapon was in jeopardy, if Vara had her way.

Ryka opened her mouth to translate Vara's emphatic refusal for Jasper, but he forestalled her. "I think we all understood that. But I'd like to know why. She does know that using the water from the Source doesn't diminish the amount in the cave? More just flows in to replace it."

Vara didn't wait for Ryka's translation. Glowering at Jasper she was off again, words flowing from her too fast for him to catch the meaning, her hands thrown around expansively, just missing Jasper's nose.

When she finally faded to a halt, Jasper, now in need of a translation, raised an eyebrow in query.

Ryka took a deep breath. "She says the water is sacred. Sent to us by the Over-god. She believes that for generations this valley was hidden to the people of the red dunes to punish them for their violence and their practice of slavery. Just when the Over-god was thinking of relenting, Davim rose up with his ideas of random rain. He reinstated slavery and went to war. However, the Over-god is merciful."

She paused, eyeing Kaneth.

"And then?" Jasper asked.

"The god sent Uthardim to show the good people of the dunes where to find water and to lead the enlightened tribesmen to victory."

"Right," said Jasper. "So what's the problem?"

"Well, she says, there is always a..." she hunted for the right word, "a caveat. A catch. For victory to be granted when the odds are against you, you have to show both your faith in the Over-god, and your appreciation of the life he has bestowed on you. The valley is a holy place and the water is sacred. It is granted to save life, not to take it. If you use this water as a weapon during the war, the way you used water up in the Warthago when you fought Davim, then you will be cursed, your cause will be lost and this valley will be hidden from you, with the water lost once more."

When Jasper opened his mouth to object, Ryka laid her hand on his arm to stop him, but it was Kaneth who actually halted his words. "She's right," he said.

Ryka blinked. Kaneth, usually so prosaic and cynical and unspiritual, was agreeing with Vara Redmane? *No, that's the Uthardim of his amnesia speaking,* she thought. *And Kaneth is a better man for having that mystical side now, never forget that.*

"We don't use the water to kill," Kaneth said to Jasper. "And that's final. No more discussion. The water of the Source is sacred."

Ryka caught Jasper's expression—frustration edged with anger—but he shuttered the look and nodded his assent.

A wise decision. If Vara's Reduners lost their faith in Uthardim and their mythology, they would lose the will to fight. Still, Jasper was worried, and rightly so. If neither he nor Rubric could use the unlimited water at hand, then they'd have to take water from the tribes. She wondered if Vara would let them take the replacement supplies from the Source after the fighting was all over.

If they won.

And during the fighting, wouldn't it slow them down to bring water from the twenty or thirty different waterholes on the next couple of dunes? Of course it would! Some of them might even have their water stirred up, which would make it inaccessible to Jasper. Vara was insisting he enter the battle with one hand tied behind his back . . .

The determined old woman, having won her fight, hobbled away oblivious to the consternation she'd left behind her.

Kaneth sat on the rock slab of the table. "Let's run through this one more time. Jasper, you were up on the top knob earlier today; what did you think?"

"Ravard's in position."

"He's waiting for us. He could besiege us, but that's not the way of the Reduners, as we discovered in the Scarpen and as I am sure Cleve would tell us." Jasper smiled in his direction. Cleve had established a reputation for impatience and love of action. The remark was friendly enough, but the young warrior scowled.

You should be more careful of that volatile warrior, Jasper, Ryka thought. Cleve tended to be edgy around the two stormlords; he regarded her and Kaneth as true Reduners, stained red as they were and with their knowledge of the language and customs, but Jasper and Rubric would forever be outlanders, no matter that they'd come to help.

"He's flaunting his presence," Jasper continued. "Riding his men up on their pedes to the dune tops, lining them up to look at God's Pellets. We may not be able to see them, but he knows I will feel their water."

"He wants us to come to them," Kaneth said. It wasn't a question.

"Yes. We would be at a disadvantage either way, of course. In a siege we might win, because they'd run out of water before we ran out of food, especially if we ate our pedes. If we attack them…" He paused, then enumerated some of the problems. "At a fast pace it's five sandglass runs across the plains. All his men and pedes would have to do is wait and rest. Once at the dune, to get at him we'd have to ride up the steepest slope, while they rained spears down on us. Or ziggers. Or both. Our pedes would be exhausted. We had been planning to move blocks of water from the Source to Dune Koumwards to hurl at them and their ziggers as we attacked. But now Vara has said her piece and you agree with her." Jasper shrugged as if to say he didn't like the implications.

A wave of sick dread hit Ryka as she imagined the slaughter. *Ziggers.* "Locating and bringing water from waterholes of the other dunes will tire you," she said.

"Yes, I'm afraid so. It will limit the amount we'll have at our disposal. It's a tough dune, or so it seemed to us when we crossed it," Jasper continued. "Higher than any of the others. With deeper valleys and steeper slopes. More vegetation, too; I suppose because there are no tribes to graze their pedes on it. The pedes get their feet tangled in the vines."

"That's true." Kaneth shot a look at Ryka. "The men have a vulgar Reduner name for it."

"I've heard. 'A woman's intimate furrows' would be a polite translation, I believe."

Jasper grinned.

"You used water in the form of clouds when you fought Davim before. Why can't you do that now?" Kaneth asked.

"I had the help of a waterpainter, for a start," he said, his grin vanishing, his voice suddenly harsh. "One of the many things she did was kill thousands of ziggers before we even began. Better still, I didn't have to worry too much about precision because her magic guaranteed it for me."

"We're stormlords, not miracle workers," Rubric added in support.

"In the Warthago battle, I used water from the cistern and ice from the clouds," Jasper said. "The enemy was bunched together, confined by the rugged walls of a narrow valley and therefore vulnerable to attack. Pulling water out of the cistern into that confined valley created a wind I could use. Here, if I drop ice on them, they can just ride off in a hundred different directions. Most would escape unscathed. In fact, they know what to look for now. They'd probably scatter before I even began. Rain alone is not a weapon." The steady stare he gave Kaneth was one of foreboding. "What about your sand shifting? Can you bring down the dune with them on it? And do it before the ziggers start coming?"

The silence that followed was uncomfortably long. Then Kaneth said, "I don't know. A small sandslide is all I've ever accomplished. The one that demolished Davim's camp was barely thirty paces wide. It's not something that I have much control over."

"You had better be a quick learner, my lord," Jasper said with a snappishness normally foreign to him, "for I won't stand still and see good men slaughtered because the water of the Source is denied to Rubric and me. That is too much to ask. We'll do our best with water from waterholes, but if disaster is looking us in the face anyway, I make no promises."

"You will not take Source water to kill! If that's your intention, then I don't want you here."

Ryka was aghast. "Kaneth!"

"I mean it. This is the Red Quarter, and we will respect their ways, or leave. Is that clear?"

Another long silence followed. Then Jasper sighed and nodded.

"Swear to it, both of you."

Jasper and Rubric exchanged a look. "No water for killing will come from the Source, I promise," Jasper said. He sounded grim.

He's not sure we'll win, Ryka thought. Her chest pained her at the thought.

"We have to avoid a frontal attack," Kaneth said. "I've no wish to be suicidal. Cleve and I have discussed this at length with Vara and some of the other more experienced warriors. We'll leave tonight at sunset, by the northernmost canyons, invisible to their sensitives because of the rock between us, or so I hope. Jasper and I go east with half our force. Rubric, you go west with Cleve, Vara and the other half. I'm giving you a driver and a bodyguard who both speak good Quartern. We mount the front slope of Dune Koumwards at dawn, to the east and west of the bulk of Ravard's forces. Then we ride inwards, attacking him from both directions along the top of the dune—two mandibles coming together to slice them up."

"Their water sensitives will feel us sooner or later, won't they?" Rubric asked. "And deploy their forces accordingly?"

"I'm hoping we can confuse things. We'll need a fog from you and Jasper. Not only can we can hide under it once the sun comes up, but it will baffle their sensitives. They don't have rainlords who might be able to sort an army's water from the water in the vapour of a fog."

Jasper brightened. "It will confuse the ziggers' sense of smell and sight, too."

"This afternoon we sleep," Kaneth continued, "while those who remain behind will pack the pedes and the panniers. It will be the last sleep we get in quite a while."

"We'll be fighting a battle tired, mounted on tired pedes," Rubric said.

"I know that." Kaneth was implacable. "Cleve, alert the men to the plan."

As Cleve left, Jasper glanced over at Rubric and raised an eyebrow. "Think we can manage a thick fog?"

Rubric considered the statement. His eyes twinkled. "Guaranteed."

Something about their exchange made Ryka uncomfortable. Two stormlords knew a lot more than she or Kaneth did about moving clouds…*Sandblast them. They're up to something.*

Jasper saw her scepticism and said, "Ryka, I won't use water from the Source to kill people. I gave my word. Excuse us," he added to Kaneth. "There are some details Rubric and I need to work on. We have to give some thought to killing ziggers." The two stormlords left together, deep in discussion.

Ryka contemplated her husband wordlessly.

"What should I have done?" he asked.

"Do you expect me to answer that?" she asked.

"No, not really."

"Since when have you believed in sacred pools and Over-gods? In curses and legends?"

"I don't. But I don't underestimate how important such things are. I'm a Reduner now, Ryka. This land speaks to me. The sands speak to me. The water of the Source speaks to me. I feel these things, like a whisper in my soul. Is there an Over-god? I've no idea, but I know this place is sacred, and that the water here is our lifeblood for all the generations to come. Kedri will grow up here. And any other children we have."

"Don't I get a say in where we live?"

He smiled at her. "Do you think I haven't asked you? I've not used words, true, but I've seen the way your eyes soften when you see the shadows on the dunes, when the sun rises and sets across the plains, when the perfume of the flowers drenches the air. I've felt your love for this place, for the sands. I feel you in ways I can't explain. I know your frowns and the way you tense and relax. You talk to me in a hundred ways you don't realise."

She swallowed, hearing the truth on his lips, loving it, thinking that the old Kaneth would never have known. "The little pieces of water..."

He nodded. "With you, it's a joy. With others, it's unsettling often, embarrassing sometimes, puzzling on occasion. I feel the anger and respect and dislike of others. It helps me anticipate problems, which is useful, but there are many times when I know too much that's intimate about those around me. Things which shouldn't be known. I'm beginning to get the hang of turning off my awareness," he said. He gave a rueful shake of his head. "Ironic, really—if I'd truly listened to Guyden, I'd have known he was going to betray us."

"You felt something?"

"He was afraid of me and he didn't like me. I shut off the feeling. You can't assume everyone likes you, after all, or that everyone who thinks you're the arse on a sand-louse is also going to betray a whole tribe." He smiled down at her. "Anyway, I do know that although you may hanker after your books and learning, you aren't hankering for Breccia. You will have your books again, I swear it."

When she was silent, pondering his words, he took up the thread of the conversation and sketched his dreams. "There'll be a great city out there on the plains, with water coming from the Source. Not a city like those of the Scarpen, or a tribal encampment, either. A tent city of learning and culture for all Reduners, a place where it'll still be possible to sleep under the skies, and sit around a campfire. A city that will move when the dunes come, as they do. You'll build your schools there, Ry. Not of mud bricks, but of learning. You'll teach again. And men and women of the dunes will come to be scholars, if that's what they want.

"There'll be trees and gardens and crops out there on the plains. When the sands cover them, the dunes folk will start again on the land that's been uncovered." He looked around them, and his voice was tender. "This valley will never be lived in again; it'll indeed be a sacred place. A place to heal the wounded soul, where the sands never come. We'll take its water, yes, to supply the encampments. We'll even build tunnels or brick pipes to our city and to the dunes if they want."

"The Reduners hate the idea of anything permanent on their dunes."

"It won't be on their dunes, but under them, lying on the solid plains. I can move sand," he said. "I think I can gently push a hollow tube through a dune from one side to the other like a pebblemouse digging its burrow. I'll ask the Alabasters to help with the pipe building. Jasper tells me they were the original engineers of all the tunnels."

"And that'll be as easy as finding sand on a dune, eh?"

He chuckled. "When are the dunes ever easy? For the moment it's just a fancy, a wraith of an idea, something that may never happen."

She moved closer to him, put her arms around his neck. "If that's your future, then you must not die tomorrow. You must live to fulfil it."

He dipped his head, his cheek to hers so she could not see his face. "There are no guarantees. I'll be frank, Ry. I have a bad feeling about what's going to happen. What I sense out there touches me with dread. I cannot interpret it all, but Ravard has plans and they please him. He's laughing at me. That I know. Tomorrow one of us must die, and he doesn't believe it'll be him. He's confident and amused."

Her body fitted to his, as if they had always belonged that way: her curves, his muscles. Water to water. She whispered, "I can't imagine a world without you."

"You may have to live in it."

"How could I ever start again? You were all I ever wanted from the day I turned thirteen."

"And I was so stupid." He shook his head as if he

couldn't credit his idiocy. "If—if I don't come back, then my vision is passed on to you." He kissed the tip of her nose. "Take my dream and live it, for me."

She shook her head. "I cannot dream it without you."

"Yes, you can. And you would, too. For Kedri, you'd have those dreams, part of them, anyway, whether I'm here or not." He looked around. "I love you, Ryka, and I'll do my best to survive this coming day—for you as much as for myself. And for Kedri, and the children as yet unborn. And where is that son of ours, anyway? I need to hold him."

"Robena is looking after him. It was the only way I could stop her from hovering over Cleve like a sandgrouse guarding its eggs."

He grimaced. "I really can't stand that woman. By the way, I'm putting you in charge of the valley when we ride out."

"But I'm a rainlord—I'll be fighting." She leaned back so she could see his face and gripped his upper arms, digging her fingers in. "You can't do that to me!"

"God's Pellets needs the protection of a rainlord, should we lose. What you do then will be up to you. I did consider leaving Vara behind too, but she's already told me what she thinks of *that* idea."

"And you think I won't tell you what *I* think—?"

He gave a lopsided grin. "I'm sure you will. Nonetheless, it's your task to defend this place and keep the women and the children safe. You won't have many able-bodied men, I'm afraid. You're the only person I can trust to do a good job with very little. To take care of Kedri. And that's not just a statement from a fond father who wants his son to live. You know that."

She tried to push away the horror of what might be,

tried not to think of the possibilities. He was right. Some-one did have to stay behind. And it had to be her.

Because I'm a rainlord. Because Kedri matters, and not just because he is our son. He's the Quartern's future stormlord.

"Blighted eyes," he muttered suddenly. "What's both-ering Cleve now?"

They both turned, and sure enough, there was Cleve approaching with a determined frown that was almost a glower.

"Kher Uthardim," he said without preamble. "Before this battle, I want to know if you will declare me Master Son."

Kaneth stared at him in surprise.

Ryka expected him to rip into the young man for his presumption, but it didn't happen. Kaneth turned away, hands behind his back, to stare out over the camp. Then, astonishingly, he nodded. "Very well. I'll announce it later today."

"Thank you, Kher. I will not fail you."

"You will not fail the people of the dunes," Kaneth cor-rected as he turned, his voice as sharp as a scimitar edge.

Cleve nodded. "I will not fail the people of the dunes." He turned on his heel and left.

Ryka raised an eyebrow. "What happened just then?"

"You heard. If I die, use your judgement about whether to have him killed or not."

She gaped. "*What?*"

"If I hadn't granted him what he wanted, he would have betrayed us, perhaps in the middle of the battle. We couldn't afford that. I just gave him the extra bait he needed to be loyal."

"Kaneth, what the salted hells are you talking about?"

"Those little pieces of water of mine. If I read them right, they spoke to me of treachery. So I did what I could to prevent a betrayal we cannot afford. It seems we had two spies, not one. And this one didn't know about the other."

"*What?*"

"Two sons of Davim. Ravard must have approached them both. I felt something change in Cleve the moment Guyden disappeared. Remember how he figured out Guyden was probably Islar, the eldest of Davim's legitimate sons? I suspect he realised then that Islar is Ravard's favoured heir. I suspect he felt betrayed and began to wonder if he's not better off here."

"Are you sure? *Can* you be sure?"

"No and no, but it is an explanation that fits what my senses tell me."

"Do we want such a man as Master Son? Kaneth— what if he turns on you in the midst of the battle? A misthrown spear . . . and he'd be the new dunemaster. And you'd be dead! Can you trust him?"

"For the moment. When he left here he wasn't planning to stab me—or anyone—in the back. Except maybe Ravard." He smiled at her in reassurance. "I'll keep a watch on his little pieces of water, I promise. Even in the heat of battle. *Especially* in the heat of battle."

She took a deep breath. "You can rely on me. If ever there is a need for Cleve to die by my hand for a greater good, it will happen. I'd even murder his mother if necessary."

And that, she thought, *is what war does to decency. Sunblast you, Ravard.*

As they parted, she felt water vapour leaving the Source at a rate heavy enough to tell her it wasn't a natural loss. She halted. Those two blasted stormlords: they were going to *steal* the water to use? Sneak it out as thin vapour so no one except a rainlord would notice?

While she was hesitating, wondering what to do, Jasper came up behind her to whisper in her ear. "I don't want either Rubric or me to start the night exhausted because we've had to haul blocks of water from all over the dunes. I won't break my promise. Fog never killed anyone. For killing water, we will raid the waterholes. I made that promise and I intend to stick to it, unless the result of doing so is too terrible to contemplate."

"Blighted eyes, Jasper—that's splitting sunbeams. People will die because they don't see you coming!"

"And we'd die if they saw us coming. Which is better? Ry, neither you nor I believe in dune gods and Over-gods. There's not going to be seven cycles of bad luck because of this. If we lose this battle, it'll be because we don't have as many warriors and because we listened to superstitions. However, Rubric and I will respect Reduner culture and beliefs. If armsmen see and feel streams of water coming in, it will be from the south, after we reach Dune Koumwards."

She was unable to meet his gaze. "I suppose I'd rather you played with words than with lives."

"I wonder who taught me to do that?" He walked away and didn't look back.

That sunblasted man; he knew she wouldn't say anything.

Ryka climbed to the top of the highest of the Pellets that evening, just before sunset. Kaneth and his army had already left the valley to assemble under the northern wall of God's Pellets. She knew they must be there still, as it wasn't dark yet, but the rock walls cut off all sense of their water.

The two sentries at the top of the knob were older men, beyond an age to fight. She was surprised that they could still manage such a stiff climb. "Old man I may be," one of them said, "but I can still do my bit for the people of the dunes and Kher Uthardim." He patted her hand in a kindly fashion. "Don't worry, lady; the Over-god is watching over your lord. There will be a great victory tomorrow."

Yes, but whose?

She gazed towards Dune Koumwards. She thought she could discern smoke from cooking fires smudging the air above the red sand hills, but she might have been imagining it. If she concentrated hard, she could feel water on the dune, but her sensitivity told her nothing more than that. Men, pedes, water in panniers, it all blurred together into a mere suggestion of abundant moisture, and the dune was far too distant for anyone to be seen.

Just then, unexpectedly, she felt water on the move, but not on the dune. "There's something out there," she said. Panic pounded her heart, although she hoped she kept it from edging into her voice. "That way." She pointed out to the west. Neither her eyesight nor her water-sense was good enough for her to identify the source.

The sentries swung around to stare across the plains. "Oh, it's the wild pedes. See? Look towards those pointed rocks. They've been hanging around for days. A large family group of cleanskin packpedes, including three pre-moult young. Kaneth had someone check them out. Must have come this far north because Ravard's army scared them withering witless. If they reckon on drinking from the Source in the next day or two, though, they're going to be disappointed. We've got this place staked up tight."

She nodded, knowing that in normal conditions pedes ate dew-drenched plants at night, needing to drink at a waterhole only every ten days or so.

"Maybe the battle will be over by tomorrow's end," the old sentry said. "Then we can let them into the valley." His smile gleamed with an anticipatory joy. If the premoults entered the valley, Ryka doubted they'd ever be wild again.

"Maybe," she agreed, but her thoughts were more savage. Maybe Kaneth could be dead by the end of the day. Or Jasper. Or Vara. Or one of the other friends she had made among the Reduners.

Or all of them.

Him, too. Ravard.

She had no idea how she felt about that. Glad? Indifferent? Sad? She could not have said. All she knew was that she never wanted to see him again, and she never wanted him near her son again.

CHAPTER THIRTY-NINE

Red Quarter
God's Pellets to Dune Koumwards

Jasper, with Dibble seated directly behind him, and Kaneth on his own pede with five of his men, drove through the night at the head of their part of the army. While there was still light in the sky, Jasper had sent the cloud messages out to the southern portion of their army, and now he caught vague snatches of their water as they too moved through the darkness.

They rode in silence, twice stopping briefly to rest. Many of the men used that time to nap and he wondered how they could. He was too tense; his stomach roiled. He didn't even want to sit still. Besides, he needed to keep his mind on the cloud.

He looked up to where it blocked out the stars. He wasn't *happy* about messing with the water out of the Source, he had to admit. And if he was wrong and there really was a vengeful Over-god guarding the stuff, well, he and Rubric would be no more than pebbles and sand by the end of the night.

Towards dawn, they worked together, although they

were miles apart, to drag the cloud. They settled it over the dune like a blanket covering a sleeping red giant. Only the dune wasn't asleep. It seethed with Ravard's men.

He felt them. Dreaming, eating, drinking, sleeping, patrolling, sitting by their pede-pellet fires, doubtless thinking of the death that could be theirs in the coming day. Men, like those he led: the frightened and the brave, the cautious and the foolhardy, the compassionate and the bloodthirsty. Men like any others. Like him. It was a travesty that they should come to this, he and Mica. They had loved one another, supported one another. They had *cared*.

Sunblast you, Mica, why couldn't you listen?

He pushed the thought away. Choices had been made and he would abide by them. *Hold on, Amberlyn, Terelle. I'm coming, I promise. I just have to do this first, and hope that Taquar is lulled into thinking he has me beaten…*

The one thing he didn't fear yet was death. Waterpaintings in Breccia showed him still alive and cloudshifting, paintings he hadn't yet made true. *I wonder if the Khromatians use waterpaintings to prolong lives?* He'd have to ask Lord Jade sometime. He suspected she'd say no, that there were too many variables to make it a good idea.

Power is like that, and it's probably just as well.

It was true, Rubric thought, what Terelle had told him. These folk didn't care that Rubric Verdigris had once been Ruby Verdigris. Rubric hadn't tried to hide it from them, but they simply weren't interested. They judged him, yes—but not on that. No one worried that he wouldn't be able to fight because he'd been born a woman;

blighted eyes, he was a *stormlord,* wasn't he? That was enough. No one tried to bed him as they might a woman, mocking him because of it.

A sprinkling of the forces were even women. Vara Redmane had done her best to break down old customs about a woman's place in tribal society. He smiled, finding it ironic that on the dunes he would have faced more prejudices as a woman than as a man who had been born a woman.

Would he have come if he'd known that the first thing that would happen to him was that he'd be involved in a war? He wasn't sure. He should be angry. Back in Khromatis, Jasper had glossed over a few details that he ought to have made clear, but somehow Rubric was enjoying himself too much to be enraged. It was one thing to be ordered by his father to commit a murder, quite another to help end a revolt that was tearing the dunes apart, had devastated two cities and destroyed the trade-caravan routes. This, perhaps, was why he'd wanted to be in the army of the Southern Marches to begin with.

After the battle, would he stay?

He wanted to see the Scarpen. He wanted to see his mother again, to find out how she was coping. He wanted to see Terelle and build on his friendship with her. He thought briefly of his father and Jet and Hue and of returning to Khromatis. He was still amazed at his lack of grief over his brothers. They had tormented him too long and too often; and now, when they were no more, he was more relieved than grieving. One part of him even felt grateful to Jasper for causing their deaths. He hadn't expected that, and it shook him.

He decided then that if he could persuade his mother to

stay in the Quartern, he would stay too. If she returned to Khromatis, well, he wasn't sure what he'd do. His lips twisted in self-mockery: all his plans might end within a few runs of a sandglass and a scimitar slash across his throat, or a spear in his chest, or a zigger in his ear, although Jasper seemed confident enough that Terelle's waterpainting of him would keep him alive.

Touching the leather and metal of the vest he had been lent, he worried; it was such primitive armour by Khromatian standards. *Please God, care for this your son today, who carries your sacred water within... And forgive me for praying only when I am in danger, all right? I know I'm a hypocrite...*

Damn it, how do you pray when you aren't sure you believe in anything at all?

Just then he felt a change in the fog covering the dune ahead of him. Jasper was reworking it. He followed the alterations with his senses; the Cloudmaster was clearing a hole free of the mist, shifting it away from Ravard's men. They were still ringed by the white shroud of it, but the Watergatherer army itself was out in the open, its warriors able to see the sky and each other, yet not knowing what was going to come at them out of that mist. He chuckled.

They'll feel hunted, vulnerable, unable to know how close their enemy is or from which direction we'll come. They'll be uneasy, nervous, as jumpy as the dunnarts we startled on our way across the plains tonight.

They reached the dune just then, and the driver of his pede urged their mount up an impossibly steep slope. Rubric gripped tight to the saddle handle, leaning forward to keep his balance. *No wonder they don't use alpiners;*

they would have been floundering knee-deep in sand after the first few steps.

They entered the fog, and at a signal from Kaneth he cleared a way for them. When they reached the flatter areas of the dune, they waited a quarter of a sandglass run for most of the men to top the first slope. Then Kaneth gestured to start the advance. Another signal, and drivers prodded the pedes into fast mode, while Rubric tore the fog away from immediately in front of them as they raced across the tangled vegetation of the dune surface.

The run of a sandglass, he thought, judging the distance to the first Watergatherer warriors. *A single sand-run to the battle.*

When Kaneth set his pede at the front slope of Dune Koumwards, he grinned. The dune sang beneath his mount, welcoming him. Ryka could talk about sand shifting and explain how one grain rubbed against another to set up resonance; Vara could speak of the voice of the dune god; Kaneth didn't care. He just knew how it made him *feel:* welcome.

Should he continue to look for a man capable of being the dunemaster of all the dunes, as Makdim, Vara's husband, had been—or should he look to himself? When he brought changes to make their future less insecure, would the people of the dunes follow him even though he was an outsider? Could he lead men to a new future and rule them justly?

Kaneth Carnelian: he'd never amounted to much, unless he was on the back of a pede with a sword in his hand. Perhaps he'd started to grow up, a little, once he'd married Ryka. But then someone had creased his skull with a spear and someone else had thrown him onto a funeral fire, and everything had changed. He'd become Uthardim. Even then, he hadn't been much of a man, until Vara's burning herbs and incantations had fused the two men together, Scarpen Lord and Reduner Kher, cynic and mystic, lover and aesthete.

And there was Kedri…He swallowed back a lump in his throat. How was it possible to love someone that much? To feel so responsible? So protective? Kedri had changed everything. A child had made him into a man who cared about people and the world more than he cared about himself. A man who wanted to build a legacy for others to enjoy long after he had gone.

But first, he had to live through this day. In the run of a sandglass he would confront a man who hated him, who wanted nothing more than his death. *Oh Ryka, when I think of what he did to you, I burn. Ravard must die today. I don't care if he is Jasper's brother. He has to die, and by my hand.*

Perhaps this new Kher Kaneth wasn't such a good man, after all.

But please, let me live through this day.

What the withering spit's going on?

Dibble was driving now, so Jasper glanced around, struggling to understand the unexpected. Their pede was in the middle of a row of pedes flowing over the landscape, their natural fluidity interrupted by the occasional jerk when their feet tangled in the creepers. Moving towards them from the east came Vara, Rubric and their men; he could feel them, a block of living water, the other side of the pincer to close around his brother. With

Rubric's help, he kept the mist thick where it surrounded Ravard's encampment, or where he felt the presence of sentries and scouts. Somewhere below, he heard the dune thrumming in answer to the pattering of myriad feet. Not a sound he was comfortable with and, sunblighted hells, this dune made for a difficult ride anyway. They had to plough their way up slopes, then plunge down them, half falling from their saddles, lurching this way and that. He'd seen several fall.

Still, all that was as he expected. It was something else that was terrifying him.

Nothing was as he'd expected. That was it.

Ravard's armsmen were fleeing to the south. All of them, wheeling their pedes and charging away to avoid the pincer. Why would they not stay to fight?

Another strangeness: he couldn't feel Mica. Perhaps that was to be expected in the confusion, but still ...

I thought a fight was what he wanted. A chance to kill Kaneth. And me, too, perhaps. A desire to wipe rainlords and stormlords from the face of the Quartern. Yet they were definitely racing off. Jasper could feel the pedes flowing away in a number of distinct lines of pedes down the long fissured slope of the dune to the south.

And he couldn't feel Mica among them.

Kaneth was aware of the fleeing men more as a set of emotions. Conflicting emotions bombarding his senses from a hundred different directions and from thousands of men ... Far too many, far too much. Jostling together in lines of four abreast, pouring down the slope. Sand-brains. They should have spread out. They were a perfect target, if he could shift the sand beneath them. If.

Not so easy.

Jasper yelled out to him, telling him what was happening. And then asking, "Why? Why would he do that? What's he up to?"

"Scared of what I will do to the sand!" he shouted back. It was the only reason that made sense. Their assumption might be that Uthardim could not move the solid soil of the plain, and they were right. It was odd, though; from what he remembered, Ravard had been sarcastically sceptical of the idea that Uthardim could move the sands at all.

Well, he'd learn, the raping bastard.

They were heading away, down the southern slope of the dune towards the plains. Yet if they were scared, why had they been on the dune in the first place?

He projected his senses forward, delving deep into the sand. He pulled, twisted. The sands began to sing. It was difficult. Too much vegetation held the dune together. And he was moving too fast. He couldn't concentrate. As he and his men hit the now-empty camp where the bulk of Ravard's men had been, they were joined by the leading riders of the other half of his forces. He could see Rubric and Vara and Cleve. Cleve was grinning happily.

Blast the lad. This isn't a game, you blithering sand-worm.

Vaguely aware that Jasper and Rubric were pilfering moisture as they ploughed their way through the abandoned encampment, he noted strands of water twisting through the air in all directions, shining in the sun.

He tugged at the sand ahead, pulling more of it from under the plants and the Watergatherer pedes. Dust billowed, staining the mist, obscuring the view still further.

He wasn't sure how successful he'd been, but Rubric gave him a thumbs-up. From the slivers of information imping-ing on his mind, he knew Watergatherer pedes had stum-bled and fallen, tumbling their drivers and riders. It wasn't enough, but it was a start.

The two pincers of his army, now on a broad front, rode on into the dust and flowed after Ravard's men. The first clashes occurred as they caught up with stragglers and those who had fallen. Men died. He felt their deaths in their last exhalation; the water of their breath changing from animation to...emptiness. His pede rippled on.

When they reached the edge of the dune, Kaneth indi-cated to Fassim, the man with the bullroarer who rode behind him, that he was to sound a halt. The undulating whuuurrr started and was taken up by others up and down the front line of their army. Drivers heard and hauled on their reins. Pedes dropped their heads, looping their feel-ers backwards, grateful for the rest. Rubric cleared the air of mist and the dust settled.

Kaneth surveyed the downward slope, scored where he'd moved it. It was dotted with bodies, some of them visible only as a hand or a leg sticking out of the red sand. Damaged pedes struggled out of the soil. Wounded men tried to right themselves. And died as they shrivelled, water taken.

No mercy here. They had agreed on that beforehand, and Rubric was playing his part.

Battle is the ugliest thing any man will ever see.

Down on the plains, about a mile away, those who had escaped joined the bulk of Ravard's men who had appar-ently never been on Dune Koumwards in the first place.

They were all spreading out in their lines, facing the dune. A battle array.

Kaneth said quietly to Fassim, "Signal the 'ware ziggers'." The man fitted a different board to his twine and began to swing. The sound it made was higher pitched, whiny. Around them, men adjusted their headgear to cover all but their eyes and rearranged their tunics to swaddle their necks.

Dibble drove up and lined Jasper's pede, Chert, beside Burnish. Jasper waved a hand at some sheets of water hanging in the air above their heads like rows of curtains. "We've brought in more water from the two nearest waterholes down on Singing Shifter. If anything happens to Rubric and me, make sure you replace it afterwards, all right?"

Nodding his acknowledgement, Kaneth asked, "Will you have enough?"

"Not as much as I'd like. We're joining the sheets up into one big one. We're building a wall of water, about half a hand-span thick, in front of us all. Any zigger trying to fly through that will ruin its wings. But neither Rubric nor I are certain how long we can maintain the integrity of the sheet once we start moving. Kaneth, do you think it's wise to attack him before our southern forces put in an appearance? Half of our armsmen could be dead by zigger before our front men reach them, and down there we'll have lost our main advantage—your ability to move sand. Out on the plains, it's mostly compacted soil. Can you move that?"

He shook his head. "Where are our southerners? Can you sense them yet?"

"Yes. They aren't as close as I'd hoped they'd be.

They've met with some resistance from more of Ravard's men and are still a couple of sandruns off. It feels as if they're unable to break through. The longer we delay, the better. Listen, Ravard's men left most of their water and food behind in the camp. Our men could do with a rest and something to eat."

"With ziggers coming at us all the time?"

"Leave that to Rubric and me. We'll deal with them. It might help if you could compact the armsmen a bit more so we don't have such a large area to protect."

Hearing his name mentioned, Rubric dismounted and walked over. "I've been killing bumble bees for practice," he said in his usual off-hand way. "I felt a bit like a mean lad who pulls the wings off butterflies, but I'm quite good at it." He shrugged. "Not sure why I should still feel bad about bees when I've been killing men."

Kaneth felt foolish, suddenly made aware he was failing to make decisions based on the larger picture. "Stand the men down," he said. "Raise your water wall at the beginning of the slope. You two stay in front of it to give warning. Select some sentries to help you—and tell them to dive back inside the water wall yelling louder than an irate snuggery madam if they hear a zigger."

Only later, once he was certain that everything was in order, did he accept the food and water his driver thrust into his hands. He was hungry and attacked the roasted goat meat tucked inside cold damper with gusto. But he wasn't happy. Something didn't smell right—and it wasn't his nose that was failing him, nor was it just his sense of little pieces of water informing him of danger. It was his logic, his reasoning. He couldn't sort out why Ravard would come all the way to Koumwards only to flee when the force from God's Pellets confronted him. Somehow he couldn't accept that it was just Ravard's fear of Uthardim's sand-moving abilities, not when the man had been so scathing about those same abilities to Ryka and others.

He stepped through the water curtain to check on the stormlords. Rubric was munching his way through his meal as if he was enjoying a picnic with friends. Kaneth continued on some distance away to where Jasper was stoically eating looking more as if he was being poisoned. Something about his stance didn't sit well with Kaneth. An uncertainty. A troubled pain. Because he didn't want to confront Ravard? He almost let it ride, but some instinct, or perhaps those little pieces of water, told him it wasn't just that.

He walked over to the stormlord and squatted next to him. "What's wrong?" he asked.

Jasper smiled slightly. "You mean other than the fact that there's an army out there twice our size and better equipped, bent on slaughtering us?"

"Yes, other than that."

"I can't sense Mica."

Mica. Not Ravard. "Just now, or from when we left the Pellets?"

"I had a vague sense of him early last night. After we left the Pellets. Now we're so much closer and that's still all I'm getting—a faint hint of his water."

"And you thought it would be stronger by now."

Jasper nodded. "Although, well, you remember what it's like. Sometimes other things overwhelm what you ought to feel."

"I remember."

Jasper ran a hand over his forehead in a gesture of concern. "I'm tense and worried. And scared too, I suppose, if I'm honest. Maybe all that affects my water-sense."

Kaneth stayed rock still. Behind him the sheet of water shimmered and shifted. In front, Ravard's army had settled down too. No sound of ziggers rent the air. Not yet. "You think we ought to be worried about where he is?"

"I don't know. Maybe he's with the smaller force that's fighting our southern supporters right now. Or he could be hiding somewhere else along the dune to attack us from the side once we engage the forces down there." There was doubt in his tone. "If so, it'd have to be only a small scattered force because I can't sense them."

Kaneth felt himself growing cold. His thoughts were racing, and the horror of what he was thinking momentarily paralysed him. Finally he asked, his voice soft, his tone wooden to his ears. "What about one man? Or two or three, taking care to keep apart? Men approaching the back of God's Pellets so you couldn't feel their water through the rock? Guyden will have passed on that little fact to him, the traitorous louse."

"Traitor—or brave-hearted spy, depending on which side of the coin you are paying," Jasper said. Then he added flatly, "You think Mica might be inside God's Pellets."

"I—yes. Think, Jasper. I'm his worst enemy. I have the woman he purports to own and the son he wanted to steal. I'm the man he blames for his humiliation when he lost Davim's slaves. I defeated him in a fight on the back of a pede. Men think I'm Uthardim, come to lead the tribes to a renewed prosperity; he thinks I'm the usurper. If he holds my wife and child, *he can force me to do whatever he wants.*"

CHAPTER FORTY

Red Quarter
God's Pellets
Dune Koumwards

"Hold on," Jasper said calmly. "Firstly, if you are right, and Ravard plans to kidnap Ryka and—or—your son, how could he possibly get into the valley? During the day, even a single man would be seen. There's no cover out on the plains. All the canyons are guarded anyway. Every single one. In fact, all but one are blocked or trapped as well. A night approach? Not on a pede. The sentries on top would spot a pede even in the starlight."

"On foot at night," Kaneth said, fighting his horror. "It's possible."

Jasper raised an eyebrow. "That would be a very long walk over several days, hiding during daylight hours. Just possible, with luck, I suppose. But Ryka is taking the night watch and she's a rainlord. She doesn't have to *see* someone to know they are there."

"She can only guard one aspect." Jasper's composure had its effect; Kaneth was gathering his wits. Even so, his certainty grew, matched by rage. "Guyden—he was always up on the knobs. I put him on sentry duty for half a withering cycle. He used to climb about up there all the time. I thought he was just having a lad's fun. What a sun-fried fool I was; he was checking how to *climb in!*"

"You could be right. But it wouldn't be easy. Possibly one man, or two or three. Any more than that—difficult." He shook his head just thinking about it. "And is Ravard the kind of man to abandon an army on some sand-brained scheme of revenge all by himself? Anyway, if he'd been hidden close to God's Pellets, I think I would have sensed him the moment we left the valley. There was that meddle of wild pedes hanging around, not particularly close—but you sent men to check them out, didn't you?"

"Yes. The meddle fled into the scrub to the west, but my men got a good look first. Cleanskins, definitely no one with them. They'll hang around until they get thirsty enough to brave entering the valley. When we get back we'll have to open up a canyon for them."

If we get back.

"Then it's probably just my sensing that's at fault. It has limitations."

The effort to stop himself from shaking, to appear rational and composed, knotted Kaneth's muscles. He said, mustering confidence in his tone if not in his thoughts, "And Ryka's got the better of Ravard before. If he turns up alone, or with Guyden and a couple of others, she'll stuff him full of stones and toss him off one of the knobs."

Jasper whitened around the mouth, but he didn't speak. Only then did Kaneth remember they were talking about the Cloudmaster's brother.

Well, you'll have to forgive me, Jasper, if I don't exactly care.

Anyway, the man must know how he felt; his own daughter was being used as a hostage for his good behaviour. How the salted hells did he stay so withering calm about that? Kaneth wanted to tear Ravard apart just thinking of him coming anywhere near Kedri and it hadn't even happened yet. That he knew of.

"What do we do?" he whispered.

The silence was painful.

Finally Jasper said, his words deliberately formal, "Lord Kaneth, you lead an army on its way to battle. What you should be thinking about is how to even up the odds so we don't get slaughtered on our way down there." He pointed in the direction of the waiting Watergatherer army.

Kaneth pushed away his fear—no, his terror. He stood and signalled Rubric to join them. Jasper was right. He had to have faith in Ryka to look after herself and their son. His task was still in front of him. What had come over him? *It's this business of being a father. It changes you. It makes a blithering dryhead out of a warrior. Ry, I'm sorry. I'll be there as soon as I can…*

When Rubric arrived, he addressed them both, glad to hear the calm of his voice, "I'd like to know why they haven't used their ziggers yet. We are vulnerable up here, and they must know it."

"If we were dealing with my father," Rubric said after some thought, "I'd say he wanted us to be plunging down that slope at full speed."

"Some sort of trap?" He regarded the slope doubtfully. "It looks normal enough."

Jasper scanned the slope with his water-senses. "A lot of plants holding the surface stable, which means I can feel more water and insect life than usual. Nothing odd that I'm aware of."

"*Insect* life?"

They looked at one another.

"Salted damn!" Jasper said.

"You two take a look," Kaneth ordered. "Split up."

He watched as they began to walk along the top of the slope in opposite directions. They hadn't gone very far before Dibble, ever protective of the Cloudmaster, burst through the wall of water and ran after Jasper. Kaneth smiled as the two men had a short argument, which Dibble must have won because, when they stopped talking, he followed in Jasper's footsteps.

Kaneth went to find Vara. She was behind the water wall, haranguing a stoic Cleve about how he should treat his mount with more respect. Cleve rolled his eyes, which Kaneth took as an invitation to interrupt. He wanted to talk to the two of them about just how they should approach the Watergatherers below. Anything was better than thinking of the danger his family might be in.

"I have an idea of how Jasper and Rubric can use these water walls when we ride on," he said. "Listen."

The Watergatherer tribesmen had buried cages of ziggers on the slope, the lids of each level with the ground. It was cleverly done; the sides and base of the cages were solid enough and large enough to contain ten or so of the beetles, but the tops was made of loosely woven leaves. Strewn with a few strands of the succulent thick-stemmed, thick-leaved creeper common on the dune, the cages became invisible, both to the eye and to a casual search by the water-senses.

When Jasper sensed the first ziggers and knelt with Dibble to uncover it, he was reluctantly impressed by the simplicity and potential effectiveness of the trap. The cage top was so fragile a pede leg would wreck it easily to release the irate and hungry beetles. Thoughts grim, he covered the top with his palmubra to make sure none could escape, then stamped on the cage until the contents were crushed

Mica. Mica had done this.

Between them, he and Rubric cleared the slope of cages, about a hundred of them. A thousand ziggers. When nothing remained but dried-up husks, they returned.

No sign of agitation marred Kaneth's face now. When Jasper told him that the southern force had still not managed to break through, he was coldly calm, his orders logical and clear and firm. He was once more the consummate warrior who'd taught Jasper the rudiments of sword play, who'd defended Breccia almost to the moment of death.

He spoke to the army, his words echoing over the dune, promising them victory, predicting a new future in which water would be certain and their culture safe from the vagaries of unpredictable drought.

When he finished, they cheered him, calling out his name: Uthardim! Uthardim! Uthardim!

Who would ever have thought?

Jasper watched, and wondered how many of them would still be alive at the end of the day.

They mounted then and, lined up at the top of the slope, waited for the signal to ride. Below, Ravard's men had moved still further away. He pondered the reason and decided it was to tire out the pedes from God's Pellets. They had ridden all night long, and now they had still further to go.

One more moment of hesitation, then Kaneth gave the order.

Ryka spent the night up on the Great Knob, the highest lookout on God's Pellets. By morning there was even less to see than there had been the day before. Rubric and Jasper had covered Dune Koumwards with fog, a great bank of it hugging the land like wind-blown seed cotton. The armies lay invisible under that cloak.

Around God's Pellets, the plains were quiet. She could see the wild pedes now, grazing much closer, pulling at the plants with their mouthparts, then pausing to masticate. She felt the water of a windhover in the air nearby, so still it could have been pinned to the sky, until it abruptly folded its wings and dropped like a spear from above on some hapless creature. Crouched amongst the creepers, it tore at the flesh of its victim. A feeling of foreboding raised the hair on her arms.

"Keep an extra sharp watch today," she told the relief sentries. "You see anything that is unusual, anything at all, you send word. And don't assume that anyone you see is one of ours."

Descending to the valley floor, she mounted her pede and rode around the valley, visiting each of the canyon entry points, checking the alertness of the guards. All was as it should be. Yet somewhere this day, a battle would begin. Her pulse speeded up unpleasantly and seeded a sick feeling in her stomach that no amount of rational thinking could quell. Men would kill and be killed. And this time she was one of the women who waited, unable to influence the result.

I'm not patient enough for this. I hate it.

By midday she was back in the main camp. Robena had been looking after Kedri, a task she delighted in but which exhausted her. Kedri was rarely still, and turning your back on him usually guaranteed he'd be into mischief, especially since he'd learned to shift water. Fortunately most sources of water were kept tightly covered, but on one memorable occasion he had pulled hot water out of a pot over the fire. Luckily, the only damage he'd done was to extinguish the flames. But since then everyone watched him with the same wariness they gave to a spindevil wind. It was tiring.

He toddled across the tent to her, arms held aloft. "Up, up!" She swung him into her arms as Robena left. "Want Dada! Dada!"

"He'll be back tomorrow," she said. *I hope. Because I don't know how I'd live without him. Dreams, Kaneth? Trouble is, you've been part of my dream since I was just a girl.*

Kaneth turned to look back at Fassim. "Give the signal."

He waited until the board was whirring and the circles it made were steady, then prodded Burnish. He stood up, hooked his feet under the saddle handle and slipped the butt of his throwing spear into its notch to give him stability. Standing made him a target, but it also gave him the overall view that he needed to control the progress of the battle.

The pede lurched forward, then gathered speed. At his

side Cleve, Vara and other tribal leaders headed the front edge of the wedge; behind them the lines of men gradually widened out to provide the bulk. Rubric was positioned about one quarter of the way along one side and Jasper on the other. They were tasked with controlling the two panels of water to protect the front and edges of the wedge from zigger attack.

The mile over the plains seemed endless.

The front line of Ravard's army loomed larger, men and pedes shimmering through the distortion of the water like sand-dancers. Warriors wavered, spears glimmered, antennae whipped and undulated.

I hope ziggers won't think to go over the top of the water wall...

About half a mile from the army, they hit a wave of the little beasts. Most of them flew straight into the water and fell, wings sodden, to the ground where they were trampled underfoot. But not all. Kaneth heard the sounds of screams somewhere behind. Ahead, he noted in the calm part of his mind, the Watergatherers had not moved. They wanted the ziggers to do as much damage as possible before the two armies clashed. Once there was fighting at close quarters, ziggers were dangerous for everyone, especially when each tribe had perfumes that protected them from only their own beetles.

The second wave, about a quarter of a mile further on, was worse. By that time, Rubric and Jasper were no longer able to maintain the integrity of the water barrier and pieces were flying off in sprays of droplets.

All the more likely now that a trained zigger was aiming for his eye or ear or the soft tissues of his throat...

He saw one of Vara's men fall, clutching his face, his

scream a banner to his agony. He heard others behind, but did not turn to see. There was nothing he could do, so he shut them out, grateful he wasn't one of them. He ordered Fassim to give the bullroarer signal for fast mode. Burnish raised itself, speed doubled.

The front row of the Watergatherers turned their pedes sideways to the charge, forming a solid barrier.

Now, he thought. *Jasper, Rubric, for pity's sake: now!*

As if they heard him, the two wings of water sheltering their attack swung forward into a straight line and smashed into the barrier of pedes. Startled, pedes reared and panicked, thrashing about with their feelers. Men fell, swept from their saddles by water and the whipping antennae, creating pockets of chaos in the orderly Reduner formation.

Kaneth readied his throwing spear. Launched, it thudded into the side of one of the Watergatherer leaders trying to rally his men. With a deft twist of the reins Kaneth edged his pede into a gap. Then, scimitar in one hand and with the other clutching a thrusting spear he'd snatched from the rack on the side of his pede, he was among the enemy and whatever order there had been vanished into the chaos and horror of slaughter, the stink of death, the screams of battle. The only thing that mattered was to stay alive. It was impossible to direct the fight. There was no way to make order out of the disarray.

Seething, unpatterned turmoil. Clamour in his ears. Blood on his scimitar, his spear, his clothes, his face. His cheek pierced by something. *Pull it out.* Sharp slivers piercing his mind as men screamed their agony or their fear.

The stench of pierced guts, voided bowels, pumping

blood, hot urine, pede shit. The scream of men and zigger and animal.

Then...

Something's wrong.

Jasper was keeping close to him. Chert, his mount, was swinging its serrated antennae at Dibble's command. Wisely, Jasper was confining himself to flinging water at the enemy, making them easier for others on his pede to kill.

Nothing wrong there. But still, something's not right. What is it?

His sense of small pieces niggled at him.

No time to concentrate on it. He thrust with his spear, once, twice, three times. Connected each time. Ducked under an enemy pede's feeler. Slashed a rider from behind. Booted a man in the mouth when he tried to jump onto his mount. Rubric was ducking and weaving as he used his stormlord power. Blighted hells, he was quick. And deadly. Using a combination of stormlord powers and a fast blade. Nothing wrong there, either.

Something missing.

That was it. Something he should be feeling.

And then Jasper was yelling at him, "Ravard's not here!"

Too few pieces. That was it. Too few pieces. Not just Ravard's pieces.

A battlefield. Should be so many emotions...

He hadn't seen Guyden either, or whatever the little louse's real name was. People were missing. Not just Ravard. Not just Guyden. People who had been there, now gone. Hundreds. Some dead. Couldn't all be dead, surely?

A spear flashed between his arm and his body. Too

withering close. The man who had thrown it had pulled his packpede alongside. Eight riders. *Pedeshit*. For a wild moment the men on his pede and the men on the other animal were locked in a bloody scrimmage—jabbing, ducking, slashing. Whipped by the serrations on flailing feelers. A piece of fear and excitement abruptly gone— that was a man lost from Burnish's last segment. Dead.

Someone hit Kaneth's leg with his blade, but the blow was muted because it also connected with the saddle handle. He ignored the pain. The enemy pede began to pull away. Before they separated he wedged his spear under the mounting slot leaving his hand free to grab one of their warriors by the leg.

"Fassim, give me a hand!"

Together they hauled the man out of his saddle and pulled him across the growing space between the mounts onto Burnish.

"Don't kill him," Kaneth said as Fassim pulled a knife while the man behind him held the Watergatherer warrior face down across the saddle. The other pede and its riders disappeared into the melee. Kaneth sheathed his sword and extracted his own dagger. He bent over the captured man and laid the tip of his blade against his eyelid. "You have three heartbeats to tell me where Ravard is or the point of this digs out your eye."

When the man didn't reply, Kaneth began to cut his eyelid off.

"He's fucking your bitch of a rainlord wife!" the man screamed at him.

He died then, with a blade into his brain. Fassim tossed him off the pede.

"Kaneth!" Vara rode up, yelling. "They're fleeing!"

He stood tall and looked around. She was right. He hadn't heard a retreat sounded, but far fewer of the foe were left on the battlefield. The odds were now definitely in his favour.

His unspoken question was answered by a voice calling out to him. "Some of their men charged straight through us!" He looked around to see who had spoken. Jasper.

Sunlord blast them to a waterless hell. A number of Ravard's armsmen were heading to God's Pellets.

He yelled back. "How many?"

"A thousand maybe!"

"Where are our southerners?"

"Still half a sandrun out! But on the move now."

"Then we're splitting up." He pulled his pede closer to Vara's, head to rear, and shouted at her to make himself heard over the noise of the fighting around them. "Vara, you and Cleve deal with the ones left here. You'll have the southern reinforcements in half a sandrun." He turned to Fassim. "Signal retreat for my section only. Jasper, get Rubric—you two are coming with me."

The bullroarer sounded. "All of you, off my mount. Find a loose pede and follow me."

He turned Burnish and jabbed it hard in the neck as his men scrambled to leave the beast. Outraged, the animal took off, straight towards Dune Koumwards.

As Kaneth burst through the perimeter of the fighting, he could see part of Ravard's army as a cloud of dust, nearing the base of Koumwards. A thousand men between him and God's Pellets.

The fighting had been the fiercest around Jasper and Kaneth. For Jasper, there'd been no time to think, no moment to focus on the battle as a whole. All he'd been able to do was fight the best way he knew how—with water, as a team with the men on his pede. One moment he'd been battling to survive, his breath coming in ragged gasps, his fear so constant it was part of him; the next, the ferocity around him had melted away.

What the—?

He concentrated on the water he could feel. And the water that wasn't where it should be. That was when he yelled at Kaneth to tell him part of Ravard's army had gone. Kaneth gave the orders and he obeyed, glad it wasn't him who had to make the decisions. He looked around for Rubric and told the riders behind him on his own pede to dismount.

"I'm not going anywhere," Dibble said. He was driving and kept a hold on the reins. Jasper didn't argue.

Rubric was in the midst of the fighting, using his water-power to blind and maim rather than kill. Tossing a ball of water in his direction so that it hit him on the shoulder, Jasper attracted his attention and signalled they were leaving.

"Ride for home like you have fifty spindevils on your tail," he ordered Dibble. "This whole thing must have been just a diversion to get us out of God's Pellets so they can seize the Source and hostages. Hurry, man!"

Rubric rode up in time to hear his words. "We'll never catch them," he said. "Our beasts are dead tired. Theirs were much—"

But Dibble had already prodded the pede into action and Jasper had to guess the rest of the words as Chert sprang forward.

"We have Kaneth," he yelled back over his shoulder. "Follow me!"

*   *   *

Kaneth rode with a focus that allowed no distraction. He saw nothing to either side. He could only hope that the men ahead did not have any more ziggers to release, because if they did, he was probably dead. But that must not happen. He had to stop them. *I have to get back.*

Weeping hells, why had they been so sand-brained stupid? Ravard didn't give a damn about winning a battle. The wilted bastard knew everything that Guyden knew, and his conclusion had been simple and logical. Whoever occupied God's Pellets and controlled the Source was the sandmaster of all the dunes. Dunemaster. He wouldn't need a stormlord or a cloudmaster. He wouldn't even need random rain. He'd have the water, and he'd control Kaneth and those from God's Pellets because he'd have their womenfolk and their children. For the future, he'd have Kedri, a stormlord—if he wanted one.

It was as simple as that.

And the bastard was ruthless enough to leave part of his forces behind to be decimated by me, while he seized God Pellets . . . The concept was so foreign to his own idea of honour, he could scarcely believe Ravard had done it. Brutal, cold-blooded—and brilliant. *Damn you to waterless hell, Ravard.*

Still, Ravard hadn't won yet. He'd have to enter God's Pellets, and Kaneth couldn't see how he'd manage that. Not with Ryka there.

I have to get there before Ravard's army does. I have to have faith in Ryka. I have to assume that she can handle him. She's a rainlord. She's Ryka Feldspar.

But then, if Ravard got anywhere near her he had a lever to use against her. *Kedri.*

Withering spit, he had to be there. He leaned low over the pede's neck and spoke to Burnish, murmuring praise and encouragement.

And Burnish did try. It streamlined its feelers back along its body, ducked its head lower and raced across the plains towards the dune. But how would it have the energy to climb the steep slopes and valleys of Koumwards? The sunblighted dune was so staggeringly high. He couldn't ask Burnish to hurry up those slopes again.

Ravard's men were already on the dune. As he approached, he could see that the tail end of them had stopped at the top of the first slope to look back. To release more ziggers? He wouldn't be surprised. Hatred rose within him. He hadn't come this far just to be eaten alive by one of those despicable creatures.

His anger reached out ahead of him, to whatever he could grasp. Not ziggers. Not men. No, he seized those tiny pieces that dwelt beneath the dune sand. The soul of the dune. The essence of the dune god. The lifeblood of a living, moving dune. Or just tiny pieces of water. It didn't matter. He touched them with his fury, whispered his needs to them—and blew them apart with his rage.

Some way behind Kaneth, Jasper's jaw dropped. One moment he was feeling sick at the thought that Kaneth had no protection from ziggers, the next he almost fell off Chert in shock. What he saw, what he heard, what he felt—all his senses were assailed. The sands screamed and howled and wailed. The earth shuddered. Threaded through it all was the extraordinary movement of water, water in people, in pedes, in ziggers, in plants, inside the dune…All of it being ripped away from its foundations and flung in different directions.

Kaneth's power slammed into the first slope of the dune like the bore wave of a rush slapping into the bend of a settle drywash. The power furrowed into the dune, deep, deep inside—and exploded. On the surface, pedes, men and ziggers were tossed aside like leaves in a spindevil wind. The earth erupted. Sand was flung up and out to the left and right, two huge waves channelled to each side. The land roared. Even as far away as they were, they could hear it. The impact resonated under the feet of their mount. Chert balked, antennae trembling.

Dibble slowed the pede down. The devastation in front of them continued. Still the sand fountained and parted, pushed aside as if the breath of an invisible, monstrous giant was blowing a path through the dune from one side to the other.

"I'll be shrivelled," Dibble whispered. "Wait till I tell Elmar about this! Is—is it Lord *Kaneth* doing that?"

"I rather think he is."

The floor of the plain was being laid bare in a broad ribbon, wide enough for three pedes to ride abreast, slicing through the sand as straight as the path of an Alabaster spear.

A moment later Rubric's pede drew up beside Chert. Rubric's eyes were wide with amazement. "I'll be blown flat!" he said. "I reckon Pa would like to get his hands on the secret of doing *that* trick." He too was using a driver and had abandoned the other men sharing his pede. "What happened?"

"Kaneth happened."

"I hope you're joking."

"I'm afraid not. Dibble, I think we can follow now. The beginning of this . . . road looks stable enough." He wound his head cloth around his face, and Dibble urged the pede to shutter its eyes and rely on its feelers as dust whirled through the air.

In the distance, on the newly made road, Kaneth drove Burnish still, and the bow wave of sand rose on either side of his mount, curving up high above the level of the dune hills before cascading back to form steep, loose valley slopes on either side.

"He did mention driving a water tunnel under the dunes, to bring water from the Source to the other dunes," Rubric shouted as they raced on towards the base of what was left of Koumwards. "I wondered how he was going to do that. Reckon I know now."

"I don't think he quite had *this* in mind," Jasper shouted back.

"I suppose the dune god might be a tad, er, *upset.*"

"You know—I don't think Kaneth bothered to ask."

Rubric gave him an amused look. They rode on until they arrived at the beginning of the freshly made road. And there, they stopped. They could no longer see far ahead as dust silted through the air. A few moments later, more armsmen from Kaneth's section began to arrive. They too halted, staid warriors trembling and white-faced with shock. Behind them a thousand more followed, scattered over the plains. Still further back, the clashes between the remnants of the two armies raged on.

We abandoned our men, Jasper thought. *And we won't know if what we did was right until we find out exactly what's ahead of us.*

He pointed at the nearest sub-overman he could find. "You. Get these men moving! Your homes and your families are in danger. Ride on to God's Pellets!"

But just as Dibble was about to prod Chert, an unarmed man appeared out of the dust cloud, wading through loose sand up to his knees. His hair was gritty, his skin abraded and pinpointed with tiny blood pricks. He'd lost his mount, his armour and much of his clothing. Sand showered in rivulets of red from the rags he wore.

They stared at him in shock, uncertain of who he was or where he'd come from. He spat, hawking sand out of his mouth as he groped for the water skin still tied at his side. He drank and spat again. Blinking painfully, he looked up at Jasper through red-rimmed lids.

"Dryheads," he rasped. He spoke as if his throat pained him. "Dryheads to think we could fight Kher Uthardim. The hero of the dunes has returned!" He shuddered and sank to his knees. Jasper wasn't sure that the man even knew who he addressed, or cared.

He signalled to one of the waiting armsmen from God's Pellets. "Help him," he said. "I don't care who he is. There have been enough deaths here today."

Once again he had the odd feeling that had first plagued him when Taquar had told him he was a stormlord: the feeling that he was an impostor. A settle wash-rat, an illiterate boy with soles as hard as iron, matted hair and ragged clothes. And now here he was, using pompous language to pretend he could command others twice his age. Yet, when he looked at Dibble, the man was waiting for his orders, respect in his eyes.

"Let's move," he said, curbing a desire to sigh. "The day is not finished yet, not nearly."

As they entered that unnaturally smooth road, sand slithered down the fresh-made slopes singing sweetly, softly. The sun was already low in the sky, the slanted beams filtering through the dust so the very air glowed red around them.

Ryka, he thought, *so much depends on you. Mica, don't hurt her, or Kedri. Remember Wash Drybone. Remember Citrine. Remember when we were boys, the only thing we had was the fact that we cared about each other. It was all that counted.*

The trouble was, Mica had come a long way since then. Sweet water, it looked as if he'd stop at nothing now. Nothing.

CHAPTER FORTY-ONE

Red Quarter
God's Pellets

Once he'd realised Guyden's treachery, Kaneth had altered all the times of the sentry changeovers, and even which knobs were to be used as sentry posts, with one exception. Because it had the best view, the Great Knob—the highest of all—was still in use. When the sun set on the day of the battle, Ryka was already at her post on the knob. This time there was no smoke or fog over Dune Koumwards, but there was a huge cloud of red dust smudging the air. Just the dust from the battle? Or dust from Kaneth moving sand? She had no idea.

"Any sign of the wild pedes?" she asked the man she was relieving.

"No, m'lord. Last I saw of them was early this morning. They disappeared around the back wall of the valley." He nodded towards Koumwards. "Don't you worry none. Your man will be home soon." With those words, meant to be comforting but ultimately meaningless because he knew no more than she did, he left the knob.

The second sentry, who still had some hours to the end

of his duty watch, was only fourteen, newly beaded but still too young to ride to war. His name was Wallus. While there was still light in the sky it was pleasant enough, and the two of them chatted and watched the evening skeins of birds as they bunched up or stretched thin, patterning the sky before they dropped to roost on the cliffs of God's Pellets. Ryka checked the equipment and supplies: knives and swords in the unlikely event they were attacked; pitch-soaked torches and two tinder boxes to light them; water, food and blankets for warmth.

That done, she settled down to watch. To pass the time, she asked Wallus about Guyden, as the two lads were about the same age. "Kept himself to himself," Wallus said. "Good fighter. Always practising. Hard worker, never complained, not even when Kher Uthardim banned him from dune patrols and he was stuck with sentry duty."

"But you didn't like him."

He thought about that. "Wouldn't say that, m'lord. Was more that he didn't like us. Never mixed with us. Y'know, never fooled around, never teased. Aloof." He thought about his own words. "Reckon it was 'cause he didn't *want* to get close to us. Not if one day he'd have to fight us. Hard to kill a fellow you've had a game of chala with." He shrugged. "Reckon he was brave after all, coming here like that, spying on us."

"I reckon he was at that," she agreed. *Damn you, Rav-ard, sending him at all. A child . . .*

The sun set and the night grew steadily colder. They lit a small fire of pede pellets, and warmed their hands. She kept her water-sense roving, especially towards Dune Koumwards, but found nothing. Nor could she see the glow of fires. The battle was probably over, won or lost, and there was nothing she could do about the outcome. She just wished her water-senses were better.

Closer at hand, within the valley, she could feel the water of a couple of pedes with drivers; a changeover of sentries, she assumed. When one stopped at the foot of the Great Knob, she told Wallus his replacement had arrived. He bade her goodnight and started on his way down. From his grin, she guessed he was already dreaming of a warm bed. Holding a burning brand, she lit his way through the pipe at the top; after that he lit his own smaller torch.

At the foot of the rock wall, another myriapede rode up, also with only the driver on its back. Idly she wondered why, but nothing seemed amiss. When disaster struck a few moments later, it happened so suddenly she wasn't sure whether she'd imagined it or not. There had been two living men, then only one. She could feel the water of the other, but in that oddly changed way, the way that signalled a death.

She screamed then, shouting to Wallus to come back. And turned to thrust the torch straight into the unlit signal bonfire of oil-soaked fuel. The volatile mix burst into leaping flames to tell the camp guards and the watchers on the other lookouts that there was trouble. Dropping first a jabbing spear, and then the burning brand down the pipe to light her way, she slipped on her small backpack and headed down. Not the measured descent she usually undertook, but half frantic scramble, half uncontrolled slither. Her sword banged at her side.

Inside the rock of the pipe she could feel nothing. Emerging at the base onto a ledge, she cast her water-senses wide. Wallus was still climbing down. Hadn't he heard her? Further away she was aware of several other pedes with single riders. Ordinarily she would have assumed they were sentries riding between their posts and the encampment; now she was not so sure. She wished she could identify people by their water the way storm-lords could, but she couldn't even tell women from men.

She cried out to Wallus again, yelling for him to stop and wait for her. His puzzled voice floated back, telling her he was already at the base. And then, once again, that horrible change. Instantaneous. Living water to lifeless water, the snuffing out of a human spirit. A sob caught in the back of her throat. Wallus was gone. Someone was down there, killing the men of God's Pellets.

How the wilted hells had they sneaked up to the valley?

Keeping low, she picked up the still-burning brand and heaved it over the edge. It fell, flaring brightly, and landed near the pedes where it continued to burn. The bodies of two men lay on the ground nearby, one of them on his stomach. A spear stuck up out of his back. She could feel the living water of the remaining man in among the tumble of rocks around the base of the knob, out of her line of sight. *The murderer.* She reached out to take his water.

And failed. It was like trying to suck water from a stone; he was a water sensitive. Fear settled into her gut. He must know exactly where she was. *Gods, how many of them were there? Was he the only one? Had they been invaded?* She glanced around, expecting to see other fires lit in answer to her own; there was only blackness on the knobs. Even the camp guards had not responded by light-ing their fire. No point shouting to them; they were too far away to hear.

She slipped the jabbing spear into the straps of her

backpack and scrambled down the steep slope of the path. In the dark and in her rush, she fell and then skidded on her back, out of control. As she veered off the track, an avalanche of stones fell with her, bouncing noisily over the rocks. She dug her palms and fingers in to halt her slide, scraping the skin and tearing the nails. It seemed an eternity before she secured a grip and ceased to slither downwards. Panting heavily in her shock, she realised that her lower legs were hanging over the edge of a cliff. She was still about three or four times her own height above the ground.

Carefully she edged back and knelt. Her warm clothing and backpack had protected her from worse scrapes, but she had broken the spearhead from the spear haft. She stared through the gloom to where she could sense the person standing waiting for her at the bottom of the narrow zigzagging trail. Her heart thumped. How the withering spit was she going to avoid him if he was a sensitive?

She looked to her left where she could make out the two pedes, one of them unhobbled, grazing side by side. They were close to the wall of the knob. If she could get to one of them before the murderer could...Eyeing the height, she contemplated jumping straight down. Possible, just. But also quite possible she'd break a leg or an ankle. The burning brand had sputtered and died in the damp grass. In the dark she couldn't even be sure whether she'd land on rock or meadow.

"Garnet, is that you?"

She froze.

"Garnet? I know you're there."

Sweet water, I'm shrivelled. That's Ravard!

*No, wait...Ravard? Here? Surely not. He'd have led
the Watergatherers into battle. He couldn't have got here
so fast...*

But she knew that voice. She knew it so well. Ravard.
Mica Flint. She stared down into the darkness but couldn't
see much more than his outline.

"It's you, isn't it?" he asked. "You're the only rainlord
in the valley and one of the folk back in the camp told me
you'd be here."

She remained silent, immobile, terrified.

Kedri is back in the camp. We're withered. Her terror
for her son was all-encompassing.

"Yes," he said in answer to her unspoken words. "We
got Khedrim. I've got the proof, right here."

He held something up but she couldn't make it out.

"Some sort of blanket. He was wrapped in it. 'Broidery
all round the edge. Pebblemice, by the look of it." He
waved it at her.

Robena had sewn it...

Her knees wobbled and she almost fell. *If you've
touched one hair of his head, I'll kill you, Mica...*

"Come on, Garnet. I know it's you. I'm not going t'hurt
you. Look at you, I can feel you're trembling like a leaf
touched by a spindevil's child. There's no need."

She glanced down at the pedes. Forced herself to
think. Smiled without mirth as the seed of an idea took
root. With deliberate slowness so he would not notice the
movement of her water, she swung the pack from her back
into her arms.

"How do I know you won't kill me the moment I'm
within reach of your blade?" she asked. She didn't have to
fake the breathless fear making her voice ragged. She dug

into her pack for the food she had brought with her for a snack.

"My honour as a sandmaster. I just want t'talk t'you. I won't hurt you so long as you don't fight me. And Khedrim'll be safe too. He's with Islar at the moment, in your tent. Guyden, that is."

With exquisite care and tiny, imperceptible movements, she edged over to the rim of the cliff, while her hands unwrapped the baked yam and held it out on her palm towards the pedes below. Both showed an immediate interest, their great heads craning upwards. The antennae of the unhobbled animal swung in search of the origin of the delectable smell.

Please don't let Ravard feel the movement.

She didn't think he would. His water skills were minimal. "How can I trust you?"

As she spoke the pede came closer and a feeler appeared over the rim of the cliff to touch the yam. Just the lightest of caresses, but it was enough to tempt the beast. And yet the food was out of reach of its mandibles.

"I don't need t'hurt you. I've the means t'make you or your Lord Kaneth do what I want—I have Khedrim."

Without hesitation, the pede scrabbled at the cliff, rising up on its back feet until its head was resting on the ledge. Ravard yelled, but she didn't catch the words.

She didn't hesitate either. She took a flying leap, using her water-senses more than her eyesight to plant one foot on the strong outer mandible and to vault from there onto the top of the head and hence to the saddle. She fumbled for the reins and pulled the beast around, forcing it to drop back down to the ground. Groping for the pede prod, she was relieved to find it where it should be, racked along the side. She seized it and jabbed it into the tough skin between head and body, and the animal leaped away in response.

In the gloom she glimpsed Ravard rounding the rocks towards her, and then he receded into the darkness. She knew what was at stake; she had to get to the tents first. A glance at the saddlecloth told her the pede she'd taken was one of theirs, and therefore an ageing beast, too old to go to battle. It was slow. Her hope that Ravard had stolen a similar beast was soon shattered; before she was halfway to the encampment, he had overtaken her on a packpede.

She saw him grin across at her as his beast drew level. "There's nothing you can do, Garnet!"

But they were passing the Source, and there *was* one thing she could do. She dragged a block of water out of the pool and flung it at him. He felt it coming, and yanked his reins hard to dodge. His pede screamed its pain and snapped its antennae in annoyance. Ryka ducked, but too late. She had a glimpse of the black whip of chitin whipping through the air towards her, followed immediately by the shock of a blow slamming into her shoulder and neck. She tried to maintain her grip on the saddle handle, tried to manipulate the water, but the force of the impact ripped her from the saddle and hurtled her to the ground. Jagged pain, heart-stopping panic, all encased in the certain knowledge that there was nothing she could do to halt the calamity about to happen...

She released her hold on the water as she hit the ground and all the breath was driven from her body. Her last coherent thought was that if this was dying, then it was sandblasted agony...

*   *   *

Jasper figured that Kaneth's roadway through Dune Koumwards more than halved the time of the journey from one side to the other. The consequences of his alteration of the landscape were sickeningly obvious.

A head or an arm or half a torso, sticking out of the slope bordering the road, like one of a series of macabre decorations from a murderous artist. A live pede, its long body three-quarters buried, its feelers and legs snapped, struggling to free itself from the sand. A group of men, lost and wandering, faces stark with horror, bleeding from their eyes and noses and ears. A strange toneless wail, uttered without end, from a large Reduner warrior standing on the roadway. As they rode by, he did not appear to see them. A meddle of confused and riderless pedes huddled together nearby, skittish, their antennae whipping this way and that in pointless frenzy. Jasper shuddered.

By the time he and Rubric reached the other side, ahead of the remaining armsmen because of their lighter loads, it was dusk. They still had to cross the plains in the deepening night, on weary, hungry pedes. Their return route was direct, but fatigue would add several more sandglass runs to the time it should have taken.

To Jasper's mild surprise, Kaneth was waiting for them at the edge of the plains, resting his pede where his newly made road ended. Even in the fading light he looked terrible. His face was grey, his mouth pinched, his eyes sunken. He was still on his pede, drooping on the saddle as though he had doubled his age in a matter of hours.

Oh sandhells, Jasper thought. *He's expended far too much of his power. He's killing himself.*

Kaneth's intense fear for his family was bridled tightly, but Jasper didn't doubt it was still there. "I waited because

I need you two stormlords. I don't think I can do it without you. Water your pedes and let's get going." They had no water with them, so Jasper pulled as much as he could gather from the remains of the mist and cloud, much of which was now dampening the dune plants as evening dew, and Rubric gathered the water of the dead pedes and men who lay in the sand behind them. They hovered the water into a large block over the ground and the pedes drank deeply, unfazed by its lack of containment. Burnish dipped its feelers into the water and flung spray over his back to cool down.

"They'll be dropping dead under us if we push them too hard," Jasper warned Kaneth as Dibble and Rubric's driver dismounted and inspected the pedes for damaged feet and nicked segments.

In the dying light of dusk, Kaneth's eyes were wild with grief, begging Jasper not to tear him in two. "Better that than Ryka and Kedri die, or that the Source falls into the hands of a man who will use his possession of it as a weapon to control the dunes. He's in the valley, Jasper. I know it."

"From what I can see, none of Ravard's army are riding to God's Pellets any more," Jasper said dryly. "I suspect we only have a handful of men to worry about in the valley." *One of whom is doubtless Mica…sweet water save me.*

"I killed some of his army ahead of me, but there's still the remainder behind us."

Some? Jasper blinked. Did Kaneth not know what he had done? "I suspect they decided they didn't want to mix with Kher Uthardim; not when he throws a dune around as if it was a bucketful of sand cast in the path of a spindevil. Those that could, rode away. Headed home, I guess. Have you no idea how spectacular what you did was?" *Or how many men died in there?*

"I didn't think about it," he confessed. "I just had to prevent them getting to God's Pellets, and they were ahead of me. And I wanted to cross the dune as quickly as possible, without taxing Burnish with the steep hills. Poor fellow is so tired."

"The pedes all should rest." Chert was plunging its whole head into the water in obvious relief.

Kaneth gave Jasper a look then that he knew he would never forget. The lines of his face were cut so deep with such raw pain that Jasper wondered if he might not collapse under the enormity of it. His words were no more than a whisper. "Getting there fast may mean the difference between life and death for Ryka and Kedri and those we left in the valley." The agony in his tone was so intense it took Jasper's breath away. "Don't you understand? If he has taken them hostages, I will have to make a choice. Think, Jasper. The Source and the future of the dunes—or the lives of my family? Ravard is confident he knows which way my choice will fall—and he could be *wrong!*"

The dread in Kaneth's voice was wrenching. He glanced to where the Pellets were, now no more than dark shapes in the falling night. "I think we're already too late. You may not be able to feel their water through the rock, but this—this I feel: he's there somewhere. In that direction."

Jasper swallowed, realising the full horror of the words. Kaneth thought he may have to let his family die—in order to save the dunes.

"Lighten your load," Kaneth ordered, his voice harsh. "Leave your drivers behind."

Rubric gave a grimace. He had handled a pede on the way to God's Pellets, but he was hardly experienced.

Jasper glanced across at him. "Can you do it?"

"I think so. My animal will doubtless just follow yours anyway." With a gesture of resignation, he edged forward onto the saddle vacated by his driver.

"Dibble, I'll leave the water here for the armsmen behind us," Jasper said, "but tell them not to linger. We need them at God's Pellets as soon as possible."

They were still a full run of a sandglass away from the Pellets, and dawn had not yet begun to edge into the eastern sky. The pedes were labouring, so Kaneth—his reluctance overridden by necessity—slowed Burnish down to a gentle run. Jasper and Rubric, their pedes one on either side of Kaneth, followed his example.

"Trouble," Jasper called across to him. "There were supposed to be two sentries on each knob, right?"

"Yes." The tightness in his chest grew worse. What now?

"I can't sense through the rock, but when the sentries were in the open, I could feel them. Then they disappeared. I thought they were just being relieved, but no one has replaced them. The tallest knob has one person. Ryka."

"You can tell that much from here?" Of course he could. He was a stormlord, wasn't he? Kaneth glanced up in the direction of the Great Knob, and as he did, flames leaped up from its peak. A signal fire. The valley's wall had been breached.

"Sunlord save her." He signalled Burnish to quicken the pace, and reluctantly the beast obliged. "We'll assume Watergatherer men control the valley," he shouted over his shoulder as the other two mounts struggled to keep up. "Ravard and Guyden and an unknown number more." His voice sounded coldly calm to his ears. It lied.

In reply, Jasper yelled, "And then what?"

"We'll loose our pedes at the entrance to the open canyon. They know their way in and will go straight through. Any normal water sensitive won't know the difference between a pede with a rider and one without. While they are chasing pedes to find out, we'll sneak in through the narrower canyon just to the east, close to the camp."

"Is it guarded?"

"It was, inside, yes. And we set a trap on the outer side too, a deadfall, but I know how to circumvent that."

They rode on in silence, but a bare quarter of a sandrun later, Kaneth gasped as he felt Ryka himself. Not her usual self, but a woman in terror. Those little pieces of her, all panicked. Pieces racing, rushing, nothing calm. No more than that, but it was enough. He had never felt her that way before. She was in terrible danger, and she knew it.

He jabbed his prod deep. Burnish, gasping, plunged forward. Concentrating on Ryka, only on Ryka, Kaneth hunched low to the carapace for the least wind resistance as the animal raised itself to fast mode and sped off into the night. He didn't look behind to see if the other two could keep up. All he cared about was getting there, to be with her and Kedri.

And killing Ravard. He cared about that as he had never cared before about the death of anyone. Especially when the little of pieces of Ryka vanished from his consciousness.

When they emerged on foot from the narrow winding of the canyon, they found the guard dead at the other end. He'd been knifed. Rubric turned him over. *God have mercy, he was an old man.*

"Gundi Hurdle," Kaneth said, kneeling at his side and touching the old man's face. "I'd recognise his nose anywhere, even in the dark."

God's voice, the man's reeling, Rubric thought. *He can barely stand. He's used too much of this strange power of his*... He doubted Kaneth would live through the night unless he rested, and the thought disturbed him. He was part of them now, these Quartern folk. He'd fought alongside them, for a cause. And yes, he'd killed, although he'd once shrunk from it. *There are things worth fighting for,* he thought. *And dying for, too.* Ironic that he had found that out in a land far from his own.

Kaneth looked across at Jasper. "What can you sense? Where's Ryka? I know she's alive, though I think—I think—" But he couldn't complete the sentence.

Oh, God be voiceless, he's trying to say he thinks she's dying.

"Ryka's in your tent with Kedri. With Mica," Jasper said quietly.

The rage in Kaneth was momentarily a physical emanation, which Rubric felt like a physical blow in his chest, just before the man strode off towards the encampment. Rubric glanced at Jasper's face, sheened by starlight, and knew he too had felt the rage.

Jasper grabbed Rubric's arm and pulled him along

after Kaneth, whispering, "Help me bring some water out of the Source."

"But—"

"We'll try not to use it to kill anyone, but I'll make my own decisions."

"Agreed."

"How do you figure this? I don't know who's friendly and who's not."

"Small groups fleeing in twenty directions, most with children. Thirty or so dead bodies, scattered. One of which is in Kaneth's tent."

"I know. That's Cleve's mother. She was looking after Kedri. There's four men in the camp moving around purposefully. Can you feel them? Searching the tents and herding people together and sitting them down near the main fireplace. Some of those I recognise. I think the fighting's over and I think they are the only ones we have to concern ourselves with at the moment. Could you deal with them, while I help Kaneth? He'll need it. Mica has help there and Kaneth is exhausted."

He began to pull water out of the Source. "I can try." Inwardly, he smiled even as his heart pounded. Jasper was confident he could handle four of Ravard's men? On his own?

"If any of them are sensitives, you can't take their water and they'll feel you coming. If worse comes to worst, dump a lot of water on them."

Fear and excitement mingled, heightening his awareness.

They covered the last fifty paces in silence. At the first tent they split up, Jasper gripping his shoulder in a gesture of comradeship. Rubric turned in the direction of the group of people huddled together. All but two of them were seated. He figured he need not worry about the seated ones; they would be the prisoners. Carefully, he familiarised himself with the two who were standing. When he was sure he would recognise their water again, he homed in on the other two, who were still walking around. They were not together; one was on the northern edge of the encampment; the other appeared to be walking back to where the prisoners were. He would pass close by.

How good were Reduner water sensitives? Jasper had told him once that their skills were elementary, usually not much use in areas where there was plenty of water about, like a camp. Water in pots and people and food and pedes tended to overwhelm and confuse the best of sensitives anyway. Just as people stopped hearing the individual sounds in a noisy environment, a water sensitive stopped noticing the movement of water. He hoped so, because there was a block of water hovering directly over his head, high up, that he didn't want anyone to wonder about. *Maybe they'll think it's a cloud...*

He shivered, suddenly less excited. He could die if he made a mistake. And so could innocent people. *Remember all the dead bodies out there scattered around the valley. These are killers.* He crouched behind a family jar of water under the veranda of a tent and waited for the man to come by.

Then he carefully dumped the block of water on the man from about twenty paces up. It flattened him. Rubric strolled over and put a foot onto the small of the man's back and a sword point to his neck even as he was gathering the water together again. "Hello there," he said softly. "I'm Lord Rubric, a stormlord, working for the Cloudmaster. Just in case we haven't met. Ye want to be friendly, or shall I take your water? Ye know, as in kill ye?"

The man made up in bravery for what he lacked in brains. Spluttering, he raised himself up onto his elbows, then made a wild grab at Rubric's knees. Rubric cursed, stepped back and tripped over a guy rope. On his way down, his sword scored the man's neck, but didn't kill him. *Pedeshit.*

He pulled at the man's water. Nothing happened. Unaffected, the fellow was already scrabbling to his feet, knife in hand. Rubric jammed water into his face instead. While his assailant tried to cope with that, he slit his throat.

Blood pumped out, and Rubric's stomach heaved. He wiped his mouth on the back of his sleeve and scrambled to his feet with a sigh. *I'll never get used to killing people. Why, oh why, wasn't I born a waterpainter?*

"Sand-brain," he told the corpse as he evaporated the water from the blood on his blade and shook the powdered remnants to the ground. "That really wasn't necessary." He cast around for the man on the far side of the encampment, to find him herding several women his way. After cutting a piece of guy rope loose, Rubric waited until they appeared. The women, clutching one another, were silent and scared. The man foolishly carried a burning brand, which may have helped him to pick his way over the tent ropes, but which also made him night-blind.

Rubric carefully dropped a packet of water on his head, avoiding the women. *Neatly done*, he congratulated himself. The women squealed and ran. This time Rubric took no chances. He had the man roped up like a deer for gutting, then gagged before the fellow had worked out what was going on. *Almost too easy*, he thought. No blame the armed forces in Khromatis had such strict rules about using water-power. With so many stormlords, it would be a madhouse if waterlords used it in every skirmish.

He made for where the other hostages were being held. A burning torch lit the area. Peeping between two tents, he saw fifty or sixty prisoners sitting on the ground, mostly women and children. Some of the children were sound asleep and he envied them. His last sleep seemed a long time ago. The two men guarding them were armed with both knives and scimitars, the latter weapons sheathed. Rubric's lip curled. Scimitars were not the best weapon for a fight on foot.

One of them must have sensed him because he stared, frowning, into the darkness between the tents. "Who the waterless hells are you?" he asked. At least, that was what Rubric thought he might have said. The words were incomprehensible. There was no mistaking the tone, though. Or the drawn scimitar.

"Lord Rubric," he said politely, stepping forward into the light. "Stormlord. Ye know, the person who can leave ye looking like a bit of dried-up lizard that's been dead for a least half a cycle."

The man looked blank, and so did his equally well-armed companion.

Rubric heaved an obvious sigh and addressed the prisoners. "Maybe one of ye good people could translate what I just said to these two dryheads? And ye had better tell them that their two friends are already taken care of, Lord Jasper and Kher Uthardim are dealing with Ravard right now, and the rest of our forces will enter the valley any minute."

One of the women seated on the ground obliged with a

translation, grinning. Rubric recognised her as a Scarper-woman and ex-slave he'd met before.

The two Watergatherers were badly rattled, but the braver of the two advanced on Rubric anyway, his weapons at the ready, saying, "We're water sensitives. You couldn't take our water if you tried."

The woman continued to translate.

"He's lying anyway," the other man said. "There's only one withering stormlord and this is not him."

"I can prove it, if ye like," Rubric said cheerfully.

"Go ahead," one of the men said, grinning when he heard the translation. The two of them approached him, one from the left, one from the right.

"Sure," said Rubric and tossed a ball of water from behind his left shoulder straight into the first man's face. He followed up with a second block of water dropped from above on the other. Expecting he would then be in the middle of a fight for his life, Rubric tensed for attack.

It never came. One of the younger women flung herself at the back of the knees of the first man. He fell over her body, crashing onto his back, where several of the other prisoners promptly sat on him and a third disarmed him. His companion, torn between attacking Rubric alone or helping his companion in the face of a number of irate women, dithered. A girl flung a blanket over his head from behind and in an instant he too was on the ground, squashed under a hugely pregnant woman.

"I suggest ye tie them up," Rubric said to her, impressed, "and stay here until we get all this mess sorted out."

"What happened to the others?" someone asked, fearful. "We're not all here. Most of the folk ran."

He prevaricated, not wanting to mention the dead. "I'm not sure. There are people scattering everywhere. Do you know how many of these Watergatherers there were?"

Someone began to sob quietly.

"We don't know," the woman doing the translating said. "What about the army?"

"Well, we won the fight. The Watergatherers were routed." He hoped he was right about that. There was no jubilation at the news. They all knew there would be plenty to make them weep.

Rubric left them and went to find Jasper.

CHAPTER FORTY-TWO

Red Quarter
God's Pellets

So much pain. She couldn't be dead. Anyone who was dead wouldn't feel all this, surely.

She couldn't decide which was worse: the splitting, throbbing headache or the appalling pain in the front of her shoulder. And that was just the start. Her whole body was shrieking for her attention. Her stomach was telling her to throw up. The agony in her shoulder radiated into her neck with every step. Or maybe the stabbing jabs into her neck were something separate?

Steps. Not her steps. Someone was carrying her, but for a moment she couldn't think who it might be, or even what had happened. She wanted to open her eyes, but couldn't seem to part the eyelids. Pain was blocking out coherent thought. *Ryka Feldspar, think. What happened?*

Sliver by sliver, she began to collect her last memories. She'd been on a pede.

Another pede had slashed her across the neck with the serrated edge of its feeler. Ah, that explains the neck. She'd fallen. And that explained the pain just about everywhere else. She'd be one big bruise after a tumble like that. The shoulder: she couldn't move her arm without terrible pain. She hazarded a guess: a broken clavicle. Anything else?

And then it all came rushing back. Ravard.

Her eyes flew open.

He was carrying her. It was still dark and she was looking up at the underside of his chin. A wave of awful dizziness drowned her. She moved her head slightly and vomited.

"Welcome back," he said.

And then he was ducking his head to enter a tent and lay her down on the central carpet. *Her tent.*

Kedri!

She looked around, ignoring the agony every move caused her. The tent was lit with the oil lamp and the first thing she saw was Robena, lying on the floor facing her. The woman's eyes stared lifelessly. A bloody tear had been ripped through her throat and the front of her clothing was drenched with blood. Blood soaked into the carpet, so much it looked almost black. Sticky.

Sunlord save us.

Kedri.

Her panic was total, yet every movement she made was deliberate, considered. She couldn't afford to feel dizzy again. She turned her head the other way and saw another man. Guyden, with his white beading. He stood in the doorway of the room where Kedri usually slept. He held a knife, too. Wise move; better than a scimitar in this confined space. *Don't underestimate the lad, Ryka. He has the instincts of a killer.* He was alert and poised. *Don't forget, he knows you are a rainlord, and he's a water sensitive.* Worse, the knife was bloodied.

She couldn't see her son, but she could feel him. He still lived. The panic subsided a notch, enabling her to think. Slowly she began to move her good arm until her hand was close to the handle of the dagger still strapped to her side under the cover of her tunic.

She looked back at Ravard, noting his eye-patch for the first time. It should have made her aware of his deformity, but all she could think of was that it made him look dangerous. "I've broken some bones," she said. "I can't move. I think I'm dying."

He looked stricken, and she hardened her heart. *You've have no rights here, Ravard. None.*

"Kedri," she said.

He moved then, to the room where Kedri slept, and a moment later brought the boy back. Kedri, asleep in the crook of his left arm, lips twitching into a smile.

"He's grown into a fine boy," he said.

His gaze was fond and he handled Kedri tenderly, as if the child was his own. She felt ill.

"He's not your son, Mica." Sunlord bless him, Kedri was still sound asleep and showed no signs of waking.

"He is t'me," he said simply. "I'll look after him, I swear, Garnet. He'll be like my own son. And you . . ." He swallowed. "You can recover; be his mother."

"No. My—my insides are all in a mess. I can tell. I'm a rainlord, remember?"

Her mind was racing, fighting to push the pain into the background, to work out what was within her capabilities. She pushed her senses outwards. She had to seek a source of water. All the jars in the tent were closed tight. There was Robena, of course—but taking hers would be too obvious. Scanning the surrounding tents she could find nothing accessible. *No wait, what's that?* When she tugged at the water in the kettle on the table in the communal kitchen, it responded. The spout had been carelessly left uncovered. She pulled out a thin stream, hardly wider than a grass blade. Not too much or too fast, or even someone of Ravard's weak talent would sense it. But oh, it was sapping her strength, her tenuous hold on her consciousness.

He gave her a look of dismayed guilt and sorrow. "I didn't mean t'hurt you. I—I thought we could start again—"

"Too late. If you want to make amends, give Kedri to his father. His real father." She winced as she eased her arm into a more comfortable position. "Guyden will tell you how Kedri loves his father."

Ravard nodded at Guyden. "This is Islar, Sandmaster Davim's son. He's my Master Son. Sorry, Garnet, but we're taking over God's Pellets. And I'm keeping you and Khedrim. Your sand-witted husband must get out of the Red Quarter, along with all Scarpen warriors. Your stormlord's been preventing us from getting random rain by stealing all the natural clouds, so what can we do? We have a right t'lead the kind of life we choose. With the Source in our hands, we can. We can be independent."

Her head ached and talking was painful, but she refused to give in. She wanted to scream at him, to stab him with her knife. She wanted Kedri out of his arms. She wanted Kaneth. "We're working towards the same thing! Don't you see?" she asked. "You *can* have it all. Kaneth—all of us here—we're working to achieve this. A time when the Quartern does not have to rely on Scarpen stormlords."

She trailed the water from the kettle through the air alongside the tent. When it reached the veranda, she began to bundle it together into a ball. It was so hard to focus on Ravard, on Kedri's safety, on the water...So hard not to feel the pain. Not to slip away where she wouldn't feel it all.

Keep him focused on you.

She took a deep breath. "All your tribe has to do is to stop raiding and killing others. To swear that trade caravans will never be attacked and that the White Quarter will be safe from your raids. Promise that, and we can rebuild a prosperity for the dunes together."

"With me as your sandmaster, and Islar as the Master Son, not just of the Watergatherer, but of all dunes?"

The sneering disbelief behind the words was more hinted at rather than obvious, but she heard it anyway. She thought about his words, about his proposal, if indeed it was that. *Kaneth will never agree. Neither will Vara. They both want Ravard dead. Many of the other dunes won't agree, either. They suffered too much under Davim and Ravard. They don't trust him. And now Islar has linked himself to Ravard. And unlike Cleve, he was raised by Davim. No, there would be no peace there. Not now.*

The time had come and gone for Ravard to have a place in the new order. Surprising herself, she felt only pity.

"I think it's too late for that," she murmured.

"You're right. Our armies fought yesterday, and your man and Vara were defeated."

Her heart struggled to beat normally. Her thoughts were so tangled by pain she wasn't sure she was making sense. "You can't know that. You may have ziggers, but Kaneth and Vara had two stormlords with them."

He looked shocked. "Two?"

"Yes."

Ravard looked at Islar. "Know anything 'bout that?"

Screams shredded the calm of the night outside. Neither of the men took any notice. *Someone trying to raise the alarm. Too late. Ravard must have brought more men with him . . .*

"No," the lad said. "Although I told you the Cloudmaster had another Gibber grubber with him."

"So you did."

She stared at Ravard. She knew him well enough to know he was shaken. But he wasn't going to admit it. He waved Islar out of the tent. "Keep watch," he said. "Warn me of trouble. And drag that body out of here."

As fast as Ryka could, she zipped the water ball to hover immediately over the roof of the veranda. Islar left, and she followed him with her senses. He went to stand at the front corner of the veranda where he would have a good view of people coming and going, if there were any.

When they were alone, Ravard continued, "I won't force you, Garnet, not this time. What I did . . ." He hesitated, evidently finding the words hard to say. "It wasn't right."

"So?" she asked, not making it easy for him. "There's not going to be another time, Mica. I'm dying."

Outside, someone screamed, but the sound was cut short. She jumped. The wave of pain that followed almost demolished her fragile hold on clarity and coherence.

"I'll get the best healers for you," he was saying when she focused again. "It was just a fall. I think you've broken the bone here." He tapped his shoulder and continued, stubbornly refusing to believe she was seriously hurt.

"Once your man's army has dispersed and he's dead or gone back where he belongs, you're free t'go, if y'want. Your rainlord's a street-groveller, used t'hard floors underfoot and a roof overhead t'hide the sun and stars. You want that life? Go with him."

She didn't believe him. *You'd kill Kaneth if you had half a chance.* Another calming breath. *Don't slaughter the mount under you, Ry. Keep your temper.* Under the cover of a fold in her tunic, she groped for the handle of her knife and edged it out of its holder. *Sunlord help me, even my fingers hurt.*

"And Kedri?"

"I claimed Khedrim as my own when his father rejected him. He's my son, born in the Red Quarter. He stays."

Her arms ached to take Kedri from him. "He was born in the Warthago. His father did not reject him; he just couldn't remember who he was, or who I was."

"Kedri was born north of the divide. That's the Red Quarter."

By all that's sun holy, this has got to be the weirdest conversation ever. Her glance flicked to Kedri. How was she going to keep him safe if she attacked? Worse, she couldn't let Ravard make a sound, or Guyden-Islar would come to his aid. Waterless damn, why did this irritating man always present her with these frustrating dilemmas? *Think, Ryka. Concentrate.*

Just then, Islar poked his head back into the tent, thankfully without noticing the ball of water now hovering over the door under the veranda roof. "Timwith says a lot of the folk in the camp fled and they've scattered all over the place. Wants to know what they should do."

"Make sure they don't leave the valley. We have Ryka and Khedrim—nobody's going to try anything. Tell him to round up those he can and keep them under guard."

Islar withdrew and she said, "I don't understand how you entered the valley. The canyons are blocked. The guards are everywhere. You should've been seen or your approach felt by the water sensitives."

He grinned, suddenly boyishly puffed up like a sand-grouse. "We came in with the wild pedes. Only they weren't really wild at all. We brought them from the Watergatherer, just t'fool you."

Her mind cried out against the possibility. "They weren't carved. We sent riders to check!"

"My men have been too busy to carve any of the spare pedes we captured after Uthardim stole or killed ours. We brought 'em here and allowed them t'roam free, so you could take a look, get used to them. Then, starting at midday yesterday, we sneaked in as far as the rock wall. Under them."

"Under?" Her mind wasn't working. That made no sense.

"In net cradles woven t'be hung under their bellies. What water sensitive can feel the water of a man when he has t'pass through the water of a pede t'do it? We were there, right under the gaze of your sentries, impossible to see in the grass and scrub."

He laughed, charmed by the simplicity and success of his plan. Ryka wanted to hit him.

"By dusk we were at the back of God's Pellets," he continued, "and you had no idea we were there."

"There can't have been many of you." Only a few could safely hide in a small meddle of pedes, surely.

"Twelve others. All water sensitives. From there we climbed in. Islar showed us the way."

She went cold. "And what are the others doing right now?"

"Herding together your people under guard. Killing your sentries. We aren't harming women and children. We want them as hostages."

You spitless louse! She had to do something. But what?

She didn't think he would hurt Kedri. Her, yes. Pushed into a corner, he'd kill her now and maybe grieve a little later. She could hear the anger and bitterness in his voice; he had not forgiven her for...what? The fact that she hadn't loved him? That she'd gone back to Kaneth? No, she didn't think that was it. He was furious because all along she was a rainlord and she'd hidden it from him. She could have drowned him in his sleep at any time, but instead she'd waited and, in the end, he'd looked a fool before his men. A leader who'd slept with a rainlord without knowing what he was doing. That was what he couldn't forgive: being made to look as if he had no more brains than a wilted sand-tick. It would have cost him credibility.

"And your army on Koumwards?" she asked.

"T'entice yours away. T'allow Islar and me the chance t'enter and find ourselves the hostages that'd keep your so-called Uthardim away."

You really don't know Kaneth, you water-waster.

He continued, "Our army is so much larger than yours, and we got ziggers. My Warrior Son is dealing with your forces. His orders are t'send half the army after us soon as possible and t'leave t'other half t'keep you armsmen occupied."

Oh, frizzled hells, let them be all right...

She moved, trying to find a way to lie that helped the pain, but it was impossible. There just was no way she could get comfortable. "Put Kedri back where you got him," she said. "He'll get cold like that."

To her surprise, he did as she asked, taking Kedri into the sleeping room. In the brief moment he was away, she sneaked the water inside and brought it down behind the family jar in the corner. It was a risk, she knew. If his senses were attuned to water just then, he would feel the movement easily. But when he stepped back into the main room, he was smiling softly. "He's so beautiful. So like you." He came to stand beside her, looking down at her. "I loved you," he added. "But I didn't know how t'say it. Not sure when it happened, either, but it did. I loved you. And you betrayed me."

"No, I didn't. You never had my loyalty to start with." Her hand tightened around the handle of her dagger. "Sit down and talk to me. I don't have much time left..." Her voice trailed away weakly.

"If I do, what says you won't use your rainlord abilities against me?"

"You know I can't take your water."

"I know there's more than one way rainlords can snuff someone."

"The lid is tight on the family jar," she said, waving weakly towards the large vessel standing in the corner of the room behind him. "And on every jar in the tent, as I am sure you know."

"Garnet, I'm not stupid. The only reason I'm safe from you is 'cause you're hurt." The smile he gave her was a strange mix of longing and sadness. "Try t'sleep. I'm going t'see how our takeover of the valley is going, and if our army is approach—" He didn't finish.

She whipped the water across the room and into the back of his head. When he jumped in shock and instinctively began to turn she forced herself up, knife in hand. The pain that ripped through her body was excruciating. Even as she propelled herself forward, angling the knife upwards to take him between the ribs, she sobbed.

But nothing happened the way she thought it would. The tent burst open. Ravard was hit by the figure that burst through the wall and was sent staggering out of her reach. She fell back down to the floor, crying out in her agony. She dropped the knife. Forgot that she'd been about to kill a man. Forgot everything in her desperate attempt to stay conscious and subdue the pain.

Nightmare images shot across her vision between shards of scarlet pain vision. Kaneth, sword in hand—he was the one who'd burst through the canvas wall. The back wall of the tent was slashed from top to bottom. Her mind was still several steps behind the events. Shouts outside. Guyden's voice. Jasper's voice. Ravard rolling out of the way of Kaneth's attack. Sunlord save him, Kaneth looked *awful*. He looked as if he wasn't in any better shape than she was. Gaunt. Aged. Ill.

The two men were fighting; both had swords and daggers and hatred for one another.

She had barely grasped the enormity of what was about to unfold when she saw Jasper standing in the doorway of the tent. His sword was held to the throat of Guyden, who was struggling and cursing and in danger of slitting his own throat as a consequence.

Dizzy, clasping her left arm tight to her body so the

bones in her shoulder wouldn't grate, she edged herself to her feet, but then immediately had to sit on the wooden chest in the corner to avoid falling down. When her head stopped spinning, the first thing she saw was Kedri's blue eye staring out of a narrow gap between the wall and the hanging canvas of the door to his sleeping room and the wall. The noise had finally awoken him. His gaze, wide-eyed, was fixed on his father. She desperately wanted to go to him, but she would have had to cross between the two skirmishing warriors.

Stay there, Kedri. Just stay there, please...

A small room where two warriors were skirmishing was not the place for a toddler. His gaze, wide-eyed, was fixed on his father. She didn't dare call to him, worried that might prompt him to cross between the men.

She turned to Jasper. "Stop them! That's your brother and my husband."

"I don't know how to stop them. Do you? Or more to the point, how do we stop them for good? The moment we turned our backs, they'd be at it again!" Guyden was twisting and squirming in his grip, and Jasper said, exasperated, "Look, you sand-brained tick, I can drown you in water or kill you with my sword. Or you can stop struggling and accept the fact that your part in this fight is over. Which would you prefer?"

Guyden stopped struggling. In his frustration, he was close to sobbing. Jasper pushed him to the floor on his stomach.

Ryka was overcome with a sense of futility. *I know what Kaneth is fighting for. It's me, and Kedri and the people he led away from slavery, and his dream. But Ravard? Does he even really know any more? It will only end when one of them is dead...*

She didn't know how to stop them. They were evenly matched, neither able to gain the advantage. Ravard was quicker, more powerful and more reckless, willing to take chances to gain an advantage, but the lack of an eye must surely have affected his depth perception. Kaneth was wily and cool and seasoned, but obviously exhausted. The edge of desperation about him shattered her. When he attacked and Ravard countered, his blade slid upwards so that the two men were caught in a clinch, breast to breast, swords locked perpendicular between them, dagger blades crossed above their heads in a struggle for ascendancy.

Ryka's gasp remained imprisoned in her throat, her terror total. She wanted to intervene, but what if her intervention distracted them and Kaneth was killed?

Their ragged breathing was the only sound. The moment dragged on, the time stretched, each man knowing he could so easily kill the other—or die himself. And into the silence, Kedri spoke.

"Naughty man," he said from where he stood. "Hit Dada."

"Yes, naughty," she said, hearing hysteria in her voice.

Ravard moved first, flinging Kaneth away from him then attacking brutally hard, driving him back until he was braced against the pole in the back corner of the tent. Fortunately it was one of the main supports, fashioned from the trunk of a small fallen tree. It offered solidity at his back, and protection, but he was also trapped, unable to manoeuvre. Ravard, on the other hand, could vary his attack. He didn't miss the chance. Eagerly savage, he rained blow upon blow on Kaneth with his sword, even as his dagger wove through the air to divide his opponent's attention. And yet Kaneth was smiling, parrying the blows almost effortlessly, as if suddenly inspired.

As though he knew what would happen before it occurred. Ravard's fury grew.

Sunlord save us, Ryka thought. *He's reading Ravard like words on a scroll.* Those tiny pieces of water. *Ravard doesn't have a chance.* She should have felt joy; instead she was overwhelmed with a sense of the stupid pointlessness of it all.

She forced herself across the room to the family jar, reeling under the combined effects of her bruises, her aching head and her broken bone. She knocked the lid off but couldn't find her power to use the uncovered water. Sliding down to the base of the jar, she looked back at Jasper.

"You do it," she said. "I can't."

Even as she spoke, he was pulling the water out. When he had all of it up in the air he flung it at the fighting men. Ravard didn't see it coming. Kaneth did, and flinched, distracted. Ravard's dagger slid into Kaneth's upper arm, tearing open his tunic sleeve and opening up a shallow cut on his biceps. And then they were both spluttering and blinking under the deluge.

"Naughty man!" Kedri shouted at Ravard. "Naughty!" He ran with surprising speed across the room. Everyone moved to grab him, but Ravard was the closest and he was the one who succeeded in swinging the boy up into his arms, dropping his sword in the process. Ryka and Kaneth and Jasper all stopped dead. Ravard stepped back. He still held his dagger. To Ryka, it hovered appallingly close to Kedri's wriggling body.

"Keep your distance," Ravard said.

Kedri, facing him, pounded him on the chest with his tiny clenched fists, crying, "Naughty, hurt Dada!"

Guyden used everyone's moment of distraction to ram the back of Jasper's knees. Jasper staggered and fell onto his back, and Guyden punched him in the stomach. Jasper doubled over in pain. Some of the water rose up in the air and rushed towards Guyden. He twisted away, but the water followed him. Guyden fought, but his fists passed through it. It was like fighting the wind.

Ryka screamed at Ravard, "What are you going to do? Kill a child? Is that the kind of man you are?"

Jasper staggered to his feet, not even looking at Guyden. "Mica. Remember Citrine. She was his age…"

Behind him, Rubric stepped into the room. He grinned at Guyden. "That's me doing that, not Jasper. Shall I stop?" Guyden glared and lunged at him. Rubric side-stepped, jamming the water gag across his face again. Guyden gasped, breathed in water and choked.

"The first of our army is here," Rubric said to no one in particular. "They're hunting the valley for the remnants of Ravard's men now."

Kaneth wiped his face dry with a hand. He still held his sword at the ready. "It's over, Kher Ravard. Your men lost the battle and turned for home. There's just you now. You and Guyden. And we have two stormlords in this room."

"You're lying," Ravard spat the words at him. "You're both lying."

Kaneth shook his head. "They're not coming, your army. I swear, on the honour of Uthardim, the real Uthardim. It's over. And the young man playing with water at the moment is not Jasper, but the fellow behind him, Lord

Rubric Verdigris. Now put the boy down before one of us kills you."

"He's my son!" Ravard clutched the squirming child tighter.

Kaneth's rage flared in his eyes. Ryka knew his fear for Kedri was the only thing keeping him from slicing Ravard to pieces right then. On the other side of the room, Rubric released his hold on the water, and it found its own shape and level, flowing away to soak into the carpets. Guyden gasped and coughed, then rolled over and vomited. No one took any notice. Jasper and Ryka waited for Kaneth's explosion of ire.

Instead, he turned to Ryka. "You're hurt. Did *he* do that?"

"No. I fell off a pede and broke my collarbone." She touched the rip across her neck. "This was a feeler. The rest is just bruising. Give me a week or two, and I'll be all right."

"Why you—" Ravard began, realising for the first time that her injuries were not severe. He let out a breath. "I should have known. You never give up. But I still have Khedrim."

The point of Kaneth's sword shivered as his hand shook in anger. "Ask him," he said. "Ask Kedri who his father is."

Guyden made a feeble abortive move to sit up and passed out instead. No one else moved, waiting to see what Ravard would do. Unexpectedly, he collapsed to his knees. The dagger fell from his hand. He was panting, drawing in great gasps of air.

They all stared at him.

Kedri pushed his way out of Ravard's arms and sat

down with a thump on the carpet in front of him. "Don't like you!" he said, glaring.

Ravard grabbed at the boy's shoulder before Kaneth could get to him.

"Hurt Dada!"

Perspiration poured from Ravard's forehead. He looked at Jasper. "I'm a water sensitive," he protested in shock. "You can't kill me like this."

None of them moved. None of them understood.

Ryka was confused. She felt Ravard's water leaving him. She felt it being pulled. *He's right. We can't do this.*

His face began to change. His cheeks sank, his lips thinned. His skin glistened. Rivulets of sweat dripped from him. His breath came raggedly, the dragging intakes of a dying man. His fingers thinned and clutched at empty air. Ryka looked at Jasper, shocked. Only to find him looking at her, equally appalled.

It was Kaneth who realised the truth. He said firmly, "Kedri!" The boy turned his gaze from Ravard to his father. "Stop it, son." Kaneth's tone was gentle, but firm. He stepped forward and picked Kedri up. "No more, all right?"

Ravard made no move to stop him. He was gasping for air, for life. The pull on his water vanished; they all felt it go. He still knelt on the carpet, gulping deeply, his head bowed.

Kaneth ignored him to focus on Kedri. "Dada's hurt not so bad. See? Just a little blood now."

"*Naughty* man."

"Yes, I know. Now how about you go back to bed, eh? Tell you what, just for tonight, you can sleep in Mama and Dada's bed, all right?"

The boy nodded enthusiastically. "Want!"

Kaneth walked to the door that led to the main bedroom. He paused just before stepping through, and his gaze swept the room.

They stared at him, all of them silent. He was calm, half-smiling, all his anger leeched away, his exhaustion real but his stress assuaged. First, he asked Rubric to find someone who could strap up Ryka's arm and tend to her injuries. When the stormlord left, he addressed the others. "I found out today what really matters. Ry, Jasper, I think I'll leave Ravard's fate for you both to decide. Ry, because you were the one he hurt; not me. Never me, because you are by my side still, and we have Kedri." The smile he gave her made her shiver with love for him. "Jasper, because he's your brother. And you're the Cloudmaster of all the Quartern." One side of his mouth quirked up. "And do dry out the carpets before you leave, won't you?" He lifted the canvas door and stepped through with one last look at Ryka.

Still stunned, she looked back to where Ravard was hugging his stomach in agony. *Kedri* did that? But not even a stormlord could steal a water sensitive's water. *Sunlord save us, what is this son of ours?*

Jasper took the dipper hanging on the wall over the water jar, filled it and gave it to Ravard. "Mica, drink. You have to drink to replace the water he took."

Ravard took the dipper and drank deeply. "Khedrim?" he rasped finally. "It was *Khedrim*?"

"So it seems," Jasper said, taking Ravard's weapons and throwing them outside the tent. "It certainly wasn't me."

"Nor me," Ryka said, swallowing her shock.

Ravard was stricken. All the fight, the hate, the passion

had drained from him. "All I wanted...was...t'love him."

Ryka shook her head, speechless. She looked away from him, to Jasper. "I think this is your decision." She gave a slight smile. "For once, I have nothing to say."

She turned her back on them both and went to join her husband and son.

CHAPTER FORTY-THREE

Red Quarter
God's Pellets

The two brothers stared at one another. Pale-faced, Guyden crawled to prop himself up against a tent pole and was ignored by them both.

Ravard, recovering, raised the dipper in salute. "So, you give me water now, 'n' kill me later?" He drank again, draining the vessel.

Jasper took it to refill, then gave it back to him. "What do you want, Mica? I doubt that there's a man alive who will follow you as tribemaster now."

"I will," Guyden said suddenly. He pulled himself to his feet. "I'll follow you."

"Sit down!" Jasper growled at him, waving his sword in his direction. "Otherwise I'll stuff water down your throat."

Guyden sat down abruptly—but only after Ravard made a gesture for him to do so.

"Give me back my pede," Ravard said, "water, food, my weapons. And I'll leave."

"To do what?"

"What you've all said—it's true, isn't it? It's all over? You've won."

"Yes."

"Don't pity me. I couldn't bear that."

Jasper shrugged. "All right, but please don't ask me to kill you. I'm not going to live with that for the rest of my life."

"If what you say is true, about the battle..."

"It is."

Ravard's gaze flickered briefly to the door Ryka had used. "I—I lost everything I ever cared about t'night. I'm despised by the people I wanted t'love. I've no plans t'upset your world. Not any more." He swallowed. "I believed in something, and it came t'nothing. I tried t'make it happen, but I know now it's not going t'be. You're too strong for me, for us. You either got t'kill me and Islar or let us go. Your choice, littl'un.' He looked across at Guyden. "Are you all right, lad?"

The youth nodded, but there was fear lurking at the back of his eyes.

Jasper asked quietly, "If I let you go, then what?"

The reply was a long time coming.

"There's no going back, is there?" Ravard may have phrased the words as a question, but both of them knew it wasn't. It was a truth. "So... let's say I'll ride out into the unknown. A wanderer. A hunter. A fossicker of gems, perhaps. And see where it all ends for me." He shrugged. "I really don't care."

"I'll ride with you," Guyden said.

Ravard smiled faintly. "Two pedes," he told his brother.

Jasper shook his head. "I can't set you free to roam the Red Quarter, Mica."

"Understood. There are other parts of the world."

"I can have men escort you to the coast. There are lands enough on the other side of the Giving Sea—"

"No. I'm not a man for soft, water-filled city dwellers and a roof over my head. I'll go north."

The Burning Sand-Sea. "That's certain death."

"Been there, have you?" he mocked. "I'll take my chances."

They stared at each other.

Then Jasper nodded. "Don't ever come back, Mica. I can't vouch for what would happen if you did."

Ravard stood, still groggy, and walked over to Guyden. The young warrior scrambled to his feet, his eyes shining with a mixture of admiration and resolution. Ravard draped an arm around his shoulders to support himself. "Shale, right now I think I need t'sleep. If you've more natter, can we make it later?"

Jasper nodded. In his heart, he didn't think he had anything to say. Not any more.

Ryka let the canvas door close behind her. Kaneth was lying with Kedri, the child's head supported in the crook of his good arm. He'd wound a makeshift bandage around the biceps of the other.

"He's asleep," he said. He edged out from under his son and stood. "Gods, Ryka—I was terrified I'd lost you. Both of you. Are you really all right? I rode back feeling your pain and despair. And then—sweet water, Ryka, my touch on you was all wrong. I thought you were dying!"

"I was unconscious."

The ache in him: it seared her senses. She came to stand within the circle of his arms and for a long moment they didn't move. Her chest tightened under the weight of her love. She was the first to speak. "You should get all those cuts seen to properly."

His lips brushed her hair. "So should you. I have to go now and straighten out the mess outside. So many people are dead, Ry. And they weren't armsmen."

"I didn't feel them coming. It happened on my watch." She started to sketch the details of how Ravard had smuggled himself and his men inside the valley.

He placed a finger over her lips. "We do our best. That's all we can ever hope for. Our best, and it will never be perfect." He touched her cheek in understanding, in love. "Lie down and wait for the healer. You'll feel better with your arm in a sling, and a pain draught. You have blood on your hair—did you hit your head?"

"I have a colossal headache."

"Make sure you tell the healer that. I have to make certain all is well outside. Stay here with Kedri, while I check." He looked back at the sleeping boy and shook his head in profound wonder. "We have a lot of things to discuss about that little lad."

Kedri looked so small and normal, lying there. He'd found his thumb and was sucking it. "What are we going to do?" she whispered. "Not even stormlords can do what he did."

"I think—be grateful. And watch him very, *very* carefully for the next few years." He gave a lopsided smile. "We will have our hands full, methinks."

About sunset, the remainder of the army they had left behind returned. Bloodied, weary, many of them wounded or carrying their dead—but victorious. In the lead was

Vara, still alive, utterly triumphant, grinning to display the gaps in her yellowing teeth.

"Watergatherer won't be bothering us again," she said. Kaneth helped her clamber down to the ground. If he hadn't supported her, she would have fallen. She felt frail and tiny in his grip, yet when she poked him with her bony finger, she still had the power to make him wince. "I'm going home to Scarmaker," she said. "My dune is going to be the first one to have a woman sandmaster!"

He grinned back at her.

"What happened here?" she asked.

He was about to tell her when another pede was ridden past and he saw Cleve's body strapped across the last of the segments.

"Ah, yes," she said. "Died well, in the end. Leading the army. Had my doubts, I did, but he deserves a hero's burial in the sands." She fixed Kaneth with a look as sharp as a spear tip. "No doubt about it now, Kher. You're the heir to my Makdim. You're sandmaster of all the dunes. Heard people calling you that new word after what happened yesterday: Dunemaster. Dunemaster Uthardim of the Red Quarter. The man who commands all dune gods to do his bidding. No going home now, Scarperman!"

She straightened and hobbled away to her tent leaning on the arm of her driver, her wheezing laughter audible even above the wails of grief from those discovering loved ones returning lifeless across the back of a pede.

Kaneth turned—and saw Ryka standing watching him from the veranda of their tent, her arm in a sling and with Kedri clinging to her trousers. The boy laughed and waved to him.

Why would I want to return, Vara? I have everything I want right here...even a budding cloudmaster.

He didn't even want to *think* about the trouble his son was going to give them on his way to manhood.

Two days later, at dawn, Jasper climbed the Great Knob to watch his brother leave. He'd given the pede, Chert, back to Mica, bestowed another mount on Guyden-Islar and allowed them to take one of the cleanskin packpedes they had brought to God's Pellets. It carried panniers packed with plentiful supplies and water for their journey. He'd said goodbye, with no great hope that either of them would survive. No one had ever crossed the Burning Sand-Sea and returned.

"You always were a good littl'un, Shale," Mica had said as he'd mounted up, a momentary flash of satisfaction on his face as he noted which pede had been brought for him. But he hadn't hugged his brother, or said any words of love, and neither had Jasper. Love was too long in the past to be resurrected.

Instead the next words were all Ravard's, not Mica's. "Look after the dunes, Lord Jasper. Don't let that false Uthardim turn them into another Scarpen midden heap. This should always be a place where people are free to wander."

"It will be. D'you ever remember Wash Drybone Settle? I'm going back there to live. I'll make it better, I swear, all of it." He knew Mica would know what he meant. A better place for boys to grow up, a place where children didn't have to scrounge for their water, or fear their parents would sell them—one way or another—to a passing caravan.

And now, as he watched Mica turn his pede north towards the Burning Sand-Sea and pass beyond the world they knew, he felt hollow, bereft anew of something long since gone.

I wonder if you think to kill yourself, Mica. Well, there are ways a stormlord can make sure two men and their pedes don't die of thirst, even crossing a burning desert. Whether you want it or not.

But then there was a limit too, and he had no idea how far the Burning Sand-Sea extended. He reconciled himself to never knowing if his brother survived.

Goodbye, Mica Flint. Remember me sometimes, just as I'll remember you the way you once were.

CHAPTER FORTY-FOUR

"I'm ravenous." Terelle's head emerged from a tangle of bedding, part of which appeared to be on the floor, and the rest wound around her legs.

"I thought I took care of that last night," Jasper said. He sounded smug.

If a pillow had been within reach, she would have flung it at him.

He'd arrived back in Breccia the night before. Alive. In one piece. Rubric was safe too, and the Red Quarter would eventually settle down under the rule of Kaneth and Ryka. Mica was gone from his life and Ravard had gone from the dunes.

Maybe now we can get on with our lives...

Except there's still Amberlyn. And Taquar. Her heart gave a sick lurch as it always did when she thought of Jasper in confrontation with Taquar. She glanced to where he was pulling on his clothing. He was thinner, and there was pain in his gaze. Grief at his acknowledgement of his final parting from his brother, and far, far more. Amberlyn was in the care of his worst enemy. To attempt a rescue was to risk her life; he knew that and would do it nonetheless. If the attempt failed he would have to live with the consequences for the rest of his days.

God save him, how is it even possible to make that decision?

They finished dressing and went downstairs to have breakfast at the bread shop next door. It was already mid-morning, so the place was empty and some of the varieties of stuffed buns had sold out, but neither of them minded that. They were together again. And, for the moment, safe.

"I suppose you have to go up to Breccia Hall this morning," she said, spearing a bun with her knife. "Do you want this one? It has kumquat jam inside."

"Thanks." He took the bun, broke it in half and gave half back to her. "I am not taking you to the hall, though. I don't want you near Senya or Laisa, not after what Umber told me last night."

She shrugged, licking her fingers. "I'm still alive, and Laisa has kept Senya on a tight leash since it happened. How long will it take you to complete the stormshifting?"

"Ten days and I'll be done."

"Were you serious about going to live in the Gibber?"

"Yes. If—if you'll come with me. It won't be like it was when you were a child, I promise you."

"I hope not. And I am glad you're doing this, Shale. I don't mind leaving the Scarpen, truly. It's time the Gibber became a better place."

"Umber told me he was going to stay in the Scarpen, at least for a few years. Possibly forever."

"Yes, I know. He's already courting a seamstress down on the fourth."

She wondered why he didn't speak of Amberlyn. He hadn't mentioned her name since he'd come back. Not once. Yet surely her situation was haunting his every waking moment and probably his dreams as well. She said, "I think Umber rather likes the idea of becoming a highlord. He has his eye on Scarcleft if you can get Taquar out of there."

He nodded. "Bet Lord Ouina will have something to say about that. The city will be his if he wants it, though. Who is going to say no to a stormlord when there are only three of us? Oh, another thing—I want to see Jade today."

"She's opened a healer's hospice on Level Ten. I go there every day to help her with translations. Now that Rubric's here, he can do that."

"We can set up the scene that will leave them both free to go home."

"Will Rubric leave?"

"I think he would, if Jade does. But I don't think he wants to. In fact, I'm sure he doesn't. But Jade has lost two of her sons..."

"I think she'll decide to stay if Rubric tells her he wants to. She'll probably grizzle about it, but she actually wants an excuse. She's enjoying being a much sought after healer."

"Good!"

"I've learned a lot from her about healing using water-painting. I hope I can put it to good use in the Gibber." When he looked at her with an odd expression on his face she asked, "What?"

"Just thinking. It's ironic. Nealrith dreamed of a more

united Quartern with strong stormlords and a powerful cloudmaster. Instead we have a land more splintered than it ever was. Nothing has turned out the way I thought it would. And yet everything seems to be, well not exactly easy, but at least functioning."

"Remember the Lords and Shells game? There's a Wild Lord who can change everything."

He pondered that. "Kedri?"

She nodded.

"Who knows?"

That's it, she thought. *No one ever does know.*

And still he didn't mention Amberlyn. He stood and dropped some tokens on the table in payment. "Here's Rubric to escort you. I have to go up to the hall. I'll be back tonight."

She grinned at him. "You'd better be."

As he reached the door, he turned back to her. "It's difficult to talk about her when I can't do anything about it. Yet."

A tear edged out of the corner of her eye to wet her lashes. She gave a tiny nod, which he returned, and then he left.

Rubric smirked knowingly as he entered.

Highlord Laisa visited Senya every morning after she'd completed her morning's workload. She'd come to hate those visits. Senya loathed the restrictions that had been placed on her. First, she was only allowed to leave her apartment for the city under guard, and Laisa made sure the head of the guard was always Elmar Waggoner because he was the one person she could trust to have the Cloudmaster's personal interests at heart. Nor would he ever be swayed by any approach from a waterpriest. The second restriction imposed was that Senya could have no visitors unless her mother was present.

The result was that every day Senya assailed Laisa with a one-way litany of complaint and abuse. And never, not once, did she acknowledge that anything she'd ever done was unjustified or worthy of condemnation.

On the day Laisa told her Jasper was back but had not yet come to Breccia Hall, the visit was even more unpleasant than usual. Senya, quite rightly, assumed that Jasper had elected to see his lover rather than his wife, and she was incandescent with rage, her ire spilling out in the form of foul language that Laisa had been unaware Senya would ever have heard, let alone known how to use.

At the end of her diatribe, she said, suddenly amiable, "But never mind. I know how to get my own back on that snuggery slut."

"Oh, how?" Laisa asked, not expecting to hear anything much.

"Oh, poison her, of course. You thought you were so clever, taking that poison from me, but we'll see who has the last laugh." She folded her arms. "And I'm not going to say another word. You'll just have to wait and see."

Laisa smiled pleasantly, even as her stomach churned in sudden apprehension. "Oh? I don't believe you've done anything at all. You're just making it up."

It took her the run of a sandglass, but eventually she had the whole story. Senya had bribed her maid, Inya, with a piece of her jewellery, a pearl necklace, to procure another vial of the same poison, label it as essence of sweet vanillin, then wrap it and have it delivered to Terelle's lodgings as a present from Jasper. It was supposed to be a flavouring to be added a few drops at a time to any drink.

Senya was smiling triumphantly as she related her vision of Terelle's painful death.

Laisa heard her out without comment. Within, she was raging. The stupid girl would bring both of them down with her irrationality. Thank the Sunlord, Terelle had changed her lodgings several times since the last attempt on her life, ensuring that such a present would have been delivered to the wrong address. Not that Laisa could imagine Terelle being so gullible as to accept unknown presents. Every word Senya uttered drove Laisa's despair deeper. Her daughter was not only naïve and irrational, she was sandcrazy.

Perturbed, Laisa left her alone and cornered Inya to find out the details. At first the girl pretended innocence, but Laisa wasn't fooled. Inya broke down under further questioning and added another layer to the sordid tale. Yes, she'd taken the jewellery, but she hadn't wanted to poison anybody. Instead she'd sold the pearls to a pawnbroker, then used the money to buy an apprenticeship for her brother. She'd come back and lied to Senya, telling her that she'd bought the poison and safely delivered it to Terelle.

Laisa had the Overman of the Guard lock Inya up for theft and sent one of her trusted servants to check the information. When he reported back to her later that day, it was clear Inya had told the truth. Laisa thanked him, then dismissed the maid on the spot, but took no further action on the promise of her silence.

The next morning Jasper came to the hall for the first time after his return to the Breccia. When he met Laisa, he was chillingly polite and distant as he gave her a brief outline of all that had happened in the Red Quarter. In return, she told him she'd insisted on regular reports from Zirca and Crystal about Amberlyn. "Your daughter is well and thriving," she said and showed him the latest message she had received, written in Zirca's childlike script.

He read it and slipped it into his pocket. Calmly, he repeated the words he'd sent by cloud message, "If she dies, so do you."

That was the only reference he made to her treachery, but she felt she was living poised on the edge of a knife blade. Perfectly poised at the moment, but knowing that sooner or later she would fall and impale herself because Senya would bring her down, if nothing else. *He's going to kill me, the first time I put a foot wrong, I know it.* She'd betrayed him, sold his daughter to Taquar. His anger was there, it must be, even though he never showed it. His gaze was cold and dispassionate, but one day . . .

The strain of waiting made her sick. She couldn't eat or sleep. A few days later, after Jasper had been coming to Breccia Hall every day to stormshift, he told her he would soon be finished and would be able to go to the Gibber with Terelle. She knew she'd run out of time. She had to do something to show her new loyalties.

She sat for a long while that morning, deep in thought. Then she went to her jewellery case and took out the poison Senya had got from the waterpriest, still in its pretty onyx container. It was pale green, with strands of brown through the polished stone like tresses of hair spread out on a pillow . . .

*   *   *

Early the next morning, before Jasper arrived at the hall, Laisa went to see Senya.

As usual, Senya was in a fury. "When do I get a new maid? I hate that old hag of yours you've been sending me! She's as sour as an unripe kumquat. And I don't understand why Inya left anyway."

"I'll find you someone new and young," she replied. "Senya, I was thinking, tomorrow why don't we go and buy some new clothes? I heard there was a pede caravan in from the ports full of the latest fashions. There's a shop down on Level Four that has promised to show them to us first, in the morning."

Senya clapped her hands. "Oh, wonderful! Why can't we go now?"

"They're still unpacking. Tell you what, why don't we look at your wardrobe and see what you need?"

They spent an hour discussing clothing and what Senya required. *No, it's more a list of what she demands,* Laisa thought, sighing inwardly. She fingered the vial in her dress pocket.

When they'd finished dissecting Senya's wardrobe, she ordered a jug of Senya's favourite juice and they sat down in her sitting room. When the drink came, Laisa dismissed the servant and went to pour the juice herself. With her back to Senya, she asked, "Tell me, do you ever think of your father?"

"No, why?"

Laisa glanced over her shoulder, the juice still unpoured. "Don't you miss him?"

Senya laughed. "Of course not! It's because he was so sun-fried that we're in this horrid city. Him and grand-father. Tell me, do you think they have any pearls in the shipment? I really need some more, seeing as I sold the ones I had. Have you heard if Terelle's dead yet?"

"No. Not yet."

She pouted. "I'm beginning to wonder if Inya really did buy the poison. Maybe she just ran away with my pearls."

"Maybe she did."

"I'll have to think of something else, then. Mama, we have to do *something*."

"We will. Here's your juice."

Senya took the glass and drank it all. "I was thirsty," she said. "Can I have some more?"

"Of course." Laisa smiled at her. "Drink as much as you want. And think about what fun we'll have tomorrow."

"The highlord is waiting for you," the guard told Jasper when he arrived that day. "She asks that you see her first before going to the stormquest room. She said to conduct you to Lord Senya's apartments, m'lord."

Jasper hid a grimace. The last person he wanted to see was his wife. He braced himself, aware that he had been putting the meeting off longer than was wise. Better to get it over and done with and comfort himself with the knowledge that he'd soon be able to leave and shake off the corrosive memories of Breccia Hall.

It was Laisa who bade him enter Senya's apartment, and he walked on in, closing the door behind him.

And stopped in shock.

Senya was lying on the divan, her eyes closed. Unmoving. Her hair was loosened to cover the cushion under her head. And her water was no longer alive. Laisa sat beside her on a hassock, holding her hand. On a table close by there was a jug of juice and two glasses, one full, one empty.

For a long while he stood stock still, taking in the scene.

Finally he said, "You—you *do* know she's dead?" *Inane question; of course she knows.* He felt nothing. No sorrow, no relief, no regret. Just...a neutral interest. As if he'd scarcely known Senya Almandine.

Laisa fumbled in her skirt and withdrew an onyx vial. She held it up, then placed it carefully on the table. "I found out she'd hatched another plan against Terelle. I scolded her and told her I'd tell you. She took the poison she'd intended for Terelle."

He eyed the two glasses. "I see." No other words came to him. Murder, of course. Laisa's—what? Propitiation? Her atonement for her wrongs, reparation to him? For a moment he felt ill. She had killed Senya to regain his trust? To ensure her position? He stared at her.

"You know what my biggest mistake was, Jasper?"

He shook his head, not moving from where he stood.

"Not appreciating Nealrith nearly enough."

"A lot of people made that mistake."

"Yes. Would an apology mean much?"

"To me?" He gaped, robbed of further speech. It wasn't what he'd expected.

"Yes."

It was a moment before he managed to say, "Not much. In fact, nothing at all. Not while my daughter is held by Taquar. Truth to tell, probably never. And somehow I doubt that an apology would make Nealrith feel any better."

She nodded, accepting his words without apparent distress, awaiting his decision on her future. His approval for what she'd done? That was when he glimpsed something he'd thought he would never see in her eyes: resignation. Even, perhaps, a little regret.

When he said nothing, she asked, "So what's next?"

"Somehow I don't think I want to see too much of you in the future, Laisa. In fact, I don't want to see you ever again if I can help it. I even regret that I still have to use your stormquest room for another three days."

"You're welcome."

"The Scarpen has a stormlord in Umber. I suggest you all treat him very well indeed and continue to search for other water talents to train. Start accusing Umber of blasphemy, and you will find yourselves without water, because I'm through with the Scarpen. I'm through with you all. You can tell Lord Gold that. Actually, I think I take great delight in leaving him for you to manage."

She frowned, as if she didn't understand what he was trying to say. "You're not bringing storms for us any more?"

"Not once I leave, no. It will all be Umber's task. He's both skilled enough and happy to manage the Scarpen by himself."

"The Red Quarter?"

"Rubric—that's Lord Jade's son—has undertaken to send storms there, possibly with the help of Jade if he needs it. But the Red Quarter has found another source of water and may gradually become independent under Dunemaster Kaneth."

She looked at him blankly.

"I doubt that the Red Quarter will ever bother you again."

"I have difficulty thinking of an irresponsible woman-iser like Kaneth ruling all the dunes with the slightest competence."

"He will. With Ryka's help." He wasn't sure she was taking it all in. *No wonder, I suppose, with Senya's body lying there.* He continued, "The White Quarter expects to be able to persuade Khromatis to supply their water from now onwards. If that doesn't work out, Terelle and I will do it."

"And me?"

"Laisa—I don't care."

She looked at him, dubious.

"I simply don't care," he repeated. "Somehow I don't think there is a Quartern any more, not as an entity, let alone one with a cloudmaster. Rule your city as best you can. Work with other cities to keep the roads and caravan-saries open. If you want to do something to help me, then continue to keep an eye on Amberlyn. I understand Umber has already informed Taquar that if she is hurt, Scarcleft will get no water from him. And you can tell Taquar from me that if she's hurt, I'll hunt him down, no matter where he goes. But I'll not risk her life by attempt-ing a rescue, especially as—" He halted and blushed. "Terelle is not keen on raising Senya's child."

She tried and failed to hide a cynical smile. "I imagine not. That is—wise of you. Doubtless Terelle will have your children in due course."

"It is my hope."

"I don't communicate with Taquar any more, though. You'll have to send your own messages."

He snorted, not believing her, then took one last look at Senya. "Nealrith asked me to look after her. In the end, it seems I failed him."

"I don't think there could have been any other ending. She was no longer quite...sane."

Laisa stood and he noted that her silks were faded and patched. *Things do change,* he thought.

Another knock sounded at the door. "That will be the waterpriests to take her body to the House of the Dead," she said. She was abnormally pale and her fingers trembled. He couldn't bring himself to care, or to try to decide if she was grieving, shocked, or just worried about what action he would take.

He said calmly, "I'll leave now. Please do all that is proper for the taking of her water. I'll attend, of course."

"Of course."

In the doorway, he paused. "My condolences."

She flushed.

You murdered her daughter, he thought, *and I am not going to do anything about it.*

He passed the priests on his way out.

Sandhells, Rith, I am sorry. I am so sorry.

CHAPTER FORTY-FIVE

Scarpen Quarter
Scarcleft City
Gibber Quarter
Wash Drybone

A light wind skittered through the bab grove, scurrying dust and rattling the dried underskirt of the palms. In near silence, a pack pede carrying three people slipped through the darkness of the night in the direction of the Scarcleft city walls. It wasn't following the road and it wasn't heading towards any of the gates, either. They would have been closed anyway, at this time of the night. Three hours before dawn, with the night at its darkest.

When they drew level with the grove's main water cistern, Jasper, who was driving, halted the pede and jumped across onto the stone slab top. Terelle and Rubric followed.

"No guards," Rubric remarked as he lit the single candle in a small shutter lantern.

"They clear everyone out of the groves and close the city up tight," Jasper explained. "Not much out here to be stolen."

"Or broken," added Rubric, selecting a prybar from his

pack. He inserted it at the edge of the cistern lid and proceeded to use it to break the lock. "Scared?" he asked Terelle.

"Of course I'm scared."

We all are, Jasper thought. *What if Taquar is waiting for me?* All they could do was hope that Laisa had told Taquar that he and Terelle were heading for a new life in the Gibber. Most of their party, led by Dibble and Elmar, were indeed doing just that. Laisa might not have relayed the message, and if she had, Taquar might not have believed it.

They worked on in silence, each step unfolding according to plan.

They'd been over it so often. They'd practised and experimented and discussed every aspect. With Jasper's help, Terelle had drawn maps of Scarcleft and its hall from memory and they'd studied them together. Even so, being here again, in the bab grove outside the gates of Scarcleft, Jasper felt vulnerable. Not like a stormlord at all. Not like a man who'd fought battles and held the fate of thousands in the magic of his power. He felt like Shale Flint, helpless in the clutches of a rainlord. And how must Terelle be feeling? She'd once been imprisoned within these walls, threatened with death by the man he was about to confront.

In the distance, night-parrots boomed. If he looked through the trees he saw the walls of the city, dark and formidable, patrolled by armed sentries. From all that Jasper had been able to find out about the way Taquar now ran his city, it was a place difficult both to enter and to leave. All who passed the gates were questioned and searched. Jasper had no doubt that everyone was on special lookout for him.

Together he and Rubric dealt with the cover of the cistern, edging it open. Together they pulled a large block of water out. They had to work quickly now. The longer there was an unusual movement of water the more chance that Taquar or one of his rainlords would notice it.

Please let them all be asleep...

Once the block was the size Jasper wanted, and had been shaped to suit his needs, they lowered it until its upper surface was level with the back of their mount. Terelle had already uncovered their unwieldy baggage to reveal a single boat-shaped segment taken from a dead pede.

He turned to Terelle and kissed her lightly on the lips. "I have to do this."

"I know."

"I may not succeed."

"I know that too."

"If I fail—" he began.

"Just remember that only Amberlyn matters. Take her and ignore Taquar if you can. Why should we care enough about him to see him dead?" Her voice trembled with passion.

He didn't reply.

She added, her tone telling him she was resigned but not defeated, "No matter what, if I can, I will look after Amberlyn."

"I love you."

She smiled. "I know that as well. And I so need you back in one piece."

He nodded to Rubric. "I'll throw some water at you if I'm successful, then send someone to open the gate. No water by dawn—get out of here, both of you."

Rubric and Terelle manoeuvred the segment until it floated on top of the water. Cautiously, with Rubric stabilising the surface for him, Jasper stepped aboard and sat down. The "boat" wobbled alarmingly, then tipped to one side. He distributed his weight more evenly and sat still.

"I think that's got it," Rubric muttered. "Jasper, take care. Terelle's right, ye know. Taquar doesn't matter."

He didn't reply. Taquar had been behind the attack on his settle that had killed his family and his baby sister. Taquar had imprisoned him. Taquar had kidnapped and threatened the woman he loved. Taquar had brought the whole land to the brink of disaster. Taquar had manipulated him into a marriage he didn't want and was threatening to torture his daughter.

What he did matters to me.

The rage behind the thought—he felt that deep in his being, searing and corrupting his inner peace. It had been there so long it was almost part of him. He needed to expunge it. Terelle thought he could do it by dismissing Taquar, as if the man didn't matter. Well, he'd tried that and failed miserably.

Now he had a better idea. It wasn't nice, it probably didn't reflect well on him, but he didn't care. *If Taquar and I both die, at least Amberlyn will be safe. And the Quartern will survive, with Umber and Rubric and Jade and Terelle and the Source. I'm not so important any more.* The thought was oddly liberating.

"Time to go," he said. He took a deep breath. It didn't do anything to stop the pounding of his heart. He was about to fly.

The block of water began to lift, the boat rocking in the middle. This was the part that they had practised the most; this was the reason he'd needed Rubric along. He'd tried to do it on his own, but found he just wasn't powerful enough to lift himself and the water and guide it as well. He hadn't wanted to bring Terelle either, but she had asked him loftily just how he and Rubric were going to take care of a baby on the way to the Gibber, and that was that.

Slowly, carefully, they lifted the water, sending it higher and higher.

If he lost his hold on it . . .

Don't think about that.

If a rainlord sensed it and yanked it from under him . . .

Don't think about that either, you sand-head.

Rubric concentrated on holding the integrity of the block of water intact; Jasper focused on moving it where he wanted.

Which was straight up, at least at first. The higher it went, the better the chance that none of the guards along the walls would notice as he slid silently overhead. *Rubric, whatever you do, don't drip water on the sentries' heads.*

Or worse still, drop Jasper and his vessel on the city from a considerable height. Jasper tried not to imagine that. If they failed, he died. At least it would be quick.

He sat motionless. When he glanced over at Scarcleft, he gasped.

I'll be weeping waterless, this is like being a bird!

For one wild moment he wished it was daylight so he could see it all. At this time of the night, there were hardly any lights; just the occasional flicker of a candle in a window, a lantern wending its way up through the city, grasped, perhaps, in the hand of a drunken reveller on his way home. The brightest points of light were occasional inn windows opening onto a courtyards. Still, there was enough starlight to outline the buildings in a silvery glow.

He edged the water still higher, resisting the impulse to go faster, or to go closer before he was high enough. He wanted to be on a level with Scarcleft Hall when he drifted over the walls. As he reached the right height, he scooped up a handful of water and tossed it over the edge; his warning to Rubric to be ready. A moment later it returned as a shower of droplets on his head.

He's a withering fine stormlord. Those drops had barely started to fall before Rubric had become aware of them and sent them back. He smiled as he began to edge his craft towards the heights of the city. Terelle's meeting up with her cousin—with both her cousins—was the best thing that had happened in Khromatis.

He passed over the wall, directly below. Everything was so dark that he had no way of telling if a guard was looking upwards. At least no one shouted an alarm. Wilted damn, it was a long way down...

He looked ahead to the hall where it squatted on the second highest level, just below the waterhall. Easy enough to orient himself because the main Sun Temple of the city poked its tower up above all the surrounding buildings on Level Three, not far from the main gates on Level Two. He knew exactly which balcony belonged to Taquar.

But first he had to enter the hall unseen.

He used his senses to pinpoint guards. More difficult than he'd thought, blast it. The water of his craft blocked the details of people further away. He thought there could have been as many as fifteen men up on the ramparts of the wall around the hall and the waterhall above. In addition, guards patrolled the gardens. He smiled slightly, remembering. Guards had almost caught him there the day he had arrived in Scarcleft, when he'd been thirteen or fourteen years old. How different things would have been if they had! He never would have met Terelle, for a start...

He brought his mind back to his task.

Deal with Taquar first. If Taquar was dead, then everything else would fall into place. He started to descend, speeding up as he went. Rubric, bless him, kept the raft's integrity, no small feat from his distant perch on the cistern.

He guided the raft to Taquar's balcony. The room beyond was shuttered tight, no light showing. He hovered level with the balcony railing and climbed out of the pede segment. Then, to make sure it didn't float off the edge of the water block and go crashing somewhere below, he pulled the front end up onto the balcony railing just enough to anchor it.

He paused. Everything inside was quiet. *If he's awake, he'll know who it is.* He'd be waiting. And Taquar was a skilled swordsman, even handicapped as he was now. His knee was a mess after their last encounter, and by all accounts he walked with a pronounced limp and a lurching gait. It must have affected his ability to fight. Jasper had no compunction at all about taking advantage of that, not with this man.

Stepping away from the water, he used his senses to tell him Taquar was supine. Good. Probably still asleep. He tried the door, but it was barred. He unhooked his prybar from his belt and inserted the hooked end between doorjamb and door lock, then levered it savagely. The door splintered. He wrenched it open, sword in one hand, prybar still in the other, and launched himself into the room like a low-flung spear, not directly ahead, but off to the left.

Wise move. Taquar had been faking sleep. The highlord came off the bed already holding his sword and slashing the place where logically Jasper would have been. Jasper rolled and leaped upwards onto the bed. He feinted with his sword to cover the savage swing of the prybar with his left hand. Taquar ducked at the last moment and the metal hook did no more than rip off his ear in a spray of blood.

At that moment, the damaged door swung shut, sweeping the meagre starlight from the room as it closed. It wasn't quite pitch dark—briquette coals glowed in the fireplace—but mostly they had only their sense of sound and their feel for the other's water to guide them.

I hope I'm better at this than he is. Jasper had the disadvantage of never having been in the highlord's bedroom before. As he moved across the bed, he kicked something with his foot. Silently he reached down to pick it up, thinking it was a pillow. To his delight his hand closed around the harder, more manageable shape of a cushion.

Senses wide to every nuance of Taquar, he was aware that the highlord had stepped back, away from the bed. He had one hand to his ear, in an attempt to stem the copious flow of blood that Jasper could sense. Taquar's breath had quickened. Air in, damper air exhaled. His hand held his sword at the ready, weaving it to and fro in the air.

"Jasper." His tone was amused and apparently unworried. He must have been in agony, but there was no trace of it in his voice.

Still arrogantly confident, sunblast the wilted bastard.

Jasper's courage shrank. How could he fight a man like that? He was no swordsman. All his battle successes had been with water, but now he was up against the most powerful of all the rainlords.

"I might have known you couldn't just leave while you were ahead."

Jasper's mouth was dry and he had to lick his lips before he could speak. "You have my daughter." He made a small slit in the cushion cover, a heavy bab-fibre cloth, and slid the prybar crossways inside. It fitted firmly through the packed stuffing, wedged from corner to corner.

"So? I won't hurt her if you leave me alone." Taquar said. "I thought you'd be sensible and stay away to keep her safe. I underestimated your foolishness. Or is it your desire for revenge? I was prepared to give up my schemes of a greater, united land under my rule in exchange for a prosperous future for Scarcleft. But no, you couldn't let it rest, could you? Never mind, at least we have other stormlords now to manage the water. Your death will mean nothing."

His contemptuous dismissal was strangely hurtful. Jasper said, "You have a price to pay for what you've done." He made another two slits, in the back cover of the cushion this time, and slid his arm into one and out of the other, so that the cushion fitted snugly over his forearm like a buckler. A cushion was a poor substitute, but this one had a tough iron prybar in it as a nasty surprise. It could be both a weapon and a shield. In the dark, he felt sure that Taquar would not realise what he'd done.

"The truth is, you can't save Amberlyn from me, any more than you could save your little sister—can't recall her name—from Davim. Still, it's not too late. I'm prepared to be magnanimous. Leave now, the same way you came in, and I swear she'll be well cared for as long as you stay away and encourage anyone else with a grudge to stay away from my city."

Jasper pretended to consider the idea. "Why should I accept that assurance? You can hardly expect me to think of you as an honourable m—"

Someone knocked at the door. Ordinarily the man's water would have warned them both, but not now. Their focus was on each other.

When Taquar opened his mouth to say something, Jasper leaped from the bed in his direction, lunging with his sword from above. His stroke was almost successful. Almost. Taquar's parry carried Jasper's sword past, but it was close enough to rip his sleeve. The highlord followed up with a flurry of strokes that Jasper only just managed to turn. Twice the improvised buckler saved his life. The strain of concentration formed sweat along his brow, but he didn't dare wipe it away. *Blighted hells, I think I am going to die. Concentrate, Jasper. Make sure that you take him with you when you go. This is for Amberlyn...And Citrine.*

The knocking at the door continued. Neither Taquar nor Jasper paid any attention.

It was hard to know just where the point of the sword was in the dark. The lack of light gave Taquar an advantage because he was the better swordsman. The confines of the room meant that his injured leg was not much of a disadvantage.

I must have more light.

The knocking became pounding. "My lord! My lord! Are you all right?" Several voices.

Withering spit, reinforcements. Jasper disengaged and back-pedalled, fast, until he was back at the door to the balcony.

"Break it down!" Taquar shouted to those on the other side of the door. "And get the child!"

Jasper flung open the balcony door and wrenched the water inside. He didn't care what happened to the pede segment and didn't wait to see. He stepped aside to let the water shoot into the room. Taquar felt it coming, but his damaged knee did not allow him to move quickly. He pushed against it with his power instead. Water shot off in all directions. Jasper gathered it together again, and the two men struggled to wrench control of it away from each other.

Your mistake, Taquar. I may be a lousy stormlord, but I'm more powerful than you are when it comes to water.

He eased off the pressure of his power slightly to encourage Taquar to give it his all, then jerked the water away. Taquar staggered, caught off guard. Jasper had control now and slammed a stream upwards into Taquar's face. While the man was coping with that, Jasper moved to hook a leg behind Taquar's knee and toss him to the floor. It must have hurt his wounded ear, because he gave a short cry of pain. Yet he still managed to parry Jasper's next sword cut while he struggled to rise.

Jasper stamped on his damaged knee, then further hampered his movements by flinging water into his face. Taquar retaliated, jabbing at his leg with his blade. It cut into the fleshy part of his calf, hurting more than incapacitating. He jumped back and kicked Taquar, this time grinding the toe of his sandal into his raggedly torn earhole.

Taquar screamed. As he faltered, Jasper pounced on

his sword and twisted it out of his hand. With a swing he tossed the weapon out of the room, over the balcony and into the garden below.

"My lord, my lord, are you all right?" The door was juddering now as those outside battered at it with something heavy.

Taquar scrambled to his feet, butting Jasper in the stomach with his head as he came up. As Jasper doubled over, dragging air into starved lungs, Taquar wrested his sword out of his hand. Then he lunged at him. Jasper swung his buckler blindly upwards to deflect the blow. The curved end of the pry iron slammed into Taquar's cheek, piercing the skin and pushing into his mouth, knocking out several teeth on the way. The sword blade scraped Jasper's ribs in passing. *That was close.*

Taquar gasped and stumbled back against the wall, finally realising that there was something more than just a cushion tied to Jasper's arm. He still held Jasper's sword.

The door to the passage burst open and three armsmen plunged into the room, weapons drawn, followed by another carrying a lantern. Behind them, a guard was holding the arm of a woman clad in a voluminous nightgown, hugging a bundle to her shoulder. Amberlyn's nurse, Zirca, her eyes wide with fear.

And Amberlyn.

Taquar spat out a tooth. "My game after all, I think," he said, straightening up.

Jasper bundled water together in the centre of the room. "Don't come any closer," he said to the armsmen, "or you're all dead."

"That's the Cloudmaster!" one of the men exclaimed, holding the lantern high.

The room was stilled, the men looking from one to the other in startled shock. No one needed to explain to them the danger they could be in if they challenged a storm-lord.

"He won't hurt you," Taquar said, dabbing at the jagged tear in his cheek with his sleeve. "We have his daughter." His next remark was addressed to Jasper. "Touch any of my men, and one of them will kill the child, I swear it, and I'll kill you as well. You can't drown us all. Let's talk about what we want in a civilised manner."

A long, tense silence swallowed them all. No one moved. No one spoke. Then a guard shuffled uneasily and darted an uncomfortable look at Amberlyn.

A spike of terror drove into Jasper's heart. *Can I risk it?*

All it would take would be one man who had it in him to kill a child. One man. And these were enforcers.

"Whoever harms my child dies in the very next instant," he said.

"They'll follow my orders," Taquar said. Blood streamed down his face and his speech was distorted by the damage to his cheek, but his gaze never wavered from Jasper's.

"Are you sure?" Jasper asked grimly.

More shuffling at the door was followed by the guards parting to let someone else through: Harkel Tallyman, once again the seneschal of Scarcleft Hall and the man in charge of the guards and the water enforcers.

Jasper shifted his focus to stare at him, and their gazes met briefly, before Harkel's look moved on to Taquar. "My lord?" he asked. "Your orders?"

Taquar repeated what he'd already said.

Harkel looked at his men. "Any volunteers to kill the Cloudmaster's daughter if the need arises?"

No one moved or spoke.

"Wise men. I don't think that person would be alive a moment afterwards," Harkel told Taquar apologetically. "I don't think you would be, either, m'lord."

Taquar's rage exploded, his hatred spilling out in his voice, in his glare. He advanced on Jasper, his sword raised. "Get rid of that water through the balcony door, Jasper, or both Amberlyn and you die, *right now.*"

"I think not," Jasper said quietly. He nodded to Harkel. The seneschal tossed him a sword, which he caught by the hilt.

Taquar swung his head in bewilderment to stare at his seneschal.

"Sorry, my lord," Tallyman said. "It's over. A sensible man knows when it's time the change masters." He made a gesture with his hand and the armsmen surrounded the highlord, swords at the ready.

"*What?*" Taquar's tone was pure disbelief.

"Wise decision," Jasper told the seneschal. "This is the end, Taquar. For what I am about to do, I don't have the slightest compunction." He stepped between two of the armsmen, flung a small amount of water at Taquar's face to distract him, and used the moment to jam his blade home, upwards between the ribs, into Taquar's body. "I shan't ever be sorry at all. Remember Citrine?" He stepped away, withdrawing the sword. The steel slid out easily. Surprising little blood followed the blade out of the flesh.

Taquar tried to speak, but no sound came. One of the armsmen plucked the sword he held from his fingers. For a moment the highlord remained standing, then slowly he slid to the floor where he sat, propped up against the wall. He looked down at his chest. His fingers touched the small wound there, as if he was surprised by its negligible appearance.

Jasper, coldly calm, removed his buckler and cleaned the sword with the cushion cover. Taquar raised his face to look at him. His last coherent expression before he died was one of utmost astonishment.

"Welcome back, m'lord," Harkel said. He fumbled in his pocket and drew out a small piece of parchment. "I thought this must have come from you. Made me think, it did." He tossed it into the fireplace.

"I was banking on your survival instincts, Harkel. We shall discuss terms later. In the meantime, get this mess cleaned up, send a message to Lord Umber in Breccia notifying him of Taquar's death, and inform the Rainlord Council that a new highlord is needed. I will be suggesting Lord Umber. Oh, and send someone to the south gate. They will find the waterpainter Terelle Grey there, with another stormlord, Lord Rubric Verdigris. They are to be made welcome." Even as he spoke he bundled up a ball of water and pitched it through the open door towards Rubric and Terelle.

"And you, my lord? Is there something you need? You're bleeding—"

"Yes, never mind, it's nothing much. I need you to leave me alone. With my daughter."

He beckoned to Zirca. She entered the room with a broad grin. "My lord, it's good to see you again." She deposited the child she held into his waiting arms. Amberlyn stirred and smiled in her sleep. He touched her hand and she curled her fingers around his.

Amberlyn. Her hair was soft and curly and so *long*. How she'd grown!

He didn't even noticed as the armsmen carried Taquar's body away and the room emptied, leaving him and his daughter, together.

He whispered, "We are going home soon, Amber. To the Gibber." The child stirred, then nestled more comfortably. He nearly wept. "With your mother. Her name is Terelle, and she's the most beautiful woman in the Quartern."

In the fireplace, a tiny piece of paper began to brown around the edges and the unsigned writing on it darkened:

> *Harkel,*
> *saving the life of a child*
> *will earn you the undeserved right*
> *to a long and comfortable old age.*

Sometimes, Jasper reflected, it paid to be known as an honourable man, one who kept his promises. On such little details could hang the fate of the most important things in the world.

Jasper stood next to Terelle at the top of the crack across the land and looked down on the floor of the wash. Wash Drybone. Where he had been born and grown up, where he'd been abused and kidnapped. The settle was still there, two parallel streets of stone houses, each surrounded by its stone wall with the narrow gap facing upstream to catch the water rush. Once it had been all of Shale Flint's world, all that he knew. Now it was a tiny fragment of Jasper Bloodstone's past life.

The bab-palm thatching had long since gone, but the stone walls remained, largely as they had been the day he'd left. Not his house, of course; that had been on the bank, poorly built and now no more than a heap of uncut stones covered in dust sprinkled through with the sparkle of mica from the Gibber Plains. Some of the bab trees of the wash had survived too, but none were thriving. The cisterns and slots remained; it was just a matter of cleaning them out. The trees would fruit again...

He looked along the edge of the wash, now crowded with people gazing down on what was to be their new home: Elmar, Dibble, Zirca and Crystal were among the forty Gibber families, mostly people who'd been waterless in the Scarpen. He'd sketched a vision for them of a different future. He hoped they were thinking of that now, seeing beyond a dusty drywash with its dilapidated houses and cisterns to a different sort of wash: a wetter place than it had been for centuries, a place where trees would grow along the edges of its natural pools, where there was greenery and water birds and wild fish. A place where their children could play and be carefree in a way he'd never been. He'd promised them hard work, yes, but he'd also promised them a better world. The buzz of their conversation and their laughter cheered him.

In a moment they would ride on down. Perhaps he and Terelle would sleep the night in the ruins of what once had been Rishan the Palmier's home. A humble house for a stormlord, but neither of them cared. He had smaller ambitions now: to be a man who brought unity to the Gibber and supplied its water. No more would Gibber folk be the lowest of the low, the dust along the hem of the Quartern. They would be independent-minded folk who earned their living as miners and traders and fossickers, perhaps even a nation in the way that Khromatis was a nation. A people who had the water and the pedes to do it. And the stormlord and the waterpainter healer to seed the beginnings of a better life. A dream? Yes. But he was content to start small. They were young, and their lives stretched before them yet.

Beside him Terelle slipped a hand into his. She was carrying Amberlyn on her hip. "Look, Amber," she said. "That's your new house down there. One day you'll run along those streets with your friends."

"Mama," said Amberlyn. "Mama."

Terelle's face lit up. "Oh! You precious thing!" She planted a kiss on the child's head and, glowing in her delight, turned to look at Jasper. "Her first word!"

He grinned at her. 'You cheated, I swear. You've been coaching her."

"Her second word will be Papa, I promise."

Next to Jasper, Dibble drank from his water skin and then offered the skin to Elmar. Amberlyn waved her hand at him in supplication.

"Water," she said. "Water!"

Jasper threw back his head and roared with laughter.

GLOSSARY OF CHARACTERS AND TERMS

(Note: Characters and terms introduced for the first time in this book are not included.)

ALABASTER: Name given to the White Quarter by its inhabitants. Also the name given to the white-skinned, white-haired people who live there.

ASH GRIDELIN: The Watergiver's real name. The Alabasters claim he was merely a promiscuous Khromatian Watergiver explorer.

BAB PALM: Palm tree grown extensively in the Scarpen and Gibber; also found in small numbers around waterholes in the Red Quarter. The trunk is the main source of wood for the Quartern; the fruit, shoots and roots are edible; the leaves are used for thatch, baskets, mats.

BASALT, Lord: Rainlord and High Waterpriest of the Quartern. After the death of the last Sunpriest, or Lord Gold, Basalt was the logical successor to that post.

'BASTER: Derogatory shortening of Alabaster.

BLOODSTONE (also known as MARTYR'S STONE): Green jasper flecked with red droplets, supposedly the blood of the Watergiver; particularly valued by the priesthood. Jasper, when a boy, found a particularly valuable piece.

BRECCIA CITY: Scarpen city, traditional seat of the Cloudmaster.

BURNISH: Name of Sandmaster Davim's myriapede.

CHALAMEN: Spear-carrying Reduner warriors.

CHERT: One of the sons of Rishan the palmier, the head of Wash Drybone Settle in the Gibber. Killed by Mica Flint to prove his loyalty, on the orders of Sandmaster Davim.

CITRINE FLINT: Shale's baby sister; murdered by Sandmaster Davim.

CLOUDMASTER, The: A stormlord who also rules the Quartern through his fellow stormlords and a Council of Rainlords. The temporal power of a cloudmaster is limited largely to water matters, taxation and maintenance of trade routes, achieved through consensus with his or her water-sensitive peers. The last Cloudmaster, Granthon Almandine, died during the siege of Breccia.

DAVIM, Sandmaster: Sandmaster of Dune Watergatherer and leader of the Red Quarter until his death at the hands of Iani Potch and Jasper Bloodstone during the battle for the Qanatend mother cistern. Father to three sons.

DAYJAR: A container which holds exactly the amount of water gifted as a free daily ration to those entitled to such an allowance.

DIBBLE HORNBLEND: A young Scarcleft armsman who supported Jasper long before it was safe to do so. Now acting as his personal bodyguard and pede driver.

DROVER: Colloquial term for a Reduner, originating in their herding of pede meddles.

DUNE GOD: Each dune of the Red Quarter is believed to have a god who lives at the heart of the dune.

ELMAR WAGGONER: A Breccian armsman, friend and battle comrade of Lord Kaneth Carnelian. Was a slave of the Reduner Watergatherer tribe at the same time as Kaneth, with whom he is in love.

ERITH GREY: Terelle's Khromatian father, killed by Russet Kermes before she was born.

FEROZE KHORASH: An Alabaster salt trader once rescued from death by Jasper Bloodstone. Led the Alabasters who fought alongside Scarpen troops against Sandmaster Davim.

GIBBER QUARTER: One of the four quarters of the Quartern. Gibber folk live mainly in settles in the drywashes, eking out a living from bab-palm cultivation and fossicking.

GOLD, Lord: Title given to the Sunpriest, the most senior of the Quartern's priests; always at least a rainlord.

GRANTHON ALMANDINE, Cloudmaster: Highlord Nealrith's father; recently dead of apoplexy and exhaustion suffered when Breccia was attacked by Reduners.

HANDMAIDEN: A female sex worker in a snuggery.

HARKEL TALLYMAN: Once Seneschal of Scarcleft Hall and head of Highlord Taquar's Scarcleft Enforcers, now imprisoned by Iani Potch as a traitor to the Scarpen.

HIGHLORD: A rainlord or stormlord who rules one of the eight cities of the Scarpen Quarter.

HOUSE OF THE DEAD: Religious building where water is extracted from the dead for re-use, as part of the funeral service.

IANI POTCH, Rainlord: Husband of Highlord Moiqa, father of Lyneth who died when kidnapped by Tarquar Sardonyx; partially paralysed by apoplexy.

JASPER BLOODSTONE: Name used by Shale Flint after his arrival in Breccia. Has water skills greater than a rainlord, but is a flawed stormlord, incapable of handling water contaminated by salt or other impurities. Cannot therefore kill the rainlord way.

KANETH CARNELIAN, Rainlord: Bladesman, husband to Ryka Feldspar, father to her son, injured and enslaved by the Reduners at the fall of Breccia, when he suffered loss of memory. Called Lord Uthardim by the superstitious Reduners because of his resemblance to their legendary hero. Has lost his rainlord powers but appears now to have an unreliable ability to move the sand of dunes.

KHEDRIM CARNELIAN: Infant son of Kaneth Carnelian and Ryka Feldspar. Also called Kedri.

LAISA DRAYMAN, Rainlord: Widow of the late Highlord Nealrith Almandine, mother of Senya Almandine.

MAGENTA KERMES: Deceased daughter of Russet Kermes; wife of the Pinnacle, mother of Sienna, grandmother of Terelle Grey.

MASTER SON, The: Title given to the heir of the sandmaster of each dune; not necessarily a blood son of the sandmaster.

MEDDLE: A herd of pedes.

MEDRIM: Warrior Son to Davim, and now to Ravard.

MICA FLINT: Shale's older brother; disappeared during a Reduner raid only to re-emerge as a Reduner warrior called Ravard.

MOIQA, Highlord: Highlord of Qanatend, wife to Lord Iani; died during the siege of her city.

MOTHER CISTERN: A cistern, supplied by mother wells, that in turn supplies water to a city through tunnels.

MOTHER WELL: Wells dug down into the water table, from which water runs into a mother cistern.

MOTLEY, The: The multi-coloured mixture of paint-powders that forms a base coat for a waterpainting, necessary to fix the future of the scene depicted.

MYRIAPEDE: The smaller of the two species of pedes. Has six segments behind the head/thorax, three pairs of feet per segment. Can seat five to six riders if there is no baggage, but manages better with only two to three riders. Feelers are as long as the body.

NEALRITH ALMANDINE, Highlord: Cloudmaster Granthon's son, rainlord and former Highlord of Breccia. Died by the hand of Jasper after being severely tortured by Davim.

OTHER SIDE, The: Anywhere across the Giving Sea.

OUINA, Highlord: Middle-aged Highlord of Breakaway.

OVER-GOD: Deity of the Reduners, said to supply water to the Source.

PACKPEDE: Length variable, three to five times the length of a myriapede, with eighteen segments and fifty-four pairs of legs. Feelers generally no longer than a myriapede's.

PALMUBRA: Sun hat used in the Scarpen, woven from the leaves of the bab palm.

PEDE: Large desert herbivore native to the Red and White Quarters. Black pedes now used throughout the Scarpen, Red and Gibber Quarters, and white pedes in the White Quarter, as personal hacks (*see* MYRIAPEDE) and beasts of burden (*see* PACKPEDE). Tearing, cutting and crushing mouthparts masticate food externally. Poor eyesight, excellent sense of smell.

PEDEMASTER: Man given responsibility for the care of a stable (Scarpen Quarter) or a meddle (Red Quarter) of pedes.

PINNACLE, The: Ruler of Khromatis. Always a Watergiver.

QANATEND: The Scarpen city closest to the Red Quarter, taken and held by the Reduners.

QUARTERN, The: A loose confederation of four distinct quarters (pebble plains, sand dunes, stony drylands and salt plains). In the past, ruled by a Cloudmaster with limited powers, each quarter largely independent except for water concerns and matters involving trade routes, for which they are centrally taxed.

RAINLORD: A water sensitive who can sense the presence of and move small bodies of water and who can kill in the "rainlord way," i.e. take a person's water from their body. Both men and women rainlords are addressed as "Lord."

RAVARD: Sandmaster of Dune Watergatherer on the death of Davim. Born Mica Flint; brother to Shale Flint. Enslaved Ryka Feldspar as a concubine, and asserted his rights as a father to her unborn son before her escape.

RED QUARTER: That section of the Quartern consisting of lines of red sand dunes, peopled by Reduners.

REDUNER: Anyone born in the Red Quarter, or who has chosen to adopt the dune culture and lived long enough on the dunes to be stained red.

REEVE: A water sensitive who can sense but not move water.

RUSSET KERMES: A waterpainter born in Khromatis, father of Magenta, grandfather of Sienna, great-grandfather of Terelle Grey. Murdered Terelle's father before she was born.

RYKA FELDSPAR, Rainlord: A short-sighted Breccian rainlord of limited water-power; a scholar and teacher. Married to Lord Kaneth Carnelian. Was taken from Breccia after the siege to become Ravard's slave and concubine. Gave birth to her son, Khedrim, while escaping. Was recaptured by Ravard, then rescued by her husband.

SAMPHIRE: The only city in the White Quarter.

SANDMASTER: The ruler of a dune, commanding all the tribes found on that dune. Usually a water sensitive.

SCARCLEFT: The Scarpen city ruled by Highlord Taquar Sardonyx until he was deposed.

SCARPEN QUARTER: The most prosperous of the Quartern's four quarters. Consists of five stepped cities of the Escarpment, two port cities and one northern city on the other side of the Warthago Range.

SENYA ALMANDINE, Rainlord: Daughter of Highlord Nealrith and Rainlord Laisa. An unskilled rainlord. Seducer of Jasper Bloodstone.

SETTLE: Gibber village, usually located inside a drywash.

SHALE FLINT, Stormlord: Gibber-born, identified and trained as a stormlord by Taquar Sardonyx, then by the rainlords of Breccia and Cloudmaster Granthon. Also known as Jasper Bloodstone. His claim to the rank of stormlord or the title of Cloudmaster is debatable. Obtains water for the Quartern only with the aid of Terelle Grey's waterpainting.

SHUFFLE UP, To: The process that changes a waterpainting from a mere artwork to a work of magic, fixing the future of the scene and people portrayed in it. It entails the use of the motley by a waterpainter of talent.

SIENNA: Terelle Grey's mother, a woman of Khromatis who died in a Gibber settle after running away with her lover, Erith Grey. Daughter of Magenta Kermes, granddaughter of Russet Kermes.

SNUGGERY: Higher-class brothel (with either manservants or handmaidens as sex workers).

STORMLORD: Water sensitive with higher powers than a rainlord. Can move fresh water or water vapour over long distances in larger quantities than a rainlord. Can make and move clouds.

TAQUAR SARDONYX, Rainlord: Once Highlord of Scarcleft City until defeated by Jasper in a swordfight. Now a prisoner of Iani Potch. Unmarried and childless.

TERELLE GREY, Arta: Great-granddaughter of Russet Kermes. Born in the Gibber Quarter, related to the ruling family of Khromatis. Waterpainter. Placed under a coercion by Russet's waterpainting which ensures that she will have to travel to Khromatis within a year. Helps Jasper to supply rainclouds to the Quartern.

TIME OF RANDOM RAIN: Period before the rise of water sensitives, about a thousand years ago, when rain was uncontrolled and scarce. Reduners were the major force in the Quartern during this period.

TRIBEMASTER: A man who leads a tribe of any dune of the Red Quarter; usually a water sensitive.

UTHARDIM, Kher: Mythical leader of the Reduners who led them from servitude to freedom on the dunes at some time in the distant past. Now the name is sometimes given to Lord Kaneth Carnelian.

VARA REDMANE: Elderly widow of the Sandmaster of Dune Scarmaker and leader of a rebellion, first against Sandmaster Davim, then his successor, Ravard.

VIVIANDRA (VIVIE): Terelle's "sister," actually unrelated. Now a handmaiden.

WARRIOR SON, The: Title given to the sandmaster's warrior leader on each dune. Not necessarily a blood son of the sandmaster.

WASH DRYBONE SETTLE: Gibber village where Shale Flint was born.

WATER-BLIND: Lacking any water sensitivity, i.e. not able to feel the proximity of even nearby water.

WATERGATHERER, The: Home dune of Sandmaster Davim, and now of Ravard and his tribes.

WATERGIVER, The: Believed by the Scarpen pious to be the intermediary of the Sunlord who taught men and women to manipulate water, thus bringing the Time of Random Rain to an end. His actual origins are disputed, even among the waterpriests. Real name believed to have been Ash Gridelin.

WATERGIVERS: Name used by the people of Khromatis to indicate the water sensitives of that land. Includes waterpainters and waterlords.

WATERLESS, The: Anyone who is not entitled to a daily free water allowance.

WHITE QUARTER: The section of the Quartern closest to Khromatis. Peopled by the Alabasters. Produces salt, and related mineral products. Samphire is the one plant that grows well. Native pedes are white in colour.

ZIGGER: Winged flesh-eating, blood-drinking beetle, native to the Red Quarter and now used as a weapon. Can be trained not to attack people wearing a particular perfume. Excellent sense of smell and eyesight.

ACKNOWLEDGMENTS

Once upon a time...in fact twice...I wrote and had a book published without the aid of a single beta reader. I have no idea how I ever achieved that miracle. I know I couldn't do it today. This book owes more than usual to four beta readers: Karen Miller, Phill Berrie, Alena Sanusi and Donna Hanson. I cannot imagine I would ever have finished *Stormlord's Exile* with my sanity (relatively) intact without these people; for sure, without their spectacular advice and input, the book would be the poorer—by far.

In addition, my heartfelt thanks to my agent Dorothy Lumley, and my editors Stephanie Smith and Bella Pagan, who were all superbly supportive when things weren't going well. I consider myself lucky to know them all.

extras

orbit

meet the author

Glenda Larke is an Australian who now lives in Malaysia, where she works on the two great loves of her life: writing fantasy and the conservation of rain forest avifauna. She has also lived in Tunisia and Austria, and has at different times in her life worked as a housemaid, library assistant, school teacher, university tutor, medical correspondence course editor, field ornithologist and designer of nature interpretive centers. Along the way she has taught English to students as diverse as Korean kindergarten kids and Japanese teenagers living in Malaysia, Viennese adults in Austria, and engineering students in Tunis. If she has any spare time (which is not often), she goes bird watching; if she has any spare cash (not nearly often enough), she visits her daughters in the United States and her family in Western Australia. Find out more about the author at www.glendalarke.com.

introducing

If you enjoyed **STORMLORD'S EXILE**,
look out for

THE SWORN
The Fallen Kings Cycle: Book One

by Gail Z. Martin

*As plague and famine scourge the Winter Kingdoms, a
vast invasion force gathers beyond the Northern Sea.
And at its heart, a dark spirit mage wields the blood
magic of ancient, vanquished gods.*

*Summoner-King Tris Drayke must attempt to meet this
great threat, gathering an army from a country ravaged
by civil war. Tris seeks new allies from among the
living—and the dead—as an untested generation
of rulers face their first battle.*

Tris turns to the Sworn, a fierce nomadic clan bound to protect ancient, legendary warriors—the Dread. But even the mighty Sworn do not know what will happen when the Dread awake. All are certain, though, that war is coming to the Winter Kingdoms.

CHAPTER ONE

Every time you go, I can't believe six months have passed already."

Prince Jair Rothlandorn of Dhasson looked up as his father, King Harrol, stood in the doorway. Jair smiled and sighed as he closed his saddlebag and secured the cinch. "And every time I get ready to leave, I can't believe I've survived six months away from the Ride." Carefully, Jair folded his palace clothing into neat piles and placed them in a drawer to await his return. For the Ride, the only clue that would mark him as the heir to the throne of Dhasson was the gold signet ring on his right hand.

Jair walked to his window and looked out over the city. Valiquet was the name of both the Dhassonian palace and its capital city. The sun gleamed from the white marble and crystalline sculptures that had earned Valiquet its reputation as "The Glittering Place." Long a crossroads for commerce and ideas, Dhasson was perhaps the most cosmopolitan of the Winter Kingdoms. Its long tradition of tolerance for all but the Cult of the Crone had spared it the conflicts that often tore at the other kingdoms and had made it a magnet for scholars and artists. Beautiful as it was, for the six months Jair was home, the city felt like a glittering prison. Jair sighed and returned to packing.

Harrol watched as Jair gathered the last of his things. For the last eleven years, ever since Jair's fourteenth birthday, he had made the Ride. Although this trip would take Jair away from the palace, Valiquet, and Dhasson for six months, Jair's belongings fit neatly into two large saddlebags. "You miss her still."

Jair turned back to look at his father. "I miss her always." He was dressed for the road, in the dark tunic and trews that were the custom in the group with which he would ride sentry for the rest of the year. Jair slid up the long sleeve of his shirt, revealing a black tattoo around his left wrist, an intricate and complicated design that had only one match: around the wrist of his life-partner, Talwyn. On his left palm was an intricate tattoo that marked him as one of the *trinnen*, a warrior proven in battle. He stared at the design on his wrist for a moment in silence. "I wish—"

"—that the Court would accept her," Harrol finished gently. "And you know it's not to be. Even if it did, Talwyn is the daughter of the Sworn's chieftain and she's their shaman. She can no more leave her people than you can renounce your claim to the throne."

"I know." They'd had this conversation before. Although every heir to the Dhasson throne made the six-month Ride, only two before Jair had married into the secretive group of warrior-shamans. Eljen, Jair's great-great-granduncle, had renounced the throne, throwing

Dhasson into chaos. Anginon, two generations removed, had worked out an "accommodation," accepting an arranged political marriage in Dhasson to sire an heir while honoring his bond to his partner among the Sworn by making it clear the Dhasson marriage was in name only. Neither option was to Jair's liking, and it was at times like these that the crown seemed to fit most tightly.

"You may find that this year's Ride leaves little time for home and hearth," Harrol said. "Bad enough that plague's begun to spread into Dhasson. What I've heard from Margolan sounds bad. I know the Sworn stay to the barren places, where the barrows lie. Please, avoid the cities and villages. And be careful. Nothing is as it should be this year. I fear the Ride will be more dangerous than it's been in quite some time. I have no desire to lose my son, to plague or to battle." Harrol embraced Jair, slapping him hard on the back. But there was a moment's hesitation and the embrace was just a bit tighter than usual, letting Jair know that his father was sincerely worried.

"Don't worry. I'll be home before Candles Night. And perhaps this time, I'll bring Kenver with me. The Court can't argue that he's my son, whether or not they recognize my marriage. Whether he can take the crown one day or not, they can get used to the fact that I won't deny him."

Harrol chuckled. "If the boy can be spared from his training, by all means, bring him. If he's half the handful you were as a lad, it should keep you busy fetching him out of the shrubbery!"

Neither Jair nor his father said more as they descended the stairs to Valiquet's large marble entranceway. There was no mistaking the two Sworn guardsmen who awaited

Jair. They were dressed as he was, in the dark clothing and studded leather armor of the Sworn, wearing the lightweight, summer great cloaks that would help to keep down the dust and discourage the flies. Jair shouldered into his own cloak.

"Good to see you once more, Commander."

Jair recognized the speaker as Emil, one of the guardsmen he had known since he'd first begun making the Ride. Emil's greeting was in Dhassonian, but his heavy accent made it clear that that language was not his native tongue. His companion, Mihei, a warrior land mage, echoed the greeting. No one would mistake either of the men as residents of Dhasson. Both wore their dark, black hair straight and long, accentuating the tawny golden cast of their skin. Their eyes, amber like the Sacred Lady's, marked their bloodline as servants of the goddess. A variety of amulets in silver and carved stone hung from leather straps around their necks. The leather baldrics that each wore held a variety of lethal and beautiful *damashqi* daggers, and the weapon that hung by each man's side was neither broadsword nor scimitar but a *stelian*, a deadly, jagged, flat blade that was as dangerous as it looked, the traditional weapon of the Sworn.

Jair was dressed in the same manner, but it was obvious to any who looked that he did not share the same blood. Tan from a season outdoors, he was still much lighter than his Sworn companions, and his dark, wavy, brown hair and blue eyes made his resemblance to Harrol obvious.

"It's been too long," Jair responded in the clipped, consonant-heavy language of the nomads. "I've been ready to leave again since I returned."

Jair knew his father watched them descend the sweeping front steps to the horses that waited for them. Even the horses looked out of place. They bore little resemblance to the high-strung, overbred carriage horses of the nobility. These were horses from the Margolan steppe, bred for thousands of years by the Sworn for their steadiness in battle, their intelligence, and their stamina. Jair fastened his saddlebags, shaking his head to dissuade the groomsman who ran to help him. Then the three men swung up to their saddles and rode out of the palace gates.

They did not speak until the walled city was behind them and they were on the open road. Mihei was the first to break the silence. "When we stop for the night, I have gifts for you in my bag."

"Oh?" Jair asked, curious. "From whom?"

Mihei smiled. "Kenver—and his mother. Kenver chased me down the road to make sure I'd packed the gifts he made for you. *Cheira* Talwyn didn't chase us, but I wouldn't care to face her displeasure if I were remiss in making sure you received your welcoming gift."

Jair smiled broadly, knowing that he had packed several such gifts for his wife and son in his bags as well. "Are they well?"

Emil laughed. "Kenver is a hand's breadth taller than when you left, and begging for a pony to ride with the guards. Talwyn's driven us all mad these past few weeks with her wishing for time to pass more quickly."

"Tell me, where do we join the tribe?"

Mihei's smile faded. "The Ride's taken longer this year than in any season for many years."

"Why?"

"Many times, we've found the barrows desecrated.

Cheira Talwyn says the spirits are unhappy. We'll join the others just across the river, below the Ruune Vidaya forest," Mihei replied.

Jair didn't say anything as he thought about Mihei's news. The Sworn were a nomadic people, consecrated thousands of years ago to the service of the Lady. They were the guardians of the barrows, the large mounds that dotted the landscape from the Northern Sea down through Margolan into Dhasson and to the border of Nargi. Legend said that long ago, the barrows had continued, down into Nargi and beyond, to the Southern Plains. But when the Nargi took up the worship of the Crone Aspect of the Lady, they destroyed the barrows and fought any of the Sworn who dared cross into their lands. The Sworn had left them to their folly, and the legends said that the Nargi had paid dearly for destroying the barrows.

Within the barrows were the Dread. What, exactly, the Dread were, Jair did not know. No one had seen the Dread in over a thousand years. Only the shamans of the Sworn, the *cheira*, ever communicated with their spirits, and then only through ritual and visions. But it was said that as the Sworn were the guardians of the barrows of the Dread, so the Dread were guardians of the deep places, and it was their burden to make sure that a powerful evil remained buried.

The three men rode single file, and Jair noted that both Emil and Mihei seemed unusually alert for danger on this leg of the trip. Normally, the two-day journey from Valiquet to meet up with the Sworn was uneventful. Now, Jair realized that the others' heightened vigilance had affected him, and he found himself scanning the horizon.

"Look there," Jair said as a small hamlet came into view

late in the afternoon. Any other year, the fields would have been full of men, women, and children working. Instead, even from a distance, Jair could see that the fields lay untended, although it was only weeks until harvest. As they drew nearer, an overpowering stench filled the air, and Jair saw shifting gray clouds hovering over the village and the pastures.

"Dark Lady take my soul, what's happened?" Jair breathed as they drew nearer. The air stank of decay, and it was clear that the gray clouds were swarms of flies. The sunken, half-rotted corpses of cows, sheep, and horses lay in the pasture. There was no noise, except for the buzzing of flies, so many that it sounded like the hum of a distant waterfall.

"It's the plague," Mihei said, as they passed the turn to the lane that led into the village. The smell was overpowering in the late-summer heat. He began to chant quietly to himself, and Jair recognized it as the passing-over ritual the Sworn said for the bodies of the dead. Jair made the sign of the Lady, adding his own fervent prayer for safe travel.

"What have you seen of plague?"

Emil shook his head. "Rarely have I been so glad to avoid cities as this season. Most of what we hear comes from the news of the travelers and tinkers we pass on the road. But it's bad enough in some of the larger towns that the dead lie stacked like cordwood because there isn't time to bury them, and the living have abandoned their sick and fled."

"Sweet Chenne," Jair murmured. "What of the other kingdoms? Have you heard?"

"There's a rumor that Principality has closed its border

to Margolan refugees. It's said that Nargi is patrolling the river more frequently, as if anyone would think about sneaking into that rats' nest. Has your father closed Dhasson's borders?"

"Not yet. But it may come to that."

"Watch out!" Mihei's shouted warning came as figures crashed through the underbrush toward the road. Jair's eyes widened as he drew his *stelian*. Four creatures burst from the forest, dressed in rags, moving in a frenzy of rage. They had been men once, but there was no reasoning in their eyes, nor sanity. They stank of waste and sweat and were covered in filth and dried blood. Three of the madmen swung tree limbs that looked to have been ripped from their trunks. One of the men wielded a large branch with finger-length thorns, heedless of the blood that flowed from his hands as the thorns tore at his discolored flesh. Their faces and arms were covered with large, red pustules and bleeding open sores. The sight of three well-armed men on horseback should have deterred even the most determined thieves. Instead, the four howled with rage and ran at them, swinging their makeshift weapons.

"What are they?" Jair shouted as his horse reared.

"Ashtenerath," Mihei replied, slashing down with his *stelian* as one of the madmen tried to lame his mount with the branch it swung. Mihei's weapon cleaved the man from shoulder to hip, but the remaining attackers pressed forward, paying no attention to their companion's fate.

Two of the madmen circled Jair, yammering and howling in their rage. The third launched himself toward Emil, and his thorny club scored a gash across the flank of Emil's horse before Emil sank his blade deep into the man's chest. The *ashtenerath* collapsed to his knees with a gurgle as blood began to pour from his mouth. Still, he swung at Emil's horse with his club until Emil's *stelian* connected once more, severing his head from his shoulders.

Jair struck at the *ashtenerath* that ventured the closest, slicing through the madman's shoulder and severing the arm that swung the club. The thing pressed on, paying no attention to the pain or to the rush of blood that soaked his tattered rags. Aghast, Jair brought his *stelian* down, slicing from the bloody stump of his attacker's shoulder through his ribs until the body lay severed in two.

With a cry, Mihei engaged the fourth man, who had advanced on Jair's horse from the left. Mihei's horse reared, and a well-placed kick tore the *ashtenerath*'s club from its hands. Blind with rage, the berserker hurled himself toward Mihei. The horse reared again, knocking the attacker to the ground and crushing him beneath its hooves as its full weight landed on the berserker's chest, spattering gore and soaking the horse's front legs to the knees in blood.

Silence filled the clearing as Jair and the others watched the tree line for another attack.

"By the Crone! What spawns those things?" Jair asked as he wiped his *stelian* clean and resheathed his weapons.

Emil and Mihei looked around the bloodied roadway. "Usually, *ashtenerath* are created by potions and blood magic, men pushed past sanity by torture and drugged into a bloodlust," Mihei replied. "They're expendable fighters, just a breath removed from walking corpses, and it's a kindness to put them out of their misery."

"A blood mage did this?" Jair asked.

Emil shook his head. "In a way. The plague began in Margolan, and it was the traitor Curane's blood mages who created it, as a way to stop King Martris's army. Only it got away from them, and it spread beyond the battle-field. Maybe it's the nature of the sickness, or maybe it's because it was magicked up, but a handful of the ones who catch the plague don't die right away. The madness takes them and they become *ashtenerath*. We've heard of attacks before, but this is the first time we've been set upon ourselves."

Jair looked down at the mangled bodies on the road-way and repressed a shiver. He'd fought skirmishes against raiders and seen men die in battle. In the eyes of his opponents, he'd seen determination and unwillingness to yield, but never complete madness.

"Come now. We've got to purify ourselves and the horses to make sure we don't spread the sickness," Emil urged.

They rode another candlemark before they found a clearing near the road with a well. Emil signaled for them to stop. They dismounted, warily watching the under-brush for signs of danger. Mihei stood silently, staring into the forest, but his hands were moving in a compli-cated series of gestures that Jair knew worked the ward-ing magic of the Sworn. As Mihei set the wardings, Emil built a fire and began to take a variety of items from his saddlebags. Jair drew a bucket of cold water from the depths of the well, and Mihei gestured for him to set the bucket near the fire. Mihei took pinches of dried plants from pouches on his belt and ground them together in his fist, then released them into the fire.

Smoke rose from the fire, heavily scented with cam-phor, thyme, and sage. Mihei bade them enter into the thick smoke that billowed from the fire and to draw the horses near as well. "Breathe deeply," he instructed, and

Jair closed his eyes, taking in a deep breath of the fragrant smoke. "The smoke wards off fever and strengthens the body's humours."

Next, Mihei took a flask from his bags and uncorked it. Jair immediately recognized the smell of *vass,* the strong drink favored by the Sworn, made from fermented honey, hawthorn, and juniper. Mihei poured a liberal draught into the bucket of water, then added crushed handfuls of fetherfew and elder leaves, finally dropping in two gemstone disks, one of emerald and one of bright blue lapis. Mihei began to chant, his fingers tracing complex runes in the air over the mixture. He gestured for each man to unfasten the cups that hung at their belts and fill their tankards with the brew. Jair tossed the noxious-tasting concoction back, stifling the urge to choke on the strong bite of the *vass.* He was gratified to note that Emil also seemed to be catching his breath.

Mihei finished his drink in a coughing fit, but held up a hand to wave off help. When he had recovered, he took three dried apples and a handful of dried fruit from his bags and soaked them for a few moments in the liquid, then offered a handful of the fruit to each of the horses, which they took greedily. Then he moved from Jair to Emil, using a rag to wipe away any blood from the *ash-tenerath* that had spattered their cloaks or clothing, tending at the last to his own cloak. Next, he bathed the horses' legs and underbellies to assure that any splattered gore was wiped away, and made a paste of the liquid and some herbs from his pouches to tend the gash on Emil's horse. Finally, he walked around the others, chanting as he went, spilling out the liquid to make a wide circle in which both men and horses could spend the night.

"And you know this works, how?" Jair asked as the wind caught the scented smoke and carried it away.

Mihei shook the last of the liquid from his hands and sat down beside the fire. "Talwyn said our great-grandfathers used these mixtures the last time a plague swept across the Winter Kingdoms. Few among the Sworn died, even though many others perished."

They settled down around the fire and Emil took lengths of hard sausage, goat cheese, and crusty bread from his saddlebags, enough for all of them. Jair rinsed the bucket well and drew up another bucket full of icy water. When they had eaten, Emil took two pouches bound in cloth and leather strips from his bag and handed them to Jair. "I promised I'd give these to you just as soon as I could," he said with a grin.

Jair smiled and took the packages, carefully unwrapping them. On the inside of the piece of bleached linen was a berry-stained handprint, just the size that might belong to a three-year-old boy. Beside it was a charcoal drawing of a horse and a man standing next to the stick figure of a smaller person, and Jair had no doubt it was Kenver's image of his homecoming. Wrapped in the middle of the linen was a disk of finely polished hematite, wound with four strings of colored leather plaited with strands of Talwyn's long, dark hair. Though Jair possessed no magic of his own, he knew it to be a powerful amulet, imbued with Talwyn's shamanic magic.

"Talwyn said it would heighten your awareness of the unseen, and guide your dreams," Emil said with a smile as Jair raised both the linen and the charm to his lips and held them tightly in his hand.

"Thank you," Jair replied, tucking the linen safely into

his pack and tying the charm around his neck. It lay against another amulet, this one forged of silver and bronze set with amethyst, a token Talwyn had given him at their wedding. She had told him then that the charm would allow her to enter his dreams, and although Jair spoke of it to no one at the palace, it was only that contact, at the border between wakefulness and sleep, that made it possible for him to endure their separation.

"We'd best get some sleep," Emil said. "We've got another day's ride to meet up with the others." He spread out his cloak beneath him, using his saddlebag as a pillow, and took his blanket from the roll behind his saddle. Jair and Mihei did the same, and Mihei shook his head when Jair moved to sit by the fire to take the first watch.

"Get some rest. I'll take this watch. Don't worry—I'll be happy to rouse you when your turn comes."

Despite the amulet, Jair's dreams were dark. The afternoon's battle replayed itself, but in his dream, throngs of *ashtenerath* pursued them, undeterred until hacked to bits. He woke with a start, relieved to find the campsite peaceful. Mihei had put another log on the fire, and from the smell of the smoke, more warding leaves. Jair settled himself back into his blanket and tried to sleep once more.

As he balanced between waking and slumber, Jair saw Talwyn's image in the distance. She smiled and beckoned for him to come closer. She was singing, and the sound of her voice cheered his heart. Finally, he stood next to her, and Talwyn welcomed him with a kiss. Then she placed a hand over the pendants at his throat. "Watch carefully, my love. The roads are filled with danger." Her eyes widened. "Wake now. Take your sword. The shadows are moving."

Jair jolted awake an instant before Mihei cried out in

alarm. Jair and Emil were on their feet in an instant, swords in hand.

"What do you see?" Emil said, scanning the night. Jair could just make out a trace of movement in the shadows.

"Spirits. *Dimonns*. Don't know which, but whatever's out there isn't friendly," Mihei replied. "I strengthened the wardings."

Jair looked down, and where Mihei had traced a large circle around them and their horses with the cleansing elixir, a ring of stones now marked the area.

"There! Can you see?" Emil pointed into the darkness where darker shapes moved swiftly across the tall grass of the clearing. Mihei nodded, raising his hands as he began to chant. As Jair watched, a phosphorescent mist rose in the clearing, first just ankle-high, then suffusing the night with an eerie green glow. In the glowing mist, the shapes became clearer. Disembodied shadows slipped back and forth in the mist, but their outlines looked nothing like men. Some were misshapen hulks with wide, empty maws. Others were wraiths with thin, grasping arms and impossibly long, taloned fingers that stretched toward the living men and horses within the wardings.

The horses shied and Jair feared they might bolt. Mihei spared the animals a moment of his attention, looking each of the horses in the eyes and murmuring words Jair did not catch. Immediately, the horses quieted.

The black shapes rushed toward the stone circle, and a curtain of light flared between the three men and the advancing shadows. The shadows howled and shrieked, spreading themselves across the glowing barrier until they blotted out the moonlight. Jair glanced at Mihei. The land mage's forehead was beaded with sweat and he was biting his lip with the effort to reinforce the strained wardings.

"Tell us what you need and we'll do it," Jair urged.

"Keep me awake," Mihei said. "My guess is that someone used this forest as a killing field, and the spirits have never left. Their anger could have drawn the *dimonns*. The deaths in the village could also make the *dimonns* stronger."

"What do they want?" Jair asked.

"Blood."

"If they're drawn by the wronged dead, can you appease their spirits, reduce the *dimonns*' power?" Jair had drawn his *stelian,* even though it was clear that it would be little protection against the shadows that wailed and tore at the gossamer-thin veil of the warding.

"I'm no summoner," Mihei replied. "I can't help the spirits pass over to the Lady. But if we survive the night, I can find where their bodies were dumped and consecrate the ground. That should satisfy the spirits, and without them and the *ashtenerath,* the *dimonns* should leave."

"Should," Emil repeated doubtfully.

Mihei looked to Jair. "I need some things from my bag." Jair listened as Mihei recited a list of powders and dried plants, and he went to gather them from the vials in Mihei's bag as Emil stood guard, weapon at the ready.

"Mix them with my mortar and pestle," Mihei instructed. "Then make a paste of it with some water." Jair did as Mihei requested, dripping water into the mortar's rough bowl until a gray, gumlike paste stuck to the pestle.

"Bring me a small wad—save the rest, we'll need it."

Jair rolled a coin-sized wad of the gum between thumb and forefinger and brought it to Mihei, who placed it under his tongue. "That should help. When I trained with the mages, there were all-night workings where we didn't dare fall asleep. The muttar gum will keep me wide awake, although I'll pay for it tomorrow."

"Anything else we can do?" Emil asked.

Mihei nodded. "The *dimonns* will try to reach my mind. They'll send visions and nightmares. If I begin to lose my focus, you have to bring me back. All our lives depend on it."

"How should we wake you?"

Mihei shrugged. "Douse me with water. Pinch my arms. If you have to, slap me across the face. Better a few bruises than to be sucked dry by the *dimonns.*"

Grimly, Jair and Emil took seats next to Mihei. Jair fingered his amulets, but his connection to Talwyn was gone. Just on the other side of the coruscating light, the *dimonns* stretched their shadows over the domed warding, mouths full of dark teeth snapping against the barrier. Talons scratched against the ground and cries like tortured birds of prey broke the silence of the night.

A motion caught Jair's eye. Something solid moved through the tall grass, and to his horror, the face of a young girl, no more than six or seven seasons old, pale and wide-eyed, rose above the mist. The image wavered, and as Jair ran his fingers over the amulets at his throat, the girl seemed to flicker and shift.

Emil started toward her, and Jair blocked his way. "She's not real."

Emil struggled against Jair, his eyes on the child. "They'll kill her."

"She's not really here."

"Let me go!" Emil broke away from Jair and stepped

through the warding. Immediately, the shadows massed and the image of the girl winked out. Emil's scream echoed in the night. With a curse, Jair dove after him, making sure to keep one foot within the warding as Mihei began to chant loudly. Jair caught the back of Emil's great cloak and pulled with all his might. Claws tore at him, slicing into his forearm and shoulder. He twisted out of the way of snapping jaws and he pulled again. This time, he succeeded, landing hard on his back as Emil tumbled through the warding.